THE ODYSSEY

THE ODYSSEY

Homer

Translation, Introduction, and Notes
by
Barry B. Powell

New York   Oxford
OXFORD UNIVERSITY PRESS

Oxford University Press is a department of the University of Oxford.
It furthers the University's objective of excellence in research,
scholarship, and education by publishing worldwide.

Oxford   New York
Auckland   Cape Town   Dar es Salaam   Hong Kong   Karachi
Kuala Lumpur   Madrid   Melbourne   Mexico City   Nairobi
New Delhi   Shanghai   Taipei   Toronto

With offices in
Argentina   Austria   Brazil   Chile   Czech Republic   France   Greece
Guatemala   Hungary   Italy   Japan   Poland   Portugal   Singapore
South Korea   Switzerland   Thailand   Turkey   Ukraine   Vietnam

For titles covered by Section 112 of the US Higher Education
Opportunity Act, please visit www.oup.com/us/he for the latest
information about pricing and alternate formats.

Published by Oxford University Press
198 Madison Avenue, New York, New York 10016
http://www.oup.com

Library of Congress Cataloging-in-Publication Data

Homer, author.
  [Odyssey. English]
  The odyssey / Homer ; translation, introduction, and notes by Barry B. Powell.
     pages cm
  Includes bibliographical references and index.
  ISBN 978-0-19-992588-9 (pbk. : alk. paper)
  I. Powell, Barry B. II. Title.
  PA4025.A5P69 2014
  883'.01--dc23

                                                        2014006009

Printing number: 9 8 7 6 5 4 3 2 1

Printed in the United States of America
on acid-free paper

To Sanford Dorbin, who knows a good story when he hears it

Contents

List of Maps and Figures

Maps

Figures

Preface

In 1956 in Sacramento, California, when I was a teenager, I saw a movie called *Helen of Troy* about some war that took place long ago—but when? Where? Who were these people, and what where they fighting about? The movie excited in me a burning desire to learn the answers to these questions. Looking back, I see the story had something to do with a beautiful blond, that was clear, but what I remember best is a warrior running across the plain and an arrow suddenly piercing his throat in a wondrous image of terrible violence. What was this war, anyway?

From that moment, I conceived my lifelong passion for what turned out to be the Homeric poems. I drifted away to other interests, but in college I came back to the story I then knew to be based on Homer's *Iliad*. I learned Greek, wrote a doctoral dissertation on the *Odyssey*, and for years taught Homer in college. I wrote several books on Homeric problems. But never did the force of these early questions disappear: When did this war really take place? Did it ever take place? What were they fighting about? Did Achilles ever live? What about Helen of Troy? Did Odysseus exist? Did he come home, sailing across the wine-dark sea, to a patiently waiting wife in order to avenge the wrong done to his house and honor? The answers were by no means obvious, and they are still hotly debated today.

Despite the interest of such historical questions, what matters most are the poems themselves—the stories they tell and the language in which they are told. Without them, we would have no Trojan War, no Helen or Achilles, no Paris, nor the homecoming of Odysseus. The poems are the thing, and when Charles Cavaliere of Oxford University Press suggested to me, rather out of the blue, that I translate the Homeric poems, I welcomed the opportunity. When I told friends about this project, they said, "But hasn't Homer already been translated many times?" Yes, sure, I tried to explain, but not by *me*—here was a chance to put into English what the Greek had come to mean to *me*, how it sounded, what the words meant, what was their power that had, indirectly, entranced me as a youth through the medium of film. Too often in modern translations the translator tries to impose a modern sensibility on the style, as if in this way Homer can be made "relevant." I have avoided such affectations, trying always to communicate in a lean, direct manner what the Greek really says, to put in English how Homer in Greek might have sounded to his contemporaries.

Because of the film *Helen of Troy* (Warner Brothers, 1956), I've been much interested in my career in studying and teaching how the Homeric poems were represented in art in the ancient world, the distant antecedent of our own cinema. After all, it was the Greeks who first told stories in art, and they did so inspired by the Homeric and similar poems. *Helen of Troy* is only a modern cinematic version of this ancient tradition. In my translation, I want to show some of these images, selecting two or three pictures from ancient art for each book in order to show how the Greeks and Romans visualized Homeric events. This translation is unique in being illustrated by ancient art.

I've also written an introduction that summarizes scholarship on the Homeric poems, a digest of over fifty years of reflection. About Homer there is somebody somewhere who thinks absolutely anything, but in the introduction and notes to my translation I have attempted to give common-sense answers to problems of Homeric interpretation. The reader's experience with the *Odyssey* is further enriched by a companion website, www.oup.com/us/powell, which includes audio files of key passages that I read aloud (indicated in the text by an icon placed in the margin), overviews and plot summaries for the poem's twenty-four books, and PowerPoint slides that include outlines and all the maps and photographs in the translation.

Homer's poems are very odd—so difficult to comprehend in their astonishing range and complexity. I hope that this translation of the *Odyssey* will open to many its beauty and glory as a song set against the background of a war fought long ago and the struggles of heroes to get back home. There is always war, and the issues are always the same: anger, glory, honor, hate, love, death, terror, violence, and forgiveness. There is always a return to life as it was lived before the war. But back home, everything has changed—changed utterly. Only the hero's experience and power can restore the world to what once it was so that new life can begin again.

Santa Fe, 2014

Acknowledgments

My thanks to Sandy Dorbin, who read the entire manuscript and made more suggestions than I can count. William Aylward and Ian Morris read the Introduction and saved me from many indiscretions. Finally, my wife, Patricia, suffered through the whole thing with characteristic good cheer.

I want to thank Christof Haussner for the drawing of the layers of Troy (Figure 0.4).

I also wish to thank the following readers, in addition to those who wished to remain anonymous, who read early samples of the translations. Their advice was excellent, for which I am very grateful, and I have attempted to make use of their many fine suggestions: Jonathan Austad, Eastern Kentucky University; Bella Vivante, University of Arizona; Luke Reinsma, Seattle Pacific University; Joel Christensen, University of Texas at San Antonio; Susan Gorman, Massachusetts College of Pharmacy and Health Sciences; William Johnson, Duke University; Rachel Ahern Knudsen, University of Oklahoma; Nicholas D. More, Westminster College; Clementine Oliver, California State University, Northridge; Joseph Pearce, Ave Maria University; Andrew Porter, University of Wisconsin, Milwaukee; Nancy St. Clair, Simpson College; Paul Scott Stanfield, Nebraska Wesleyan University; and Carolyn Whitson, Metropolitan State University.

Many have helped in the production of this book, but I would like to thank especially John Challice, vice president and publisher of Oxford University Press, who supported the book from the beginning; Marianne Paul, the production editor, who did so much to ensure a good product, for which I am very grateful; Kim Howie, who devised an outstanding design; Lynn Luecken, who has helped in many ways; and photo researcher, Francelle Carapetyan. Above all, I want to thank Charles Cavaliere, whose notion it was in the first place to bring out a new translation of the *Odyssey*. He inspired the project, then guided it with diligence and imagination.

About the Translator

BARRY B. POWELL is the Halls-Bascom Professor of Classics Emeritus at the University of Wisconsin–Madison, where he taught for thirty-four years. He is the author of the widely used textbook *Classical Myth* (8th edition, 2014). His *A Short Introduction to Classical Myth* (2001, translated into German) is a summary study of the topic. *Homer and the Origin of the Greek Alphabet* (1991) advances the thesis that a single man invented the Greek alphabet expressly in order to record the poems of Homer. *Writing and the Origins of Greek Literature* (2003) develops the consequence of this thesis. Powell's critical study *Homer* (2nd edition, 2004, translated into Italian) is widely read as an introduction for philologists, historians, and students of literature. *A New Companion to Homer* (1997, with Ian Morris, translated into modern Greek) is a comprehensive review of modern scholarship on Homer. Powell's *Writing: Theory and History of the Technology of Civilization* (2009, translated into Arabic and modern Greek) attempts to create a scientific terminology and taxonomy for the study of writing. *The Greeks: History, Culture, Society* (2nd edition, 2009, with Ian Morris, translated into Chinese) is a complete review that is widely used in college courses. His recent textbook *World Myth* (2013) reviews the myths of the world. His acclaimed translation of the *Iliad* appeared in 2013. Powell has also written novels, poetry, and screenplays. He lives in Santa Fe, New Mexico, with his wife and cats.

Maps

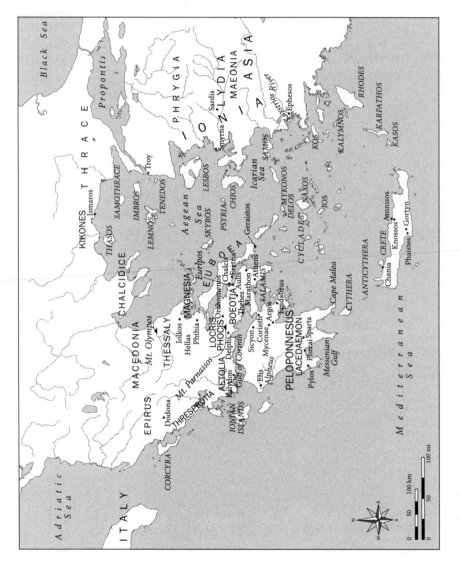

MAP 1   The Aegean

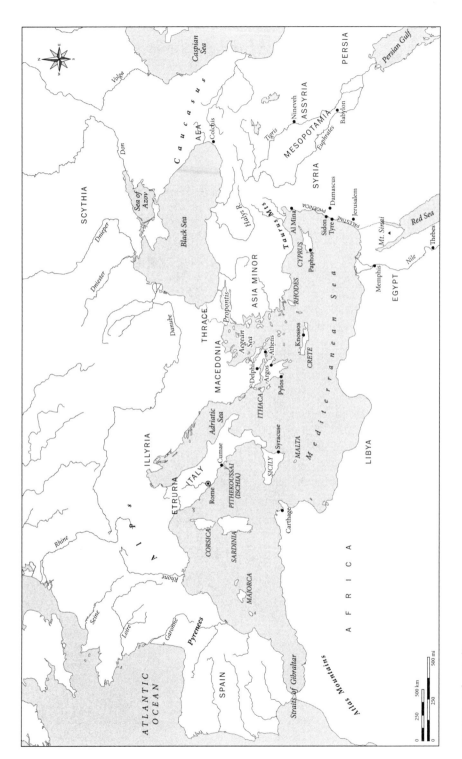

MAP II The Mediterranean

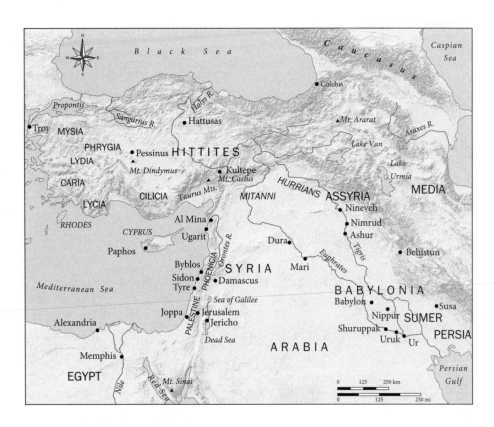

MAP III   The Ancient Near East

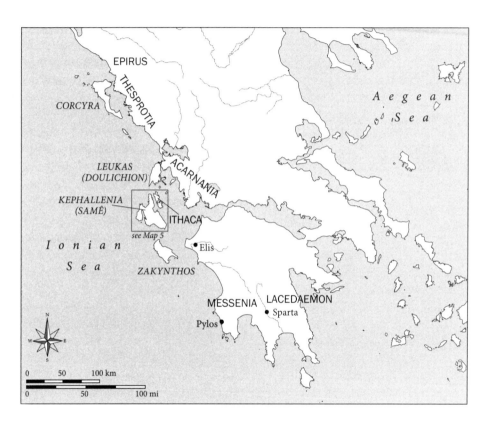

MAP IV   The Ionian Isles

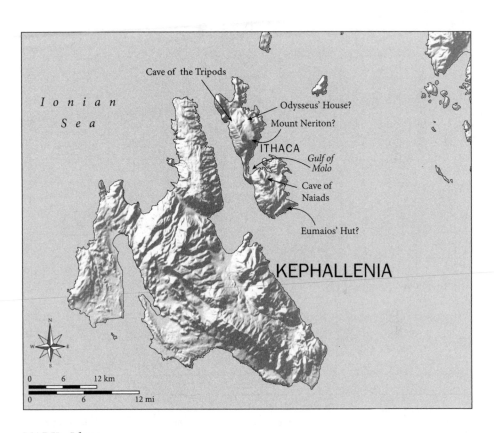

MAP V   Ithaca

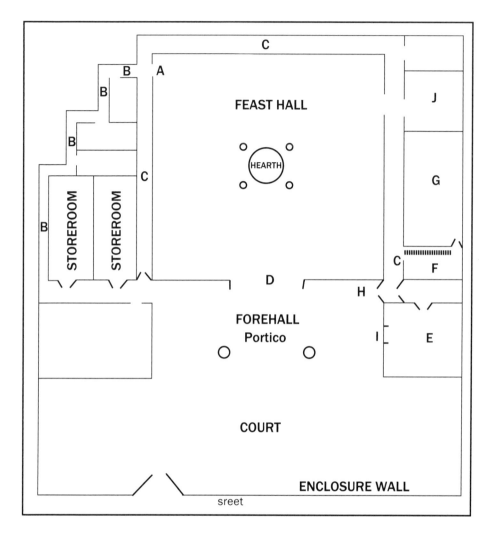

MAP VI   The House of Odysseus.   The house seems to be built on one level except for Penelope's upstairs room, G, reached by a stairwell, F. D is the threshold where Odysseus stands through almost the entire end of the poem. The "back door" at A leads to the "hall" C, which leads to the FORE-HALL and COURT. The suitors cannot escape down the "hall" because Eumaios is stationed near the doors that lead from the hall. When Melanthios sneaks through the "back door," he goes down the "side-hall" to reach one of the STOREROOMS (there seem to be more than one). The slave women's quarters is E, with doors leading to the "hall" and outside to the FOREHALL at H. They also have access to the stairwell F. At I, there is a window. J may be where Penelope sat to watch the proceedings in the other room. The "roundhouse" from which the slaves are hung is somewhere in the COURT (modified after H. L. Lorimer, *Homer and the Monuments* [London, 1950], p. 408, Fig. 59).

Homeric Timeline

c. 1200 BC	Fall of Troy
c. 800 BC	Dictation of the Homeric poems
	Invention of Greek alphabet
from 566 BC	Panathenaic festival
c. 450 BC	Herodotus
c. 200 BC	Alexandrian Vulgate
c. AD 950	Venetus A manuscript of the *Iliad* with marginal notations
c. AD 1000	Laurentianus manuscript of the *Odyssey*
c. AD 1500	First printed edition of the *Iliad* and the *Odyssey* in Italy
from 1598	Chapman's English translation of Homer
AD 1715–1726	Translation of the *Iliad* and the *Odyssey* by Alexander Pope
AD 1788	Publication of Venetus A by Villoison
AD 1795	Wolf's *Prolegomena ad Homerum*
AD 1871	Heinrich Schliemann digs at Troy
AD 1930	Milman Parry creates the oral-formulaic theory
AD 1991	Connection of invention of alphabet with recording of Homeric poems

Introduction

In 1928, Bruce Rogers (1870–1957), probably the greatest American book designer, and his associates in England contracted with the famous Lawrence of Arabia (1888–1935), writing as T. E. Shaw, to do a translation of Homer's *Odyssey*. Lawrence's military glories were in the past, and he was soon to die in a motorcycle accident. He began work in 1928, but it took much longer than he expected. Here Lawrence is explaining to Rogers in a letter why he is taking so long:

> I see now why there are no adequate translations of Homer. He is baffling. Not simple, in education; not primitive, socially . . . There's a queer naivety in every other line: and at our remove of thought and language we can't say if he's smiling or not . . . I have tried to squeeze out all the juice in the orange; or what I thought was the juice. I tried to take liberties with the Greek: but failed. Homer compels respect.
>
> I must confess he has beaten me to my knees. Perhaps if I did much more I might be less faithful. The work has been very difficult: though I'm in a Homeric sort of air; a mud-brick fort beset by the tribes of Waziristan, on a plain encircled by the hills of the Afghan border. It reeks of Alexander the Great, our European forerunner who also loved Homer.
>
> But, as I say, it has been difficult.[1]

Though Lawrence was unsure of the quality of his translation of the *Odyssey*, the backers of the project were enthusiastic. They went on to produce Lawrence's *Odyssey* in November 1932, one of the most handsome books ever manufactured.

THE DIFFICULTY OF HOMER

Lawrence was right: Homer *is* baffling. Everything about him defies expectations. He knows about too many things. It is often impossible to be sure what tone he intends. What are these gods doing here? Is he being funny? What is the joke? Why is this passage here? Where do all these names come from? Or he is savage, or sad, or beautiful.

The *Iliad* and the *Odyssey* are alternate realities. You can slip into this world of Homer and taste his food and smell his fires and endure his sufferings and enjoy his

---

1 Quoted in Joseph Blumenthal, *Bruce Rogers: A Life in Letters, 1870–1957* (W. Thomas Taylor, Austin, TX, 1989), pp. 130–131.

humor and never be afraid that it is going to end, because it seems to go on forever. It is a complete world—engulfing, like life itself, but somehow more real.

Achilles comes to question the bases for action that his society takes for granted, the heart of the story of the *Iliad*. But the *Iliad* is just as interested in the long boasting speeches of its heroes and in sudden gruesome death on the battlefield as in any moral dilemma. Some five thousand lines, or fully one third of the poem, consists of descriptions of battle. We all know the *Odyssey* from its famous stories of one-eyed giants and seductive women, but Homer is just as interested in the biting repartee between the beggar in disguise and the hostile suitors and in the alternate tales that Odysseus spins out again and again, like a singer at his craft. The action is set in a coherent world where the relationships between the characters are clearly drawn, including relationships with the gods, who are powerful characters in their own right.

But you cannot just sit down and read the *Iliad* and the *Odyssey* cold without guidance about their historical, geographical, and literary background. This I provide in the form of notes, which explain unusual usages and sometimes points of plot and character or obscure references. The purpose is to make Homer approachable, understandable.

It is a strange world, far removed in ethics and in expression from our own. It is huge, vast, a world certainly of long ago, but in every way recognizable, both socially and psychologically. It is a world in which the problems that men and women face are similar to those that we ourselves experience. In a sense, the men and women in Homer *are* ourselves, living in a world torn by violence, sexual passion, greed, and the lust for revenge. Sometimes we live in such worlds, too.

It is this curious mix of the alien and the familiar that gives Homer his special charm. For thinkers and poets in the ancient world, Homer was always the touchstone, the inspiration and model for thought and expression. But Homer *is* baffling, and one has to wonder how he ever became a classic.

In Greek, the language is extremely peculiar. As a student I was told constantly that Homer was easy to read, at least in comparison with other Greek authors, but Homer is by no means easy to read. Every ninth line contains a word that never appears again in Homer, or in many cases in the whole range of Greek literature. There are all kinds of unparalleled forms, driven by the unusually complex meter. The illusion that Homer is easy to read comes from the fact that there are many phrases and whole lines that are repeated again and again, but he is nonetheless not easy to read.

He composes in a complex meter called *dactylic hexameter*. Dactylic hexameter consists of six strong beats, each followed by either another strong beat or two weak beats, and it looks like this in a standard scheme:

"Dactylic" comes from the Greek *daktylos*, meaning finger, because it has a long joint and two short joints. "Hexameter" means that there are six of these fingerlike units per line. But the last unit is always strong-strong (——), probably because the poet feels the end of the line.

Because Greek is naturally iambic—a short beat followed by a long—it is not clear how dactylic hexameter verse can have come into being in Greek. Once the meter was thought to be adopted from a preGreek language, but this now appears uncertain. In any event, the complicated demands of dactylic hexameter, which go against the natural rhythm of Greek, seem to account for many of the puzzling and unprecedented grammatical forms found in Homer. This analysis of the Homeric meter depends wholly, however, on a written text. As an oral poet—someone who created his song without the aid of writing—Homer himself would not have been conscious of the meter, except as a feeling. (For the whole issue of oral poetry—what it was and how it worked—see below.)

You can never be free with the meaning of the Greek, as Lawrence says, because Homer casts a spell over you, compelling obedience. He beats you down. It is all very odd.

WHO WAS HOMER?

Absolutely nothing is known about the historical Homer, but he certainly existed. He composed the *Iliad* and the *Odyssey* and maybe other poems. His name looks like it means "hostage," and all sorts of fantastic biographical details have been wrapped around this etymology, and other etymologies, too. In fact, we are not sure what the name *Homeros* means. Presumably it was the poet's name. Otherwise, why was it attached to his poems?

By "Homer" in this book I mean the composer of the *Iliad* and the *Odyssey*, the oldest poems in alphabetic writing in the world. In the ancient world, poems other than the *Iliad* and the *Odyssey* were attributed to Homer, including a lost *Thebaïd* on the war at seven-gated Thebes. A group of lost poems, some anonymous, built around the saga of the Trojan War, were called the Cyclic Poems, because they were thought to be told in a circle (*kuklos*) around the *Iliad* and the *Odyssey*. We have summaries of their content. The Cyclic Poems explained what happened before and after the Trojan War and appear to have been composed later than the *Iliad* and the *Odyssey*. They were short, widely circulated and performed, and inspired the majority of illustrations with Trojan themes that appear on Greek pots from the seventh to the fourth centuries BC, some of which are included in this book. Such illustrations are one way we have of reconstructing what those lost poems said. It must be that the *Iliad* and *Odyssey* were too massive and too rarely performed *in toto*, as compared with the very much shorter poems of the cycle, which found a far wider circulation.

Other poems in a similar style were also attributed to Homer. A collection dedicated to the gods called the *Homeric Hymns* has survived, but except for the hymn to Aphrodite, which could be Homer's work, they appear to have been composed mostly later, and we do not know who the poets were. The *Iliad* and the *Odyssey* survived in their entirety, despite their inordinate length, because they were the oldest poems in the Greek alphabet, and they were the best poems—as everybody knew.

Many places claimed to be Homer's birthplace, but the Aegean islands of CHIOS and Ios and the nearby settlement of SMYRNA on what is today the west coast of

Turkey were especially popular candidates (*see* MAP I: places found on any of the maps will be indicated by SMALL CAPS the first time the name appears in a Book). Old hand-books say that he was an Ionian poet—that he lived in IONIA on the coast of central Asia Minor (in modern Turkey). The main reason for thinking this is that his language is mostly in the Ionic dialect, a form of speech spoken in Ionia, in the central Aegean islands (the CYCLADES), and on EUBOEA, the long island off the east coast of Greece.

But there are many forms in Homeric language that come from another dialect, called Aeolic, spoken north of Ionia in Asia Minor (including Smyrna), on the island of LESBOS, and on the mainland in THESSALY. Evidently the tradition of poetry that Homer inherited came through Thessaly, the homeland of Achilles, and was passed down into Euboea, where Ionic was spoken. Several features of Homeric language tie it to the West Ionic branch of the dialect, spoken on Euboea, rather than to its East Ionic branch, spoken on the coast of Asia Minor. From dialect alone the island of Euboea is the most likely location of Homer's creative activity, wherever he was born, and there are other strong reasons for placing Homer on Euboea, where his poems were probably written down.

Homer, however, was certainly familiar with Asia Minor, and even with the site of Troy. For example, he knows that you can see the peak of SAMOTHRACE over the island of IMBROS from the Troad, the area around Troy. In similes he shows a familiar-ity with Mount Mykalê on the west coast of Asia Minor, with the KAYSTRIOS RIVER that flows near EPHESUS, and with the central Cycladic island of DELOS (MAP I). Homer's geographical knowledge is wide. He knows about the northern Aegean, including the islands of Imbros, Samothrace, LESBOS, and TENEDOS, and he speaks about the HELLESPONT (or Dardanelles) and inland PHRYGIA, and regions south to LYDIA and far south to LYCIA, and even to SIDON in PHOENICIA (in modern Lebanon). He also knows about CYPRUS, CRETE, and EGYPT (MAPS I, III). In the *Odyssey* he seems to have firsthand knowledge of ITHACA and the surrounding islands and mainland THESPROTIA, and ELIS, and Nestor's kingdom of PYLOS (MAP IV).

Homer knows about all these places. He seems to have lived at the time of aggres-sive Greek sea travel out of the settlements of CHALCIS and ERETRIA on the island of Euboea in the eighth century BC. Chalcis and Eretria lay across a plain and fought the earliest *historical* war in Greece, in which many overseas communities were in-volved, even as in the *Iliad*. The Euboean port was at AULIS, located on the mainland across the very narrow EURIPOS strait. The Achaean expedition to Troy was launched from Aulis, according to Homer, not a logical port for a story in which the Greek commanders come from the plain of ARGOS far to the south in the PELOPONNESUS, but logical for a Euboean audience.

In the early eighth century BC, the Chalcidians and Eretrians were the wealthiest and most adventurous of all the Greeks. They began the tradition of Greek coloniza-tion (although other cities were involved), sailing to CHALCIDICE in northeast Greece (named after Chalcis; MAP I), evidently to an emporium at a place called AL MINA at the mouth of the ORONTES RIVER in northern SYRIA (MAP III), where their ceramics are found, and local inhabitants used West Semitic (that is, Phoeni-cian) writing, and in the other direction to far-off ITALY. There, on the island of

ISCHIA in the bay of Naples, then called PITHEKOUSSAI ("monkey island"), Greeks were involved in a multiethnic trading enclave c. 800–775 BC, from which the earliest Greek colony at CUMAE on the mainland across the bay was founded, apparently named after a settlement on the east coast of Euboea (MAP II). The natural audience for the *Odyssey*, which describes dangerous sea travel in the Far West, were Euboeans who had actually made that journey, evidently in search of iron and copper ores. "Chalcis" means copper or bronze; "Eretria" means city of rowers.

Around 800 BC, or slightly before, someone invented the alphabet on the basis of the preexisting Semitic syllabary—a writing system whose symbols indicate only whole syllables (discussed later). This invention seems to have taken place on Euboea, probably in Eretria, where Semitic speakers were living side by side with Greeks. There we have found a mixture of inscriptions in West Semitic, on the one hand, and in the oldest alphabetic writing in Greece, on the other, dated c. 775–750 BC. Other very early fragmentary inscriptions come from a nearby site called Lefkandi, which may have been an earlier settlement of the Eretrians. These very short inscriptions consist of only a few letters. Recently inscriptions from the late eighth century BC, some metrical, have been found at Methonê in MACEDONIA, an Eretrian outpost. From Ischia in Italy, from about the same time, we also find Semitic writing mixed with Greek, and c. 740 BC one of the earliest Greek alphabetic inscriptions of more than a few words, including two perfect hexameters and an apparent reference to the cup of Nestor in Book 11 of the *Iliad*. Among the earliest surviving alphabetic writing in the Greek world is a literary reference.

Here is the puzzle of the Homeric poems: You cannot have Homer without the alphabet, but in Homer's world there is no writing. He does refer to writing once, but seems not to understand what it is.

THE TEXT OF HOMER

Investigation into the origin of the text of Homer constitutes the famous "Homeric Question" (from the Latin *quaestio*, "investigation"), a central topic in the humanities for over two hundred years. When did these two very long and complex texts come into being? Where and why? How and by whom? What did the original texts look like?

The Homeric poems are improbably long: the *Iliad* around sixteen thousand lines and the *Odyssey* around twelve thousand. The *Odyssey* takes place later than the *Iliad* and shows an intimate familiarity with events in the *Iliad*: No stories told in the *Iliad* are repeated in the *Odyssey*, but several events foretold in the *Iliad* are described in the *Odyssey*, for example, the death of Achilles. The poet seems to be finishing stories in the *Odyssey* that he began in the *Iliad*. Perhaps the only element of Homeric criticism that all scholars agree on is that the *Odyssey* came after the *Iliad*. From a time during which there was no reading public, it is impossible that any poet could have been so familiar with the *Iliad* unless he were himself its composer. Both poems are by the same man—Homer—as tradition has always maintained.

In spite of much speculation, no one has been able to offer a persuasive model for the circumstances of the performance of the complete *Iliad* and the *Odyssey*, although portions of the poems were presented at the Panathenaia in Athens in the sixth century BC, nearly two hundred years after their composition. In the seventh and sixth centuries BC, the heyday of Greek lyric poetry, written texts were prompt books for memorized reperformance. They were studied in the schools but never "read" for pleasure, as we read Homer today. This is also true of the poet Pindar from the early fifth century BC. He sold written copies of his poems, some of which survive, to clients around the Mediterranean, who performed them to the accompaniment of song and dance. Herodotus and Thucydides from the mid-fifth century BC still produced works to be listened to as someone read them aloud, as far we can tell. If Homer belonged to the eighth century BC—he was always said to be Greece's oldest poet—his poems, or parts of them, could have been memorized for reperformance, but we must admit that we have no idea what these poems were for or what purpose they originally served. They appear as if from nowhere, wrapped in mystery.

THE ALEXANDRIAN VULGATE

Homer has been the object of curiosity and study since the sixth century BC, when a Greek living in southern Italy named Theagenes (whose works are lost) is reported to have explained the battles of the gods in the *Iliad* as allegories for natural phenomena. It was not until the third and second centuries BC in Alexandria, Egypt, that the first real inquiry arose regarding the Homeric texts. There, in the Mouseion, the "temple to the Muses," librarians tried to establish an official text from the many variant versions. Our text goes back to this "official" Alexandrian text and is, practically speaking, identical with it.

It is a remarkable situation. The Ptolemies, Macedonian descendants of a general of Alexander the Great (356–323 BC), ruled Egypt as a personal possession. They were rich beyond dreaming. To prove the cultural superiority of the Greeks over the subjugated Egyptians, with the Egyptians' exaggerated claims to cultural achievement, the Ptolemies funded, on foreign soil, the world's first comprehensive library of alphabetic texts. Using their power and prestige, the Ptolemaic librarians bought and otherwise obtained texts of all the famous poets of the past, including Homer. They seem to have amassed around 500,000 texts.

The Ptolemies obtained Homeric texts from various cities, from Marseilles in France to Sinopê on the southern shore of the BLACK SEA, the so called "city texts," and also from individuals. A third textual tradition is called the "common" (*koinê*) text, perhaps a generic text in common circulation, but we are not really sure. We do not know what these groups of texts were like, only that they existed

Homer is strongly represented in Egyptian papyrus finds that come from this time (third to first centuries BC), although there are many more fragments from the *Iliad* than from the *Odyssey*. (Many of these papyri were once used to mummify crocodiles!) Many fragments seem to be from school editions. They sometimes vary from the standard modern text in having different forms of words and alternate phrasings and sometimes extra or "wild" lines. The wild lines almost invariably repeat other lines or are made up from other lines. They never add to the narrative.

The origin of the wild lines seems to be scribal in nature: A scribe copying the text inadvertently adds lines or repeats other lines that he knows.

The Alexandrian scholars Zenodotus of Ephesus (active c. 280 BC), Aristophanes of Byzantium (c. 257–c. 180 BC), and especially Aristarchos of Samothrace (active c. 220–240 BC) somehow established a "clean text" that did not have the wild lines. The wild lines disappear from the papyrus fragments around 150 BC. From this time on, there is a fixed number of lines to the poems.

This "clean text" that the Alexandrians prepared we call the *vulgate*, the basis for all medieval and modern texts. We do not possess it directly, but we infer it. There is no extra-Alexandrian textual tradition for the Homeric poems. There is reason to think, on the basis of the way some words are spelled in the Athenian style, that the "clean text" was based on a text retrieved from Athens. This might also accord with the tradition that something was done to the text of Homer in Athens in the sixth century BC (discussed later).

Perhaps the librarians at Alexandria exerted so much influence and prestige that after their editorial work copyists brought the book industry into line with the scholarly exemplars, but it is not at all clear how work in the library governed the book trade. Still, there must have been some connection.

In addition to throwing out the wild lines, the Alexandrian librarians went on to question many other lines in Homer, placing a mark beside a line when they thought it suspicious, the origin of our word *athetesis*. So began the venerable tradition of wondering about the real meaning of many words in Homer and whether this or that line was "genuine." But though the Alexandrians marked lines as being suspicious, they seem never to have prepared a text that actually omitted such lines.

We might contrast the situation of Homer's text with that of the very long epic, the Sanskrit *Mahabharata*, the "great story of the Bharata dynasty," the longest epic poem in the world. It contains over ninety thousand verses, long passages in prose, and 1.8 million words. According to tradition, it was composed by one Vyasa, who supposedly also composed various sacred texts. We cannot date Vyasa accurately, although he may belong to the time when writing was introduced into India, about 600 BC. He was presumably a man who had something to do with fixing the Hindu epic poem in writing, but the *Mahabharata* contains demonstrably much later material and in fact exists in many versions. The poem did not settle down into something like its modern form until AD 400, one thousand years after Vyasa.

The *Iliad* and the *Odyssey*, unlike the *Mahabharata*, exist in single versions, not in many. Early papyri of Homer, and early quotations and misquotations, do not represent different versions of the poems. There is a single text undergoing occasional corruption in the usual manner.

BEFORE AND AFTER THE VULGATE

Unfortunately, we know almost nothing about the condition of the text of Homer's poems from the time of their composition, c. 800 BC, to the Alexandrian "clean text" of c. 150 BC. What went before the Alexandrian vulgate?

Evidence from Greek art, mostly paintings on pots, suggests that the *Iliad* and the *Odyssey* were widespread in the Greek world beginning c. 675 BC. We cannot, however, always be sure whether such illustrations depend on literary exemplars or on lost oral songs. In any event, it is clear that Homer had become a cultural yardstick by the late sixth and early fifth centuries BC, especially in the city of Athens, where most of our information comes from. From the fourth century, Plato (424–348 BC), Aristotle (384–322 BC), and other authors quote Homer frequently, but they are careless in their quotations, and their text often differs from ours. It is not clear that such writers are looking at a manuscript of Homer; the quotations are not really evidence for the text of Homer at this time. More likely, such writers are quoting from memory. Greek education consisted of memorizing passages of Homer and other poets. Every literate Greek had Homer somewhere in his head.

We cannot penetrate beyond the veil of the stabilization of the text by the Alexandrian scholars. Their text of Homer is our text; what seemed right to them is what we have. The original text of Homer cannot be recovered. It existed, but it cannot be found.

In the fifth century AD, knowledge of Greek disappeared from Western Europe and did not return until Italian bibliophiles brought Greek manuscripts from Constantinople in the fourteenth and fifteenth centuries. The learned Dante Alighieri (AD 1265–1321) knew about Homer and the Trojan War, but he knew no Greek. While we do not have the edited text of the Alexandrian scholar Aristarchos of Samothrace (third century BC), the oldest surviving complete text of the *Iliad* incorporates many marginal commentaries from his writings, called *scholia*. This text is now kept in Venice and is called *Venetus A*, which seems to have appeared in Italy sometime in the fifteenth century. It is a large, beautiful, and extremely expensive vellum (calf's hide) manuscript written in the tenth century AD in Constantinople. The manuscript also has a summary of the lost poems of the so-called Cyclic Poems. A complete manuscript of the *Odyssey*, nearly as old, comes from the tenth or eleventh centuries AD. It is held in Florence and is called the *Laurentianus*, but it has no scholia, though later manuscripts to the *Odyssey* do contain some scholia. Although the learned Demetrius Chalcondyles (AD 1423–1511), a leading light in Renaissance humanism, brought out printed editions for both the *Iliad* and *Odyssey* in Florence around AD 1488, *Venetus A* and its scholia were forgotten until 1788, when a French scholar, Jean-Baptiste Villoison, published an edition of the text and the previously unknown scholia. Villoison's publication of *Venetus A* began the modern era in Homeric scholarship.

The scholia in *Venetus A* seemed to prove that the Alexandrians had created our modern text, but, still, what was the ultimate origin of this text?

THE HOMERIC QUESTION

Before Villoison's publication of *Venetus A*, the universal assumption by scholars was that Homer had created his poems in a fashion similar to Vergil and Dante and Chaucer, all direct heirs to the technological revolution of the invention of the Greek alphabet, about which early scholars knew absolutely nothing. Homer had taken a pen to paper and composed his poetry, just as had Vergil, Dante, and Chaucer.

After the publication of *Venetus A*, a German scholar, Friedrich August Wolf (AD 1759–1824), revolutionized Homeric studies in his famous *Prolegomena ad Homerum* of 1795. Wolf was the creator of the modern science of "classical philology," the careful study of language to reveal the truth about the classical past. He presented drastic evidence about the poems that shocked his contemporaries and directly contradicted Aristarchos' conviction that the poems had a unity and a unified origin.

Wolf noticed that nowhere in Homer is there any reference to writing, except in the story of the hero Bellerophon's exile in *Iliad* Book 6, when Bellerophon carries tablets bearing "ruinous signs" (*sêmata lugra*) to his host in Lycia (namely, "kill the bearer"). But in later Greek, "writing" is never referred to as "signs" (*sêmata*). Evidently, Homer is reporting a story that contained a detail he did not understand.

Homer must have come from a time when there was no writing in Greece, Wolf argued, otherwise he would in some place have mentioned it. In fact, there are several passages that cry out for the use of writing, if Homer knew about it. Because it is quite impossible to memorize twenty-eight thousand lines of poetry, what appears to be the unity of the *Iliad* and the *Odyssey* is in reality a compilation of short, oral songs capable of being memorized, Wolf thought.

There were reports in various ancient writings that the Athenian tyrant Peisistratos (d. 527 BC) or his son Hipparchos (d. 514 BC) had brought "the Homeric epics" to Athens and ordered the rhapsodes, in their performances at the Panathenaic Festival, "to go through them in order," each taking up where the last left off. The implication is that the various episodes were accustomed to be performed out of sequence. It must have been at this time, in Athens, that the *Iliad* and the *Odyssey* were created by unknown editors from earlier, separate, short, orally preserved songs capable of memorization, Wolf thought. The poems had been "stitched together" (based on a popular but inaccurate understanding of rhapsode as meaning "song-stitcher"). This hypothetical event came to be known in Homeric scholarship, after Wolf, as the "Peisistratean Recension."

Wolf formalized the point of view, already old, that the Homeric texts must be anonymous compilations. This view is known in Homeric criticism as *Analysis*: the theory that the poems were created by different poets at different times. The theory was modeled on contemporary eighteenth-century biblical criticism, which had discovered different layers to the certainly edited first five books of the Bible (Pentateuch).

Analysis was predominant in the nineteenth century, especially in Germany, and well into the twentieth century, and it is still embraced by some scholars. For generations, scholars subdivided the poems, and even the lines, into this or that layer, ignoring or ignorant of the material conditions that would make such editorial activity improbable. There were no desks in Homer's world, or studies or libraries or a reading public. There was no scribal class dedicated to protecting a religious vision, nor record of the people, nor a bureaucratic state. If there was so much editorial interference going on, we would expect more than a single version of the *Iliad* and the *Odyssey*, as we get with the Indian *Mahabharata*. But all evidence testifies to a single version.

Analysis was opposed by the minority *Unitarian* view, which held that the poems were the creation of a single intelligence at a single time. Whereas the Analysts made use of narrative and logical inconsistencies (of which there are a good number) to establish the lines of demarcation between allegedly originally discrete poems, the Unitarian position looked past such flaws in a theory of unitary composition, although accretions and alterations were probable. Everything about the poems betrays careful design, they argued—not always the design that will pass a modern scholar's muster, but an intelligent design all the same. One never forgets when reading Homer that a single personality stands behind the plan of the plot and its arresting expression.

The Unitarians also complained that if the poems are made up of separate parts, or if they began as a core that was expanded, then why is there no agreement on where the divisions lie between the originally separate songs? And if someone makes up extra lines, or changes words, how do such additions and changes enter the textual tradition? Someone bent on interpolation must recopy the entire poem, or the portion he is altering, and then that copy must somehow become the canonical version, the one that everybody else copies, in direct ancestry to the text that the Alexandrians inherited, the vulgate.

No doubt the poems suffered various distortions in their transition between an archaic orthography to a modern one, but to copy the complete *Iliad* and *Odyssey* is no mean feat, requiring many months of sustained daily labor. It is extraordinary that after two hundred years of argument, not one single line of Homer's poems the *Iliad* and the *Odyssey* can be *proven* to be an addition to the original text (which, in any event, cannot be reconstructed).

The Unitarians tended to be poets, such as Goethe and Schiller, while the Analysts tended to be scholars. The Analyst position held all the prestige in this argument.

THE ORAL-FORMULAIC THEORY

Throughout the debate, no attention was paid to how a written text comes into being or to the nature of the writing system that made the Homeric poems possible. With dismaying naiveté, scholars assumed that Homer was like the professors themselves, toiling away in a dim light, crossing out words, improving the expression, adding favorite lines and incidents. Somehow, poems once oral became written poems, for unclear reasons; these were then manipulated further, for unclear reasons.

MILMAN PARRY AND ALBERT B. LORD

This discussion was turned on its head by the writings of a young American scholar, Milman Parry (1902–1935), who studied the creation of oral poetry in Bosnia-Herzegovina in the early 1930s. Milman Parry was born in Oakland, California, and studied classics at the nearby University of California in Berkeley, where he earned a BA and an MA.

Parry became interested in the Homeric Question as an undergraduate. How did these poems really come into being? What does the trail look like that extends backward from the *Venetus A Iliad* or the *Laurentianus Odyssey* to a manuscript that touched the poet's hand? Parry's remarkable discoveries were to revolutionize Homeric studies, as well as the study of many other literatures.

When Parry began his work, the prevailing view was the Analyst position: that the poems were the result of a long period of accretion and editorial redaction. In early academic studies Parry showed how the formulaic style, which all commentators on Homer had noticed, was simply not compatible with the theory that Homer's poetry had been created in writing. Parry was interested in such noun-epithet combinations as "Achilles the fast runner" and "wine-dark sea" and "resourceful Odysseus" that are so striking to a reader. An epithet is a descriptive term accompanying a noun. Epithets occur again and again and with little respect to the context. For example, Achilles is described by the epithet "fast runner" even when he is sitting down.

In meticulous fashion, Parry showed how the epithets vary not in accordance with the demands of the narrative but *in accordance with the position of the name in the metrical line*. So different epithets are attached to the same name in accordance with where in the metrical line the name appears, at the beginning, middle, or end.

Not only does the system show *extension*, in which there are different epithets for many characters for different positions in the line, but it shows *thrift*, because usually there is but a single epithet for a single position in the line. Such stylistic features are impossible, and in fact are unknown, in poems created in writing. Hence Homer's poetry was created without the use of writing.

In 1924, Parry traveled to Paris and enrolled at the Sorbonne, where he studied under the great linguist Antoine Meillet (1866–1936). In 1923, Meillet had written the following (quoted in Parry's first French thesis, 1925):

> Homeric epic is entirely composed of formulas handed down from poet to poet. An examination of any passage will quickly reveal that it is made up of lines and fragments of lines which are reproduced word for word in one or several other passages. Even those lines of which the parts happen not to recur in any other passage have the same formulaic character, and it is doubtless pure chance that they are not attested elsewhere.

Meillet thought that such features might be distinctive of orally transmitted epic in general and suggested to Parry that he observe a living oral tradition. In 1933–1935, Parry traveled with his assistant Albert B. Lord (1912–1991) to Bosnia-Herzegovina. There Parry made original studies of many illiterate, mostly Muslim, singers who spoke Serbo-Croatian, a southwest Slavic dialect.

Parry made many recordings on primitive recording equipment, and he took down poems by dictation, several as long as the *Odyssey*. His and Lord's collection of oral documents is at this time still the largest ever made in the field. Parry discovered that although his informants claimed that they could reproduce a song word for word at different times, in fact their songs were always different. There was no fixed text, because of course a fixed text depends on a written version.

Until the fieldwork of Parry and Lord, the theory of the oral origins of the Homeric texts had depended on Parry's rigorous analysis of the language of the text, but the theory was supported by Parry and Lord's unprecedented experiments in the contemporary world. Parry argued that Homer, like the Serbo-Croatian poets, composed orally by means of "formulas" instead of "words." Parry defined a formula as "a group of words that is regularly employed under the same metrical conditions to express a given essential idea."

For example, such phrases as "dawn with her rosy fingers" or "wine-dark sea" occupied a certain position in the metrical line and enabled the singer (in Greek, *aoidos*) to compose rapidly. Because of formulaic thrift—one formula with a certain metrical pattern occupying a certain place in the line—such a system could not be the creation of one man. It must depend on a *tradition* (from Latin "hand over") to which the singer had access. An oral tradition is a system of transmission of cultural material from generation to generation through vocal utterance without the assistance of writing, in this case of stories about heroes. Of course the formulas in oral traditional speech did allow internal substitutions and adaptations in response to narrative and grammatical needs, and eventually Parry fixed on the notion of a "formulaic system" that contained both constant and variable elements.

The purpose of such a system of ready-made diction was to enable composition in performance so that the traditional features of Homer's language became proof of its oral origins: *Such poems are not memorized, but created anew in performance from traditional material and diction every time the songs are sung.* Parry's thesis seemed to explain the highly unusual "artificial language" (German *Kunstsprache*) in which Homer composed, the so-called "epic dialect" that no Greek ever spoke. Basically, the dialect is Ionic (spoken on the central west coast of Asia Minor, on the islands, and on the island of Euboea), but as we have seen, it incorporates features from other dialects (especially Aeolic). Parry thought this epic language must have emerged over a long period of time through exposure to various dialectal forms that proved useful in the construction of the poetic line. Such features could only have come into being through generations as a collective inheritance of many singers.

Parry died before he could systematically compare the technique of South Slavic poetry with Homer's. His work attracted little attention until the publication in 1960 of *The Singer of Tales* by his assistant Albert B. Lord, the most influential work of literary criticism of the twentieth century. Lord summarized his teacher's discoveries, made original contributions of his own, and examined other non-Greek poems to discover their oral features. Lord also wrote about the singer's apprenticeship. He described the study of an aspiring illiterate singer as a young boy under an illiterate master up until the time of the apprentice's mastery of the craft. Lord went on to describe other features of oral-traditional style, for example, the story patterns that governed whole epics and the building blocks of individual epics, the *type scenes.*

Type-scenes are blocks of words in which typical events are arranged in the same order and often with the same words. Typical type-scenes in Homer include *Arming, Battle, Travel, Speeches, Sleeping, Dreams, Divine Visitation, Conference, Assembly, Supplication, Dressing, Oath-Taking, Bathing*, and *Seduction*—and there are others.

For example, in an arming scene, the warrior first puts on his shin guards and breastplate, then he takes up his sword, shield, helmet, and spear, always in that order. When somebody arrives for a feast there is always a seating of the guest, a servant brings water for washing, a table is placed before the guest, a servant provides bread and other foods, and a carver hands around meat and gold cups. Then:

> They put forth their hands to the good things set ready before them.
> But when they had cast off all desire for drink and food . . .

All such type scenes can be fleshed out or compressed in accordance with the dramatic requirements of the narrative. They are common in the South Slavic epic that Parry studied, as well as the theme of "Withdrawal and Return" that determines the overall story of the *Iliad*, a theme also attested in the traditions of medieval England, Russia, Albania, Bulgaria, Turkey, and Central Asia.

THE ORAL STYLE

The theory of oral composition was used to explain the various narrative inconsistencies of which Analysts had made so much, for the dictating poet has no way to go back and correct "errors," nor any interest in doing so. After all, there was no written text to check up on, and who cared anyway? Inconsistencies, repetition, and formulas or formulaic phrases were sure signs of the oral style.

Oral composition also explained the use of such out-of-context epithets as "blameless Aigisthos" to describe the murderer of Agamemnon, or "Achilles the fast runner" while he sits calmly in his chair. It also could explain the inordinate length of the Homeric poems, because when an oral poet dictates his text released from the exigencies of a live performance, free to elaborate his tale at will, the songs can become very long. The *Iliad* and the *Odyssey* are far longer than ordinary oral poems and were probably never performed as we have them. When Parry took down texts by dictation, the process gave the informant time to think, to expand, to add, just as we find in the *Iliad* and the *Odyssey*.

The thrust of the Parry–Lord school is that Homer was like the Serbo–Croatian singers. He was illiterate. He composed the *Iliad* and the *Odyssey* at some early time, and his words were taken down by somebody who understood how to write down Greek. The Parry-Lord model has become orthodoxy in a modern understanding of the genesis of Homer's poems.

Oral Theory was initially criticized because it appeared to make the fount and origin of Western culture a slave to a mechanical system. Where was there room for the genius of poetic invention if the lines were made up of preset expressions and preset events? The contribution of individual creativity appeared to be submerged in a collective poetic tradition. However, the units of expression that Parry and Lord identified in oral verse are no more restrictive to expression than is the large but finite store of "words" (conventionally understood) in literate traditions. The oral-formulaic language is just that: a language, subject to the morphological and grammatical restrictions of any language, which in this case happens to include metrical expression.

This is why scholars working after Parry were unable to define clearly what was meant by a "formula." Noun-epithet formulas were easy to find, but other formulaic expressions slipped away as one tried to pin them down. That could have been the only outcome, just as the attempt to define a conventional "word" has proved impossible. Language is a flexible medium depending on invisible templates that generate the form on the surface. Language is not mechanical but a human faculty whose origins and functioning are poorly understood.

We think of poems as being made up of words, but linguists cannot define a "word" except as something found in dictionaries. The concept "word" is a product of literacy. For the illiterate singers of Bosnia-Herzegovina, a "word" is a unit of meaning, not a typographical convention that depends on the technology of writing. Further questioning of the Serbo-Croatian bards revealed that by "word" the singer could mean several lines, a scene, or even a whole poem. Any spectrograph reveals that speech is a continuous *stream* of sound, with peaks and valleys, a wave, not a sequence of separable sounds. So Homer's song was a continuous stream of sound, roughly reconstructible from a system of written symbols that crudely encoded aspects of this sound.

What Parry/Lord did not explain is *how* a dictated oral song became a text, a stream of symbols on a piece of papyrus.

HOMER AND THE ALPHABET

The eastern coast of the Mediterranean—modern Lebanon and northern Syria—was a mosaic of coastal city-states like Tyre and Sidon (map III), whose inhabitants spoke a West Semitic dialect belonging to the same language family as Hebrew and Arabic. They traded with the Euboean Greeks in the late ninth and eighth centuries BC, in Syria at Al Mina, on the Greek mainland, and in Ischia in Italy, and no doubt in such other places as southern Spain, Sardinia, and north Africa and with other groups, like the peoples of Etruria.

The western Semites used a writing often called the "Phoenician alphabet," but these Semites did not call themselves Phoenicians, nor was their writing alphabetic. It was a sort of syllabary of around twenty-two signs, each of which represented a consonant, with an implied vowel to be supplied by the speaker. No doubt some western Semitic speakers intermarried with the illiterate Greeks, and their children were bilingual speakers of Greek and Semitic dialects. In Ionia, the founder of Greek philosophy Thales (seventh–sixth centuries BC) was said to be the child of an Examyes and Kleoboulinê, both Phoenician nobles.

The western Semites had a tradition of taking down texts by dictation, which may explain why all the elements in their system of writing are phonetic—that is, every sign has a sound attached to it. This is by no means true of the earlier Egyptian and Mesopotamian cuneiform systems, which contained many nonphonetic elements. There is a clear example of creating a poetic text by means of dictation in a note attached to a poem on Baal, written c. 1400 BC in the earliest attested use of West Semitic writing in the emporium of Ugarit (in so-called Ugaritic cuneiform, not in West Semitic script), on the coast in North Syria (MAP III). The appended note remarks on the names of the priest who dictated the text and the scribe who took it down.

Evidently somebody—his name may have been Palamedes, according to Greek tradition—knew the West Semitic writing and was heir to the tradition of taking down a poetic text by dictation. If for unknown reasons he tried to do this with an extremely famous poet named Homer, he soon discovered that West Semitic syllabic writing was unable to preserve the rhythm of the Greek in which the poetry resided (Semitic poetry works on different principles). If you applied the West Semitic system to write down the first line of the *Iliad* and separated the words by dots as the Phoenicians did, in Roman characters it would look something like this:

MNN·D·T·PLD·KLS

for the Greek alphabetic:

MENIN AEIDE THEA PELEIADEO AKHILEOS

You cannot pronounce a text written in West Semitic writing unless you are a native speaker because the sound of the spoken word is never given by the signs—only *hints* about its sound. West Semitic writing could not, and did not, encode Homer's poetry, which was so rich in vowel sounds and subtle rhythms.

It was the meter's dependence on the alternation of vocalic qualities that gave the Adapter, our Palamedes, his idea. He redesigned the West Semitic system into a system consisting of two different kinds of signs: one group pronounceable, the five vowels signs; and one group unpronounceable, what we call consonants. The inventor added the inviolable spelling rule *that a sign from the long unpronounceable group must always be accompanied, before or after, by a sign from the short pronounceable group.* Only in this way do you get a pronounceable syllable, though not one accurately reflecting what we think of as "long" and "short" syllables, which the vowels signs did not distinguish. The Adapter also added three new signs to the series of unpronounceable signs: F, X, and C.

The Adapter's spelling rule revolutionized human culture. It is the writing that we use today every day of our lives, but its initial purpose seems to have been to make possible a written record of poetic song. To judge from very early and unexpected inscriptional finds in hexametric verse on baked clay and stone, the Greek alphabet was from the beginning used for just this purpose, to notate the rhythms of the Greek hexameter.

We must be talking about the poems of Homer, for otherwise it is hard to explain the coincidence of the sudden appearance of a writing that encoded the approximate sound of the voice, capable of encoding dactylic hexameter, with the sudden appearance of a poetry that depended on just those sounds. As F. A. Wolf noticed in 1795, alphabetic writing is not referred to a single time in Homer, who composed verse that delights in the description of everyday life. This is because Homer lived at a time when alphabetic writing was unknown or known only to a few. Apparently the few who possessed alphabetic technology in the eighth century BC were applying its power to record the songs of oral poets, called *aoidoi* in Greek (related to our word "ode"). Hesiod, very close in time to Homer and also an oral poet, seems to have been the second singer whose songs were recorded: the *Theogony* and the *Works and Days* and, a poem that exists in fragments, *The Catalog of Women*. It only occurred to someone, perhaps in the seventh century BC, that one can create poetry from scratch *in writing* by using this same technology.

Homer comes like a shot out of the blue, at a time when most of Greece was an impoverished backwater. Instead of temples and pyramids, the decorated pot was their greatest cultural contribution. There was no state, no scribal class. Suddenly there are 28,000 lines of complicated verse inscribed on expensive papyri—more, in fact, when one counts the poetry of the near contemporary Hesiod and the Cyclic Poems that soon followed.

The invention of the Greek alphabet c. 800 BC was the third most important invention in the long history of the human species, after the discovery of fire in the primordial past and the invention of writing itself c. 3400 BC in Mesopotamia. The Greek alphabet was the first writing that could be pronounced by a nonnative speaker. It is a technology that allows the recreation of a rough phonic equivalent of speech, even if one does not know the language. The Greek alphabet was the first system of writing capable of preserving Homer, and it seems to have been designed for this very purpose. Attempts to place Homer later than the early eighth century on the basis of archaeological data are inconclusive; on balance, we must place Homer at the time of the alphabet's invention in the early eighth or late ninth century.

It is wrongheaded to be concerned with the elegance or crudeness of expression, as many commentators are, when to the composer and those who heard him sing it is all a continuum of rhythmical sound. The poet must carry his listeners along on the path of song, and nothing else matters. Palamedes' epoch-making invention transformed Homer's poems from an oral version to a cold, roughly phonetic abstraction. Gesture, intonation, and musical accompaniment, so essential to oral song, are lost. They are not part of the alphabet. So we should not imagine that we "have the poems of Homer": We have a symbolic representation of some of the phonetic aspects of the speech of Homer.

WHY HOMER IS IMPORTANT

In circumstances almost unimaginable today, probably in Eretria on the island of Euboea, among the very wealthy Euboean international traders where alphabetic writing first appears archaeologically, we should suppose that two men, the poet and his scribe, worked together for many months to create the *Iliad* and the *Odyssey*. We must remember that after the recording of the poems, only one man in the world, the Adapter, could read them. Nothing is known directly about Homer because he lived in a time when there were no records of any kind: no libraries, no readers, no archives. There were only the Homeric poems and, later, the poems of Hesiod. They were the object of study for, at first, a tiny, then a rapidly growing literary and social elite, men who understood the rules of alphabetic writing well enough to memorize portions of these poems for representation as entertainment at the feast.

At first Euboeans were this elite, leaders in wealth and international trade. Early Greek inscriptions present a remarkable unprecedented use of writing. In the East, "literacy"—the ability to manipulate a system of symbols with partial ties to speech—is entirely in the hands of a scribal class, special men who have devoted their lives to the mastery of the symbolic system. The power and wealth of these scribal classes was very great, and they are not always separable from the ruling elites themselves.

In Greece, by contrast, "literacy" is in possession of amateurs without connection to the power structure of a state, which scarcely exists. These amateurs are interested in poetry and never in business. As far as we know, Greek alphabetic writing was never used for economic purposes of any kind until about 600 BC, two hundred years after its invention. It was used preeminently for poetic expression, to judge from the inscriptional finds.

But we should be surprised that Homer ever became *the* classic. His poems are much too long, and sometimes it is hard to retain the narrative thread in them. The expression is exaggerated, with wild and improbable similes, strong emotion directly expressed, and a seemingly inexhaustible taste for gore. Yet the *Iliad* and the *Odyssey* are by far the most studied of ancient texts, then as now. Only the intersection of the invention of the Greek alphabet, the technical means that made Homer's poems possible, and the greatness of Homer himself can explain this oddity.

From the beginning of alphabetic literacy—from the beginning of the Western world—the Homeric poems have been at the core of Western education. They, or portions of these poems, were the books that one read when learning to read in ancient Greece. Still today, every course in Western Civilization begins with the *Iliad* and the *Odyssey*. The invention of the Greek alphabet in order to record the poetry of Homer, and then Hesiod, is the single most important event in the history of the Western world. That is why Homer is important.

THE FIRST TEXT OF HOMER

Texts of the Homeric poems are easy to find, in print constantly since the first printed edition of Demetrios Chalcondyles in Florence in 1488. Because it is a material thing, a text has a certain appearance, not only the texture and color of the paper or leather, but also the conventions by which the signs are made. Early printed editions of the *Iliad* were set in typefaces made to imitate Byzantine manuscripts, with its many abbreviations and ligatures (in which more than one letter is combined into a single sign). No ancient Greek could have read such a text, nor can a modern scholar do so without special training, not even a professor who has spent an entire life reading and teaching Greek.

In the nineteenth century, modern typefaces and orthographic conventions replaced typographic conventions based on manuscripts handwritten in Byzantium before the invention of printing, but in no sense did such modern conventions attempt to recreate the actual appearance, or material nature, of an ancient text of Homer. For example, the forms of the Greek characters in T. W. Allen's standard Oxford Classical Text, first published in 1908 (the second edition with D. B. Monro, 1917–1920, is the basis for this translation), imitate the admirable but entirely modern Greek handwriting of Richard Porson (1759–1808), a Cambridge don important in early modern textual criticism. Complete with lower- and uppercase characters, accents, breathing marks, dieresis, punctuation, word division, and paragraph division, such Greek seems normal to anyone who studies Greek today. Here are the first few lines of the *Iliad* from the Oxford Classical Text:

> μῆνιν ἄειδε θεὰ Πηληϊάδεω Ἀχιλῆος
> οὐλομένην, ἣ μυρί᾽ Ἀχαιοῖς ἄλγε᾽ ἔθηκε,
> πολλὰς δ᾽ ἰφθίμους ψυχὰς Ἄϊδι προΐαψεν
> ἡρώων, αὐτοὺς δὲ ἑλώρια τεῦχε κύνεσσιν
> οἰωνοῖσί τε πᾶσι, Διὸς δ᾽ ἐτελείετο βουλή,
> ἐξ οὗ δὴ τὰ πρῶτα διαστήτην ἐρίσαντε
> Ἀτρεΐδης τε ἄναξ ἀνδρῶν καὶ δῖος Ἀχιλλεύς.
> *Iliad* 1.1–7

If you study Greek today and take a course in Homer, you will be expected to be able to translate such a version. You are reading "the poems of Homer." In fact, the orthography is a hodgepodge that never existed before the nineteenth century. A full accentual system, only sometimes bearing meaning, does not appear until around AD 1000 and is never used consistently. The distinction between upper- and lower case letters is a medieval invention. Porson's internal sigma is drawn [s], but in the classical period the sigma was a vertical zigzag S (hence our "S"), and after the Alexandrian period always a half-moon shape C (the "lunate sigma"); the shape s appears to be Porson's invention. The dieresis, two dots over a vowel to indicate that it is pronounced separately (e.g. προΐαψεν), is a convention of recent printing. Periods and commas are modern, as is word division, unknown in classical Greek.

The Oxford Classical Text would have mystified Thucydides or Plato. The much earlier first text of the first seven lines of Homer, if we take account of inscriptional evidence from the eighth and seventh centuries BC, seems to have looked something like this:

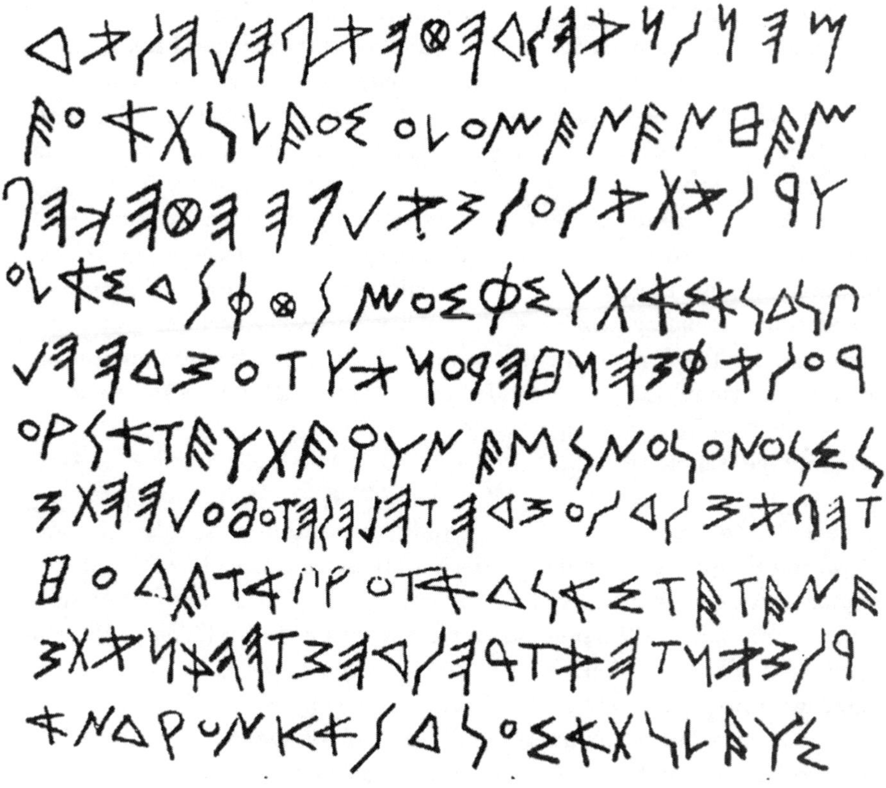

FIGURE 0.1   The first seven lines of the *Iliad*.   This reconstruction is based on what we know about the earliest Greek orthography.

In this earliest form of Greek alphabetic writing, there is no division of words (giving rise to many later false divisions) nor other diacritical devices, such as capitalization or periods, to indicate the function of a word in a sentence. In fact, there are no words, but a continuous stream of symbolic signs to match the continuous stream of sounds. There is no Homeric word for a discrete "word" (the Homeric *epea*, from which comes *epic*, means an utterance, as in "May I have a word with you?"). There are only five vowel signs, which do not indicate "length" (as the later *omega* "long o," was distinguished from *omicron*, "short o"). Doubled consonants are written as single consonants. The writing was mostly *boustrophedon*, "as the ox turns," that is, it went from right to left, then left to right, imitating both the plowing of a field and the endless road of song. There are no accents.

In reading such a text in an archaic alphabet, the exchange of meaning from the material object to the human mind takes place in a different way than when we read Homer in English or Greek today. The Greek reader of the eighth century BC decoded this writing by the *ear*, whereas we read by the eye. First the reader heard the sounds behind the signs, then he recognized what was being said. One thousand years after Homer the Greeks still did not divide their words.

When we read Greek (or English), by contrast, we are concerned with where one word begins and another ends, and how the word is spelled. The *appearance* of our texts carries meaning, as when a capital letter says "a sentence begins here" or a period says "a sentence ends here" or a space says "a word ends here." Our text is directly descended from an ancient Greek text, yes, but the alphabetic text works for us in a different way.

When modern editors attempt to recover an original text of Homer, they never mean that they are going to reconstruct a text that Homer might have recognized. Rather, they mean that they are going to present an interpretation of how an original text might be understood according to modern editorial bias. What appears to be orthography in a modern text, "the way something is written," is really an editorial comment on the meaning and syntax. If editors gave us Homer as Homer really was, no one could read it.

THE GRAPHIC REPRESENTATION OF ORAL SONG

Earlier criticism approached the text of Homer with little understanding that it is the dim mirror in alphabetic writing of a once continuous stream of sound with its own internal logic, with little respect for what we term the rules of grammar or the rules of metrics. The alphabetic representation of this stream of sound is only approximate because the relationship between systems of writing and speech are approximate. The song is like a stream, but the alphabetic signs are like a row of buckets.

We examine with intense interest the grammar and the style and the "words" of the Homeric text, but they prove surprisingly slippery. In the Greek of Homer, there are constantly grammatical constructions that make no sense, words of mysterious formation, and words whose meaning is never clear. To interpret the "language" of Homer is regularly to find reasons for exceptions to the rules—exceptions in scansion, construction, and meaning.

A tradition of textual exegesis that explains forms and usages and discusses alternatives is now over 2300 years old, but it is based on a misunderstanding of the relationship of the original text to the oral song that underlies it. The text is not the song, but a symbolic representation of phonetic aspects of the song. The many "rules of Homeric scansion" are a form of special pleading: In fact Homer only scans roughly, as with all oral poetry, and such "rules" only attempt to find regularities in a sea of flexibility.

In the very many grammatical and other irregularities of the Homeric vulgate, we glimpse behind the text the continuous stream of highly stylized sound that came from the poet's mouth. And we glimpse the many, many inaccuracies in the scribe's efforts to reduce the sound of the song to a phonetically symbolic representation. Thinking that Homer was like us, that he wrote down his big poems as Vergil wrote the *Aeneid*, laboring over every word and scene, earlier scholars were led into a labyrinth of false speculation. To Homer, the poem was a continuous stream of sound, with a rhythmical feeling behind the sound. He did not have time to think about refined effects.

For this reason it is easy to find passages in the poem that are "not very good," that do not follow the rules of grammar or scansion or even of logic. Homer is telling a story as vividly as possible within a conventional medium that evolved as a means of public storytelling. This medium, the technique of oral composition, exists for a single purpose: to tell a riveting story. Nothing else matters.

HOMER AND HISTORY

In the *Iliad*, Homer sings a tale set in the days of the Trojan War, and the *Odyssey* records its aftermath. Naturally, one wonders if there ever was a Trojan War, and if so, when, and what was it about?

GREEK HISTORY

Intensive study in the last 150 years of the archaeological and literary evidence has revealed a good deal about historical periods in ancient Greece. In rough terms, the third and second millennia BC (3000–1000 BC) are the Bronze Age, and the first millennium (1000–0 BC) is the Iron Age, named after the metals commonly used, but we may break the schema down further.

In the late third millennium BC, the earliest European civilization arose on the island of Crete, called the Bronze Age *Minoan Civilization* by its discoverer, Arthur Evans (1851–1941), after the legendary King Minos. The ethnic affinities of the Cretans are unknown, but they are often thought to come from Anatolia (modern Turkey). They certainly were not speakers of Greek. They built palaces of astonishing elegance and size, decorated with frescoes of beauty and charm. They administered their kingdoms with the help of a writing system called Linear A, inspired by writing in Mesopotamia but independent of such systems. The writing has not been deciphered, but the signs seem to represent syllables, not alphabetic letters.

The heyday of the Minoan Civilization was from about 2000 to 1400 BC, when dwellers on the Greek mainland, the Mycenaean Greeks, appear to have conquered them or to have moved in after some natural catastrophe. The Greeks' arrival on the mainland from somewhere to the east may have been around 2300 BC, and they reached a height of power between c. 1600 and 1150 BC: the Bronze Age *Mycenaean Period*. They had a system of syllabic writing called Linear B, a modification of the earlier Minoan Linear A. Linear B is preserved on a large number of clay tablets, including a cache from PYLOS, a place important in the *Odyssey*. The writing, now deciphered, is an early form of Greek, but the clay tablets record only administrative accounts and no literature of any kind. Sometimes names known from Homer appear in the Linear B writings.

From early in this period come the royal burials at Mycenae discovered by Heinrich Schliemann (1822–1890) in 1876, which contained pristine burials with intact skeletons and a huge amount of treasure in the form of gold masks, vessels, and weapons of astonishing sophistication and beauty. Agamemnon, ruler of Homer's Greeks in Homer's *Iliad*, came from Mycenae, which Homer calls "rich in gold," and in fact Schliemann was looking for Agamemnon's stronghold.

Then about 1200 BC a catastrophe of unknown nature befell the whole area around the Aegean (but not Mesopotamia or Egypt) that lasted for about four hundred years. We call this period in the Greek Iron Age the *Dark Ages* (to be distinguished from the medieval European Dark Ages!). Linear B writing disappears along with the palaces that it served. The catastrophe is somehow connected to marauding bands of seafarers called the Sea Peoples, who devastated the entire east Mediterranean and attacked Egypt around 1200 BC. Some think that the famous Philistines of Palestine were Mycenaean Greeks from Crete who belonged to the coalition of Sea Peoples and settled in the Near East at this time; in fact Philistine pottery bears a striking resemblance to Mycenaean pottery.

The invention of the Greek alphabet c. 800 BC ended the Greek Dark Ages and began the *Archaic Period*, which lasted about three hundred years, until the Persians attacked Greece in 490 and 480 BC. Both epic and lyric poetry flourished during this period, but little survives except the poems of Homer and Hesiod. The Persian invasions began the *Classical Period* in Greek culture. The great figures of Greek alphabetic culture who lived during the Classical Period include Aeschylus, Sophocles, Euripides, Socrates, Plato, Aristotle, Pericles, Herodotus, Thucydides, and others. The death of Alexander the Great in 323 BC marks the end of the Classical Period and the beginning of the *Hellenistic Period*, when, thanks to Alexander, Greek culture became world culture. The death of Cleopatra in 30 BC is usually taken as the end of the Hellenistic Period and the beginning of the *Roman Period*.

SCHLIEMANN'S TROY

If there ever was a Trojan War, it must have taken place in the late Mycenaean Period, where, in fact, ancient commentators always placed it (as if they had any way of knowing). The Greek Dark Ages were too backward and impoverished to have sponsored an undertaking of this magnitude. Homer could have known about such a war through the oral tradition, which is continuous and could easily reach back over the four hundred years of the Dark Ages to the Mycenaean Period. After all, Mycenae was a village c. 800 BC, but in 1200 BC it was the center of unimaginable power.

Heinrich Schliemann was a German businessman who set out to find Troy against the certain views of scholars who dismissed the war as folklore, no more real than the poet Homer himself. Impoverished as a youth and poorly educated as a young man, Schliemann earned a fortune in Europe and then in Sacramento, California, where in 1851 he was a banker during the gold rush. He had a talent for languages and learned fourteen of them during his life, including Turkish and Arabic. Because he was in California when it became a state, Schliemann became an American citizen.

After the gold rush, Schliemann moved to Russia (where he had lived earlier) and greatly increased his wealth through international trade. At one time, he controlled the international trade in indigo, a dye. Schliemann retired in 1858 at age 37 and thereafter devoted his life to proving the historicity of the Homeric poems, a driving passion conceived in early childhood.

Schliemann searched in northwest Asia Minor for a likely site until he met a British expatriate named Frank Calvert, whose family owned half of a promontory at a place called Hissarlik, about five miles from the Dardanelles. Hissarlik is Turkish for

FIGURE 0.2 **Sophia Engastromenos wearing the Jewels of Troy.** Having divorced his first wife in an Indiana divorce court, Schliemann married seventeen-year-old Sophia Engastromenos (1852–1932) in 1869, despite the thirty years difference in age. Here she is shown wearing jewelry that Schliemann found in 1873 in a level of the city that we now know is much too early for the Trojan War, c. 2400 BC. Schliemann called the cache "Priam's Treasure." Schliemann smuggled the jewelry out of Turkey and gave it to the University of Berlin. Feared lost after the Russian sack of Berlin in 1945, the jewelry emerged at the Pushkin Museum in Moscow in 1994, but who owns it remains a matter of international dispute.

"fortress." Calvert, who worked as a consul for the British and the Americans, was interested in the problem of the site of Troy. He was convinced that the mound at Hissarlik held its ruins, where earlier in the century others had looked for Troy. Calvert had conducted modest excavations there but had not discovered much.

Schliemann began work on Hissarlik in 1870 and continued until 1873. With his superior resources, he dug deep into the hill, uncovering massive walls and thousands of artifacts: diadems of woven gold, rings, bracelets, earrings, necklaces, buttons, belts, brooches as well as anthropomorphic figures, bowls and vessels for perfumed oils, daggers, axes, and jewelry. He declared that he had discovered Priam's Troy. Schliemann conducted later excavations at Troy between 1878 and 1890, when he died.

Though Schliemann had misdated his finds on Hissarlik, the identification of Hissarlik with the Troy of Greek legend fits fairly well with Homer's own descriptions, and in fact with ancient tradition. The first Roman emperor, Augustus (63 BC–AD 14), established a city called New Ilium that encompassed Hissarlik, a fact established even before the work of Frank Calvert and Heinrich Schliemann. After 150 years of debate, a consensus has emerged that Hissarlik is in fact Homer's Troy. Schliemann wrote many books, he warred with the professors, and he sometimes lied about his achievements; after all, he had been a trader in a turbulent time. But he discovered the Greek Bronze Age, about which nothing was known formerly.

WAS THERE A TROJAN WAR?

There are nine separate settlements on Hissarlik, one of the most complicated archaeological sites in the world. "Priam's Treasure" (Figure 0.2) belongs to the second city, evidently destroyed by fire around 2250 BC—much too early, on balance, for mythical chronology. Probably Homer's Troy was the sixth city, which

FIGURE 0.3 The Walls of Troy. The translator standing before the walls of the sixth city at Troy.

had astounding walls, or an early phase of the seventh city, apparently destroyed by enemy action around 1190 BC.

The site may be referred to in tablets from the Hittite capital near Ankara (Turkey) where it is called Wilusa, that is, Ilion, the usual name for Troy in the *Iliad*. In 1995, in the level of the seventh city, the only example of writing ever found at Troy was discovered: a biconvex bronze seal with the parts of two names written in a special Hittite writing (called "Luvian hieroglyphs")—one the name of a scribe and the other the name of a woman.

But what do we mean by "Trojan War"? If we mean a war caused by a queen's infidelity, avenged by an outraged husband whose brother, in the ninth year of the campaign, came into conflict with his best fighting man, we must confess that the question is not a historical one. We can never know whether such behavior motivated a campaign or not, or what were the fates of those who sailed home after the war. Homer lived four hundred years after the events, evidently, and had no concept of history.

In the study of oral traditions throughout the world, it is clear that patterns of folktale quickly overlay the reporting of actual events, so that "what really happened" soon becomes irrecoverable. We have in the *Iliad* a tale about the anger of a man whose honor was slighted, a story about anger and its devastating consequences. The *Odyssey* is a tale of revenge—sweet and exquisite—when one man

FIGURE 0.4   The superimposed settlements of Troy, from c. 3000 BC to c. AD 100.
The enlarged illustration shows Troy VI, c. 1300 BC. (After drawing by Christof Haussner)

returned from Troy and all the strange things that happened to him before he got home. The Trojan War is simply background to these tales.

There is an oral tradition in which one singer teaches another and so passes on old songs. The Homeric tradition seems to have centered on the Boeotia/Euboea/Thessalian circuit. The Boeotian entry in the *Iliad's* Catalog of Ships (Book 2) is by far the longest. Alphabetic writing was invented on Euboea, where Ionic was spoken. Achilles is from Phthia in Thessaly. Aulis is the Boeotian/Euboean port from which overseas expeditions to southern Italy were launched in the early eighth century BC or earlier. The Homeric formulaic language has an underpinning of the dialect spoken in Thessaly, as if the singers who carried this tradition had once been from Thessaly before their song was taken over by Ionic speakers. A tradition of stories about the Thessalian hero Achilles, the best of the Achaeans, has fallen under the spell of a probably older cycle of stories about a war fought against an overseas mercantile center of power, Troy. This other cycle of stories, with heroes from Argos in the Peloponnesus leading an Argive campaign, must go back to the time of the Trojan War itself. In ancient times, no one sings about glorious deeds performed in an imaginary war.

So there *was* a Trojan War, that is, a campaign launched from the Greek mainland against the city of Troy sometime in the Late Bronze Age. Some of the names of the fighting men may be historical, but we can know nothing of the details of the war, let alone of the pathway home of one of its heroes. The stories Homer tells are in any event older than any historical war, going back to Mesopotamian song and the story of Gilgamesh and his friend Enkidu, whose death Gilgamesh indirectly caused, as Achilles indirectly caused the death of his friend Patroklos; and about Gilgamesh's far journey through magical mountains, his meeting with a maiden at the seashore, and his journey across the waters to inquire of a prophet about the secret of eternal life. Every once in a while details from this far-distant literary and historical past peer through, but the *Iliad* and *Odyssey* are certainly not poems about the Bronze Age. Rather they appealed to the interests of the adventurous, wealthy, seafaring Euboean Greeks of the early eighth century BC.

THE HOMECOMING OF ODYSSEUS

Everything about the *Odyssey* is different from the *Iliad*. They are literary opposites, created by one of the greatest artists that ever lived.

Life is big, life is moral. There is war, there is family. The *Iliad* is about war in which families are destroyed—the women raped, the children murdered. The *Odyssey* is about a man trying to get home to his family, to protect them. On the way, he becomes a symbol for the human spirit in quest of the meaning of human life. Not that Odysseus seeks knowledge as such in his wanderings: He does not. But his wandering symbolizes the human quest for knowledge. As the *Iliad* defines the West's preoccupation with the philosophy of value—why should I do anything?—the *Odyssey* defines its restless quest for the discovery of new things.

While Odysseus is lost at sea and presumed dead, a clique of 108 well-born men from Ithaca and neighboring islands have moved into Odysseus' house, urging Odysseus' wife Penelope to marry one of them. Each wants to become the next *basileus*, "chief," or Big Man, controlling Odysseus' house and lands and his overseas flocks. Apparently, the widow of the old chief (Odysseus) determines through remarriage who will be the next chief.

In its general setting, Homer describes the historical transition from rule by petty kings in the Iron Age, the Big Men (*basileis*), to rule by aristocratic oligarchies in the early historical period in the late ninth and early eighth centuries BC. But Homer is on the side of the old order, of older men of experience with a proper contempt for those not of their class. They made up his audience, for in Homer's story about the return of Odysseus the older generation of Big Men is triumphant. In the end Odysseus kills every one of the presumptuous and arrogant youngsters who allow their amorous inclinations and political ambitions to justify rude behavior. One might contrast modern film entertainment, where the audience is between eighteen and thirty-six years old: The common plot shows the young as vigorous and in the grip of honest love, while their middle-aged parents, libidinous and corrupt, oppose them; in the end, the young triumph over the old. Entertainers in every age know their audience.

Whereas the *Iliad* is set in the heroic age, the Bronze Age, the world of the *Odyssey* (except for Fairyland) is Homer's own world, Greece of the Iron Age. Sometimes literary critics call the *Iliad* "saga" because of its pretense to be set long ago in a world peopled by a greater race, and they call the *Odyssey* "romance" because it describes a contemporary world, with allowance for embellished effects such as the presence of gods.

Why should the hero's home be the obscure island of Ithaca, to the west of the Greek mainland in the mouth of the Gulf of Corinth (*see* MAP IV)? Heinrich Schliemann, confident in the historicity of the Homeric poems, found the ruins of Troy and Mycenae and Tiryns, then searched Ithaca, but found no physical evidence. Nor has intensive later investigation found a Bronze Age palace there. That is because the *Odyssey* has nothing to do with the Bronze Age. It reflects the age of early Western Greek exploration, beginning in the late ninth and early eighth centuries BC, when Ithaca was directly on the coasting route to Italy. Still today, yachtsmen exploring the Mediterranean put into port on Ithaca before heading north to CORCYRA, from where the Italian coast is nearly visible. When Greek sailors arrived on Ithaca, back from the wild west of Italy in the eighth century BC, truly they were home again.

NOSTOS

The *Iliad* takes place over a few days in the tenth year of the Trojan War; its story is linear. First there is the quarrel of Achilles and Agamemnon, then an embassy to Achilles to persuade him to return to the fight, his refusal, then the death of Patroklos who goes in as a substitute, then Achilles' killing of Hector in revenge, then Hector's ransom and burial—the end. The *Odyssey*, too, has a linear background: First Telemachos goes to find his father, then his father comes home, then they plot together, then they kill the suitors, then they vanquish the suitors' relatives—the end. But against this linear background are spirals and flashbacks that extend the story of the *Odyssey* over ten years' time and give to the *Odyssey* a very different shape from the *Iliad*. Fully one fifth of the poem consists of Odysseus' famous *apologue*, "speech" (Books 9–12), a long flashback where he tells of his adventures on the high seas.

As a general type of song, the *Odyssey* is called a *nostos*, a "homecoming" (plural, *nostoi*, as in our *nostalgia*, "aching for home"). In addition to the homecoming of Odysseus, the poem contains several shorter *nostoi* presented as flashbacks. For example, in Book 4, Menelaos, in a long speech, describes his adventures while coming home, which sound like a foreshortening of Odysseus' own adventures. In the second half of the poem, after Odysseus returns home, comes a sequence of "false tales," fictional accounts of Odysseus' wanderings. He always claims to be a Cretan (known to be liars). Such *nostoi*, like the famous *apologue* of Books 9–12, stop the progression of the narrative cold while enriching the story by taking us back in time, real or imaginary. The *Iliad* has occasional flashbacks, but in the *Odyssey*, Homer seeks every opportunity to prolong the story through related tangential tales.

THE FOLKTALE OF THE HOMECOMING HUSBAND

Viewed as a whole, the *Odyssey* is the oldest example of a folktale modern scholars call "The Homecoming Husband," the story of the man who came home after a long absence, found his household in the hands of usurpers, and killed them to reestablish his ascendancy. The older generation, tough, smart, and wise in the insistence on just behavior is triumphant over the younger, who are brash, indolent, and self-indulgent, taking what they want. This pattern of basic good and basic evil, simple and clear-cut moral distinctions, is common to traditions of folktale all over the world. The *Iliad*, by contrast, is not a folktale, but an account of heroic behavior in crisis.

In "The Homecoming Husband" typical elements are: a contest among suitors, often including archery (this usually comes first); the husband goes away; the wife is to wait a certain length of time before remarrying; the husband is imprisoned or otherwise prevented from returning; he may visit the underworld; there are reports of his death, and his wife is at last compelled to remarry; in a magical journey during which he falls asleep he returns home in disguise; an animal first recognizes him; he reveals his identity to his family by means of tokens; the imminent new wedding is called off, or the imposter is put to death.

Homer heard a version of this folktale, and his story follows the pattern closely. Folktales commonly have strong morals, and the *Odyssey* is no exception. In the *Iliad*, Zeus metes out good and evil from the jars before his throne, or Fate is responsible for suffering. In the *Odyssey*, by contrast, one is punished not just because of the hostility of the gods, but as a direct consequence of one's own evil actions. Because the youthful usurpers threaten traditional property rights, at one level the poem is a simple tale of revenge, of human justice triumphant over wrong. Not the gods' enmity, but their own greedy behavior, brings about the suitors' destruction.

The central theme of the *Iliad* is *psychological*: the destructive power of anger, that sweet but self-destructive feeling that comes with hate. The central theme of the *Odyssey* is *moral*: the evil will pay for their evil deeds, so we need not feel sorry for the suitors cut down in cold blood. We might say that the *Odyssey* is ethically more advanced than the *Iliad*, but this is probably an illusion based on the difference in genre. In the heroic world of battle, the gods determine everything that happens; in the moral world of the folktale, evil is always punished, often exquisitely.

THE MORAL ODYSSEY

Homer announces his moral theme right at the beginning (*Od.* 1–10):

> Sing to me of the resourceful man, O Muse, who wandered
> far after he had sacked the sacred city of Troy. He saw
> the cities of many men and he learned their minds.
> He suffered many pains on the sea in his spirit, seeking
> to save his life and the homecoming of his companions.
> But even so he could not save his companions, though he wanted to,
> for they perished of their own folly—the fools! They ate
> the cattle of Helios Hyperion, who took from them the day
> of their return.

Crime never pays! That is why Odysseus' men died and he survived. His men were fools. They broke the law and died. They violated the taboo. They ate the Cattle of the Sun when they were not supposed to, but Odysseus did not and he survived. He is "resourceful"—the Greek literally means "turned in many ways"—flexible and versatile. He does what is required.

Zeus enunciates this same theme when a counci of the gods decrees Odysseus' release from the island of Kalypso (*Od.* 1.31–34):

> "Only consider,
> how mortals blame the gods! They say that from us
> comes all evil, but men suffer pains beyond what is fated
> through their own folly."

Take, for example, the House of Atreus, in the *Odyssey* a paradigm for bad behavior. The gods warned Aigisthos not to sleep with Klytaimnestra, Agamemnon's wife, while Agamemnon was at Troy, but he did so anyway. When Agamemnon returned, the adulterous couple murdered him. The price *they* paid was clear: Orestes, son of Agamemnon and Klytaimnestra, came from abroad and killed Aigisthos and Klytaimnestra. On the one hand is Odysseus, his son Telemachos, and his wife Penelope; on the other hand is Agamemnon, his son Orestes, and his wife Klytaimnestra. Klytaimnestra strayed, Penelope remained true. Find the guilty party, and do not blame the gods for your troubles.

Similarly, Odysseus' foolish men dawdle in the land of the Kikones in Thrace, where six from each ship are killed. They eat the dangerous Lotus, which sends them into forgetful narcosis. They open the bag of the winds, which unleashes a storm. They devour the Cattle of the Sun, which kills all that remain of the crew save Odysseus himself. Justice is based on restraint, on the ability to hold back and not give in to one's animal appetites. Food is good, but when forbidden by gods, on Helios' island, or when it belongs to someone else, on Ithaca, you should not eat it. Sex is pleasurable, but when your husband is absent, you must do without.

After his moralizing prologue, Homer opens his story in the dark dining halls of Odysseus' palace on Ithaca, where the boorish young bucks drink, whore, and listen to poetry. In the midst of this *grand scandale* a mysterious stranger appears. And so the story begins.

MYTHIC PATTERNS IN THE *ODYSSEY*

In the *Iliad*, many gods are prominent, but in the *Odyssey* only three play important roles: Athena, protectress of the hero; Zeus, protector of the moral law; and Poseidon, persecutor of the hero, who represents the sea and all its real and symbolic dangers; for sometimes the simple morals, typical of folktales, are contradicted by the story itself. Although Zeus explains that humans are responsible for their own troubles, Poseidon, a god, harasses Odysseus in revenge for the blinding of Polyphemos. Poseidon's enmity also seems to explain the destruction of Odysseus' men. In fact, the mythic underlying structure of Homer's folktale—the triumph of the powerful advocate of order against the forces of death and chaos—is much older than the moral posture Homer gives to his story.

The *aoidos*, the oral poet, depends on unconscious linguistic patterns in the construction of his narrative. Thus he organizes words within the hexameter line by means of formulas and builds action within such type scenes as the shared feast according to a definite sequence. An analogous process is at work in the poet's presentation of the thematic elements by which he creates his story. Having chosen his subject of the Homecoming Husband, Homer develops the grand narrative by fashioning a long series of episodes generated from a single thematic folktale pattern. Repeated again and again, this pattern, an invisible constant beneath a versatile surface, is identical to that which supports the grand narrative: Odysseus, held by a deathly antagonist, victoriously returns to life and is "recognized."

In Mesopotamian stories about the creation of the world and in Hesiod's stories of the creation, which describe the triumph of the ordered over the disordered world, of life and progress over death and stagnation, appear similar structural features to those governing the folktale of the *Odyssey*—so closely interwoven are myths of creation, of the epic hero, and of the folktale hero. After all, Homer's theme is the hero's victory over death, the affirmation of new life against the forces of chaos and darkness.

The enemies of Odysseus are death's allies: sleep (Odysseus falls asleep at crucial junctures in the stories of Aiolos and the cattle of Helios); narcosis (the Lotus Eaters); darkness (the cave of Polyphemos, the shadowy land of the Cimmerians); or forgetfulness of purpose (Kirkê). Declared by all to be dead, Odysseus travels across water, the element separating this world from the next, to the land of the Cimmerians, where he interrogates the actual spirits of the dead and sees the torments of the damned. The eternal life offered him by Kalypso, whose name means "concealer" and whose island is the "navel of the sea," is eternal death for the inquisitive man ever thirsting for experience: Death hovers in the still-central point of the boundless water, "concealing" the dead from the living. Hades means "unseen," and in truth when someone dies, he or she will not be seen again. Water is death and its god, Poseidon, is Odysseus' relentless enemy.

Like Polyphemos and the Laestrygonians, death is a cannibal, devouring the living in the tomb's dark and hungry maw. Within the dark cave of Cyclops, Odysseus is "Nobody." He is nameless, without identity, nonexistent. As dragons of death are stupid, so Polyphemos is made drunk by the potent wine, fooled by the trick of the name, then wounded by the special weapon of the pointed stake. The same pattern underlies the killing of the suitors. When Odysseus escapes from the cave, passing from darkness into light, from death into life, he gets his name back and shouts to Polyphemos, "I am Odysseus!" After he kills the suitors, Penelope sees that he is indeed Odysseus, and they retire to the wedding bed.

Triumph over death leads to rebirth. Odysseus, like a baby leaving the "navel of the sea," passes through waters to emerge naked on the shore of Phaeacia. He takes refuge in a womblike hole in the dark bushes, then is welcomed by Nausicaä, a virgin who has dreamed of imminent marriage, like the marriage that unites Odysseus and Penelope at the end of the poem. Nausicaä's role as deliverer, as new mother, is explicit as Odysseus is about to depart for Ithaca. She says to him: "Never forget me, for I gave you life" (Book 12).

In Near Eastern and Hesiodic myth that explains the origin of the world, the primordial being is female, Tiamat (the primordial waters) or Gaia (Earth), who begets monstrous dragons that oppose the establishment of the ordered world; or she is herself the enemy. But the female is ambiguous and may also conspire with the hero to overthrow the demons of chaos, as in Hesiod's *Theogony*, where Gaia conspired with her son Kronos to defeat her husband Ouranos, or as Rhea in turn conspired with her son Zeus to overthrow Rhea's husband Kronos.

The ambiguity of the female in such stories is paralleled in the extraordinary array of female types in the *Odyssey*, who oppose or help Odysseus' efforts to return home and reestablish order. At one end of the spectrum are the dangerous seductive women Kalypso and Kirkê. Kalypso, although beautiful, is the "concealer." Kirkê, although beautiful, wishes to castrate Odysseus, a symbolic death. She turns men into pigs by the irresistible female power that reduces the male to pure animal lust, snorting and groveling in the dirt and filth. The female Skylla eats Odysseus' men whole. The female Sirens, like perverted Muses, lead men to their deaths through the alluring promise of secret knowledge dressed in beautiful song.

On the positive end of the scale stand Athena, Odysseus' protector; Nausicaä, the uncorrupted maiden, cast both as potential mate for Odysseus and symbolic mother; and Penelope, who resists sexual temptation for twenty years. In Zeus's speech about human folly, Klytaimnestra is cited as an example of humans who act recklessly and pay the price. Throughout the poem Klytaimnestra is the implied opposite to Penelope. Klytaimnestra is the wicked woman who gave in to sexual desire, betrayed the strict rules of wifely fidelity, and murdered her husband. Penelope, by contrast, is the ideal woman, long-suffering, ever faithful, and ingenious in preserving the honor of her home.

The hero must slay his dragon, and in his wanderings Odysseus overcomes many deadly enemies. The 108 suitors who besiege Odysseus' house are, in a realistic mode, a kind of dragon, described repeatedly as voracious ("devouring his substance") and sexually threatening ("whoring with the female slaves") while seeking to marry his wife. In the same way, the mythical dragon devours everything in sight and sexually threatens a woman. In the myth of dragon-combat, the monster is often overcome by a trick, sometimes at a banquet, and slain with a special weapon. Even so Odysseus tricks the beast with 108 mouths by entering the palace in disguise, surprising the suitors in the dining hall, then killing them with a special bow that no one else can string. As the dragon-slayer receives a princess as reward, Odysseus too "marries" Penelope.

Beset by a dangerous crisis, Penelope courageously decides to take a second husband, thus setting up (unknowingly) the slaughter of the suitors. Clever like her husband, she cooly tests Odysseus with the token of the bed, its immovability the symbol for their own marriage, as the olive from which it is made stands for the life of the family uncorrupted by adultery. In the contrasting but parallel stories of the royal houses of Mycenae and Ithaca, Odysseus is like Agamemnon, each returning from Troy to find his house in the hands of enemies, and Telemachos is like Orestes, fighting to restore family right and honor. The difference between the parallel legends lies in the character of the woman: Odysseus survives because Penelope is woman as she should be, while Agamemnon is cut down like a dog. That, too, is a moral of the tale.

THE SINGER SINGS

The *Odyssey* is self-reflexive, curiously concerned with the art of oral verse-making of which it is itself a product. It is our principal source for information about how an *aoidos*, an oral poet, functioned in archaic Greek society. Whereas the *Iliad* has no *aoidoi*, they and their art loom large in the *Odyssey*.

There are two *aoidoi* in the Ithacan and Phaeacian courts, Phemios and Demodokos. There really is no other form of entertainment in this world, only their song. *Aoidoi* always perform after a banquet, and the audience wants the song to go on and on. King Alkinoös in the *Odyssey* begs Odysseus to continue with his tale, though it is late at night (*Od.* Book 12).

Odysseus' famous apologue, Books 9–12, the story of his journeys in the other world, is compared to the song of an *aoidos*, though it is unaccompanied by the lyre. The Sirens are like perverted *aoidoi*, whose songs about the Trojan War are so sweet that one would die to hear them. On Ithaca, Odysseus repeatedly tells lying tales in which he claims to be a traveler from Crete. These false tales are a different story each time, but vary as we would expect in accordance with the oral singer's art. Homer touchingly has Odysseus spare the life of the singer Phemios, one of his own kind.

The singers' audience is nearly all male, as was no doubt Homer's own audience. Queen Aretê is the only female to hear the song of the *aoidos*. After all, songs such as the humorous and salacious "Love Affair of Ares and Aphrodite" (Book 8), are quite inappropriate for female ears!

TRANSLATION ISSUES

The audience can absorb only so much information so fast, but the singer cannot stop his delivery, he cannot be silent for long. His task is to replace the listener's thoughts with his own words, and so the words must come constantly. Thus in Homer an audience always redundantly "listens and obeys," and to characters, "he spoke and he addressed them." The pervasive use of such amplified expression, and of epithets, enhances the audience's comprehension. To enjoy our modern Homer, we must teach ourselves to accept this repetitive, formulaic style, evolved in order to help the poet create his rhythmic line on the fly in oral composition.

THE REPETITIVE STYLE

Not only are many lines repeated, but sometimes whole passages. For example, when a message is given, the listener knows that it will be repeated word for word when delivered. The fixed epithets attached to heroes and gods lengthen the line and slows the rate of the delivery of information while reminding the audience what this character is best known for. The epithet puts the character in context. Hence "resourceful Odysseus" takes longer to say than just "Odysseus," while reminding us of what sort of man this is. The epithet is part of the meaning, a capsule biography. And there is something evocative about "wine-dark sea" that "sea" alone does not convey.

The translator faces the temptation to ignore these epithets entirely and translate "resourceful Odysseus" simply as "Odysseus." This would produce a translation that is not very fair to the poet-singer, obscuring the reality of the origin of these poems as oral compositions. Another strategy is to always translate the epithets in a different way, for example "ingenious Odysseus" or "Odysseus of many turns" or "wily Odysseus" (for the Greek *polutropos*, "turned in many ways"), again hiding the origin of the text as an oral poem.

I have followed a middle way: using the epithets, thus making clear that this poem is composed in an oral style, but sometimes allowing a different wording, or ignoring the epithet altogether, in accordance with modern taste. Still, we have to adjust to the repetitive style if we want to read a translation of Homer. Homer is an oral poet and he is singing in an oral style, a style grounded in the practicalities of oral presentation.

GETTING USED TO HOMER'S WORLD

Homer's world is a stylized world. Emotions are exaggerated or expressed in concrete imagery that strikes us as strange. Gods and goddesses zip in and out with perfect credibility. Eating is highly ritualized, and Homeric heroes do a lot of eating. Everything is strange about this world, yet recognizable. A translation must acknowledge this strangeness.

The extraordinarily long and often unexpected similes relieve the tedium of the narrative and open a window into another world, giving a different point of view. The poet feels as if he can create alternate worlds in the midst of his original alternate world. The similes abound with beautiful images from the natural world, especially of magnificent predators to whom warriors are compared. But they also delay the progress of the narrative.

Such is a hallmark of Homer's oral style, to stretch things out by interposing all kinds of delaying tactics. He inserts episodes and diversions of every kind to put off what must come. Evidently Homer was encouraged when dictating the *Iliad* and the *Odyssey* to make the songs as long as possible for reasons we can only imagine. Milman Parry seems to have had a similar experience with Avdo Mejedovich (c. 1870–1955), his best singer, who at Parry's encouragement sang *The Wedding of Smailagich Meho*, about as long as the *Odyssey*.

Words have a different range of meaning in Greek than in English, especially those referring to feelings. The Greek does not distinguish between emotional and mental categories as we do, so we must seek parallels in English that correspond to the nuance in the Greek. For example, there are several words that indicate the things that go on inside a person's chest, but Homer is very imprecise in his use of these words, and they must constantly be translated in different ways.

So *thumos* means something like the air that you breathe in, but it comes to mean the heart, as in grieved "at heart" or "in spirit," as in "he was troubled in his spirit." But at other times *thumos* means the life, the breath-soul that departs from the body when you die, like the *psychê*, really "breath," the air or "breath-soul" that leaves a dead inert body. But *thumos* can also be the seat of thought. The word *kêr* probably means the organ the "heart," but it is also commonly used to designate the place where decisions are made, like *thumos*. The word *phrên*, or in the plural *phrenes*, may also designate a specific internal organ, but whether this is the lungs or the liver or something else is never clear, and often *phrên(es)* can mean "heart," like *thumos* or *kêr*. The word *êtor* is another word that refers to the place of feeling in the chest, not thinking, as in "grieving at heart." The meaning of these vague terms varies according to the context, but it is clear that the Homeric Greeks saw the basis for thought, decision, and action as taking place in the chest. After all, it is emotion, not thought, that drives men to behave in certain ways, just as emotion lives in the stomach and in the heart still today.

ON THIS TRANSLATION

Translations reflect the taste of their times. Since the seminal translation of George Chapman (1559–1634) in iambic heptameter (seven feet, all iambs), published in full in 1615, there have been over 130 translations of Homer's poems into English. Alexander Pope (1688–1744) took 11 years (1715–1726) to complete his translation of the *Odyssey* into rhymed couplets, which suited the prevailing conviction that rhyme was what characterized poetry, raising it above pedestrian prose.

In modern poetry, rhyme is avoided as something that stands in the way of direct expression. But Homer seems wrong as prose—after all, it is a poem composed in dactylic hexameter. Again, I have chosen a middle way, adopting a rough five-beat line in this translation. My focus is on the *meaning* of Homer's words and how they would sound today in contemporary English.

Homer's style may be strange, but it is always simple, direct, and sensual. I have tried to reproduce these qualities in this new English translation. Flexibility within accuracy has been my principle. I have often added personal names to replace pronouns, because Homer's use of pronouns can be very unclear.

Translating the meaning of the text does not necessarily imply a word-for-word rendering. After all, Homer's thoughts are rendered in a different language with very different habits of expression. Still, I hope to convey the sense of each word and phrase in the Greek, without prettifying or embellishing. I am not concerned with sounding "poetic," or beautiful, or clever, because that would be to falsify the plain style of the original Greek. Yet much of the stylistic beauty of Homer's poetry comes from his use of words in unexpected or startling ways, a feature I try to preserve.

TRANSLITERATION AND PRONUNCIATION OF NAMES

There are two traditions in transliterating classical names, the Latin and the Greek. The Latin spellings come through the Latin language and impose traditional rules of Latin spelling. In Greek spellings, the names are transliterated more or less as they are written in Greek, but using Latin characters. The Latin tradition lies behind English dictionary usage, because Latin was once the language of the educated classes in England and the United States. So in dictionaries the names are "Achilles," "Priam," "Helen," and "Menelaus." In the 1950s, however, a fashion began of using the Greek spellings, so that it is "Akhilleus," "Priamos," "Helena," and "Menelaos." The trouble with using the Greek forms, however, is their lack of familiarity. The trouble with using all Latin forms is that they can look too fussy, old-fashioned.

In this translation I have followed the practice in transliteration of the superb *The Homer Encyclopedia*, edited by Margalit Finkelberg (Wiley/Blackwell, 2011). "Achilles," "Priam," "Helen," and "Ajax" are too familiar to be changed, but except for these major players, and for *place names*, I give the names of subordinate characters in the Greek spelling: "Kalypso" not "Calpyso."

Two other conventions are observed: Where the upsilon in Greek is pronounced in English as /i/, I have transliterated the upsilon as [y], not [u]. I have used a dieresis, two dots over a vowel [ï], to indicate when adjacent vowels are to be pronounced separately: Antinoös, Nausithoös. I have transliterated the Greek [x] as [ch]. When the *final vowel* of a name is to be pronounced, I write it with a circumflex on top: Mykenê, Alkmenê. Final *es* is also pronounced, as in Achillēs.

There is a fair amount of uncertainty as to how to pronounce Greek names in English, and even professionals can be unsure. Moreover, Greek names are pronounced differently in, for example, England and the United States. Certainly an ancient Greek would be puzzled at the ordinary English pronunciation of his or her name. There is little agreement on how to pronounce the vowels, so one hears the name of the Athenian playwright Aeschylus pronounced as *e*-schylus or *ē*-schylus or sometimes *ī*-schylus. Is the famous king of Thebes called *e*-dipus or *ē*-dipus? With many names, however, there is a conventional pronunciation, which I give in parentheses in the Pronunciation Glossary at the back of the book.

Another problem is the accent—where to stress the word. Greek relied chiefly on pitch and quantity, whereas English depends on stress. Because of the influence of Latin on Western culture, the English accent on proper names follows the rule that governs the pronunciation of Latin: If the next-to-last syllable is "long," it is accented; if it is not "long," the syllable before it is accented. For many it will be easiest simply to consult the Pronunciation Glossary, where the syllable to be accented is printed in **bold** characters.

BOOK 1. *Telemachos in Ithaca*

Sing to me of the resourceful man, O Muse, who wandered
far after he had sacked the sacred city of Troy. He saw
the cities of many men and he learned their minds.
He suffered many pains on the sea in his spirit, seeking
to save his life and the homecoming of his companions.   5
But even so he could not save his companions, though he wanted to,
for they perished of their own folly—the fools! They ate
the cattle of Helios Hyperion,° who took from them the day
of their return. Of these matters, beginning where you want,
O daughter of Zeus, tell to us.   10

           Now all the rest
were at home, as many as had escaped dread destruction,
fleeing from the war and the sea. Odysseus alone
a queenly nymph, Kalypso,° a shining one among the goddesses,
held back in her hollow caves, desiring that he become
her husband. But when, as the seasons rolled by, the year came   15
in which the gods had spun the threads of destiny
that Odysseus return home to ITHACA, not even then
was he free of his trials, even among his own friends.

    All the gods pitied him, except for Poseidon.
Poseidon stayed in an unending rage at godlike Odysseus   20
until he reached his own land. But Poseidon had gone off
to the Aethiopians° who live far away—the Aethiopians
who live split into two groups, the most remote of men—
some where Hyperion sets, and some where he rises.
There Poseidon received a sacrifice of bulls and rams,   25
sitting there and rejoicing in the feast.

---

8 *Helios Hyperion*: In other poets, Hyperion, which means "going over," is a Titan, the father of Helios, but Homer uses the word as an epithet of the sun god.

13 *Kalypso*: "concealer," evidently Homer's invention.

22 *Aethiopians*: "burnt-faced," usually taken to refer to Africans living in a never-never land at the edge of the world.

                              The other gods
were seated in the halls of Zeus on Olympos. Among them
the father of men and gods began to speak, for in his heart
he was thinking of bold Aigisthos, whom far-famed Orestes,
30   the son of Agamemnon, had killed. Thinking of him,
he spoke these words to the deathless ones: "Only consider,
how mortals blame the gods! They say that from us
comes all evil, but men suffer pains beyond what is fated
through their own folly! See how Aigisthos pursued
35   the wedded wife of the son of Atreus, and then he killed
Agamemnon when he came home, though he well knew
the end. For we spoke to him beforehand, sending Hermes,
the keen-sighted Argeïphontes,° to say that he should not kill
Agamemnon and he should not pursue Agamemnon's wife.
40   For vengeance would come from Orestes to the son of Atreus,
once Orestes came of age and wanted to reclaim his family land.
So spoke Hermes, but for all his good intent he did not persuade
Aigisthos' mind. And now he has paid the price in full."

      Then the goddess, flashing-eyed Athena, answered him:
45   "O father of us all, son of Kronos, highest of all the lords,
surely that man has fittingly been destroyed. May whoever
else does such things perish as well! But my heart
is torn for the wise Odysseus, that unfortunate man,
who far from his friends suffers pain on an island surrounded
50   by water, where is the very navel of the sea. It is a wooded
island, and a goddess lives there, the daughter of evil-minded
Atlas, who knows the depths of every sea, and himself
holds the pillars that keep the earth and the sky apart.
Kalypso holds back that wretched, sorrowful man.
55   Ever with soft and wheedling words she enchants him,
so that he forgets about Ithaca. Odysseus, wishing to see
the smoke leaping up from his own land, longs to die. But your
heart pays no attention to it, Olympian! Did not Odysseus
offer you abundant sacrifice beside the ships in broad Troy?
60   Why do you hate him so, O Zeus?"°

                              Zeus who gathers the clouds
then answered her: "My child, what a word has escaped the barrier

---

38 *Argeïphontes*: An obscure epithet of Hermes, usually taken to mean "killer of the monster Argos," but
    explicable in other ways as well.

60 *. . . O Zeus*: The Greek for "hate" is *ódusaô*, punning on Odysseus' name. In fact, the etymology of *Odysseus* is
    unknown; it is probably pre-Greek. In many later sources it is written *Olysseus*, giving rise to the Latin *Ulysses*.

FIGURE 1.1 Aigisthos kills Agamemnon.   Aigisthos holds Agamemnon, covered by a diaph-
anous robe, by the hair while he stabs him with a sword. Apparently this illustration is inspired by
the tradition followed in Aeschylus' *Agamemnon*, where the king is caught in a web before being
killed. Klytaimnestra stands behind Aigisthos, urging him on, while Agamemnon's daughter
attempts to stop the murder (she is called Elektra in Aeschylus' play). To the far right, a handmaid
flees. Athenian red-figure wine-mixing bowl, c. 500–450 BC. Photograph ©2014 Museum of Fine
Arts, Boston.

of your teeth! How could I forget about godlike Odysseus,
who is superior to all mortals in wisdom, who more than any other
has sacrificed to the deathless gods who hold the broad heaven?
65 But Poseidon who holds the earth is perpetually angry with him
because of the Cyclops,° whose eye he blinded—godlike
Polyphemos, whose strength is greatest among all the Cyclopes.
The nymph Thoösa bore him, the daughter of Phorkys°
who rules over the restless sea, having mingled with Poseidon
70 in the hollow caves. From that time Poseidon, the earth-shaker,
does not kill Odysseus, but he leads him to wander from
his native land. But come, let us all take thought of his homecoming,
how he will get there. Poseidon will abandon his anger!
He will not be able to go against all the deathless ones alone,
75 against their will."

        Then flashing-eyed Athena, the goddess,
answered him: "O our father, the son of Kronos, highest
of all the lords, if it be the pleasure of all the blessed gods
that wise Odysseus return to his home, then let us send Hermes
Argeïphontes, the messenger, to the island of Ogygia, so that
80 he may present our sure counsel to Kalypso with the lovely tresses,
that Odysseus, the steady at heart, need now return home.
And I will journey to Ithaca in order that I may the more
arouse his son and stir strength in his heart to call the Achaeans
with their long hair into an assembly, and give notice to all the suitors,
85 who devour his flocks of sheep and his cattle with twisted horns,
that walk with shambling gait. I will send him to Sparta and to sandy
Pylos to learn about the homecoming of his father, if perhaps
he might hear something, and so that might earn a noble fame
among men."

        So she spoke, and she bound beneath her feet
90 her beautiful sandals—immortal, golden!—that bore her
over the water and the limitless land together with the breath
of the wind. She took up her powerful spear, whose point
was of sharp bronze, heavy and huge and strong,
with which she overcomes the ranks of warriors when she is angry
95 with them, the daughter of a mighty father. She descended
in a rush from the peaks of Olympos and took her stand
in the land of Ithaca in the forecourt of Odysseus, on the threshold

---

66 *Cyclops*: "round-eye," though Homer never says that Cyclops has but a single eye.

68 *Phorkys*: Probably a pre-Greek sea deity, like Proteus or Nereus.

of the court. She held the bronze spear in her hand, taking on
the appearance of a stranger, Mentes, leader of the Taphians.°

    There she found the proud suitors. They were taking their pleasure,   100
playing board games in front of the doors, sitting on the skins
of cattle that they themselves had slaughtered. Heralds°
and busy assistants mixed wine with water for them
in large bowls, and others wiped the tables with porous sponges
and set them up,° while others set out meats to eat in abundance.   105

    Godlike Telemachos° was by far the first to notice
her as he sat among the suitors, sad at heart, his noble
father in his mind, wondering if perhaps he might come
and scatter the suitors through the house and win honor
and rule over his own household. Thinking such things,   110
sitting among the suitors, he saw Athena. He went straight
to the outer door, thinking in his spirit that it was a shameful thing
that a stranger be allowed to remain for long before the doors.

    Standing near, he clasped her right hand and took the bronze
spear from her. Addressing her, he spoke words that went   115
like arrows: "Greetings, stranger! You will be treated kindly
in our house, and once you have tasted food, you will tell us
what you need!"

    So speaking he led the way, and Pallas Athena°
followed. When they came inside the high-roofed house,
Telemachos carried the spear and placed it against a high column   120
in a well-polished spear rack where were many other spears
belonging to the steadfast Odysseus. He led her in and sat her
on a chair, spreading a linen cloth beneath—beautiful,
elaborately-decorated—and below was a footstool for her feet.
Beside it he placed an inlaid chair, apart from the others,   125

---

99 *Taphians*: Elsewhere in the *Odyssey*, the Taphians are pirates and slave traders living in some distant
    community. *Mentes* means "advisor," like the *Mentor*, the disguised Athena who accompanies
    Telemachos on his travels.

102 *Heralds*: Heralds were free-born, but of a lower social class than the aristocratic suitors whom they serve,
    performing all kinds of subordinate functions.

105 *set them up*: In Homer's world tables are not permanent furniture but are set up on folding legs when eating,
    a little like "TV tables."

106 *Telemachos*: "far-fighter," presumably named from his father's excellence as an archer.

118 *Pallas Athena*: The meaning of *Pallas* is unknown, but is often interpreted as "brandishing" (from Greek *pallô*).

so that the stranger might not be put-off by the racket and fail
to enjoy his meal, despite the company of insolent men.
Also, he wished to ask him about his absent father.

    A slave girl brought water for their hands in a beautiful golden
130 vessel, and she set up a polished table beside them.
The modest attendant brought out bread and placed it before them,
and many delicacies, giving freely from her store. A carver
lifted up and set down beside them platters with all kinds
of meats, and set before them golden cups, while a herald
135 went back and forth pouring out wine for them.

    In came the proud suitors, and they sat down in a row
on the seats and chairs, and the heralds poured out water for
their hands, and women slaves heaped bread by them in baskets,
and young men filled the wine-mixing bowls with drink.°
140 The suitors put forth their hands to the good cheer lying before them,
and when they had exhausted their desire for drink and food,
their hearts turned toward other things, to song and dance.
For such things are the proper accompaniment of the feast.
A herald placed the very beautiful lyre in the hands of Phemios,°
145 who was required to sing to the suitors. And he thrummed the strings
as a prelude to song.

        But Telemachos spoke to flashing-eyed Athena,
leaning his head in near so that the others would not hear:
"Dear stranger, will you be angry for what I say? These gatherings
are their sole concern, the lyre and epic song, especially,
150 and they devour without penalty the substance of another—
of a man whose white bones rot in the rain, lying on the land,
or a wave of the sea rolls them about. If they ever saw him
return to Ithaca, every man of them would soon pray
to be swifter of foot, not richer in gold or cloth!

155   "But as it is, my father has died a wretched death,
nor is there any comfort for us, even if perhaps some one
of the men who live on the earth were to say that he would
come. The day of his return is gone.

        "But come, tell me
and say it truly—who are you among men, and where

---

139 *with drink*: Wine was ordinarily mixed with water in a proportion of two parts wine to three parts water.

144 *Phemios*: "the man rich in tales," a speaking name, as are the names of many minor characters in Homer.

do you come from? Where is your city and your parents?
On what kind of ship did you arrive? How did sailors
bring you to Ithaca? Who did they say that they were?
For I don't think that you came here on foot! Tell me this truly,
so that I may know—whether this is the first time that you
have come here, or whether you are a guest-friend° of my father.   165
For many were the men who came to our house. He was
widely traveled among men."

        The goddess, flashing-eyed Athena,
answered him: "I will truthfully tell you all. I am Mentes,
the son of wise Anchialos, and I rule over the Taphians,
lovers of the oar. Now, as you see, I have come with a ship   170
and my companions, sailing on the wine-dark sea to men
of foreign speech, to Temesa after copper, and I bring
shining iron. My ship is beached far from the city in a field,
near the harbor of Rheithron beneath wooded Neion.° We say
that we are guest-friends of one another from a long ways back,   175
even as our fathers were. If you want, go to the old warrior
Laërtes, and ask him. They say that he no longer comes
to the city, but that he suffers pains far away in a field,
attended by an old woman as his servant who places before him
food and drink when fatigue has taken hold of his limbs   180
as he creeps along the hill of his vineyard. Now I have come.

  "They said that your father was among his people," said
flashing-eyed Athena," but I see that the immortal gods prevent
his return. And yet godlike Odysseus has not yet perished
from this earth! He is still alive, held back on an island in the broad   185
sea surrounded by water. Savage men confine him, I think,
wild men who hold him all unwillingly.

        "And now I will
utter a prophecy that the deathless ones put into my mind,
and I think it will come to pass—though I am no prophet
nor one wise in the flight of birds. He will not be absent   190
much longer from his father's land, not even if iron chains
should hold him! He will figure out how to return, for he is
a resourceful man.

---

165 *guest-friend*: A guest-friend (*xeinos*) is someone from outside the community who has exchanged gifts (*xeinēïa*)
    to establish a lasting association of friendship and support (*xeinia*). *Xeinia* is inherited, passing from one
    generation to the next. Much of the *Odyssey* is concerned with *xeinia*, its observation and its crass violation.

174 ...*Neion*: *Temesa* is probably a port on the west coast of southern Italy; *Rheithron* and *Neion* are unknown.

"But come tell me this and say it truly,
if, being so tall, you are the son of Odysseus himself?
195 In your head and your beautiful eyes you seem amazingly like him,
for we often communed together before he went off to Troy,
where others too, the best of the Argives, went in their hollow ships.
Since that day I have not seen Odysseus, nor has he seen me."

Then the shrewd Telemachos answered her: "I will tell you
200 the whole truth, stranger. My mother says that I am
his child, but I'm not so sure. No man ever knows
for sure who his own parents are. Would that I was the son
of some favored man who grew old among his own possessions!
As it is, they say that I am the son of the most ill-fated
205 of mortal men—since you ask."

Then the goddess, flashing-eyed Athena,
answered him: "But surely the gods have made your lineage
famous for the times to come, seeing that Penelope°
has borne you such as you are. But come, tell me this,
and speak truly—what is this feast, what is this crowd?
210 What is your need of it? Is this a drinking-party, or a wedding?
Obviously this is no potluck! These men appear to act insolently,
partying with arrogance throughout your house. It's enough
to make a man of sense ooze anger if he came among them,
seeing these shameful acts."

Then the shrewd Telemachos
215 answered her: "Stranger, because you ask me these things
and inquire so, you should know that this house once was rich
and fine, so long as that man was among his people. But now
the evil-devising gods have wished otherwise. They have made
that man invisible above all men. I would not grieve so much for his death
220 if he had fallen among his companions in the land of the Trojans,
or in the arms of his friends—once he had reeled up the thread of war.°
All the Achaeans would then have made a tomb for him,
and he would have won great fame for his son, too, in the days
to come. But as it is, the storm-winds have snatched him away,
225 without report. He is gone from sight and out of hearing, and has left
me only pain and weeping. And I do not weep and wail

---

207 *Penelope*: Seemingly from a Greek word meaning "duck." In Chinese and Russian folklore ducks are
famous for their marital fidelity, but there is no trace of this tradition in Greece.

221 *thread of war*: The metaphor depends on weaving: You wind up the ball of thread once the task is com-
pleted. Usually it is the Fates who do the weaving.

for him alone, because the gods have devised other pains for me.
All the leading men who rule over those islands—
Doulichion and Samê and wooded Zakynthos ° and they
who lord it over rocky Ithaca—all of them are suitors   230
to my mother, and they ravage the household. She neither refuses
the hateful marriage nor can she get rid of them once and for all.
And they consume my substance. Before long they will bring me to ruin!"

    Pallas Athena indignantly answered him: "Yes, surely
you are in need of absent Odysseus, who would surely   235
lay hands on these shameless suitors. Would that he were here now,
standing before the outer doors of his house with his helmet
and shield and two spears, just as when I first saw him
in my house, drinking and taking his pleasure when he had come
from Ephyra and the house of Ilos, the son of Mermeros.°   240
Odysseus went there on a swift ship to get a man-killing poison
so that he might dip his bronze arrows in it, but Ilos would not give
it to him. He feared the anger of the gods who never die.
My father gave the poison to him, because he loved him very much.
Would that Odysseus appeared with such strength in the midst   245
of these suitors, I say! They would find a bitter and abrupt
end to their courtship!

      "All of this rests on the knees
of the gods, whether or not he will return and take revenge
in his halls. But I urge you to consider how you can drive the suitors
from your halls. Come now, give me your ear, and listen   250
to my words . . . Tomorrow call the Achaean warriors
to an assembly and speak out your word to all, and may the gods
be your witness. As to the suitors, urge them to scatter each
to his own house. As to your mother, if she is minded to marry,
let her go back to the house of her powerful father. There they   255
will prepare a wedding and make ready the abundant gifts,
as much as is appropriate to go with a beloved daughter.

    "As for you, I will give you some good advice, if you will listen:
Fit out a ship with twenty oarsmen, the best you can find.

---

229 *Zakynthos*: Samê is probably Kephallenia, where there is still a town called Samê. In the Catalog of
     Ships in the *Iliad*, Doulichion is not in Odysseus' realm, but is ruled by one Meges. Probably Zakynthos is
     the modern Leukas. See Map iv.

240 . . . *Mermeros*: Many places were named Ephyra, but this Ephyra seems to be in Thresprotia in the mainland
     opposite Ithaca (it is not Corinth, as in the Iliadic story of Bellerophon, *Il.* Book 6: see Map iv). Ilos is a
     nonentity not mentioned elsewhere. His father Mermeros was a son of Jason and Medea.

260 Go and find out about your father who has long been away,
if some mortal will tell you. Or you may hear a voice from Zeus,
which most often brings news to men. Go first to PYLOS
and inquire of godlike Nestor, and from there go to SPARTA
to blonde-haired Menelaos. He was last of the Achaeans
265 who wear shirts of bronze to return to his house. If you hear
that your father is alive and coming home, then, though
you are hard-pressed, you can hold out for a year. If you hear
that he is dead and no longer among the living, then return to your
native land and heap up a mound and make appropriate funeral
270 offerings, as many as is fitting, and give your mother to a husband.°
And when you have accomplished these things and done them,
then take counsel in your heart and mind how you will kill
the suitors in your halls, either by a trick or openly. It is not right
that you act as a child, for you are no longer a youth! Have you not
275 heard what fame godlike Orestes won among all men when he killed
the father's killer, the treacherous Aigisthos, who killed
Agamemnon, his famous father? And you, my friend—for I see
that you are handsome and tall—be valiant so that many
of those who will live after will speak well of you.

280   "But now I will go down to my swift ship and to my
companions, who I think are impatient waiting for me. But you
give heed to my words, and pay them careful attention."

      Then the shrewd Telemachos answered her: "Stranger, truly
you have said these things with a friendly mind, as a father to his son,
285 and I won't forget them. But wait now—stay a moment, though
you wish to be on your way, so that you might have a chance to bathe
and to satisfy your heart to the fullest. Then I will give you a gift,
and you may be off on your ship, rejoicing in your heart—
a costly gift, very beautiful, which will be an heirloom to you
290 from me, such as guest-friends give to other guest-friends."

      Then the goddess, flashing-eyed Athena, answered him:
"No, don't hold me back, for I am eager to continue my journey.
As for the gift that your heart bids you give—give it to me
when I return to carry to my home, and choose a very beautiful one.
295 It will bring you a similar one in return."

---

270 *to a husband*: It is not clear how this part of Mentes' advice accords with his earlier suggestion that
     Telemachos send his mother back home to Sparta for her father Ikarios to marry her off, as many commen-
     tators have complained. Probably Mentes/Athena is speaking casually, throwing out one idea after another
     without thinking the whole plan through. Being a goddess in disguise, Mentes/Athena knows, of course,
     that Odysseus is alive and will soon return, but being in disguise she cannot reveal this.

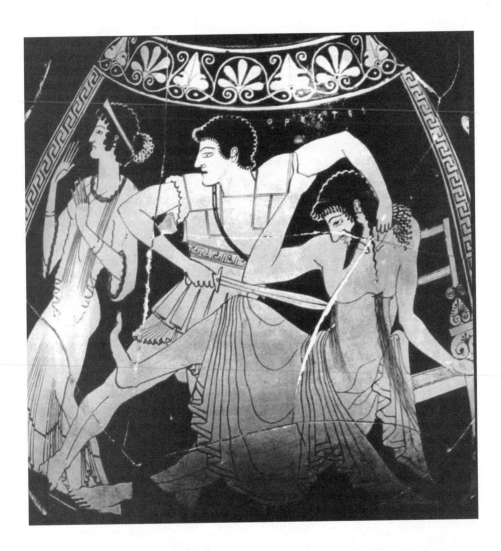

FIGURE 1.2   Orestes kills Aigisthos.   With his right hand a young, beardless Orestes, wearing armor, plunges a sword into Aigisthos' already wounded chest while with his left hand he holds the bearded Aigisthos by his long hair. Aigisthos sits on a fancy chair and a cloth covers his lower body. ORESTES is labeled. Athenian red-figure vase, c. 500 BC.

So speaking, flashing-eyed Athena
went off, flying upward as a bird. And she placed strength and daring
in Telemachos' heart. She made him think of his father more even
than he had been. In his mind he took account of her leave-taking
and he was amazed, realizing that she must be a god.

300   Immediately he went among the suitors, a man like a god.
A famous singer was performing before them, and they sat
in silence and listened. The singer sang of the miserable return
of the Achaeans that Pallas Athena imposed on them
as they headed home from Troy.° The clever Penelope, daughter
305 of Ikarios, heard the wonderful song from her chamber up above,
and she went down the high stairway from her room—not alone,
but two slaves followed along behind. When the fair lady
came down to the suitors, she stood beside a pillar of the hall,
so well constructed, holding a shining veil before her cheeks.
310 A faithful handmaid° stood on either side.

                       Then in tears she spoke
to the divine singer: "Phemios, you know many other things
that are charming to mortals, the doings of men and gods
that singers make famous. So sing one of these as you sit there,
and let them drink their wine in silence. But cease from this
315 sad song that ever tears at the heart in my breast. For a sorrow
never to be forgotten has come on me especially. I desire
and think upon the head of that dear man whose fame
is abroad throughout HELLAS and mid-ARGOS."°

                       Then the shrewd
Telemachos answered her: "My dear mother, why do you not let
320 the loyal singer bring pleasure in whatever way his mind
urges him to? Singers are not to blame, but I think it is
Zeus who is to blame! He gives to men who live
on grain just as he wishes. It is no cause for anger
if this man sings of the evil fate of the Danaäns.° Men praise
325 that song more which comes freshest to the audience.

---

304 *from Troy*: Athena sponsored the Achaean forces at Troy, but she was outraged by Oïlean Ajax's rape of
    Kassandra as she clung to the idol of Athena, according to later tradition. The *Odyssey* seems to refer to this
    incident here.

310 *handmaid*: Probably the "handmaids," "housemaids," "housekeepers," and "servants" are all slaves. There
    does not appear to be a free serving class, as far as we can tell.

318 *Hellas and mid-Argos*: *Hellas* is a territory near Achilles' realm in southern THESSALY, in northern Greece;
    mid-Argos would be southern Greece, or the PELOPONNESUS. The phrase means "all of Greece."

324 *Danaäns*: Used interchangeably with *Achaeans* and *Argives* to refer to the Greeks.

Let your heart and spirit dare to listen. Not only
Odysseus lost in Troy the day of his homecoming,
but many other men perished. So go to your chamber
and busy yourself with your own tasks, your loom and distaff,°
and order your handmaids to do their own work.   330
Speech is man's concern, for every one of us, and especially
for me, because the authority in this house is mine!"

Amazed, Penelope went back to her room, for she took
to heart her son's wise speech. Going then into her upper chamber
with her slaves, she bewailed Odysseus, her dear husband,   335
until flashing-eyed Athena cast sweet sleep upon her eyes.

The suitors broke into an uproar throughout the shady halls,
and every one of them prayed that he might lie by her side.
Then shrewd Telemachos began to address them: "Suitors
of my mother, though you are insolent, let us now take pleasure   340
in the feast. But let there be no brawling. It is a good thing
to hear a singer such as this one, whose voice is like that
of the gods. But in the morning let us take our seats in the assembly,
all of us, so that I may declare my views to you outright—
that you depart from these halls! Make up other feasts, devour   345
your own possessions, changing from house to house.
If you think it is better and preferable to destroy the substance
of one man with impunity—go ahead and do it! But I will call
upon the gods who live forever, in case Zeus may grant
that you be punished for your acts. Then you would all perish here   350
without remedy!"

So he spoke, and all the suitors bit their lips in astonishment,
for he had spoken boldly. Then Antinoös,° the son of Eupeithes, spoke
to him: "Telemachos, surely the gods themselves are teaching you
to be a man of boastful tongue and to speak boldly! May the son
of Kronos never make you the chief in Ithaca surrounded by the sea, 355
though it is your right by birth."

Then shrewd Telemachos answered him:
"Antinoös, will you be angry at what I am saying? I would be willing
to accept even this chieftainship from the hand of Zeus. Do you think

---

329 *distaff*: The distaff was a stick held between the chest and upper arm at the end of which the wool was
     bunched for spinning.
352 *Antinoös*: "hostile," the ringleader among the suitors. His father Eupeithes, "very persuasive," is the last
     man to die in the poem (Book 24).

that is the worst thing that can happen to a man? It is not a bad thing
360 to be chief. Your house becomes rich right away and you are held
in highest honor. But there are many other chiefs of the Achaeans
in Ithaca surrounded by the sea, young and old. One of these may have
this position, for godlike Odysseus is dead. But I will be the chief
of my own house and of the slaves that godlike Odysseus won in his raids!"

365   Then Eurymachos,° the son of Polybos, answered him: "Telemachos,
well, these things lie on the knees of the gods, who will be chief
of the Achaeans on Ithaca surrounded by the sea. As for your possessions,
you may have them and rule over your own house. May that man
never come who takes away your possessions by violence so long
370 as men still live on Ithaca! But, my excellent fellow, I would like
to ask about this stranger—where does he come from? From what land
is he? Where are his kinsmen and his ancestral fields?
Does he bring some news of your father's return, or does he come here
with his own purpose in mind? How he leaped up and was gone!
375 He did not wait for us to become acquainted with him. And yet
he did not seem in any way to be a base man to look upon."

     The shrewd Telemachos answered him: "Eurymachos, the homecoming
of my father is no more. I no longer believe in any news, no matter
where it comes from, nor do I put any faith in some prophecy
380 that my mother may learn from a seer when she has called him into the hall.
This stranger is a guest-friend of my father, from Taphos. He says
that he is Mentes, the son of wise Anchialos, and that he is lord
of the Taphians who love to row." So spoke Telemachos,
though in his heart he had recognized the deathless goddess.

385   Now the suitors turned to the dance and to pleasant song,
and they made merry. They partied until the evening should come.
As they made merry, the dark night fell upon them. Then
each man went to his own house to take his rest. Telemachos
went to his chamber built in the very beautiful court,
390 lofty, in a place of broad outlook. He went up to bed there,
turning over many things in his head.

                    Wise and faithful
Eurykleia went with him, the daughter of Ops, son of Peisenor,
carrying blazing torches. Once Laërtes had purchased
her with his wealth, though he was still very young.

---

365 *Eurymachos*: "widely powerful," also a leader among the suitors.

He gave the price of twenty cattle,° and he honored Eurykleia   395
in his halls as he honored his faithful wife. But Laërtes never slept
with her, avoiding the anger of his wife.

                          It was she who carried
the blazing torches for Telemachos. Of all the female slaves
she loved him the best, and she had nursed him when he was
a child. He opened the doors of the well-built chamber   400
and sat down on the bed. He took off his soft shirt and placed it
in the hands of the wise old woman. She folded the shirt
and smoothed it out, then hung it on a peg beside the corded bed.
Then she left the chamber, shutting the door by its silver
handle. She drove the bolt home with its strap. There,   405
all night long, wrapped in a woolen blanket, he pondered
in his mind the journey that Athena had shown him.

---

395 *cattle*: A high price. The father and grandfather of Eurykleia, "of wide fame," are named because she is
evidently of high birth, no doubt captured by pirates.

BOOK 2. *Telemachos Calls an Assembly*

When early-born Dawn appeared with her fingers of rose,
the dear son of Odysseus rose from his bed. He put on
his clothes and he slung his sharp sword around his shoulder.
He bound his beautiful sandals beneath his shining feet
5 and went out of the chamber, like a god to look upon.
He quickly ordered the clear-voiced heralds to summon
the Achaeans, who wear their hair long, to assembly. They made
the announcement, and the Achaeans promptly assembled.
When they were assembled and gathered together, Telemachos
10 went into the place of assembly, holding his bronze spear
in his hands. He was not alone, but two swift dogs followed
behind. Athena poured out a wondrous grace upon him,
and all the people marveled at him as he went along.

He sat in his father's seat, and the elders drew back.
15 Then the warrior Aigyptios° began to speak to them, a man
bowed with age, who knew ten thousand things.
Now he spoke, for his son had followed godlike Odysseus
to Ilion, famed for its horses, in the hollow ships—
the warrior Antiphos. The savage Cyclops had killed
20 Antiphos in his hollow cave and prepared him last
for his dinner. He had three other sons. One, Eurynomos,
consorted with the suitors, and the other two regularly
kept their father's farm. Yet Aigyptios could not forget
about Antiphos, mourning and feeling sorrow for him.°

25 Pouring down tears, Aigyptios spoke and addressed
the assembly: "Listen now, Ithacans, to what I say.
We have had no assembly or meeting since the time
when brave Odysseus went away in his hollow ships.
And now who has called the assembly? On whom has so
30 great a need fallen? On any of the young men, or on those

---

15 *Aigyptios*: "the Egyptian," a name that also appears in the Linear B tablets from the Greek Bronze Age
(c. 1200 BC) found at Pylos.

24 *for him*: But Aigyptios could have no way of knowing about his son's fate!

who are older? Has he heard some news of an invading
army that he might tell us about plainly, seeing that he has
first learned of it? Or will he speak and address us on some
other public matter? He seems to be a good man, a blessed man.
May Zeus accomplish some good thing for that man,   35
whatever he desires in his heart."

       So he spoke, and the dear son
of Odysseus rejoiced at his words of good omen. He no longer
kept his seat, but was minded, now, to speak. He stood up in the middle
of the assembly. The herald Peisenor,° a man of good sense,
placed the scepter in his hand. Taking it, Telemachos spoke   40
to old Aigyptios first: "Old fellow, that man who has called this
assembly is not far off, and now you will know who it is.
It is I! For on me more than any other has sorrow fallen.
I have heard no news of an approaching army that I can plainly
describe to you that I have learned about first, nor will I   45
speak and address you about some other public matter,
but only from my own need.

      "A double evil has fallen
on my house. First, my noble father is dead, who once
ruled among you, and was a gentle father. And now
a far greater evil has come, one which will soon ruin   50
my house and destroy all my substance. Suitors have
forced themselves on my mother, who is entirely unwilling—
the sons of men who are of the highest birth here.
They are afraid to go the house of her father, Ikarios,°
who might provide his daughter with a dowry and give her   55
to the man he wants, to whomever he finds most pleasing.
Instead they throng our house day after day,
killing the cattle and the sheep and the fat goats.
They make merry and recklessly drink the flaming wine.
These things are largely wasted! For there is no longer   60
a man, such as was Odysseus, to ward off ruin
from the house.

    "As for me, I am not such as he to ward it off.
Even if I tried, I would be found weak and wanting of valor.
I would of course defend myself—if I only had the strength!

---

39 *Peisenor*: Never mentioned again.

54 *Ikarios*: He speaks as if Ikarios lives on Ithaca, but later tradition usually placed him in Sparta.

65 Intolerable deeds have been done—my house is ruined,
    and in no pretty way. Take shame upon yourselves, and have
    some respect for the other neighbors who live nearby. Fear
    the anger of the gods, in case they turn against you in wrath
    at your evil deeds! I pray by Olympian Zeus and by Themis,°
70 who dissolves and gathers the assemblies of men—forbear,
    my friends, and leave me to waste away alone in bitter grief—
    unless my father, the noble Odysseus, badly treated the Achaeans
    with their fancy shin guards, and in revenge for this you spitefully
    do me harm by egging these men on. It would be better
75 for me if you yourselves ate up my treasures and flocks.
    If *you* were to devour them, someday there might be recompense.
    For just so long we would go up and down the city
    asking for our goods back, until all were given. But as it is,
    you cast woes upon my heart past cure!"

                                        Thus he spoke
80 in anger, and he threw the scepter to the ground and burst
    into tears. Pity seized all the people. Everyone fell silent,
    and not one dared to answer Telemachos with harsh words,
    until Antinoös alone spoke to him in reply: "Telemachos,
    you loudmouth! Unrestrained in daring! What are you saying?
85 Putting us to shame? You want to fix the blame on us?
    The Achaean suitors are in no way at fault, but it is your own mother,
    crafty above all other women. Already now it is the third year—
    soon it will be the fourth—since she has deceived the hearts
    in the breasts of all the Achaeans. To all she offers hope
90 and promises to each man, sending him messages, but her mind
    is set on other things.

                    "She devised this trick in her heart:
    Setting up a great loom in the halls, she fell to weaving.
    The web was of fine thread and very large. Right away
    she said to us: 'Young men, my suitors, because the excellent
95 Odysseus is dead, be patient, although eager for my wedding,
    until I finish this robe. I would not want my spinning
    to be for nothing. It is a shroud for the warrior Laërtes,
    for the time when the dread fate of grievous death will take hold
    of him. I would not want any of the Achaean women in the land
100 to be angry with me, if he who had won many possessions should
    lie without a shroud.' So she spoke, and our proud hearts agreed.

---

69 *Themis:* "law," a Titan. She stands for the traditional order of things, the way things should be done.

"Then by day she wove at the great loom, but at night
she unraveled that same work by torchlight. Thus by this trick
she kept the Achaeans from knowing for three years. But when
the fourth year came around as the seasons rolled along, then 105
one of her women, who well knew what was going on, told us,
and we caught her unraveling the splendid weaving. So she finished it
against her will. We made her do it.

            "And so the suitors answer
you thus, so that you might know this deceit, and all the other
Achaeans know it too: You must send your mother away! 110
Urge her to marry whomever her father orders, whomever
pleases her. But if she shall continue to annoy the sons
of the Achaeans for very long, being conscious in her heart
that Athena has given to her above all other women to be skillful
in making beautiful things, and in having an understanding heart— 115
and knowing tricks such as we have never heard of in the women
of olden times! Of the fair-tressed Achaean women of long ago,
Tyro and Alkmenê and Mykenê° with the fine crown!
Of all these, not one knew clever plots like Penelope. But *this* plot
did not come out favorably— 120

            "Well, for so long shall men
devour your substance and your possessions, as long
as that woman keeps to this plan which the gods now place
in her heart. She may bring great fame to herself, but on you
a concern for your rich substance. As for us, we will *not* go
to our farms nor any place else, before she marries 125
whichever of the Achaeans she chooses."

            The shrewd Telemachos
then answered him: "Antinoös, there is no way that I can thrust
her from this house against her will—she who bore me, who raised me.
My father is off in some other land, whether he is alive or dead.
It is an evil for me to pay back a great price to Ikarios,° if I willingly 130
send my mother away. For I will suffer evils from her father, and evil
spirits will pile on still more trouble. For my mother, as she leaves

---

118 . . . *Mykenê*: Tyro was the mother of Pelias and Neleus by Poseidon, hence the grandmother of Nestor;
     Alkmenê was the mother of Herakles by Zeus; Mykenê is the eponymous heroine of Mycenae. But none of
     these women was especially noted for her cleverness.

130 *Ikarios*: Telemachos means he would have to pay Ikarios the equivalent of Penelope's dowry, or compensa-
     tion for the slight done her. If so, this cost would in any event be less than the depredations of the suitors.
     Telemachos is rattled, and his speech is not entirely coherent.

FIGURE 2.1 Penelope at her loom with Telemachos. Telemachos stands to the left holding two spears, reproaching his mother. She sits mournfully on a chair, head bowed and legs crossed in a pose canonical for Penelope. The partially completed weaving shows a border of two winged horses (Pegasos?), a winged god (Hermes?), and a winged sphinx. Athenian red-figure cup, c. 440 BC, by the Penelope Painter.

the house, would call on the dread Erinys.° And I would have blame
from men too. Therefore I will never pronounce this command.

"As for you, if your heart is angry at these things, well, get out   135
of my house! Prepare other meals—go, devour your own possessions,
shifting from house to house. But if it seems better and preferable
to you to destroy the substance of one man's house without recompense,
go ahead and do it! But I will call on the gods that are forever,
in the hopes that Zeus will grant deeds of retribution.   140
Then all of you will perish unavenged in my halls!"

So spoke Telemachos, and Zeus with his far-reaching
voice sent two eagles to fly high from a peak of the mountains.
They flew with the breath of the wind for a time, side by side
with their wings spread out, but when they came to the middle   145
of the assembly with many voices, then they wheeled over it and flapped
their wings rapidly, and they looked down on the assembly. Their glance
was death. They tore with their claws one another's cheeks and necks
on either side,° then dashed away to the right, over the houses
and the cities of men.   150

The people were amazed when their eyes
saw the birds. They pondered in their hearts what was about
to come to pass. The aged warrior Halitherses° spoke to them,
the son of Mastor, who surpassed all men of his day in bird-prophecy
and in pronouncing words of fate. He addressed and spoke to the assembly
with good intent: "Listen now, O Ithacans, listen to what I say.   155
Especially I speak to the suitors and pronounce these things,
for on you a great calamity will soon unroll. Odysseus
will not be away from his friends for long. Already he is near
and preparing deadly fate for these men—for one and all.
Yes, and evil will come to many others of those who live   160
in bright Ithaca. But let us take counsel much before that
how we might end this. Much the best that they *themselves* end it!
That would be the best thing by far. I prophesy as one experienced,
one with full knowledge.

---

133 *Erinys*: An underworld spirit that punished crimes within the family, associated with curses (often in the
     plural, *Erinyes*).
149 *on either side*: Apparently as a gesture of mourning for the sad situation on Ithaca. Presumably the two
     eagles represent Odysseus and Telemachos.
152 *Halitherses*: "sea-bold"; his father Mastor is "seeker," a name no doubt made up for this occasion.

"And as far as Odysseus is concerned,
165 I say that everything has come to pass just as I told him
when the Argives went off to Ilion, and the resourceful Odysseus
went with them. I declared that after suffering many evils, and losing
all his companions, he would return home, unrecognized by all,
in the twentieth year. And now all these things are coming to pass."

170 Eurymachos, the son of Polybos, said to Halitherses in reply:
"Old man, get out of here! Go home and prophesy to your own children,
so that something bad doesn't happen to them in times to come.
I am much better than you to make prophecies in such matters.
There are many birds just flying around beneath the rays of the sun,
175 and I don't think they are all bird prophecies.° As for Odysseus, he is dead
in some far-away land, and I wish that you had perished with him.
Then you would not go around making up these tall-tale prophecies,
and you would not be goading-on Telemachos in his anger,
hoping for some gift for your house, if he might give it.

180 "But I am going to say something to you, and I think that
it will come to pass: If you, with so much more experience,
will drive on a younger man to anger with your deceiving words,
then that will surely be a still greater pain for him. He will never
be able to do *anything* because of these suitors here. And on you,
185 old man, we will load a penalty that will cause a ton of trouble
for your spirit to pay! Your sorrow will be bitter!

"And to Telemachos I will offer this advice here among all:
Let him order his mother to go back to her father's house!
He will arrange the marriage and prepare the wedding gifts,
190 full many as are suitable to follow a beloved daughter. I don't
think that the sons of the Achaeans will cease from their onerous
courtship before that time, and *in any case* we fear no man—
neither Telemachos, for all his fine speeches, nor do we give a hoot
for any prophesying that you, old man, deliver. It will come
195 to nothing, and you will be despised the more. And his possessions
will be wickedly devoured. They shall never be what once
they were, so long as she shall delay her marriage with one
of the Achaeans. After all, we are waiting day after day,
rivaling one another on account of this woman's excellence.
200 We do not go after other women whom any one of us might
fittingly marry!"

---

175 *prophecies*: In fact, in the *Iliad* and the *Odyssey* bird prophecies always come true.

Then the shrewd Telemachos replied:
"Eurymachos and you other proud suitors, I will not beg
these things any more from you nor speak of them,
for now the gods know all about it, as do all the Achaeans.
But come now, give me a swift ship and twenty companions   205
who will help me complete my journey there and back.
For I will go to Sparta and to sandy Pylos to learn of the homecoming
of my father, who has been gone so long—if perhaps someone might
tell me. Or I might hear news from Zeus, who more than any other
brings tidings to men. If I hear that my father is alive and will return,   210
then, though I am hard-pressed, I might still hold out here for a year.
But if I hear that he is dead and no longer among the living,
I will return to this my native land and heap up a barrow for him
and perform the funeral rites, as many as are appropriate,
and I will give my mother to a husband."   215

                So he spoke, then sat down.
Mentor, always a companion to noble Odysseus, stood up among them.
When he left for Troy, Odysseus turned over his household to him,
saying all should obey this old man, who would keep everything safe.
And so Mentor, with good intention, addressed the assembly:
"Listen to me now, Ithacans—hear what I have to say.   220
Never after this may any sceptered chief with a friendly heart
be kind and gentle, nor may he heed righteousness in his heart,
but may he always be harsh and do unrighteous things.
For apparently no one remembers godlike Odysseus—
none of the people over whom he ruled. He was gentle,   225
like a father. I do not hold it against the proud suitors that they
perform violent acts in the evil devising of their minds, for it is
at the hazard of their own lives that they brutally devour
the household of Odysseus—he who they *say* will never return.
But I am angry at the rest of you people who sit in silence   230
and speak no rebuke against the suitors, telling them to cease,
though you are many and they are few."

                Then Leiokritos,°
the son of Euenor, replied: "Mentor, you are a mischief-maker.
Crazy in your head! What have you said? Urging us to lighten up?
It's tough times to fight with men about a feast when they   235
are many more than you. Were even noble Odysseus himself
to return and find the noble suitors eating in his house,

---

233 *Leiokritos:* "chosen among the people, " a suitor, he is named only here and when he is killed by Telemachos
    (Book 22).

and be eager in his heart to drive them out of his house,
his wife would take little joy in his coming, though she longed
240 for him greatly! Right here he would meet a shameful death,
if he were to go against so many. You have not spoken what is right.

    "But come, let the people scatter each man to his farm.
As for this fellow, Mentor and Halitherses will speed him on
his journey, for they are friends of his father from a long way back.
245 But as I reckon, Telemachos will remain here in Ithaca
receiving his information, and not succeed in his journey."

    So he spoke, and hastily Leiokritos dissolved the assembly.
The people scattered, each man to his own house,
but the suitors returned to the house of godlike Odysseus.
250 Telemachos went his own way, to the seashore. He washed
his hands in the gray sea and prayed to Athena: "Hear me,
you who came yesterday as a god to our house and ordered me
to take a ship on the misty sea, to find out about the homecoming
of my father, who has been so long away. All these things the Achaeans
255 oppose, but especially the suitors in their evil insolence."

    So he spoke in prayer. And Athena came near him,
now in the guise, the form and voice, of Mentor,
and she spoke to him words that went like arrows:
"Telemachos, you will not be a base man in times to come,
260 nor without good sense, if any of the good spirit of your father
is instilled in your veins. Such a man was he, to accomplish
in both word and deed. This journey of yours will not be in vain,
not for nothing. If you are not his son and Penelope's son,
then I have no hope that you will succeed in your desire.
265 Few sons are like their fathers. The most are worse,
and only a few are better than their fathers. But because
you will not be a base man in times to come, nor without
good sense, nor has the cleverness of Odysseus entirely
failed you, there is hope that you will fulfill this task.
270 Let the attitude and the intentions of the suitors go—the fools!
They cannot foresee what will happen, and they do not know justice.
Nor do they know of the death and black fate that is near them,
that they shall all die in a single day.

                              "As for yourself,
the journey that you have in mind is not far off, so true
275 a companion am I to your father's house. I will fit out for you
a swift ship, and I myself will go with you. But go now to your

house and mix with the suitors. Make ready your provisions.
Put everything into vessels—wine into two-handled jars,
and barley, the marrow of men, in thick skins. I will go through
the town quickly and gather willing companions for you.   280
There are many ships in Ithaca, surrounded by the sea,
both new and old. Of these I will find one that is best,
and soon will we fit her out and set forth on the broad sea."

    So spoke Athena, the daughter of Zeus. Telemachos
did not wait long after he heard the voice of the goddess.   285
He went off to his house with heavy heart. He found the proud
suitors in the halls, skinning out goats and singeing pigs
in the court.

        Antinoös, laughing, came right up to Telemachos.
He clasped his hand and he spoke and addressed him by name:
"Telemachos, you braggart, unrestrained in boldness, let no more   290
evil deed or word reside in your breast! But go ahead, eat
and drink, as before. And all these many things too the Achaeans
will provide for you, the ship and chosen rowers, so that you
might quickly go to sacred Pylos in search of news about
your noble father."   295

        The shrewd Telemachos answered him:
"Antinoös, it is impossible that I sit quietly in the midst of your
arrogant company, you who dine and make merry at my expense.
Is it not enough that in earlier times you wasted my many fine
possessions, you suitors, when I was still a child? But now that
I have grown and gain knowledge hearing the speech of others,   300
and anger grows within me, I will find how I might do to you
all the harm I can—either going to Pylos, or here in this land.

    "Well, I will go, but this journey of which I speak will not
be for nothing, though I go as a passenger. For I do not
have my own ship, nor do I command a crew of rowers.   305
I suppose you thought that to be to your advantage?"

    Telemachos spoke, and without more ado pulled his hand
away from Antinoös.

        The suitors busied themselves with their
meal throughout the house. They mocked and jeered Telemachos
with their speech. Thus would one of the arrogant young men say: 310
"I suppose that Telemachos is planning our murder! I suppose

that he will bring men from sandy Pylos to help him, or even
from Sparta, since he is completely determined to go there.
Or maybe he wants to go to Ephyra,° that rich land, to get some
315 death-dealing potions that he can throw into the wine bowl
and so waste us all!"

And again another of the arrogant youths
would say: "Who knows? He may himself perish going on the hollow ship,
far from his friends, wandering around like Odysseus. That would only
cause us a lot more trouble. Then we would have to divide up
320 all his possessions, and we would give his house to his mother
to live in, and to him who should marry her."

So they spoke. But Telemachos
went down to the high-roofed chamber of his father, a wide room
where gold and bronze lay piled up, and cloth in chests,
and an abundance of sweet-smelling oil. Jars of wine stood there,
325 all in a row and fitting close together against the wall—
old, sweet wine, having within pure divine drink, in case
Odysseus were to come home after suffering many pains.
The double-doors were locked, fitted closely together, and there
a serving woman guarded them night and day in the wisdom
330 of her mind—Eurykleia, the daughter of Ops, the son of Peisenor.

Telemachos now called her to the chamber and addressed her:
"Nurse, come, draw some sweet wine for me in two-handled jars,
that which is the finest, after that wine which you keep
in constant hope for that ill-fated one, if ever he should return—
335 Zeus-born° Odysseus, escaping from death and the fates.
Fill twelve jars and fit them with stoppers. Pour out for me
barley into skins that are well sewn. Let there be twenty measures
of ground barley meal. And keep this quiet! Have all these things
brought together. At evening I will pick them up, when my mother
340 goes upstairs and lies down to sleep. I am going to Sparta
and to sandy Pylos to inquire about my dear father's homecoming,
to see if I can find out something."

So he spoke, and the dear nurse
Eurykleia cried aloud, and weeping spoke to him words
that went like arrows: "Why, O why, dear child, do you want

---

314 *Ephyra*: Probably in THRESPROTIA, where Odysseus went to get poison for his arrows (Book 1).

335 *Zeus-born*: An honorific epithet, in the sense that Odysseus is like a god.

to do this? Why do you want to go over the wide earth,   345
you who are an only child and one well loved? He has died
far from his own country, the Zeus-born Odysseus,
somewhere in a strange land. These men will work some evil
against you as soon as you are gone, so that you may perish
by their trickery—and then they will divide all your possessions.   350
Only stay here and watch over what is yours. There is
no need for you to suffer by wandering on the unresting sea."

    Then the shrewd Telemachos answered her: "Courage,
nurse! Not without a god have I devised this plan. But do not
tell my mother before the eleventh or twelfth day, or until she   355
herself shall miss me and hear that I have gone. I do
not want her to harm her beautiful flesh by weeping."

    So he spoke, and the nurse swore a great oath by the gods.
And when she had sworn and accomplished the oath, she drew off
wine into the two-handled jars, and then she poured barley into skins   360
that were well sewn. Telemachos went off into the house
to mix with the suitors.

                        Then the goddess, flashing-eyed Athena,
thought of something else. In the likeness of Telemachos she went
everywhere throughout the city, and to each man she came
near she spoke a word, urging him at evening to gather   365
beside the swift ship. From Noëmon, the glorious son of Phronios,°
she asked for a ship, and he gladly agreed. The sun went down
and all the byways were filled with shadow, and then the goddess
dragged the swift ship down to the sea. She placed all
the gear in it that well-constructed ships carry. She tied it up   370
at the mouth of the harbor. Then the noble companions assembled
around it, and the goddess gave encouragement to each man.

    Then again the flashing-eyed goddess thought of something
else. She went to the house of godlike Odysseus. There
she poured out sweet sleep over the suitors, and she made   375
their minds to wander with drink, and she cast the cups from
their hands. They got up to go to their rest throughout the city.
They did not remain seated for long, because sleepiness fell
on their eyelids.

---

366   *Noëmon . . . Phronios*: "thinking man" son of "sensible man," speaking names to distinguish these Ithacans
      from the suitors; *Noëmon* is a fairly common name, but *Phronios* appears only here.

FIGURE 2.2 Athena. The goddess holds her helmet in her left hand and a spear in her right as she looks to her right. She wears the goatskin fetish (*aegis*) as a cloak around her neck and down her back, its edges fringed with coiling serpents. Illustration on an Athenian red-figure vase, c. 490 BC.

But flashing-eyed Athena spoke to Telemachos,
calling him out of the comfortable halls, taking on the likeness
of Mentor in both form and voice: "Telemachos, right now
your companions with fancy shin guards are sitting ready
at the oar. They await your departure. So let us go!
Let us not long delay this journey!"

                    So speaking, Pallas Athena
quickly led the way, and Telemachos followed in the footsteps
of the goddess. When they came to the ship and the sea,
they found their long-haired companions on the shore. Telemachos
spoke to them: "Come, my friends, let us load the provisions.
All are gathered together in the hall. My mother knows nothing,
nor none of the female slaves. Only one heard my word."

   So speaking, he led the way, and his crew followed along.
They brought and stored everything in the well-constructed ship,
just as the dear son of Odysseus ordered. Then Telemachos
got in the ship, and Athena went before him and sat down
in the stern of the ship. Telemachos sat down beside her
while the men loosed the stern cables and got on board.
They sat down near the thole-pins.° Flashing-eyed Athena sent
a favorable wind, a powerful west wind that sang
over the wine-dark sea. Telemachos called to his men
and ordered them to take hold of the ropes, and they did what
he said. Then they set up the mast of fir in the hollow socket
and made it fast with fore-stays. They raised the white sail
with twisted thongs of ox-hide. The wind filled the belly
of the sail. The dark wave rang loudly about the keel of the ship
as it raced along. She sped through the waves, making her journey.

   When they had made fast the tackle throughout the dark swift ship,
they set out bowls brimming with wine, and they poured out
drink-offerings to the deathless gods who live forever—
but most of all to the flashing-eyed daughter of Zeus.
All night long and up through the dawn they cut their way.

380

385

390

395

400

405

410

---

397   *thole-pins*: Hook-shaped fittings to which the oars were attached by means of leather straps.

BOOK 3. *Telemachos in Pylos*

The sun rose out of the very beautiful sea, into the brazen heaven,
where it shone for the immortals and for mortal men on the earth,
giver of grain. The Ithacans came to PYLOS, the well-built city of Neleus,
where the people of the town were sacrificing all-black bulls at the edge
5 of the sea to Poseidon,° the earth-shaker whose locks are blue.
There were nine companies of townspeople, and five hundred men in each,
and in each they readied nine bulls. They were tasting the entrails
and burning the thigh bones to the god when the Ithacans put straight
into shore. The Ithacans furled the sail of the comely ship and tied it up.
10 They moored the ship and stepped forth.

                             Then Telemachos disembarked
and Athena led the way. Flashing-eyed Athena, the goddess, was first
to speak to him: "Telemachos, you have no need to be embarrassed,
not a bit. You have sailed over the sea in order that you might learn
about your father, where the earth lies over him and what fate
15 he has met. So come now, go straight to Nestor, the tamer of horses,
so that we may learn what counsel he conceals in his chest.
Inquire of him plainly, so that he may tell you the truth.
He will not tell you a lie! He is a just man."

                                 The shrewd
Telemachos answered her: "Mentor, how shall I go up to him?
20 How shall I greet him? I have no experience with clever words.
I would be embarrassed to question an older man."

                               Then flashing-eyed
Athena, the goddess, spoke to him: "Telemachos, you will think
of something all by yourself, and a spirit will help you. I don't think
that you were born and reared without the help of the gods!"

25   So speaking Pallas Athena quickly led the way, and Telemachos
followed in the footsteps of the goddess. They came to the gathering

---

5 *Poseidon*: In fact Poseidon appears as an important god in the Linear B tablets found at the Bronze Age site of Pylos.

of the companies of the Pylian men, where Nestor sat with his sons.
Around him his companions made ready the feast, roasting some
of the meat and skewering other pieces on spits. When they saw
the strangers, they all gathered around them and clasped their hands   30
in welcome and urged them to take a seat. First of all Peisistratos,°
the son of Nestor, came close and clasped the hands of each man,
and had them sit at the feast on soft fleece on the sands
of the sea, beside his brother Thrasymedes and his father.

    Peisistratos gave them a share of the entrails, and he poured   35
out wine in a golden cup. Saluting her, he spoke to Pallas
Athena, the daughter of Zeus who carries the goatskin fetish:°
"Pray now, O stranger, to King Poseidon. It is his feast
you have chanced to come upon. But when you have poured out drink
as an offering and prayed, as is proper, then give the cup   40
of honey-sweet wine to your friend to pour from, because
I think that he too prays to the deathless ones. All men
have need of the gods. However, he is younger, of a like age
with myself. Therefore I give the golden cup to you first."

    So speaking, Peisistratos placed the cup of sweet wine   45
in Athena's hand, and she rejoiced at the justice of this sensible man
for giving the golden cup to her first. Then promptly she prayed
to King Poseidon: "Hear me, O earth-holder Poseidon,
and do not fail to fulfill these things for which we pray.
To Nestor and his sons, first of all, grant glory, then give   50
to all the other Pylians a gracious return for this splendid
sacrificial offering. Furthermore, grant that Telemachos
and I return home when we have accomplished all that for which
we have come here on a swift black ship."

                    So she prayed, though
she herself was bringing all to fulfillment! She gave the beautiful   55
two-handled cup to Telemachos, and the dear son of Odysseus
prayed likewise. Then they roasted the outer flesh and drew it
from the spits. They divided the portions and had a glorious feast.

---

31 *Peisistratos*: Not mentioned in the *Iliad*, he is Nestor's youngest son and the only one who is not married.

37 *fetish*: The Greek is *aegis*, which means "goatskin," maybe in origin either a shield or a "medicine" bag
      containing power objects. In Homer, the *aegis* is an object that inspires terror. In art somewhat later than
      Homer, the *aegis* has become a cloak with snake-head tassels and a Gorgon's head in the center, worn more
      by Athena than by Zeus (see Figures 2.2, 13.2).

But when they had put all desire for drink and food from themselves,
60 then Gerenian° Nestor, the horseman, began to speak:
"Now it is right to ask and inquire of these strangers who
they are, for they have had pleasure in our food.° O strangers,
who are you? From where have you journeyed over the watery deep?
And on what business have you come? Or do you sail around recklessly
65 like pirates on the salt sea, who wander around endangering
their lives and bringing evil to men of foreign shores?"

The shrewd Telemachos, taking courage, then replied, and Athena
placed boldness in his heart to ask about his father, who was gone,
so that there might be a good report about himself among men:
70 "O Nestor, son of Neleus, great glory of the Achaeans, you ask
from where we come? I will tell you. We come from ITHACA
that is beneath Mount Neion. The business of which I speak
is personal and does not concern the people. I come for far-reaching news
of my father, in case I might hear something—I mean godlike
75 Odysseus of the steady heart, whom they say once fought by your side
and sacked the city of the Trojans. We have learned where all the others
who fought the Trojans died their wretched deaths, but of him the son
of Kronos has made even the death unknown. For no one is able to say
for sure where my father died, whether he was killed on land
80 by the enemy, or whether he died on the sea amidst the waves
of Amphitritê.° For this reason I have come now to your knees, in case
you can tell me of his wretched death, if you saw it with your own eyes,
or heard someone else tell the story of his wanderings. For beyond all
others his mother bore him to sorrow. And do not, from respect for me,
85 or from pity, speak honeyed words, but tell me how you got sight
of him. I beg you, if ever my father, the noble Odysseus,
promised you anything of word or deed and fulfilled it in the land
of the Trojans, where the Achaeans suffered evils, remember it now
and tell me the truth."

Then Gerenian Nestor, the horseman,
90 answered him: "My friend, you have reminded me of the sorrow
that we endured in that land, we sons of the Achaeans, irresistible
in daring, and all that we suffered on the misty sea, wandering

---

60 *Gerenian*: Evidently "from Gerena," perhaps a place near Pylos, but the meaning is obscure.

62 *food*: Wandering strangers are always fed first, then they are expected to reveal who they are, where they come from, and what is their mission.

81 *Amphitritê*: A daughter of Nereus, the Old Man of the Sea, and according to Hesiod (eighth century BC) the consort of Poseidon.

about in our ships in pursuit of booty, wherever Achilles led,
and all our struggles around the city of great King Priam—
there the best of us were killed. There warlike Ajax lies,   95
there Achilles, there Patroklos, the equal to the gods in giving counsel.
And there lies my own dear son, strong and handsome, Antilochos,°
superior in speed of foot and as a warrior.

                      "And we suffered many other
losses beside these. Who of mortal men could tell them all?
Not if for five or six years you were to remain here and ask   100
of all the evils that the good Achaeans suffered there . . . Well, you
would grow tired of listening and would return to your native land.

    "For nine years we plotted their ruin, contriving all manner
of tricks, and barely did the son of Zeus bring our plans to fulfillment.
There, no man was willing to pit himself against Odysseus   105
in giving advice, for godlike Odysseus was better by far
in all kinds of cunning—your father, if in fact you are his son.
I am amazed to look upon you! Your speech is just like his, and you
would not think that a younger man could speak just like him.
So long as godlike Odysseus and I were there, we never spoke   110
at cross purposes in the assembly or in the council, but having a single
mind we advised the Argives with wisdom and wise council how things
would turn out for the best. But after we had sacked the high city
of Priam and gone off in our ships, and some god scattered the Achaeans,
then Zeus devised a wretched homecoming in his mind for the Argives.   115
For we were not all respectful or just. And so many of us suffered
an evil fate through the destructive anger of the flashing-eyed goddess,
the daughter of a powerful father. She caused strife between the two sons
of Atreus.° For these two called all the Achaeans into assembly,
recklessly, and not in the way things should be done, just when   120
the sun was going down. The sons of the Achaeans came, wooly with wine.
Then the sons of Atreus gave their speech, saying why they had gathered
the army together. And Menelaos urged all the Achaeans to think
of their homecoming over the broad back of the sea, but this did not please
Agamemnon at all. He wanted to hold the company back   125
and perform holy sacrifice in order to appease the terrible wrath of Athena—
the fool! He did not know that she was not going to be persuaded.
For the mind of the gods who last forever is not quickly turned.

---

97   . . . *Antilochos*: Ajax killed himself after being denied the arms of Achilles, as told in Sophocles' play *Ajax*
    (c. 450-430 BC). Achilles was killed by an arrow from Paris' bow, guided by Apollo, an incident widely known.
    Antilochos was killed by Memnon, a son of Dawn, as told in a lost epic, the *Aethiopis* (c. seventh century BC).

118–119 *sons of Atreus*: That is, Agamemnon and Menelaos.

FIGURE 3.1   The death of Astyanax and Priam and the rape of Kassandra.   Many impieties were committed in the sack of Troy, which earned the enmity of Zeus and Athena against the Achaeans. In the central scene, Neoptolemos, son of Achilles, who has come to the war after his father's death, raises his sword for the coup de grace on Priam, who raises his hands, his shoulders and head already bloody. He sits on the altar of Zeus in the courtyard, indicated by the palm tree. On his lap lies the mangled body of Astyanax, the son of Hector, thrown from the walls. At his feet lies one of his dead sons, probably Deïphobos. On the far left, Kassandra clings to an image of Athena while she is raped by Oïlean Ajax (off the photo: *see also* Figure 4.3). The statue holds a shield and brandishes a spear. Two crouching women of Troy bewail their lot. On the far right, another Trojan woman attempts to defend herself, with a large wooden pestle, against a kneeling Greek. Athenian red-figure water jar by Kleophrades, c. 480 BC.

"So the two leaders stood there and exchanged harsh speech.
The Achaeans who wear fine shin guards jumped up in a wondrous din.   130
The opposed factions approved a double council. That night we rested,
pondering hard thoughts against one another. Zeus was fitting us out
for an evil doom. When dawn came, some of us dragged the ships
into the shining sea, and we put in them our possessions and the svelte
women. So half of the army stayed back and remained there with   135 🔊
Agamemnon, son of Atreus, shepherd of the people, while half of us
disembarked and rowed away.

        "We went very quickly, for a god
smoothed out the cavernous sea. When we came to TENEDOS
we made holy sacrifice to the gods, longing to reach our homes.
But Zeus did not yet intend our return—the rogue! He stirred   140
up wicked strife again, for a second time. Some again turned
back their ships, curved at both ends, following the wise
and crafty-minded King Odysseus, who now showed favor
to Agamemnon, the son of Atreus. But I took flight with
the full company of ships, who followed me. I knew that   145
some spirit was devising evil. Diomedes, the warlike son
of Tydeus, fled too, and he urged on his companions. At last
light-haired Menelaos came along with us—he overtook us
in LESBOS as we were arguing abut the long sea-trip, whether we
should sail north of rugged CHIOS toward the island of PSYRIA,   150
keeping Chios on our left, or whether we should sail on
the landward side of Chios, past windy Mimas. We beseeched
the god to show us an omen—and he did show it to us,
indicating we should sail through the midst of the sea to EUBOEA
as soon as possible, so that we might escape misery.   155

    "A shrill wind came up, and the ships ran swiftly over
the fishy deep. At night we put into GERAISTOS. There on the altar
of Poseidon we laid many thigh bones of bulls, in thanks for having
passed over the great sea.°

        "On the fourth day the companions
of Diomedes, the son of Tydeus, the tamer of horses, moored their   160
well-balanced ships in ARGOS, but I kept on towards Pylos. The wind
was never lessened from the time when a god first sent it forth to blow.

---

159 . . . *great sea*: The second day's sail was from Tenedos to Lesbos, about 30 miles. The shorter route of the
"long sea-trip" would take them north of Chios and Psyria, directly to Geraistos, the southernmost tip of
Euboea, a distance of about 125 miles. The safer but longer route, where there are ports of call, runs inside
Chios past a headland called Mimas on the coast of Asia Minor, then south of Chios and west through the
CYCLADES. At Geraistos, there was a temple to Poseidon. See MAP I.

"Thus, dear child, I came without knowledge of the others,
nor do I know about them—who of the Achaeans were saved and who
165 were destroyed. However, what I have learned sitting here in our halls,
you shall learn, as is right. I will not conceal any detail from you.
They say that the Myrmidons, famous for their spear-work, whom
the glorious son of great-hearted Achilles led,° came home safely.
Philoktetes, the splendid son of Poias,° came home safely too.
170 Idomeneus brought his companions home to Crete, all who
escaped the war, and the sea took not a single one.

                                            "You yourselves
have heard about the son of Atreus, though you are far away—
how Agamemnon came, and Aigisthos devised a gloomy end
for him. But Aigisthos paid the price, and in a terrible fashion.
175 It is a good thing to leave behind a brave child when a man
gets killed, for Orestes took vengeance on the murderer of his father,
the crafty Aigisthos, who killed his famous father. And you,
my friend—for I see that you are tall and well-knit—you, too,
be valiant, so that in times to come men may speak well of you."

180   The shrewd Telemachos answered him: "O Nestor, son of Neleus,
great glory of the Achaeans—truly Orestes took his revenge,
and the Achaeans will spread his fame abroad so that men who
are yet to come may know of it. Would that the gods might place
a similar power in me—to take vengeance on the suitors for their
185 arrogant depravity, who in their violent debauchery pile injuries
upon me! But the gods have spun out no such happiness for me—
for me or my father. Now I must endure no matter what."

      Gerenian Nestor, the horseman, answered him: "My friend,
since you have brought this up and spoken of it, they say
190 that many suitors for your mother's hand devise evils
for you in your halls against your will. Tell me, do you allow
yourself to be oppressed or do the people throughout the land
hate you, following the prompting of a god?° Who knows
whether some day Odysseus may come and take vengeance

---

168 ... *led*: Neoptolemos, raised on the island of SKYROS, whom according to prophecy the Achaeans needed to take the city of Troy after the death of Achilles.

169 ... *Poias*: Philoktetes was abandoned on the island of Lemnos after receiving an obnoxious wound from a snakebite. He possessed the bow of Herakles, without which Troy could not be taken. In the last year of the war, he was retrieved from Lemnos, his wound healed, and with Herakles' bow he killed Paris.

193 *prompting of a god*: That is, are Telemachos' troubles caused by the suitors' individual ill-will ("allow yourself to be oppressed") or by the anger of the gods revealed by the hostility of the people of Ithaca.

on them for their violence, either alone or with all of the Achaeans?   195
Ah, if only flashing-eyed Athena were willing to love you
even as she cared for glorious Odysseus in the land
of the Trojans, where the Achaeans suffered so greatly—for never
yet have I seen the gods so plainly love a man
as did Pallas Athena, standing clearly by his side. If she   200
were willing to love and care for you in her heart in the same way,
those suitors would quickly forget all about marriage!"

The shrewd Telemachos answered him: "O old man, I can't
expect this ever to happen. What you have said would be too great
a thing. I am astonished! These things will never come to pass,   205
no matter how much I wish it, not even if the gods should want it."

Then flashing-eyed Athena, the goddess, said to him:
"Telemachos, what a word has escaped the barrier of your teeth!
A god who wanted to could easily bring a man home safely,
even from a far distance. As for my part, I would rather endure   210
much pain before I reached home, and saw the day of my homecoming,
than be killed at my hearth as Agamemnon was killed by the treachery
of his wife and Aigisthos. But truly, not even the gods
can ward off death that is common to all men, even when they love
the man, once the dreaded fate of dismal death has laid hold of him."   215

Then the shrewd Telemachos answered her: "Mentor,
let us no longer speak of these things, though we are grieving.
For Odysseus a homecoming is no longer possible! For him
the deathless ones devised death and black fate a long time ago.
Now I want to ask Nestor another troubling question,   220
because he knows many things and is wise beyond all others.
They say that he has been king, in the generations of men, three times.
He seems like a deathless one to look upon.

"Nestor, son of Neleus,
tell me the truth. How did the son of Atreus, wide-ruling Agamemnon, die?
Where was Menelaos? What manner of destruction did the crafty   225
Aigisthos devise for him so he could kill a man much better than he?
Was Menelaos not in Achaean Argos,° but wandering elsewhere
among men so that Aigisthos dared to kill Agamemnon?"

---

227 *Argos*: Not the city of Argos, which was Diomedes' capital, but either the Argive plain, where Mycenae was,
     or the whole Peloponnesus.

Then Gerenian Nestor, the horseman, answered him: "Well,
230 my child, I will tell you the straight truth. I think that you
yourself know this, how things would have turned out
if the light-haired Menelaos, the son of Atreus, had come from Troy
and found Aigisthos alive in his halls! Then nobody
would have heaped-up a pile of earth over Aigisthos when dead,
235 but the dogs and birds would have ripped him apart as he lay
on the plain, far from the city. Nor would any of the Achaean
women have cried for him. What he did was monstrous!
While we were there in Troy sweating out our many trials,
he sat at his ease in a corner of Argos that nourishes horses,
240 beguiling the wife of Agamemnon with his words. At first
she put off the evil deed, the beautiful Klytaimnestra,
for she had a good heart. Furthermore there was a singer at her side
that the son of Atreus had set to look closely after his wife
when he left for Troy. But when the fate of the gods determined
245 that she should be overcome, then Aigisthos took the singer to a desert
island and left him there to be the prey and booty of birds.
Then Aigisthos took her to his house where she gladly gave in.
He burned many thigh pieces on the sacred altars of the gods,
and he hung up many pleasing gifts as offerings, woven cloth and gold,
250 for he had accomplished such a deed that he had never really believed
would fall to him.

"Then we were sailing along from Troy,
Menelaos the son of Atreus and I, in perfect friendship to one
another, when we came to holy Sounion,° the cape of Athens.
There Phoibos Apollo struck down Menelaos' helmsman,
255 hitting him with his painless arrows as he held the steering-oar
of the swift ship in his hands—Phrontis the son of Onetor,°
who excelled among the tribes of men in guiding a ship when
the storm-winds rage. So Menelaos stopped there, though eager
to continue, until he could bury his companion and perform
260 the funeral rites.

"But when Menelaos, traversing the wine-dark sea,
came to the steep peak of Malea in his hollow ships,
then Zeus, whose voice is heard from a long way off, devised
a hateful road for him. He poured blasts of the shrill winds

---

253 *Sounion:* The southeastern tip of Attica, where a temple to Poseidon still stands.

256 *... Onetor: Phrontis* means "wise"; *Onetor* means "beneficial." A sudden death for no obvious reason was
explained as caused by Apollo, for men; for women, Artemis was responsible.

on him, and the waves swelled up huge, like mountains. Then
splitting his fleet into two parts, he drove some ships to CRETE,   265
where the Kydonians live beside the streams of Iardanos. There is
a smooth cliff that goes down steeply to the misty sea on the border
of GORTYN. There South Wind drives a great wave against
the headland, on the left toward PHAISTOS, and a small rock holds
back a great wave.° Those ships came there, and with much trouble   270
the men escaped injury, but the waves smashed the ships
against the reef. And the wind and water carried the five other
dark-prowed ships along, bearing them to EGYPT.

                        "So Menelaos
was drifting there with his ships, gathering up goods and gold among
men of foreign speech. During this time Aigisthos, back at home,   275
worked out his dire plan. He ruled for seven years at Mycenae,
rich in gold, after he had killed the son of Atreus, and the people were
oppressed by him.

                "On the eighth year the good Orestes came, bent on
vengeance, back from Athens,° and Orestes killed his father's murderer,
the treacherous Aigisthos, because Aigisthos had killed his glorious father,   280
Agamemnon. After Orestes killed the man, he made a funeral feast
for the Argives over his hated mother° and the cowardly Aigisthos.
On that same day, Menelaos, good at the war cry, returned,
bearing rich treasure, all the burden that his ships could carry.

  "And you, my friend, do not wander for a long time away   285
from your house, leaving your treasure behind with such insolent
men in your house! They will divide up and devour all your wealth
and you will have gone on a fruitless journey. But I encourage
and urge you to go to Menelaos. He has recently° come
from a foreign land, from men where one would hope   290
in his heart never to return to—he whom the storm winds had once
driven off his course into a sea so vast that not even birds
may cross it in an entire year, so great and terrible it is.

---

270 ...*great wave*: The Kydonians lived around modern CHANIA in the northwest of the island (near the
      modern river Platanias, ancient Iardanos). Homer seems to mean that Menelaos' ships approached Crete
      from the western end, then sailed around to the southern side of the island where Phaistos is. Gortyn lies
      nearby. Probably the headland is the southernmost tip of Crete, but the topography is obscure.

279 *Athens*: But the later Greek tragedians place Orestes' exile in PHOCIS.

282 *hated mother*: The only reference in Homer to Orestes' matricide, famous from Aeschylus' play, the *Oresteia*
      (458 BC).

289 *recently*: In fact, nearly three years before.

"But go now with your ship and your companions, or if
295   you wish to go by land, there is a chariot and horses here,
and my sons who are here to serve you and be your guides
to shining LACEDAEMON, where light-haired Menelaos lives.
Entreat him to tell you the truth himself. He will not lie to you.
He's a wise and just man."

                        So Nestor spoke, and then the sun
300   went down and the darkness came on. The goddess, flashing-eyed
Athena, said to him: "Old man, you have said these things in accordance
with what is right. But come, cut out the tongues of the victims°
and mix the wine so that we may make a drink-offering to Poseidon
and to the other gods, then take thought of sleep. It is the time for that.
305   The light has gone down beneath the darkness. It is not right that we sit
long at the feast of the gods. We need to get on our way."

    So spoke the daughter of Zeus, and they hearkened to her voice.
Heralds poured out water over their hands and young men filled
the wine bowls brim full with drink. They served it out to all,
310   first pouring wine into the cups for the drink-offerings.
Then they threw the tongues into the fire and, standing, they poured
out the drink-offerings over the tongues. And when they had poured
out the drink-offerings and had drunk to their heart's content, then Athena
and godlike Telemachos wished to return to the hollow ship.

315   But Nestor wanted to hold them back, and he spoke, saying:
"May Zeus and the other deathless gods forbid you to go to your hollow
ship from my house as from one utterly without spare cloth!—
someone poor who does not have an abundance of cloaks and blankets
in his house on which both he and strangers may softly sleep.
320   Surely the dear son of Odysseus will never lie down on the deck°
of a ship so long as I am alive and children are left behind
in my halls to entertain strangers, whoever comes to my house."

    The goddess, flashing-eyed Athena, then said to him:
"You have spoken well, dear old man. It is right that Telemachos
325   heed you. It is better by far. While he will now follow along
with you and sleep in your hospitable halls, I will go to the black ship
and tell my companions everything that has happened, and so

---

302   *of the victims*: The tongues are those of the bulls sacrificed earlier in the day.

320   *deck*: Homeric ships did not have decks, but Nestor seems to mean a kind of platform at the rear of the ship
used by the helmsman.

reassure them. For I alone among them am the older man.
The others are younger men who follow in friendship,
all of a like age with great-hearted Telemachos. I will now lie down   330
to sleep, there, beside the black ship, but in the morning I will be off
to the great-hearted Kaukones.° They owe me a debt, neither recent
nor small. But provide this man, Telemachos, who has come
to your house, with a chariot and send along your son Peisistratos.
Give them horses, too, the fastest and strongest you have."   335

                                             So speaking,
flashing-eyed Athena went off in the likeness of a vulture.
Amazement seized all who saw this! Old Nestor was astonished
as he saw it with his own eyes. He took the hand of Telemachos,
and he spoke a word and called him by name: "My friend,
I don't think that you will prove to be a base man or without valor,   340
not if the gods shall continue to guide you in this fashion.
Truly this is none other of those who have their houses on Olympos
than the daughter of Zeus, most glorious Tritogeneia,° who honored
your noble father among the Argives. Be gracious, O Queen,
and give noble fame to myself and my children and my revered wife!   345
In return, I will sacrifice an unbroken yearling cow with a wide brow
to you, one which no man has ever put beneath the yoke.
I will sacrifice her after covering her horns in gold."

   So Nestor spoke in prayer, and Pallas Athena heard him.
Then the horseman Gerenian Nestor led them, his sons and sons-in-law,   350
to his beautiful palace. When they came to the glorious palace
of the king, they sat down in rows on the seats and chairs. The old man
mixed sweet wine for them in a wine bowl, wine that the housekeeper
opened, now in its eleventh year when she loosed the string on the stopper.
The old man mixed the wine in a wine bowl, and he prayed   355
to Athena as he poured out a drink-offering to the daughter
of Zeus who carries the goatskin fetish.

                        When he had poured
the drink-offering and they had drunk to their hearts' content, they went
to lie down, each to his own home. The horseman Gerenian Nestor
then bid Telemachos, the dear son of godlike Odysseus,   360
to take his rest on a corded bed beneath the resounding portico,
and beside him lay down Peisistratos of the fine ashen spear,

---

332 *Kaukones*: An obscure group who seem to have lived someplace in ELIS, north of Pylos.

343 *Tritogeneia*: An epithet of Athena of unknown meaning.

a leader of men, who of Nestor's sons was still unmarried
and at home. Nestor himself slept in the innermost chamber
365 of his high house. Beside him lay his wife, the mistress of the house,
who had turned down the covers.

                                When the early dawn appeared,
spreading her fingers of rose, the horseman Gerenian Nestor
arose from his bed. Coming outside, he sat down on the polished
stones that stood before his high doors, white, glistening with oil.°
370 Neleus had sat on these before, the equal to the gods in counsel.
But before this time he was overcome by fate and had gone
into the house of Hades. Now Gerenian Nestor sat there,
holding a scepter, the guardian of the Achaeans. His sons gathered
closely around him as they came out of their rooms—Echephron
375 and Stratios and Perseus and Aretus and godlike Thrasymedes.
To these Peisistratos then came as the sixth warrior.
They brought in Telemachos, like a god, and sat him beside them.

    The horseman Gerenian Nestor spoke: "Quickly, my dear
children, help me fulfill this desire—that first of all the gods
380 I might appease Athena, who came to me visibly at our rich feast.
Someone needs to go to the field and quickly get a cow,
and have the cow herder bring her here right now. Let someone,
too, go to the black ship of great-hearted Telemachos and bring all
his companions, leaving only two. And have someone order
385 Laerkes° the goldsmith to come so that he might gild the cow's
horns with gold. The rest of you should stay here together,
but ask the women slaves inside the glorious house to make ready
a feast, and to set out chairs and firewood on either side of the altar,
and to bring shining water."

                            So he spoke, and they all bustled about.
390 They brought a cow from the plain. The companions of great-hearted
Telemachos came from the well-balanced ship.° Then the metal-worker
arrived with the bronze tools in his hands, the means of accomplishing
his art—the anvil and hammer and the well-made tongs by which
he worked the gold. Athena came to witness the offering.

---

369 *with oil*: This seat of judgment is anointed with oil to mark its sanctity.

385 *Laerkes*: "defender of the people," a rather grandiose name for a man who is probably a slave.

391 *well-balanced ship*: Now follows the most elaborate description of sacrifice in Homer, of great interest to his-
torians of religion. Sacrifice was what actually happened in Greek religious practice. There was no elaborate
priesthood, as in Egypt. Ritual was always in the hands of a local family, as here in Homer's descriptions.

The old man Nestor, the driver of horses, gave gold, and the metal-worker   395
skillfully gilded the horns of the cow so that the goddess might
rejoice when she saw the offering.

                              Stratios and the good Echephron
led the cow by the horns. Aretos came from the chamber holding
water for their hands in a basin with a floral decoration,
and in the other hand he held barley in a basket. Thrasymedes,   400
staunch in war, stood by with a sharp ax in his hands to cut down
the animal. Perseus held the bowl for the blood. The old man Nestor,
driver of horses, began the rite: the washing of hands and the sprinkling
of barley, and he prayed earnestly to Athena, cutting off the hair
from the cow's head and throwing it into the fire as the first offering.   405
When they had prayed and cast the barley grains, quickly the bold
Thrasymedes, the son of Nestor, moved in close and struck. The ax
cut through the tendons of the neck and loosed the strength of the cow.
Then the women gave a cry—the daughters and the sons' wives
and the revered wife of Nestor, Eurydikê, the oldest daughter of Klymenos.   410

    The men raised the cow's head from the broad-wayed earth and held it.
Peisistratos, the leader of men, cut her throat. When the black blood flowed,
the life left its bones. At once they butchered the body, cutting out the bones
from the thighs, all in accord with proper ritual. They covered them with
a double layer of fat and on top lay raw flesh. The old man   415
burned the thigh bones on some split wood and poured flaming wine
on top. Beside him the young men held forks with five prongs
in their hands. When the thigh pieces were completely burned
and they had eaten the entrails, they cut up the rest and placed it
on spits and roasted it, holding the pointed spits in their hands.   420

    In the meanwhile, the lovely Polykastê, the youngest daughter
of Nestor, the son of Neleus, bathed Telemachos. And when
she had bathed him and anointed his flesh with oil, she placed
a beautiful cloak and shirt around him. He came out of the bath
near in form to the deathless ones. Then he went and sat beside Nestor,   425
the shepherd of the people. When they had roasted the outer
layer of flesh and had drawn it from the spits, they sat down and ate.
Noble men waited on them, pouring wine into golden cups.

    When they had put from them all desire for drink and food,
the horseman Gerenian Nestor began to speak: "My children,   430
bring out the horses with beautiful manes for Telemachos, and yoke them
to a chariot so that he might get started on his journey."

FIGURE 3.2 Telemachos and Nestor.   Telemachos, holding his helmet in his right hand and two spears in his left, a shield suspended from his arm, greets Nestor. The bent old man supports himself with a knobby staff, and his white hair is partially veiled. Behind him stands his youngest daughter (probably), Polykastê, holding a basket filled with food for the guest. South-Italian red-figure wine-mixing bowl, c. 350 BC.

                                                  So he spoke
and they happily hearkened to his words and obeyed. Quickly they yoked
the swift horses beneath the car, and the housemaid placed bread and wine
in it, and delicacies such as god-nourished chiefs are accustomed to eat.   435
Telemachos mounted the beautiful car and Peisistratos, the son of Nestor,
leader of the people, climbed in beside him. Peisistratos got into the car
and took hold of the reins in his hands, and he lashed the horses
to get them going. And not unwilling, they sped over the plain,
leaving behind the steep city of Pylos.°   440

                                    All day long the horses shook
the yoke they had about their necks. The sun went down
and all the ways were covered in shadows. They came to PHERAI,°
the home of Diokles, son of Ortilochos, whom the river Alpheios
had fathered. There they passed the night. Diokles placed the entertainment
due to strangers before them. When early Dawn appeared and spread   445
her fingers of rose, they yoked the horses and mounted the inlaid car.
They drove out of the gate and the resounding portico. Peisistratos
touched the horses with the whip to make them go, and they flew,
not unwilling. The men came to the wheat-bearing plain, and from there
sought to finish their journey, so well their swift horses carried them.   450
The sun went down and all the ways were covered in shadow.

---

440   *city of Pylos*: In fact the chariot was never used for long-distance travel. Such a journey would take
      Telemachos over high Mount Taygetos, which lies between Pylos and Sparta, but there was never a road
      there suitable for wheeled traffic in ancient times. Furthermore, the journey would require considerably
      more time than the two days here given. Homer is not at all well informed about the topography of the
      southern Peloponnesus.

442   *Pherai*: The same as modern Kalamata, on the coast in southern Greece.

BOOK 4. *Telemachos in Sparta*

They came to LACEDAEMON,° hemmed in by mountains, crisscrossed
with ravines, and they drove to the house of brave Menelaos.
They found him celebrating the marriage of his son and lovely daughter,
with his many retainers in his house. He was sending his daughter
5   to the son of Achilles, breaker of the ranks of men.° At Troy Menelaos
had first promised her to Neoptolemos, agreeing he would give
her up, and the gods now brought this marriage to pass.
He was sending her forth with horses and chariots to go
to the famous city of the Myrmidons,° over which Neoptolemos ruled.
10 For his son, the powerful Megapenthes, much-beloved child
of a slave, he brought the daughter of Alektor° from Sparta. To Helen
the gods granted no offspring after she first bore the beautiful
child Hermionê, who had the appearance of golden Aphrodite.

And so they were dining in the high-roofed great house,
15 the neighbors and the clansmen of brave Menelaos, taking their pleasure.
A divine singer was singing among them, plucking his lyre,
and two tumblers whirled through their midst as the singer
began his song. The two men, Prince Telemachos and the fine son
of Nestor, stood outside the doors of the house with their two horses.

20 The lord Eteoneus, the busy follower of brave Menelaos,
came outside and saw them, and he went through the house to announce
them to the shepherd of the people. Standing near, Eteoneus spoke
words that went like arrows: "There are two strangers here,
O Menelaos nourished of Zeus, two men who are like the seed
25 of great Zeus. But tell me whether we should unharness their two
swift horses for them, or whether we should send them off
to find someone else to entertain them."

---

1   *Lacedaemon*: A district in the Eurotas Valley between Mount Taygetos on the west and Mount Parnon on
the east, of which SPARTA was the chief city.

5   *ranks of men*: Neoptolemos, raised on the island of SKYROS, came to Troy after Achilles' death.

9   *Myrmidons*: In PHTHIA, far to the north in THESSALY.

11 *Megapenthes ... Alektor*: *Megapenthes* means "of great sorrow," no doubt named for Menelaos' grief at Helen's
betrayal. *Alektor* means "defender," evidently a son of Pelops.

Then, greatly annoyed,
light-haired Menelaos answered him: "Well, you were no fool
before, O Eteoneus, son of Boethoös! But now you talk
drivel like a little child! Surely we enjoyed the hospitality of many   30
as we made our way home in the hope that Zeus would put an end
to our sorrows in the days to come! So—unyoke the strangers' horses
and bring them here, so that they may feast!"

Thus he spoke
and Eteoneus hurried through the hall, and he called out to the other
busy aides to follow him. They loosed the sweating horses from   35
the yoke, and they tied them up at the manger. They flung wheat
before them, mixed in with white barley. Then they leaned the chariot
against the white-painted brick walls of the stall and led the men
into the splendid house.

Telemachos and Peisistratos were amazed
as they passed through the house of the Zeus-nourished chieftain.   40
There was a gleam of a sun or moon over the high-roofed house
of glorious Menelaos. When they had gazed to their heart's content,
they went into the polished baths and bathed. When the female slaves
had bathed them and anointed their flesh with olive oil, they cast
woolen cloaks and shirts around them. Then the guests sat down   45
on chairs next to Menelaos, the son of Atreus. A servant brought
in water for their hands in a beautiful golden pitcher. She poured
it out over a silver basin for them to wash, and she set up a polished
table beside them. The worthy housemaid then brought in bread
and set it down before them, and she added an abundance   50
of foodstuffs, giving freely from her store. A carver lifted up
and placed down platters of all kinds of meats, and put golden goblets
before them.

Then greeting them, light-haired Menelaos said:
"Take the bread, and enjoy it. But when you have eaten the meat,
we will ask who you are among men. For the seed of your parents   55
has not been lost in the two of you! You seem to be of the breed
of Zeus-nourished chieftains—of men who wield the scepter!
Men of the lower classes could never father men such as you."

So he spoke, and he placed before them the rich backbone
of an ox, taking the roast meat in his hands, which they had put   60
before him as a prize of honor. The two men set their hands
to the delightful refreshment lying before them. But when
they had put aside the desire for drink and food, then Telemachos

spoke to the son of Nestor, holding his head close to him so that
65 the others would not hear: "Son of Nestor, most dear to my heart,
note the flashing of bronze through the echoing halls, and the gold
and amber and silver and ivory! This is like inside the hall
of Zeus on Olympos, so untold is the wealth. I am amazed
when I look upon it!"

              And light-haired Menelaos heard him as he spoke,
70 and he said words that went like arrows: "My dear children,
I don't think any mortal would care to compete with Zeus!
His house is deathless and his possessions forever. However,
of men, few or none may rival me in wealth. For after suffering
many things and wandering far, I brought my wealth home
75 in my ships in the eighth year, having wandered to CYPRUS
and PHOENICIA and EGYPT, and I came to the Aethiopians
and the Sidonians and the Erembi and LIBYA,° where the lambs have
horns when they are born. For the sheep there bear their young three
times in the course of a year. There, neither master nor the shepherd
80 is lacking for cheese and meat, nor of sweet milk, for the flocks
yield milk the whole year long. While I wandered around in those
lands gathering much substance, my brother was killed by stealth,
unawares, through a trick of his damned wife! So you see that I have
no joy in ruling over this wealth. You are likely to have heard of this
85 from your fathers, whoever they may be, for I suffered plenty,
and I let a very well-established house fall into ruin,
one containing much treasure. Would that I dwelled in my house
with but a third of this wealth, and that those men stayed safe
who perished in the broad land of Troy far from horse-pasturing Argos!

90   "All the same, although often I sit in my halls weeping and wailing
for all of them—at one moment I satisfy my heart with lament,
but in the next I give it up, for men quickly come to a surfeit of cold
sorrow—yet I do not grieve for them all in spite of my pain, as much
as for one who makes me hate my sleep and food when I think of him.
95 For no one of the Achaeans suffered so much as Odysseus
suffered, and took upon himself. To himself, as it seems,
there was to be nothing but trouble, and for me sorrow not to be
forgotten. He is so long away, and we do not know whether
he is alive or dead. I suppose that old man Laërtes mourns him,

---

77 ...Libya: The Aethiopians, "of burned face," are usually taken to be Africans, but where they lived is unclear.
Homer's separation of Phoenicians, "the red-handed ones" (probably because they harvested purple dye
from a shellfish) from Sidonians, "men of SIDON," is odd because the Sidonians are Phoenicians. Who the
Erembi are is completely mysterious.

and the faithful Penelope and Telemachos, whom he left
as a newborn child in his house."

So he spoke, and he moved
in Telemachos the desire to weep for his father. He let tears fall
from his eyes to the ground when he heard the name of his father.
With both hands he raised up his purple cloak before his eyes.
Menelaos noticed this, and he pondered in his mind and heart whether
he should let Telemachos speak of his father himself or whether
he should question Telemachos first and put him to the test.

While he was thus pondering in his heart and in his spirit,
Helen came out from her fragrant high-roofed chamber,
like Artemis of the golden distaff.° Adrastê set up a well-made
chair for her, and Alkippê carried a rug of soft wool,
and Phylo carried a silver basket, which Alkandrê, the wife
of Polybos, had given her. She lived in Egyptian THEBES°
where the most wealth lies in men's houses. Polybos
gave to Menelaos two silver bathtubs, two tripods, and ten talents
of gold.° In addition his wife gave Helen very beautiful gifts:
a golden distaff and a wheeled basket made of silver,
its rim finished with gold. This the female slave Phylo now
brought, stuffed with finely spun yarn, and sat down beside her.
Across it a distaff was laid, loaded with dark violet wool.

Helen sat down in the chair, and below was a footstool
for her feet. At once she questioned her husband on every matter:
"Do we know, Menelaos nourished of Zeus, who these men
say that they are who have come to our home? Shall I make up
a story or speak the truth? My heart urges me to speak. I have
never seen anyone so like another, neither man nor woman—
amazement holds me as I look! Why this man looks *just like*

100

105

110

115

120

125

---

110 *distaff:* It is not clear why Artemis should be associated with weaving because she is a goddess of the fecundity of the wild.

113 *Thebes:* The splendid capital of New Kingdom EGYPT about 400 miles south of modern Cairo. The name is a puzzle: none of the Egyptian names for this city sounds like "Thebes." Apparently it was so called in Greek by analogy with the seven gates of Boeotian THEBES in Greek myth; the pylons—ceremonial temple gateways in Egyptian Thebes—are to this day astounding for their size and magnificence. Homer's knowledge of Egypt is in any event vague, based on rumor. All the names of Egyptians given in this and following passages (except Thôn) are Greek.

115–116 *... talents of gold:* None of these gifts is typically Egyptian. Tripods were highly valuable Greek artifacts made usually of bronze; important examples from the eighth century BC have been found dedicated at the sanctuary to Zeus at Olympia. *Talent* means "balance," that is the scale that measured out a certain portion. In Homer, only gold was measured in talents, but the weight of a talent is unknown.

FIGURE 4.1   Helen and Menelaos.   Menelaos wears a helmet and breast-guard. His right hand is poised on top of a shield while his left, holding a spear, embraces Helen. She wears a cloth cap, a necklace with three pendants, and a bangle around her arm. Her cloak slips down beneath her genital area, emphasizing her sexual attractiveness. Decoration on the back of an Etruscan mirror, c. fourth century BC.

the son of great-hearted Odysseus, Telemachos, whom that man
left as a newborn child in his house when on my account—
bitch that I am!—the Achaeans went up under the walls   130
of Troy, laying down ferocious war . . .'"

             Light-haired Menelaos
answered her: "Yes, now I see the resemblance, wife,
as you point out the likeness. Why, his feet and hands are just the same
as that man's, and the cast of his eyes, and his head and his hair above!
And just now when I was talking about Odysseus, and was telling   135
about all the pain and suffering that he endured for my sake—
why, he let a bitter tear fall from beneath his brows, holding up
his purple cloak before his eyes."

          Peisistratos, the son of Nestor,
answered him: "Menelaos, son of Atreus, nourished by Zeus,
leader of the people, truly this *is* the son of that man,   140
just as you say. But he is a prudent man, and feels in his heart
that it is wrong to come before you and to make a show
of uninvited speech, in whose voice we take delight as in a god's.
But the horseman Gerenian Nestor sent me forth to come
with him as a guide. Telemachos wanted to see you   145
so that you could tell him of some word or deed. For a son
has many sorrows in his halls when his father is away,
when there are no others to help him, even as now Telemachos'
father is gone, and there are no others among the people
who might ward off ruin."   150

       In reply to him light-haired Menelaos said:
"Well, wonderful! The son of a man much-beloved has come
to my house, a man who suffered many trials on my account.
I always thought that if he returned I would treat him best
among all the Argives, if Zeus whose voice is borne afar
gave us two a homecoming in our swift ships over the salt sea.   155
And in Argos I would have given him a city to live in, and built
him a house, leading him out of Ithaca with all his possessions,
and his son, and all his people—cleaning out one city
among those that lie nearby and obey me as their chief.
Then living here we would often have got together,   160
and nothing would have kept us apart, entertaining one another
and taking delight, until the black cloud of death engulfed us.
But I suppose that some god was jealous of this, who to that
wretched man alone gave no day of return."

So he spoke,
165 and he stirred all to a desire for lament. Argive Helen, daughter
of Zeus, wept. Telemachos wept, and Menelaos, the son
of Atreus, too. Nor was the son of Nestor able to keep
from weeping. In his heart Peisistratos thought of his handsome
brother Antilochos, whom the brilliant son of Dawn° had killed.

170   Thinking of him, Peisistratos spoke words that went
like arrows: "Son of Atreus, old man Nestor always said
that you were wise above all men, whenever you were mentioned
in our halls as we questioned one another. And now, if it is
in any way possible, listen to me, for I take no joy
175 in weeping during mealtime, and soon early dawn will be here.
I see no wrong in weeping for a mortal who has died
and met his fate. In fact, this is the only prize we give
to miserable mortals—to cut our hair and let a tear fall
from our cheeks. For my brother has died, and in no way was he
180 the worst of the Argives. You must know about him. I never met him
nor saw him, but they say that Antilochos was better than all
the rest, superior in both speed of foot and in battle."

Light-haired
Menelaos then answered him: "My friend, you have spoken such
as a wise man would say and do, even one that was older than you.
185 You are your father's son, and so you speak with wisdom.
It is easy to recognize the offspring of a man to whom
the son of Kronos spins out the thread of good fortune, both
when he is born and when he marries. Even so he has given
to Nestor throughout all his days that he reach a fine old age
190 in his halls, and that his sons should be clever and valiant with the spear.

"But we will give up this weeping that we have indulged in.
Let us think again of dinner, and let them pour water over our hands.
At dawn there will be stories for Telemachos and me to tell one
another at length!"

So he spoke, and Asphalion, the busy follower
195 of glorious Menelaos, poured out water over their hands.
They put forth their hands to the delightful refreshment lying
before them. Then Helen, the daughter of Zeus, had another idea.

---

169   *son of Dawn*: Memnon, important in post-Homeric stories about the Trojan War. Achilles' killing of
        Memnon is often represented on Greek pots.

At once she cast a drug into the wine they were drinking,
to quiet all pain and anger and bring forgetfulness of evils.
Whoever would drink this down once it was mixed in the bowl   200
would not in the course of that day shed a tear from his cheeks—
not if his mother and father should fall down dead, nor if
before his eyes a brother or a beloved son should be stabbed
to death and he should see it with his own eyes. The daughter of Zeus
had such cunning drugs, healing drugs, which Polydamna had given her,   205
the wife of Thôn,° an Egyptian woman. In Egypt the bountiful
earth grows the best drugs, many that are healing when mixed,
and many that are deadly. For there every man is a doctor,
learned above all men: They are of the race of Paieön.°

    After she had cast in the drug, and urged them to pour forth   210
the wine, at once she answered and said: "Menelaos, son Atreus,
nourished of Zeus, and you who are here, children of noble men—
now the god Zeus gives good and now evil, for he can do
all things—well, sit in our halls and feast and take delight
in telling tales. I will myself tell a story suited to the occasion.   215

    "I could tell all the labors of Odysseus of the steadfast heart,
and what a thing that mighty man dared to do in the land of the Trojans,
where the Achaeans suffered such pains. Raking his body
with cruel blows and throwing a cloth about his shoulders,
looking like a slave, he entered the broad-wayed city   220
of the enemy. He hid himself, looking like another man,
a beggar, such as there were none in the Greek camp.

    "In this likeness he entered the city of the Trojans, and no one
recognized him. I alone saw through his disguise, and I questioned him.
In his cleverness he avoided me. But when I was bathing him   225
and rubbing him with olive oil,° and putting clothes on him, and swearing
a great oath not to expose him as Odysseus among the Trojans
before he returned to the swift ships and the huts—then he told me
all the plans of the Achaeans. After he had killed many Trojans

---

206 ... Thôn: The only name that appears to be Egyptian: Thôn was a place in the delta. *Polydamna* means
     "much-conquering." The drug is often thought to be opium, but there is no evidence that opium was ever
     added to wine.

209 *Paieön*: A healing god mentioned in the Linear B tablets, later identified with Apollo (but Apollo has lim-
     ited healing functions in Homer).

226 *olive oil*: A function usually reserved for the female slaves of a house, here surprisingly performed by
     Helen herself. Helen, of course, tries in her story to show herself as a fifth column, working secretly for the
     Achaean cause.

230 with his long sword, he returned to the Argives, bringing back
much information.

                "Then the other Trojan women shrilly wailed,
but my spirit rejoiced. Already my heart was turned to go
back home! I groaned for the blindness that Aphrodite gave me
when she led me there, far from the beloved land of my fathers,
235 abandoning my child and my wedding chamber and my husband,
a man who lacked nothing, either in wisdom or looks."

                                 Light-haired
Menelaos then said in reply: "Yes, wife, surely you have spoken
rightly! Before this I have come to know the council and mind
of many fighting men, and I have traveled the wide earth, but not ever
240 did my eyes behold a man such as was Odysseus of the steadfast heart.
Why, what a thing that powerful man daringly performed
in the wooden horse, where all the best men of the Argives were seated,
bringing death and fate to the Trojans! Then you came out there.
I suppose some spirit urged you, who wished to give the Trojans glory—
245 and handsome Deïphobos° followed along with you! Three times
you went around the hollow ambush, feeling it with your hands,
and you called by name the chieftains of the Danaäns, making your
voice like that of the wives of all the Argives. Now Diomedes, the son
of Tydeus, and I, and Odysseus, were sitting in the middle of the men
250 and heard how you called out. Diomedes and I were eager
to rise up and come out, or else to answer right away from inside.
But Odysseus held us back, he prevented us, although we were eager
to go. All of the other sons of the Achaeans kept silent, but Antiklos°
alone wanted to answer your call. Odysseus continually
255 squeezed his jaws tight with his powerful hands, and so saved
all the Achaeans. He held him in this fashion until Pallas
Athena led you away."

                The shrewd Telemachos
said in reply: "Menelaos, son of Atreus, nourished of Zeus,
leader of the people—it is really all the sadder! For in no way
260 did any of this deflect grievous destruction from him,
not even if the heart within him had been of iron. But come,

---

245 *Deïphobos*: A brother of Hector with whom Helen took up after the death of Paris, according to
post-Homeric tradition.

253 *Antiklos*: Not mentioned in the *Iliad*.

FIGURE 4.2 The Trojan Horse and Greek soldiers.   One of the earliest certain representations of Greek myth. The Greeks look out from little windows in the body of the wheeled horse, one holding out his shield, another a scabbard with sword. Some Greeks have climbed out of the horse. A warrior with two spears and shield walks on top of the horse and three other warriors walk on the ground. Other scenes on the pot show the rape of women, the killing of children, and general mayhem. Relief from the neck of an earthenware amphora, c. 640 BC.

send us off to bed, because it is through sweet sleep that
we can take our pleasure in rest."

　　　　　　　　　　　So he spoke, and Argive Helen
ordered the female slave to set out beds in the portico
265　and to lay on beautiful purple blankets, and to spread covers
on top, and on these to place woolen cloaks to wear.
The slaves went out of the hall carrying torches in their hands,
and they set up the beds, and a herald led out the guests. And so
they slept there in the fore-hall of the house, the prince Telemachos
270　and the glorious son of Nestor. The son of Atreus slept in an inner
chamber of the high house. Beside him Helen with the long gown
took her rest, matchless among women.

　　　　　　　　　　　When early born Dawn
spread out her fingers of rose, Menelaos, good at the war cry,
rose from his bed. He put on his clothes and around his shoulders
275　he cast his sharp sword. He bound his beautiful sandals beneath
his shining feet and went forth from the chamber like a god.
He sat down beside Telemachos, and he spoke, calling his name:
"What need brings you here, Prince Telemachos, to shining Lacedaemon
over the broad back of the sea? Is it a public matter, or private?
280　Tell me the truth."

　　　　　　　　　　The shrewd Telemachos then answered him:
"Menelaos, son of Atreus, nourished of Zeus, leader of the people,
I come here in the hope that you might give me some news
of my father. My home is being eaten up, my rich farm lands
are going to ruin, and my house is filled with men who devour
285　my herds of sheep and cattle with shambling walk—the suitors
of my mother—powerful, insolent men. I come now to your knees
on this account, to see if you might be willing to relate to me
his miserable death. Perhaps you saw it with your own eyes
or heard from another the story of his wanderings. For his mother
290　bore him to be wretched above all others. Please, don't sweeten
your words out of respect or pity for me, but tell me straight
how you came to behold him. I beg you, if ever my father, the noble
Odysseus, promised you anything in word or deed and fulfilled
it in the land of the Trojans, where the Achaeans suffered pains—
295　be mindful of these things, and tell me the truth."

　　　　　　　　　　　Greatly grieved,
light-haired Menelaos then answered him: "Well, they want
to sleep in the bed of a man valiant of heart, they who are

themselves base cowards! As when a deer has lain down
her newborn suckling fawns to sleep in the lair of a mighty lion,
then gone to explore the mountain° slopes and the grassy valleys   300
seeking pasture, and then the lion comes to his lair and on the two
fawns lets loose a cruel doom—even so Odysseus
will loose cruel doom on these men. I wish, O father Zeus,
and Athena and Apollo, that with such strength that he had
when he rose up in rivalry in well-settled Lesbos and wrestled   305
Philomeleïdes° and threw him powerfully, and all the Achaeans
rejoiced—I wish that in such strength Odysseus might deal
with the suitors! Then would they all be destroyed, and bitterly
married! But as for this matter that you ask and inquire about,
I will not shade the true story to speak of other things, nor will   310
I deceive you. Of all that the unerring Old Man of the Sea
told me, I will not hide or conceal one word.

"The gods
had held me in Egypt, though I was eager to return here,
because I did not perform the sacrifices that guarantee fulfillment.
The gods require that we be always mindful of their commands.   315
Now there is an island in the surging sea outside of Egypt,
and they call it Pharos,° as far as a hollow ship runs
in a full day's sail when a stout wind blows behind her.
There is a harbor there, a good place to put into land,
from where men launch well-balanced ships into the sea   320
once they have drawn a supply of black water. The gods
held me there for twenty days. No breezes arose that
blow over the deep, that speed men over the broad back
of the sea. And all the stores and the strength of my men
would have been spent then, except some god took pity on me   325
and saved me—Eidothea,° the daughter of the powerful Old Man
of the Sea. I had moved her heart above all others.

"She met me as I wandered alone, apart from my companions
who were sauntering about the island fishing with bent hooks
as hunger tore at their stomachs.° Standing next to me   330
she spoke and addressed me: 'Are you such a fool, O stranger,
and poor in understanding? Or are you deliberately so neglectful?

---

306 *Philomeleïdes:* This story is otherwise unknown, as is Philomeleïdes.

317 *Pharos:* An Egyptian name, *pr-hr*, "the house of Horus." It is the name of an island just a few hundred yards
     from the coast, the site of the famous lighthouse of Alexandria, not a full day's sail.

326 *Eidothea:* Probably "the knowing goddess," unattested elsewhere and no doubt Homer's invention.

330 *stomachs:* Normally Homeric warriors ate roasted flesh, not fish (in reality, the Greeks always ate a lot of fish).

Do you take pleasure in suffering pain? You are penned-up
in this island for a long time, and you cannot find a sign
335 of your deliverance. And the hearts of your companions grow faint.'

    "So she spoke, but I said in reply: 'I will speak out
and tell you, whoever you are among goddesses, that I am not
held here willingly. I must have offended the deathless ones
who live in the broad sky. So tell me—for you gods
340 know all things—who of the immortals ties me up here
and hinders my journey? Tell me of my homecoming,
how I might go over the fishy deep.'

        "So I spoke,
and the beautiful goddess immediately replied: 'Well
stranger, I will tell you everything straight out.
345 The Old Man of the Sea used to come here, the deathless
Proteus° of Egypt, the servant of Poseidon who knows
all the depths of the sea. They say that he is my father,
they say he begot me. If somehow you could lie in ambush
and capture him, he might tell you of your way, the measure
350 of your path, and of your homecoming—how you might
cross the fishy sea. And surely he will tell you, O Zeus-nourished
one, if you want to know, what evil and what good
has been done in your halls while you have been away
on your cruel long journey.'

        "So she spoke, and I said
355 in reply: 'Can you yourself think of a way I might ambush
the divine old man so that he will not see me in advance
and, seeing my purpose, avoid me? That is a tough project,
for a mortal to overcome a god!'

        "So I spoke, and the beautiful
goddess answered at once: 'Well, stranger, I will tell you exactly.
360 When the sun comes into the middle of the sky, then the unerring
Old Man of the Sea comes forth from the salt sea beneath
the breath of West Wind, hidden in a black ripple. He comes
out and takes his rest in a hollow cave and, around him,
seals, the offspring of the beautiful daughter of the sea,
365 sleep in a bunch, coming forth from the gray water,
exhaling the bitter smell of the deep salt sea. I will take
you there at the break of dawn and lay you down in a row—

---

346 *Proteus:* Probably "prophetic god."

you select three of your companions who are the best
in your well-benched ships.

         " 'I will tell you all the tricks
of this old man. First he will count the seals, going over them all.   370
Then, when he has counted them off by fives and seen them,
he will lie down in their midst like a shepherd among his flocks
of sheep. As soon as you see that he is asleep, then
may you be filled with strength and courage. Hold him
down there, though he will be vigorous, striving to escape.   375
He will try everything, taking on the form of all creeping things
on the earth, and of water, and wondrous blazing fire.
But hang on!—be unshaken and grip him still more tightly.

  " 'When at last in his own form—in the shape he had when you
saw him lie down to sleep—he will speak and question you.   380
Then, my warrior, give up your violence and let the old man go.
Ask him who of the gods is oppressing you so much,
and ask him about your homecoming, how you might cross
over the fishy sea.'

        "So speaking, Eidothea plunged beneath
the surging sea. Then I went off to the ships, where they stood   385
in the sand, and many things my heart pondered darkly
as I went. But when I came to the ship and the sea,
we made ready a meal, and the refreshing night came on.
Then we lay down to sleep on the shore of the sea.

  "When early-born Dawn spread out her fingers of rose,   390
I went along the shore of the sea with its broad ways,
praying mightily to the gods, and I took with me three companions
whom I trusted most in any circumstance. In the meanwhile,
the goddess had plunged beneath the broad bosom of the sea
and brought forth four skins of seals from the deep. All were newly   395
flayed, for she devised a trick against her father. She had scooped
out beds in the sea sand and sat there, waiting. We came very near her,
and she had us lie down in a row. Then she covered each one
of us with a skin. Our ambush would have been most terrible,
for the horrible stench of the sea-bred seals afflicted us   400
awfully—for who would lie down with a monster of the deep?—
But she saved us and devised a great relief: She brought
ambrosia and placed it beneath the nose of every man.
The ambrosia had a very sweet fragrance and stifled the smell
of the seals.   405

"So throughout the entire morning we waited
with resolute hearts, and, finally, the seals came out
of the sea. They lay down in a row along the shore. At midday
the old man came out of the sea and saw the fat seals.
He went over all of them and counted their number.
410 Among the number of the beasts he counted us first, and he never
suspected in his heart that there was trickery in the works.

"Then he himself lay down, and we rushed on him
with a shout and threw our arms around him. But the old man
did not forget his clever wiles. First he became a lion with
415 a splendid mane, then a snake and a leopard, then a huge sow.
He became a stream of cold water, then a tree—high and leafy.
However, we hung on with steady heart, never flinching.

"The old man grew tired, though skilled in his destructive arts.
Then he spoke and questioned me: 'Who of the gods, O son
420 of Atreus, has concocted this plan—that you seized me against
my will while I was asleep? And what do you want?'

"So he spoke, but I said in answer: 'You know, old man!
Why do you try to put me off with this question?
How long am I stuck on this island? I can find no sign
425 of deliverance and my heart grows faint within me.
But please tell me—for the gods know all things—who
of the deathless ones ties me up here and delays my journey
and my homecoming, that I might travel over the fishy deep?'

"So I spoke, and right away he answered me:
430 'Well now, you should have made appropriate sacrifice
to Zeus and to the other gods before setting out,
so that you might have arrived as quickly as possible to the land
of your fathers, sailing over the wine-dark sea. It is not
your fate to see your friends and to arrive at your finely built
435 house and to the land of your fathers before you return
to the Zeus-nourished waters of Egypt,° and there perform
appropriate sacrifice to the deathless gods who inhabit
the broad sky. And then the gods will give you the journey
that you desire.'

"So he spoke, but my heart was shaken
440 within me because he commanded me again to go

---

436 *Egypt*: Homer does not know the name of the Nile River, but calls the river Egypt.

over the misty deep to Egypt, a long and hard road.
Nonetheless, I answered him: 'I will do these things, old man,
just as you say. But come, tell me this and tell it straight:
Did all the Achaeans whom Nestor and I left when
we set out from Troy come home safe in their ships?   445
Or did any perish by a cruel death on his ship
or in the arms of his friends, once he had rolled up
the thread of war?'

      "So I spoke, and right away he answered me:
'Son of Atreus, why do you ask me these things?
There is no need to know, or to learn my mind. I don't   450
think you will be without tears long when you have
heard it all. Many of them were killed, and many survived.
Of the captains, two alone of the Achaeans who wear shirts
of bronze perished on their way home—as for what happened
on the field of battle, you were there yourself. And one,   455
I think, is still alive, held back on the broad sea. Ajax, son
of Oïleus, was overcome in his ships with their long oars.
Poseidon first drove him on the great Gyraean Rocks,
but saved him from the sea. Although Athena hated him,
he would have escaped his doom if he had not spoken an insolent   460
word in his great blindness of heart.° He said that he had escaped
the great gulf of the sea in spite of the gods. Poseidon
heard his boastful speech, and right away he took his trident
in his powerful hands and struck the Gyraean Rocks,
splitting them in half. One half stayed in place, but the other half   465
on which Ajax was then sitting dropped into the sea, for
he fell into blindness. It carried him down into the boundless
restless deep, and so he died, when he had drunk the briny water.

      " 'As for your brother Agamemnon, he fled the fates
and escaped in his hollow ships. The revered Hera saved him.   470
But when he was about to reach the steep height of CAPE MALEA,
a storm wind caught him and drove him, moaning deeply,
over the fishy deep to the border of the land where Thyestes
used to live in earlier times, but where now Aigisthos,

---

461   *... blindness of heart*: Ajax, the son of Oïleus, or Little Ajax, was a Locrian and unrelated to Big Ajax, the son
     of Telamon, who ruled over Salamis, though they often fought together. After the sack of Troy, Oïlean Ajax
     raped Kassandra as she clung to a statue of Athena, so incurring the goddess's wrath (see Figures 3.1, 4.3).
     The Gyraean ("round") Rocks were usually placed in the CYCLADES north of MYKONOS, but later tradition
     places them at Kaphareus at the southeast promontory of EUBOEA. The word translated as "blindness" here
     and in line 447 is *atê* (a-tā), a word of unknown etymology that means the force that leads one to act in ways
     that prove disastrous, or sometimes it refers to the disaster itself.

FIGURE 4.3 Oïlean Ajax rapes Kassandra.   Kassandra clings to an idol of Athena. The idol holds a shield and spear and wears a helmet. Kassandra has on only a flimsy gown, exposing her nakedness. The helmeted Oïlean Ajax is "heroically nude" (an artistic convention of uncertain meaning) but carries a spear and shield with the blazon of the forepart of a horse. His left foot stands outside the frame of the picture. Because of this outrage, Oïlean Ajax is destroyed on his homeward journey. Athenian red-figure wine cup by the Kodros Painter, c. 440–430 BC.

Thyestes' son, lived. When a safe return from there was showed   475
Agamemnon, and the gods changed the course of the winds,
and he reached home, then he stepped out on the land of his fathers
with joy.° Laying hands on the land, he kissed it, and many
hot tears poured from him, so welcome the land appeared.

  " 'But a lookout whom crafty Aigisthos had placed there,   480
promising him a reward of two talents of gold—that lookout
saw Agamemnon. So that he would not pass by unseen
and invoke his furious valor, the watchman went straight
to the house, to the shepherd of the people, to tell what
he had seen. Right away Aigisthos worked out a treacherous plan.   485
Choosing twenty of the best men throughout the land,
he set up an ambush. On the other side of the hall he ordered
that a feast be prepared. Then he went with chariot and horses
to summon Agamemnon, the shepherd of the people, intending
a foul deed. Thus he brought him up unawares of his doom.   490
He killed him after he had dined, as one kills an ox
in its stall. Not one of the comrades who followed the son
of Atreus survived, and not one of Aigisthos' men,
but they were all killed in his halls.'

                                   "So he spoke, and my heart
was crushed within me. I sat down on the sand and wept.   495
I no longer wanted to live and see the light of the sun.
But when I was sated with weeping and writhing around,
then the unerring Old Man of the Sea said to me:
'Do not, O son of Atreus, weep for a long time without end.
We achieve nothing by it. But strive as quickly as is possible   500
to return to the land of your fathers. You may find Aigisthos
alive, or perhaps Orestes will have already killed him,
and you may come upon his funeral feast.'

                                   "So he spoke,
and my heart and manly spirit were again warmed in my breast,
in spite of my anguish. I spoke and said words that went   505
like arrows: 'Of these men now I know. But what is the name
of the third man who is held back alive on the broad sea,
or else is dead? I would like to know, even though I am distressed.'

---

478   ...with joy: It is hard to sort out the topography of this passage. If Agamemnon was making for the Argolid, it
        is strange that he should come near Cape Malea, the southernmost tip of the Peloponnesus (although that is
        where storm winds regularly blow ships off course, including Odysseus' ships). Usually storm winds blow to
        the south, but in this case they would have to blow north. The passage also seems to imply that Thyestes lived
        somewhere in the south, perhaps in Sparta, but at this time he was living in Mycenae, in the north.

"So I spoke, and right away he answered: 'The son
510 of Laërtes, who lives in Ithaca. I saw him on an island, pouring
down hot tears in the halls of the nymph Kalypso, who holds
him by force. He cannot come to the land of his fathers, for he
has no oared ships and companions who might send him
on his way across the broad back of the sea.

                                        " 'But for you,
515 O Menelaos, it is not ordained that you die and meet your fate
in horse-pasturing Argos, but the deathless ones will send you
to the Elysian fields at the ends of the earth, where
light-haired Rhadamanthys lives,° where life is easiest for men.
No snow, nor heavy storm, nor rain, but always does Ocean°
520 send up breezes of the shrill-blowing West Wind to refresh men.
For you have Helen to wife and you are the son-in-law of Zeus.'

      "So saying, Proteus plunged beneath the surging sea,
and I went off to the ships and my godlike companions, and my heart
darkly pondered many things as I went. When I came to the ship
525 and the sea, we prepared our meal. Refreshing night came on
and we lay down to sleep on the shore of the sea.

                                  "When early born
Dawn appeared and spread out her fingers of rose,
we dragged our ships into the shining sea. We set up the masts
and the sails in the well-balanced ships. We got in the ships
530 and sat down on the benches. Sitting in a row, we struck
the gray sea with our oars. I sailed back to the waters of Egypt,
the river fed by Zeus, and moored my ships there. Then we
performed sacrifices sure to bring fulfillment. When we had put
an end to the anger of the gods who live forever, I heaped up
535 a mound to Agamemnon so that his fame might be everlasting.
Having done this, I sailed away. The deathless ones
gave me a good wind. They sent me quickly to the land
of my fathers.

---

518 ...*Rhadamanthys*: Probably a preGreek Cretan name. The notion of the Elysian Fields, so contrary to the
Greek notion of the dark and cheerless House of Hades, is also probably Cretan, though it may derive ul-
timately from Egypt. *Elysian*, if it is Greek, might mean "struck by lightning," because any place or person
struck by lightning was considered to be blessed. Menelaos is promised entrance to this paradise not be-
cause he has led a good life, but because of his family connections.

519 *Ocean*: Ocean is a river that runs around the world. The word is probably not Greek but Semitic. Ocean is
the husband of Tethys, probably a Greek form of the Mesopotamian Tiamat, the primordial waters from
which the world has sprung. Likewise, Ocean is the "origin of gods" (*Il.* Book 14), and also the origin of all
"rivers, springs, the sea, and wells" (*Il.* Book 21).

"But come, stay awhile in my halls, until the eleventh
or twelfth day. Then I will send you on your way with honor,
and I will give you glorious gifts—three horses and a well-polished   540
chariot. And I will give you a beautiful cup so that you might
pour out drink-offerings to the deathless gods and remember
me for all your days."

      The shrewd Telemachos
then answered: "Son of Atreus, don't hold me back
for so long a time. I could easily remain for a whole year,   545
sitting with you, and never would the desire for my home
and parents overcome me, for I take great delight listening
to your stories and your words. But already my companions
grow impatient in sandy Pylos. You keep me here for a long time.   550
Whatever gift you would give me, let it be something
that I might treat as a treasure. I will not, however,
take horses to Ithaca but will leave them here as a delight
to you. You rule over a broad plain where there is much clover
and marsh-grass and wheat and spelt and white barley with
wide ears. But in Ithaca there are neither wide-running courses   555
nor meadowland. It is pastureland for goats, more pleasant than one
that nourishes horses. Not one of the islands that slopes down
to the sea is fit for horses or rich in meadows, and in Ithaca
least of all."

      So Telemachos spoke, and Menelaos, good at the war cry,
smiled and he stroked him with his hand and addressed him: 560
"You are of good stock, dear child! I can tell by what you say.
So I will change the gifts—I can do it! Of all the gifts
that lie stored as treasure in my house, I will give you one
that is the most beautiful and the most valuable. I will give you
a finely made bowl, entirely of silver, and its rims are finished   565
in gold, a work of Hephaistos. The warrior Phaidimos, king
of the Sidonians,° gave it to me when his house gave me
shelter as I returned here. And now I wish to give it to you."

    And so they spoke to one another, while the banqueters came
to the house of the divine chieftain. And they brought sheep, and they   570
carried wine, good for men. Their wives with beautiful hair-coverings
sent them bread. And so they made busy with feasting in the halls.

---

567 *Sidonians*: That is, the Phoenicians.

Meanwhile the suitors in front of Odysseus' palace
took pleasure in throwing the discus and javelin over a level space
575   they had made, and as they had before, behaved insolently.
Antinoös and handsome Eurymachos, the leaders of the suitors,
were sitting there—in valor they were by far the best.

Noëmon, the son of Phronios, came up close to Antinoös
and spoke to him, questioning him in these words:
580   "Antinoös, do we know in our hearts, or do we not know,
when Telemachos returns from sandy Pylos? He took
my ship on his trip, and I need her now to cross over
to spacious ELIS, where I have twelve mares, and sturdy mules
at the teat, still unbroken. Of these I would like to drive
585   one off and break him in."

So he spoke, and they marveled at heart,
because they did not think that Telemachos had gone to Neleian
Pylos,° but that he was still there on his lands, or among the flocks,
or with the pig herder.

Antinoös, the son of Eupeithes,
spoke to him: "Tell me the truth! When did he go? Did some
590   youths go with him? Were they chosen youths of Ithaca,
or laborers and slaves of his own? He would be able
to accomplish at least that. Tell me this truly so that I may know.
Did he take away your black ship by force, or did you give it
willingly because he pressed you about it?"

Noëmon, the son
595   of Phronios, answered him: "I myself freely gave it to him.
What else could any man do when a man like that,
burdened with care in his heart, makes such a request?
It would be hard to deny the gift. The youths who are the noblest
in the land—after us!—are those who went along with him.
600   I notice that Mentor went along as their leader—or it was a god,
but like Mentor in all respects. Still, I marvel at this,
because I saw the good Mentor yesterday at early dawn,
at the same time that he was setting off to Pylos!"

So speaking,
Noëmon went off to the house of his father,° but the arrogant

---

587   *Neleian Pylos*: Because Nestor's father was Neleus.
604   *house of his father*: The last we ever hear of Noëmon.

hearts of Antinoös and Eurymachos were angered. Right away
they made the suitors sit down and leave off their games.
Antinoös, the son of Eupeithes, spoke to them
out of great anger. His heart, blackened on every side,
was wholly filled with rage, and his eyes were like blazing fire:
"Well, Telemachos has arrogantly brought a great deed to pass—
this journey! We thought that he would never bring it off.
In spite of all of us, the young man is gone anyhow,
launching a ship and picking out the finest men in the land.
He will soon be a big problem! But Zeus may ruin his strength
before he reaches the full measure of manhood. Come,
give me a swift ship and twenty companions so that I may
set an ambush for him as he returns. I will guard the strait
between Ithaca and rugged Samos.° Thus will his voyage
to find his father be to his considerable cost!"

                   So Antinoös spoke,
and they all assented to his words and urged him to act.
Then they got up and quickly went into the house of Odysseus.
But Penelope was not ignorant for long of the plans that the suitors
were plotting in their hearts, for the herald Medon told her.°
He learned of their plot standing outside the court while they
wove their designs. He went straight through the house
to tell Penelope.

         As he stepped over the threshold, Penelope spoke
to him: "Herald, why have the noble suitors sent you forth?
Perhaps to tell the female slaves of godlike Odysseus to cease
from their labor and prepare a feast for them? Would that this
might be an end to their courtship! May they gather together
someplace else and feast here for the very last time! For scheming
together in a crowd you have wasted the abundant substance,
the property of clever Telemachos.° You listened not at all
to your fathers in past times when, being yourselves but children,
they told you what sort of man Odysseus was among those
who begot you. He never did anything unjust to anyone,
nor spoke against any man in the land, as godlike chieftains
usually like to do. They are sure to hate one and love another.

605

610

615

620

625

630

635

---

618   *Samos:* That is, Kephallenia, where to this day there is a town called Samê.

623   *Medon told her:* Medon is the only suitor to be spared in the massacre, in addition to the singer Phemios.

633   *... clever Telemachos:* Though Medon betrays the suitors' plans to Penelope, he is a suitor himself.

Yet that man never treated anyone wickedly. But your mind
640 and foul deeds are obvious to all. There is no gratitude
for good deeds in after times."

Medon, with wisdom in his heart,
then answered her: "My queen, I would that this were the worst evil.
But the suitors are planning one much greater and more painful.
May the son of Zeus not bring it to pass! They plan to kill
645 Telemachos with the sharp bronze as he makes his way homeward!
He has gone to sandy Pylos and shining Lacedaemon, seeking
news of his father."

So he spoke, and her knees and heart
were loosened where she sat. For a long time she said nothing.
Her eyes were filled with tears, and the swelling of her voice
650 was stopped. At last she answered, and said: "Herald,
why has my son gone? There was no need for him to mount
the swift-faring ship—for men, the horses of the sea—
and cross over the wide waters . . . so that not even his *name*
should remain among men?"

Medon, wise in his heart,
655 then answered: "I do not know whether some god stirred him
to go, or whether his own heart impelled him to travel to Pylos
to learn about the homecoming of his father, or what fate
he encountered."

So speaking, Medon went off
through the house of Odysseus. An anguish that consumes
660 the spirit fell on Penelope. She no longer had the heart to sit
on one of the many seats that were in the room, but she sat
on the threshold of the firmly built chamber, moaning pitifully.
All her female slaves wailed around her, as many as were
in the house, both young and old.

Weeping copiously,
665 Penelope spoke to them: "Listen, my darlings . . . Surely
the Olympian has given me pains beyond all the women who
were bred and born with me. Long ago I lost my noble husband
whose heart was like a lion's, superior in every kind of excellence
among the Danaäns—a noble man whose fame reached throughout
670 HELLAS and mid-ARGOS.° And now the storm-winds have snatched

---

670 *Hellas and mid-Argos:* That is, throughout all of Greece.

away my beloved son unannounced from my halls, nor did I hear
that he had set out . . .

"You cruel women! Not a single one
of you gave thought to rouse me from my bed, though you
had complete knowledge that he had gone forth on a black
hollow ship. If I had known that he was thinking about this trip,   675
I should have seen to it that he stayed here, however eager
he was for the journey—either that or he would have left me
dead in my halls!

"But now call the old man Dolios° here,
my slave, whom my father gave me before I came here, he who
keeps my garden with its many trees. He might go to Laërtes   680
and sit down beside him and tell him all these things, in the hope
that Laërtes may weave some plan in his heart. That man could
go forth and make a lament before the people who are eager to destroy
the race of Odysseus, who is like a god!"

Then the beloved
nurse Eurykleia said to her: "Dear lady, either kill me   685
with the pitiless bronze or let me stay in the house!
In any event I will not hide my thoughts from you. I knew
all this, and I gave Telemachos everything he asked for,
bread and sweet wine. He made me swear a great oath
that I would not tell you before the twelfth day had passed,   690
or you yourself should miss him and hear that he was gone—
so that you would not harm your beautiful skin with weeping.

"Now take a bath and put clean clothes on your body
and go to your upper chamber with all of your handmaids
and pray to Athena, the daughter of Zeus who carries   695
the goatskin fetish. She might save Telemachos even from
death. Don't trouble a troubled old man. I do not think
that the race of Arkeisios° is hated by the blessed gods!
There will always be someone to occupy the high-roofed house
and the rich fields far away."   700

---

678   *Dolios*: He is mentioned numerous times (Books 4, 17, 18, 24). Dolios is on Odysseus' side, but he is also the
      father of the wicked Melanthios and his sister Melantho, as we will see (if it is the same Dolios). We learn in
      Book 24 that he is married to an old Sicilian woman and, though a slave, seems to own his own slaves.

698   *Arkeisios*: Laërtes father, Odysseus' grandfather. Nothing else is known about him.

So she spoke, and she put to rest
Penelope's complaints, and she caused her eyes to stop weeping.
Penelope then bathed. She put clean clothes about her body
and went into her upper chamber with the women, her handmaids,
and she placed barley grains in a basket° and prayed to Athena:
705 "Hear me, O child of Zeus who carries the goatskin fetish,
you who never tire: If ever the resourceful Odysseus
burned the fat thigh bones of ox or sheep to you in his halls,
remember these now and bring my son to safety,
and ward off the suitors in their evil insolence." So speaking,
710 she cried out, and the goddess heard her prayer.

But the suitors broke into an uproar throughout the shadowy halls.
Thus one of the prideful youths would say to another: "Well, our
much-wooed queen is preparing her marriage, but she does
not know that death is made ready for her son!" So they
715 would say, but they did not know how these things
would come out.

Then Antinoös spoke and addressed them:
"My good friends, please avoid such prideful speech of any kind,
so that no one in the house may report what you say. But come now,
let us stand up in silence and put into effect our plan, which pleases all."

720 So speaking, he picked out twenty of the best men,
and they went to a swift ship on the shore of the sea.
First of all they dragged the ship down toward the deep water.
They set up the mast and the sail in the black ship, then they fitted
the oars in the leather thole-straps—everything as it should be.
725 They spread the white sail. The dutiful retainers brought them
their weapons. When they had dragged the boat into the water
near the shore, they tied it up and disembarked. They prepared
a meal and awaited the coming of night.

But she, the clever
Penelope, lay there in her upper chamber without bread,
730 without food or drink, wondering whether her brave son
would escape death, or whether he would succumb to the insolent
suitors. Even as a lion in fear wonders in the midst
of a crowd of men when they draw their ring of cunning
about them, so she wondered as sweet sleep came upon her.

---

704   *basket*: It is not clear what Penelope does with the barley grains or what is their purpose in the ritual.

She sank back and slept, and all her limbs were relaxed.   735
Then the goddess flashing-eyed Athena had another thought.
She made a phantom, likening it in form to a woman—
Iphthimê, the daughter of great-hearted Ikarios, whom Eumelos
had married, who lived in Pherai.° She sent the phantom
to the house of godlike Odysseus—to Penelope as she wept   740
and wailed, to put a stop to her lament and her tearful moaning.
The phantom went into the chamber past the thong of the bolt°
and stood over her head, and she spoke to her this word:
"Are you are asleep, Penelope, troubled at heart? The gods
who live forever do not want you to weep or mourn.   745
Your son will return. In no way has he transgressed
against the gods."

Then the clever Penelope answered her
as she slumbered very sweetly in the gates of dreams: "Why,
my sister, have you come here? You have not been accustomed
to come here before, because you live in a house far away.   750
And you bid me to cease from grief and the many pains
that afflict my heart and spirit. I lost my noble husband
with the heart of a lion long ago, preeminent
among the Danaäns in every excellence, a noble man,
whose fame is wide throughout Hellas and mid-Argos.   755
And now my beloved son has gone in a hollow ship—the fool!—
knowing nothing of the labor or of the gatherings of men.
I sorrow for him even more than for my husband.
I tremble for him, and I am afraid that something bad
may happen to him, whether in the land of the men where   760
he has gone, or on the sea. Many are the enemies who plot
against him, desiring to kill him before he reaches the land
of his fathers."

The dark phantom then spoke in reply:
"Take courage and do not be afraid in your heart.
Such a guide goes with him whom other men pray   765
to stand at their side: She is powerful, Pallas Athena.
She has taken pity on you in your pain and has sent me forth
to say these things to you."

---

739 ...*Pherai*: Iphthimê, the sister of Penelope, is not mentioned elsewhere. Eumelos of Pherai in Thessaly is
a son of Admetos and Alkestis, referred to in the *Iliad's* Catalog of Ships (*Il.* 2) and in the funeral games of
Patroklos (*Il.* 23).

742 *thong of the bolt*: Doors in Homeric houses are locked by means of a bolt drawn by an attached thong.

Then the clever Penelope
said to her: "If you are a god and have heard the voice of a god,
770 then tell me of my luckless husband, whether he is still alive
and sees the light of the sun, or whether he has died
and is in the house of Hades."

Then the dark phantom
answered her: "I may not speak of him at length,
whether he lives or not. It is unwise to say words empty
775 as the wind."

So saying, the phantom glided past
the bolt of the door into the breath of the winds. The daughter
of Ikarios started up from sleep. Her heart was warmed
that so clear a dream had come to her in the dread darkness
of the night.

As for the suitors, they embarked, sailing over
780 the watery ways, contriving in their hearts the vile murder
of Telemachos. There is a rocky island in the middle of the sea
between Ithaca and rugged Samos, Asteris,° not a large island.
There is a harbor there where ships may tie up, with two
entrances. There the Achaeans lay in wait for Telemachos.

---

782 ...Asteris: There is, in fact, a small island between Ithaca and Kephallenia, though it is low-lying and has no
anchorage. Homer is not here concerned with topographical precision any more than in his description of
the Egyptian island of Pharos.

BOOK 5. *Odysseus and Kalypso*

D awn arose from her bed beside the noble Tithonos°
in order to bring light to the deathless ones and to mortals.
The gods were sitting in council, and among them was Zeus
who thunders on high and whose strength is greatest.°

Athena was speaking to them of the many sufferings   5
of Odysseus, as she called them to mind. It was troubling to her
that he was in the house of the nymph: "Father Zeus and you other
blessed gods who live forever, let no other scepter-bearing
chieftain ever be kind and gentle and with a ready heart,
but always harsh. May he perform unjust deeds! For no one   10
of the people that he ruled remembers godlike Odysseus,
how he was gentle like a father. And now he lies on an island
suffering terrible pains in the halls of great Kalypso,°
who holds him against his will. He is not able to come to the land
of his fathers. For he has no oared ships, nor companions   15
who might send him over the broad back of the sea. And now
men scheme to kill his beloved son as the son returns
home, for he has gone to holy Pylos and to shining
Lacedaemon to see if he can learn news of his father."

Zeus the cloud-gatherer said in reply to her: "My child,   20
what a word has escaped from the barrier of your teeth!
Did you yourself not devise this plan so that Odysseus
could take vengeance on these men when he returned?
As for Telemachos, guide him in your wisdom.
You can do it! That way he will return to his native land   25
unscathed, and the suitors will return in their ship, thwarted
in their purpose."

1   *Tithonos:* A son of Laomedon, hence a brother of King Priam. Dawn snatched him away to be her husband
and gave him eternal life, but not eternal youth, according to the usual story.

4   *…greatest:* The narrative now returns to the council at the beginning of Book 1: As Athena went off to
Ithaca, Hermes goes off to the island of Kalypso. The action of Books 1–4 takes place at the same time as the
action of Book 5. A council of the gods often begins a new narrative element.

13   *Kalypso:* "concealer," no doubt Homer's own creation. She is like a goddess of death, concealing Odysseus
from human eyes, as Odysseus' return is like a rebirth. "Hades" means "the unseen."

Thus Zeus spoke, then said to Hermes,
his dear son: "Hermes, you are our messenger in many
matters—do go and tell the fair-haired nymph our fixed
30 resolve, the homecoming of long-suffering Odysseus:
that he might return without the guidance of gods or mortal men,
on a tightly bound raft, suffering many pains, and come
to rich Scheria on the twentieth day, to the land
of the Phaeacians, who are born near to the gods.
35 They will honor him like a god and send him forth
on a ship to the beloved land of his fathers. And they will give
him much bronze and gold and a abundant woven things,
much more than Odysseus would ever have taken from Troy
if he had escaped without trouble with his due share of booty.
40 For it is his fate to see his friends and arrive to his high-roofed
home and to the land of his fathers."

So Zeus spoke, and the messenger
Hermes Argeïphontes did not disobey. Immediately
he bound his beautiful sandals beneath his feet—immortal,
golden!—that carried him over the watery deep
45 and the boundless land with the blasts of the wind.
He took up his wand with which he enchants the eyes
of those he wishes, while he awakes others from their sleep.
Holding it in his hands, the powerful Argeïphontes
flew away. Stepping from the upper air onto Pieria°
50 he swooped onto the sea, and he sped over the wave
like a bird—a seagull that in search of fish over the dread
gulfs of the unresting sea wets its thick plumage in the brine.
Hermes rode like that on the numberless waves.

But when
he came to the island far away, then he raced forth
55 from the violet sea onto the land. He came to the great cave
in which the nymph with her plaited hair dwelled.
He found her there inside. A great fire was burning
on the hearth, and the scent of split cedar and juniper wafted
over the island as they burned. Within she was singing
60 in her beautiful voice, going back and forth before her loom
with a golden shuttle. A luxuriant wood grew near the cave,
birch and poplar and sweet-smelling cypress. Long-winged birds
nested in them, owls and falcons and chattering cormorants
whose business is upon the sea. A vigorous vine was stretched

---

49 *Pieria*: The mountain range north of OLYMPOS.

FIGURE 5.1 Hermes weighing souls (*psychostasis*).   Hermes is the god of boundaries, and as such he is *Psychopompos*, or "soul-guide": He leads the souls of the dead to the house of Hades. In a sense, Odysseus *is* dead, imprisoned on an island in the middle of the sea by Kalypso, the "concealer." Hence it is appropriate that Hermes deliver the message that he be released. Here the god is shown with winged shoes (in Homer they are "immortal, golden") and a traveler's broad-brimmed hat, hanging behind his head from a cord. In his left hand he carries his typical wand, the caduceus, a rod entwined by two copulating snakes. In his right hand he holds a scale with two pans, in each of which is a *psychê*, a "breath-soul," represented as a miniature man (scarcely visible in the picture). Usually the weighing is given to Zeus, as when he weighs the fates of Hector and Achilles (*Iliad*, Book 22), but here Hermes weighs the *psychai* of Achilles and Memnon, to see which will die. Memnon is the famous warrior, the son of Dawn, who killed Nestor's son Antilochos (referred to in Book 3), whom Achilles killed after the action described in the *Iliad*, according to post-Homeric tradition. Athenian red-figure amphora from Nola, c. 460 BC, by the Nikon Painter.

65 there around the hollow cave, blooming with clusters
    of grapes. Four fountains all in a row, close by one another,
    ran with white water, turned in four different directions.
    All around soft meadows of violets and parsley bloomed.
    There even a deathless one might come and wonder and be amazed
70 and take delight in his heart.

                                    Just so the messenger Argeïphontes
    stood and was amazed. But when in his spirit he had marveled
    at everything, he went right into the wide cave.
    Kalypso, the beautiful goddess, seeing him face to face,
    recognized him, for the deathless gods are not unknown
75 to one another, not even if one lives a long ways away.
    But he did not find great-hearted Odysseus inside,
    for he sat on the shore weeping, as had become his custom,
    racking his heart with tears and moans and agony.
    He would look over the restless sea and pour down tears.

80   Kalypso, the beautiful goddess, questioned Hermes, having him
    sit down on a bright shining chair: "Why have you come,
    O Hermes with the golden wand, an honored guest,
    a welcome guest? In the past you have not come at all often.
    Tell me what you have in mind. My heart bids me to fulfill it,
85 if I am able and it is possible. But follow me, so that I may place
    entertainment before you."

                                    So speaking the goddess set before him
    a table filled with ambrosia, and she mixed the red nectar.°
    Then the messenger, Argeïphontes, drank and ate.
    When he had dined and satisfied his heart with food,
90 then he answered and said: "You, a goddess, ask me about
    my coming—I who am a god. I will speak my words truthfully,
    because you ask. It was Zeus who ordered me to come,
    although I did not want to. Who would willingly cross over
    so great an expanse of endless salt water? Nor is there any city
95 of mortals nearby who sacrifice to the gods and make choice
    offerings. But there is no way that a god may get past or avoid
    the plan of Zeus who carries the goatskin fetish. He says
    there is a man here, most wretched of all those men
    who fought around the city of Priam for nine years—

---

87 *ambrosia . . . nectar*: "ambrosia" seems to mean "undying" and is the food of the gods, though it has other
    functions; "nectar" has no known etymology: It is the drink of the gods.

then they sacked the city in the tenth year and went home.   100
But on the homeward journey they transgressed against Athena,°
who sent an evil wind and high waves against them.
There all the other noble companions perished, but as for him—
the wind and waves brought him here. He it is whom Zeus
now urges you to send on his way as quickly as possible.   105
It is not his fate to perish here far from his friends, but it is
his portion to see his friends and to arrive to his high-roofed
home and the land of his fathers."

                    So he spoke, and Kalypso,
the beautiful goddess, shuddered, and she spoke to him
words that went like arrows: "You are cruel, you gods,   110
envious above all others! You have it in for any goddess
who sleeps openly with a mortal man, if any should take one
as her dear bed-fellow. Just so when Dawn with her fingers
of rose took Orion as a lover,° you gods who live at ease
envied her until chaste Artemis of the golden throne   115
killed him in Ortygia,° attacking him with her gentle arrows.
Or when Demeter of the plaited hair, giving into passion,
mixed in love with Iasion in the thrice-plowed fallow field,
Zeus was not long ignorant of it: He killed Iasion,
striking him with his flashing thunderbolt.° Even so   120
you are now envious, you gods, that a mortal man should be
with me. I saved him when he was riding the keel and all alone,
when Zeus struck his swift ship with his flashing thunderbolt
and shattered it in the midst of the wine-dark sea! There
all his noble companions perished, but the wind and the waves   125
drove him here. I held him dear and I nourished him, and I said
that I would make him deathless and ageless for all time.

    "But because it is not possible for a god to get beyond or avoid
the plan of Zeus who carries the goatskin fetish—let him go back

---

101 ...Athena: By Oïlean Ajax's rape of Kassandra at Athena's altar. Hermes speaks generally, or loosely: In
     fact, Poseidon wrecked Oïlean Ajax's ship (*Od.* 4), and Zeus wrecked Odysseus on the request of Helios, as
     we will see (*Od.* 12).

114 ...*a lover*: A son of Poseidon and a daughter of Minos, Orion was a great hunter and famed for his beauty,
     beloved by Dawn.

116 *Ortygia*: "quail island," usually said to be DELOS in the center of the CYCLADES. The reasons for Artemis'
     killing of Orion are variously given elsewhere, but never because of his affair with Dawn.

120 *thunderbolt*: The offspring of the union of Iasion and Demeter was said to be Ploutos, god of wealth
     (of the land). The reference is to a fertility rite whereby sexual intercourse in a thrice-plowed field
     increased the yield.

130 over the restless sea, if Zeus so urges and commands!
But it is not I who will send him, for I have at hand neither
oared ships nor companions who might conduct him over
the broad back of the sea. But I will gladly give him counsel,
and I will conceal nothing, so that he might arrive unscathed
135 at the land of his fathers."

                              Then the messenger Argeïphontes
answered her: "So release him now, and avoid the wrath
of Zeus, so that he does not grow angry with you
and in time to come do you harm."

                              So speaking, the powerful
Argeïphontes went off. And the revered nymph
140 went to great-hearted Odysseus, because she had heard
the message of Zeus. She found him sitting on the shore.
His eyes were never dry of tears. His sweet life
ebbed away as he longed in sorrow for his return,
for the nymph no longer pleased him. At night he slept
145 beside her in the hollow cave, under duress, unwilling
beside the willful nymph, but during the day he sat
on the rocks and the sand racking his heart with tears,
with moans and agonies, looking out over the restless
sea, pouring down tears.

                              Coming close to him, the beautiful
150 goddess spoke: "Sad man, I wish that you would sorrow here
no more, wearing away your life. Now I shall send you
forth with a ready heart. Come now, cut long beams
with an ax and build a broad raft. Fasten on it cross-planks
above so that it might carry you over the misty sea. In it
155 I will put bread and water and red wine that satisfies the heart,
that will stave off hunger. I will put clothes on your back
and send a breeze behind you, so that you might arrive unscathed
in the land of your fathers, if the gods who live in the broad sky
are willing—those who are more powerful than I, and have such
160 a desire to fulfill their intent."

                              So she spoke, and the much-enduring
Odysseus shuddered. He said to her words that went like arrows:
"You have some other purpose in mind, goddess! It is not
to send me away, seeing that you urge me to cross the great
gulf of the sea—in a raft! That is a dread and grave thing!

Not even shapely swift-traveling ships that enjoy a breeze   165
from Zeus can cross it. I would never set foot on a raft
against your will° . . . unless you, O goddess, will undertake
to swear a great oath not to devise any other further
evil against me."

      So he spoke, and Kalypso,
the beautiful goddess, smiled, and she stroked him with   170
her hand and spoke and addressed him: "You're a rascal.
And no fool, that you have thought to say this word! Well, let
earth and the wide heaven above be witness, and the cascading
waters of the Styx,° which is the greatest and most dread
oath of the blessed gods: *I will not plot any further evil*   175
against you. My thoughts and contemplations are such as I
would devise for myself, if I were in your position.
For my mind is just. This heart of mine is not made of iron.
I am compassionate."

      So saying the beautiful goddess quickly
led the way, and Odysseus followed in the footsteps   180
of the goddess. They came to the hollow cave. Odysseus
sat down on the chair from which Hermes had just arisen,
and the nymph placed before him every kind of food and drink,
such as mortal men eat. She herself sat down opposite
godlike Odysseus, and female servants set out for her   185
ambrosia and nectar.

      They opened their hands to the good board
lying before them, but when they had put the desire for
food and drink from them, Kalypso, the beautiful goddess,
began to speak: "Son of Laërtes, sprung from Zeus,
most clever Odysseus, so you want to go home to the land   190
of your fathers, right away? Well then, farewell. If you only knew
how many more sorrows that fate requires you to endure
before you come to your homeland—you would stay here
with me in this house and be immortal, although you desire
to see your wife, whom you long for all your days. I don't   195
think that I am worse than she in looks or beauty! Well,
it really is not fitting that mortals compete with the immortals
with respect to comeliness."

---

167 *against your will*: That is, he will not go if she does not *really* want him to go; Odysseus thinks that Kalypso's
     suggestion is ironic, that she does not mean it.

174 *Styx*: An oath sworn by the gods on the underworld river of the Styx can never be broken.

Then the resourceful Odysseus said
to her in reply: "Revered goddess, don't be angry about this.
200 I myself well know that the clever Penelope is less
to look upon than you in attractiveness and physique.
For she is a mortal, and you are an immortal and will never
grow old. Nonetheless, I wish and I want every day
to go home—to see the day of my homecoming. And if
205 some god shall strike me on the wine-dark sea, I will endure it.
I am a stout-hearted man. I can stand every affliction.
I have already suffered many things. I have labored much
on the waves, and in war. Let this, then, be added to all that."

So Odysseus spoke, and the sun went down and the darkness
210 came on. The two went into an inner recess of the hollow cave
and took their pleasure in love-making, lying side by side.

When early born Dawn appeared with her fingers of rose,
Odysseus quickly put on his cloak and shirt, and the nymph
clothed herself in a long white robe—finely woven, charming—
215 and around her waist she tied a beautiful golden belt,
and placed a veil on her head. And then she set out
to plan the return of great-hearted Odysseus.

She gave him
a large ax made of bronze, fitted to his hands, sharp
on both sides. It had a very beautiful well-fitted handle
220 of olive wood. Then she gave him a well polished adze.
She led the way to the edge of the island where the trees
grew tall—birch and poplar and fir, reaching to the sky.
The trees were long dried-out and well-seasoned and would float
lightly on the water.

When she had shown him where the tall trees
225 grew, the beautiful goddess Kalypso went back to her house.
Odysseus cut the timbers, and his work proceeded swiftly.°
He cut down twenty trees in all, trimming them with the ax.
He smoothed them out—he knew just what he was doing,
making them true to the line. Meanwhile Kalypso,
230 the beautiful goddess, brought him drills. He drilled all the pieces
and fitted them to one another. He hammered them together

---

226 *proceeded swiftly:* The following passage is one of the most difficult in Homer, filled with words that occur
a single time, and their meaning is unclear. Odysseus appears, however, not to be constructing a raft,
but a boat, though many of the details elude us.

FIGURE 5.2   A ship from the days of Homer.   On the right, a man seizes a woman by the wrist, evidently to abduct her. She holds a wreath in her left hand (barely visible). The ship he is about to board has 40 (or 39) rowers. In Homer, the ships generally have 20 rowers, but some have 50. The rowers are shown above one another, but really they would sit on either side of the ship. The prow, on the right, is curved, and a shield and sword hang from it. The stern, on the left, would have had a kind of half deck for the helmsman to sit on. Not shown is the mast, which stood in the center and was hinged so it could be folded down into the body of the ship. The mast had a single sail that allowed the boat to run before the wind, but it had no jib and so could not tack into the wind: Hence much travel by ship was powered by rowers. Geometric vase from the 8th century BC.

with pegs and fastenings. As wide as a highly skilled man makes
the floor of a broad merchantman, even so wide did Odysseus
make his raft. He set up the deck-beams, fitting them to the close-set ribs.
235 Then he continued his labor, finishing the raft with long gunwales.°
He set up a mast and yardarm° fitted to it. He also made
a steering oar so that he might guide the craft. He closed-in
the whole craft with wickerwork, from stem to stern, as a defense
against the waves, and he strewed much brush upon it.°

240   In the meanwhile Kalypso, the beautiful goddess, brought
cloth to make a sail, and Odysseus made that too with skill.
He made fast the upper lines attached to the yardarm, and the lines
for raising and lowering the sails and for changing the sail's position,
and then used levers to lower the craft into the shining sea.
245 The fourth day came, and all the work was done.
On the fifth day Kalypso the beautiful goddess sent him
away from the island after she had bathed him and clothed him
in a scented garment. The goddess placed a skin of dark wine
on the raft and another, larger one of water, and provisions
250 in a knapsack. She put in it many delicacies sure to satisfy his heart,
and she sent forth a warm and gentle wind.

Gladly godlike

Odysseus spread his sail to the breeze. Sitting down,
he skillfully guided the craft with the steering oar. Sleep
did not fall upon his eyelids as he watched the Pleiades
255 and the late-setting Boötes and Arktos, which men also call
the Wagon, which turns in place, ever on the lookout for Orion,
and alone has no part in the baths of Ocean.° This star Kalypso,
the beautiful goddess, had told him to keep on the left
as he traveled over the sea.

For seventeen days he sailed,

260 but on the eighteenth appeared the shadowy mountains of the nearest

---

235 *gunwales*: The upper edges of the sides of a vessel, if that is what the Greek word means.

236 *yardarm*: A horizontal support for the sail.

239 *upon it*: Apparently the wickerwork and brush are to support cargo, but their function is obscure.

257 *. . . Ocean*: The Pleiades, probably "doves," are tightly grouped, the most obvious star cluster in the
     heavens, consisting of seven stars (only six are usually visible). Boötes, the "plowman," sets late in the
     month of October, perhaps giving a time for Odysseus' journey, a warning of stormy weather to come.
     Arktos, the "bear" (*Ursa Major*), is the Big Dipper that never sets, perhaps a corruption of a Near Eastern
     word for "wagon," an alternative name that Homer also gives; the bear is appropriately in proximity to the
     hunter Orion, a constellation bearing the same name today, as the name "Wagon" is suitable to the
     nearness of the Big Dipper to Boötes, the "plowman." These stars may have suggested specific navigational
     directions to Odysseus, but we cannot untangle the details.

FIGURE 5.3 Odysseus and Kalypso. The goddess presents a box of provisions for the hero's voyage. The box is tied with a sash. The bearded Odysseus sits on a rock on the shore holding a sword and looking pensive. Athenian red-figure vase, c. 450 BC.

part of the land of the Phaeacians. It looked like a shield on the misty sea.°
But the lord, the earth-shaker, coming back from the Aethiopians,
saw him from afar, from the mountains of the Solymi.° He saw
Odysseus sailing over the sea, and he grew more angry in his heart,
265 and he shook his head and spoke to his spirit: "Well, I see that
the gods have changed their minds concerning Odysseus
while I was among the Aethiopians! And now he is near the land
of the Phaeacians, where it is his fate to escape the trial
of misery which has come upon him. But even yet, I think,
270 I will give him his fill of evil!"

So saying he gathered together
great clouds. Taking his trident in his hands, he stirred up the sea
and he roused all the blasts of every kind of wind, and he hid
the earth together with the sea in clouds. Night rushed down
from heaven. East Wind and South Wind dashed together,
275 and the wild-blowing West Wind and North Wind, born in a clear sky,
rolled out a gigantic wave.

And then Odysseus' limbs were
loosened and his heart shivered, and, groaning, he spoke
to his great-hearted spirit: "Alas, wretched me, what is going
to happen to me at last? I am afraid all that the goddess said is true
280 when she said that I would suffer terribly before I came
to the land of my fathers. And now all this is coming to pass!
Zeus overcasts the broad heaven with such mighty clouds,
and he has stirred up the sea, and the blasts of all kinds of winds
drive on. Now dire destruction is near. Three-times blessed,
285 and four times, are the Danaäns, who died in broad Troy, bringing
pleasure to the sons of Atreus.° Would that I had died and followed
my fate on that day when gangs of Trojans hurled their bronze
spears at me as I fought over Achilles, the dead son of Peleus.
Then I would have received proper funeral rites, and the Achaeans
290 would have spread my fame. As it is, I am doomed to be taken
by an unhappy death."

As he spoke, a great wave drove upon him,
coming down from on high. It rushed on him with terrible strength,

---

261 *misty sea*: That is, a shield lying on its inner side, because Homeric shields were concave and bossed.

263 *... Solymi*: Poseidon had gone to the land of the Aethiopians before the action of the *Odyssey* begins.
The Solymi lived in LYCIA in southwest ASIA MINOR, an odd location from which to see Odysseus,
who seems to be sailing in Western seas.

286 *sons of Atreus*: Bringing pleasure by defending their honor, violated when Helen ran off with Paris.

whirling his raft round and around. He was thrown far from the raft,
and he let go the steering oar from his hands. The mast was broken
in two by a ferocious blast that came on the mingled winds.   295
The sail and the yardarm fell far out in the sea. For a long time
he was held underwater, and he could not rise at once from beneath
the onrush of the great wave. His clothes that Kalypso, the beautiful
goddess, had given him weighed him down.

                    At last he came up
and he spit up the bitter brine that gurgled in torrents from his mouth.   300
But even though he was worn down, he did not forget about the raft
but he sprang after it in the waves—he grabbed on to it, and he sat down
in the middle, avoiding the finality of death. A great wave shunted
the raft here and there along its course, as when in late summer
North Wind carries thistles across the plain and closely they cling   305
to one another—even so did the winds carry the raft here and there
over the sea. Now South Wind would throw it to North Wind
to carry along, now East Wind would yield it to West Wind to pursue.

    The daughter of Kadmos saw him, Ino with the pretty ankles,
who became Leucothea. Earlier she had been a mortal of human speech,   310
but now in the depths of the sea she won a portion of honor among the gods.°
She took pity on Odysseus as he wandered, suffering agonies. She rose up
from the deep like a seabird on the wing. She sat down on the strongly
bound raft and said: "Poor man, why is Poseidon the earth-shaker
so terribly angry with you that he devises so many evils against you?   315
Even so he shall not destroy you, though he would very much like to.

    "But do this, for you seem to me a man of understanding:
Take off your clothes and leave the raft. Let it be carried by the winds.
Swim with your hands and try to reach the land of the Phaeacians—
for it is your fate to escape there. Here, take this immortal veil   320
and tie it beneath your breast. You need not fear you will suffer
anything. And when you get hold of the dry land with your hands,
untie the veil and throw it into the wine-dark sea, far from land.
Then turn away."

                    So speaking, the goddess gave him the veil
while she dove into the swelling sea like a seabird and was hidden   325

---

311   *among the gods*: Leukothea, the "white goddess," was the name that Ino took, a daughter of Kadmos of
      Thebes, after she leapt into the sea with her baby Melikertes in her arms. He became a sea-god too. Ino is
      otherwise known as the malignant stepmother of Phrixus and Hellê in the saga of the Argonauts, and she
      was the nurse of Dionysos.

by the dark wave. But godlike, much-enduring Odysseus
pondered, and in grief he spoke to his great-hearted spirit:
"O no, I hope that one of the deathless ones is not again
preparing a deception, because she encourages me to leave the raft.
330 But I will not yet obey. I saw with my eyes the land far off
where she said there was a chance of escape. I will do this,
which seems to me to be the best: So long as the beams
hold together in their fastenings, I will stay and endure my affliction.
But when the wave shatters my raft, I will swim. There is
335 no better plan."

While he was pondering these things in his heart
and spirit, the earth-shaker Poseidon caused a great wave to rise—
awesome and savage and overhanging!—and Poseidon drove the wave
on him. As when a powerful wind scatters a heap of dried straw,
and some of it blows here, some there, even so the wave scattered
340 the long beams of the raft. But Odysseus rode on a single plank,
driving it as though it was a race horse, and he discarded the clothes
that the divine Kalypso had given him. Immediately he tied the veil
beneath his breast and threw himself headlong into the sea.
He spread out his arms, eager to swim.

The lord, the earth-shaker,
345 saw him, and shaking his head he spoke to his own heart:
"Go now, wanderer over the seas, having suffered many trials,
go until you come among men who are nourished by Zeus.
Even so, I don't think you will make light of your suffering!"
So speaking, he lashed his horses with beautiful manes and he came
350 to Aegae,° where his glorious house is.

But Athena, the daughter
of Zeus, had another idea. She bound the paths of the other winds
and ordered them all to stop and to take their rest. Then she roused
the swift North Wind, and broke the wave before it until Zeus-born
Odysseus could come among the Phaeacians who love the oar,
355 and so avoid death and ruin.

And so for two nights and two days
he was driven over the heavy waves, and often his heart
looked death in the face. But when Dawn with her fine tresses
brought the third day to birth, then the wind stopped and there
came a windless calm. He caught sight of the nearby land,

350 *Aegae*: Various places had this name; its location is unclear.

and he cast a quick glance forward as he was lifted up   360
by a broad heaving swell. As when the life of a father appears
very welcome to his children when he has lain in sickness,
suffering terrible pains, wasting away for a long time
because a malevolent spirit has assailed him, but then
to their joy the gods release him from evil—so welcome   365
did the earth and the woods appear to Odysseus.

   He swam on, eager to set his foot on the dry land. But when
he was as near a distance as a man can make himself heard
when he shouts, and he heard the thud of the waves against the reef
of the sea—for the great wave roared against the dry land,   370
belching terribly, as everything was wrapped in the foam
of the salt sea, and there were no harbors, no anchoring places
for ships, nor places of shelter, but only projecting headlands
and reefs and cliffs—then the knees of Odysseus were loosened
and his heart shivered, and, groaning, he spoke to his own   375
great-hearted spirit: "Alas, now that Zeus has allowed me
to see the land, beyond all hope, and I have cleaved my way across
this gulf, I can see no way out of the gray sea. There are steep cliffs
on the shore side, and around them the waves break roaring,
and the rock runs up sheer, and the water is deep in close,   380
and there seems no way to take a stand on both feet and escape ruin.
I fear that if I try to escape the water a great wave may seize
me and dash me against a jagged rock, and my trouble
will be for nothing. But if I swim on farther in hopes of finding
a sloping beach and harbors of the sea, I fear that a storm wind   385
will snatch me up again and carry me groaning heavily
over the fishy sea. Or some spirit may set a sea-monster on me
from the deep, such as glorious Amphitritê breeds in great number.
For I know that the famous shaker of the earth is angry with me."

   While he pondered these things in his heart and spirit, a great wave   390
bore him toward the rugged shore. His skin would have been ripped
off there, and his bones smashed, if the goddess, flashing-eyed Athena,
had not put a thought in his mind. Rushing on, he seized the rock
with both hands and held on to it, groaning, until the great wave
went past. And so he escaped it in that fashion, until flowing backward   395
the wave broke on him again and carried him far off into the sea.
As when an octopus is dragged from its lair, many pebbles stick to its
suckers, even so the skin was ripped from his powerful hands
against the rocks, and the great wave covered him over.

400   Then wretched Odysseus would have died, contrary to what
was fated, if flashing-eyed Athena had not given him a plan.
Making his way forth from the wave where it belched against the land,
he swam outside it, looking landward, to see if maybe he could find
a sloping beach and a harbor of the sea. And then as he swam
405 he came to the mouth of a beautifully flowing river. That seemed
to him the best place, smooth of stones and also there was shelter
from the wind.

          He recognized the river as it flowed forth
and he prayed in his heart: "Hear me, O king, whoever you are!
I come to you as to one most welcome, fleeing from out of the sea
410 from the threats of Poseidon. Respected is a man, even to the immortal
gods, who comes as a wanderer—as now I come to your stream
and to your knees, having suffered greatly. Take pity on me,
O king. I am your suppliant."

              So he spoke, and promptly the river
stopped its flow, and held back the wave, and the river
415 made a calm before it and it brought Odysseus safely
to its mouth. Odysseus bent his two knees and his powerful
hands. For his heart had been overcome by the sea. His flesh
was swollen and torn. The sea water flowed from his mouth
and nostrils. He lay breathless and speechless, with barely the strength
420 to move, and a terrible weariness came over him. But when
he had caught his breath and his spirit was gathered in his breast,
then he untied the veil of the goddess from him, and threw it
into the river that murmured toward the sea. The great wave
carried it down the stream, and Ino quickly took it in her hands.

425   Odysseus, having turned away from the river, sank down
in the reeds and kissed the rich earth. Groaning, he spoke
to his great-hearted spirit: "Alas, what has happened to me?
What will happen to me in the end? If I pass a miserable night
in this river bed, I fear that the chilling frost and the soaking dew
430 together will overcome me, and from weakness I will have breathed forth
my spirit. For the breeze from the river blows cold in early morning.
But if I go up the slope into the shady wood and lie down
to rest in the thick brush, in hopes that the cold and weariness
will leave me, and if sweet sleep comes upon me, I fear
435 that I might become prey and sweet booty to wild animals."

    As he pondered, this plan seemed to him to be best: He went up
into the woods and found a clear space near the water. He crept beneath

two bushes that grew from the same spot. The one was a thorn bush,
and the other olive. The cold strength of the damp winds could never
blow through these, nor could the bright sun strike with its rays,   440
nor could the rain come through, so closely did they grow
to one another, intertwined together. Odysseus crept beneath them,
and with his hands he put together a broad bed. There were many
fallen leaves there, as many as could shelter two or three men
in the winter season, no matter how bad the weather.   445

  Seeing them, the much-enduring godlike Odysseus rejoiced,
and he lay down in the middle of the leaves, and he heaped
over himself a mass of them. As when a man hides a brand
beneath the dark embers in an outlying farm, where there are
no neighbors, preserving the seed of fire so that he won't have to   450
kindle it from someplace else—just so, Odysseus hid himself
in the leaves. Athena shed sleep on his eyes, enfolding his lids, so that
sleep might make an end to his awful fatigue as quickly as possible.

BOOK 6. *Odysseus and Nausicaä*

And so the much-enduring godlike Odysseus lay there,
overcome by sleep and weariness. But Athena went to the land
and the city of the Phaeacians, who earlier had lived in Hypereia°
with its broad places for dancing—near the arrogant Cyclopes°
5 who were greater in strength and constantly plundered them.
From there Nausithoös, who was like a god, had removed them
and settled them in Scheria,° far from men who labor
to raise barley. He built houses and he built a wall around the city.
He made temples for the gods and divided the farm lands.
10 But after this time, Nausithoös was overcome by death
and went to the house of Hades. After that Alkinoös° ruled,
made wise in his counsel by the gods.

                        Now the goddess,
flashing-eyed Athena, went to his house, to devise a homecoming
for great-hearted Odysseus. She went to the brightly decorated
15 chamber in which the daughter of great-hearted Alkinoös slept—
Nausicaä,° like to the deathless ones in beauty and form.
Two handmaidens, made beautiful by the Graces, slept close by,
one on either side of the doorway, and the shining doors were shut.

    Like a breath of air, Athena hastened to the couch
20 of the young girl. She stood over her head and she spoke,
taking on the appearance of the daughter of Dymas, famed
for his ships and of a like age to Nausicaä, dear to Athena's heart.

---

3 *Hypereia*: The "land beyond far beyond," a fanciful name emphasizing the Phaeacians' distance from human habitation.

4 *Cyclopes*: The "round-eyes," presumably the same as the beastly Cyclopes in *Od.* 9.

6-7 *... Scheria*: *Nausithoös* mean "swift in ships," and most of the Phaeacians have ship names. *Scheria* is of unknown etymology. By the fifth century BC, however, it was identified with the island of CORCYRA (modern Corfu) north of the IONIAN ISLANDS.

11 *Alkinoös*: Perhaps "strong in his mind."

16 *Nausicaä*: "excelling in ships."

In her form flashing-eyed Athena spoke: "Nausicaä, how is it
that your mother bore you to be such a careless girl? Your bright
clothes are lying there all uncared for, yet your marriage   25
time is nearing, when you really ought to be wearing nice clothes,
and to give similar garments to those who will accompany you.
It's from things like this that your good reputation goes up
among men, and your father and revered mother will rejoice.
So let us do some washing as soon as the sun rises. I'll go along   30
as your helper, so you should get ready as soon as possible.
You will not be a virgin much longer! Already all the best men
in the land of the Phaeacians court you, from whom comes your
own lineage. So come, ask your famous father to fit out mules
at dawn, and a wagon that can carry the shirts and robes   35
and shining clothes. It is much better for you, too, to go in this fashion,
for the washing tanks are far from the city."

                                        So speaking, flashing-eyed
Athena went off to Olympos, where they say is the eternal seat
of the gods. Neither is it shaken by the winds, nor is it ever wet
with rain, nor does it snow there, but it is spread out clear   40
and cloudless, and over it hovers a brilliant whiteness.
There the blessed gods take their pleasure for all their days.
That is where the flashing-eyed one went, after she had spoken
to the young girl.

                        At once Dawn came along on her lovely throne.
She woke up Nausicaä with her beautiful robes. Nausicaä marveled   45
at her dream and went off through the house to tell her parents,
her dear father and mother. She came upon them inside the house.
Her mother sat at the hearth with her handmaids, spinning
purple yarn, the color taken from the sea, and she met her father
as he was going outside to join the glorious chieftains in the place   50
of council, to where the noble Phaeacians had called him.

    Standing close to her father, she spoke to him: "Papa dear,
do you think you could fit out a wagon—a high one with good wheels—
so that I may take my fine clothes to the river to wash them?
They are very dirty! You too should have clean clothes when   55
you are at council with the leading men. And you have five sons
in your halls, two of them married, but three are sturdy bachelors.
They ought to put on clean clothes when they go to the dance.
I've been thinking about these things—"

                                           So she spoke, too embarrassed
60 to mention her blooming marriage to her dear father.

    But he understood everything and answered her: "You can
    have the mules, my child, and anything else you want. Go then!
    The slaves will fit out a wagon for you—a high one, with good wheels,
    fitted with a box above."

                                        So speaking, he called to his slaves,
65 who obeyed him. Outside the palace they fitted out a light-running
    mule wagon. They led up the mules and yoked them to the wagon.
    The girl brought the shining clothes out of her chamber and placed
    them in the well-polished wagon. Her mother loaded a chest
    with all kinds of food adequate to satisfy the heart. She loaded
70 it up with dainties and poured wine in a goatskin, and the girl
    mounted the wagon. Her mother also gave her gentle olive oil
    in a golden oil-flask so that she and her handmaidens might
    anoint themselves with it after a bath.

                                           Nausicaä took up
    the lash and the shining reins, and she lashed the mules
75 to get them going. The mules clattered as they eagerly sped
    along, carrying the clothing and the girl. She was not alone,
    for her ladies went with her. When they came to the very
    beautiful flow of the river, where the washing basins were
    that never failed—much beautiful water flowed out from beneath
80 them to wash clothes no matter how soiled—there they freed
    the mules from the wagon and drove them along the swirling
    river to feed on grass sweet as honey. They removed
    the clothes from the wagon by hand and carried them
    to the black water. They trampled them in the trenches,
85 busily vying with one another.

                                    When they had washed the garments
    and cleansed them of all stains, they spread them out in a row
    along the shore of the sea, where the sea washed against the land
    and cleaned most of the pebbles. After bathing and richly anointing
    themselves with olive oil, they prepared a meal on the river's banks
90 while waiting for the clothes to dry in the rays of the sun.

    When Nausicaä and her ladies had had their pleasure of food,
    they cast aside their veils and began to play ball. White-armed
    Nausicaä was their leader in the song. Even as Artemis,
    who takes joy in arrows, runs over the mountains, either

high Taygetos or Erymanthos,° delighting in the chase   95
after boars and swift deer, and with her play the woodland
nymphs, the daughters of Zeus who carries the goatskin fetish,
and Leto° rejoices in her heart, and high above them all
Artemis holds her head and brow, easy to recognize,
though they all are beautiful—even so Nausicaä, the young virgin,   100
untamed by marriage, stood out among her handmaidens.

But when she was about to fold the beautiful clothes
and yoke the mules to return home, the goddess, flashing-eyed
Athena, had another idea—that Odysseus might awake
and see the young girl with the fair face, and she might lead him   105
to the city of the Phaeacians.

                   The princess Nausicaä tossed
the ball to her ladies, but she missed the handmaiden and the ball
fell into the deep eddying water. The girls all screamed aloud
and godlike Odysseus awoke. He sat up and pondered
in his heart and spirit: "Alas, to the land of what mortals   110
have I now come? Are they violent and savage? Unjust?
Or are they hospitable, fearing the gods in their minds? I thought
I heard the voices of young girls, of nymphs who haunt the tall
peaks of the mountains and the springs that feed the rivers
and the grassy meadows. Could I be among folk of human speech?   115
But come, let me check out the situation, to see what's what."

So speaking, the godlike Odysseus emerged from the bushes.   🔊
With his powerful hand he broke off a leafy branch from
the thick woods to cover his flesh, to hide his male parts.
He came out like a lion reared in the mountains, trusting   120
in its strength, who goes forth beaten with rain and wind-tossed,
and with eyes ablaze he goes into the midst of the cattle
or the sheep or after the wild deer, and his belly orders him
to go even into a closely built farmstead to attack the flocks.
Just so, Odysseus was about to mingle with the young girls   125
with fine hair, even though he was naked, for necessity drove him.

But he appeared hideous to them, all besmirched with brine!
They ran every which way—one here, one there—across

---

95   *Taygetos or Erymanthos*: Taygetos is the high range of mountains between MESSENIA, where PYLOS is, and
    LACEDAEMON, where Sparta is. Erymanthos is a mountain range in the northwest PELOPONNESUS between
    ARCADIA and ELIS, site of Herakles' famous pursuit of the Erymanthian Boar.

98   *Leto*: Artemis' mother.

FIGURE 6.1 The virgin goddess Artemis.   Wearing an elegant dress and a band about her hair, Artemis carries a torch in her left hand and a dish for drink offerings in her right hand (*phialê*), not her usual attributes of bow and arrows. She is labeled POTNIAAR, "lady Artemis." An odd animal, perhaps a young sacrificial bull, gambols at her side. Athenian white-ground lekythos, c. 460–450 BC, from Eretria.

the jutting spits of the beach. Only the daughter of Alkinoös
held her ground, for Athena placed courage in her breast   130
and took fear from her limbs. She stood and faced him. Odysseus
wondered whether he should clasp the knees of the young girl
with the fair face and beseech her, or stand apart just as he was
and implore her with honeyed words to give him some clothing
and show him her city. As he was pondering in this manner,   135
it seemed to him to be best to stand apart and implore her
with simple words. If he seized her knees, the young girl
might grow angry!

      Immediately he spoke a honeyed, cunning
word: "I entreat you, O queen—are you a goddess, or a mortal?
If you are a goddess, one of those who inhabit the broad heaven,   140
I would compare you in beauty and stature and form
to Artemis, the great daughter of Zeus. If you are a mortal,
one of those who live upon the earth, then your father and
revered mother are three-times blessed, and three-times blessed
are your brothers. Their hearts must always be warmed with joy   145
on account of you, when they see you entering the dance—
a plant so fair. But that man is blessed in his heart
above all others who prevails with his bridal gifts and
leads you to his house. For I have never yet beheld
with my eyes such a mortal as you, neither man nor woman.   150
I am amazed, looking at you!

      "In Delos once I saw
such a sight—the young shoot of a palm springing up beside
the altar of Apollo. There I went, and many people followed
me on that journey when evil pains were my lot.° Just so,
when I saw that palm, I marveled long in my heart,   155
for never yet did such a shaft emerge from the earth.
In like manner, O lady, I do wonder at you and am amazed,
and I fear awfully to touch your knees. But painful anguish
has come upon me. Yesterday, after twenty grim days,
I escaped from the wine-dark sea. Until then waves   160
and the swift winds bore me far from the island of Ogygia.°
And now some spirit has cast me forth here, that here too

---

154 *my lot*: Apparently on the voyage to Troy, but nothing is known otherwise about a stop on Delos, the small
    central island of the Cyclades. In classical times Delos was a center of the cult of Artemis and Apollo,
    and a palm tree grew there that Leto supposedly held onto when she gave birth to the twins Artemis and
    Apollo.

161 *Ogygia*: Kalypso's island.

FIGURE 6.2   Odysseus, Athena, and Nausicaä.   The naked Odysseus holds a branch in front of his genitals so as not to startle Nausicaä and her attendants. On the right, near the edge of the picture, Nausicaä half turns but holds her ground. Athena, Odysseus' protectress, stands between the two figures, her spear pointed to the ground. She wears a helmet and the goatskin fetish (*aegis*) fringed with snakes as a kind of cape. Clothes hang out to dry on a tree branch (upper left). Athenian red-figure water-jar from Vulci, Italy, c. 460 BC.

FIGURE 6.3 **Nausicaä and a frightened attendant.** Nausicaä, on the left, holds her ground while one of her ladies runs away with laundry draped about her shoulders (this is the other side of the vase shown in Figure 6.2). Athenian red-figure water-jar from Vulci, Italy, c. 460 BC.

I may suffer some sorrow. For I think my troubles will not yet
be over. The gods will cause me much pain before then.

165   "But O Queen, take pity! I have come to you first
of all after suffering many evils. I know no one of the other men
who inhabit this city and this land—no one! Show me the city,
give me a rag to cast about my body if perhaps you
brought some wrapper for the clothes, when you came here.
170 As for yourself, may the gods grant all that you desire
in your heart—a husband and a house, and harmony of mind,
a noble gift! For there is nothing greater or better than this,
when a husband and wife live in a house with like minds,
thinking like thoughts, a great annoyance to their enemies
175 and a joy to those who wish them well—and they themselves
are aware of their happy situation."

                              Then white-armed Nausicaä
answered him: "Stranger, you do not seem like an evil or stupid
man. But Zeus the Olympian gives good fortune to men,
both to the good and the bad, to every man as he wishes.
180 So he has given this lot to you, as I see it, and you have no choice
but to endure it. But now, because you have come to our land
and city, you shall not lack clothing nor anything else appropriate
to a suppliant who has suffered a long time and then come our way.
I will show you the city, and I will tell you the name of the people:
185 The Phaeacians occupy this city and land. I am the daughter
of great-hearted Alkinoös, on whom the strength and power
of the Phaeacians depend."

                              Thus she spoke, then ordered her handmaids
who have lovely tresses: "Stop where you are, my ladies! Why are
you running at the sight of this man? Surely you do not think
190 that he is an enemy? No such man lives or exists who will
come to the land of the Phaeacians with hostile intentions,
for we are dear to the deathless ones. We live far away
in the stormy sea at the ends of the earth, and no other mortals
have dealings with us. But this is some wretched wanderer
195 who has come here. We must take care of him, for all strangers
and beggars are from Zeus, and a small gift is a dear one.
So come then, my ladies, give this stranger food and drink
and wash him in the river, where there is shelter from the wind."

     So she spoke, and the girls stopped and called to one another.
200 Then Odysseus sat down in a sheltered place, as Nausicaä, the daughter

of great-hearted Alkinoös, had said. Beside him they placed
a cloak and a shirt to wear, and they gave him gentle olive oil
in a golden oil-flask, and they urged him to bathe himself in the river.

Then godlike Odysseus spoke among the young ladies:
"Ladies, stand apart over there so that I can myself   205
wash away the brine from my shoulders and anoint myself
with olive oil. It has been a long time since my flesh has felt oil.
But I won't bathe in front of you. I would be ashamed to be naked
in the midst of young girls with lovely tresses."°

So he spoke,
and the maidens moved away, and told Nausicaä. And godlike   210
Odysseus washed the brine that covered his back and broad
shoulders from his flesh, and he wiped off the foam
of the restless sea from his head. And when he had washed himself
and anointed himself with oil, he quickly put on the clothes
that the unmarried virgin had given him. Then Athena the daughter   215
of Zeus made him taller to look upon, and stronger,
and she made the locks from his head to fall in curls,
like the hyacinth flower. As when a man overlays silver
with gold, a skilled worker whom Hephaistos and Pallas
Athena have trained in every kind of craft, and he produces   220
work filled with grace—even so she poured out grace
on his head and shoulders.

Then he sat apart, going a little along
the shore of the sea, where he shone with handsome grace.
And Nausicaä marveled at him. Then she spoke to her ladies
with the fine tresses: "Listen to me, my white-armed ladies,   225
attend what I say. This man has not come to the godlike
Phaeacians without the will of all the gods who live on Olympos.
He seemed to be rather coarse before, but now he seems
like the gods who live in the broad heavens. Would that
such a man, living here, might be called my husband,   230
and that it might please him to remain here! But my ladies,
give food and drink to this stranger."

So she spoke, and they listened
and happily obeyed. They placed food and drink beside Odysseus,

---

209 *lovely tresses*: Odysseus' modesty is remarkable, because it was the custom for the young ladies of the
house to bathe guests, as Telemachos and Peisistratos are bathed by Nestor's daughters (Book 3). Perhaps
Odysseus is ashamed because of his filthy condition.

and that much-enduring godlike man avidly drank and ate.
235 It had been a long time since he had anything to eat.

　　But white-armed Nausicaä had another thought. She folded
the clothes and placed them in the beautiful wagon. She yoked
the mules with their powerful hooves and mounted the wagon.
Then she called to Odysseus and spoke and addressed him:
240 "Now get up, stranger, and come to the city, so that I may escort you
to the house of my wise father. There, I say, you may come
to know all the best of the Phaeacians. Only do this—for you seem
to me to be a man of sense: So long as we go through the fields
and farms of men, keep up quickly with the ladies behind the mules
245 and the wagon. I will lead the way. But when we come into the city,
around which a high wall runs, a beautiful harbor lies
on either side of the city, and the entrance is narrow,
and ships with curved prows are drawn up along the way,
for each man has a station for his ship—there, too, is the place
250 of assembly around the beautiful temple to Poseidon.
The place is fitted with huge stones set down into the earth.
There the men are busy with the tackle of their black ships,
the ropes and sails, and they shape oars there. For the Phaeacians
are not concerned with bow or quiver, but with masts and oars
255 and with shapely ships. Rejoicing in them, they travel the gray sea.

　　"But it is their unkind speech that I want to avoid, in case
someone should hereafter taunt me. For there are unpleasant
people in the land. And thus some scoundrel might say,
if he were to meet us: 'Who is this tall handsome stranger
260 who follows Nausicaä? Where did she find him? I suppose
he will be her husband now! No doubt she has brought some
wanderer from his ship—from men who live far away, because
nobody lives nearby! Or maybe it is some god for whom
she has long prayed, come down from the sky, and he will have
265 her forever. Well that is better, if she has gone forth to find
a husband from somewhere else. For she scorns those Phaeacians
in the land, the many noble men who pursue her!'

　　　　　　　　　　　　　　　　　　　"So some
might say, and this would be a reproach to me. And I myself
would reproach another girl who acted in this way, one
270 who should associate with men against the wishes of her own
father and mother, while they were still living, before
she should be openly married.

"So, stranger, please quickly heed
my words, so that with every speed you might obtain an escort
from my father for your homecoming. You will find a splendid
grove of Athena near the road, a grove of poplars. In it a spring   275
wells up, and around it is a meadow. There is my father's park,
and a blooming vineyard, as far from the city as a man's voice
carries when he shouts. Sit down there and wait awhile,
until we come into the city and arrive at the palace of my father.
Then when you think that we have reached my father's house,   280
go into the city of the Phaeacians and ask the way to my father's
house, the great-hearted Alkinoös. It is easy to recognize—even
a little child, a baby, could lead you there. For the houses
of the Phaeacians are not built like the palace of Lord Alkinoös.

"Then when you reach the courtyard and the house itself,   285
go rapidly through the great hall until you come to my mother.
She will be seated on the hearth near the blaze of the fire,
spinning purple yarn, a color taken from the sea. She'll be leaning
against a column, and female slaves will be seated behind her.
My father's great throne rests against this same column.   290
There he sits and drinks his wine, like a god. Pass him by
and throw your arms around the knees of my mother, so that
you might with rejoicing quickly see the day of your homecoming—
even if you come from very far. If you receive favor in her sight,
then there is hope that you will see your friends and arrive   295
at your well-built house and the land of your fathers."°

                                        So speaking
she struck the mules with the shining whip, and they moved
smartly, leaving the streams of the river. They moved along
nimbly, placing their hooves with speed and care. Nausicaä
drove carefully so that her ladies and Odysseus might follow   300
closely on foot, and she applied the lash judiciously.

                                        The sun went
down and they came to the glorious grove sacred to Athena
where godlike Odysseus took a seat. He immediately prayed
to the daughter of great Zeus: "Hear me, child of Zeus
who carries the goatskin fetish—hear me, unwearied one!   305
Hearken to me now, for earlier when I was shipwrecked

---

296 *your father*: No one has ever convincingly explained why Odysseus should approach Nausicaä's mother
   rather than her father to request his return.

you never did attend to me, when the glorious earth-shaker
wrecked me! But grant that I may come to the Phaeacians
as one to be welcomed and pitied."

So he spoke in prayer, and Pallas
310 Athena heard him. But she did not yet appear face to face,
for she feared her father's brother:° Furiously Poseidon raged
against godlike Odysseus until he reached his own land.

---

311 *father's brother*: Poseidon, angry because Odysseus blinded the Cyclops Polyphemos, his son (Book 10).
But Athena abandoned Odysseus before this encounter. She does not appear in her own person before
Odysseus reaches Ithaca (Book 13), though she intervenes constantly from the moment of the shipwreck
off Phaeacia.

BOOK 7. *Odysseus in the Phaeacian Court*

So he prayed there,° godlike much-enduring Odysseus,
and the two strong mules brought the young girl to the city.
When she came to the glorious house of her father, she stopped
in the forecourt, and her brothers thronged around her, men like gods.
They unyoked the mules from the wagon and carried the clothing   5
inside. She herself went to her chamber. The old woman from Apeirê,
her maid-in-waiting Eurymedousa,° lit a fire for her. Ships curved
at both ends had brought her from Apeirê long before,
and men had chosen her as a prize for Alkinoös because
he ruled over all the Phaeacians, and the people listened to him   10
as if he were a god. She had reared white-armed Nausicaä
in the halls. Now she lit a fire and prepared a meal for Nausicaä
in the chamber.

Then Odysseus arose to go the city. Athena,
with kindly purpose toward Odysseus, poured a thick mist
around him, so that none of the great-hearted Phaeacians,   15
coming upon him, might ask him mockingly who he was.
And when he was about to enter the lovely city, the goddess,
flashing-eyed Athena, met him in the likeness of a young girl
carrying a pitcher. She stood in front of him, and godlike
Odysseus asked her: "Child, would you lead me to the house   20
of the man named Alkinoös, who rules among these men?
I have come here from far away as a stranger who has
undergone many trials in a far country. For this reason I do
not know any of the people who live in this city and country."

The goddess, flashing-eyed Athena, then answered him: 25
"Well, I will show you the house that you ask about,
sir stranger, for he lives near my own noble father's house.
But go in silence, please, and I will show you the way.
Do not turn your eyes toward any man or ask anyone questions,
for the people here do not like strangers, and they do not welcome   30

---

1 *prayed there*: In the grove of Athena, outside the city.

7 *Apeirê . . . Eurymedousa*: Apeirê means "without bounds," a fictional location. *Eurymedousa*, "wide-ruling,"
is an odd name for a slave.

men who come from another land. Trusting in their swift ships
they cross over the great gulf of the sea. This the earth-shaker
has given them, and their ships are as swift as a bird, or a thought."

So speaking, Pallas Athena quickly led the way, and Odysseus
35 followed in the footsteps of the goddess. The Phaeacians,
famous for their ships, did not notice him as he went
through the city in their midst, for Athena, the dread goddess
with lovely tresses, would not permit it. With kindly thoughts
in her heart, she cast a wondrous mist around him.
40 Odysseus was amazed at the harbors and the well-balanced
ships and at the meeting places where men gathered, and the long
high walls, crowned with battlements—a wonder to behold.

But when they came to the glorious house of the chieftain,
the goddess, flashing-eyed Athena, began to speak: "This is the house,
45 sir stranger, that you asked me to show you. You will find the Zeus-nourished
chieftains feasting at the banquet. Go inside, do not be afraid. A bold
man is better in all matters, even if he comes from some other land.
You must first approach the mistress in the halls—her name is Aretê,°
sprung from the same line as the chieftain Alkinoös. Poseidon
50 the earth-shaker first begot Nausithoös on Periboia—of women
the most beautiful, the youngest daughter of great-hearted Eurymedon,
who ruled over the insolent Giants. But Eurymedon destroyed
his reckless people, and was himself destroyed. You see,
Poseidon slept with Periboia and fathered the great-hearted
55 Nausithoös, who ruled over the Phaeacians, and Nausithoös
fathered Rhexenor and Alkinoös. Apollo of the silver bow
struck down Rhexenor in his halls° when he was newly married,
without sons. Rhexenor left a single child, a daughter, Aretê,
whom Alkinoös made his wife, and he honored her as no
60 other woman on earth is honored, of all those who today command
their households in subjection to their husbands. She is honored
from the heart both by her children and by Alkinoös himself,
and by the people, who look upon her as a goddess, greeting her
as she goes throughout the city. She has very good sense, and she

---

48 *Aretê*: a-**rē**-tē, "prayed for," that is, from the gods. Also, she is the recipient of Odysseus' prayer for a safe
return. She is Alkinoös' niece, a descendant of the mysterious Giants. Homer betrays no knowledge of the
battle between the gods and the Giants ("earth-born ones") prominent in later Greek myth, mentioning
the Giants only three times (twice in this book, once in Book 10) and presenting them only as a violent and
savage people.

57 *. . . in his halls*: Untimely deaths of males were attributed to Apollo (of females, to Artemis). Eurymedons
("wide-ruling") and Rhexenor ("breaker of men") are otherwise unknown.

FIGURE 7.1   Head of Odysseus.   In the first century BC, the Roman emperor Tiberius (42 BC–AD 37) built a villa at Sperlonga between Rome and Naples. There in a grotto, sculptors from Rhodes created various scenes from Greek myth, including the blinding of the Cyclops Polyphemos. Fragments of the sculptural group survive, including this evocative head of Odysseus, bearded and wearing a traveler's cap (*pilos*) as he plunges a stake into the giant's eye. Marble, c. AD 20.

65 dissolves quarrels among those to whom she is well disposed.
    If you win her favor, there is hope that you might see your friends again
    and arrive at your high-roofed house and the land of your fathers."

    After speaking so, flashing-eyed Athena left lovely Scheria
    and went away, across the restless sea. She came to MARATHON
70 and to wide-wayed ATHENS, where she went into the sturdy house
    of Erechtheus.°

            Odysseus went to the glorious house of Alkinoös.
    In his heart he pondered many things as he stood there,
    before he reached the bronze threshold. The brilliance
    over the high-roofed house of great-hearted Alkinoös
75 was like that of the sun or moon. There were bronze walls
    that extended on both sides of the threshold into the interior,
    and the topmost row of stones was made of lapis-lazuli.
    Golden doors shut in the sturdy house, and silver doorposts
    were set in a bronze threshold. The lintel above was of silver,
80 the ring on the door was gold. There were gold and silver
    dogs on both sides of the door that Hephaistos had made
    with cunning skill, to guard the house of great-hearted Alkinoös,
    deathless and ageless for all their days. Inside,
    seats were propped along the walls running into the interior
85 from the threshold. Finely woven fabrics, skillfully fashioned,
    covered the chairs—the work of women. The leaders of the
    Phaeacians liked to sit on these, drinking and eating,
    for there was an abundant store. Youths made of gold
    stood on finely chiseled pedestals, holding burning torches
90 in their hands, lighting up the night for the banqueters
    in the halls. Fifty slave women in the house ground yellow
    grain on a millstone; others wove on looms and, sitting
    down, spun yarn, like the leaves of a tall poplar tree.°
    The soft olive oil dripped down from the warp attachments
95 of the finely woven wool.° As the Phaeacian men are superior
    to all in their knowledge of speeding a swift ship over the sea,
    so their women are handy in working the loom,

---

71 *Erechtheus*: A legendary early king of Athens. In historical times, Erechtheus and Athena were worshipped
    together in the Erechtheion, a celebrated temple on the Acropolis near the Parthenon, probably built on the
    ruins of a Mycenaean king's house. Marathon is a plain northeast of Athens across from EUBOEA, site of the
    famous battle against the Persians in 490 BC.

93 *tall poplar tree*: The point of comparison is between the rapid fingers of the workers and the flickering leaves
    of the tree.

95 *woven wool*: The "warp" are the vertical strings of the loom. This very obscure reference seems to be to the
    use of oil to make the weaving of the "woof"—the horizontal threads—smoother.

for Athena has given them skill in beautiful handiwork,
and noble hearts.

              Outside the courtyard, near the doors,
was a large orchard, four acres in size. A hedge   100
ran around it on two sides. Within, tall trees
grew blooming—pears and apples with shining
fruit, and sweet figs and luxuriant olives. Of these,
the fruit never perishes or fails in the winter or summer,
but lasts all year round. West Wind, ever blowing,   105
brings some fruit to life, and it ripens others. Pear ripens
on pear, apple on apple, grape on grape, fig on fig.
There Alkinoös' fruitful vineyard is planted. In one part of it,
a warm place on level ground, grapes are being dried
in the sun. At another site, men gather grapes, at another   110
they are treading them. And immature grapes shed
their blossoms, while other grapes are turning purple.

    There, by the last row of vines, trim garden beds of every
kind grow, and they bloom all year round. There are two springs
there: One sends its stream throughout the whole garden,   115
the other, on the other side, runs beneath the threshold of the court
toward the high house, from which the citizens draw their water.
Such were the glorious gifts of the gods to the house of Alkinoös.

    Much-enduring godlike Odysseus stood there and marveled.
But when he had wondered at all of this in his heart,   120
he quickly crossed the threshold and went into the house,
where he found the leaders and the counselors of the Phaeacians.
They were pouring out a drink-offering to sharp-sighted Argeïphontes,
to whom they poured the last of the wine before going to bed.°

    Much-enduring godlike Odysseus went through the hall   125
wrapped in the thick mist that Athena had poured around him.
He came up to Aretê and the chieftain Alkinoös. With his hands
Odysseus seized the knees of Aretê, and immediately the wondrous
mist melted away from him. All who saw that man in the room
fell into silence—they were amazed seeing him.   130

                  Then Odysseus
made his entreaty: "Aretê, daughter of godlike Rhexenor,
I come to your husband and your knees after suffering many pains,

---

124   *to bed*: Hermes is so honored because he is the bringer of sleep.

and I come to these banqueters—may the gods grant them happiness
in life! And may each man hand down to his children
135 the wealth in his halls and the prize of honor that the people
have given to every one. But for me, may you send me an escort
so that I arrive quickly to the land of my fathers, for I have long
endured trials apart far from my friends."

So speaking he sat down
on the hearth, in the ashes beside the fire. All were hushed
140 in silence. At last the old warrior Echeneos spoke, an elder
among the Phaeacians and excellent in speech. For he knew
all the ancient wisdom. With good intent he spoke and addressed
them: "Alkinoös, this is not a good thing. It is not fitting
that a stranger sit on the ground in the ashes of the hearth!
145 These others only hold back awaiting your word.
But come, raise up the stranger and seat him on a chair
with silver studs. And order the heralds to mix wine
for him so that we may make an offering to Zeus who delights
in the thunder, for Zeus attends on honored suppliants.
150 And let the housekeeper give the stranger a meal from the stores
that are in the house."

When the strong Alkinoös heard this,
he took wise and cunning-minded Odysseus by the hand
and made him rise from the hearth. He sat him down on a shining
chair, making his son arise, the welcoming Laodamas.
155 For Laodamas sat next to Alkinoös, being the most beloved.
A female slave brought in water for washing in a beautiful golden
vase and poured it over Odysseus' hands into a silver bowl.
Then she set up a polished table beside him. The revered
housekeeper brought in bread and many delicacies, drawing
160 generously from her stores.

But when much-enduring godlike
Odysseus had drunk and eaten, the strong Alkinoös spoke
to the herald: "Pontonoös, mix some wine in a bowl and give
it to all who are in the hall, so that we might pour out
an offering to Zeus who delights in the thunderbolt, who attends
165 on honored suppliants."

So he spoke, and Pontonoös mixed
the honey-hearted wine, and he distributed it to all, beginning
the ritual by pouring wine in the cups. And when they had
poured the drink-offering and drunk as much as each one wished,

Alkinoös spoke to them and said: "Listen to me, leaders
and counselors of the Phaeacians, while I say what the heart   170
in my breast urges me to say. Now that you have finished
dining, go to your houses and take your rest. At dawn we will
call more of the elders together. We will entertain the stranger
in our halls and offer beautiful sacrifices to the gods.
Then we will take thought of sending him home, so that under   175
our guidance this stranger shall come to the land of his fathers,
speedily and with rejoicing, without pain and woes, though
he comes from very far away. And he will not suffer any evil
or pain on his way, before he arrives to his land. Once there
he will suffer whatever Fate and the dread Spinners wove   180
for him with their thread when he was born—when his mother
gave birth to him.

        "But if he is one of the deathless ones
who has come down from the sky, then the gods have devised
some new thing! In the past the gods have always appeared
in person before us when we perform glorious sacrifices   185
and they feast among us, sitting here in our company.
And if one of us going as a lone wayfarer meets them,
they do not hide themselves, for we are close to them,
like the Cyclopes and the wild tribes of Giants."

                                        Then resourceful
Odysseus said in reply: "Alkinoös, may that thought be far   190
from you. I am not like the deathless ones who live in the broad sky,
neither in form nor nature, but like mortal men. Whomever
you know among men who has most endured misery, I might
liken myself to them in my sorrows. Yes, and I could tell
a still longer tale of all the evils that I have suffered through   195
the will of the gods. But as for me, let me eat now, despite
sorrow's pangs. There is nothing more shameless than a belly
that demands that one think about her, even worn out with grief
and with sorrow in one's heart, just as I have sorrow
Even so, my belly urges me to eat and drink, and helps   200
me forget about all that I have endured. She commands me
to stuff myself. And at daybreak hasten to send me
to the land of my fathers, wretched as I am after suffering
many torments. Life may leave me then, once I have
seen my possessions—my slaves and my high-roofed house."   205

    So he spoke, and they all praised what he said and urged
that the stranger be sent home, for he had spoken in a fitting way.

And when they had made their drink-offerings and drunk to their
heart's content, each man went off to his house to take his rest,
210 leaving godlike Odysseus in the hall. The slaves cleared away
the furniture of the feast. Aretê sat beside him, and godlike Alkinoös.

White-armed Aretê began first to speak to them, for as she looked
on his beautiful clothing, she recognized the cloak and shirt that she had
herself made together with her women slaves. She spoke, saying words
215 that went like arrows: "Stranger, this question I will put to you
first of all: Who are you among men? And *who* gave you these clothes?
Didn't you say that you came here wandering over the sea?"

The resourceful Odysseus said in reply: "It would be hard,
O lady, to tell my sufferings to the end, because the gods
220 in the heaven have given me many. But this I will tell you,
because you ask and inquire. There is a certain island,
Ogygia, that lies far away in the sea, where the daughter
of Atlas, guileful Kalypso with fine hair, lives—
a dread goddess. No one has anything to do with her,
225 neither gods nor mortals. But some spirit led miserable me
alone to her hearth, for Zeus had shattered my swift ship, striking
it with a bright thunderbolt in the midst of the wine-dark sea.
All my noble companions perished then, but I seized
the keel of the curved ship in my arms and was carried along,
230 drifting, for nine days. On the tenth day, in the black night,
the gods bore me to the island of Ogygia, where Kalypso dwells,
the dread goddess with fine hair. She took me up
and welcomed me kindly. She nourished me and said that she
would make me deathless and ageless for all my days.
235 But she did not persuade the heart in my breast. There
I remained continually for seven years, always wetting
the immortal clothes that Kalypso gave me with my tears.
But when the eighth year came around, then she roused me
to return, either because of a commandment from Zeus
240 or because she had had her fill of me. She sent me off on a raft
with tight bindings, and she gave me many things, bread
and sweet wine, and she put immortal clothing on me.
And she sent forth a gentle, warm wind.

"For seventeen days
I sailed, traversing the sea, and on the eighteenth the shadowy
245 mountains of your land appeared. My heart rejoiced,
ill-fated as I was, for I was soon to be companion to
much misery, which the earth-shaker Poseidon set upon me.

FIGURE 7.2 Caricatures of Odysseus, Aretê, and Alkinoös.   In a lost literary tradition, characters from Greek epic were parodied in comic theater productions that flourished in South Italy in the fourth century BC. Scenes from such theater pieces, in which all the characters wore masks, were often reproduced on vases. Here Aretê is shown as an obese hag asking Odysseus about his clothes, an incident based on the seventh book of the *Odyssey*. Odysseus wears the felt cap typical of travelers (compare Figure 7.1). He wears a grotesque mask and supports himself with a staff. Alkinoös, similarly masked, stands behind his wife, agreeing with her every word. South Italian red-figure wine-mixing bowl, c. 375 BC.

He stirred up the winds against me and shut down my journey.
He roused the sea against me wondrously. I bemoaned my state,
250 but he would not let me make headway on my raft. The storm
shattered the raft and then I swam, cutting through the gulf
of the sea, until wind and water, as they swept me along,
drove me to your land. If I had tried to come out of the water
there, the wave would have dashed me against the land
255 and thrown me against the huge rocks and a joyless place.
But I drew away and swam back until I came to a river
free of rocks, protected from the wind, which seemed
to me to be the best place. I fell down there, collecting
the life in me. Immortal night came on. I went forth from
260 the Zeus-fed river and lay down to sleep in the bushes. I gathered
leaves around me. Some god poured endless sleep over me.

"There in the leaves I slept the whole night through,
my heart stricken, and through the dawn and into the middle
of the day. The sun was ready to set when sweet sleep released me.
265 Then I heard your daughter's ladies playing on the beach,
and among them your daughter was like a goddess. I beseeched her,
and she did not fail in noble understanding. She did not act as
one would expect, being so young and coming across me so.
For most young are ever without good sense. She gave me
270 a good portion of bread and gleaming wine, and she washed me
in the river and gave me this clothing. In this I have spoken the truth,
although I am filled with sorrow."

Alkinoös answered him:
"Stranger, my daughter did not act rightly in this matter,
for she did not bring you to our house along with her ladies
275 when it was to *her* first that you made prayer."

Then resourceful
Odysseus answered him: "Sir, do not rebuke your daughter
in this matter. In fact she urged me to follow along with her ladies,
but I was not willing, for fear and shame. What if your heart
were to darken when you saw me? We are quick to anger,
280 we tribes of men upon the earth."

Alkinoös then answered him,
saying: "Stranger, my heart is not like that, to become angry
without good cause. Measure is better in all things. Why,
I would wish—by Zeus and Athena and Apollo!—that, being
so good a man as you are, and being of a like mind as

FIGURE 7.3   Parodic image of Odysseus.   A pudgy grotesque hero (labeled ODYSEUS), naked except for a cape, with a comically dangling phallus, rides a raft made of wine jars (he is a drunkard!). He holds a trident like Poseidon while North Wind (labeled BORIAS) blows from the right. Such parodic images of Greek myths were a standard theme in Greek art. Black-figure drinking vessel from Thebes, Greece, c. 350 BC.

285 myself, you would take my daughter and remain here
and be called her husband! I would give you a house
and possessions, if you were willing to remain. But no one
of the Phaeacians would hold you back against your will—
let this not be the design of father Zeus! As for your leaving,
290 just so that you may know, I hereby appoint a time for it—
tomorrow! Then you shall lie down overcome by sleep,
and the Phaeacians shall row you across the calm sea
until you come to the land of your fathers and to your house,
or to whatever place you want, even if it is much farther
295 than Euboea, which they say is the farthest of all lands.
Some of our men saw it when they carried light-haired
Rhadamanthys there to visit Tityos, the son of Gaia.°
They went there and accomplished their journey without fatigue,
then returned on the same day. You will yourself know
300 in your heart how far my ships are the best and how much
my men excel at tossing the brine with their oars."

So he spoke, and much-enduring godlike Odysseus
rejoiced. He spoke in prayer and said: "Father Zeus,
I hope that Alkinoös will bring all these things to pass.
305 Thus his fame shall be unquenchable over the earth,
the giver of grain, and I will reach the land of my fathers."

So they spoke to one another in this fashion. White-armed
Aretê called to her slaves to set out a bed in the courtyard
and place beautiful covers of purple on it, and to spread
310 blankets over it and place woolen cloaks on it for clothing.
The slaves went forth from the hall holding torches in their hands.

When they had made the bed comfortable, they came to Odysseus
and called to him: "Up now, O stranger, your bed is prepared."
Thus they spoke, and sleep was welcome to him.

315 So the much-enduring godlike Odysseus slept there
on the corded bed in the echoing courtyard. And Alkinoös lay
down to sleep in the innermost chamber of the high house,
and beside him slept the lady his wife, who had made their bed.

---

297 *son of Gaia*: This myth is otherwise unknown. Rhadamanthys is an enigmatic figure; his name is certainly
not Greek, perhaps Cretan. He is a son of Zeus and Europa and a brother of Minos. He is the archetypal
just man, a judge in the underworld or resident of the Elysian Fields. According to *Od*. 11, Tityos was
tormented in Hades for an assault on the pregnant Leto, evidently in PHOCIS across the EURIPOS from
EUBOEA. The *Odyssey* seems to have been composed and written down on Euboea, so the statement that
Euboea is the farthest of lands (it is obviously not as far as Troy, with which the *Odyssey* is familiar) may be
an appeal to an audience of Euboean sailors, looking homeward from the far Western seas.

BOOK 8. *The Stranger in Town*

When early-born Dawn appeared with her fingers of rose,
the powerful Alkinoös arose from his bed, and so did
Zeus-nourished Odysseus, the sacker of cities. The powerful
Alkinoös led the way to the place of assembly of the Phaeacians,
built beside the ships. They came and sat down beside   5
the polished stones set close to one another. Pallas
Athena went through the city in the likeness of the herald
of wise Alkinoös, devising the homecoming for great-hearted
Odysseus. Standing by each man, she spoke to him:
"Come now to the place of assembly, leaders and counselors   10
of the Phaeacians, so that you might learn about the stranger
driven over the seas, in aspect like to the deathless ones,
who has recently come to the palace of wise Alkinoös."

So saying, she roused the strength and spirit of every man,
and quickly the seats in the place of assembly were filled   15
with the men gathered there. Many marveled when they saw
the wise son of Laërtes. Athena poured out a wondrous
grace on his head and shoulders and made him appear
taller and stronger so that he would be welcomed by all
the Phaeacians and win awe and admiration, and so that   20
he might compete in the many contests by which the Phaeacians
were going to put Odysseus to the test.

                              And when they were assembled
together and in a group, Alkinoös spoke and addressed them:
"Listen to me, leaders and counselors of the Phaeacians,
so that I may speak what the heart in my breast bids.   25
This stranger—I know not who he is!—has come to my house
in his wanderings, whether from men of the East or the West.
He wants to be sent on his way, and he begs for it constantly.
Let us speed-on his sending, as we have always done in the past.
For no man, whoever comes to my house, waits here long   30
in sorrow for his sending forth. So let us draw down
a black ship into the shining sea for her first voyage,
and let us choose fifty-two young men throughout the people,
those who earlier have proved the best. When all of you

35 young men have lashed the oars to the thole-pins, come ashore.
Then we'll quickly make ready a feast at my house,
and I will provide well for everyone. I make these orders
to the youths, but as for the others, the scepter-bearing chieftains—
you also come to my beautiful palace so that we might entertain
40 the stranger in my halls. Let no man refuse me! And call here
the divine singer Demodokos.° For the god has given him
above all the gift of song, to delight in whatever his heart
impels him to sing."

So speaking, he led the way
and the other scepter-bearing chieftains followed. A herald
45 went to find the divine singer. Chosen young men,
fifty-two in all,° went to the shore of the restless sea,
just as he ordered. And when they had gone down to the ship
and sea, they dragged the black ship down into the deep water.
They set up the mast and the sail in the black ship. They fitted
50 the oars in the leather thole-loops, all as it should be,
and they spread out the white sails. They anchored the ship
well out in the water, then made their way to the great palace
of wise Alkinoös. The porticoes and courtyards and the rooms
were filled with the gathering men. They were many, both
55 young and old. Alkinoös slaughtered twelve sheep for them,
eight swine with white tusks, and two cattle with shambling gait.
They skinned them out, then dressed them, and made ready a pleasant
feast. The herald came in, leading the trusty singer, whom the Muse
loved above all men, giving him both good and ill-fortune:
60 She deprived him of sight, but gave him sweet song.

Pontonoös
set out a silver-studded chair for Demodokos in the middle of the diners,
leaning it against a tall pillar. The herald hung the clear-voiced
lyre from a peg above his head and showed him how to reach it
with his hands. He placed a basket and a beautiful table beside him
65 and put a cup of wine on it so that he could drink whenever he wanted.

And so they reached out their hands to the refreshment
lying before them, and when they had put the desire for food
and drink from them, the Muse impelled the singer to sing
of the famous deeds of men, of that song whose fame had reached

---

41 *Demodokos*: "welcome to the people," a speaking name like the earlier *aoidos* Phemios on Ithaca, a "man rich in tales."

46 *fifty-two in all*: Fifty would be rowers, one man the captain, and one man the helmsman—a very large ship.

the broad heaven—the quarrel of Odysseus and Achilles, 70
the son of Peleus, how once they fought with savage words
at a banquet of the gods, and the king of men Agamemnon was glad
in his heart because the best of the Achaeans were quarreling.
For thus had Phoibos Apollo foretold him, when he answered him
in holy Pytho, when Agamemnon passed over the threshold of stone 75
seeking an oracle. For that moment was the beginning of calamity
for the Trojans and the Danaäns through the will of great Zeus.°

The famous singer sang this song. But Odysseus
took up the purple cloak in his thick hands and covered his head,
and he covered his handsome face. For he was ashamed that 80
the Phaeacians should see the tears falling from beneath his eyebrows.
And as often as the divine singer would leave off his singing,
Odysseus would wipe away his tears and draw the cloak
away from his head, and taking up the two-handled cup he would
pour out drink-offerings to the gods. But when Demodokos 85
would begin again, and the Phaeacian nobles would urge him
to sing because they delighted in his words, then Odysseus would
again cover his head, groaning.

He concealed his weeping
from all the others, but Alkinoös alone noticed him, for he sat at his side
and heard him groaning heavily. At once he spoke to the Phaeacians 90
who love the oar: "Hear me, leaders and counselors of the Phaeacians!
We have taken our fill of the equal feast° and enjoyed the lyre,
the companion of the rich feast. But now let us go forth
and try our hands at all sorts of games, so that the stranger
may tell his friends when he returns home how much we surpass 95
others in boxing and wrestling and jumping and in running."

So speaking, he led the way and the others followed.
The herald hung the clear-toned lyre from the peg, and he took
Demodokos by the hand and led him from the hall, taking him
by the same path as the other nobles of the Phaeacians 100
had taken in order to watch the games. They went to the place
of assembly, and a great crowd past counting followed along.

---

77   *...great Zeus*: This quarrel is otherwise unknown. *Pytho* is Delphi, the only time that the Delphic oracle is
     mentioned in the Homeric poems. *Danaäns* is another name for "Achaeans," the Greeks.

92   *equal feast*: A feast in which everyone receives exactly the same portion, thus not slighting the honor of
     anyone.

FIGURE 8.1   Phaeacian banquet in honor of Odysseus.   A Phaeacian nobleman lies back on his couch (an inscription identifies him) and drunkenly puts his right hand to his head. In his left hand, his arm supported by pillows, he holds a wine cup (*kylix*). On the same couch, to the right, lies another diner playing the double flute (really a kind of oboe with a double reed mouthpiece; such instruments never appear in Homer). A naked young boy, a cupbearer, lifts a wine cup from the table in front of the couch, a leather pouch suspended from his right arm (containing oil?). To the far left is another diner. A wine cup and an unidentifiable object covered by a cloth hang from the wall. Athenian red-figure wine-mixing bowl, c. 475 BC.

Many noble youths stood then, including Akroneos
and Okyalos and Elatreus, Nauteus and Prymneus and Anchialos
and Eretmeus and Ponteus and Proreus, Thoön and Anabesineos   105
and Amphialos, the son of Polyneus, son of Tekton.
Then Euryalos, the son of Naubolos, arose, the equal
to man-killing Ares and the best in form and stature
of all the Phaeacians after the handsome Laodamas.
And the three sons of the handsome Alkinoös also   110
arose, Laodamas and Halios and godlike Klytoneos.°

These men first contested in the foot race. A course was set up
for them with start and finish lines, and they all sped swiftly,
raising up the dust with their feet. Handsome Klytoneos was
by far the best in running, and by as far as is the distance   115
of a team of mules in the fallow land,° by so far did he run
out ahead and reach the spectators, leaving the others behind.
Then they tried wrestling, exhausting, and here Euryalos
surpassed all the other nobles. In the long-jump Amphialos
was the best of all. In the discus-throw Elatreus was by far the best, 120
and in boxing Laodamas, the good son of Alkinoös.

                                        When everyone
had taken pleasure in the athletic events, Laodamas, the son
of Alkinoös, spoke to them: "Come, friends, let us ask the stranger
if he knows—if he is familiar with any athletic event. In build,
he is no mean man, in thighs and calves and in his two arms   125
above and in his powerful neck and great strength. He does
not lack in the power of youth, but he has been broken
by his many troubles. I don't think that anything else is worse
than the sea in breaking a man down, no matter how strong he is."

Euryalos answered him and said: "Laodamas, you have said   130
all this aright. Go ahead, call him out, make your word known."

And when the good son of Alkinoös heard this, he took
his stand in the middle and said to Odysseus: "Come now, you too,

---

111   ... *Klytoneos*: All these names are speaking names, referring mostly to various aspects of the nautical life:
      Akroneos, "sharp-ship"; *Okyalos*, "sea-swift"; *Elatreus*, "rower"; *Nauteus*, "ship-man"; *Prymneus*, "steersman";
      Anchialos, "near-the-sea"; *Eretmeus*, "oarsman"; *Ponteus*, "seaman"; *Proreus*, "prow-man"; *Thoön*, "swifty";
      Anabesineos, "ship-boarder"; *Amphialos*, "of two seas"; *Polyneus*, "many ships"; *Tekton*, "builder"; *Euryalos*,
      "of the broad sea"; *Naubolos*, "ship-attacker" (?); *Laodamas*, "subduer of peoples"; *Halios*, "of the sea";
      Klytoneos, "famous-ship."

116   *the fallow land*: That is, Klytoneos was as far ahead of the other runners as a standard area of plowland that
      a mule team would traverse, apparently around 90 feet.

old stranger, try your hand at the contests, if you have ever learned any.
135 It seems to me that you must know some, for there is no greater
glory for a man, so long as he lives, than what he achieves
by his feet and hands. So come, give it a try, cast away
all troubles from your heart. Your journey won't be long now,
for already the ship is launched and the crew is ready."

140   The resourceful Odysseus then said in reply: "Laodamas,
why do you mock me with your challenge? Misery is more
in my mind than athletic events, for before this I have suffered
and labored very much, and now I sit in the midst of your assembly,
desiring my return, entreating your chieftain and all your people."

145   Euryalos answered then, abusing him to his face:
"Well now, stranger, you don't look to me like a man
skilled in athletic contests, which are popular among men.
I liken you to one who sails about in his benched ship,
a skipper of traders who think only of cargoes, in charge of
150 homeward-bound freight, and thinking only and always
of filthy profit. You don't look like an athlete at all!"°

Then the resourceful Odysseus answered him, looking
from beneath his brows: "Stranger, you have not spoken well.
You seem to me a fool. Truly, the gods do not give
155 gracious gifts to everyone, neither of build nor mind—
nor skill in speech. One man is poor in appearance,
but the god puts the crown of charm on his speech and men
delight to look upon him. He speaks with honeyed modesty
and he stands out in a gathering among the people. Men look
160 on him as on a god as he passes through the city. Another
is like the deathless ones in looks, but then no crown
of grace is set upon his words—as is the case with you!
In looks distinguished—a god could not do better—but your
words are empty. You have stirred the spirit in my breast
165 by speaking ungraciously. I am not unskilled in athletics, despite
your prattle. I think I was among the first, so long as I trusted
in my youth and my hands. Now I am bound by evil
and pain. I have dared many things, passing through the wars
of men and the savage seas. Even so, though I have suffered
170 many evils, I will try my hand at the contests. For your little speech
has stung me to the heart. You have provoked me with your talk."

---

151 *athlete at all*: Aristocracies, such as the British aristocracy today, traditionally despise men who have made
their money in business.

Thus Odysseus spoke, then leaped up, cloak and all.
He seized a large, thick discus, as heavy as those with which
the Phaeacians competed against one another. Whirling
this around, he let it go from his stout hand. The discus boomed   175
as it flew, and the Phaeacians with the long oars, men famous
for their nautical skills, crouched down to the earth
beneath the rush of the stone. It flew lightly from his hand
past all the others' marks, and Athena, taking on the likeness
of a man, noted where it had fallen. "Stranger," she said,   180
"even a blind man feeling about with his hands could distinguish
this mark, for it is beyond all the others, by far the first.
So be of good cheer about this contest. No one of the Phaeacians
will reach this, or throw beyond it."

                So she spoke,
and much-enduring godlike Odysseus rejoiced, glad   185
to see a friendly face in the crowd. Then he spoke
to the Phaeacians with lighter heart: "Reach this now,
you youngsters! I think I will soon throw another one
as far as this one, or farther. As for the other events,
if anyone's heart and spirit urges him on, let him come here   190
and give it a try, either in boxing or wrestling or the footrace—
I don't care, for you have angered me greatly. Let any one
of the Phaeacians come, except for Laodamas alone. He is my host—
who would quarrel with one who entertains him? That man
is a fool and without value who challenges his host   195
to a contest in a foreign land. He only cuts short his good
fortune. But of the others I refuse no one, nor make light
of him. But I want to know them and to make trial of them
face to face. In all matters I am no base man, in as many
contests as men practice. I know well how to handle   200
the polished bow, and I would be first to hit my man
with one shot in a crowd of enemies, even if my many
companions stood nearby and loosed their arrows at him.
Only Philoktetes° alone excelled me in archery in the land
of the Trojans, when we Achaeans were making war.   205
But of all others I say that I am by far the best of all the men
who live on the earth, eating bread. Of course I am not willing
to vie with the men of earlier generations—with Herakles

---

204 *Philoktetes*: Mentioned once in the *Iliad* (Book 2) and one other time in the *Odyssey* (Book 3). He killed
    Paris with Herakles' bow, according to post-Homeric tradition. In fact, in the *Iliad*, Odysseus fights with
    the spear, not the bow. Perhaps his boasting here looks forward to his slaughter of the suitors by means of
    the bow later in the poem.

or Eurytos of Oichalia, who competed even with
210 the immortals in the use of the bow. And so great Eurytos
died early, and old age did not come upon him in his halls.
Apollo killed him in anger because Eurytos challenged him
in a contest of the bow.° And I can throw the spear farther
than anyone else can shoot an arrow. In the footrace alone
215 I fear that someone of the Phaeacians could beat me. I have
been cruelly broken on the many seas, for there were poor
provisions in my ship. For this reason my limbs are loosened."

So he spoke, and they all fell into silence. Alkinoös alone
spoke in reply: "Stranger, because you have said these things
220 among us not without a certain grace, and you wish to show us
that excellence which attends you, being angry because this man
standing beside you in the contests has insulted your excellence
in a way that no sensible man would—a man who knew in his heart
how to speak correctly—well, come now, attend to my word
225 so that you might tell another warrior when you are feasting
in your halls beside your wife and your children. Remember our
excellence and the feats that Zeus has given us from the days
of our fathers up until now. For we are not faultless boxers
nor wrestlers, but we run swiftly in the race and are the very best
230 with ships. The banquet and the lyre are always dear to us.
And dancing, and a change of clothes, and warm baths, and the couch.

"Come now, all who are the best dancers of the Phaeacians—
dance! Then when he gets home the stranger can tell to his friends
how we surpass all others in seamanship and the footrace,
235 and in dance and song. Let someone quickly get the clear-voiced
lyre for Demodokos that lies somewhere in our halls!"

So spoke Alkinoös like the gods, and the herald got up
to fetch the hollow lyre from the house of the chieftain.
Then nine judges selected from the people stood up, those
240 who arranged everything in the gathering. They leveled a place
for the dance, a beautiful round space. Then the herald came,
carrying the clear-voiced lyre for Demodokos, who went into
the center. And the young men in the full bloom of youth, those
skilled in the dance, stood around him, and they struck the fine

---

213 *of the bow*: The bow (not the club) was the characteristic weapon of Herakles in Homer. According to
post-Homeric tradition, Eurytos offered his daughter in marriage to whoever could beat him in an archery
contest. Herakles won the contest, but Eurytos would not surrender his daughter. Therefore, Herakles
sacked Oichalia, variously located in MESSENIA, THESSALY, and EUBOEA. Eurytos' bow descended through
his son Iphitos to Odysseus, as reported in *Od*. 21, the bow he uses to kill the suitors.

dancing floor with their feet. Odysseus watched their twinkling feet   245
and he was amazed in his heart.

                    Then Demodokos struck up the beautiful
song on his lyre, the love song of Ares and fair-crowned Aphrodite,
how they first mingled in love, in secret,° in the house
of Hephaistos: "Ares gave her many gifts, and he shamed
the bed and couch of King Hephaistos. But Helios came to him   250
as a messenger, and he saw them as they made love. When Hephaistos
was told the dire tale, he went into his forge, pondering evil
thoughts in his heart. He placed his huge anvil on the anvil-block,
and he forged bonds that could not be broken or loosed,
that the lovers might remain fixed just where they were.   255
And when he had fashioned his trick, in his anger at Ares,
he went into the chamber where his bed lay, and everywhere
he spread around the bedposts the bonds, and many he hung
from the roof-beams above, as fine as spider webs so that no one
could see them, not even one of the blessed gods, so cunningly   260
were they made. And when he had suspended his snares all
around the couch, he pretended that he was going to LEMNOS,
a well-founded city, which to him was much the dearest
of all lands.°

    "Nor did Ares, whose reins are of gold, fail
to notice when he saw the marvelous craftsman Hephaistos   265
going away. He went straight to the house of glorious
Hephaistos, craving the love of beautifully crowned Kythereia.°
She had just come from the house of the mighty son of Kronos.
She sat down. Ares came into the house and he took her
by the hand and spoke and addressed her: 'Come here, my dear,   270
let us go to bed and take our pleasure, lying together, for Hephaistos
is no longer in the land, but has gone off to Lemnos, to the Sintians°
of wild speech.'

    "So he spoke, and she liked the thought
of going to bed with him. So they went to the bed and lay down,

---

248 *in secret*: The marriage of Hephaistos and Aphrodite is scarcely attested outside the present passage:
     In the *Iliad*, Hephaistos is married to Charis ("grace"). Nonetheless, this famous story has inspired artistic
     representations even to the present day.

264 *all lands*: The island of Lemnos had a cult to Hephaistos, and its principal town was called Hephaistia.

267 *Kythereia*: "she of CYTHERA," the island off the southernmost tip of the Peloponessus, where Aphrodite was
     born according to some traditions.

272 *Sintians*: Early inhabitants of Lemnos, probably from THRACE.

275 and around them fell the cunning bonds of the wise Hephaistos.
They could not move—could not lift their limbs—
and then they saw there was no escape. The famous god
with two powerful arms came up near them, for he had turned
back before he reached the land of Lemnos. Helios had been
280 his lookout and had brought word to him.

                         "He went off
to his house, troubled in heart, and he stood in the doorway
as a savage anger seized him. He cried out terribly, and he called
to all the gods: 'Father Zeus, and you other blessed gods
who last forever, come here!—to see a laughable business,
285 a matter not to be endured! Aphrodite the daughter of Zeus
always scorns me because I am lame. She loves this pestilent
Ares because he is handsome and strong of foot,
whereas I was born a weakling. But who is to blame?
My two parents,° who ought never to have begotten me!
290 But you will see where these two have gone up to my bed
to make love, and I am troubled to see it. But I doubt that they
will lie in this fashion for long, no, not for a minute, even though
they enjoy the sex. Soon they will both lose the desire
to sleep! The snare and the bonds will hold them until her father
295 gives back all the wedding gifts that I gave him for his bitch
daughter. She may be good-looking, but she can't contain her lust!'

   "So he spoke, and the gods gathered at the house
with the bronze floor. Poseidon the earth-shaker came,
and Hermes the helper, and King Apollo came, who works
300 from a long ways off. (But the lady goddesses stayed at home
for shame, each in her own house!) The gods, givers of good
things, stood in the forecourt, and an unquenchable laughter
arose among the blessed gods when they saw the art
of wise Hephaistos.

            "Thus would one say, glancing at his neighbor:
305 'Evil deeds never prosper! The slow catches the swift! as even
now Hephaistos, though slow, has caught Ares, the swiftest
of the gods who live on Olympos. Though he is lame, Hephaistos
has caught him by guile, and Ares owes an adulterer's fine!'

   "They said things like this to one another. Then King Apollo,
310 the son of Zeus, said this to Hermes: 'Hermes, son of Zeus,

---

289 *two parents*: Here Hera and Zeus; in other traditions, Hephaistos was the child of Hera alone.

FIGURE 8.2 The adultery of Ares and Aphrodite.   Clad only in a gown that comes just above her pubic area, Aphrodite holds a mirror while her half-naked lover, Ares, sitting on a nearby bench, embraces her and touches her breast. The device that imprisoned them is visible as a cloth stretched above their heads. Such paintings were especially popular in Roman brothels in Pompeii. Roman fresco from Pompeii, c. AD 60.

messenger, the giver of good things, wouldn't you like to share
a couch with golden Aphrodite, even though bound
in powerful chains?'

       "The messenger Argeïphontes answered him:
'Would that this might come about, O King Apollo who shoots
315 from afar, that three times as many endless bonds might bind me,
and all you gods look on and all the goddesses too, if only
I might lay beside golden Aphrodite.'

       "So he spoke
and laughter arose among the deathless gods. But Poseidon
did not laugh. He begged Hephaistos, the famous craftsman,
320 to let Ares go. And he spoke to him words that went like
arrows: 'Release him! And I promise this to you, just as
you bid, that he will pay all that is right in the presence
of the immortal gods.'

       "The famous god, strong in both arms,
then said: 'Do not ask this, O Poseidon, shaker of the earth.
325 Pledges given on behalf of a worthless fellow are worthless!
How could I put you in bonds among the deathless gods
if Ares should avoid the debt and the bonds and escape?'°

    "Poseidon the holder of the earth then said to him:
'Hephaistos, even if Ares avoids the debt and runs off,
330 I will pay it for him.'

       "The famous god of two strong arms then replied:
'All right, I cannot refuse you.'

       "So speaking, the mighty Hephaistos
loosed the bonds, and the two lovers, when the strong bonds
were relaxed, leaped up. Ares went off to THRACE
and laughter-loving Aphrodite went off to CYPRUS,
335 to PAPHOS,° where her estate and her fragrant altar are.
There the Graces bathed her and anointed her flesh with
immortal oil such as gleams on the gods who are forever,
and around her they placed lovely clothing, a wonder to see."

---

327 *and escape:* Hephaistos' point is that Ares would be sure to default on the pledge, but Hephaistos could not
very well move against Poseidon, the older god who stands up for respectability and due process while the
younger gods, Hermes and Apollo, find the situation a cause for laughter.

335 *Paphos:* Where Aphrodite had a famous shrine.

This song the famous singer sang, and Odysseus was delighted
to hear it, and so were all of the oar-loving Phaeacians, men   340
famous for their ships.

　　　　　　Then Alkinoös urged Halios
and Laodamas to dance alone, because no one could compete
with them. After they had taken the beautiful purple ball in their
hands that the clever Polybos° had made for them, then one
would lean backward and throw it toward the shadowy clouds   345
while the other leaped up from earth and easily caught it
on the fly before his feet again reached the ground.

　　　When they had shown their skill in throwing the ball
straight up, then they danced on the much-nourishing earth,
throwing the ball back and forth, again and again, to one another.   350
Meanwhile the other young men stood along the edge
of the gathering and beat time, and a great roar arose.

　　　Then Odysseus spoke to Alkinoös: "Lord Alkinoös,
most excellent of all peoples, you boasted that your dancers were
the best, and I have to agree that they are. I'm seized with wonder   355
as I look upon them."

　　　　　　So he spoke, and the mighty Alkinoös
was happy. Right away he said to the oar-loving Phaeacians:
"Hear me, leaders and counselors of the Phaeacians: This
stranger seems to me to be a man of good will. So come,
let us give him a gift of guest-friendship, one that is fitting.   360
Twelve excellent chieftains rule as leaders among our people,
and I am the thirteenth. Let every one of these bring out
a robe that is recently washed and a shirt and a talent
of precious gold. Let us quickly bring all these things together
so that the stranger may have them in his hands when he goes   365
to dine, rejoicing in his heart. And may Euryalos make amends
to the stranger with words and a gift, because he has stepped out
of line in what he said."

　　　　　　So he spoke, and everybody praised
this suggestion and said it should be so. Each man ordered
his herald to bring forth the gifts. Euryalos answered and said: 370
"Lord Alkinoös, most excellent of all the peoples,

344　*Polybos*: A common name in the *Odyssey*: the father of the suitor Eurymachos (Book 1); the king of
　　Egyptian Thebes (Book 4); one of the suitors (Book 22).

I will make amends to the stranger now, just as you ask.
I will give him this sword all made of bronze with a haft
of silver, and a scabbard of fresh-sawn ivory. It will be
375 an object of great value."

             So saying, he placed the silver-studded
sword in Odysseus' hands and spoke words that went like arrows:
"Hail, sir stranger! If any word has been spoken that is harsh,
may the storm-winds snatch it and bear it away. And may the gods
grant you a return to your wife and the land of your fathers,
380 for you have suffered pain far from your friends for a long time."

    The resourceful Odysseus then spoke to him in reply:
"And hail to you, my friend, and may the gods grant you happiness.
And in times to come may you never long for this sword
that you have given me, making amends with your speech."

385   He spoke and placed the silver-studded sword around his shoulders.
The sun went down, and the glorious gifts were brought to him.
The bold heralds brought them to the palace of Alkinoös,
and the sons of the excellent Alkinoös took the very beautiful gifts
and placed them beside their honored mother. The mighty Alkinoös
390 led the way, and coming in they sat down on high-backed chairs.

    Then the mighty Alkinoös spoke to Aretê: "Come here,
woman, and bring a good chest, one of the best, and put this
freshly washed cloak in it, and a shirt. Heat up a cauldron
on the fire for the stranger, and warm some water so that once
395 he has bathed and seen all these gifts lying before him that
the good Phaeacians have brought here, then he might take pleasure
in the feast and in hearing the strains of the song. And I will give him
my own very beautiful cup, made of gold, so that remembering me
all his days he may pour out drink-offerings in his halls to Zeus
400 and to the other gods."

             Thus he spoke, and Aretê ordered
her female slaves to set up a large tripod on the fire as soon
as possible. They set a tripod filled with water for the bath
over the blazing fire, and they poured water in it, and took wood
and stoked it beneath. The fire licked around the belly
405 of the tripod, and the water was warmed. In the meantime Aretê
brought out a very beautiful chest from her chamber, and she placed
in it beautiful gifts, cloth and gold that the Phaeacians
had given her.

She herself put in it a beautiful cloak
and a shirt, and she spoke words to Odysseus that went
like arrows: "Now see that you secure the lid. Quickly put a cord   410
on it so that someone does not rob you on the way
when by and by sweet sleep has fallen upon you as you
travel on the black ship."

When the much-enduring godlike
Odysseus heard these words, he immediately fitted on the lid
and quickly put a cord around it—a clever knot that once   415
the lady Kirkê had taught him. And now the housekeeper urged
him to get into the tub and bathe, and he was glad to see
the warm bath, because he was unaccustomed to being
so well cared for since he left the house of Kalypso with
the fine tresses. Up until then he was cared for continually,   420
as if he were a god.

When the female slaves had washed him
and anointed his flesh with olive oil, they put a beautiful cloak
and shirt around him. When he came out of the bathtub,
he went forth to the men who were drinking wine. Nausicaä,
gifted with beauty by the gods, stood beside the doorpost   425
of the well-built hall, and she marveled at Odysseus when she
saw him. She spoke to him words that went like arrows:
"Dear stranger, remember me when you return to your native land,
and thereafter, because to me first of all you owe the price
of your life."   430

The resourceful Odysseus then answered her:
"Nausicaä, daughter of great-hearted Alkinoös, even so may Zeus,
the loud-thundering husband of Hera, bring it to pass that I return
home and see the day of my homecoming. There I will pray to you
as to a goddess always, for all my days. For you, young girl,
gave me life."°   435

So he spoke and sat down on a chair beside
the chieftain Alkinoös. They were serving out portions and mixing
the wine. The herald came near, leading the fine singer Demodokos,
honored by the people. Demodokos sat down in the middle
of the diners, leaning his chair against a tall pillar. Then

---

435   *me life*: But in the summary of his wanderings told to Penelope in Book 23, he does not even mention
Nausicaä.

440 the resourceful Odysseus spoke to the herald, cutting off
a piece of the backbone of the white-tusked boar°—there was still
plenty left—and there was rich fat on either side: "Herald,
here, give this meat to Demodokos, so that he might eat of it,
and I will greet him, though I am sad at heart. For to all men
445 upon the earth singers are endowed with honor and reverence
because the Muse has taught them the pathway of song.
She loves the tribe of singers."

Thus he spoke, and the herald
carried the lyre and placed it in the hands of the good man
Demodokos. He took it, glad in his heart. Then they put out their
450 hands toward the refreshment that lay before them. But when they
had put aside all desire for food and drink, then the resourceful
Odysseus asked Demodokos: "Demodokos, I praise you above all men,
whether the Muse, Zeus's child, has instructed you, or Apollo.
For you sing well and accurately the fate of the Achaeans—
455 all that they did and suffered, and all the pains that the Achaeans
endured, as if you yourself were present or had heard the story
from someone who was. But come now, change your theme
and sing of the building of the wooden horse that Epeios° made
with Athena's help, that godlike Odysseus once dragged up
460 to the acropolis as a deception, having filled it with men who sacked
Ilion. If you can tell me this tale truly, I will at once tell all men
that the god has readily given you the gift of divine song."

So he spoke, and Demodokos began with an appeal to the god,
then let his song be heard. He took up the story where the Argives
465 had embarked on their well-benched ships and were sailing off,
having cast fire into their huts. In the meanwhile, a remaining band,
led by famous Odysseus, sat in the place of assembly of the Trojans,
hidden in the horse. For the Trojans themselves had dragged the horse
up to the acropolis. And there it stood, while the Trojans talked long
470 as they sat about it, but could reach no firm conclusion. There were
three opinions: that they should smash the hollow wood with
the pitiless bronze, or that they should drag it to the rampart and throw
it down on the rocks below, or that they should leave it alone
as a great offering to the gods. The third view was the one brought to pass,
475 for it was the Trojans' fate to perish when the city should enclose

---

441   *white-tusked boar*: The backbone (chine) was the cut of honor.

458   *Epeios*: He appears otherwise in Homer only as a boxer and weight-thrower in the funeral games for
Patroklos (*Il.* 23).

the great horse of wood. In it were the best of the Argives,
bringing death and doom to the Trojans.

So Demodokos sang of how
the sons of the Achaeans poured out of the horse and, leaving
their hollow ambush, sacked the city. Some went this way,
some that, to waste the steep city, but Odysseus went to the house   480
of Deïphobos° together with godlike Menelaos. There, he said,
Odysseus braved his most bitter battle, but was victorious
with the help of great-hearted Athena. These things the famous
singer sang, and Odysseus was melted. He wet the cheeks
beneath his eyelids with tears.   485

As a woman falls on her dear husband
and wails, a man who has fallen before his city and his people,
warding off the pitiless day from the city and from his children—
as she sees him dying and breathing his last, she shrieks
aloud and throws herself about him while the enemy
behind her strike the middle of her back and shoulders   490
with their spears, and lead her away into slavery to bear pain
and calamity while her cheeks are wasted with the most
pitiful grief—even so Odysseus poured a torrent of tears
from beneath his brows. Only one noticed him weeping—
Alkinoös alone saw it and marked it, because he sat   495
next to him, and he heard him groaning deeply.

Quickly he spoke to the oar-loving Phaeacians: "Listen
to me, O leaders and counselors of the Phaeacians! Let Demodokos
leave off the clear-voiced lyre. For his singing is not pleasing
to everyone here. Ever since we began to dine and the divine   500
singer began to sing, the stranger here has not ceased
from sad lament. Surely grief has encompassed
his heart. But come, let Demodokos cease his singing
so that we might all take delight alike, both hosts and guest,
for it is better this way. On the honored stranger's account   505
all these things are made ready, his sending forth and the gifts
of friendship that, lovingly, we have given him. A stranger
and a suppliant is like a brother to a man who has some little
grasp of wisdom.

---

481 *Deïphobos*: A son of Priam and Hekabê and brother of Hector, who took up with Helen after the death
of Paris.

"Therefore do not hide with crafty thoughts
510 what I shall now ask you. The better course is to speak plainly.
Tell me the name by which your mother and father called you,
and the people of the town and those who live round about.
For no one of all mankind is altogether without a name,
neither base man nor noble, when he is first born, but parents
515 give a name to everyone when they are born. And tell me
your country, your people, and your city, so that our ships
may send you there, telling the course by their wits.
For the Phaeacians have no pilots, nor steering oars such as other
ships have, but their ships know the thoughts and minds
520 of men, and they know the cities and rich fields of all peoples,
and they quickly travel over the gulf of the sea covered
in a mist and a cloud. They do not fear harm or destruction.

"But this story I once heard my father Nausithoös say—
he said that Poseidon is indignant with us because we give
525 safe transport to all men. He said that once, as a well-made ship
of the Phaeacians returns from an escort over the misty sea,
that Poseidon would strike here and heap-up a great mountain
around our city.° So spoke the old man. Either these things
the gods will bring to pass or will leave unfulfilled, as is pleasing
530 to the heart of the god.

"But come, tell me this and say it truly.
Where have you wandered? To what countries of men have you come?
Tell me of the thickly populated cites themselves, both of those
who are cruel and savage and unjust, and of those who love strangers
and are god-fearing in their minds. Tell me why you weep
535 and wail in your spirit when you hear the fate of the Argives
and the Danaäns at Ilion. This the gods brought about.
They spun the thread of destruction for men so that there might
be song for those yet to come. Did some family member die
before Ilion—a good man, your daughter's husband, or your wife's father,
540 who are nearest to one after his own flesh and blood? Or was it
some revered comrade, a man most dear, a good man? For a comrade
with an understanding heart is in no way less than a brother."

---

528 *around our city*: Apparently so they could no longer offer safe transport to strangers.

BOOK 9. *Odysseus in the Cave of Cyclops*

Then resourceful Odysseus spoke to him in reply:
"Lord Alkinoös, renowned above all men, truly
it is a lovely thing to listen to a singer such as this man is,
like to the gods in his voice. I don't think that there is
a greater fulfillment of delight than when joy holds 5
all the people, and while dining seated side by side
in the house they listen to a singer, and beside them
the tables are filled with bread and meat and the cupbearer
draws wine from the mixing bowl and carries it around
and pours it into the cups. This seems to my mind 10
to be the fairest thing of all. But your heart is turned
to ask about my grievous pains, that I might
weep and groan still more.

"What then should I say first of all,
what last? For the gods in heaven have given me many
afflictions. Now I shall tell you my name so that you too 15
may know it and I, once I have escaped the pitiless day
of doom, may be a guest-friend to you, although I live far away.
I am Odysseus, the son of Laërtes, known among men
for my many deceits, and my fame reaches to the sky.
I live in clear-seen ITHACA. There is a mountain there, Neriton, 20
covered with forest, conspicuous. Round about are many other
islands close to one another—DOULICHION and SAMÊ
and wooded ZAKYNTHOS.° Ithaca itself is low-lying
in the sea and is the furthest toward the west. The others
lie apart toward Dawn, and the sun. It is a rugged island, 25
but a good nurse for young men. As for me, I can see nothing
sweeter than one's own land.

"Truly Kalypso, the beautiful goddess,
tried to keep me there in her hollow caves, desiring
that I be her husband. Likewise did Kirkê, the crafty lady

---

23   *Zakynthos*: Evidently, Doulichion is modern Leucas; Samê is Kephallenia; Zakynthos is Zakynthos; Ithaca
is Ithaca, but it is not the furthest "toward the west" (see MAP IV). As usual, Homer is somewhat cavalier
about geography.

30 of Aiaia,° tried to hold me back in her halls, desiring that I be
her husband. But they could not persuade me in my heart.
For there is nothing sweeter than one's homeland and one's parents,
even if he lives far away in a rich house in a foreign country,
apart from his parents.° But come, let me tell you of my painful
35 homecoming that Zeus set upon me as I returned from Troy.

"Coming out of Ilion, a wind drove us to the KIKONES,
to Ismaros. There I sacked the city and destroyed the men.
We took the women and much wealth from that city
and divided it up that no one might be cheated of an equal share.
40 I urged that we flee on swift foot, but the others would not
be persuaded—the great fools! There we drank much wine,
and we slaughtered many sheep beside the shore and cattle
with shambling walk. In the meanwhile the Kikones went
and called to other Kikones in the neighborhood, more numerous
45 and braver ones. They lived inland, experienced in fighting
the enemy from chariots and, where necessary, on foot.
They came in the morning, as many as there are leaves and flowers
in their season. And then an evil fate from Zeus fell upon us
ill-fated men, that we might suffer many sorrows. The Kikones
50 took their stand and fought beside the swift ships, and each side
threw spears of bronze at the other. So long as it was morning
and the sacred day progressed, for so long we held out
and fought them off, although they were more. And when
the sun turned to the time of the unyoking of oxen, then
55 the Kikones turned the tide of battle and overcame the Achaeans.
Six companions with fancy shin guards perished from each ship,°
but the others fled from death and fate.

"Then we sailed farther,
grieving in our hearts, saved from death, though we lost
our dear comrades. Nor did I allow the curved ships to travel
60 on farther before we had called out three times to each
of our wretched companions, those who died on the plain,
overcome by the Kikones.° But Zeus the cloud-gatherer

---

30 *Aiaia*: "earth," the name of Kirkê's mythical island.

34 *parents*: He does not mention his wife, whose loyalty is, in fact, the focus of the story.

56 *from each ship*: Odysseus commands 12 ships, so he lost 72 men to the Kikones. The usual complement of rowers to each ship was 20, though sometimes this could reach 50, as with the ship of the Phaeacians. It is never clear how many men Odysseus has in each ship.

62 *by the Kikones*: A reference to the religious practice of calling out the names of the dead three times to assist their transition into the other world.

roused North Wind in an astounding tempest against
our ships, and North Wind hid the land and sea alike in cloud.

"Night rushed down from the heaven. Our ships were borne   65
sidelong—the strength of the wind tore the sails to shreds,
so we let down the sails into the ships, fearing death,
and we hastily rowed the boats toward the land.
There we lay continuously for two night and two days,
eating our hearts out from exhaustion and torment. But when   70
fair-tressed Dawn brought the third day to birth, we raised
the white sails on the masts and took our seats. The wind
and the helmsmen steered the ships.

                            "And then I would have
reached unscathed the land of my fathers, but as we
rounded MALEA° the wave and the current of North Wind   75
beat me back and drove me off course past CYTHERA.

"Then we were carried by deadly winds over the fish-rich
sea for nine days, but on the tenth we came to the land
of the Lotus Eaters, who feed on a flowery food.° There we went
ashore and drew water, and quickly we took our meal   80
beside the swift ships. But when we had tasted food and drink,
I sent forth some of my companions to find out who were
the men who ate bread in this land. I picked out two men,
and sent with them a herald as the third. Quickly they went
and mingled with the Lotus Eaters, who did not plan death   85
for my men, but gave them to eat of the lotus. Whoever ate
of the honey-sweet fruit of the lotus no longer wished
to bring back word or to return home, but wanted to remain
there with the Lotus Eaters, feeding on the lotus, forgetful
of their return home.   90

                    "I drove them, weeping, to the ships,
by force, and I dragged them beneath the benches
and bound them in the hollow ships. I ordered my other
trusty companions to depart with speed on the swift ships

---

75 *Malea*: The winds and powerful currents off Malea, on the southeast coast of the PELOPONNESUS, are still a
    problem for seafarers. Menelaos, too, was driven off course here (Book 3).

79 *flowery food*: Beginning in the ancient world, and continuing today, commentators have attempted to trace
    Odysseus' wanderings on a map, but he is no longer in the real world and all such efforts are fruitless. "We're
    not in Kansas anymore," as Dorothy says in the movie *The Wizard of Oz*. Similarly, attempts to identify the
    lotus plant are misconceived. The plant is like that magical food in the other world that, once consumed,
    prevents one from returning to this world (in the myth of Persephone, it is the seed of the pomegranate).

so that none of them could eat of the lotus and forget his homeward
95   journey. Quickly they went on board and sat at the thole-pins,
and seated in a row they struck the gray sea with their oars.

"From there we sailed on, grieving in our hearts. We came
to the land of the arrogant and lawless Cyclopes.° Trusting
in the deathless gods they neither plant with their hands nor
100   do they plow, but all these things spring up for them unsown
and unplowed—wheat and barley and vines that bear grapes
for a fine wine. And the rain of Zeus makes them grow.
They do not have assemblies where they discuss policy, nor do
they establish rules, but they live on the peaks of high mountains
105   in hollow caves, each man laying down the law to his own
children and wives—nor do they care about one another.

"There is a fertile island that stretches outside the harbor,
not close, not far from the land of the Cyclopes, wooded.
Countless goats live there, wild goats. The comings
110   and goings of men do not drive them away, nor do hunters
go there, men who suffer jeopardy in the woods as they tramp
upon the peaks of the mountains. The island is not occupied
by flocks, nor covered by plowland, but unsown and unplowed.
The island is every day empty of men, and it feeds
115   the bleating goats. For the Cyclopes have no red-cheeked ships,°
nor do builders of ships live among them who might build
ships with fine benches to provide them everything
they want, journeying to the cities of men, as men often
cross the sea in ships to visit one another. Such men would
120   have made of this island a pleasant place. It is by no means
a poor place, but would bear every fruit in season. There are
meadows in it, watered and soft, beside the shores of the gray sea.
Vines will never fail there. The land is level and suitable
for plowing. One could harvest a bumper crop every season,
125   for the soil is rich.

"There is a secure harbor where there is
no need of mooring ropes, nor need of throwing out
anchor stones, nor of making fast the sterns of ships.

---

98 *Cyclopes*: Probably originally meaning "with round face" or "with round eyes," but in Homer, Cyclops is
taken to mean "round-eye," that is, having only one eye. Homer never says that Cyclops has only one eye,
but the story depends on it. In art, he is often shown with three eyes. The relationship between Homer's
Cyclopes and the Cyclopes (in Hesiod), who were Titans and the smiths of Zeus, forgers of the thunder-
bolt, has never been clarified.

115 *red-cheeked ships*: Because their sterns are painted red.

You need only draw the ships up on the shore, then wait
for the time that your spirit urges you again to put to sea,
when the winds blow fair.   130

        "At the head of the harbor
a spring of shining water flows from beneath a cave.
Poplars grow around it. There we sailed—some god
guided us through the dark night, for there was no light
by which to see. A thick mist covered the island all around,
and the cloud-hidden moon did not appear in the night sky.   135
No one had seen the island, nor the long waves rolling
onto the dry land until we ran our ships with fine benches
up onto the shore. When we had beached the ships,
we took down the sails and ourselves went ashore
on the edge of the sea. There we fell asleep and awaited   140
the bright dawn.

        "When early-born dawn appeared, who has
fingers like roses, we wandered over the island, wondering
at it. Nymphs, the daughters of Zeus who carries the goatskin
fetish, roused up the mountain goats so that my companions
could have something to eat. Immediately we took out our bent   145
bows and javelins with long sockets from the ships. We split up
into three groups and set to throwing our missiles. Soon
the god had given us enough game to satisfy our hearts.
Twelve ships followed me,° and to each nine goats fell
by lot. For me alone they chose out ten.   150

        "Then we spent
the whole day dining on endless flesh and sweet wine
until the sun went down. The red wine from our ships had not
yet run out. Some was still left, for we had taken a lot of it
in jars for each crew member when we sacked the sacred
city of the Kikones. We looked across to the land   155 🔊
of the Cyclopes, who lived nearby. We saw smoke and heard
voices and the sound of sheep and goats. When the sun went down
and darkness came on, we lay down to rest on the edge of the sea.

"When early-born dawn appeared, whose fingers
were like roses, I called an assembly and spoke thus to all: 160
"The rest of you stay here, my trusty companions, while

---

149 *followed me:* The first time we learn how many ships were in Odysseus' contingent.

I take a ship and some comrades and appraise these men,
to see who they are, whether they are violent and savage
and unjust, or whether they are friendly to strangers and have
165 minds that fear the gods."

          "So speaking I got in my ship
and commanded my men to embark, to release the stern-cables.
They quickly got in and sat down on the benches.
Sitting in order, they struck the gray sea with their oars.
And when we had reached the place nearby, there,
170 at the edge of the land, we espied a cave close to the sea,
high up, overgrown by laurels. Many flocks were
accustomed to sleep there. A high wall surrounded
the cave, made of stones set deep in the earth, and tall
pines grew there, and high-crowned oaks. A huge man
175 slept alone in that place and herded his animals there,
all alone. He had no doings with others, but lived
in solitude, without laws. For truly he was an unearthly
monster, not like a man who lives by bread, more like
a wooded peak of a high mountain range that stands
180 out alone above all others.

          "I ordered the remainder
of my trusty companions to stay by the ship and to guard it
while I went off, having selected twelve of my best men.
I had with me a goatskin of dark sweet wine that Maron
had given me, the son of Euanthes, a priest of Apollo
185 who used to watch over Ismaros.° He gave it because
out of respect we protected him, along with his wife and child.
He lived in a wood of Phoibos Apollo, and he gave me
splendid gifts. Of finely worked gold he gave me
seven talents, and he gave me a silver wine-mixing
190 bowl, and beside these he filled twelve jars with wine,
a divine drink—sweet, unmixed. No one in his household
knew about this wine, neither slave nor servant,
only his wife and the housekeeper. Whenever they drank
honeyed red wine, he would pour one cup of the wine
195 into twenty of water, and a wondrous odor would come up
from the mixing bowl. Then one could hardly resist
drinking it.

---

185 *. . . Ismaros:* Maron is named after Maroneia, a wine-growing district in southern THRACE. His father is
aptly named "blooming" (Euanthes). This is the only time in the *Odyssey* that a priest is referred to.

FIGURE 9.1   Maron gives the sack of potent wine to Odysseus.   Wearing a Phrygian cap
(though he lives in Thrace), net leggings, crossed belts on his chest, and a cape, the beardless
Kikonian priest Maron gives the sack of wine to Odysseus by which Cyclops is overcome. In his left
hand, he holds a spear pointed downwards. His crowned wife stands behind him with a horn
drinking cup. The very long-haired Odysseus wears high boots, a traveler's cap (*pilos*), and holds a
spear over his shoulder with his right hand. To the far left stands a Kikonian woman. South Italian
red-figure wine-mixing bowl by the Maron Painter, 340–330 BC.

"With this wine I filled a large skin and took
it along, also provisions in a leather sack. For my proud
spirit imagined confronting a man clothed in mighty strength,
200 a savage, not subjecting himself to laws or regulations.
We quickly arrived at the cave, but did not find him inside,
for he was shepherding his fat flocks in the fields.
Coming into the cave we marveled at everything—there
were crates filled with cheeses, and pens groaned with sheep
205 and kids. Each kind were penned separately—the older
by themselves, the younger by themselves, the newborn
by themselves as well. Vast jars were brimful of whey,
and the milk pails and bowls, finely made, into which he milked.

"Then my comrades begged me to grab the cheeses and to leave
210 that place—to drive the kids and lambs quickly out of the pens
to our swift ship, and to sail away across the salt water.
But I was not persuaded—it were better if I had been!—
because I wanted to see him, in case he might give me gift-tokens.°
As it happened, his appearance was not to be a pleasing one
215 to my companions!

                    "We made a fire and offered
sacrifice. We took some of the cheeses and ate them.
We sat inside and waited until he should return from
herding his flocks.

                    "He finally arrived with a large load
of dried wood, useful at dinner time.° He threw the wood inside
220 the cave with a crash. In terror we shrank back into a deep recess
of the cave. He drove his fat flock of sheep, all those
he needed to milk, deep into the wide cavern, leaving
the males outside—the rams and the billys—in the deep
courtyard. Then he placed a huge boulder in the opening
225 of the cavern, lifting it on high, gigantic. Twenty-two
fine four-wheeled carts could not have dislodged it from
the ground, such a towering mass of rock he placed
before the door.

---

213 *gift-tokens*: To establish *xenia*, "guest-friendship." As we have seen with Odysseus' experience on Scheria,
the aristocratic traveler could expect to be entertained and given a gift, often precious, that would ever
thereafter bind the traveler and his descendants to the host.

219 *dinner time*: But for heating and light. He does not use the fire for cooking.

"Then he sat down and milked his sheep
and the bleating goats, all in turn, and he placed
a suckling beneath each. And he smartly curdled half   230
the white milk,° gathered it and stored it in woven baskets,
and the other half he put in vessels so that he could use it
for drink, so that it might serve him for dinner.

                                   "When he had
finished his tasks, he built a fire and, finally, he saw us—
and he asked: 'Strangers, who are you? From where do you sail   235
the watery paths?° Are you on some mission, or do you cross
the sea at random, like pirates who wander around endangering
their lives while doing evil to men of other lands?'

   "So he spoke—and our hearts were frozen in fear of his
rumbling voice and his immense size. Nonetheless I answered   240
in this way: "We are Achaeans returning from Troy.
We have been buffeted by winds from every direction across
the great depth of the sea. Longing to go home, we have travelled
on a false course, by many stages. For so Zeus devised.
We are followers of Agamemnon, the son of Atreus,   245
whose fame is now the greatest under the heaven.
He has sacked a city of great size and destroyed its many
people. We come to you on our knees, as suppliants,
in the hope you might give us a gift-token or some other
present, as is the custom among strangers. Respect the gods,   250
O mighty man! We are your suppliants, and Zeus
is the avenger of suppliants and strangers—Zeus the god
of strangers, who always stands by respectable voyagers.'

   "So I spoke, and he answered me immediately with a pitiless
heart: 'You are a fool, stranger, or you must come from faraway,   255
inviting me to fear or shun your gods. The Cyclopes have no care
for Zeus who carries the goatskin fetish, nor for any other
of your gods, because we are more powerful than they.
Not to avoid the hatred of Zeus would I spare you
or your companions, if my spirit did not so urge me.   260
But tell me, so that I may know—where did you anchor
your well-made ship, far away, or nearby?'

---

231   *white milk*: Presumably by adding a fermenting agent, such as fig juice.

236   *watery paths*: Cyclops inverts all the rules of *xenia*. In polite society, the host entertains and feeds the guest
      before asking the stranger's identity. Cyclops immediately wants to know who these men are, then instead
      of feeding them, he eats them!

"Thus he spoke, testing me, but he did not fool
my great cunning. I answered him with crafty words:
265 'Poseidon, the rocker of the earth, shattered my ship,
throwing it against the cliffs at the edge of your land,
driving it onto a headland. For a wind arose
from the sea, but I, along with my men, escaped
dread destruction.'

"So I spoke. He did not answer from his
270 pitiless heart, but leaping up he seized two of my companions,
raised them high, then dashed them to the ground as if
they were puppies. Their brains ran out onto the ground,
wetting the earth. Cutting them limb from limb, he readied
his meal. He ate them like a lion raised in the mountains,
275 not leaving anything—not the guts nor the flesh nor the bones
rich with marrow.

"Wailing, we held up our hands to Zeus,
seeing this vile deed and helpless to do anything about it.
But when Cyclops had filled his great belly by eating the flesh
of two of our men, and then drinking pure milk, he lay stretched
280 out among the sheep in the cave. I contemplated in my great
heart going up close to him, drawing my sharp sword
from my thigh, and stabbing him in the chest where the belly
shields the liver, feeling along with my hand to find
the right place. But a second thought came to me—
285 we would then die a grisly death! For our hands would be
incapable of budging the heavy stone he had set in place
against those high doors. So, groaning miserably, we awaited
the bright dawn.

"When early-born dawn appeared
and spread her fingers of rose, Cyclops stirred up
290 the fire and milked his glorious herds, all in order,
again setting the young to each dam. When he had
finished his tasks, he again seized two of my men
for his meal. After he had made his meal, he drove out
the fat herds, easily lifting away the huge stone.
295 Then he put it back again, as if shutting the lid
on a quiver. With a loud whistle Cyclops turned
his flocks toward the mountains.

"I was left there devising evil
in the depths of my heart, wondering how I could take

revenge, if Athena would grant me glory. Thinking on it,
I devised the following plan: A great club of Cyclops lay   300
beside a sheep pen, green, made of olive wood.
He had cut it to carry, once it dried out. Looking at it,
we considered it to be as big as a mast of a black
ship with twenty oars—a big merchantman that
crosses over the great gulf, so great it was to look at   305
in length and in breadth.

           "I went up to it and cut off
about six feet and gave the length to my companions.
I told them to strip off the bark and make it smooth,
while I stood by it and sharpened the point. Then I at once
placed the stake in the blazing fire to harden it.   310
Then I laid it away, hiding it beneath some dung
that was spread in big heaps all over the cave.° I ordered
the others to select by lot who would dare to assist me
in hoisting the stake and grinding it into his eye,
when sweet sleep overcame him. They selected the very   315
ones I myself would have chosen, four solid men,
and I the fifth among them.

           "At dusk Cyclops returned
from the fields, leading his herds with their beautiful fleece.
He drove the fat sheep into the broad cave, all of them
this time, leaving none of them outside in the deep court,   320
either because he had a foreboding, or some god urged him to.
Then he lifted high the huge rock and set it back in place.
He sat down and milked his ewes and bleating goats,
all in order, again placing each young beneath the teat
of every mother. When he had finished his tasks, he snatched   325
two of my men and prepared his meal.

           "Then I spoke
to Cyclops, standing near him, holding in my hands
a bowl of ivy wood filled with black wine: 'Cyclops,
take this wine, drink it after your meal of human flesh,
so that you might know what manner of drink our ship   330

---

312 *the cave*: Odysseus has forgotten all about his sword, which could have served as a lethal weapon, but the
folktale hero needs a special weapon by which to overcome his adversary. In this case, the weapon is the
olive stake. Just such primitive fire-hardened spears were used in primordial times to separate man from
nature, so the stake is a fitting symbol of civilization triumphant over barbarism.

contained. I was bringing it to you as a drink offering,
in hopes you would take pity on me and send me homeward.

  " 'But as it is you are mad past bearing! Vile monster!
How will anyone else from all the multitudes of men
335 ever come here again when you have behaved so badly?'

  "So I spoke. He took the wine and drank it.
He was tremendously pleased, quaffing the sweet drink,
and again he asked me: 'Give me some more, be a good
fellow. And tell me your name right away so that I may give
340 you a gift-token that will make you happy. Surely the rich
plowland bears a fine grape for the Cyclopes, and the rain
of Zeus makes the grape grow. But this is equal to the food
of the gods!'

  "So he spoke, and again I poured for him
the flaming wine. Three times I brought it and gave it to him,
345 three times he drank it in his mindless folly.

                                    "When the wine
had gone to his head, I spoke to him with honeyed words:
'Cyclops, you ask about my famous name, so I will tell
you and then you will give me a gift-token, just as you
promised. *Nbdy* is my name. My mother and my father
350 and everyone else calls me *Nbdy*.'

                          "So I spoke, and he at once
answered me from his pitiless heart: 'Nbdy, I will eat you
last among your comrades, and the others first. *That* will be
your gift-token!'

                    "He spoke and then, reeling over, fell on
his back. He lay there, bending his thick neck, and sleep,
355 which overcomes all, took hold of him. From his throat
dribbled wine and bits of human flesh. Drunk, he vomited.°

  "I then pushed the stake I'd made into the hot ashes
until it glowed hot. I encouraged my companions, so that no man
would hold back from fear. Then, as soon as the stake was nearly
360 afire—although it was green, and glowed terribly—then

---

356 *vomited:* The demonic being in a folktale is often killed when drunk or at a banquet.

I went up close and took it from the fire, my comrades
attending me. A god breathed into us strong courage.

"They took the stake of olive wood, sharp on
its point, and thrust it into his eye. I threw my weight
on it from above and spun it around, as when   365
a man drills a ship's timber with a drill, and those
beneath keep the drill spinning with a thong, holding
the thong from either end, and the drill runs around
unceasingly—just so we took hold of that fiery stake
and spun it around in his eye, and his blood streamed   370
all around the heated thing.° The flame singed his
eyelid and eyebrow and the eyeball popped and its roots
crackled in the fire.

            "As when a bronze-worker dips
a great ax or an adze in the cold water and the metal hisses
as he tempers it—from there comes the strength of iron—   375
so did Cyclops' eye hiss around the olive stake.°
He screamed horribly, and the rock echoed his cry.

"In terror we drew back as he ripped out the stake
from his eye, mixed with a huge amount of blood. He wrenched
it from his eye and threw it away, throwing his hands about wildly.   380

"Cyclops called aloud to the Cyclopes who lived
nearby in caves in the windy heights. Hearing his cry,
they assembled from here and there, and standing
outside his cave they asked him what was the matter:
'What is so bothering you, Polyphemos, that you cry out   385
through the immortal night and wake us all up? Can it be
that some man is driving off your flocks against your will?
Or is someone killing you by trickery or by might?'

---

371 *heated thing*: The stake is like a bow drill digging a hole. The forward thrust comes from the weight of the
     user as he leans against it, while the twist of the drill comes from a thong wrapped in a single turn around
     the drill. Men at each end of the bow push and pull so the drill turns, now clockwise, now counterclock-
     wise, like the drill of someone starting a fire by friction. Still, it is hard to see how Odysseus could both put
     pressure on the stake and twist it, especially if its weight was carried by four other men.

376 *olive stake*: At the time that Homer was composing, iron was replacing bronze, so the bronze-smith is said
     to quench an ax, and "from there comes the strength of iron." In Homer, weapons are always of bronze, but
     everyday implements can be iron. For centuries the effectiveness of tempering iron (immersion does noth-
     ing for bronze) was thought to come from substances dissolved in the water into which the hot metal was
     plunged, not from the sudden cooling of the metal: The word translated "tempers" really means "to treat
     with a drug," that is, with something dissolved in the water.

FIGURE 9.2   The Blinding of Polyphemos.   Odysseus and two of his men thrust the stake into the bearded giant's eye. In his right hand, Polyphemos holds the cup of wine by which Odysseus had made him drunk. Odysseus is shown in white to distinguish him from his companions. This is the earliest representation of Cyclops' blinding, a popular subject in Greek art. Athenian black-figure two-handled jug, c. 660 BC.

"The powerful Polyphemos answered them from the cave:
'My friends, Nbdy is killing me by trickery, not by might!' 390

"And they answered with words that went like arrows:
'If nobody is assaulting you in your loneliness—well,
you cannot escape a sickness sent by great Zeus. Pray
to our father Poseidon, the king.'

                                "So they spoke and went away.
My heart laughed! My made-up name and my cunning 395
device had deceived him. Cyclops, groaning, in terrible pain,
fumbled around with his hands, then took away the stone
blocking his door. He sat down in the doorway with arms
outstretched, to catch anyone who might try to get out
of the door along with the sheep—so much did he hope 400
in his heart to find me a fool!

                                "But I considered what
would be the best plan to devise a sure escape
for my companions and for myself. I considered
every kind of trick and device, as is usual in matters
of life and death. A great evil was near . . . Now this 405
seemed to me to be the best plan: Here are his well-fed
rams with thick wool, handsome and large, with fleece
dark as violet. In silence I bound these together,
taking up three at a time, with twisted stems
on which the huge Cyclops, who knows no laws, 410
used to sleep.° The sheep in the middle would carry a man,
the two on the outside would go along, saving
my comrades. Thus each three sheep bore a man.
"As for me—there was a ram, by far the best of the flock,
and I climbed up on his back and then squirreled around 415
to his shaggy belly, where I lay, my hands clinging
constantly, with a steady heart, to the wonderful fleece.

"Thus we waited, wailing, until the bright dawn.
When early-born dawn appeared and stretched forth her fingers
of rose, the rams hastened out to pasture. But the ewes, 420
unmilked, bleated in the pens, for their udders were full
to bursting. Their master, worn down by savage pain,
felt along the backs of all the sheep as they stood before

---

411 *used to sleep*: Threaded in a bed-frame, the twisted stems would make a kind of mattress.

FIGURE 9.3 Odysseus clinging to the belly of a sheep. Here Odysseus is tied by three straps, around his knees, middle, and shoulders. He holds his sword in his right hand drawn against the giant. Meaningless alphabetic characters are scattered around the scene. Athenian black-figure oil jar from c. 590 BC.

him—the fool! He did not realize that my men were bound
beneath the breasts of the wooly sheep.   425

                              "Last of all
the ram went out the door, burdened by the weight
of its fleece and my own devious self. Feeling along
his back, the mighty Polyphemos said: 'My dear ram,
why do you go out of the cave last of the entire flock?
In the past you would never lag behind the sheep,   430
but you always went out the very first to graze on
the tender bloom of the grass, taking long strides.
You always came first to the flowing rivers, and you were
always the most eager to return to the fold at evening.
But now you are the last of all. Perhaps you regret   435
the eye of your master that an evil man blinded,
along with his miserable companions, overcoming
my brain with wine! Nbdy, who has not yet, I think,
escaped destruction! If you could think as I do,
and you had the power of speech to tell me where   440
that man flees from my wrath, then would his brains
be smeared all over the ground of this cave when I hit him,
and my heart could take rest from the agony that this
good-for-nothing Nbdy has brought!'

                              "So saying
he sent the ram forth from the door. When we had gone   445
a short distance from the cave and the fold, I was first
to loose myself from the ram, and then I cut free my
companions. Quickly, turning constantly around, we drove
off the long-legged sheep, rich with fat, until we came to the ship.
Our friends who had escaped death were glad to see us, but they   450
bewailed those who were lost. I would not let them weep.
I nodded at each, ordering them to load aboard the herds
with beautiful fleece so we might sail away over the salt sea.
Then they boarded and sat down on their benches, and sitting
all in a row they struck the gray sea with their oars.   455

   "But when we were so far away you can barely hear
a man when he shouts, then I called to Cyclops with these
contemptuous words: 'Cyclops, it turns out that you did not eat
the companions of a man without strength in your hollow cave,
taking them by might and by violence. Surely your evil   460
deeds were bound to come back to you, wretch! You did not
shrink from devouring strangers in your own house.

FIGURE 9.4 **Polyphemos talks to his lead ram.** Blinded, holding his club, leaning against the cave wall, the giant reaches out to stroke his favorite ram, under which Odysseus clings. Athenian black-figure wine cup, c. 500 BC.

For this Zeus and the other gods have punished you.'

"So I spoke, and more anger boiled from his heart. He ripped
off the peak of a high mountain, and he threw it. The peak landed   465
just forward of our ship with its dark prow. The sea surged
beneath the rock as it came down and the wave carried
our ship back toward the shore on that flood from the deep—
driving it onto the dry land. But I seized a long pole
in my hands and thrust the ship off land again. I nodded   470
to my comrades, directing them to fall to their oars
so that we might escape this evil. They set to their oars
and rowed.

            "When we were twice as far away,
traveling over the sea, then I wanted to speak
to Cyclops again, but my comrades, one after the other,   475
tried to stop me with gentle words: 'Reckless man!
Why do you want to stir up this savage? Just now
he has thrown a rock into the sea and brought our ship
back to the dry land, and, truly, we thought we were
done for. If he had heard just one of us uttering   480
even one sound, he would have thrown a jagged rock
and smashed our heads and all the timbers of our ship!
He's a mighty thrower!'

                "So they cowered, but they did not
persuade my great-hearted spirit. I shouted back
at him with an angry heart: 'Cyclops, if any mortal man   485
ever asks about the disgraceful blinding of your eye,
you can say that Odysseus, sacker of cities, did it,
the son of Laërtes, whose home is in Ithaca.'°

                    "So I spoke,
and groaning he gave me this answer: 'Yes, yes—!
Now I remember an ancient prophecy. A prophet once   490
came here, a good man, a tall man, Telemos, the son of Eurymos,
who was better at prophecy than anyone. He grew old
among the Cyclopes. He told me that all this would happen
sometime in the future, that I would lose my sight at the hands   495

---

488   ....Ithaca: Homer is following a narrative pattern that repeats many times in the poem: danger;
         defeat of an enemy; recognition. Following this pattern, Odysseus here gives his name as a sign that
         he is recognized. But knowledge of Odysseus' name gives Cyclops power over Odysseus, as in the curse
         Cyclops is about to give.

of 'Odysseus.' I always thought that some big man, and handsome,
would come here, dressed in mighty power. As it is,
a little man, a man of no consequence, a feeble little guy—
he has blinded my eye after he got me drunk on wine!

"'But do return, O Odysseus, so that I can give you some
500 gift-tokens. And I can ask Poseidon, the famous shaker
of the earth, to give you a good trip home. I am his son,
you know, and he is my father. He himself will heal me, if he
wishes it: None of the blessed gods, nor mortal human can.'

"So he spoke, and I said in reply: 'Would that I might
505 rob you of your breath-soul and your life and send you
to the house of Hades, as surely as the earth-shaker
shall never heal your eye!'

"So I spoke. He then raised
his hands into the starry heaven and prayed to Poseidon
the king: 'Hear me, Poseidon, holder of the earth,
510 you with the dark locks—if truly I am your son
and you are my father, grant that Odysseus, the son of Laërtes,
the sacker of cities, never reach his home, which he says
is in Ithaca. But if it is fated that he see his friends
again, and arrive to his well-built house, returning to the land
515 of his fathers—may he come after a long time and after many
troubles, having lost all his companions, on someone
else's ship, and may he find grief in his own house!'

"So he spoke in prayer, and the dark-haired one
heard him. Right away Cyclops picked up a much bigger
520 stone, twirled it around, and put all his strength
into the throw. The rock this time fell behind the ship
with its dark prows just a little bit, missing the blade
of the steering-oar. The sea surged as the stone submerged,
and its wake drove the ship forward and onto dry land.

525 "But when we came back to the island,° the other ships
with fine benches were waiting, grouped together. Around
sat our comrades, wailing, awaiting us constantly.
We dragged the ship up onto the sand. We ourselves
got out of the ship and onto the shore of the sea. Then
530 we took the sheep out of the hollow boat and divided

---

525 *the island*: Goat-island opposite the Cyclops' cave, from where Odysseus set out.

them up so that no man, as far as I was able, would go
deprived of an equal share. My companions, who wear fancy
shin guards, gave the ram to me alone as a special gift
when the division took place. I sacrificed the ram
on the shore to Zeus of the dark thundercloud, the son   535
of Kronos, who rules over all, and I burned the thigh pieces.
He did not heed the offering but pondered how all
the ships with their fine benches might be destroyed,
along with my trusty companions.

                        "So we spent the whole day
until the sunset, dining on endless flesh and sweet wine.   540
When the sun went down and darkness came on, then we went
to bed on the shore of the sea. When early-born dawn
came and spread her fingers of rose, I roused up my companions
and ordered them to embark, to loosen the stern-ropes.
Quickly they boarded the goats and sat down on the benches,   545
and all in a row they struck the gray sea with their oars.
From there we sailed farther, grieving at heart—glad to have
escaped death, but sorry for our dear companions who did not.

BOOK 10. *Odysseus and Kirkê*

"We arrived at the island of Aiolos, where Aiolos lives,
the son of Hippotas,° dear to the deathless gods—
a floating island, and all around it is an unbreakable wall
of bronze, and the cliff runs up sheer. He has twelve children
5 in his halls, six daughters and six sons in their prime,
and he gave his daughters as wives to his sons.
These feast continually at the side of their dear father
and diligent mother, and endless refreshment lies beside them.
The house, full of steam from cooking, resounds all day long
10 even in the outer court, and at night they sleep beside
their chaste wives on blankets and corded beds.

"Well, we came to their city and their beautiful palace,
and for a full month he entertained me and asked me about everything—
about Ilion and the ships of the Argives and the homecoming
15 of the Achaeans. And I told him everything in proper order. But when
I asked that I might leave and I pressed him to be sent on my way,
he did not deny me anything, and he arranged my sailing.
He gave me a skin made from a nine-year-old ox that
he had flayed and in it he bound the paths of the howling winds,
20 for the son of Kronos had made him the keeper of the winds,
both to stop and to rouse them, whichever he wished.°

He bound the bag in my hollow ship with a shining silver cord
so that not even the slightest bit of wind might escape. Then he sent
forth the breath of West Wind to blow so that it might carry the ships
25 and my men.° But West Wind was not to bring this to pass,
for we were ruined through our own foolishness.

---

2 *son of Hippotas*: Unrelated to the hero Aiolos, founder of the house of the Aiolids, in which Jason and Nestor were to appear.

21 *he wished*: Aiolos acts as the proper host, in contrast to Cyclops: first a friendly welcome; the host's questions; the guest's reply; the request for a sending forth; the bestowal of a gift-token.

25 *my men*: We cannot, of course, say where the island of Aiolos is because it is a floating island, but it must be somewhere in the west if West Wind will blow them homeward.

"We sailed on
for nine days without stopping either night or day,
and on the tenth day we caught sight of our native land.
We were so close that we saw men tending the watch fires
when, being exhausted, sweet sleep came over me. I had   30
constantly kept the rope for tightening the sail in my hand,
and had not given it to another of my comrades, so that
we might arrive more quickly to the land of our fathers.

"Now my companions began to speak to one another,
saying that I was carrying home gold and silver,   35
a gift from great-hearted Aiolos, the son of Hippotas.
Thus one would say, glancing to someone sitting nearby:
'Think about it—this man is *so* dear and honored
by all men whose city and land he comes to!
And he is loaded with fancy treasure that he has taken   40
as booty from Troy, while we go home with empty hands,
though we have made the same journey. And now Aiolos
has given him this, showing kindness from friendship's
sake. But come, let us quickly see what this is here,
how much gold and silver this bag contains.'   45

"So they spoke,
and the wicked counsel of my comrades prevailed. They opened
the bag and the winds escaped. The storm wind instantly
took hold and carried them, wailing, out to sea away from
the land of our fathers. I woke up and wondered in my heart
whether I should throw myself from the ship and perish   50
in the sea, or whether I should endure in silence and remain
among the living. But I endured and held on, and covering
my head lay down in the ship.

"The ships were blown back
by the evil blast of wind again to the island of Aiolos,
and my comrades groaned. We went ashore to draw water,   55
and my companions quickly made ready a meal beside
the swift ships. But when we had tasted food and drink,
then I took a herald and a companion and went to the famous
palace of Aiolos. We found him feasting side by side with his
wife and children. Coming into his house we sat down beside   60
the doorposts on the threshold.

"They were amazed in their hearts
and questioned us: 'How have you come here, Odysseus?

FIGURE 10.1   Aiolos, king of the winds.   Roman mosaic from the House of Dionysos and the Four Seasons, 3rd century AD, Roman city of Volubilis, capital of the Berber king Juba II (50 BC–24 AD) in the province of Mauretania, Morocco. The Romans loved to decorate their floors with themes taken from Greek myth, and many have survived.

What evil spirit has assailed you? I believe we sent you forth
with kindly care so that you might arrive at the land
of your fathers, and your house, and whatever place you wanted.'   65

   "So they said, but with a sorry heart I spoke among them:
'With blind folly my evil companions injured me, and in addition
to that, accursed sleep. But make us well, my friends. For you
have the power.'

              "So I spoke, addressing them with gentle
words, but they fell silent. Then their father answered: 70
'Quickly get off this island, you most vile of living men!
It is not right that I help or send that man on his way
who is hated by the blessed gods. Go, for you come here
as one hated by the gods!'

                    "So saying he sent me out
of his house, as I deeply groaned. We sailed away from there,   75
grieving in our hearts. The spirits of the men were worn out
by the harsh rowing, all because of our own foolishness.
No longer did any breeze come up to bear us on our way.

   "We sailed for six days, night and day without stopping,
and on the seventh we came to the steep city of Lamos,   80
to Telepylos of the Laestrygonians, where herdsman calls
to herdsman as he drives in his flocks, and the other answers
as he drives his out. There a man who never slept could earn
a double wage, one by herding cattle, the other by pasturing
white sheep, for the paths of night and day are close.°   85

   "When we had come into the famous harbor, around which
steep cliffs ran continuously on both sides, and projecting headlands
opposite each other reach out at the mouth, and the entrance
is narrow—there all the others steered their curved ships inside.
They moored them within the hollow harbor close together.   90
There no wave ever swelled, neither great nor small,
but a white calm prevailed all around. I alone moored

---

85   ... *are close*: Apparently Lamos ("gluttonous") founded the city of which, as we learn, Antiphates ("killing in
return") is king. The etymology of *Laestrygonian* is quite obscure. *Telepylos*, the name of the Laestrygonian
settlement, means "far-gated," associating it with the underworld. Because the Laestrygonians seem to live
in a land of perpetual light, perhaps we are to think of this land as lying in the Far East where Dawn arises;
certainly Odysseus' next landfall on Kirkè's island is set in the East. Or it is like the Far North with its bright
summer nights, and the harbor is like a northern fiord. But this is a fairytale realm where directions are
topsy-turvy, confused, and normal rules of existence do not apply.

my black ship outside the harbor, on the border of the land,
tying the ship to a rock. Then I climbed up to a rugged
95 place of outlook and I took my stand. I could see neither
the works of men nor oxen. We saw only smoke rising
from the land. Then I sent forth some of my comrades
to find out who these men were who ate bread here on this land.
I selected two men, and a third as herald. When they had gone
100 ashore they went along a smooth road over which wagons
brought wood to the city from the high mountains. They met
a young girl in front of the city, drawing water, the excellent
daughter of the Laestrygonian Antiphates. She had come down
to the lovely flowing spring of Artakia, from where they carried
105 water into the city.

          "My men stood around her and spoke to her
and asked who was the king of this people and who they were
over whom he ruled. And she at once showed them the high-roofed
house of her father. When they entered the glorious palace, they found
his wife, as big as the peak of a mountain, and they were aghast
110 at the sight of her. She quickly called the famous Antiphates
from the place of assembly, her husband, who devised a hateful
death for one of my men. At once he seized a companion of ours
and prepared his meal, but the other two leaped up and came
fleeing to the ships. Then Antiphates raised a cry in the city,
115 and the brutish Laestrygonians, hearing it, came running from
all sides, ten thousand of them, not like men but Giants.
From the cliffs they hurled rocks at us, as huge as a man can lift.

    "At once an evil din arose throughout the company of dying men
and smashed ships. Spearing my men like fishes, they carried
120 them off—a disgusting meal. While they were destroying my men
inside the deep harbor, I drew my sharp sword from my thigh
and cut the cables of the blue-prowed ship with it. Calling quickly
to my crew, I ordered them to fall to their oars so that we might flee
from this evil. They tossed the sea with their oars, fearing destruction.
125 Joyfully my ship fled the overhanging cliffs into the sea,
but the others were destroyed there, every one.

                          "From there
we sailed on farther, grieving in our hearts, saved from death
but bemoaning our dear companions. We came to the island of Aiaia,
where Kirkê° with the fine tresses lived, a dread goddess

---

129 *Kirkê*: "hawk," for some reason.

FIGURE 10.2 **Laestrygonians attack Odysseus' ships.** In this somewhat dim Roman fresco there are ten of Odysseus' oared ships with single masts in the middle of the narrow bay, three near the shore, half-sunk, and a fourth half-sunk near the high cliffs on the right. Five of the Laestrygonian giants stand on the shore and spear Odysseus' men or throw down huge rocks. A sixth giant has waded into the water on the left and holds the prow of a ship in his mighty hands. From a house on the Esquiline Hill decorated with scenes from the *Odyssey*, Rome, c. AD 90.

130　of human speech,° the sister of Aietes of a destructive mind.
　　　Both were the children of Helios who brings light to mortals,
　　　and Persê was their mother, whom Ocean begot.° Here we put into
　　　shore in silence, into a harbor safe for ships—some god led us.
　　　There we disembarked and lay low for two days and two nights,
135　eating out our hearts from weariness and sorrow. But when Dawn
　　　with her lovely tresses brought the third day to birth, then I took
　　　my spear and sharp sword and quickly went up from the ship
　　　to a place of wide outlook, in the hopes I might see the works
　　　of men and hear their voices. I climbed up to a rugged place
140　of outlook and there took my stand. And I saw smoke rising
　　　from the wide-wandered earth, from Kirkê in her halls, through
　　　the thicket of oaks and the woods. I pondered then in my heart
　　　and spirit whether I should go to investigate, because I saw
　　　the fiery smoke. And as I pondered, this course seemed to me
145　to be the better: first to go to the swift ship and the shore of the sea
　　　and give my companions a meal, then to send them out
　　　to make a search.

　　　　　　　　"But when I came near to the curved ship,
　　　some god took pity on me, being all alone, and sent a great
　　　high-horned stag into my path. He was coming down
150　to the river from his pasture beside the wood, to get a drink,
　　　for the power of the sun oppressed him. I hit him
　　　with my spear in the middle of the back as he came out
　　　of the wood, and my bronze spear pierced straight through.
　　　Down he fell in the dust with a moan. His spirit fled
155　from him. I put my foot on him and pulled the bronze spear
　　　out of the wound and left it there lying on the ground.
　　　I plucked out sticks and willow-twigs. Weaving a rope
　　　about five feet in length, I bound the feet of the monstrous
　　　beast and went off to the black ship, carrying him on my back
160　and supporting myself with my spear. In no way could I carry him
　　　on my shoulder with one hand, for he was a very huge beast.

　　　"I threw him down in front of the ship, and I cheered up
　　　my companions with honeyed words, coming to each man in turn:
　　　'My friends, we shall not yet go down into the house of Hades
165　before the fated day shall arrive, although we grieve. But come,

---

130　*human speech:* The meaning of this mysterious phrase is unclear.

132　*Ocean begot:* The story seems to owe a lot to the tradition of an *Argonautica,* in which Jason travels to the
　　　Far East to Aia, "earth," and there seduces Medea. Aietes (ē-ē-tēz), Medea's father, Kirkê's brother, was
　　　Jason's enemy who subjects him to various trials.

so long as there is still food and drink in our swift ship,
let us think of them, so that we do not waste away with hunger.'

"So I spoke, and they hastily obeyed my words. Drawing
their cloaks from their faces, they wondered at the stag beside
the shore of the unwearied sea, for it was a huge beast. When they had   170
gladdened their eyes with looking, they washed their hands and made
ready a glorious meal. So until the sun went down we sat there dining
on the endless flesh and sweet wine. But when the sun went down
and the darkness came on, we went to take our rest on the shore
of the sea.   175

"When Dawn appeared with her fingers of rose,
then I called my men together and spoke among all:
'Listen to my words, comrades, although we are suffering.
My friends, we do not know where the darkness is, nor where
the light, nor where the sun that brings light to mortals
goes beneath the earth, nor where it rises. But let us   180
quickly consider whether there is still any plan left to us.
I don't think there is. For I climbed up to a rugged place
of outlook and looked over the island, about which the endless
sea is set as a crown. The island itself is low-lying, and my eyes
saw smoke in the middle of it, through the oak thickets   185
and the woods.'

"So I spoke, and their hearts were crushed, thinking
of the deeds of the Laestrygonian Antiphates and of the violence
of great-hearted Cyclops, the eater of men. They wept shrilly,
pouring down hot tears. But no good came of their wailing.
I divided up all my companions with fancy shin guards into two   190
groups, and I appointed a leader to each. Of one I was the leader,
of the other godlike Eurylochos. Quickly we cast lots in a bronze
helmet, and out leapt the lot of great-hearted Eurylochus.
He went off, and with him, weeping, went twenty-two companions.
They left us behind, groaning.   195

"In a low place they found
the house of Kirkê, made of polished stone, in an open meadow.
There were wolves around it from the mountains, and lions
whom Kirkê had herself enchanted by giving them potions.
They did not rush up to the men, but waving their
long tails fawned about them. It was just as when   200
hounds will fawn about their master when he returns
from feasting, knowing he will bring them tidbits

to appease their hunger—so did these lions and wolves
of mighty paws cringe around them.

                    "The men were terrified
205 beholding what seemed terrible monsters. They stood
outside the doors of Kirkê, a goddess with beautiful
hair. They heard Kirkê sing within in a lovely
voice as she went back and forth before a great loom,
immortal, weaving a delightful, shining design
210 to please the gods.

         "Polites spoke first, a natural
leader, whom I loved before all others, and trusted most:
'My friends, someone sings as she goes back and forth before
a wondrous loom, making the floor echo all around.
It is either some goddess or a woman. But let us make
215 ourselves known.'

        "So he spoke, and they all called out
to her. Promptly she came forth and flung open the shining
doors. She invited them in. In their ignorance they all
obeyed, except for Eurylochos, who suspected a trap.

      "She gave them seats on lovely couches and chairs.
220 She mixed up a drink of Pramnian wine° and cheese
and barley and bright honey, pouring in dangerous potions
so that they might forget their native land. When she
had served them, and they had drunk, she struck them
with her wand, then penned them up in her sties.
225 They now had the heads of swine, and a pig's snort
and bristles and shape, but their minds remained the same
as before. They wailed as they were penned up, but Kirkê
threw them acorns, both sweet and bitter, and the fruit
of the dogwood, the food that pigs, slithering in slime,
230 so love to eat.

       "Eurylochos came back quickly
to the swift black ship, to tell what happened
to his companions and what was their intolerable fate.
But at first he could not speak a word, though he wished to,
so overcome with grief was he in his great heart.
235 His eyes filled with tears and he gave forth

---

220 *Pramnian wine*: A wine of high quality, evidently named after an unknown place.

a deep sigh. Then when all of us questioned him,
amazed, at last he told of the doom of his comrades:
'We went through the forest, noble Odysseus, just
as you ordered. We found the house of Kirkê,
in a low place made of polished stone, in an open   240
meadow. There, someone was going back and forth before
a great loom, singing sweetly, either goddess or woman.
They all called out to her. Promptly she came forth
and flung open the shining doors. She invited them in.
In their ignorance all of them agreed, but I alone   245
remained outside, suspecting a trap. Then they
vanished all together, and not one of them appeared
again, though I sat there for a long time and watched.'

   "So he spoke, and I cast my silver-studded sword
around my shoulders, huge, made of bronze, and I shouldered   250
my bow too. I urged him to lead the way.
But he seized my knees and begged me, wailing, and spoke
words that went like arrows: 'Don't make me go there again,
you who are nurtured by Zeus, but leave me here!
For I doubt that you yourself will return, nor will   255
you bring back any of our comrades. But let us who
remain swiftly flee. There is still chance for escape!'

   "So he spoke, but I answered him: 'Eurylochos,
you stay here beside the hollow black ship, eating and drinking.
I shall go alone, for go I must.'   260

                    "So speaking
I went up from the ship and away from the sea. But as
I journeyed through the sacred forest to the great house
of Kirkê, a connoisseur of drugs, Hermes of the golden
staff met me in the form of a youth who is just getting
his beard, in the comeliest time of life. He took   265
my hand and he said to me: 'Where are you going,
unhappy man, traveling alone through the hills,
knowing nothing of the country? For Kirkê has
penned-up your companions behind thick bars,
and turned them all into pigs! Do you plan on letting   270
them go? I'm telling you that you yourself will not return,
but will remain there in their company. But come,
I will free you from danger—I will save you. Here, take
this powerful herb and go to Kirkê's house. It will ward
off the evil day from you.   275

"'Now let me tell you
the deceptions that the goddess Kirkê has in store.
She will make a potion for you, and mix drugs
with your food. But she will not be able to enchant
you because of the herb that I will give you. I will
280 tell you the whole story. When Kirkê strikes you
with her long wand, then you must draw your sword
from your thigh and rush at Kirkê as if you wished
to kill her. She, in fear, will then urge that you sleep
together. Don't refuse the goddess's bed, if you wish
285 to free your companions and entertain yourself. But first
force her to swear a great oath to the blessed gods
that she will plot no further evil against you. Otherwise,
when your clothes are off, she will unman you.'

"So speaking, Argeïphontes drew the herb from the ground
290 and gave it to me, showing me what it looked like.
At the root it was black, but its flower was like milk. 'The gods
call this *moly*. It is difficult for mortals to dig,
but there is nothing the gods cannot do.' Then Hermes
went off to high Olympos through the wooded island,
295 and I went on to the house of Kirkê, my brain boiling
with thoughts.

"I stood before the doors of the goddess
with beautiful hair. Standing there, I cried out, and the goddess
heard my voice. Promptly she opened the shining doors
and invited me in, and I followed, disturbed in my mind.
300 She suggested I sit on a lovely chair with silver rivets,
finely made, with a footstool attached. She prepared
a potion for me in a golden goblet, bidding me drink it.
But she placed drugs within it, wishing me ill.

"She gave it, and I drank it, but was still not enchanted,
305 so she struck me with her wand and said, 'Go now to the sty!
Lie with your companions!'

"So she spoke. I drew
my sword from my thigh and rushed on Kirkê as if
I wished to kill her. But she with a loud cry
ducked beneath the sword and seized my knees,
310 and wailing spoke words that flew like arrows:
'Who are you? Where is your city? Who are your parents?
I can't believe that you drank my potion and yet

FIGURE 10.3 Kirkê enchants the companions of Odysseus. A seductive Kirkê stands naked in the center, stirring a magic drink and offering it to Odysseus' companions, already turning into animals—the man in front of Kirkê into a boar, the next to the right into a ram, and the third into a wolf. A dog crouches beneath Kirkê's bowl. The figure behind Kirkê has the head of a boar. On the far left is a lion-man beside whom Odysseus comes with sword drawn (but in the *Odyssey* they turn only into pigs). On the far right, Eurylochos escapes. Athenian black-figure wine cup, c. 550 BC. Photograph ©2014 Museum of Fine Arts, Boston.

were not entranced. No other has withstood this drug,
once he has drunk it and it has passed the barrier of his teeth.
315 The mind in your breast cannot be enchanted! Surely
you are the trickster Odysseus. Argeïphontes of the golden
staff always said you would come, returning from Troy
in your swift, black ship. But come, put away your sword
in your scabbard. Let us go to my bed, there to mingle
320 in love. Let us learn, lying together, to trust one another.'

   "So she spoke, and I answered her in turn.
'Kirkê, how can you think that I would be gentle
with you, who in your halls have turned my men
into pigs? You would keep me here, bidding me
325 with deceitful thoughts to go to your room and there
to have sex with you. But when I am naked you would
unman me! I don't think I want to bed with you until
you swear, goddess, a great oath that you will not plan
further evil against me.' That's what I said, and right away
330 she swore as I asked. And when she had sworn,
then we went to her bed and I mingled with the very
lovely Kirkê.

   "Meanwhile the four servants busied
themselves in the house, where they did all the housework.
They were children of the springs and the forests
335 and holy rivers that flow to the sea. One of them
spread purple cloth on the chairs, and beneath the cloth
white linen. Another set up tables of silver in front
of the chairs and placed golden baskets upon them. A third
mixed honeyed wine in a silver bowl, and set out
340 golden cups. The fourth drew water and lit a
fire beneath a large tripod, and warmed the water.
When the water had boiled in the brilliant bronze, she sat
me in a tub and bathed me from the great tripod,
mixing the water so that it was just right. She poured
345 it over my head and shoulders until she had taken
all the dispiriting weariness from my limbs. And when
she had bathed me, and rubbed rich oil in my skin,
she cast a shirt and a beautiful cloak over my shoulders.
She brought me into the hall and sat me down in a chair
350 with silver studs, wonderfully made, and a footstool
was fixed beneath it. A servant brought in a beautiful,
golden vase, and poured water over my hands into
a silver basin for me to wash. Beside the basin

FIGURE 10.4 Odysseus threatens Kirkê with his sword. He wears a broad-brimmed
traveler's hat (different from the *pilos* or skullcap that he commonly wears). Kirkê has dropped the
cup containing the magic potion and flees in terror before the armed Odysseus who has leapt from
his chair. Athenian red-figure oil vase, c. 440 BC.

she set up a shining table, and on it, the bashful
355 servant placed bread and all kinds of meats, making
free use of what she had on hand. She urged me to eat,
but I was not at ease in my mind. I sat with other thoughts,
as I considered the evil that might come.

                                  "When Kirkê saw me
sitting but not eating, in deep sorrow, she stood beside me
360 and spoke words that flew like arrows: 'Why do you sit,
Odysseus, as if you were dumb, eating out your heart?
Nor do you touch your food or drink. Do you suspect
some other deceit? But you should not be afraid,
for I have sworn to you a mighty oath.'

                                  "So she spoke,
365 and I answered: 'Kirkê, what sort of man, if he did
his duty, would dare to partake of food or drink before
he had freed his companions and beheld them before
his eyes? But come, if you urge me with true good will
to drink and eat, let them go, let me see my trusty
370 companions with my own eyes.'

                                  "So I spoke, and Kirkê stalked
from the chamber, holding her wand in her hand. She opened
the door to the sty and drove them out. They were like
nine-year old porkers. As they stood around her, she went
among them and anointed each with another charm.
375 The bristles fell from their limbs that earlier a harmful
charm of Queen Kirkê had caused to grow. They were men
again, but younger than before, and more handsome, and taller.
They recognized me, and clung each one to my hands.
A passionate sobbing took hold of them, and a tremendous
380 sound reverberated throughout the hall. Even the goddess took pity.

   "She came near to me and spoke: 'Son of Laërtes, nurtured
by Zeus, much-devising Odysseus, go now to your swift ship
and the shore of the sea. First of all, drag your ship onto the shore,
and conceal your possessions and your weapons in a cave.
385 Then come back, and bring all your trusty companions.'

   "So she spoke. I was content with her advice. I went
to the ship and the shore of the sea. I found my trusty
companions wailing piteously around the swift ship, warm
tears poring down their cheeks. Even as calves, lying in a field,

jump up and prance around their mothers as they come 390
in a herd into the yard, having grazed their fill—for the pens
no longer hold the calves, but mooing constantly
they run about their mothers—even so did those men
crowd around me when they saw me, weeping copiously.
It seemed as if we had reached our native land, and the city 395
itself of rugged Ithaca where we were born and raised.

"With a hearty cry they spoke to me words that went like
arrows: 'Seeing you return, you who are nurtured by Zeus, we are glad
as if we had returned to Ithaca, our native land. But come,
tell us of the fate of our other companions.' So they spoke. 400

"I answered with gentle words: 'First of all, drag the ship
up onto the land, and place our possessions, and our armor,
in a cave. Then let us all hurry up to Kirkê's holy house
where you may see your companions both eating and drinking.
They have everlasting store!' 405

"So I spoke. At once they obeyed
my words. Eurylochos alone held back my companions and spoke
to them words that went like arrows: 'What? Are you crazy?
Where are you going? Are you in love with death? You would go
to the house of Kirkê, who will change you to pigs or wolves
or lions that you might be forced to guard her house? Just what 410
Cyclops did when our companions went to his fold,
and this *brave* Odysseus followed with them! He killed them
with his reckless behavior.'

"So he spoke. I weighed in my mind
whether I should draw my sword from my strong thigh
and cut off his head, rolling it on the ground, though he was 415
a close relation, my brother-in-law.° But my companions
held me back with sweet words, saying: 'You who are
nurtured by Zeus, we will leave him behind, if you order it,
to remain beside the ship and guard it. Lead us to the holy halls
of Kirkê.' 420

"So saying, they went up from the ship and the sea.
Nor did Eurylochos remain beside the hollow ship,
but he followed along, unnerved by my savage rebuke.

---

416 *brother-in-law*: But we never learn to whom Eurylochos is married.

"In the meanwhile, Kirkê kindly had bathed my other
companions and anointed them with rich oil, and cast shirts
425 and fleecy cloaks about their shoulders. We found them feasting
away in Kirkê's halls. When they saw and recognized one
another, face to face, the men burst out crying, and the hall
rang with their sobs.

          "Standing near me, the beautiful goddess
said: 'No need for all this weeping any longer. I know
430 the great sorrows you have suffered on the briny deep, and how
many pains cruel men have shown you on land. But come,
eat and drink! Let your spirits rise, as they were when
you first left your native land, rugged Ithaca. As it is,
you are feckless, discouraged, thinking always of the hardship
435 of travel. It's hard to be happy when you have endured so much.'

    "So she spoke, and we did as she suggested.
Then we remained there all of our days for a full year eating
the abundant meats and drinking the delicious wine.
But when a year had passed, and the seasons turned
440 as the months passed along, and the long days came to an end,
then my trusty companions called me out, and they said:
'Odysseus, you are behaving strangely! We must think
of our native land, and whether destiny grants that we be
saved, and whether we will return to our high-roofed homes
445 in the land of our fathers.'

          "So they spoke, and my proud
heart agreed. We sat all day long until the sun went down,
dining on endless flesh and sweet wine. And when the sun went
down and the darkness came on, they took their rest throughout
the shadowy halls.

          "But I went up to Kirkê's very beautiful bed
450 and beseeched her, clinging to her knees, and the goddess
heard my voice. I spoke words that went like arrows:
'O Kirkê, complete the promise that you made for me,
to send me home. My spirit is anxious to be gone,
and the spirit of my companions too, whose grief breaks
455 my heart as they surround me, mourning whenever
you are somewhere else.'

          "So I spoke, and the beautiful goddess
answered me: 'Zeus-nourished son of Laërtes, resourceful

Odysseus, don't remain longer in my house if you are unwilling.
But first you must complete another journey—to go
to the house of Hades and dread Persephone, to ask   460
for a prophecy from the breath-soul of Theban Tiresias,
the blind prophet, whose mind remains unimpaired.
To him even in death Persephone has granted reason,
that he alone maintains his understanding. But the others
flit about like shadows.'   465

     "So she spoke, and my heart was shattered.
I wept, sitting on the bed, and my heart no longer wished
to live and see the light of the sun. But when I was surfeited
with weeping and flailing about, I answered her then with
the following words: 'O Kirkê, who will guide us on this journey?
No one has ever gone to the house of Hades in a black ship.'   470

  "So I spoke, and the beautiful goddess at once answered:
'Zeus-nourished son of Laërtes, resourceful Odysseus,
don't be concerned with your desire for a pilot to guide
your ship. Set up your mast and spread your white sails
and take a seat. The breath of North Wind will carry you there.   475
When you have passed over the river Ocean in your ship,
where there is a level beach and the grove of Persephone—
tall poplars and willows that shed their fruit before fully ripe—
beach your ship there by the deep-swirling river Ocean
and go yourself into the fetid house of Hades. There into Acheron   480
flow Pyriphlegethon and Kokytos, a branch of the water of the Styx.
There is a rock there, the meeting place of the two roaring rivers.°
There, my prince, approaching very near as I command you,
dig a pit an arm's length this way and that, and around it
pour a drink-offering to all the dead, first with milk and honey,   485
then with sweet wine, and finally with water. Sprinkle white
barley on top of it. Vow on the strengthless heads of the dead
that when you come to Ithaca you will sacrifice a barren cow
in your halls, the best you have, and will sacrifice on your altar
many good things, and that to Tiresias alone you will separately   490
sacrifice a ram, entirely black, that stands out in your flocks.
And when you have supplicated the glorious tribes of the dead
with prayers, then sacrifice a ram and a black ewe,

---

482 ...*roaring rivers*: Acheron ("affliction") may be a lake; Pyriphlegethon ("burning with fire") and Kokytos
  ("wailing") flow into it. Kokytos is a branch of the Styx ("hateful"). An oath sworn by the gods on the Styx
  can never be broken. The two "roaring rivers" are Pyriphlegethon and Kokytos.

turning them toward Erebos°—but yourself, turn your face
495 backward toward the streams of Ocean. The many breath-souls
of the dead will come forth. Call to your companions. Order
them to flay and burn the sheep that lie there, killed
by the pitiless bronze. Pray to the gods, to mighty Hades
and dread Persephone. Draw your sharp sword
500 from beside your thigh. Take a seat, and do not allow
the strengthless heads of the dead to come near the blood
before you have made inquiry of Tiresias. Right away
the prophet will come, the leader of the people, who knows
the road you will take and the measures of your journey
505 and your homecoming—how you may cross the fish-rich sea.'

   "So she spoke, and immediately Dawn sat on her
golden throne. She cast a cloak and a shirt around me
as clothing. The nymph herself put on a great silvery robe,
finely woven and filled with charm, and around her waist
510 she placed a beautiful golden belt, and on her head
she put a veil.

      "And I went through the halls rousing up
my companions. I stood beside each man and spoke with honeyed
words: 'Sleep no longer! Awake from your sweet slumber!
Let us go—the revered Kirkê has told me all.'

            "So I spoke,
515 and their proud hearts were persuaded. But even so I was unable
to lead my men from there unscathed. There was a man,
the youngest of all, not especially distinguished in war
nor endowed with good understanding—he had lain down
apart from his companions in the sacred halls of Kirkê, heavy
520 with wine, desiring the cool air. He heard the noise and the bustle
of his companions as they moved about, and he suddenly
jumped up. He forgot to go to the tall ladder to climb back down
and fell headlong from the roof. His neck was broken away
from the spine, and his breath-soul went off to the house of Hades.

525   "As my men were getting ready to go, I spoke
to them: 'You think that you are going home to the beloved
land of your fathers, but Kirkê has devised another road

---

494 *Erebos*: "darkness," a general term for the land of the dead. In Hesiod's *Theogony*, Erebos is the fifth primor-
dial element that came out of Chaos. Conjoined with Nyx (Night), Erebos fathered Aither (Upper Air)
and Hemera (Day).

for us: to go the house of Hades and dread Persephone
to seek a prophecy from Theban Tiresias.'

                    "So I spoke—
and their hearts were shattered. They sat down where they   530
were and moaned and tore at their hair. But no good came
of their lamenting. When we were on our way to the swift ship
and shore of the sea, grieving and pouring down hot tears,
and in the meanwhile Kirkê had gone to the black ship
and bound a ram and a black ewe there. She had gone   535
on ahead, easily. For who with his eyes could see
a goddess against her will, either going or coming?"

BOOK 11. *Odysseus in the Underworld*

"When we came down to the ship and the sea, we dragged
the ship first of all into the shining sea, and we set up
the mast and the sail on the black ship. We took on
the flocks and embarked. We went off mourning
5 and shedding warm tears. Kirkê, with the lovely tresses,
dread goddess of human speech, sent a wind that came
behind the ship with its dark prow and filled the sails,
a noble companion. Once we made all the tackle
on the ship secure, we took our seats. Wind favored us
10 and the helmsman kept her on a straight course.

"All day long the ship's sail was stretched
as she sped across the sea. The sun went down
and the ways grew dark. We came to the limits
of deep-flowing Ocean. We came to the people and the city
15 of the Cimmerians,° hidden in mist and cloud, nor does
the shining sun look down upon them with its rays,
not when he mounts toward the starry heaven, nor when
he turns again to the earth from the heaven, but total
night is stretched over wretched mortals.

"We came there
20 and dragged up our ship on the shore and off-loaded the sheep.
We walked along the stream of Ocean until we came to the place
that Kirkê had described. There Perimedes and Eurylochos° held
the sacrificial animals. I drew my sharp sword from my thigh
and dug a trench an arm's length wide in both directions.
25 Around it I poured an offering to all the dead, first
with milk and honey, then with sweet wine, and then
with water. I sprinkled white barley. Powerfully I entreated
the strengthless heads of the dead, saying that when

---

15 *Cimmerians:* A historical people who descended over the Caucasus Mountains in the eighth century BC and
for a hundred years terrorized Asia Minor. Either Homer's Cimmerians are a translation into myth of this
people, or the historical Cimmerians were named in Greek after Homer's mythical Cimmerians, a word that
might in Greek mean "those living in misty darkness."

22 *Perimedes and Eurylochos:* Perimedes is mentioned only once later in this book but we have already seen
Eurylochos as a rival to Odysseus' power, and he is important in later episodes.

I came to Ithaca I would sacrifice in my halls a barren cow
to them the best I had, and that I would pile the altar   30
with excellent gifts, and that to Tiresias—to him alone—
I would sacrifice a ram, all black, an outstanding
one from our flocks.

                    "When with vows and prayers
I had supplicated the tribes of the dead, I took the sheep
and slit their throats over the pit, and the black blood   35
flowed. Then the breath-souls of the dead who had passed
away gathered from Erebos—brides, and unwed youths
and miserable old men, and tender virgins with hearts
new to sorrow, and many others wounded by bronze spears,
men killed by Ares° wearing armor spattered with blood.   40
These came thronging around the pit, coming from here
and there, making a wondrous cry.

                    "A sickly fear gripped me.°
I ordered my companions to flay and burn the sheep that lay
there, their throats cut with the pitiless bronze, and that
they pray to the gods, and to mighty Hades and dread   45
Persephone. I myself drew my sharp sword from my thigh
and took a seat, not allowing the strengthless heads of the dead
to come close to the blood before I had made inquiry of Tiresias.

    "First came the breath-soul of my companion Elpenor,
for we did not bury him beneath the earth with its broad   50
ways but left his corpse in the hall of Kirkê unwept
and unburied because another task drove us on.° I wept
when I saw him and took pity in my heart, and spoke to him
words that went like arrows: 'Elpenor, how did you come
beneath the misty darkness? You've gotten here faster   55
on foot than I in my black ship!'

                    "So I spoke, and he answered me
with a groan: 'Son of Laërtes, from the line of Zeus, resourceful
Odysseus, the evil decree of some spirit, plus endless wine
has killed me. When I lay down to sleep in the halls

---

40 *by Ares*: That is, killed in war.

43 *gripped me*: Odysseus is at the edge of the world, standing beside the primordial waters where the sun never
    shines. Now he acts as a necromancer, a magician who summons the spirits of the dead so he can learn from them.

52 *drove us on*: That is, the need to go to the underworld to consult Tiresias. Elpenor can talk without drinking
    the blood because he is still unburied. Once his ghost is "laid"—when he is properly lamented and buried—
    then his breath-soul will lose its memory of past events and its reason.

60 of Kirkê I did not think to go back down the long ladder
    but fell headlong from the roof, and my neck was torn
    away from the spine—my breath-soul went down to the house
    of Hades. Now I beg you by those we left behind,
    those not present, by your wife and father who reared you
65 when you were little, and by Telemachos, whom you left
    as an only son in your halls. For I know that when
    you leave the house of Hades and go back, you will
    put-in to the island of Aiaia in your well-built ship.°
    There—I beg of you, O captain!—I urge you to remember me.
70 Do not go off home and leave me unwept and unburied.
    Do not turn away from me, or I may become a cause
    of the gods' anger!° Burn me together with my armor,
    all that is mine, and heap up a tomb on the shore
    of the gray sea, in memory of a wretched man, so that
75 men yet to be born may learn of me. Do these things
    for me and fix on the tomb the oar that I rowed
    when I was alive among my companions.'°

                                "So he spoke,
    and I answered: 'I shall accomplish these things for you,
    my wretched friend, and bring them to pass.' Then the two
80 of us sat, exchanging melancholy words, I on one side holding
    the sword over the blood, the phantom of my companion
    on the other, who spoke at length.

                        "Then there came the breath-soul
    of my dead mother, Antikleia, the daughter of great-hearted
    Autolykos,° whom I left alive when I went to sacred Ilion.
85 I wept when I saw her and took pity in my heart, but I would
    not let her come close to the blood, though I was deeply
    sorrowful, before I had made inquiry of the wise Tiresias.

    "Then the breath-soul of Theban Tiresias came to the pit,
    holding a golden scepter. He recognized me and spoke:°

---

72 *gods' anger*: He will become a malevolent spirit if his corpse is not treated with respect and his ghost is not "laid."

77 *companions*: Elpenor wants a hero's burial, although he is only a rower!

84 *...Autolykos*: Antikleia means "opposed to glory," perhaps because she had little enthusiasm for Odysseus' exploits. *Autolykos* means "true-wolf," a thief and a trickster who gave Odysseus his name and entertained him as a youth on Mount Parnassos where in a boar hunt Odysseus received the scar by which he is later recognised. Autolykos is mentioned in the *Iliad*: He had once stolen the boar's tusk helmet that was loaned to Odysseus in a night-exploit against the Trojans (*Il.* Book 10).

89 *spoke*: Only Tiresias, because of his prophetic powers, can speak without first drinking from the blood (except for the unburied Elpenor).

FIGURE 11.1 **Odysseus summons the spirits of the dead.** Odysseus sits on a rock, sword in hand. Beneath his booted feet lie the skins of the flayed sheep whose blood fills the pit. Elpenor stands to the left, in heroic nudity except for his cloak, boots, and traveler's cap. He holds a spear. Up from the ground (lower left) comes the head of Tiresias. Athenian red-figure vase, c. 460 BC.

90 'Son of Laërtes, from the line of Zeus, resourceful Odysseus,
why, poor thing, have you left the light of the sun and come
down here? So that you could see the dead and this
joyless land? But stand back from the pit. Put up your sharp
sword so that I may drink of the blood and speak the truth.'

95   "So he spoke, and I drew back and thrust my
silver-studded sword into its scabbard. When he had drunk
the black blood, then the faultless seer said: 'You seek
to know about your honey-sweet homecoming, O glorious
Odysseus? Well, the god will make it harsh for you.
100 For I do not think you will escape Poseidon, the earth-shaker,
who has laid up anger in his heart, enraged because you blinded
his son. Still, you might arrive home after suffering many evils,
if you are willing to restrain your spirit and that of your
companions when you put your well-built ship ashore
105 on the island of Thrinakia,° escaping the violet-colored sea.
There you will find the cattle and good flocks of Helios,
who sees all things and hears all things, grazing. If you leave them
unharmed and remember your return journey, then you might
arrive at Ithaca, though suffering many evils. But if you harm them,
110 I predict the destruction of your ship and your companions.

     "'If you yourself escape, you will arrive home late,
on someone else's ship, in a bad way, having lost all your
companions. You will suffer trouble in your house from arrogant
men who consume your substance and try to seduce your godlike
115 wife with gifts. Surely you will take revenge for their violence
when you arrive! But when you have killed the suitors
in your halls either by trickery or openly with the sharp bronze,
then take a well-fitted oar in your hand and travel until
you come to where they know nothing of the sea, nor do
120 they eat food mixed with salt. They do not know
about ships with purple cheeks or well-shaped oars,
which are the wings of a boat. I will tell you a sign
that is very clear and cannot escape you: When another
wayfarer who meets you says that is a winnowing-fan°
125 on your strong shoulder, right there fix your well-shaped oar
in the ground. Make a generous sacrifice to Poseidon the king—

---

105 *Thrinakia*: Of unknown meaning, the mythical island of Helios—Thrinakia—was at an early time identified with
     "Trinacria," or "three-cornered island," another name for Sicily. Even today, Sicily is called the Island of the Sun.

124 *winnowing-fan*: A wooden implement used to throw the harvested grain into the air so that the wind blows
     away the chaff (inedible seed casings) from the heavier edible grain, which falls to the ground.

a lamb and a bull and a pig and a boar that mates with sows—
then go home and offer great sacrifice to the deathless
gods who hold the broad sky, to each of them in turn.

    " 'For you a very gentle death will come from the sea.   130
It will kill you when you are overcome with spruce old age.
Your people will live in happiness around you. Now I have
told you the truth.'

                "So he spoke, and I answered: 'Tiresias, the gods
themselves have spun the thread of all this. But come,
tell me, and tell me truly—I see the breath-soul of my dead   135
mother. She sits there in silence near the blood in the pit,
nor does she dare to look on her son just opposite,
or to speak to him. Tell me, O master, how can she
recognize who I am?'

                "So I spoke, and he at once
answered: 'I shall tell you an easy word. Do fix it   140
in your mind. Whomever of the dead and gone you allow
to come close to the black blood, that one will speak
and tell you the truth. Whomever you refuse, he will
surely withdraw from the pit.'

                "So saying, the breath-soul
of lord Tiresias went to the house of Hades. He had spoken   145
his prophecies, but I remained steadfast where I was until
my mother came and drank the dark blood. Immediately
she knew who I was, and moaning she spoke words that went
like arrows: 'My child, how have you come beneath the shadowy
dark, being still alive? It is hard for the living to see these things.   150
For there are great rivers between the living and dead, and mighty
floods—first of all Ocean, which no one can cross on foot
but only with a well-built ship. Have you come here after long
wanderings from Troy with your ship and companions? Have you
not yet come to Ithaca, nor seen your wife in your halls?'   155

    "So she spoke, and I said in reply: 'O mother,
my urgent need has been to go down to the house of Hades
to seek an oracle from the breath-soul of Theban Tiresias.
So I have not yet come close to Achaea,° nor have I walked
on my own land, but always I wander in misery, ever since   160

---

159 *Achaea*: Probably he means the PELOPONNESUS.

I first followed the good Agamemnon to Troy with its fine
horses, that I might help fight the Trojans. But come,
tell me and report it truly—what fate of grievous death
overcame you? Was it a long illness, or did Artemis, the shooter
165 of arrows, come and with her gentle shafts bring you down?
Tell me too of my father and my son that I left behind.
Do they still hold power, or does some other man have it,
and do they say that I shall never return? Tell me of the plans
and intentions of my wedded wife—does she stay beside
170 her child and keep all things steady? Or has someone already
married her, whoever is best of the Achaeans?'

                              "Thus I spoke,
and at once my revered mother answered: 'Yes, yes,
your wife remains with a steady heart in your halls. Miserable
do the nights and days wane for her, weeping tears. No one else
175 yet holds your power, but Telemachos rules over your
domains without harassment, and he hosts the equal feast
as is fitting for one who gives judgments. And all men
invite him.° °Your father lives in the country and does not
come to the city. For bedding he has no bed, no cloaks nor bright
180 covers, and in the winter he sleeps with the slaves in the house,
in the dust near the fire, and the clothes on his flesh are filthy.
But when summer comes and the rich autumn, then everywhere
across the slope of his vineyard leaves are scattered on the ground
as a bed. There he lies, sorrowing, nursing great anguish
185 in his heart and longing for your return. A harsh old age
has come upon him. Even so did I perish and follow my fate,
for Artemis, who sees from a long way off, who showers
arrows, did not strike me down in my halls with her gentle
shafts. Nor did a sickness come upon me, which often
190 takes away the spirit from the limbs with grievous wasting.
It was my longing for you and your counsels and gentleness,
glorious Odysseus, that took away my honey-sweet life.'

    "So she spoke, but I pondered in my heart and wanted
to take in my arms my mother's breath-soul, which had passed

---

178 ... *invite him*: To host an "equal feast," where everyone receives the same portion, is a sign of social power.
Telemachos is also welcome at feasts given by others. Antikleia seems to be speaking of the present, when Odys-
seus has been away from home, say, eleven or twelve years (ten years at the war; one year on Kirkê's island, plus
time for other adventures). Odysseus does not return home until the twentieth year. We learn elsewhere that
the suitors arrived in the house only three or four years before Odysseus' return, which is why Antikleia does
not mention them (though Tiresias does). If Telemachos was an infant when Odysseus went to Troy, he should
be very young now, only eleven or twelve, not even a teenager. It is remarkable that at this age he attends the
"equal feast" and "gives judgments." Sometimes Homer is as casual about chronology as he is about geography.

away. Three times I leaped toward her, for my heart   195
urged me to hold her. Three times she flew away, out
of my arms, like a shadow or a dream.

                           "A still sharper pain
came to my heart, and I spoke to her words that went
like arrows: 'My mother, why do you not await me?
I am eager to hold you, so that even in the house of Hades   200
we may delight in icy wailing, throwing our arms about one another.
Or are you just a phantom that the illustrious Persephone
has sent up so that I may groan and lament all the more?'

    "So I spoke, and at once my revered mother answered:
'Ah me, my child, most ill-fated of all mortals—Persephone   205
the daughter of Zeus does not deceive you, but this
is the way of mortals when someone dies. The tendons
no longer hold together the flesh and the bones, but the mighty
force of fire destroys all that, when the spirit first leaves
the white bones and the breath-soul flies off like a dream,   210
hovering here and there.° But hasten to the light as quickly
as you can. Remember all these things so that hereafter
you might tell them to your wife.'

                      "So we conversed
with one other, but other women came to the blood.
Illustrious Persephone sent them, whoever were the wives   215
and daughters of the chiefs. They gathered in a crowd around
the dark blood, and now I took thought how I might question
each one. This seemed the best plan to my mind. Drawing
my long sword from my strong thigh, I did not permit
all of them to drink together from the dark blood. One after   220
another they came, and each told me of her lineage.
I questioned them all.°

               "First I saw Tyro of high birth,
who said she was the offspring of excellent Salmoneus,
and she said she was the wife of Kretheus, the son of Aiolos.°

---

211 *here and there*: Homer knows only cremation as a way to treat the dead, never inhumation. This accords
     with late Iron Age practice, when cremation has replaced the inhumation common in the Bronze Age.

222 *them all*: By drinking the blood, the ghosts temporarily regain the power of speech. Now follows a Catalog
     of Women, a genre of oral poetry in the days of Homer. Book 11 is a series of catalogs: first of women; then
     of heroes; then of the denizens of the underworld.

224 *Aiolos*: No connection with the wind-king.

225 She fell in love with the divine river Enipeus,° by far
the most beautiful of the rivers that go upon the earth. She went
often to the beautiful waters of the Enipeus. Taking on the likeness
of the river god, Poseidon, the earth-holder, the shaker
of the earth, lay with Tyro at the mouth of the swirling river.
230 A dark wave stood around them, like a mountain, arched over,
and it hid Poseidon and the mortal woman. Poseidon
loosed the virgin belt, and he poured out sleep upon her.

"But when the god had finished his work of love,
he took her by the hand, and he spoke and addressed her:
235 'Rejoice, woman, in our lovemaking! As the year rolls around,
you will bear glorious children, because the embraces of a god
are not without effect.° You will attend and rear them. Now go
to your house. Be quiet. Tell no man. Know that I am Poseidon,
the shaker of the earth.'

"So speaking he descended beneath
240 the waves of the sea. Thus Tyro conceived and bore Pelias
and Neleus, who both became powerful servants of great Zeus.
Pelias lived in spacious IOLKOS and had many flocks,
Neleus lived in sandy PYLOS. And the queen of women
bore other men to Kretheus—Aison and Pheres and Amythaon,
245 who rejoiced in chariot-fighting.°

"And after Tyro I saw Antiopê,
the daughter of Asopos, who boasted that she had slept
in the arms of Zeus, and she bore two children—Amphion
and Zethus, who first founded the seat of seven-gated Thebes,
and they built its walls. Without walls they could not live
250 in spacious Thebes, though the twins were strong.°

---

225 *Enipeus*: A river in Thessaly, where this incident takes place.

237 *of a god*: Intercourse with a god, or goddess, always produces a child.

245 *... chariot fighting*: Pelias, who ruled in Iolkos in MAGNESIA in southeastern THESSALY, was a tyrannical ruler. In the post-Homeric legend of the Argonauts, Pelias sent Jason on his quest for the Golden Fleece. Neleus ruled in Pylos in the southwestern Peloponnesus and had many sons, all, except for Nestor, killed by Herakles. Aison was the father of Jason, whose throne Pelias usurped. Pheres was the father of Admetos, who married Alkestis, a daughter of Pelias, famous from the play *Alkestis* by Euripides (438 BC) in which Alkestis dies for her husband. Amythaon was the father of the famous prophet Melampous (see below).

250 *... were strong*: In post-Homeric accounts, Zethus used brute force to move the stones of the walls of Thebes into place, but Amphion merely played his lyre, enchanting them into place.

"After her I saw Alkmenê, the wife of Amphitryon,
who gave birth to Herakles, staunch in the fight, with a heart
like a lion, mixing in love in the arms of great Zeus.°

                                              "And I saw
Megara, the daughter of proud Kreon, whom Herakles married,
the son of Amphitryon, always stubborn in his strength.°   255

"I saw the mother of Oedipus, beautiful Epikastê, who
committed great evil when in ignorance she married her own son.
And Oedipus married her after killing his own father.
The gods made all these things known to men right away.
Oedipus remained as king in lovely Thebes, though   260
suffering agonies through the destructive designs of the gods.
But Epikastê went down to the house of Hades,
the powerful warden of the gate. She fitted a noose on high
from a lofty beam, overcome by her pain. She left
behind many sorrows for him, as many as the Erinyes   265
of a mother can bring to pass.°

                                 "And I saw the most beautiful
Chloris, whom Neleus once married because of her beauty
after he gave her innumerable bridal gifts—Chloris, the youngest
daughter of Amphion, the son of Iasos,° who once ruled
with power in ORCHOMENOS of the Minyans. Chloris was   270
queen of Pylos, and she bore splendid sons, Nestor
and Chromios and lordly Periklymenos. In addition she bore
Pero, a marvel to men. All those men who lived nearby
sought Pero's hand in marriage, but Neleus would give
her only to the man who rustled from Phylakê the obstinate   275
cattle with curly horns and broad faces of powerful Iphiklos.
The prophet Melampous undertook to drive them off,

---

253 *great Zeus*: Alkmenê slept with Zeus and her husband Amphitryon in the same night and so conceived
     twins: Herakles, the son of Zeus, and Iphikles, the son of Amphitryon.

255 *his strength*: According to later tradition, Herakles killed Megara and all of their children in a fit of mad-
     ness, the subject of Euripides' play *Heracles Insane*, c. 420 BC.

266 *. . . bring to pass*: This is the oldest version of the myth of Oedipus, having all the essential elements: marriage
     between a son and his mother; the son's murder of the father; the suicide of the mother (named Jocasta in later
     tradition). However, unlike in later versions, Homer's Oedipus remains as king after the exposure of his crime,
     and there is nothing said of his self-blinding as in Sophocles' celebrated play *Oedipus the King* (c. 428 BC). Also,
     Epikastê and Oedipus have no children. Epikastê curses Oedipus when she dies; the Erinyes (Furies) prevail
     on the gods to fulfill these curses; and the punishment itself comes from the "destructive designs of the gods."

269 *son of Iasos*: As distinct from the Amphion, son of Antiopê and Zeus, just mentioned.

but a cruel decree of the gods ensnared him—herdsmen
carted him off in grievous chains. But when the months
280 and days were complete as the year rolled onward, and the seasons
came around, then powerful Iphiklos freed Melampous
after he told of all the gods had decreed.° Thus was the will
of Zeus fulfilled.

"And I saw Leda, the wife of Tyndareos,
who gave birth to two children, strong of heart, by Tyndareos—
285 horse-taming Kastor and Polydeukes, good at boxing.
These two the earth, giver of life, covers over, but beneath
the earth they have honor from Zeus, living one day
in turn, then dead the next. They have won honor like
that of the gods.°

"After Leda, I saw Iphimedeia, the wife
290 of Aloeus, who they say lay in love with Poseidon
and bore him two children, but to a short life—godlike
Otos and far-famed Ephialtes, whom the earth that brings
forth grain raised up as the tallest and much the most beautiful
beings, after the celebrated Orion.° When only nine,
295 they were fourteen feet wide and fifty-four feet high, yes,
and they threatened to bring the din of furious war to Olympos.
They were eager to pile Ossa on OLYMPOS, and Pelion
with its waving forests on Ossa so they would have a way
to heaven. And they would have done it, had they reached their
300 maturity, but Apollo son of Zeus, whom Leto had borne,

---

282 ... *decreed*: Chloris ("greenfinch"), wife of Neleus, is the mother of twelve sons, of whom three are named
here (Nestor, Chromios, Periklymenos), and of a daughter Pero. Phylakê is some place in the far north in
Thessaly. Iphiklos, the son of Phylakos after whom the town of Phylakê is named, had earlier stolen some
cattle from Pylos (but Pylos is a long way from Phylakê!). Neleus will permit his daughter Pero to marry
only the man who retrieved the stolen cattle from Iphiklos. Melampous, celebrated in Greek legend as the
founder of a family of prophets, undertook to recover them from Iphiklos on behalf of his brother Bias, who
wanted to marry Pero, but the herdsmen of Iphiklos caught him, threw him into chains, and imprisoned
him for one year. When Melampous unraveled the mystery of Iphiklos' sexual impotence, and Iphiklos
begot a child, Iphiklos allowed Melampous to return to Pylos with the cattle. Neleus then permitted Bias,
Melampous' brother, to marry Pero. Iphiklos fathered a second son, Protesilaos, the first man to die at
Troy. Homer alludes to this story obliquely without giving details because he assumes that his audience
already knows it, and he refers to the story again in *Od.* 15.

289 *of the gods*: As the wife of Tyndareos, Leda is the mother of Kastor and Polydeukes. She is not named as the
mother of Helen because in Homer Helen is the daughter of Leda and Zeus. Kastor and Polydeukes are the
Dioscuri, the "sons of Zeus," so in some tradition Zeus must have been their father too. Later, especially in
Roman times, the Dioscuri became the protectors of sailors and of the Roman state.

294 *Orion*: Famed for his handsomeness, the hunter Orion was a lover of the goddess Dawn until Artemis killed
him with her arrows (various reasons are given). The nymph Kalypso, in *Od.* 5, used the incident as an
example of the gods' hostility toward goddesses who take on mortal lovers.

laid waste to them both before down blossomed on their
cheeks and covered their chins with blooming beards.°

"I saw Phaidra and Prokris and beautiful Ariadnê,
the daughter of cruel Minos, whom once Theseus bore from
Crete to the hill of sacred Athens, but he had no pleasure   305
from her. Before that Artemis killed her on wave-swept
Dia, on the testimony of Dionysos.°

                              "I saw Maira and Klymenê
and hateful Eriphylê, who took gold as the price of her own lord.°
I could never tell all the women I saw, nor give all their names,
so many wives of the heroes, and their daughters, did I see   310
before that immortal night would be gone.

                              "But it is time that
we slept, either with the crew of your swift ship or here
in your own house. My voyage home will rest with the gods,
and with you."°

                  So he spoke. All were hushed in silence,
and were held enchanted throughout the shadowy halls.   315
Then white-armed Aretê° began to speak: "Phaeacians,
how does this man seem to you in comeliness
and stature and in his well-balanced mind? Moreover
he is my guest, though each of you has a share

---

302 *blooming beard*: This famous myth of mortal presumption against the divine seems to imply that the gods
     live in the heaven, in the sky, and not on Olympos, but Homer is vague about divine geography too. All
     these mountains—Ossa, Pelion, Olympos—are in Thessaly in northern Greece.

307 *of Dionysos*: Homer names three unhappy women with Cretan connections: Phaidra, a daughter of Minos
     and wife of the Athenian Theseus, who fell in love with her stepson Hippolytos, then committed suicide;
     Prokris, wife of Kephalos of Athens, who had an affair with Minos and was killed by her husband Kephalos
     in a hunting accident; and Ariadnê, about whom Homer gives a different story from the usual later ver-
     sion according to which Ariadnê married Dionysos on the Cycladic island of Naxos and bore him many
     children. Dia is a small island north of Crete. What is meant by "on the testimony of Dionysos" cannot be
     reconstructed. This is one of the few places where Homer mentions Dionysos.

308 *. . . of her own lord*: There were many figures in Greek myth named Maira and Klymenê; perhaps this
     Maira is one of the daughters of the Argive king Proitos and Klymenê is the wife of Phylakos. Eriphylê
     is important in the legend of the Seven Against Thebes. She was the mother of Alkmaion and the wife
     of Amphiaraos ("her own lord"). Eriphylê persuaded Amphiaraos to take part in the Seven Against
     Thebes, though she knew he would die, persuaded by Polynikes, who bribed her with a valuable necklace.
     Amphiaraos charged Alkmaion to avenge his certain death, and after Amphiaraos died in the war
     Alkmaion killed his mother. See Figure 15.1.

314 *with you*: Odysseus interrupts his speech to the Phaeacians after dinner.

316 *Aretê*: Aretê is apparently the only woman in the room.

320 in this honor. So don't be in a hurry to send him off,
and don't cut short your gifts to one in such need.
For you have much treasure in your houses, thanks to
the favor of the gods."

                The old warrior Echeneos,
one of the Phaeacian elders, then spoke to them:
325 "My friends, not wide of the mark or of our own thought
are the words of wise Aretê! Do act on them, though
it is on Alkinoös that the word and deed depend."°

    Alkinoös answered and said: "This word shall come
to pass as surely as I am alive and rule over the oar-loving
330 Phaeacians. Let our guest, who longs so for his return,
remain until tomorrow, so that we may make our gift-giving
complete. His safe passage will be the concern of all men,
but especially mine, for I hold the power among the people here."

    Resourceful Odysseus answered him: "King Alkinoös,
335 most excellent of all people, even if you encouraged me
to stay here a whole year, and would arrange my escort,
and would give wonderful gifts—why, I would do it! Much
better to return to the land of one's fathers with a full hand.
I will receive more respect from men and be dearer to all
340 of them when they see me returning to Ithaca."

                 Alkinoös
answered and spoke to him: "O Odysseus, when we look
upon you, we would never liken you to an imposter or a cheat,
such men as the black earth nourishes in great numbers,
scattered far and wide, making up lies from things that no man
345 can even see. But you understand the charm of words,
and your mind is noble. You speak as when a singer
speaks with knowledge, telling the sorrows of all the Argives
and of you yourself.

        "But come, tell me this
and do so truly—whether you saw any of your godlike
350 companions, who followed you to Ilion and there met
their fate? The night is very long, endless really. It is not

---

327 *word and deed depend*: Alkinoös, who holds the highest power, must bring to fulfillment Aretê's sugges-
tion, supported by Echineos. The addition of more gifts to Odysseus will necessitate the postponing of his
departure by one more day.

time for you to go to sleep in the hall. Tell me, please,
more of your wondrous deeds! I could hold out until
the bright dawn, if you were willing to sit here in our hall
and tell of your many woes." 355

       Resourceful Odysseus said in reply:
"King Alkinoös, renowned among all people, there is a time
for talk and a time for sleep. If you want to hear still more,
I will not hold back from telling you things still more pitiful
than these—the sorrow of my companions, who perished
after we escaped from the shrill war cry of the Trojans, 360
and those who were destroyed on their return through
the will of an evil woman.°

       "When the holy Persephone
had scattered the breath-souls of the women here and there,
up came that of Agamemnon, the son of Atreus, groaning.
The breath-souls of all those who died and met their fate 365
in the house of Aigisthos were gathered around him.
Agamemnon right away knew who I was, after
he had drunk the black blood. He complained shrilly,
pouring down hot tears, throwing out his hands toward me,
longing to embrace me. But there was no lasting strength 370
or vitality, such as once dwelled in his supple limbs.

    "I wept when I saw him and took pity in my heart,
and spoke to him words that went like arrows: 'Most glorious
son of Atreus, king of men, Agamemnon, what fate
of grievous death overcame you? Did Poseidon overcome you, 375
raising up the dreadful blast of savage winds among
your ships? Or did enemy men do you harm on the dry
land as you cut out their cattle or their beautiful
flocks of sheep, or fought for a city, or for women?'

    "So I spoke, and he answered me at once: 'O son 380
of Laërtes, of the line of Zeus, resourceful Odysseus—
it was not Poseidon who overcame me, raising up the dreadful
blast of savage winds among my ships, nor enemy
men who harmed me on the dry land, but Aigisthos°

---

362 *evil woman*: Klytaimnestra, who murdered her husband Agamemnon when he returned home.

384 *Aigisthos*: Agamemnon's cousin and the lover of Klytaimnestra. He is the son of Thyestes, the brother
     of Atreus, Agamemnon's father. In other versions (most famously Aeschylus' play *Agamemnon*, 458 BC),
     Agamemnon is killed in the bathtub, not during a banquet.

385 contrived my death and fate and killed me with the help
of my accursed wife. He invited me to his house and gave
me a meal, as you kill an ox at the manger. So I died
a wretched death, and my companions died in numbers
around me, like pigs with white teeth who are slaughtered
390 in the house of a rich and powerful man at a wedding feast,
or a potluck, or a thriving symposium. You've witnessed the death
of many men, either in single combat or in the strong press of battle,
but in your heart you would have pitied the sight of those things—
how we lay in the hall across the mixing-bowl and the tables
395 filled with food, and the whole floor was drenched in blood.

    " 'But the most pitiful cry I heard came from Kassandra,
the daughter of Priam, whom the treacherous Klytaimnestra killed
next to me. I raised my hands, then beat them on the ground,
dying with a sword through my chest. But the bitch turned away,
400 and although I was headed to the house of Hades, she would
not stoop to close my eyes nor to close my mouth! There
is nothing more shameless, more bitchlike, than a woman
who takes into her heart acts such as that woman devised—
a monstrous deed, she who murdered her wedded husband.
405 I thought I'd return welcomed by my children and slaves,
but she, knowing extraordinary wickedness, poured shame
on herself and on all women who shall come later, even on those
who do good deeds!'

        "So he spoke, but I answered: 'Yes, yes,
certainly Zeus with the loud voice has cursed the seed of Atreus
410 from the beginning through the plots of women. Many of us
perished for Helen's sake, and Klytaimnestra fashioned
a plot against you when you were away.'

         "So I spoke,
and he answered at once: 'And for this reason, be not
too trusting of even *your* wife! Don't tell her everything
415 that you know! Tell her some things and leave the rest unsaid.
But I don't think you will be murdered by your wife—
she is too discreet and carries only good thoughts in her heart,
this daughter of Ikarios, the wise Penelope. We left
her just a young bride when we went to war. She had
420 a babe at her breasts, just a little tyke, who now must be
counted among the number of men. How happy he will be
when his father, coming home, sees him, and he will greet
his father as is the custom! My own wife did not

allow me to feast my eyes on my son. She killed me
before that.   425

      "'And I will tell you something else,
and please consider it: Secretly, and not in the open, put your
boat ashore in the land of your fathers! For you can no longer
trust any woman. But come, tell me this and report it
accurately, whether you have heard that my son Orestes is alive
in Orchomenos or in sandy Pylos, or even with Menelaos   430
in broad SPARTA. For Orestes has not yet died on the earth.'

   "So he spoke, but I answered: 'Son of Atreus,
why do you ask me these things? I don't know the truth of it,
whether he is alive or dead. It is an ill thing to speak words
as empty as the wind.'   435

               "And so the two of us stood there exchanging
lamentations and pouring down warm tears. Then came
the breath-soul of Achilles, the son of Peleus, and of the good
Patroklos, and of Antilochos, and of Ajax,° the best in form
and stature of all the Danaäns after Achilles, the good son of Peleus.

   "The breath-soul of Achilles, the fast runner, recognized me,   440
and, groaning, he spoke words that went like arrows: 'Son of Laërtes,
of the line of Zeus, resourceful Odysseus—poor thing! How will
you top this plan for audacity? How have you dared to come
down to the house of Hades where the speechless dead live,
phantoms of men whose labors are done?'°   445

               "So he spoke,
but I answered him: 'O Achilles, son of Peleus, by far
°the mightiest of the Achaeans, I came here out of need
for Tiresias, to see if he had advice about how I might come
home again to craggy Ithaca. I have not yet come to Achaea,
nor walked on my own land—always I'm surrounded   450
by misfortune. But Achilles, no man in earlier times or in those
that came later is more fortunate than you. When you were alive

---

438   ...Ajax: Patroklos was Achilles' friend; Antilochos was a son of Nestor; this Ajax was the son of Telamon
        (not the unrelated Ajax, son of Oïleus). In the *Iliad* Patroklos died trying to help the Achaeans; in the post-
        Iliadic tradition, Antilochos fell to Memnon, a Trojan ally from the East; in the *Odyssey*, Telamonian Ajax
        killed himself for shame (see just below), as dramatized famously in Sophocles' play *Ajax* (c. 450-430 BC).

445   *labors are done*: Although Odysseus is standing beside a pit of blood on the shore of Ocean in the land of
        the Cimmerians, the ghosts speak as if he were actually in the underworld; and soon this will be Odysseus'
        own point of view.

we honored you like the gods, and now that you are here, you rule
among the dead. Therefore do not be sad that you are dead,
455 O Achilles.'

    "So I spoke, and he answered me at once:
'Don't sing praise to me about death, my fine Odysseus!
If I could live on the earth, I would be happy to serve as a hired
hand to some other, even to some man without a plot of land,
one who has little to live on, than to be king among all the dead
460 who have perished. But come, tell me of my good son,
whether he followed me to the war and became a leader or not.
Tell me of my father Peleus, if you know anything,
whether he still holds honor among the many Myrmidons,
or whether men deprive him of honor throughout Hellas
465 and PHTHIA ° because old age has taken possession
of his hands and feet. For I am not there to bear him aid
beneath the rays of the sun in such strength as I had
when at broad Troy I killed the best of their people,
defending the Argives. If in such strength I might come
470 even for a short time to the house of my father, I would
give pain to those who do him violence and deny him honor—
reason to hate my strength and my invincible hands!'

    "So he spoke, and I answered: 'Yes, I know nothing of Peleus,
but I'll tell you everything I know about Neoptolemos, your son,
475 just as you ask. I brought him in a hollow well-balanced
ship from SKYROS to the Achaeans who wear fancy shin guards.
Whenever we took council about the city of Troy, he always
spoke first. His words were on the mark. Only godlike Nestor
and I surpassed him. But when we fought with bronze
480 on the plain of the Trojans, he did not remain in the mass
of men, not in the throng, but he ran forth to the front,
yielding to none in his power. He killed many men
in dread battle. I could never tell them all nor give their
names, so many people did he kill defending the Argives.
485 But what a warrior was that son of Telephos whom he slew
with the bronze, I mean Eurypylos! And many of that man's
companions, the Keteians, were killed because of gifts desired

---

465 ... *Phthia:* The Myrmidons ("ants," for unknown reasons) are the followers of the house of Peleus. HELLAS
is a territory in southern Thessaly near Phthia, Achilles' homeland. By the Classical Period, *Hellas* had
come to designate all of Greece, but no one is sure why.

by a woman!° Eurypylos was the best-looking man I ever saw,
after the good Memnon.°

       "When we, the captains of the Argives,
were about to go down into the horse that Epeios made,°   490
and I was given command over all, both to open and close the door
of our strongly built ambush, then the other leaders and rulers
of the Danaäns wiped away their tears and their limbs trembled
beneath them. I never saw your son with my own eyes
either turning pale in his beautiful skin nor wiping   495
away a tear from his cheeks. He constantly begged
me to let him go out of the horse. He kept handling the hilt
of his sword and his spear heavy with bronze. He wanted
to lay waste the Trojans. And when we sacked the steep city
of Priam, after taking his share, a noble reward, he went up   500
into his ship unharmed, not struck with the sharp spear
nor wounded in the hand-to-hand, such as often happens in war.
For Ares rages in confusion.'

       "So I spoke, and the breath-soul
of Achilles, grandson of Aiakos the fast runner, went off,
taking long strides across the field of asphodel, thrilled   505
because I said his son was preeminent. Other breath-souls
of the dead and gone now stood in a crowd. Each asked
about what was important to them. Only the breath-soul of Ajax,
son of Telamon, stood apart, angry on account of the victory
that I won over him in the contest for the armor of Achilles.   510
Thetis, his revered mother, had set them as a prize.°
The sons of the Trojans were the judges, also Pallas
Athena. I wish that I had never won in that contest
for such a prize! On account of this armor the earth
covered over so great a head, Ajax, who in comeliness   515

---

488   *...desired by a woman*: Eurypylos was the son of King Telephos in the territory near Troy called Mysia.
     Achilles had previously wounded Telephos. After Achilles' death, King Priam bribed Telephos' wife, Eury-
     pylos' mother, with a golden vine made by Hephaistos ("gifts desired by a woman") to get Eurypylos to join
     the Trojan side. The Keteians, mentioned only here, are plausibly the *Hittites* of central Asia Minor, a great
     power in the Aegean Bronze Age.

489   *Memnon*: A son of the Dawn goddess and Tithonos, brother of Priam. He was king of the Aithiopians, who
     lived someplace in the East. Achilles killed Memnon after he entered the fight as a Trojan ally in the time
     after that covered in the *Iliad* (where Memnon is not mentioned).

490   *Epeios made*: The carpenter Epeios built the Trojan Horse at Athena's instruction (though Odysseus takes credit
     for the plan). Epeios does not figure in the fighting but participates in the funeral games for Patroklos (*Il.* 23).

511   *as a prize*: The prize was awarded to whoever helped the most in recovering the body of Achilles. That is
     why Trojans serve as judges—they knew best.

and in the deeds of war was superior to the other Danaäns,
except for Achilles.°

        "I spoke to him with honeyed words:
'Ajax, son of excellent Telamon, even in death you
won't give up your anger on account of those accursed
520 arms? The gods placed them as a calamity to the Argives.
We lost such a tower of strength in you. The Achaeans
lament your death ceaselessly, like that of Achilles,
son of Peleus. There is no other cause but Zeus, who thoroughly
hated the army of the Danaän spearmen, who set your doom
525 on you. But come now, King, so that you might hear
my honest speech. Conquer your anger and your proud spirit!'

    "So I spoke, but he did not answer me. He went
his way to Erebos among the other breath-souls of men
who are dead and gone. He might have spoken to me
530 even though he was angry, or I to him, but the spirit
in my breast wanted to see the breath-souls of others
who had died.

        "I saw Minos, the glorious son of Zeus,
holding his golden scepter, giving laws to the dead
from his seat, while they sat and stood around the king throughout
535 the house of Hades with its wide gates, asking for his judgments.°

    "I saw huge Orion driving wild animals together
across the plain of asphodel, ones that he had himself
killed on the lonely mountains. He held in his hands
a club all of bronze, forever unbreakable.°

        "And I saw
540 Tityos, the son of Gaia, lying on the ground, sprawled
over nine acres. Two vultures sitting on either side
gnawed at his liver, plunging their heads into his intestines,

---

517 *for Achilles*: Although Ajax deserved the armor—he carried the body of Achilles from the battleground—Odysseus
somehow won the contest and received Achilles' armor. Ajax went mad for shame and attacked a herd of sheep,
thinking they were the Trojan captains. When he recovered his senses and saw what he had done, he threw himself
on his sword, the only example in Greek myth of a practice common in the Roman period (see Figure 11.2).

535 *... for judgments*: At this point Odysseus seems no longer to be standing by the pit of blood, but to be in the
underworld itself. Homer makes this transition without explanation as he launches into a new catalog, the
Denizens of the Underworld. Minos, son of Zeus and Europa, was a legendary king of Crete and a judge in
the underworld. He continues in death doing what he did in life: issuing fair judgments to supplicants.

539 *unbreakable*: Orion too is portrayed as doing in death what he did in life, even hunting the same animals, or
presumably their ghosts.

FIGURE 11.2 **The suicide of Ajax.** The naked hero has fixed his sword in a pile of sand and thrown himself on it. His shield and breastplate are stacked on the left, his club and the scabbard to his sword on the right. His name *AIWA* is written above him. Athenian red-figure wine-mixing bowl, from Vulci, Italy.

for he could not ward them off with his hands. For Tityos
tried to carry off Leto, the glorious wife of Zeus, as she
545 went toward Pytho through Panopeus with its beautiful places.°

"And I saw powerful Tantalos, suffering agony,
standing in a pool. The water came up to his chin. He stood
as if thirsty, but he could not take a drink. Every time
the old man stooped over, eager to drink, the water would
550 be guzzled up and disappear, and the dark earth would appear
all dry around his feet, as if as some god had made
it so. High leafy trees poured down fruit above his head—
pear trees and berry trees and apple trees with their shining
fruit, and sweet figs and luxuriant olive trees. But whenever
555 the old man would reach out to snare them with his hands,
a wind would hurl them to the shadowy clouds.°

"And I saw
Sisyphos suffering terrible agonies, trying to raise a huge
stone with both his hands. Propping himself with hands
and feet, he tried to thrust the stone toward the crest
560 of a hill. But when he was about to push it over the top,
its mighty weight would turn it back, and the brutish
stone would roll down again to the plain. Then straining
he would thrust it back, as sweat flowed down from his
limbs and dust rose from his head.°

"Afterward I saw
565 the mighty Herakles, or maybe a phantom of him—he who takes
his pleasure with the deathless gods at the banquet and has Hebê
to wife, the child of great Zeus and Hera, she whose ankles
are beautiful in her golden sandals.°A clanging of the dead

---

545 *beautiful places*: Tityos, a giant son of Gaia (Earth), was killed by Apollo and Artemis after he attempted
     to rape their mother, Leto—Leto was not the "wedded wife" of Zeus, who is Hera, but his mistress. Pytho
     (DELPHI) and Panopeus are in PHOCIS, on the mainland.

556 *shadowy clouds*: According to later tradition, Tantalos, from PHRYGIA or LYDIA near Troy in Asia Minor,
     chopped up his son Pelops and served the cannibal stew to the gods to test their omniscience. Pelops was
     reassembled and fled to southern Greece where he gave his name to the Peloponnesus ("island of Pelops").

564 *from his head*: It is not clear why dust should rise from Sisyphos' head. As with Tantalos, Homer does not
     give the crime of Sisyphos, a son of Aiolos of Thessaly and a king of Corinth, known as the wiliest man that
     ever lived. Sisyphos was the real father of Odysseus (not Laërtes) according to a post-Homeric tradition,
     having seduced Odysseus' mother on her wedding night. Later writers gave a variety of reasons for Sisy-
     phos' punishment, one being that he bound Death so that (for a while) no one died.

568 *golden sandals*: Homer wants to show Herakles in the underworld, but must deal with a strong religious tra-
     dition that Herakles became a god after death, hence lives on Olympos where he married Hebê, "youth"—
     that is, he never got old. Homer reconciles the two traditions by saying that the Herakles in the underworld
     was only a "phantom."

FIGURE 11.3 Punishment of Sisyphos. The naked Sisyphos pushes the rock up a hill while a winged demon clings to his back. From a metope (sculptured relief) from the Temple of Hera at Foce del Sele in southern Italy, near Paestum, c. 510–500 BC.

arose about him, like birds driven everywhere in terror.
570 Herakles was like the dark night, holding his bare bow
and an arrow on the string, glaring dreadfully, a man
about to shoot. The baldric around his chest was awesome—
a golden strap in which were worked wondrous things,
bears and wild boars and lions with flashing eyes, and combats
575 and battles and the murders of men. I would wish that the
artist did not make another one like it!°

                          "He knew who I was,
and weeping he spoke words that went like arrows:
'Son of Laërtes, of the line of Zeus, resourceful
Odysseus—Ah wretch, do you too lead an evil life such as
580 I bore beneath the rays of the sun? Though I was the son
of Zeus, I had pain without limit. For I was bound to a man
far worse than I, who lay upon me difficult tasks.
Once he sent me to bring back the hound of Hades,
for he could think of no contest mightier than this. I carried
585 off the hound and led him out of the house of Hades.
Hermes was my guide, and Athena with the flashing eyes.'

    "So speaking, Herakles went again to the house of Hades,
but I held my ground where I was, to see if another
of the warriors who had died in the days of old might come.
590 I would have seen men of earlier times—and I wanted
to see them, Theseus and Peirithoös, the glorious offspring
of the gods, but before that the tribes of ten thousand dead
gathered around with a wondrous cry. Pale fear seized me—
perhaps the illustrious Persephone would send the Gorgon's
595 head upon me, that great monster out of the house of Hades!°

    "I went at once to the ship and I ordered my companions
to embark, to loosen the stern cables. Quickly they
got on board and sat down on the benches. The wave
of the stream bore the ship down the river Ocean. At first
600 we rowed, then we ran before a fair breeze."

---

576 *like it*: That is, so lifelike are the terrible images on the belt that a second example would be unendurable—
but the Greek is extremely obscure here.

595 *house of Hades*: According to the familiar legend, there were three Gorgons, but only Medusa was mortal.
The hero Perseus cut off Medusa's head, and anyone who looked at it was turned to stone. But Homer does
not seem to connect the Gorgon with the legend of Perseus.

BOOK 12. *Odysseus on the Island of the Sun*

"When the ship had left the stream of the river Ocean
and had come to the wave of the broad sea and the island
of Aiaia, where is the house of early-born Dawn,
and her dancing ground and her risings of the sun°—
coming there we beached our ship on the sand.   5
We got out on the shore of the sea, then fell asleep
and awaited the shining Dawn.

                   "When early-born Dawn
appeared with her fingers of rose, then I sent my
companions off to the house of Kirkê to retrieve
the corpse of the dead Elpenor. We at once cut logs   10
and, mourning, pouring down hot tears, buried him
where the headland projects farthest into the sea.
When the corpse and the armor of the corpse were burned,
we heaped up a barrow and set up a memorial column.
On top of the mound we planted his finely shaped oar.   15

  "While we busied ourselves with these various tasks,
Kirkê was aware that we had returned from the house
of Hades. She spruced herself up and quickly came along,
and her servants brought bread and abundant meat
and flaming red wine with her. Standing in our midst,   20
the beautiful goddess said: 'Poor things, who have gone
down alive to the house of Hades—men who will die
twice, while other men die but a single time. But come,
eat of this bread and drink this wine, staying here all day
long. At the coming of dawn you shall sail away. I shall   25
show you the way and make clear each matter so that
you do not suffer pain and misfortune through the wicked
and terrible designs of either sea or land.'

               "So she spoke,
and our proud spirits agreed. So all the day until the sun

---

4   *of the sun*: Aiaia is therefore in the extreme East, although Odysseus has evidently been traveling in the
   Far West.

30 went down we sat dining on endless meat and sweet wine.
When the sun went down and the darkness came on,
my men lay down to take their rest beside the stern cable
of the ship. But Kirkê took me by the hand and led me apart
from my dear companions. She made me sit down
35 and herself lay down beside me and asked me about
everything.

      "I told her all in proper order, and then
the revered Kirkê spoke to me and said: 'Thus have all
these matters been brought to completion. Now listen
to what I shall say. A god himself will remind you.
40 First you will come to the Sirens° who enchant all men
who come near them. Whoever comes close to them
in ignorance and hears the Sirens' voice, he will never
return to his home for his wife and little children
to stand by his side and rejoice. For the Sirens, sitting
45 in a meadow, enchant all with their clear song.
Around them there is a great heap of the bones
of rotting men, and the skin shrivels up around
those bones. But go on past them, and then seal
the ears of your companions by kneading sweet wax
50 so that none of them may hear. If you yourself want
to hear, let them bind your hands and feet in the swift
ship, upright in the hole for the mast, and let the ropes
be fixed to the mast itself° so that you might take delight
in hearing the voice of the two Sirens. If you beseech
55 and order your companions to release you, they must
bind you with still more bonds.

             " 'Now when your companions
shall have rowed past these beings, then I won't exactly
say which course you should take, but you must
consider it yourself in your own mind. I will describe both.

60   " 'On the one side are overhanging cliffs, and against them
a great wave of blue-eyed Amphitritê roars. The blessed
gods call them the Planktai.° Not even winged things,

---

40 *Sirens*: The origin and meaning of the name are unknown.

53 *mast itself*: It is not clear how Odysseus is to be tied in the "hole for the mast," but probably Figure 12.1 gives
a good image of what Homer has in mind.

62 *Planktai*: The "clashing (rocks)."

nor timid doves that carry ambrosia to father Zeus,
can pass them, but the smooth rock always snatches
away one, and the father sends out another to make up   65
the full number. So no ship of men that ever came here
has escaped intact, but the waves of the sea and the blasts
of ruinous fire whirl the planks of ships and the bodies
of men in confusion. Only one seafaring ship has
ever sailed through the Planktai—the Argo, an object   70
of everyone's interest, sailing back from Aietes.
And even her the wave would have quickly dashed
against the great rocks, but Hera sent her on through
because she loved Jason.°

        "'On the other path are two cliffs,
one of which reaches to the broad heaven with its cragged   75
peak, and a dark cloud surrounds it that never ebbs away.
Nor is the clear sky ever seen around that peak, neither
in summer nor harvest time. No mortal man could ever
climb it or set his foot on top, not if he had twenty hands
and feet. For the rock is smooth, as if it were polished.   80
And in the middle of the cliff is a shadowy cave turned
toward the west, toward Erebos—it is likely that you should
steer your hollow ship past it, glorious Odysseus.
Not even a strong man could shoot an arrow from his
hollow ship so that it reached into the hollow cave.   85
Skylla° lives there, barking terribly. Her voice is like
that of a new-born puppy, but she herself is an evil
monster. No one would ever take pleasure in seeing her,
not even if it was a god who met her. She has twelve feet,
all of them twisted, and six long necks, and on each one   90
a horrific head, and in each three rows of teeth, set close
together in great numbers, full of black death. She hides
up to her middle in the hollow cave, but she holds out her heads
from the terrible cavern and fishes there, greedily groping
around the cliff for dolphins and seals, or, if she can, catch   95
any other beast of those that deep-moaning Amphitritê
rears in great multitudes. No sailors can boast that they

---

74 *loved Jason*: The clearest proof that the *Odyssey'*s account of Odysseus' adventures owes something to a
     traditional poem about Jason's wanderings, but we cannot be sure of the details. Aietes, the son of Helios
     and Persê. the daughter of Ocean, was the father of Medea and the brother of Kirkê, but Homer never
     mentions Aietes' position as king of Kolchis, land of the Golden Fleece, or the role of evil opponent that
     Aietes played in the story of Jason.

86 *Skylla*: "puppy," hence the dogs' heads and the barking.

have fled unscathed past her in their ships. With each head
she carries off a man, snatching him from the ship with its
100 prow painted blue.

        "'Odysseus, you will notice that the other cliff
is lower—they are so close to one another, you could shoot
an arrow across. A large fig tree with many leaves is on it.
Beneath it the divine Charybdis° sucks down the black
water. Three times a day she vomits it forth, three times
105 she sucks it down—terrible! Don't be there when she sucks
it down! No one could save you from that evil, not even
the earth-shaker. Rather, go close to the cliff of Skylla
and drive your ship past. It is better by far to mourn
for six comrades than for all together!'

        "So she spoke, and I said
110 in reply: 'But goddess, tell me this truly—is there some way
I can escape the foul Charybdis and ward off that other, too,
when she plunders my companions?'

        "So I spoke, and the beautiful
goddess right away answered me: 'Poor man, all you think
about are the acts and the grind of war! Will you never yield
115 to the deathless gods? She is not mortal, but an immortal
evil—a dread terror, savage and unmanageable!
There is no defense. It is best to flee from her. If you take
the time to arm yourself beside the cliff, I fear that she will
leap out again and attack you with her many heads and seize
120 as many men as before. Drive past her aggressively
and call out to Krataiis,° the mother of Skylla, who bore
her as a curse to mortals. Krataiis will stop her from
leaping forth again.'

        "'Next you will come to the island
of Thrinakia.° The many herds of Helios' cattle graze there,
125 and the good flocks of sheep—seven herds of cattle
and as many beautiful flocks of sheep, fifty animals
to each. They have no offspring, nor do they ever die.
Goddesses are their shepherds, nymphs with fine tresses—

---

103 *Charybdis:* Looks like it might mean "swallower," but it is probably not Greek.

121 *Krataiis:* "powerful one," otherwise unknown.

124 *Thrinakia:* That is, Sicily.

Phaëthousa and Lampetië°—whom the beautiful Neaira   130
bore to Helios Hyperion. Their revered mother bore
and raised them, then sent them off far away to live,
to Thrinakia, where they look over their father's flocks
and the sleek cattle. If you leave these unharmed
and remember your homecoming, you may all arrive
still to Ithaca, though suffering terribly. But if you harm them,   135
then I foretell ruin for your ship and your companions.
Even if you alone escape, you will come to your home
late and in evil plight, having lost all your comrades.'

   "So she spoke, and promptly then golden-throned Dawn
arose. The beautiful goddess took her way up through   140
the island, while I went to the ship and roused my
companions, ready to set sail, to loosen the stern cables
and leave. Speedily they climbed aboard and sat
down at the thole pins. They sat all in a row
and struck the gray sea with their oars. Fair-tressed   145
Kirkê, the dread goddess of human speech, sent a fair
wind that filled the sail behind the ship with painted
blue prow, our fine companion. When we had stowed all
the tackle in the ship, we took our seats. Wind arose
and the helmsman steered her along.   150

                              "Then, sad at heart,
I spoke to my companions: 'My friends, it is not right
that one or two alone know the oracles that Kirkê
the beautiful goddess delivered. I will tell you all,
so that either in full knowledge we may die, or avoiding
death and fate we may escape. First of all she urged   155
that we avoid the voice of the wondrous Sirens from their
flowery meadow. She advised me alone to hear their
voice. But you must first bind me in tight bonds so that
I remain fast where I am, upright in the hole for the mast,
and let the cables be made fast to the mast. If I beg you   160
to let me go and order you to do it, then you must bind
me with more bonds.'

            "And so I went over everything and told
all to my companions. Meanwhile the well-built ship
came quickly to the island of the two Sirens, for a fair

---

129   *Phaethousa and Lampetië*: Significant names, "shining" and "radiant," appropriate to their father's nature.

165 wind bore her along. Then the wind stopped and there
was a windless calm—some spirit lulled the waves to sleep.
My companions arose and furled the sail and stowed it
in the hollow ship. Sitting at the tholes, they made the sea
white with their polished oars of pine. And with my sharp
170 sword I cut a great round cake of wax into small pieces,
then kneaded it in my powerful hands. The wax
quickly grew warm from the great strength of my hands
and the rays of King Helios Hyperion. I anointed the ears
of all my comrades in turn with it. They bound my hands
175 and feet alike in the ship, upright in the hole for the mast,
and they fastened the cables to the mast. Then they sat
down and struck the gray sea with their oars.

                            "But when
we were as far away as a man can be heard when shouting,
driving swiftly on our way, the Sirens noticed the fast ship
180 as it came near, and they began to intone their clear song:
'Come here, O storied Odysseus, great glory of the Achaeans,
bring your ship over here so that you can hear the voices
of the two of us. For no man yet has passed
this island in his black ship before hearing the sweet
185 voice from our lips, but he takes pleasure in it and goes
on his way, knowing more. For we know all that the Argives
and the Trojans suffered through the will of the gods
in broad Troy, and we know all things that take place
on the much-nourishing earth.'

                         "So they sang, sending
190 out their beautiful voices. My heart wanted to hear them,
and I ordered my companions to set me free, nodding
with my brows. But they fell to their oars and rowed on.
Right away, Perimedes and Eurylochos stood up and bound me
in more ropes and pulled them tighter. When they had rowed
195 past the Sirens and could no longer hear their voices nor song,
my trusty companions quickly removed the wax with which
I had stuffed their ears, and they released me from my bonds.
When we had left the island, I immediately espied smoke
and a great wave and heard a roar. The oars flew from the hands
200 of my frightened men and fell in the water with a splash,
and the ship stood still where it was when they stopped
driving it on with their hands on the sharp blades.

FIGURE 12.1   Odysseus and the Sirens.   In Homer, there are only two Sirens, but here there are three. They are represented as Egyptian *ba*-birds, the Egyptian souls of the dead. One Siren seems to fall to her death from the right-hand cliff in accord with a post-Homeric tradition that the Sirens committed suicide from chagrin when Odysseus withstood their enchantments. Odysseus is tied to the mast while his men row on. Notice the helmsman to the right with his two steering oars, and the apotropaic eye painted on the ship's prow. Athenian red-figure vase, c. 460 BC.

"I went
through the ship and encouraged my companions with
honeyed words, standing by each man in turn: 'My friends,
205 we have not been ignorant of evils before this, and surely this evil
is no worse than when Cyclops trapped us in his hollow cave
by brute strength! But even then we escaped, thanks to my
courage, counsel, and intelligence. I think that one day
we will remember this sorrow too. But come now, let us all
210 obey what I say. Keep your seats on the benches and strike
the deep surf of the sea with your oars in the hope that Zeus
may somehow grant us to escape and to avoid destruction.
To you, helmsman, I make this command, and do take it
to heart, because you control the helm of the hollow ship:
215 Keep the ship far away from this smoke and these waves.
Hug the cliff so that the ship does not swerve off to the other
side and cast us into destruction.'

"So I spoke, and swiftly they
obeyed my words. I did not mention Skylla—an incurable curse!—
so that my companions would not take fear, cease from their
220 rowing, and huddle together in the bottom of the ship. And I
forgot all about the hard warning of Kirkê—that she ordered
me not to arm myself—for I put on my famous armor and took
up two long spears in my hands and went onto the fore-deck
of the ship. I thought that Skylla of the rock, who was about to
225 bring catastrophe on my companions, would first appear here first.
But I could glimpse her nowhere, and my eyes grew tired
looking everywhere across the foggy rock. We sailed on up
through the narrow passage, lamenting as we went. On the one
side was Skylla, on the other the divine Charybdis sucked
230 down the salty water of the sea. And when she vomited it forth,
like a cauldron on a huge fire, she would foam right up
to the top, seething, in chaotic confusion, and high overhead
the sea-spray would fall on the tops of both cliffs. As often
as she sucked down the salty water of the sea, all within
235 was seen seething, and all around the rock was a terrible roar,
and down deep the earth appeared black with sand.

"Pale fear seized my men. We looked towards her, terrified
of destruction. In the meanwhile Skylla seized six of my men,
the best in strength and power, from the hollow ship.
240 Looking across the swift ship and toward my companions,
I saw their feet and hands above me as they were lifted
into the air. They cried aloud to me and called me by name

for the last time, in anguish of heart. As a fisherman sits
on a jutting rock and throws in his bait as a snare to the little
fishes and with his long pole lets down into the sea the horn   245
of an ox of the field,° and then as he catches a fish and
pulls it out as it writhes for air—even so they were pulled
toward the rocks gasping for air, and there at her doors
she ate them as they screamed and held out their hands
toward me in the dread death-struggle. It was the most pitiful   250
thing that my eyes ever saw of all that I experienced while
exploring the paths of the sea. When we had fled from the cliffs
of dread Charybdis and Skylla, we soon came to the good island
of the god were where the beautiful broad-browed cattle
and the many fat flocks of Helios Hyperion. While I was still in my   255
black ship out to sea, I heard the lowing of the cattle being penned
in stalls, and the bleating of sheep, and on my heart fell the words
of the blind seer Theban Tiresias and of Aiaian Kirkê, who strongly
encouraged me to avoid the island of Helios, who gives joy to mortals.

    "Grieving at heart, I spoke to my companions: 'Hear my words,   260
though you are suffering, my companions, so that I may tell you
the oracles of Tiresias and of Aiaian Kirkê, who most strongly urged
me to avoid the island of Helios, who gives joy to mortals.
She said that there is the grimmest affliction for us. So drive
the black ship beyond the island.'"   265

               "So I spoke, and the hearts
within them were crushed. Right away Eurylochos spoke
with loathsome words: 'You are a hard man, Odysseus.
Your strength is superior and your limbs never tire. You are
made entirely of iron—you will not let your companions,
worn out with labor and lack of sleep, set foot on the land,   270
where we might make a delicious meal on this island surrounded
by the sea. Instead you ask us, even as we are, to wander on
throughout the night on the misty sea. But rough winds, the wrecker
of ships, come from the night. How might anyone avoid
total destruction if somehow, suddenly, the blast of the wind   275
should come—either South Wind or blustering West Wind—
which most often ruins ships in spite of the will of the ruling gods?
Let us yield to black night and prepare a meal, remaining
at the side of the swift ship, and in the morning we will
embark again on the broad sea.'   280

---

246 *ox of the field*: A tube of horn was set above the hook to prevent the line from being bitten.

FIGURE 12.2 Skylla devours one of Odysseus' men. From the same complex of sculptural representations of Greek myths as Figure 7.1, in a cave at Sperlonga, Italy, constructed by the Roman emperor Tiberius (42 BC–AD 37), comes this fragment showing the death of one of Odysseus' men in the talons of Skylla. One arm reaches up while the other grips a dog's head: Homer says that Skylla's "voice is like that of a new-born puppy," and Skylla means "puppy." A fishlike tail represents one of the monster's twelve feet. Fragment of a marble group showing the ship of Ulysses attacked by Skylla, c. AD 20.

"So spoke Eurylochos, and my
other companions assented. I realized that some spirit was
designing evil, and I spoke words that went like arrows:
'Eurylochos, you force my hand, for I stand alone. But come now,
may everybody swear a powerful oath: If we come across a herd
of cattle or a great flock of sheep, let no one in evil folly   285
kill either cow or sheep, but be happy to eat the food
that deathless Kirkê has provided.'

    "So I spoke, and they
all promptly swore, just as I urged. And when they had sworn
and accomplished the oath, we moored our well-built ship
in the hollow harbor close by the sweet water, and my companions   290
climbed out of the ship. Skillfully they prepared a meal,
and when they had put the desire for food and drink from
themselves, they fell to weeping, remembering their companions
whom Skylla snatched from the hollow ship and devoured.
Sweet sleep came upon them as they wept. But then,   295
in the last third of the night, as the stars had passed to the other
side of the sky, Zeus the gatherer of clouds sent forth
a savage wind in an astounding tempest, and it hid the earth
and the sea alike in clouds, and night rushed down
from the heaven.°   300

    "When early-born dawn appeared with her
fingers of rose, we dragged our ship out and made her fast
in a hollow cave, where were the beautiful dancing places
and seats of the nymphs. Then I called my men to an
assembly and I said to them: 'My friends, there is food
and drink in our swift ship, so let us stay away from these   305
cattle so that we do not come to harm. These are the cattle
and fat sheep of a dread god, Helios, who oversees all things
and hears everything.'

    "So I spoke, and their proud hearts
agreed. Then for a full month South Wind blew incessantly,
nor was there any other wind except for East Wind   310
and South Wind.° So long as my companions had food
and red wine, they kept their hands off the cattle,
being anxious to save their lives. But when all the provisions
from the ship were exhausted, and they were compelled

---

300 *heaven:* That is, the clouds covered the stars so that there was total darkness.

311 *South Wind:* That is, the wind blowing incessantly is south-easterly.

315 to wander around in search of game—of fish and birds
and whatever might come to their hands, fishing with
bent hooks. Meanwhile, hunger gnawed their bellies.°

"Then I went up on the island so that I might pray to the gods,
to see if they would show a way to go. When I had come
320 away from my companions as I went through the island,
I washed my hands in a place where there was protection
from the wind, and I prayed to all the gods who live
on Olympos. They poured out sweet sleep over my eyelids.

"In the meanwhile, Eurylochos began to give wicked
325 counsel to my crew: 'Hear me, my companions, while we
are all in an evil plight. All death is hateful to wretched mortals,
but most pitiful is to die of hunger and so meet one's doom.
So come, let us drive off the best of the cattle of Helios
and sacrifice them to the deathless ones who hold the broad
330 heaven. And if we ever arrive to Ithaca, the land of our fathers,
we will build a rich temple to Helios Hyperion, and place many
fine offerings in it. And if he is angry because of his
straight-horned cattle and wishes to destroy our ship,
and the other gods agree, I would rather die of a sudden,
335 gulping down a wave, than to waste away slowly
on a desert island.'

"So Eurylochos spoke, and all the other
companions agreed. Immediately they drove off the best
of the cattle of Helios, who were nearby. The beautiful
sleek broad-browed cattle were grazing not far from
340 our blue-prowed ship. My men stood by these and prayed
to the gods, plucking the tender leaves of a high oak,
for there was no white barley in our well-benched ship.

"When they had prayed and had cut the throats of the cattle
and stripped off their skin, they cut out the thigh bones
345 and covered them with a double layer of fat and placed
raw flesh on them. They had no wine to pour over the blazing
sacrifice, but they poured drink-offerings of water and roasted
the guts. When they had burned the thigh bone and eaten
the entrails, they cut up the rest and put it on spits. It was
350 then that sweet sleep fled from my eyes, and I went down
to the swift ship and the shore of the sea.

---

317 *their bellies*: Epic heroes eat only beef, mutton, and pork, except in extreme circumstances.

"When I came near
to the beaked ship, then the sweet smell of the fat surrounded
me. Groaning, I cried out to the deathless gods: 'Zeus Father,
and you other blessed gods who live forever, you have
ruined me by lulling me with pitiless sleep. And now my   355
companions have devised a great wickedness in my absence.'

"Quickly Lampetië, who wore a long robe, came as a messenger
to Helios Hyperion, saying that we had killed his cattle.
Then quickly Helios spoke in anger to the deathless ones:
'Zeus, father, and you other blessed gods who live forever,   360
take vengeance on the companions of Odysseus son of Laërtes!
Arrogantly they have killed my cattle in which I rejoiced as I
journeyed into the starry heaven, and when I turned back again
to the earth from the heaven. If they do not pay me a suitable
recompense for the cattle, I will descend into the house of Hades   365
and shine among the dead!'

"Zeus the cloud-gatherer said to him
in answer: 'Helios, please, continue shining among the deathless
ones and among mortal men who live on the earth, the giver of grain.
As for his men, I will soon hit their swift ship with a shining
thunderbolt and shatter it into small pieces in the middle   370
of the wine-dark sea.' I heard about all this from Kalypso
with the lovely tresses, who herself heard it from Hermes
the messenger.

"When I came down to the ship and the sea,
I reproached all my men, standing in front of each one individually,
but we were unable to find a remedy. The cattle were already dead.   375
The gods then showed forth omens for my men. The skins crawled
along the ground and flesh, roast and raw, lowed on the spits,
and there was a mooing as of cattle. For six days my trusty
companions dined on the best of the cattle of Helios that
they had driven off. But when Zeus the son of Kronos brought   380
the seventh day on us, then the wind stopped blowing like a tempest.

"We immediately went aboard and put out into the broad sea,
setting up the mast and spreading out the white sail. When
we had left the island, and no other land appeared, but only sky
and sea, then the son of Kronos set up a dark cloud over the hollow   385
ship, and the sea grew black beneath the cloud. She did not run
on for long, for quickly the shrill West Wind came on, blowing
with a great blast, and the storm wind snapped the front ropes

that held the mast so the mast fell backwards and all the rigging
390 was scattered in the bilge. In the stern of the ship the mast hit
the head of the helmsman and smashed together the bones
of his head. Like a diver he fell from the foredeck and his proud
spirit left his bones.

"Then Zeus thundered and hit the ship
with lightning. The whole ship shook when struck by the lightning,
395 and it was filled with sulfur. My companions fell from the ship.
They were borne like sea-crows on the black waves around
the ship—the god had taken from them their day of return.
But I kept going up and down the ship until the surge tore
the sides from the keel, and the wave bore her on bare, and snapped
400 off the mast at the keel. But one of the ropes holding the mast,
made of the hide of an ox, was flung over the mast. I bound the two
together with this, keel and mast, and sitting on these was carried
along by the ferocious winds. Then West Wind ceased
to blow her tempest, and South Wind came up swiftly,
405 bringing sorrow to my heart.

"I feared that I might once
again cross destroying Charybdis. All night long I drifted,
and when the sun came up I came to the cliff of Skylla
and dread Charybdis, who still sucked down the salty
water of the sea. But I sprang up high, to the tall fig tree.
410 I clung to it like a bat. But there was no way to plant my feet
firmly, nor to climb it. Its roots were far away, its branches
out of reach, long and great, and they cast a shadow over
Charybdis. I clung to the tree steadfastly until she should
vomit forth the mast and the keel, and to reward my longing
415 they did come up again. At the time when a man rises up
from the market-place, where the many quarrels of contending
young men are judged—at that time those timbers reappeared
from Charybdis.

"I let go hands and feet from above and plunged
downward and fell with a thud into the middle of the water
420 beyond the long timbers. Sitting on these I rowed forward
with my hands. As for Skylla, the father of men and gods
did not allow her to see me. Otherwise I would not have
escaped sure destruction!

"Then I was carried for nine days,
but on the tenth night the gods brought me to the island

FIGURE 12.3 Shipwreck in the days of Homer.   In this eighth century BC, painting, a man clings to the keel of an upturned ship while nine of his companions perish in the sea around him. There seems to be one other survivor, who clings to the prow of the boat. The upright figure seems to reach out to touch him. Some have taken this picture as an illustration of the shipwreck in *Odyssey* 12, but the second survivor is a problem; in fact, it is a generic scene. From an Athenian wine jug, c. 720 BC.

425 of Ogygia, where fair-tressed Kalypso lives, the dread goddess
of human speech. She welcomed and took care of me.

"But why should I tell you these things? I told it
only yesterday in your home, to you and to your noble wife.
It is an unpleasant thing to repeat a tale plainly told."

BOOK 13. *Home at Last*

S o spoke Odysseus, and they all fell into silence,
held in a spell throughout the shadowy halls.
Then Alkinoös answered him and said: "O Odysseus,
because you have come to my house with its high-roofed
floor of bronze, I do not think that you will return home   5
with further misfortune, even though you have suffered much.
And to every man of you who always likes to drink
the flaming wine of the elders in my halls while listening
to the singer—I lay on you this charge: There is
clothing for the stranger in the polished chest along with   10
gold, finely worked, and all other kinds of gifts that
the counselors of the Phaeacians have brought here.
So come, let us give him a great tripod and a cauldron too—
every man of you!° We will recoup the cost from among
the people. It is hard for one man to give generously   15
without recompense."

        So spoke Alkinoös, and what he said
pleased them. Each man went to his house to lie down
to sleep. When Dawn with her fingers of rose appeared,
they hurried to the ships and they brought the bronze,
giver of strength to men. The powerful Alkinoös   20
himself carefully stowed the treasure beneath the benches
in the ship, so that it might not get in the way
of the crew while they were rowing, when they hurried
to ply the oars. Then they went to the house of Alkinoös
and prepared a feast. The powerful Alkinoös   25
sacrificed a bull for them, to Zeus the son of Kronos,
god of the dark cloud who rules over everything.
They burned the thigh pieces, then took high pleasure
in a fine feast. The divine singer, Demodokos, sang to them,
honored by the people.   30

---

14 *of you*: He seems to be referring to the twelve chieftains of the Phaeacians, each of whom would donate
   a tripod and cauldron, and presumably the thirteenth would be the gift of Alkinoös. These are valuable
   gifts.

But Odysseus turned his head
toward the bright sun, eager that it set, for he longed so
for his return. As a man wants his dinner, for whom
two wine-dark oxen have drawn the jointed plow through
the fallow land all day long, and the setting of the sun
35 is a welcome sight so that he may prepare his dinner,
and his knees grow weary as he goes—even so welcome
to Odysseus was the sight of the setting sun.

                              Quickly
he spoke to the oar-loving Phaeacians, and he especially
addressed Alkinoös: "King Alkinoös, renowned above
40 all people, pour out drink offerings and send me safely
on my way—Farewell! All that my heart desired has been
brought to fulfillment, an escort and gift-tokens of friendship.
May the gods in heaven bless these gifts! And when I return,
may I find my excellent wife in my house and those
45 I love safe and sound. And you, staying here, may you
make your wedded wives and your children joyous.
May the gods give you every kind of prosperity, and may
no evil come to your people."

                        So Odysseus spoke, and they all
agreed and urged that the stranger be sent off, for he had
50 spoken in accordance with what is right. And then
the mighty Alkinoös spoke to his herald: "Pontonoös,
mix the sweet wine in the wine-mixing bowl and give it
out to everyone in the hall so that, praying to father Zeus,
we might send the stranger on his way to the land
55 of his fathers."

                    So Alkinoös spoke, and Pantonoös mixed
the honey-hearted wine. Coming up to each in turn he poured
it out. From where they sat, they poured drink offerings
to the gods—the blessed gods who hold up the broad sky.
Then godlike Odysseus stood up, and he placed
60 the twin-handled cup in Aretê's hands. He spoke and addressed
her with words that went like arrows: "May you fare well,
O queen—throughout the years until old age and death
that hangs over every mortal comes. As for me—I go my way,
but you must take pleasure in your house and your children
65 and your people and in chief Alkinoös."

So speaking, godlike
Odysseus crossed the threshold. With him the mighty Alkinoös
sent a herald to lead him to the swift ship and the shore
of the sea. Aretê sent her women slaves with him, one
carrying a newly washed cloak and a shirt, another carrying
the strong chest, and another carried bread and red wine.   70
When they came down to the ship and the sea, all the brave
young men who were his escort took these things and stowed them
in the hollow ship—all the drink and food. They laid out
a rug and a linen cloth for Odysseus on the deck of the hollow
ship, at the stern where he could get a good night's sleep.   75
Odysseus went on board and lay down in silence. The crew
sat down, every one at his thole pins, all in order, and they
loosed the mooring rope from the pierced stone. As soon
as they leaned back and tossed the brine with their oar blades,
then sweet sleep fell on Odysseus' eyebrows, a deep sleep,   80
most sweet, like unto death.

As when on a plain four yoked
stallions all leap forward under the strokes of the lash,
and leaping up high they quickly traverse their path,
even so the stern of the ship was lifted, and a great purple
wave of the loud-resounding sea ranged behind it, and she sped   85
safe and steady on her way. Not even the circling hawk,
the fastest of winged birds, could have kept pace with it.

And so she sped on swiftly and cut the waves of the sea,
bearing a man like the gods in giving advice, a man who
in earlier times had suffered many pains in his heart   90
and in the wars of men, and on the terrible waves. But now
he slept soundly, having forgotten all that he suffered.

When that brightest of stars arose,° which comes to announce
the light of early-born Dawn, finally the sea-faring ship
came close to the island. There is a harbor of Phorkys,°   95
the Old Man of the Sea, in the land of ITHACA. Two projecting
headlands strike the sea and slope downwards on the side
toward the harbor. These headlands keep back the great
waves raised by unfriendly winds outside, but, inside,
the well-benched ships lay calm without mooring ropes,   100

---

93   *of stars arose*: Probably the planet Venus.

95   *Phorkys*: Probably a preGreek sea god, comparable to Proteus or Nereus, said to be the grandfather of
     Polyphemos.

once they have reached the place of anchorage. At the head
of the harbor there is an olive tree with long leaves,
and near to it a lovely cave where vapors linger. The cave
is sacred to the nymphs, who are called Naiads.° In the cave
105 are mixing bowls and stone jars with two handles.
The bees store their honey there. There are stone looms,
very tall, where the nymphs weave cloaks dyed with the purple
of the sea, a marvel to behold, and ever-flowing water
within. There are two doors to the cave, one to the north
110 where men go down. The entrance to the south is for the gods.
Men would never come in there, for that is the path
of the deathless ones.°

           They drove in to the harbor, knowing it
from before. They were going so fast that they ran the boat
up on the beach to half the boat's length, for the arms
115 of the rowers were driving her that hard. They disembarked
from the finely benched ship onto the land. First of all
they raised up Odysseus from the hollow ship together
with his linen cover and shining rug. They set him down
on the sand, overcome by sleep. They lifted out the goods
120 that the noble Phaeacians gave him for his journey home,
thanks to the efforts of great-hearted Athena. These they set
all together beside the trunk of the olive tree, out of the path,
so that some passerby might not come upon them and do them
harm before Odysseus awoke.

           Then the Phaeacians returned home.
125 But the earth-shaker did not forget the threats that he had first
made against godlike Odysseus. He therefore asked Zeus about
his plan: "Father Zeus, I will no longer be honored among
the deathless gods, for mortals do not honor me at all—

---

104 *Naiads*: From a verb meaning "to flow." The Naiad nymphs are spirits of fresh water—springs, rivers, lakes
(see Figure 13.3).

112 *... deathless ones*: Sometimes Homer seems to speak from personal knowledge of the island; sometimes he
gets things wrong. Ithaca (MAP V) is entirely mountainous and in the rough shape of an hourglass. Com-
mentators imagine that Odysseus landed in the GULF OF MOLO on the right side of the island, enclosed by
two steep headlands, and that he stored his loot in a nearby cave (CAVE OF THE NAIADS) that in fact has
two entrances. He then proceeded to the northern portion of the island and his house. Parts of thirteen
tripods dated to the late ninth century BC, possibly the time of Homer's activity, were found in modern
times in the so-called CAVE OF THE TRIPODS near a harbor on the west side of the island. In Hellenistic
times, this cave was associated with Odysseus, and it seems to correspond with the Homeric mention of
tripods as gift-tokens to Odysseus, but the connection is controversial. Tourists to present-day Ithaca will
be told that the pig herder EUMAIOS' HUT was at the south of the island near a cliff where crows gather, but
little evidence supports this conclusion.

I am talking about the Phaeacians, who as you know
are of the same bloodline as myself. Just now I promised
that Odysseus would come home only after suffering
many evils. I did not *wholly* take away the day of his return,
for you once promised it to him and nodded your head
in affirmation. Yet in his sleep they have brought him
across the sea in their swift ship to Ithaca, and they have
given him gifts past telling, bronze and gold and all sorts
of woven clothes—more than Odysseus would ever have
got for himself from Troy if he had escaped unmolested,
taking his due share of the loot."

130

135

                    Zeus the cloud-gatherer
then said in reply: "Ah me, my earth-shaker, wide-ruler,
what a thing you have said! The gods do not dishonor you
at all. It would be a hard thing to attack with insult the oldest
and the best! As for men, if anyone gives in to violence
and force, and does not do you honor, you may take subsequent
vengeance on that man forever. Do what you will, whatever
is pleasing to your heart."

140

145

                    Poseidon, the shaker of the earth,
then answered Zeus: "I would quickly have accomplished
what you say—O you of the dark cloud!—but I always fear
and avoid your anger. As for now, I would like to smash the very
beautiful ship of the Phaeacians as she returns from this convoy
on the misty sea. In this way the Phaeacians will be warned to quit
giving safe passage to men. I would also like to throw up a mountain
around their city!"

150

                    Answering him, Zeus the cloud-gatherer said:
"Well Poseidon, this seems to me to be the best plan. When all
the people are watching from the city to see the ship speed
on its way, then turn it to stone near the shore—a stone
in the shape of a fast ship so that all men may wonder.
And heap a great mountain around the city."

155

                    When Poseidon
the earth-shaker heard this, he went off to Scheria where
the Phaeacians had their home, and there he waited. The seafaring
ship came close, traveling fast. The earth-shaker came near her
and turned her to stone, and he rooted her from beneath
by striking with the flat of his hand. Then he was gone.

160

FIGURE 13.1 Poseidon holding a trident.   The god is long haired and bearded and wears a band around his head. The trident may in origin have been a thunderbolt, but it has been changed into a tuna spear. Corinthian plaque, from Penteskouphia, 550–525 BC.

The Phaeacians, famous seamen, with their long oars, spoke
winged words to one another—thus would one say, glancing   165
at his neighbor: "O my, who has fixed this swift ship
in the sea as it journeyed home? I mean, she was in plain sight!"

So one would say, but they did not know how this
had come to pass. Then Alkinoös spoke to them and addressed
them: "Yes, I see how the ancient prophecies of my father   170
have come to pass. He said that Poseidon was angry with us
because we give safe transport to everyone. He said that
one day, as a most beautiful ship of the Phaeacian men returned
from a convoy, he would smash her on the misty sea, and heap up
a great mountain around the city. So the old man prophesied.   175
And now all is being brought to pass.° But come, let us all
be persuaded by what I say. Let us cease to provide escort
for mortals, when one happens upon our island. And let us
sacrifice twelve choice bulls to Poseidon in hopes that he will
take pity on us and not bury the city in a high mountain."   180

So he spoke, and they were frightened. And so the leaders
and counselors of the Phaeacians prayed to King Poseidon
as they stood around the altar.

                    In the meanwhile Odysseus
awoke from sleep in the land of his fathers. He recognized nothing,
for he had been gone a long time. The goddess Pallas Athena,   185
daughter of Zeus, had poured a mist around him so that she might
make him unrecognizable and then tell him everything,
and so that his wife and townspeople and friends would not
recognize him before he had taken full punishment on the suitors
for their transgressions. And so everything seemed strange   190
to the king—the unbroken paths and the harbors suitable for anchorage
and the steep cliffs and the blooming trees.

                    He sprang up
and beheld the land of his fathers. Then he groaned and struck
his thighs with the flat of his hands, and gloomily he said:
"Oh no! To the land of what men have I come? I wonder if they are 195

---

176 ...*to pass*: Once the island of CORCYRA was equated with Scheria, an identification that Thucydides
     (c. 460–395 BC) takes as commonplace, then a rock formation in the harbor of Corcyra was said to be
     this very ship. The myth does seem to describe some specific rock formation, but in the story the incident
     functions to cut off the Phaeacians from the world we now live in, placing a barrier between us and them,
     explaining why no one really knew where the Phaeacians lived and why you could not go there. Odysseus
     has put that enchanted world behind him, and there is no going back.

violent and savage, unjust, or are they a friend to strangers?
Do they respect the gods? Where shall I put all these things?
Where will I go now? I wish I had stayed there with the Phaeacians.
Then I would have come to some other of the mighty chieftains.
200　He would have entertained me and sent me on my way home.

　　"But now I do not know where I should put these things.
I can't leave them here or they will become the spoil of others.
Yes, the leaders and counselors of the Phaeacians were not
altogether wise—nor just! They have left me off in a strange land
205　when they said they would take me to clear-seen Ithaca!
But they have not done it. May Zeus the god of suppliants
take vengeance on them! He watches over all men and exacts
punishment from the man who misses the mark.

　　　　　　　　　　　　　　　　　　　　　"But come,
let me look closely and inventory my goods, to see if these
210　men have taken away anything in their hollow ship . . ."

　　So speaking, he counted the very beautiful tripods and cauldrons
and gold and beautiful woven cloth. Nothing of these was missing.
Then, pacing beside the shore of the loud-resounding sea,
he mourned for the land of his fathers and complained bitterly.

215　　But Athena came close to him in the form of a young man,
a shepherd, young and handsome, such as are the children of kings.
Around her shoulders she had doubled a finely made cloak.
Beneath her shining feet were sandals, and she held a spear.

　　Odysseus was glad to see her and came up close and spoke
220　words that went like arrows: "My friend, you are the first man
I have come to in this land. Greetings to you! I hope that you
will be friendly to me. Help me save my goods—and me!
I pray to you as if to a god, and I beg you by your knees.
Tell me this truly so that I may know—What land? What people?
225　What men live here? Is this some island, clearly seen, or a headland
of the mainland with its rich soil that rests upon the sea?"

　　The goddess flashing-eyed Athena answered him: "You are
a fool, sir stranger, or you come from far off if you ask about
this land. It is not *so* without a name—very many know it,
230　both those who live toward the dawn and the rising of the sun
and those who live behind, toward the misty darkness.
It is a rugged island not fit for raising horses, but not so poor,

though it is narrow. It grows prodigious quantities of wheat,
and there is wine. The rain never fails, nor the blooming dew.
It is a good land for pasturing goats and cattle. There is forest 235
everywhere and watering holes that last all year round.
For this reason, stranger, the name of Ithaca has reached even Troy,
which they say is a land far from ACHAEA."

                       So she spoke,
and much-enduring godlike Odysseus was glad, and he rejoiced
in the land of his fathers as he heard the words of Pallas Athena, 240
the daughter of Zeus who carries the goatskin fetish. And he spoke
to her words that went like arrows, but he did not speak the truth—
he took back the words he was about to speak, always storing up
cunning thoughts in his breast: "I have heard of Ithaca,
even in broad CRETE,° far over the sea. Now I have come here 245
with my goods. And I left just as much with my children when I fled,
because I killed the dear son of Idomeneus,° Orsilochos
swift of foot, who surpassed in fleetness of foot all men who live
by labor.° For he wanted to take away all the loot from Troy
on account of which I had suffered so many pains in my heart, 250
passing through the wars of men over the savage waves.
I was unwilling to show favor to his father and be his father's
aide in the land of the Trojans but, well, I commanded other men
of my own!

    "Yes, lying in ambush near the road with my companions,
I hit Orsilochos with my bronze spear when he came from the fields. 255
A very dark night covered the sky, and no man saw us. I took
away his life in secret. When I had killed him with my sharp bronze,
I went immediately to a ship and begged passage from some brave
Phoenicians, and I gave them booty enough to satisfy their hearts.
I urged them to take me aboard and let me off at PYLOS or in shining 260
ELIS, where the Epeians are strong. But the power of the wind
drove them away, much against their will. They did not intend
to deceive me. Driven from there, we arrived here during the night.
We eagerly rowed into the harbor. There was no thought of a meal,

---

245 *Crete:* For some reason, Odysseus always claims to be from Crete in the series of false tales that begins here.
     Perhaps the philosophical paradox was already current in a folk saying: "All Cretans are liars," spoken by a
     Cretan: The statement refutes itself (first credited to the Cretan Epimenides, sixth century BC). If all
     Cretans are liars, then so is Odysseus, as in fact he is.

247 *Idomeneus:* Leader of the Cretan contingent at Troy.

249 *labor:* The theme of the murderer forced to go on the run is common in Homer. The same was true of an
     anonymous Aetolian (*Od.* 14); of Theoklymenos (*Od.* 15); of Medon (*Il.* 13); of Lykophron (*Il.* 15); and
     of Patroklos (*Il.* 23).

265 although we badly needed food. All of us then went forth
from the ship just as we were and lay down. Exhausted,
sweet sleep came upon me. They took my things from
the hollow ship and placed them down where I lay on the sand.
Then they boarded their ship and went off to SIDON ° with its
270 dense population. And I was left here, sorrowing in my heart."

 So Odysseus spoke, and flashing-eyed Athena, the goddess,
smiled, and she stroked him with her hand and changed her shape
to that of a woman, beautiful and tall and skilled in glorious
handiwork. And she said to him words that went like arrows:
275 "He would have to be clever and thievish in fact if he was going
to surpass you in every sort of trickery, even if a god encountered you!
Rascal! Fancy-thinker! Insatiate for deception!—you were *not* about
to leave off your deceiving tales and thievish lies even in your own country,
which you love from the bottom of your heart. But come, let us not
280 speak further of these things. We are, the two of us, masters of deception.
Of mortals, you are by far the best in counsel and in telling tales,
and I among all the gods am famous for my wisdom and devices.

 "And yet you did not recognize Pallas Athena, daughter of Zeus—
me!—who stands beside you in all your troubles, and watches over you!°
285 I made you welcome to all the Phaeacians. And now I have come
here so that we can weave a plan. We need to hide the treasure
that the noble Phaeacians gave you on your way home—this also
thanks to my design and will. I also want to tell you about the trials
you are fated to endure in your own well-built house. But you must
290 bear it, I'm afraid, and not tell anyone, neither man nor woman, that
you have returned from your wanderings. You must suffer your trials
in silence and submit yourself to the abuse of men."

            In answer
to her the resourceful Odysseus said: "It is a hard thing, goddess,
for a mortal just coming along to recognize you, even if he knows
295 a lot—why, you take on whatever shape you wish! I know this well,
that you were friendly to me when we sons of the Achaeans
fought at Troy. But once we sacked the high city of Priam
and went off in our ships, and some god scattered the Achaeans,
I never saw you a single time, O daughter of Zeus. Nor did I notice
300 you coming onto my ship so that you might fend off danger

---

269 *Sidon:* A city in Phoenicia often mentioned in Homer. Oddly, he never mentions Tyre, in Homer's day the
   preeminent Phoenician town. Homer may reflect a Bronze Age tradition, when Sidon was great.

284 *watches over you:* In fact, this is the first time that Athena has appeared in her own person to Odysseus.

FIGURE 13.2   Odysseus and Athena.   The goddess meets Odysseus on Ithaca. He wears a cloak and carries a spear. Athena wears the goatskin fetish (*aegis*), which has a gorgon's head in the middle. She points to the ground as if to say, "This is Ithaca."

from me. No, but always I wandered with a heart torn by misery,
until the gods released me from evil. At least until you cheered me
in the rich land of the Phaeacians with your words and personally
led me into the city.° But now I beg of you, by your father—
305 I don't think I have arrived in clear-seen Ithaca! I have been diverted
to some other land. I think you speak with mocking words to trick
my mind. Tell me if truly I have come to the land of my fathers?"

The goddess flashing-eyed Athena then answered him:
"Always the same, that is the mind within you! And so I cannot
310 leave you in misery, because you are courteous and have a keen
intelligence, and you are shrewd. Another man, returning from
a long journey, would want to go to see his children and his wife
in his halls, but you are not yet minded to know and discover
anything until you have made trial of your wife, who sits as of old
315 in her halls and, ever sad, pours down tears as the nights and days
wear on. I never doubted this, but knew in my heart that you
would return home after losing all your companions. But I was
not willing to quarrel with my father's brother Poseidon, who
bore wrath in his heart, angry that you blinded his beloved son.°

320 "But come, I will show you the land of Ithaca, so that you may
become familiar with it. This is the harbor of Phorkys, the Old Man
of the Sea. Here is the long-leafed olive at the head of the harbor.
Near it is the lovely misty cave, sacred to the nymphs, who are
called Naiads. This is a high-roofed cave where you were accustomed
325 to make abundant sacrifice of perfect victims to the nymphs. Over there
is MOUNT NERITON, clothed in forest."

So speaking the goddess scattered
the mist, and the land appeared. Then much-enduring godlike Odysseus
was glad, and he rejoiced in his land, and he kissed the earth,
the giver of grain. Immediately he prayed to the nymphs, raising
330 high his hands: "O Naiad nymphs, daughters of Zeus, I never thought
I would behold you again, but now—hail, with loving prayers!
And I will give gifts as in earlier times, if the daughter of Zeus,
the gatherer of loot, allows with a good will that I continue to live
and that my son grow to be a man."

Then flashing-eyed Athena
335 spoke to him: "Take courage! Don't worry about any of this.

---

304 *into the city*: In fact Odysseus did not recognize her.
319 *son*: The Cyclops Polyphemos.

FIGURE 13.3 A Naiad. A roman floor mosaic from an immense villa in central Sicily, perhaps once owned by an emperor. This nymph is simply a young woman, nude from the waist up, wearing a pretty necklace and elaborately coiffured. Above her head is a sea urchin to emphasize her association with water. Late third to early fourth century AD, Piazza Armerina, Sicily.

But let us put the treasures in a nook in the wondrous cave
right away, so that they may remain safe for you. Then let us
take thought for what will be our best course of action."

So speaking, the goddess went into the misty cave
340 and searched out hiding places in the cave while Odysseus
brought all of his loot nearby, the gold and the unwearying
bronze and the finely made woven things that the Phaeacians
had given him. All these things he carefully laid away,
and Pallas Athena, the daughter of the god who carries
345 the goatskin fetish, placed a stone over the door. Then the two
of them sat down near the trunk of the sacred olive tree
and took thought for how they would kill the insolent suitors.

The goddess flashing-eyed Athena was first to speak:
"Son of Laërtes, of the line of Zeus, resourceful Odysseus,
350 consider how you will place your hands on the shameless
suitors who for three years have been lording it in your halls,
wooing your godlike wife and giving bridal-gifts. She, ever
mourning for your homecoming in her heart, gives hope
to all and promises to each man, sending them messages.
355 But her mind dwells elsewhere."

The resourceful Odysseus spoke
in reply to her: "Yes, I might have perished in my halls
by the same fate as Agamemnon, the son of Atreus, if you,
O goddess, had not told me all this! But come, let us weave
a plan so that I might take vengeance on them. Now, you yourself
360 stand by my side and infuse me with a bold power, such as
when we loosed the shining veil of Troy.° If you were to stand
beside me with a similar enthusiasm, O flashing-eyed one,
I would fight against even three hundred men—with you,
revered goddess, if you would come to my aid with an eager heart."

365 Then the goddess flashing-eyed Athena answered:
"I will be very much with you when we are busy with
this work. And I think that many of the suitors who devour
your substance will spatter the vast earth with their blood
and their brains. But come, I will make you unrecognizable
370 to all mortals. I will shrivel the beautiful flesh on your
supple limbs, I will destroy the blond hair on your head
and cover you in a rag so disgusting that seeing a man

---

361   *veil of Troy*: To "loose the veil" is to rape a woman, hence "sacked the city."

wearing it would make you shudder. I will dim your two
eyes that before were so beautiful, so that they appear
a disgrace to the suitors, and to your wife and child   375
whom you left behind in your halls.

              "But first of all you must go
to the pig herder who watches over your pigs and who
is kindly disposed toward you, who loves your child
and the prudent Penelope. You will find him tending
the swine who are grazing beside the rock of Korax   380
and the fountain of Arethousa,° eating acorns that satisfy
the heart and drinking black water, which cause the rich
fat on pigs to increase. Stay there and sit by his side
and question him about all matters while I go to Sparta,
land of beautiful women, to summon Telemachos,   385
your beloved son, O Odysseus. For he went to the house
of Menelaos in Lacedaemon with its broad dancing places
in order to learn news of you, if you were still alive."

   The resourceful Odysseus answered her: "Why didn't
you just *tell* him? You know everything! I suppose you wanted   390
Telemachos to suffer sorrow, wandering over the restless sea,
while others devoured his substance . . ."

              Then the goddess
flashing-eyed Athena said: "Don't worry overmuch
about him. I myself guided him so that he might achieve
a noble reputation by going there. He does not labor,   395
but he sits at his leisure in the house of the son of Atreus,
and immeasurable good cheer is set before him. It is true
that young men lie in wait for him in their black ship,
hoping to kill him before he reaches the land of his fathers.
But I don't think it will happen. The earth will cover many   400
of the suitors who devour your substance before that happens!"

   So speaking to him, Athena touched Odysseus
with her wand. She shriveled his beautiful skin on his supple
limbs, and she transformed his blond hair, and around all
his limbs she put the skin of an aged old man. She dimmed   405
his two eyes that before were so beautiful, and around him
she put other clothes—a disgusting cloak and shirt,

---

381 *...Arethousa*: Korax means "Raven's Rock," perhaps a common name; there were eight springs named
    Arethousa in ancient Greece, the name of a nymph.

ragged and filthy, befouled with dirty smoke. She put
the large skin of a swift deer with all its hair removed
410 around him. She gave him a staff and a wretched pouch,
riddled by holes, hung by a twisted cord.

                                             Having taken
counsel together in this fashion, they parted. And the goddess
went to shining Lacedaemon to find the son of Odysseus.

BOOK 14. *Odysseus in the Pig Herder's Hut*

Odysseus went up from the harbor by the rough path,
up through wooded terrain and through the heights
to where Athena had told him the excellent pig herder
lived, Eumaios, the one who cared about Odysseus' well-being
more than any other of the slaves that Odysseus had   5
acquired. He found him sitting in the forehall of his house.
His courtyard wall was built high in a place of wide
outlook, and a fine and great courtyard it was, with an
open space around it. The pig herder had built it himself
for his king's pigs during his absence. He built it unbeknownst   10
to his queen and to old man Laërtes—built it of huge stones
and bramble bush all along the top. Outside he had driven
stakes in for its whole length in both directions, huge
and set close together, which he made by splitting oak
logs and using their black cores.   15

                  Inside the courtyard wall
Eumaios built twelve sties beside one another, beds for the pigs,
and in each fifty wallowing swine were confined, all females
for breeding. The boars slept outside, being fewer
in number, for the godlike suitors were forever eating them
and diminishing their number. The pig herder was always   20
sending in the best of all the fatted hogs, which numbered
three hundred and sixty. Four dogs slept at their side,
savage like wild beasts, that the pig herder had raised,
a leader among men.

                  Eumaios was fitting boots around his feet,
cutting the skin of an ox of fine color. Three of his boys   25
were off with the droves of swine—one here, one there—
and a fourth he had sent to town to take a porker to the arrogant
suitors, under compulsion, so that they could sacrifice it
and stuff themselves with flesh. Suddenly the baying hounds
saw Odysseus and they ran at him, barking. But Odysseus   30
cleverly sat down and dropped the staff from his hand.
And even then in his own farmstead he would have suffered
cruel hurt, but the pig herder swiftly ran up on his fast feet

and hurried through the doorway, dropping the hide from
35 his hand. He called aloud and drove the dogs this way
and that with a shower of stones.

He spoke to his king and said:
"Old man, the dogs all of sudden nearly tore you apart,
and then you would have poured reproach upon me. Yes,
and the gods have already given me plenty of sorrow!
40 I wait here, mourning and grieving for my king,
who is like a god, while I rear fat swine for others to eat.
In the meanwhile he wanders through the people and cities
of men of foreign speech, wanting food—if in fact
he is till alive and sees the light of the sun. But come,
45 let us go into my hut, old man, so that you can tell me
where you are from and what sorrows *you've* suffered,
once we've satisfied our spirit with bread and wine."

So speaking, the excellent pig herder led the way
into the hut, and he made Odysseus sit down, and he spread
50 out thick brushwood and on top he spread the skin
of a shaggy wild goat, large and hairy, on which he
himself used to sleep. Odysseus was glad to receive it,
and he spoke a word and addressed him: "May Zeus
and the other deathless gods give you whatever you want,
55 stranger, because you have received me so courteously."

Then—O Eumaios my pig herder!°—you answered him:
"Stranger, it would not be right for me to dishonor one
even more foul than you, for all strangers and beggars
are under the protection of Zeus. A gift, though small,
60 is welcome from the likes of us. This is the lot of slaves—
ever in fear when young masters rule over them. Truly
the gods have bound up the homecoming of that man.
He loved me best and he would have given me possessions—
a house and a parcel of land and a woman whom many
65 wooers wanted—all those things that a kindly king gives
to his slave who has worked hard for him, one whose
work a god makes to prosper even as my own labor
prospers, to which I give every effort. My king would
have rewarded me abundantly if he had grown old here.

---

56 *my pig herder*: Sometimes Homer addresses his own characters (for example, Menelaos and Patroklos in
the *Iliad*) when he wants to heighten the feeling in a scene, but it is hard to see exactly why he does so with
Eumaios (fifteen times). Perhaps for metrical reasons!

But he perished—would that Helen and all her family   70
had perished utterly! Surely she has loosed the knees
of many men. He, too, went on account of Agamemnon's
honor to Ilion with its beautiful horses so that he might
fight the Trojans."

       So speaking, Eumaios quickly bound
up his shirt with his belt and went off to the sties where   75
the tribes of pigs were penned. Selecting out two,
he brought them in and butchered both. He singed them
and cut them up into pieces and threaded the meat on spits.
Once he had roasted the pig, he placed the hot pieces
on the spits in front of Odysseus, and he sprinkled white   80
barley on top. He mixed honey-sweet wine in a bowl
made of ivy wood.

       Then sitting down opposite Odysseus,
Eumaios urged him to eat his food, and said: "Eat now,
stranger, such food as is available to slaves—piglets!
The suitors eat the big porkers, caring nothing in their hearts   85
for the anger of the gods, nor having any pity. But the blessed
gods do not love dirty deeds. They honor justice and the good
deeds of men. Even malicious and dangerous men who go
to a foreign land where Zeus grants them booty, and they fill
their ships with it and go off home—even on the hearts   90
of such men falls the powerful fear of the anger of the gods.

  "But these men must know something, or they've heard
some voice of a god declaring the sad death of that man.
They are not willing to court as it *should* be done, nor do
they go off to their own houses, but take their ease, arrogantly   95
consuming our substance. There is no sparing of it! Every day
and night that comes from Zeus they sacrifice not one,
nor two alone. They arrogantly draw off the wine and waste it.
Truly, the king's substance was great past telling. No man
had so much neither on the black mainland, nor here   100
on Ithaca itself. Nor did twenty men have wealth so great.

  "Here, I will tell you a story. He has twelve herds of cattle
on the mainland, and as many of sheep, and as many droves
of pigs. Foreigners and his own herdsmen pasture as many
wide-roaming herds of goats there. Here, too, he grazes   105
eleven wide-roaming herds of goats on the far end of the island.
Trusty men watch over them. Every day one of these drives up his

herd of fat goats for the suitors to select from, whichever seems
the best. In the meanwhile I watch over and protect these
110   pigs and I pick out the best of the swine and send it to them."

So he spoke as Odysseus eagerly ate the flesh and greedily
drank the wine in silence, for he was sowing the seeds of evil
for the suitors. And when he had eaten and satisfied his spirit
with food, then the pig herder filled the bowl full of wine
115   from which he himself drank, and he gave it to Odysseus.

Odysseus took it and rejoiced in his heart, and he spoke
words that went like arrows: "My friend, who was it who
bought you with his wealth? He must have been rich and powerful,
just as you say. You say that he perished for the sake
120   of Agamemnon's honor—tell me, maybe I know him,
if he is so great. Zeus and the other gods will know if I've seen
him and could give you some news, for I have wandered far."

Then the pig herder, a leader among men, answered:
"Old man, no wanderer could come here and persuade
125   his wife or his son. Wanderers, wanting attention, often
will lie at random, and they have no interest in telling
the truth. When a wanderer comes to Ithaca he always goes
to my mistress and tells her a lot of foolishness. She receives
him well and entertains him and questions him about
130   everything, and in her sorrow tears fall from her lids,
as is the way with a woman whose husband has died
in a far land. You too, old man, would quickly fix up
a story, if someone were to give you a cloak and a shirt
for clothes. As for the king, dogs and swift birds are likely
135   to have ripped the flesh from his bones, and his breath-soul
has long ago left him. Or the fish ate him in the sea, and his
bones lie on the shore wrapped in thick sand. For he has perished
someplace. Sorrow is made for all his friends, but for me
most of all. I shall never find another king equally gentle,
140   no matter how far I go, not even if I went to the house
of my father and my mother where I was begotten
and they raised me. But it is not for them so much that
I grieve, although I long to see them with my own eyes
and to be in the land of my fathers. No, it is my desire
145   for *Odysseus* who is gone that seizes me . . . I speak his name
with awe, sir stranger, though he is not present, for he
loved me exceedingly and cared for me in his heart.
I call him 'my dear master,' though he is not here."

Much-enduring godlike Odysseus then said: "Friend,
because you altogether deny that he will ever come again,   150
and insist on this, and your heart has lost its trust—let me tell
you no idle prattle, but swearing an oath: Odysseus
will return! And let me be rewarded for bringing good news.
Give me a cloak and a shirt, some fine clothes. Before that,
no matter how great is my need, I will not take anything.   155
Hateful to me as the gates of Hades is that man who gives
into poverty and tells a prattling tale. Zeus be my witness
above all the gods and this hospitable table—and the hearth
of blameless Odysseus to which I have come—all things
shall come to pass of which I speak. Odysseus will return   160
here during this very month, as the old moon wanes
and the new appears. He shall return and take vengeance
on whomever has shown disrespect to his wife and his
glorious son."

And you answered him, O Eumaios my pig herder:
"Old man, I shall not pay you any reward for bringing good news.   165
Nor will Odysseus come home again . . . But drink up in peace,
and let us think of other things. Do not recall these things to my mind,
for the spirit in my breast is most grieved when someone mentions
my valiant king. As for your oath—we will let it be.

"Of course I really hope that Odysseus *will* come,   170
and Penelope does too, and old man Laërtes, and Telemachos
who is like a god. It is for Telemachos, the son whom
Odysseus begot, that I grieve constantly. The gods made him
spring up like a sapling, and I thought that among men
he would be as good as his own beloved father, admirable   175
in appearance and stature. But some one of the deathless ones,
or some man, has wrecked his wise heart within: He went to holy
Pylos to gather news about his father! In the meanwhile,
the noble suitors wait for him in ambush as he returns home.
The line of godlike Arkesios° might disappear, nameless, from Ithaca. 180
But, let us leave him now. He may be taken, or he may escape,
if the son of Kronos stretches out his hand over him.

"Come now, old man, tell me about *your* troubles,
and do tell me truly so that I may know—who are you
among men, and where do you come from? Where is your city   185
and your parents? On what kind of ship did you come here?

---

180 *Arkesios:* The father of Laërtes, about whom nothing else is known.

How did sailors bring you to Ithaca? Who did they say they were?
For I don't think you came here on foot!"

Resourceful Odysseus
said in reply: "Well then, I will tell you these things as they are.
190 Would that there were sufficient food and sweet wine
here in your hut for the time we'd need, so that we could
dine in peace while others did the work—then we
might go on for a full year and still I would not finish
telling you all the troubles of my spirit, all the things
195 that I suffered through the will of the gods.

"I come from
the line of broad CRETE, the son of a wealthy man.
Many other children were raised and begotten in the house,
true sons of a lawful wife, but my mother was a whore,
a bought woman. Still, Kastor the son of Hylax,° my father,
200 respected me as if I were one of his legitimate sons.
He was honored at that time among the Cretans as if
he were a god because of his estate, his wealth, and his
glorious sons. But then the fates of death carried him off
into the house of Hades. The arrogant sons divided up
205 his wealth and they cast lots for it. They gave me little,
but allotted me a place to live. I took to wife a woman
from a house with many possessions, winning her through
my qualities. I was no weakling, nor did I flee in battle.
Now all that is gone, but still I think that, seeing the stubble,
210 you can guess what once was the grain. For great misery
has overcome me.

"But at that time Ares gave me courage,
and Athena power, to break the ranks of men. When
I chose the best men to go into an ambush, sowing
the seeds of evil for the enemy, my proud spirit never did
215 have foreboding of death, but by far the first I leaped on
the enemy and killed with my spear anyone who ran away.
Such I was in war! Field work didn't appeal to me, nor taking
care of a house and raising glorious children. Oared ships
were always dear to me, and war, and the well-polished
220 spear, and arrows—terrible things which to others are entirely
shivery. To me was dear what the god placed in my heart—
for different men are disposed to do different things.

---

199 *Kastor son of Hylax*: "beaver" son of "barker."

"Before the sons of the Achaeans went off to Troy, I had
nine times led men and seafaring ships against foreign men,
and luck had favored our undertakings. I would choose what   225
pleased me out of the loot and I obtained much more by lot.
My house quickly grew rich, and I became feared
and honored among the Cretans. But when Zeus whose voice
is heard from a long ways off devised that hateful journey
that loosened the knees of many men, then the Cretans   230
urged me and famous Idomeneus to lead the ships to Ilion.
There was no way to refuse, because the voice of the people
was strong. There the sons of the Achaeans fought for nine years,
and on the tenth we sacked the city of Priam and went off
in our ships. But a god scattered the Achaeans, and Zeus   235
the counselor had evil plans for wretched me.

                    "On Crete I spent
one month taking delight in my children and in my wedded wife
and in my possessions. Then my spirit impelled me to sail
to Egypt with my godlike companions, once I had prepared
my ships with care. I fitted out nine ships, and the people   240
gathered quickly. Then for six days my trusty companions
feasted, for I had provided many animals to sacrifice
to the gods and to make fine meals for themselves. On the seventh
day we embarked from broad Crete and sailed with a north
wind sharp and strong.   245

                "We were carried on easily as if
going downstream. No harm came to any of my ships,
and we sat there unscathed and free from sickness as the wind
and the helmsmen guided the ships. On the fifth day
we reached fair-flowing Egypt and moored our curved
ships in the river Egypt.   250

                "I ordered my trusty companions
to remain beside the ships and to guard them, and then I
sent out scouts to go to places of outlook. But giving
in to violence, obedient to their own might, they
plundered the very beautiful fields of the Egyptians
and they drove off the women and the little children   255
and killed the men. Quickly the cry went up to the city.
Hearing the shouting, the people came forth at the break
of dawn. They filled all the plain with foot soldiers
and chariots and the flashing of bronze. Zeus who delights
in the thunderbolt sent an evil panic among my companions,   260

and no one dared to stand his ground. Evils stood around us
everywhere. They killed many of us with their sharp bronze,
and others they led up to their city, alive, to work for them
by compulsion. But Zeus placed this thought in my breast—
265 would that I had died and met my fate there in Egypt!
For much pain awaited me.

              "Promptly I took the well-made
helmet off my head and the shield from my shoulders,
and let the spear fall from my hand. I went toward
the car of the king and took holds of his knees and kissed
270 them. He lifted me up and took pity on me. Placing me in
his chariot, he took me, weeping, to his home. Yes!
many rushed at me with their spears, desiring to kill me—
for they were very angry—but he fended them off,
for he had regard for the anger of Zeus, the protector
275 of strangers, who more than any grows angry over evil deeds.

  "There I remained for seven years, and I gathered
much wealth from the Egyptian men. For they all gave to me.
But when the eighth year circled around, a Phoenician
man came, practiced in deception—a rat! who had already
280 done too much evil among men. He succeeded in persuading
me through his cunning, and he took me with him until
we arrived in Phoenicia, where his house and his possessions were.
I stayed with him there for a full year. But when the months
and the days came to completion as the year rolled around
285 and the seasons came on, he put me on a seafaring ship
to LIBYA, having told me a bunch of lies that I should
transport freight with him—but, in truth, so that when we got
there he could sell me for a high price!

              "I went with him
on the ship, under compulsion, for I was suspicious. He ran
290 with North Wind blowing sharp and strong through
the open sea, south of Crete. But Zeus devised destruction
for the men. When we had left Crete, no other land appeared,
but only sky and sea. Then the son of Kronos set a black cloud
over the hollow ship, and the sea grew dark beneath it.
295 Zeus at the same time thundered and threw his bolt at the ship,
and the whole of it spun around when struck. It filled with
sulfur smoke and everybody fell from the ship. Like gulls
they were carried on the wave around the black ship,
for the god had taken away the day of their homecoming.

"But Zeus placed the huge mast of the blue-prowed ship   300
in my hands, so that I might again escape destruction,
though I was in sore distress. Wrapped around it,
I was carried by the hostile winds. I was borne for nine days,
but on the tenth black night a great wave rolled me onto
the land of the THRESPROTIA.   305

                    "The warrior Pheidon,° chief
of the Thresprotians, took care of me and did not ask for
ransom. His dear son had come upon me, overcome with cold
and exhaustion. He raised me by the hand and led me
to the house of his father. And he covered me in a cloak
and shirt as clothing. It was there that I learned about Odysseus. 310
The chief said that he had welcomed and entertained him
as a guest-friend as he was going home to the land of his fathers,
and he showed me all the wealth that Odysseus had gathered—
bronze and gold and iron worked with great labor. It would
easily feed his children after him up until the tenth generation, 315
so much treasure lay in the house of the king. The chief said
that Odysseus had gone to DODONA to hear the advice of Zeus
from the high oak of the god, whether he should return to the rich
land of Ithaca, after being gone for so long, in the open
or in secret.° Pheidon swore to me myself, while pouring out   320
a drink offering in the house, that the ship was launched
and the men ready who would transport him to the beloved
land of his fathers.

                 "But then Pheidon sent me off first, for there
happened to be a ship of Thresprotian men setting out
for DOULICHION,° rich in wheat. So he asked them to give   325
me safe passage to the chieftain Akastos.° But they devised
an evil plan concerning me, that I might come to the end of misery!
When the seafaring ship was far out to sea, the Thresprotians
at once thought to bring about the day of my slavery.
They stripped off my clothes, my cloak and shirt, and threw   330

---

305   *Pheidon*: Otherwise unknown.

320   *in secret*: In an ancient oracle at the remote location of Dodona in northwest Greece, the storm-god spoke
       through the rustling of the leaves of an oak tree, an ancient cult, perhaps imported from northern Europe
       where the oak was sacred to the storm-god (Thor). At Dodona, Zeus's consort was Dionê (the feminine of
       "Zeus"), not Hera.

325   *Doulichion*: The identity of Doulichion ("long-island") is much debated, but probably it is LEUKAS. Fifty-
       two suitors came from Doulichion, more than from any other island.

326   *Akastos*: A leader on Doulichion, otherwise unknown.

FIGURE 14.1 Odysseus. This statue was found in the famous shipwreck off the islet of
ANTICYTHERA in 1900–1901 by sponge divers. Excavated with the assistance of the Greek Royal
Navy, the shipwreck was the first major underwater archaeological expedition. The wreck is dated
approximately 60–50 BC, but this is probably a Roman marble copy from the first century BC from a
Greek bronze original of the fourth century BC. Bearded, wearing a traveler's cap, the badly eroded
statue is probably dressed in rags.

an evil rag and shirt around me—putrid, the very garments
that you see before you now. When it was evening,
we came to the plowed fields of clear-seen Ithaca.
Then they bound me in the well-benched boat—
tightly, with a well-twisted cord, and they themselves   335
got out on the shore of the sea to prepare a hasty meal.
But the gods themselves easily undid the bonds, and covering
my head in the tattered cloak° I slid down the rudder oar
and dropped myself to the sea. I rowed with both hands,
swimming, and soon I was out of the water and away   340
from them. I went up to where there was a thicket
of leafy wood, and I crouched, then lay down. They went
back and forth looking for me, yelling loudly. But when there
appeared to be no advantage in looking further, they went
back again into their hollow ship. The gods easily hid me.   345
They led me and brought me to the farmstead of a man
of knowledge. It was my fate still to live."

                         Then you answered him,
O Eumaios my pig herder: "Alas, wretched stranger,
you have stirred my spirit deeply by telling me all these
details of the suffering and wanderings that you have endured.   350
But I don't think you have spoken rightly in this, and you
shall not persuade me in what you say about Odysseus—
but what is the point, being in such a state, for you to lie
to no purpose?° I myself know well about the homecoming
of my king—that he was very much hated by all the gods   355
because they did not subdue him among the Trojans,
or in the arms of his friends, once he had wound up
the thread of war. Then all the Achaeans would have
heaped up a tomb for him, and he would have left great
fame behind for his son. But as it is, spirits of the storm   360
have snatched him up without glory. I spend my time
in seclusion with the pigs, and I do not go into the city
unless the wise Penelope urges me to come, when news
arrives from somewhere. Then men sit around the bearer
and ask about every little thing, both those who grieve   365
for their absent king and those who happily devour
his substance without recompense.

---

338   *cloak*: To keep it dry as he swam ashore.

354   *to no purpose*: That is, "no need to lie about Odysseus, because you don't need such lies to win my good
     graces."

                              "But it is not my way
to ask questions or to inquire. Once, a man from
Aetolia came here, one who thoroughly deceived me.
370 He had killed a man and wandered over the wide earth
when he came to my house. I received him warmly. He said
he had seen Odysseus among the Cretans at the house
of Idomeneus, fixing up his ships that storm winds had
damaged. And he said that he would return during the summer
375 or the fall, bringing much wealth, and with his godlike
companions. And you, old man who has suffered so much,
because some spirit has brought you to me—do not try
to please me with lies, and do not try to enchant me! I do not
respect you and offer you entertainment for such reasons,
380 but from respect for Zeus the protector of strangers. That's why
I take pity on you."

              The resourceful Odysseus answered him:
"Well, you have a disbelieving spirit in your breast, if by swearing
I cannot convince you or persuade you. But come, let us make
an agreement, and the gods who hold Olympos may be our
385 witnesses in times to come. If your king returns to his house,
you will give me a cloak and a shirt as clothing and send me
to Doulichion, where I would like to go. And if your king
does not come as I predict, set your slaves on me and throw
me from a great cliff, a warning to any other beggar about
390 speaking deceptively!"

              The good pig herder said in reply:
"Stranger, surely I would win great glory and repute
among the people, not only now but in the future, if I should
kill and take away the spirit of a man whom I brought
into my hut and entertained! Oh, then I would pray to Zeus
395 the son of Kronos with a ready heart!

                              "But now it is time
for a meal. I hope that my comrades will soon be here
so that they can prepare a tasty meal."

                          Thus they spoke
to one another, and the pigs and the other pig herders came
close to the hut. The men shut up the pigs in the sties where they
400 were used to sleeping. A loud clamor arose from the pigs
as they were penned, and the good Eumaios called
out to his companions: "Bring up the best of the swine so that

we can butcher it for the stranger who comes from afar.
We too shall gain some benefit from it, who have suffered
misery for so long on account of these white-toothed pigs   405
while *others* devour our labor without compensation."

So speaking Eumaios split wood with the pitiless bronze.
The other pig herders brought in a very fat five-year old pig.
They stood it next to the hearth, nor did the pig herder forget
about the deathless ones—he had an understanding heart!   410
First he cut off some hair from the head of the white-toothed pig
and threw it in the fire, and he prayed to all the gods
that wise Odysseus would come home to his house.
Then he stood up and hit the boar with an oak club left over
from when he split the kindling. The breath-soul of the pig   415
flew off. The others cut the boar's throat and they singed him.
Quickly they cut him up. The pig herder cut pieces of raw flesh
from all the limbs as first offerings and he laid them
in the rich fat. These he cast into the fire after sprinkling
them with grains of barley. They cut up the rest and placed   420
it on spits. They roasted the meat carefully and then pulled
it off the spits and placed it in a pile on platters. Then
the pig herder gathered himself up to carve, for he knew well
in his heart what was fair. Cutting up the meat, he divided it
into seven portions. The one part he set aside with a prayer   425
for the nymphs and for Hermes, the son of Maia, and the others
he distributed to each. He honored Odysseus with the long
back-bone of the white-tusked boar, and he glorified the spirit
of the king.

Speaking to him the resourceful Odysseus
said: "May you be as dear to father Zeus, O Eumaios, as you   430
are to me, because you have honored me with a good portion,
although I am in such a state."

And you answered, O Eumaios
my pig herder: "Eat, my bad-luck stranger, and take pleasure
in these things such as I have. The god gives one thing
and withholds another, as he wishes in his heart. For he can   435
do all things."

He spoke and sacrificed the first-cut pieces
to the gods that are forever. After pouring out a drink-offering
of flaming wine, he placed the cup in the hands of Odysseus,
sacker of cities, then he sat down before his own portion.

440 Mesaulios,° whom the pig herder had purchased out of his own
funds when his king was gone, without the knowledge
of his mistress and old Laërtes, served them bread. Laërtes
bought Mesaulios with his own funds from the Taphians.°

And so they put forth their hands to the good food that lay
445 before them. When they had put the desire for drink
and bread from them, Mesaulios took away the food.
Sated with bread and meat, they wanted to go to their rest.
The evil night came on without a moon, and Zeus rained
the whole night through, and West Wind, always rainy,
450 blew strong.

Odysseus spoke to all in the hut, testing
the pig herder, to see if perhaps he would take off his cloak
and give it to him, or he would urge another of his companions
to do the same because he loved him so much: "Hear me now,
Eumaios and all you other companions, and I will tell you
455 a boasting tale. This crazy wine bids me, which impels
a man even though sensible to want to sing and to laugh
softly, and it makes him stand up and dance and say something
better left unsaid. But because I have already cried out,
I will conceal nothing. I wish I had the strength of my youth
460 and were as steady as when we made ready our ambush
and went under Troy. Odysseus and Menelaos, the son
of Atreus, were the leaders and I was third in command,
for they had so ordered it. But when we came to the city
and the steep wall, we lay in the thick brushwood around
465 the city, in the reeds and the swamp, crouching beneath
our armor. Evil night came on and North Wind fell, frigid,
and snow came down on us from above like hoar frost—
bitter cold!—and ice formed on our shields. All the others
had cloaks and shirts and they slept in peace, their shoulders
470 wrapped in their shields. But I had thoughtlessly left
my cloak with my companions when I set out, because
I did not think that I would be cold without it. Thus I came
along, having only my shield and my shining apron.°

---

440 *Mesaulios:* "yardman," probably made up for this scene.

443 *Taphians:* A mysterious but probably historical people, perhaps from northwest Greece, known for their
piratical habits. Athena/Mentes in *Od.* 1 claimed to be a Taphian.

473 *apron:* It is unclear what part of equipment the *zoma*, "apron" (?) really was.

"But when it was the third part of the night, and the stars
had turned their course, then I asked Odysseus, nearby,
nudging him with my elbow in the ribs. And he heard me
immediately: 'Zeus-nurtured son of Laërtes, resourceful
Odysseus, I shall soon no longer be among the living.
The cold overcomes me, for I have no cloak. Some god fooled
me into coming out with only a shirt . Now there
is no escape.'

    "So I spoke, and he then devised this plan
in his heart, such a man he was both to make plans
and to fight. Speaking in a low voice, he said: 'Be quiet
now! One of the other Achaeans will hear you.' Then he
raised his head up on his elbow and he said: 'Listen to me,
friends—a divine dream has come to me while I was
asleep. We have come very far from the ships and I wonder
if there would be somebody to tell Agamemnon, son of Atreus,
the shepherd of the people, that he should order more
men to come up from the ships?'

        "So he spoke,
and Thoas, the son of Andraimon,° immediately got up
and threw down his purple cloak, and he went off running
toward the ships. I gladly lay down in his garment.
Then Dawn arose in her seat of gold. I wish that I had
the strength of a young man and that I was yet steadfast!
Then one of the pig herders in your farmstead would give
me a cloak—both from friendship and from respect
for a brave man. As it is, they give me no respect
because I am covered in foul garments."

            Then you said in reply,
O Eumaios my pig herder: "Old man, you have told
a good story, and in no way have you so far spoken
a word amiss or unprofitably. Therefore you shall not
lack for clothing nor for anything else of what is suitable
for the much-suffering suppliant that we come across—
at least for now. But when dawn comes you will again
have to set those same rags about you. For we have
no cloaks or shirts to change into here, but each man
has one only. When the dear son of Odysseus comes,

475

480

485

490

495

500

505

---

491   *Thoas, the son of Andraimon*: From AETOLIA, mentioned several times in the *Iliad*.

he himself will give you a cloak and a shirt as clothing,
510 and he will send you off to wherever you want to go."

So speaking he stood up, and he placed a bed near
the fire, and he put the skins of sheep and goats on top.
And there Odysseus lay down. The pig herder threw
a great thick cloak about him that he kept as a change
515 of clothing whenever a savage storm should arise.

And so there Odysseus slept, and the young men slept
around him. But the pig herder did not like to sleep
there away from his pigs, and he made ready to go outside.
Odysseus rejoiced that Eumaios was taking such good
520 care of his substance while he was away. First Eumaios
threw a sharp sword in a belt around his strong shoulders,
then he put on a very thick cloak that wards against the wind,
and he took up the fleece of a big fat goat and a sharp spear
to fend off dogs and men. He went off to sleep with the white-tusked
525 pigs beneath a hollow rock, a shelter against North Wind.

BOOK 15. *The Pig Herder's Tale*

Pallas Athena came to LACEDAEMON of the broad dancing
places to remind the glorious son of great-hearted Odysseus
of his return home, and to urge that he go. She found
Telemachos and the fine son of Nestor sleeping in the forehall
of bold Menelaos. Gentle sleep had overcome the son   5
of Nestor, but sweet sleep did not hold Telemachos.
Throughout the ambrosial night thoughts of his father
kept him awake.

        Standing near him flashing-eyed Athena
spoke: "Telemachos, you can no longer go wandering around
far from your home, abandoning your wealth and leaving   10
such insolent men in your house. I hope that they do not
devour all your wealth, dividing it up, while you return
from a pointless trip. But urge Menelaos, good at the war cry,
to send you off as quickly as possible, so that you can find your
blameless mother still at home. Her father and her brothers   15
already encourage her to marry Eurymachos, who has
exceeded all the other suitors in the presents he's given, and he has
poured on the bridal-gifts. I hope that she does not carry off
some treasure from your house against your will! For you know
the way it is with a woman—they want to give everything   20
to the man who marries them, and she no longer remembers
nor asks about the children she has earlier borne, nor her dear
husband who has died.

        "When you get to ITHACA, put all your
possessions in charge of the female slave who seems best
to you, until the gods show you a noble wife. I will tell you   25
something else, and do take it to heart: The best of the suitors
have set up a deliberate ambush in the strait between Ithaca
and rugged SAMÊ. They want to kill you before you get home,
but I don't think that they will. The earth will cover many a one
of the suitors who devour your substance! So sail your well-built   30
ship out beyond the islands,° and sail at night as well as by day.

---

31 *islands*: It is not clear what islands are meant, perhaps Ithaca and Samê (= KEPHALLENIA).

One of the deathless ones who guards you and watches over you
will send a breeze behind your ship. When you arrive
at the nearest shore of Ithaca, send your ship with all your
35 companions up to the city, but you yourself go first to the dwelling
of the pig herder, he who looks out for your pigs. He is well
disposed to you. Spend the night there. Send him up to the city
to tell the shrewd Penelope that you have returned safely
from Pylos."

        So speaking, she went off toward high Olympos.
40 Telemachos stirred the son of Nestor from his sweet sleep
by nudging him with his heel, and Telemachos said: "Wake up,
Peisistratos, son of Nestor! Yoke our single-hoofed horses
beneath the chariot so that we may get going."

                    Peisistratos the son
of Nestor said: "Telemachos, we cannot set out on our journey
45 through the misty night, though we are eager to do so. Soon
it will be dawn. Wait until the warrior son of Atreus, Menelaos
famous for his spear, shall bring gifts and place them in our car
and send us on our way with kindly words. For a guest-friend
remembers all his days another guest-friend who has received
50 him and entertained him."

           So he spoke and promptly the golden-throned
Dawn rose up. Menelaos, good at the war cry, came close to them,
rising from the couch that he shared with Helen, whose hair
is beautiful. When the dear son of Odysseus saw him, he hastened
to put his shining shirt over his skin, and the prince threw
55 a cloak around his strong shoulders, and he went forth.

                  Standing next
to him, Telemachos, the dear son of godlike Odysseus, said:
"O Zeus-nourished Menelaos, son of Atreus, leader of the people,
please send me now to the land of my fathers. For my spirit
urges me to go home."

        Menelaos, good at the war cry, replied:
60 "Telemachos, I will not hold you for long if you want to go
home. I would scorn any man who received guests and loved
too much, even as one who hated too much. Measure
is best in all things. It is equally evil to send a guest-friend
on his way who wishes to stay, and to hold back someone

who wants to go. It is right that you love a guest-friend   65
when he is with you, and when he wants to go—send him
on his way!

"But stay until I bring beautiful gift-tokens
and place them in your car so your own eyes see them,
and until I tell the women in the house to prepare a meal
from the abundant store within. It is a double advantage—   70
it brings glory, and honor, and profit—that the traveler
has a good meal before he journeys over the wide
and boundless earth. If you want to travel through HELLAS
and mid-ARGOS, well then, I can follow along myself!
I will yoke horses for you, and lead you to the cities   75
of men. Nor will anyone send us off empty-handed,
but everyone will give us something to carry off, either
some kind of tripod all made of bronze, or a cauldron,
or two mules, or a golden cup."

Then shrewd Telemachos
said in reply: "O Zeus-nourished Menelaos, son of Atreus,   80
leader of the people, I would rather go to my home
immediately, for when I came here I did not leave
a guardian over my possessions behind. I would rather
that I not perish myself in looking for my father,
or that some fine treasure disappear from my halls."   85

When Menelaos good at the war cry heard this,
he ordered his wife and the female slaves to prepare
a meal in the halls from the abundant supply
that was within. Eteoneus, the son of Boethoös,
who lived nearby, arose from his bed and drew   90
near. Menelaos, good at the war cry, urged him
to kindle a fire and to roast some meat. Hearing
the command, he obeyed.

Menelaos himself went down
into his fragrant treasure-chamber, not alone, but Helen
and Megapenthes° went with him. When they came to where   95
the treasure lay, the son of Atreus took up a cup
with two handles, and he gave a silver bowl to Megapenthes
to carry. Helen came up to the trunks where the highly

---

95 *Megapenthes:* "mournful," Menelaos' only son, by a slave-girl.

embroidered robes were that she herself had made.
100 Helen—a goddess among women!—took up one and bore
the robe away, the one most beautiful and elaborately
embroidered and largest—it shone like a star! It lay at the bottom,
beneath all the others.

They went out through the house
until they came to Telemachos. Light-haired Menelaos
105 spoke to him: "Telemachos, may Zeus, the long-thundering
husband of Hera, bring your homecoming to pass, just as
you desire. I will give you the most beautiful and valuable
of the gifts that lie stored up in my house. I will give you
a wine mixing-bowl, well made, entirely of silver, and it has
110 gold running around the lip, a work of Hephaistos.
The warrior Phaidimos,° king of the Sidonians, gave it to me,
when his house gave me shelter as I returned home. And now
I want to give it to you."

So speaking the warrior son of Atreus
placed the two-handled cup in his hands. Strong Megapenthes
115 brought the shining mixing-bowl made of silver and placed it
in front of Telemachos. And there Helen, whose cheeks
are beautiful, stood by, carrying the gown in her hands,
and she said: "I give you this gift, my child, in memory
of the hands of Helen, for the day of your wedding
120 that you long for. Your bride may wear it. Until then
store it in the house under the care of your dear mother.
And may you reach your well-built house and the land
of your fathers with joy."

So speaking, she placed the gown
in his hands, and he gladly received it. The warrior
125 Peisistratos took the gifts and lay them in the wicker basket
in the car, and he gazed at them with wonder in his heart.
Light-haired Menelaos led them to the house, and then they
sat down on chairs and benches. A female attendant brought
up a beautiful golden vase and poured out water over a silver
130 basin to wash their hands. She drew up a polished table
beside them. The honored housewife brought in bread
and placed it down, and many other sorts of food, drawing
them freely from her store. The nearby son of Boethoös

---

111 *Phaidimos*: "famous," made up for this story.

cut up the meat and distributed the portions. The son
of glorious Menelaos poured out wine.   135

                        Then all set
their hands to the good food before them, and when
they had put from them the desire for drink and food,
Telemachos and the good son of Nestor yoked the horses
and got in the decorated car. They drove out
of the forecourt and the echoing portico. Light-haired   140
Menelaos, the son of Atreus, went after them, holding
in his right hand honey-sweet wine in a cup of gold so that
they could pour drink-offerings before setting out.

    Menelaos took his stand in front of the horses
and bidding them goodbye he said: "Farewell, my young men!   145
And give my greeting to Nestor, the shepherd of the people.
He was gentle as a father to me when the sons of the Achaeans
made war at Troy."

                    The prudent Telemachos answered:
"Truly, O Zeus-nurtured one, we will tell him all that you say
when we arrive. And if, when I come home to Ithaca,   150
I find Odysseus in my house, I will tell him that I received
from you every kindness before I departed, bringing with me
many fine treasures."

                    When Telemachos said this, a bird
flew up on the right, an eagle carrying a huge white
goose in its claws, a tame goose from the farmyard,   155
and the men and women followed behind, shouting.
But the eagle flew near them, then soared off to the right
in front of the horses. When the men saw this, they rejoiced,
and the spirit in their breasts was cheered. Peisistratos,
the son of Nestor, began to speak: "Tell me what   160
you think, O Menelaos, nourished by Zeus, leader
of the people—did a god send this omen for the two
of us, or for you yourself?"

                    So he spoke, and war-loving
Menelaos pondered how he might rightly adjudge
the matter. But Helen with the long gown anticipated   165
him with this word: "Listen to me, and I will prophesy
how the deathless ones put it in my heart, and how I think

it will turn out. As the eagle seized the goose that was raised
in the pen, coming from the mountains where its family
170 and its parents are, even so Odysseus, having suffered
many evils and wandering far, will come home and take
revenge. Or he is even now at home, and he sows the seed
of evil for all the suitors."

The shrewd Telemachos then said:
"May Zeus the loud-thundering husband of Hera make this
175 come out so. Then, home in Ithaca, I will worship you as if
you were a god!"

He spoke and struck the two horses
with the lash. Quickly they sprang forth, eager to get
to the plain beyond the city. All day long they shook the yoke
they carried around their necks. The sun went down
180 and the roads were covered in shadow. They came
to PHERAI and the palace of Diokles, the son of Ortilochos,
whom ALPHEIOS bore as a child.° There they spent
the night, and Diokles set before them the entertainment
appropriate to strangers. When early born Dawn appeared,
185 they yoked the horses and mounted the decorated car.
They drove out of the forecourt and the echoing portico.
Peisistratos touched the horses with the lash to get them
going, and, not unwilling, they sped onward. Quickly they
came to the steep city of Pylos.

And then Telemachos addressed
190 the son of Nestor: "Son of Nestor, will you make me a promise
and keep it? We are guest-friends of old because of our fathers'
friendship, and we are of the same age. This journey of ours
has strengthened our oneness of heart. Do not lead me past
my ship, O Zeus-nourished one, but leave me there! I fear
195 that the old man will hold me back against my will,
wishing to entertain me. But I need get home quickly."

So he spoke, and the son of Nestor thought about how he
might promise and then keep the promise. As he thought it over,

---

182 *as a child*: They stayed here on the journey out to Sparta (Book 3). Presumably Pherai is modern Kalamata.
Homer seems to know nothing about the high and rugged Mount Taygetus between the plain of Sparta and
the plain of Messenia. Alpheios is the longest river in the Peloponnesus (about 90 miles). It is one of the
rivers diverted by Herakles in later tradition to clean the stable of Augeias.

this seemed to him to be the best course. He turned his horses
toward the swift ship and the shore of the sea. He offloaded
the beautiful gifts into the stern of the ship, the cloth and the gold
that Menelaos had given.

Urging Telemachos on, Peisistratos
spoke words that went like arrows: "Now get on board quickly,
and order all your companions to board too, before I get home
and tell the old man we've arrived. For I know this well
in my breast and heart—the spirit of that man is so proud that
he will not let you go, but he will come here himself to invite
you to remain. And I don't think his efforts will be in vain.
Otherwise he will be very angry, in spite of everything."

So speaking, Peisistratos drove his horses with their
beautiful coats back to the city of the Pylians. He swiftly
arrived at the palace. But Telemachos ordered his companions
in a commanding tone: "Load up all the gear, my comrades,
into the black ship, then let us all get on board so that
we may be on our way."

So he spoke, and they listened
and obeyed. Quickly they got on board and sat down
before the thole pins.

Telemachos was still busy praying
and sacrificing to Athena beside the stern of the ship
when a man came up from a far land—fleeing from Argos
for killing a man. He was a prophet, a descendant of Melampous,
who used to live in Pylos, the mother of flocks. Melampous
was rich among the Pylians, and he lived in a fancy house.
Then he went to the land of strangers, fleeing his fatherland
and fleeing great-hearted Neleus, the noblest man alive,
who for a full year had been taking much of Melampous' wealth
by force. Then he was bound in tight bonds in the house
of Phylakos, suffering pain on account of the daughter of Neleus,
and due to a heavy blindness of heart° that the terrible
Erinys laid upon him. But he avoided fate and drove off
the deep-lowing cattle from Phylakê to Pylos. He took vengeance

200

205

210

215

220

225

230

---

228 *blindness of heart:* The Greek is *atê,* which means the irrational inability to see the consequences of one's
behavior.

FIGURE 15.1 Oïkles, Amphiaraos, Eriphylê, Alkmaion, and the necklace. Oïkles, father of the prophet Amphiaraos, greets his son who rides in a chariot off to the war at Thebes, driven by a man named Baton. Amphiaraos, on the far right, wears a helmet and carries a shield. On the left side of the picture stands Eriphylê, her name written over the horses' heads. She holds the fateful necklace (a sort of ring) in her hand, and in front of her is written the word "necklace" (HORMOS). Her son, the child Alkmaion, stands before her. Because Amphiaraos knew he would die at Thebes, he instructed Alkmaion to kill Eriphylê for forcing him to go to the war, which Alkmaion does. Athenian black-figure jug, c. 575–550 BC.

on godlike Neleus for his awful deed and brought the woman
home to be his brother's wife.° Melampous himself went
then to the land of strangers, to horse-pasturing Argos.
For it was his destiny to live there as king over the many
Argives. In Argos he took a wife and built a high-roofed house,   235
and he begot Antiphates and Mantios, powerful sons.
Antiphates begot great-hearted Oïkles, and Oïkles begot
Amphiaraos, rouser of the people, whom Zeus, carrier
of the goatskin fetish, and Apollo loved with every kind of love.
But Amphiaraos did not reach the threshold of old age: He perished   240
in the war against Thebes on account of a woman's gifts.°
His sons were Alkmaion and Amphilochos. Now Mantios
begot Polypheides and Kleitos, but Dawn of the golden
throne snatched away Kleitos because of his beauty
so that he might dwell among the gods. Apollo made   245
Polypheides to be a proud prophet, by far the best among
men after Amphiaraos had died. Angry with his father,
he had gone to Hyperesia,° where he lived and prophesied
to all mortals. He had a son, who was named Theoklymenos,
who stood just then at the side of Telemachos.   250

                                  Theoklymenos came
up to Telemachos when he was making drink-offerings beside
the fast black ship, and Theoklymenos spoke to him
words that went like arrows: "My friend, because I come
upon you as you are sacrificing in this place, I implore you
on behalf of the sacrifices and the spirits, and on your own   255
life and that of the comrades who follow you—tell me

---

232   ... *wife*: Homer also refers to the story of Melampous in Book 11 (line 281), and it must have been well
known to his audience. We can piece it together: Melampous' brother, Bias, wooed Pero, the daughter
of the Pylian King Neleus, but Neleus insisted on a bride-price of some cattle, then in the possession of a
Thessalian prince, Iphiklos, or his father Phylakos. Melampous went up to Thessaly to get the cattle but was
caught and put in prison. Melampous was a prophet and could understand the speech of beasts and birds.
He overheard the woodworms talking overhead, saying that the beam they were working on was about to
fall through. Melampous told a servant who told Phylakos. Melampous escaped just before the building fell
in, and Phylakos was so impressed by Melampous' powers that he said he would give him the cattle if only he
cured his son Iphiklos of his impotence. This Melampous did, took the cattle, and drove them to Pylos.
Then Bias married Pero. The role of Erinys in Homer's version—the underworld spirit that punishes false
oaths and offenses against the family, but here the sender of a heavy "blindness of heart" (*atê*)—is not clear.

241   *woman's gifts*: Polyneikes, leader of the expedition of the Seven Against Thebes, persuaded Eriphylê, the
wife of Amphiaraos, to force her husband to go to Thebes by giving her a special necklace. Amphiaraos had
earlier agreed to allow Eriphylê to decide any dispute between him and Adrastos, the king of Argos, who in
this case wanted Amphiaraos to join the campaign. Amphiaraos, being a prophet, knew that he would die if
he went to the war.

248   *Hyperesia*: In the northern Peloponnesus, according to the *Iliad*'s Catalog of Ships (*Il.* 2).

truly what I ask, and do not conceal the truth: Who are
you among men? Where do you come from? What is
your city and who are your parents?"

The shrewd Telemachos
260 said in reply: "Well, stranger, I will tell you straight out.
I am from the Ithacan race, and my father is Odysseus—
if he ever existed! As it is, it looks as though he has died
a terrible death. For that reason I have assembled
my companions and come in my black ship to find out
265 about my father, who has been gone for so long."

Theoklymenos, with the form of a god, then said
to him: "Even so, stranger, have I fled from the land
of my fathers because I killed a man—a relative. He has
many brothers and family in horse-pasturing Argos,
270 and they are powerful among the Achaeans. Escaping
death and black fate at their hands, I am on the run.
I'm afraid that it is my fate to be a wanderer among men.
But let me go on your ship, because I come here
in flight as your suppliant. I fear that they will kill me,
275 and I think they are in pursuit."

The shrewd Telemachos
then said: "If you want to go on our well-balanced ship,
I won't prevent you. So come aboard. We will entertain you
in our home as well as we can."

So speaking he took
from Theoklymenos the bronze spear and he lay it on the deck
280 of the ship curved at both ends, and Telemachos boarded
his seafaring ship. He sat down in the stern and he made
Theoklymenos sit down beside him. The crew loosened
the stern lines. Telemachos ordered that his companions
take hold of the tackle, and they quickly obeyed. They raised
285 up the mast of fir and stood it in the hollow mast-post,
and they tied the ropes that held the front of the sail,
and they hauled up the white sail on ropes made of twisted
oxhide. Flashing-eyed Athena sent a favorable wind,
which blew rushing through the sky, so that the ship went
290 on its way as quickly as could be, running over
the salt water of the sea. They ran past Krouni and Chalkis,°

---

291 *Krouni and Chalkis:* These seem to be the names of small streams.

with their beautiful streams. The sun went down and all
the ways were covered in shadow. They came near to Pheai,°
driven on by the wind of Zeus, and on past shining Elis,
where the Epeians are strong. From there he steered   295
for the sharp islands,° wondering whether he would
escape death or be captured.

                In the meanwhile, Odysseus
and the good pig herder were dining in the hut. Beside
them the other men were dining too. But when they had
put from themselves the desire for drink and food,   300
Odysseus spoke to them, putting the pig herder to the test,
to see if he would still entertain him in a kindly fashion,
and whether he would urge him to remain there in the hut,
or whether he would send him up to the city: "Hear me
now, Eumaios, and all you other men! At dawn tomorrow   305
I want to go up to the city and do some begging, so that
I won't be the ruin of you and your companions. Now give
me some good advice and give me a good leader who will
take me there. Otherwise I will have to wander through
the city, to see if somebody will give me a cup of water   310
and a loaf of bread. And once I get to the house of godlike
Odysseus, I would give my message to the wise Penelope,
and I would like to mix with the insolent suitors to see
if they will give me a meal—they have ten thousand
delicacies! I would do them good service on the spot,   315
in any way they wished.

            "And I will tell you this,
and you take it to heart and listen: Thanks to Hermes
the messenger, who lends grace and glory to the works
of all men, there is no one who could compete with me
in service, in heaping up a fire or in splitting dry kindling,   320
or in carving the meat and roasting it and in pouring
out the wine—all the things that base men do for those
of a better class."

          Then you answered him, O Eumaios
my pig herder: "Oh, my stranger, why has this thought
come into your mind? I think that you want to get   325
yourself killed there if you enter the crowd of the suitors,

---

293 *Pheai*: Location unknown.

296 *sharp islands*: Not clear what islands are meant, or why they are "sharp."

whose arrogance and violence reaches the iron heaven!
The serving-men of these men are not like you, but they
are young men, well-dressed in cloak and shirt, and their
330 heads are bright and their faces handsome, the men
who serve them. Their polished tables are filled with bread
and meat and wine.

          "But stay—no one resents your presence,
not I and not another of the comrades who are with me.
And when the dear son of Odysseus comes, he will give
335 you a cloak and a shirt as clothes to wear, and he will
send you wherever your heart desires."

                 The much-enduring
godlike Odysseus answered him: "I hope that you will
be as dear to Zeus, Eumaios, as you are to me, for you
have put an end to my wandering and my grievous hardship.
340 There is nothing worse for any mortal man than to be homeless.
But men endure terrible pains because of their ruinous
bellies when wandering and sorrow and pain come
on them. Because you hold me here and bid me wait
until your master comes, tell me—what about the mother
345 of godlike Odysseus and his father, whom he left
on the threshold of old age? Are they still alive beneath
the rays of the sun, or have they died and gone to the house
of Hades?"

     Then the pig herder, the leader of the people,
said: "Well, stranger, I will tell you exactly. Laërtes still lives,
350 but he prays to Zeus every day that the spirit in his limbs
may waste away in his halls. For he is in utter grief
for his son who is absent, and for his wise wedded wife,
who saddened him when she died and brought him
to a premature old age. She died of grief for her bold son,
355 a terrible death. I hope that none of those who live around
here as my friends and do me kindness may die such a death.
So long as she was alive, though suffering, for so long
it was a pleasure to me to make inquiries and to ask about
her health. It was she who reared me along with Ktimenê
360 with the long gown, her noble daughter, whom she bore
as her youngest child.° She reared me together with her,

---

361 *youngest child*: The only time that we hear about a sister of Odysseus. He was an only son.

and she honored me only slightly less than her. But when
the two of us reached the maturity that is so longed for,
they gave her over to island Samê to marry, and accepted
countless bridal-gifts for her. Odysseus' mother gave a cloak   365
and shirt to me, very beautiful clothes. Then binding
sandals beneath my feet, she sent me to the fields.
Still, she loved me the more, from her heart. But now
I lack all these things.

        "Yet the blessed gods make prosper
the work that I pay attention to. From these things   370
I eat and drink, and give to respectable strangers.
But I hear nothing pleasant from my queen, neither
word nor deed. Evil has fallen on the house—those insolent men!
Servants greatly desire to speak in the presence of their
mistress and to learn of everything, and to eat and drink,   375
and then to carry something off to the field—such things
warm the heart of any servant."°

        The resourceful Odysseus
then said in reply: "I see that when you were just a tyke,
pig herder Eumaios, you wandered far from the land
of your fathers and your parents. But come, tell me this   380
and tell it truly, whether your city with its broad streets
was sacked, where your father and revered mother lived?
Or whether, while your were alone with your pigs and cows,
pirates took you into their ships and sold you to the house
of this man, who gave a good price for you?"   385

        Then the pig herder
spoke, the leader of the people: "Stranger, because you ask
me these things and make inquiry, you can listen in silence,
you can enjoy yourself. Drink your wine as you sit here!
These nights are enormously long. There is a time to sleep,
and a time to take pleasure in listening. There is no need   390
to take our rest before it is time. There is trouble in too
much sleep. As for the others, if their heart and spirit urges—
go outside and sleep! At dawn, they can eat and follow
after our king's swine. But let us two take our pleasure,
drinking and eating in the hut, recalling to mind each other's   395
horrendous experiences. Later on, a man delights in his

---

377 *servant*: That is, in ordinary circumstances, such relaxed relationships would characterize the servants'
    lives, but not under the present dangerous conditions.

earlier pain, a man who has suffered much and wandered far.
I will tell you this because you ask and make inquiry.

"There is an island called Syriê, if you have heard of it,
400 above Ortygia, where are the turnings of the sun.° It is not
so very filled with people, but it is a good place, rich in herds,
rich in flocks, with abundant grapes for wine, and much wheat.
Famine never comes to this land, nor does any other hateful
disease fall on wretched mortals. And when the tribes of men
405 grow old throughout the city, Apollo of the silver bow comes
with Artemis, and attacking with his gentle arrows, he kills them.
There are two cities there, and all the land is divided between
them. My father was chief over both—Ktesios son of Ormenos,
a man like the deathless ones.

"Phoenician men came
410 there, famous for their ships—the rats! They had countless
trinkets in their black ship. There was a Phoenician
woman in my father's house, beautiful and tall and skilled in fine
handwork. The crafty Phoenicians tricked her. First,
one of them had sex with her as she was washing clothes
415 beside the hollow ship. This beguiles the mind
of a woman even when she is upright. Then he asked her
who she was and where she came from. At once she showed
him the high-roofed home of my father, and she said:
'I am from Sidon, rich in bronze. I am the daughter
420 of Arybas, awash in wealth. But Taphian pirates snatched
me up as I was coming from the fields, and they brought
me here and sold me to the master of this house. And he
paid a big price.' Then the man who had slept with her
in secret answered: 'Well, do you want to come with us
425 and go back home so that you can see the high-roofed
house of your father and mother? For surely they are still
alive and remain wealthy.' Then the woman answered:
'I would like this very much, if you sailors will swear
to me an oath that you will take me safely home.' So she
430 spoke, and they all swore the oath just as she asked.

"When they had sworn and finished the oath, then the woman
spoke to them again and answered: 'Now you must keep

---

400   … *turnings of the sun*: Probably a confused reminiscence of inland Syria, here thought to be an island.
Ortygia, "quail-island," is often equated with DELOS in the central Cyclades, or with a small island in the
harbor at SYRACUSE in SICILY. But there is no support in Homer for these identifications.

quiet. Let no one of you speak to me if he happens on me
on the road or at the fountain. Let's not let anyone
go to the house and tell the old king. If he get suspicious,   435
he will bind me in tight bindings and he will put you to death.
So keep my words in mind, and hasten on the bartering
of your wares. When your ship is filled with goods,
then quickly send a message up to the house. I will also
bring whatever gold is at hand. And I would give you still   440
something else as my fare. I am in charge of the son
of the house in these halls. Such a clever child, and he always
runs with me outside the house. I would bring him on board,
and he will bring you a high price wherever you might take him
for sale among people of strange speech.'   445

        "So speaking,
she went off to the beautiful palace. The Phoenicians remained
for a whole year among us, amassing by trade many goods
in their hollow ship. But when the hollow ship was laden
for their return, then they sent a messenger to the woman.
A man filled with cunning came to the house of my father   450
bearing a gold necklace, strung with amber beads in between.
The female slaves and my revered mother were handling it
and examining it and offering a price when he nodded
to her in silence. Once he had nodded, he went off to the hollow
ship, and the Phoenician woman took me by the hand   455
and led me outside. In the forehall she found the cups
and table of the diners who waited on my father. They had
gone off to the council and the place of the people's debate.
Quickly she hid three cups in her bosom and carried them out,
and I in my folly followed along.   460

        "The sun went down,
and the ways were filled with shadows. We went speedily,
moving fast, and came to the famous harbor and the swift
ship of the Phoenicians. They put us both aboard.
They embarked and sailed over the watery paths. Zeus sent
a favorable breeze behind us. We sailed for six nights and days,   465
but when Zeus the son of Kronos brought us the seventh day,
Artemis, holder of arrows, struck the woman, and she fell
into the hold the way a seagull plunges. They threw her
out to be the prey of seals and fishes, and I was left, stricken
in my heart. The wind and water bore us to Ithaca   470
where Laërtes bought me from his own wealth. And thus
I first saw this land with my eyes!"

Zeus-nourished Odysseus
answered him with this word: "Eumaios, truly you stir
the spirit in my breast, telling me all these thing that you
475 have suffered. But Zeus has given you good to go along with
the bad, though you have suffered much—because you have
come into the house of a kingly man who gives you food and drink
aplenty, and you live the good life. But I come here having
wandered through the many cities of men."

Thus they spoke
480 to one another. Then they lay down to sleep, but not for long—
for only a little while, because Dawn soon appeared
seated on her lovely throne.

In the meantime the comrades
of Telemachos, were drawing into the shore. They furled the sail,
and quickly took down the mast. They rowed with their oars
485 to the place of anchorage, threw out the mooring-stones,
and tied up the stern. Then they themselves got out on the shore
of the sea. They prepared their meal, and mixed the flaming
wine. But when they had put the desire for drink and food
from themselves, the shrewd Telemachos began to speak
490 to them: "Now, you row the black ship to the city while
I go to the fields and the herdsmen. I will come to the city
toward nightfall, after I have seen my farms. At dawn
I will provide, as wages for your trip, a good feast of meat
and sweet wine."

Theoklymenos, like a god, then spoke to him:
495 "Where, dear child, should I go? To whose house shall I go,
of those who rule in rocky Ithaca? Or should I go straight
to your mother's house and yours?"

The shrewd Telemachos
answered him: "Ordinarily I would urge you to come
to my house, for there is no lack of entertainment for strangers,
500 but under present conditions it would not be wise for you.
I will be away, and my mother will not see you. She does
not often appear to the suitors in the hall, but works at her loom
in an upper room, apart from them. But I will tell you
of another man to whom you might go—Eurymachos,
505 the glorious son of shrewd Polybos, whom now the Ithacans
look up to as if he were a god. He comes from the *best* social
class and wants especially to marry my mother, to have

the prize of Odysseus. Nevertheless, only Zeus the Olympian
who lives in the sky knows if, before the marriage,
he will fulfill an evil day for the suitors."   510

                                   As he spoke, a bird flew
on his right hand, a hawk, the swift messenger of Apollo.
The hawk had in his talons a pigeon that he plucked with
his beak, and feathers floated to the earth between the ship
and Telemachos.

                        Theoklymenos, calling him apart from
his companions, took Telemachos by the hand and spoke   515
these words: "Telemachos, not without a god has this bird
flown on the right hand. I recognized right away that it was
a bird of omen. There is no family more suited for the chieftainship
than yours in the land of Ithaca, for you are the strongest."

    The clever Telemachos then answered: "May your word   520
come to pass, O stranger. Then you would soon recognize
my friendliness to strangers and receive gifts from me
such that someone meeting you would call you blessed."

    Telemachos spoke and then he addressed Peiraios, his noble
companion: "Peiraios, son of Klytios, you of all my companions   525
who followed me to Pylos are the most obedient to my words.
Take, then, this stranger to your house and entertain him
in a kindly way and give him honor until I come."°

    Peiraios, famous for his spear, replied to him: "Telemachos,
even if you stay here a long time, I will care for him. There will be   530
no lack of what is due a guest."

                           So speaking Peiraios went on board
the ship, and he gave orders to his companions to get aboard
and to loosen the stern ropes. They sat down at the thole pins
and made ready to embark. But Telemachos bound
his beautiful sandals beneath his feet and took up his mighty   535
spear with its point of bronze from the deck of the ship.
Then they pulled in the stern ropes and, pushing off, they sailed

---

528   *until I come*: Telemachos' advice to Peiraios does not so much correct his early instructions to Theoklyme-
      nos about going to the house of Eurymachos as show that he had never seriously meant the stranger to go to
      the house of Telemachos' worst enemy.

to the city, just as Telemachos, the dear son of godlike
Odysseus had ordered.

His feet swiftly carried Telemachos
540 forward until he came to the court where his countless
pigs were, among which his good pig herder customarily
slept, who held such a high opinion of his masters.

BOOK 16. *Father and Son*

Meanwhile in the hut, Odysseus and the good pig herder
had started a fire and at dawn were making ready their
breakfast. They had sent forth the herdsmen with the droves
of swine, but the baying hounds fawned around Telemachos
and did not bark as he drew near. Godlike Odysseus noticed   5
this, the groveling of the dogs, and he heard the sound
of footsteps.

He at once spoke to Eumaios words that
went like arrows: "Eumaios, I think that one of your
companions has arrived here, or somebody you know,
because the hounds are not barking. But they grovel around   10
the man. I hear the sound of his footsteps."

But he said no more,
because his own dear son stood in the doorway. Stunned,
the pig herder sprang up, and the jugs in which he was
busy mixing the flaming wine fell from his hands. He came
up to his king, he kissed his head and both his beautiful   15
eyes and his two hands, and a hot tear fell from Eumaios.
As when a father is overjoyed to welcome back his son
in the tenth year who has gone to a far land, an only son
and well beloved for whom he has cried again and again, even
so did the good pig herder clasp godlike Telemachos in his arms   20
and kiss him all over, as if he had escaped from death.

Complaining, Eumaios spoke words that went like arrows:
"You have come, Telemachos, my sweet light! I thought
I would never see you again after you had gone to Pylos
in your ship. But come inside my house now, my dear child,   25
so that I might delight my heart in looking at you, recently
arrived from foreign lands. For you do not often come
to the fields to visit the herdsmen, but you remain in town.
I suppose that is pleasing to your heart, to watch over
the ruinous crowd of the suitors!"   30

The shrewd Telemachos
answered him: "That's right, old friend. But I have come
here on account of *you*, so that I might see you with
my own eyes and find out whether my mother is still
in the house, or has some other man married her while
35 the couch of Odysseus lies open without bedding, covered
with foul spider webs."

The pig herder, a leader
of men, answered him: "Yes, she remains in your house
with an enduring heart. The nights and days wear away
with agonizing pain as she weeps."

So speaking, Eumaios
40 took the bronze spear from Telemachos, and Telemachos
went inside, crossing over the stone threshold. As he
drew near his father, Odysseus rose from his seat to give
him a place, but Telemachos stopped him from his side
and said: "Sit, stranger, and I will find someplace else
45 to sit in our farmstead. There is a man here who will
set up a chair."

So he spoke, and Odysseus went back
and sat down. And for Telemachos the pig herder strewed
green brush beneath and a fleece above, and there the dear
son of Odysseus sat down. The pig herder set out platters
50 of roast meats left over from the meal the day before,
and quickly he piled bread in baskets, and mixed honey-sweet
wine in an ivy-wood bowl. Then he himself sat down
opposite godlike Odysseus. They reached forth their hands
to the good things that lay before them.

And when they
55 had put all desire for drink and food from themselves, then
Telemachos addressed the good pig herder: "My friend,
where does this stranger come from? How did sailors
bring him to Ithaca? Who did they say they were?
For I don't think that he came here on foot!"

Then you said
60 in reply, O Eumaios my pig herder: "Well, child, I will tell
you the whole truth. He says that he comes from a family
on broad Crete. He says that he has wandered through
many cities of mortals in his travels, for some spirit

decreed that such be his fate. Now he has run away from
a ship of the Thresprotians and come to my farmstead.   65
I hand him over to you. Do what you want. He declares
himself to be your suppliant!"

Then the shrewd Telemachos
said in reply: "Eumaios, what you have said greatly
troubles me. How shall I receive this stranger in *my* house?
I am young and I cannot rely on my power to defend myself   70
against a man if he becomes angry without any reason.
My mother is of two minds—whether she should stay
with me and take care of the house, respecting the bed
of her husband and the voice of the people, or whether
she should follow whoever is the best of the Achaeans   75
who courts her in her halls, and offers the most gifts.

"But as for the stranger, because he has come to your
house, I will give him fine clothes, a cloak and a shirt,
and I will give him a sword sharp on both sides,
and sandals for his feet. And I will send him wherever   80
his heart and spirit desires to go.

"And if you are willing,
keep him here in your steading and take care of him.
I will send the clothing here, and plenty of bread to eat
so that he doesn't ruin you and your companions. I would
not let him go up to the house to mix with the suitors!   85
They are consumed by a wicked insolence. I fear that they
would mock him, which would pain me greatly. It is so hard
for one man to achieve anything against many, no matter
how strong he is, for they are much stronger."

Then the much-enduring good Odysseus answered: 90
"My friend, I think it is right that I make an answer.
My heart is torn when I hear you say these things—
that these suitors devise mad deeds in the hall in spite
of you, who are so good a man. Do you allow yourself
to be so abused? Or do the people throughout the land   95
hate you, following the voice of some god? Or do you
blame your brothers, on whom you can depend as helpers
in a fight even if a great quarrel should arise? In my
present state of mind, I wish I were as young as the son
of blameless Odysseus—or that I were Odysseus himself!   100

Then some foreigner might cut the head from my shoulders
if I did not become a fearsome scourge to those men
once I entered the hall of Odysseus, the son of Laërtes.
And if they should defeat me by their numbers, I being all
105 alone, I would still prefer to die cut down in my own halls
than to see these filthy deeds every day—strangers mistreated,
and the female slaves rudely dragged through the beautiful
rooms, and wine spilled all around, and men recklessly eating
my bread without limit—a bad business that will never end."

110   The shrewd Telemachos answered: "Well, stranger,
I will tell you straight out. By no means do all the people
hate me, nor are they angry with me. Nor do I blame
my brothers, on whom you can depend as helpers in a fight,
even if a great clash should arise. You see, the son
115 of Kronos has made this house to run in a single line:
Arkeisios fathered a single son, Laërtes, and he fathered
Odysseus as his only son, and I was Odysseus' only child.
He left me behind in his halls and had no joy in me.
Now countless evil men inhabit the house. Many are among
120 the most powerful men in the islands of DOULICHION,
SAMÊ, and wooded ZAKYNTHOS—and as many as lord it
over rocky Ithaca—just this many court my mother and they
devour our store! And she won't refuse the hateful marriage,
nor is she able to bring it to fulfillment. Meanwhile
125 they eat up all my substance. Soon they will bring me to ruin!

     "But all this lies on the knees of the gods. Now, my dear
Eumaios, go up quickly and tell the prudent Penelope that I am
safe and that I have returned from Pylos. I will stay here.
Then come back. Only tell *her*! I don't want any other
130 of the Achaeans to find out, for many of them wish me ill."

     In reply you said, O Eumaios my pig herder: "I know,
I have the same thoughts. You are giving orders to one
who already understands. But come, tell me this and tell it
straight out—shall I go with the same news to the wretched
135 Laërtes, who in the past, though greatly mourning Odysseus,
still watched over his own fields and ate and drank with
the slaves in the house whenever the spirit moved him?
But now, ever since you went off in your ship to Pylos,
they say that he has not eaten nor drunk as before, nor does
140 he watch over the fields, but in agony and complaint
he sits weeping, and the flesh shrivels around his bones."

Then shrewd Telemachos answered him: "It is bitter,
but we must let it go, though we feel bad about it. If anything
could be had for the wishing, we would first of all choose
the day of my father's homecoming! No, after giving   145
your message, come back here, and do not go over the fields
looking for Laërtes. Tell my mother to send out the slave who
is the housemaid as soon as possible, in secret. *She* can tell
the old man."

  Thus he spoke and roused the pig herder.
Eumaios took his sandals in his hands, and binding them   150
beneath his feet he went off to the city. Athena was aware that
Eumaios the pig herder had left the farmstead, and she
came near in the form of a beautiful, tall woman, learned
in glorious handiwork. She stood outside the door of the hut,
revealing herself to Odysseus alone. Telemachos did not   155
see her or notice her standing before him, for the gods
are not visible to everyone. But Odysseus and the dogs
saw her, and the dogs did not bark but, whining, they slunk
to the other side of the farmstead. The goddess nodded
with her brows, and godlike Odysseus saw it. He came   160
out of the house, past the large wall of the court,
and he stood before her.

  Athena spoke to him, saying:
"Zeus-nourished son of Laërtes, resourceful Odysseus,
reveal your scheme to your son *now*, and don't hold back.
When you have planned how you will bring death   165
and fate to the suitors, you can go up to the famous city.
I myself will not be apart from you for long. I am eager
for the fight!"

  She spoke, and then Athena touched him
with her golden wand. First she put a well-washed cloak
and a shirt around his chest, and she made him tall   170
and youthful. Once again he grew suntanned, and his cheeks
filled out, and the beard around his chin grew dark.
After doing this, she went away, and Odysseus went
into the hut. His son was astonished to see him!

  In fear he turned his eyes aside, thinking he was some god.   175
He spoke to Odysseus words that went like arrows: "You seem
different, stranger, than a while ago . . . And you have different
clothing on, and your skin is no longer the same. You must

be some god who lives in the broad heaven! Be kind, so that
180 we might give you welcome sacrifices and golden gifts,
nicely made. But please spare us!"

                              Then the much-enduring good
Odysseus answered him: "I am no god. Why do you think I am
like the deathless ones? I am your father, on whose account
you have groaned and suffered many pains—a victim
185 of the violence of men."

                              Having so spoken, he kissed his son,
and tears flowed down his cheeks to the ground, tears
Odysseus had steadfastly held back.

                              But Telemachos
did not yet believe that he was his father, and he again
answered and said: "You are not Odysseus, my father,
190 but a spirit enchants me so that I might groan in agony
still more. For no mortal man has devised these things
in his own mind. Only the gods themselves can do this
easily—can make an old man young again if they wish.
For just now you were an old man dressed in rags, but now
195 you seem like the gods who hold up the broad sky!"

     Much-enduring resourceful Odysseus answered him:
"Telemachos, you ought not to wonder too much that your father
is here in this house, nor be so amazed. Be sure that no other
Odysseus will ever come here. I am that man, such as you see me.
200 I have suffered evils and I have wandered far, and now
in the twentieth year I have arrived in the land of my fathers.
You should know this is all the doing of Athena, who gathers booty,
who makes me just as she wants. She has the power! First like
a beggar, then like a young man wearing nice clothes upon
205 his body. It is easy for the gods who live in the broad heaven
either to glorify a mortal man or to debase him."

                              Having so spoken,
he sat down. Then Telemachos threw his arms around his noble
father and wept, pouring down tears, and the desire for lament
arose in the two of them. They wailed shrilly, more vehemently
210 than the wail of birds—of ospreys or vultures with crooked
talons whose young the country people have taken
from their nest before they could fly. Even so they poured
forth pitiful tears from beneath their brows.

And the light
of the sun would have gone down as they wept if Telemachos
did not suddenly say to his father: "On what kind of ship,   215
my dear father, did sailors transport you to Ithaca? Who did
they say they were? For I don't think you came here on foot!"

    The much-enduring good Odysseus then said: "Well, my son,
I will tell you the truth. Phaeacians, famed for their ships,
brought me here. They give safe convoy to other men too,   220
whoever comes to them. They brought me, asleep,
in their swift ship over the sea, and set me down on Ithaca.
They gave me glorious gifts, bronze and gold and a pile
of woven cloth, which now lie in caves, thanks to the favor
of the gods. I have come here at Athena's instruction so that   225
we can plan the destruction of our enemies. But tell me,
what is the number of the suitors? I need to know how
many they are and what kind of men they are. Then I can
ponder in my faultless mind to decide whether we two will be
able to take them alone without help, or whether we should   230
recruit others."

    Then the shrewd Telemachos answered him:
"Father, surely I have always heard of your great fame,
that you are a warrior in the strength of your hands and that
your counsel is excellent. But what you say is too much for me!
I am overwhelmed! Two men cannot fight against men who are   235
many and strong. There are not just ten suitors, nor twice
that, but many more. Here, learn their number: From
Doulichion there are fifty-two choice youths, and six servants
in attendance. From Samê there are twenty-four men, from Zakynthos
there are twenty youths of the Achaeans, and from Ithaca   240
itself there are twelve, all best men, and there is the herald Medon,
and the divine singer, and two aides skilled at cutting
meats.° If we were to take on all of them inside, I fear
that your coming to take revenge for their outrages
will be bitter, dread. But think, if you can find some helper—   245
one who will help us with an eager heart—"

    Then the much-enduring
good Odysseus answered him: "Well, I will tell you, and you

---

243 . . . *at cutting meats:* the servants (*drêstêres*) are probably slaves; a *herald* (*kêrux*) was a gofer, a runner,
    a messenger, an assistant not of the same social class as the "best men" (*aristoi*) but free and of high rank.
    The *aides* (*therapontes*) were free too, but also of a lower social rank than the "best men."

FIGURE 16.1 Odysseus and his son Telemachos. A bearded Odysseus wears his typical felt traveler's cap. The young Telemachos is unbearded. The third figure in the lower right may be Eumaios, the pig herder. Roman mosaic, first century AD.

take it to heart, and hear what I say. Tell me whether Athena
with the help of father Zeus will be sufficient for us two, or should
I still take thought of another helper?"   250

                    The shrewd Telemachos
spoke to him: "These *are* fine helpers that you speak of,
though they take their seats high in the clouds. Surely
the two of them have power over all men and the other
deathless gods!"

                    Then the much-enduring good Odysseus
spoke to him: "And those gods will not be absent from   255
the terrible contendings for long, once the might of Ares
is put to the test between ourselves and the suitors
in my halls. But for the present, go to the house at the break
of dawn and mix with the arrogant suitors. Later on,
the pig herder will lead me to the city in the likeness   260
of an old man, a wretched beggar. If they disrespect me
in the house, let the heart in your breast endure to see me
suffering vile things, even if they drag me by the feet
through the house to the door, or strike me with missiles.
If you see this, bear up! Urge them to give up their foolish   265
behavior. Speak with gentle words. But you will not persuade
them, for the fated day stands near.

                    "I will tell you
something else, and you reflect on it in you breast.
When the counselor Athena puts it in my mind, I will
nod to you with my head. When you see this, then pick   270
up the warrior gear that lies in the hall and put it
in a secret place of the uppermost chamber—absolutely
all of it. As for the suitors, when they miss the armor
and ask you about it, then trick them with gentle words
and say: 'I have put the armor out of the way of the smoke,   275
for they no longer look as they did when Odysseus left them
and went to Troy. They are corroded by the breath of the fire
that has reached them. And furthermore, the son of Zeus
has placed this greater fear in my head, that when you get
drunk a quarrel may break out among you so that you wound   280
one another and put shame on the banquet and your courtship.
For iron draws a man to itself.'°

---

282 *to itself*: This proverb must have come into being after iron became standard for weapons, c. 900 BC.
Ordinarily in the stylized world of epic battle, weapons are made of bronze.

"But for us alone, leave two
swords and two spears and two shields to take up in our hands,
so that we can rush on these weapons and seize them.° As for
the suitors, Pallas Athena and Zeus the counselor will cast a spell
over them. And I will tell you something else, and please turn
this over in your mind. If you are truly my son and of my blood,
let no one know that Odysseus is in the house. May Laërtes
not know it, nor the pig herder, nor any of the household
slaves—not Penelope herself! By ourselves you and I
will learn the way it is with these women. And let us put
your male slaves to the test too, to see which ones fear us
and honor us at heart, and which ones do not care for us
and dishonor you, excellent as you are."

The glorious son
said in reply: "O father, you will come to know my spirit soon,
I think, for I am bound by no slackness of will. But I don't
think that this plan will be to our advantage, so I urge you
to think about it. It will take a long time for you to go about
the fields, vainly putting every man to the test while
in your halls these other men arrogantly and at their ease
devour your wealth, sparing nothing. As for the women,
I urge you to find out who among them disrespects you,
and who is without guilt. As for the men in the farmsteads,
I would not want to put these men to the test, but to work
on that later, if truly you know of some sign from Zeus
who carries the goatskin fetish."°

So they spoke such things
to one another, but the well-built ship that bore Telemachos
and all his companions from Pylos came into Ithaca.
When they came inside the deep harbor, they dragged
the black ship up on the land, and the high-spirited aides
off-loaded the gear, and then carried the very beautiful
gifts up to the house of Klytios.° They sent a herald
to the house of Odysseus to give a message to the prudent
Penelope, saying that Telemachos was off in the fields
but had ordered the ship to sail to the city so the strong
queen might not take fright and pour down soft tears.

---

284 *seize them*: In fact this never happens, as we will see.

306 *...goatskin fetish*: Twice earlier Odysseus has claimed that Athena and Zeus would help against the suitors, so in that case they will not need helpers from the farms.

312 *Klytios*: The father of Peiraios, one of Telemachos' trusted followers.

Thus the herald and the good pig herder met on the same errand,
to tell the news to the lady. When they came to the house of godlike
Odysseus, the herald Medon spoke in the midst of the female
slaves: "Even now, my queen, your son has returned!"   320

Then the pig herder went close to Penelope and spoke
all that her dear son had instructed him to say. When he
told all that he was commanded, the pig herder withdrew
from the hall and its enclosure, and went off after his pigs.

But the suitors were disturbed and depressed in their spirits.   325
They came outside the hall past the large wall of the court
and they sat down in front of the gates. Eurymachos the son
of Polybos began to speak to them: "My friends, it looks as though
Telemachos has arrogantly accomplished this great deed
in making his journey. We thought he would not accomplish it!   330
But come, let us launch a black ship, the best we have,
and let us gather seamen as oarsmen who as soon as possible
can announce to our fellows° that they should come home
immediately."

He had not finished speaking when Amphinomos,
turning from his place, saw the very ship within the deep harbor.   335
The men were furling the sails, or they had oars in their hands.
Laughing sweetly, Amphinomos spoke to his companions:
"No need for such a message—they are here! Either some god
told them, or they themselves saw the ship of Telemachos
as it sailed by, but were unable to overtake it."   340

                                          So he spoke,
and they stood up and went to the shore of the sea. Quickly
the men dragged the black ship up on the land and their
high-spirited aides off-loaded the gear. Then they went
in a bunch into the place of assembly, and they would allow
no other of the young men, or of the old, to sit with them.   345

Antinoös, the son of Eupeithes, spoke to them: "Well,
it seems that the gods have rescued this man from evil.
Watchmen sat on the windy heights during the day,
one after the other, always on the watch. Then when the sun
went down, we did not go ashore to spend the night,   350

---

333 *fellows*: Antinoös and his companions, believed still to be hiding in ambush.

but we awaited the shining dawn, sailing on the sea
in our swift ship—on the watch for Telemachos so that
we might take him and kill him. Some spirit must have
guided him home.

        "So let us here devise a different destruction
355 for Telemachos—and may he not escape this one! For I do not
think that our work will prosper so long as he is alive.
He is shrewd in counsel and planning, and the people
no longer show friendly feelings toward us. But come,
we must act before he assembles the Achaeans into the place
360 of gathering—for I do not think he will be slow to act.
He will be filled with anger, and he will stand up
and tell everyone that we tried to kill him but could not
catch him. And when the people hear of these evil deeds,
they will not praise us! I fear that they will do us some evil
365 and drive us out of our land, so that we have to settle
in a foreign country.

        "So let us take him in the countryside
and kill him, far from the city or on the road. Then we
will posses his livelihood and property, dividing it fairly
among ourselves, and we will give the house to his mother
370 and to whomever she marries. If this plan does not please
you, and you want him to live and keep his patrimony,
well, let us then no longer devour his pleasant things
in our gatherings here, but let each man continue his courtship
from his own hall, pursuing Penelope with bridal gifts.
375 Let her then marry whoever gives her the most gifts
and whoever comes as her fated master."

        So Antinoös spoke
and they all fell into silence. Then Amphinomos spoke
and addressed them, the glorious son of King Nisos,
the son of Aretias, who led the suitors from Doulichion,
380 rich with wheat and covered with grass. He pleased Penelope
with his words more than the others, for he had a keen mind.

    Wishing them well, Amphinomos spoke and addressed them:
"My friends, I would rather not kill Telemachos. It is a grave matter
to kill a member of the chief's family. Let us first try to find out
385 the will of the gods. If the oracles of great Zeus approve it,
I will kill him myself and I will urge everybody else to become

involved. But if the gods turn us from his act, I urge you
to let it go."

So spoke Amphinomos, and his advice was pleasing
to them. The suitors promptly stood up and went into the house
of Odysseus, and after entering they sat down on the polished chairs.   390

Then the prudent Penelope had another thought—to appear
before the suitors, so overbearing in their insolence. She had
learned of the threat to her son's life in her own halls,
for the herald Medon told her, who had heard of the suitors'
plans. She went to the hall with her women attendants.   395
When the beautiful lady came to the suitors, she stood
beside the door-post of the well-built house, holding
her shining veil before her cheeks.

She rebuked Antinoös—
speaking out she said: "Antinoös, you doer of evil!
filled with insolence! They say that you are the best   400
in counsel and in speech among the people of your age
in Ithaca. Madman! Why do you weave plans for the death
and fate of Telemachos? And you have no care
for suppliants—Zeus is witness of this! It is a foul thing
to plot evil against one another. Or could you not know   405
of the time that your own father came here as a fugitive,
in terror of his people? They were very angry because
he had followed the Taphian pirates and attacked
the Thresprotians with whom we were allied. They wanted
to kill him, to take away his life and to devour his great   410
and pleasant livelihood. But Odysseus held them back
and stayed them, although they were eager.° And now
you devour Odysseus' substance without compensation,
and you court his wife and conspire to kill his son. You grieve
me greatly. And now I am commanding you to stop and to tell   415
the others to stop too!"

Eurymachos, the son of Polybos,
then answered her: "Daughter of Ikarios, wise Penelope,
take heart. Don't let any of this be a matter for your concern.
The man does not exist, nor will he ever exist, nor *could* he exist,
who might raise his hands against your son Telemachos   420

---

412 *were eager*: Antinoös' father is still on Ithaca, as we learn in *Od.* 24.

so long as I am alive and look upon the face of the earth.
I will tell you this, and I know it would come to pass—
in an instant that man's black blood would run down my spear!
For Odysseus, the sacker of cities, often hoisted me onto
425 his knees and placed a piece of roasted meat in my hands,
and he held the red wine up to my lips. Therefore Telemachos
is the most dear of all men to me, and I bid him not to have
a fear of death—at least from the suitors! But when it comes
from the gods, no man can avoid it."

So Eurymachos spoke cheerily,
430 but in his heart he still plotted Telemachos' death. Then
Penelope went upstairs to her shining rooms. She wept
for Odysseus, until flashing-eyed Athena sent sweet sleep
over her eyelids.

At evening the good pig herder came to Odysseus
and his son. They were busy making their dinner, having killed
435 a one year old boar.° But Athena, standing nearby, struck
Odysseus the son of Laërtes with her wand and made him
again an old man, and she put miserable clothes around
his flesh so that the pig herder, seeing him up close, would
not know who he was and tell Penelope and fail to hold
440 the secret in his heart.

Telemachos first spoke to Eumaios:
"You have come, good Eumaios. What is new in the city?
Have the bold suitors returned from their ambush, or do they
still await me as I travel homeward?"

In reply you said, O Eumaios
my pig herder: "I didn't really have time to go around the city
445 asking and inquiring about things. I wanted to come back
as soon as I had delivered my message. A swift messenger
from your companions chanced on me, a herald, who was first
to deliver the message to your mother. I know this too, for I
saw it with my own eyes. I was above the city as I went on
450 my way on the hill of Hermes,° and I saw a swift ship

---

435 *one year old boar*: This would provide Eumaios with the choicest pork available.

450 *hill of Hermes*: Evidently a hill on which there was a shrine of Hermes, unless "hill of Hermes" means the pile of stones that wayfarers built for good luck, called a *herm*.

coming into our harbor. There were many men in it, and it
bristled with shields and two-edged spears. I think these
were the men, but I do not know."

        So he spoke and the powerful
Telemachos smiled, looking at his father. but he avoided
the pig herder's eyes. When they had ceased from their   455
labor and had prepared the meal, they fell to feasting,
nor did they lack anything in the equal feast. And when
they had put all desire for food and drink from themselves,
they thought of rest, and took the gift of sleep.

BOOK 17. *The Faithful Dog Argos*

When early-born rosy-fingered Dawn appeared, then Telemachos,
the dear son of godlike Odysseus, bound his beautiful sandals
beneath his feet and he took up his powerful spear,
which fitted his hands, for he wanted to go to the city.

5   Telemachos spoke to the pig herder: "My friend, I am going
into the city so that my mother may see me. I don't think
that she will give up her weeping and wailing and tearful
sorrow until she actually sees me. But I give you this charge—
lead this wretched stranger up to the city so that he can beg
10 for his supper there. Then whoever wants can give him some
bread and a cup of water. As for me, there is no way that
I can care for every man, having as I do so many pains
in my heart. If the stranger is angry with this, that will be
his own problem! I like to speak the truth."

                                                The resourceful
15 Odysseus said in reply: "Friend, I have no desire to be left here.
Yes, it is better for a beggar to go to the city than through the fields
begging for food. Whoever wants will give me something,
for I am no longer of such an age as to remain at the farm
and obey in all things the commands of an overseer. But go!
20 This man will lead me, just as you bid, once I've warmed
myself at the fire and the sun grows warm. These clothes I wear
are shamefully poor, and I am afraid that the morning
frost may wipe me out. For you say that it is far to the city."

       So Odysseus spoke. Telemachos went through the farmyard,
25 going quickly on his feet, ready to sow seeds of evil
for the suitors. And when he came to the busy household,
he carried his spear and placed it against a tall pillar. He himself
went inside over the stone threshold. The nurse Eurykleia
was the very first to see him as she was spreading fleeces
30 on the fancy chairs. Weeping, she came straight to him,
and the other female slaves of much-enduring Odysseus gathered
around him. They kissed Telemachos' head and shoulders in loving

welcome. Then the judicious Penelope came from her chamber,
like Artemis, or golden Aphrodite. She burst into tears and threw
her arms around her dear son. She kissed his head and both   35
his beautiful eyes, and, wailing, she spoke words that went
like arrows: "You have come, Telemachos, sweet light! I thought
that I would never see you again after you set off in a ship to Pylos,
in secret, against my will, seeking to hear some news of your dear
father. But come, tell me, what sight did you have of him?"   40

The shrewd Telemachos answered her: "My mother, don't stir
up lament or get the heart in my breast beating! Yes, I escaped
steep destruction. But take your bath and put on some clean
clothes, and go into your upper chamber with your lady attendants
and pray to all the gods, telling them that you will perform   45
perfect sacrifices if only Zeus will grant you revenge. And I
will go into the place of assembly so that I can call a stranger
to the house who followed me when I came here from Pylos.
I sent him on ahead with my godlike companions, and I asked
Peiraios to take him to his house and give him a kind welcome   50
and honor until I should come."

So Telemachos spoke, and his
words flew just like arrows. She took a bath, and she put
clean clothes against her skin, and she prayed to the gods,
saying that she would sacrifice perfect sacrificial animals in hopes
that Zeus would help accomplish her revenge. Telemachos   55
then went from the hall to the place of assembly with his spear in hand.
Two swift dogs followed with him. Athena poured out a wondrous
grace on him, and all the people who saw Telemachos coming
were amazed. Around him the noble suitors gathered, saying
noble things, but hiding in their hearts hostile intentions.   60

Telemachos avoided the thick crowd of the suitors. He took
his seat where Mentor had sat and Antiphos and Halitherses now sat—
his father's companions in the old days. He went over there
and took his seat. And they asked him about everything.

Then Peiraios, famous for his spear, came close to them, bringing   65
the stranger, Theoklymenos, through the city to the place of assembly.
Nor did Telemachos turn away from the stranger, but stood
beside him. Peiraios spoke first: "Telemachos, quickly send some
of your women to my house so that I can send you the gifts
that Menelaos gave you."   70

     The shrewd Telemachos answered:
"Peiraios, we do not know how these matters will turn out.
If the noble suitors succeed in killing me in secret in the halls
and dividing up all my father's wealth, I'd rather that you
had these things rather than one of them. But if I can sow
75 the seeds of death and fate for these men, then please do bring all
these things to my house, and I shall be glad."

        So speaking he led
the much-suffering stranger Theoklymenos toward the house.
And when they came to the busy household, the two men laid their
cloaks over some chairs and seats, and went into the well-polished
80 bathtubs and bathed. When the female slaves had washed them
and anointed their skin with olive oil, they cast about them woolen
robes and shirts. The men came forth from the bathtubs and sat
down on their chairs. An attendant brought water for their hands
in a beautiful golden pitcher and poured it into a silver bowl
85 for them to wash. Then she arranged a polished table beside them.
The revered housewife brought in bread and placed it down
before them, and many meats too, sharing freely of what she had
on hand. His mother sat opposite Telemachos, leaning
her chair against a door-post of the hall, spinning out fine wool.

90 They put forth their hands to the good things ready before them,
and when they had satisfied all desire for drink and food,
the judicious Penelope began to speak: "Telemachos, surely
I will go into my upper chamber to lie down on the bed,
which has become a bed of wailing for me, ever wet with my tears,
95 ever since Odysseus went off to Troy with the sons of Atreus.
But you have not made plain to me—before the noble suitors come
into the house—concerning your father's homecoming, whether
you have heard something."

      Then shrewd Telemachos answered:
"Well mother, I will tell you all of it. We went off to Pylos
100 to Nestor, the shepherd of the people. He received me in his lofty
house and entertained me appropriately, as if a father were to greet
his own son who had been gone a long time, then recently returned
from a far land. Thus did he extend to me gracious hospitality,
in the company of his bold sons. But he said that he had heard
105 nothing of the much-enduring Odysseus from any man
on the earth, whether he was alive or dead. Then he sent me off
in a jointed chariot drawn by horses, to the son of Atreus—
Menelaos, famed for his spear-work. There I saw Argive Helen,

on whose account both the Argives and the Trojans had contended
for so long a time. For that was the will of the gods.   110

                                          "Then Menelaos,
good at the war cry, at once asked why I had come to shining
Lacedaemon, and I told him the whole truth. And then he said,
replying to my words: 'Egad! These men want to lie in the bed
of a man with a powerful heart, although they are themselves
cowards? As when a doe lays her newborn suckling fawns   115
down to sleep in the thicket of a powerful lion while she
wanders feeding on the mountain slopes and grassy valleys,
and then the lion returns to his lair and unleashes
a cruel doom on the two—even so Odysseus will visit
a cruel doom on the suitors! O father Zeus, and Athena   120
and Apollo, I only wish that Odysseus were the man he was
when he stood up and wrestled Philomeleides on well-founded
Lesbos, and threw him down mightily, and all the Achaeans
rejoiced—if he were in such strength Odysseus might mix
among the suitors, and they would soon meet a swift   125
and bitter end to their wooing!

                          " 'But as for these matters
you ask and beg to know, I will not swerve aside to speak
of other things—nor shall I deceive you. I will not hide
or conceal anything that the unerring Old Man of the Sea
told me. He said that he had seen Odysseus on an island,   130
suffering sad constraint in the halls of the nymph Kalypso,
who holds him by force. And he cannot come home to the land
of his fathers because he does not have a ship at hand with oars,
nor companions who could send him home over the broad back
of the sea.'   135

      "So spoke the son of Atreus, Menelaos, famous
for his spear work. When I had finished these matters, off I went.
The deathless ones gave me a friendly breeze, and quickly
the winds brought me to my dear native land."

                                    So Telemachos
spoke, and he stirred the heart within Penelope's breast. Then
godlike Theoklymenos spoke to them: "O revered wife of Odysseus,   140
the son of Laërtes, surely Menelaos knows nothing, but listen
to what I have to say—I will prophesy to you truly and I will
conceal nothing. May Zeus—the first of all gods!—be my witness.
And this table, friendly to strangers, and this hearth of blameless

145 Odysseus to which I have come: That even now Odysseus is in
the land of his fathers, either at rest or on the move, learning
of these evil deeds and sowing the seeds of destruction
for the suitors. So clear a bird of omen did I see when I was
seated on the well-benched ship—and I told it to Telemachos."°

150 Then judicious Penelope said: "I only wish that your word,
sir stranger, might come to pass. Then you would quickly know
of my kindness, and receive many gifts from me, so that if one
met you he would call you *blessed*."

So they spoke to one another
while the suitors took their pleasure with the discus outside
155 Odysseus' hall, and with throwing the javelin in a course
they had laid out, where they were accustomed to indulge
their insolence. But when it came time for dinner and the flocks
returned from all over the fields, and the same men led them
as usual, then Medon—the herald who most pleased the suitors,
160 who always joined them for dinner—Medon said to them:
"Young men, now that you have taken pleasure in the contests,
come into the house where we will prepare dinner. It is not
a bad thing to take your dinner on time."

So he spoke and the suitors
stood up and went inside, obeying his word. When they came
165 to the busy household, they took off their cloaks and put them on seats
and chairs. Then they butchered large sheep and fat goats, and they
butchered fat pigs and a cow from the herd, making ready the feast.

In the meanwhile, Odysseus and the good pig herder
were making haste coming up from the fields to the house.
170 The pig herder, a leader of men, began first to speak: "Stranger,
although you want to go to the city today, as my king advised,
I would rather that you stayed here to guard the farmstead.
But I respect him and I am afraid that he might blame me
in the future, and the reproaches of kings are hard to bear.
175 So come now, let us go. The day grows old, and it gets chilly
when it gets toward night."

The resourceful Odysseus then said in reply:
"I know, I understand. You are giving advice to one who already

---

149 *Telemachos*: Actually, he and Telemachos had disembarked and were on the shore when the omen appeared
(Book 15).

knows. So let us go, and you lead the way. But give me a staff
to lean on, if you have one cut, because you said that the path
is treacherous."   180

Odysseus spoke and he cast about his shoulders
his wretched pouch, riven with holes, suspended from a twisted cord.
Eumaios gave him a staff that pleased him, and the two set out.
The dogs and the herdsmen stayed behind to protect the farmyard.
Eumaios led King Odysseus to the city, looking just like
a beggar and an old man, hobbling on his crutch. Miserable   185
clothing hung about his skin. They went along the rugged path
and came close to the city. They arrived at the spring—
nicely worked, beautifully flowing—from which the inhabitants
of the city drew their water. Ithakos and Neritos and Polyktor
had boxed it in.° Around the spring was a wood of water-nourished   190
aspen, wrapping all the way around, and cold water flowed down
from high on the rock above. On top was built an altar
to the nymphs, where all passersby made sacrifice.

At the spring
Melanthios, the son of Dolios,° met them, driving his she-goats,
by far the best of all the herds, as a meal for the suitors.   195
And two herdsmen followed him. When he saw Odysseus
and Eumaios, he spoke to them with violent and abusive insults,
and he greatly riled Odysseus' heart: "Now, surely a stinking
man leads another stinking man! As always, the gods brings like
and like together! Where are you leading this glutton,   200
you miserable pig herder? this annoying beggar, this wrecker
of banquets? He is just the man to stand at many doorposts,
rubbing his shoulders against them, begging for scraps,
not swords or cauldrons. If you were to give me this man
to protect my farmsteads, to clean out the pens and to carry   205
young shoots to the kids, then by drinking whey he *might*
grow himself a strong thigh. But because he has learned
only evil deeds, he will not wish to busy himself with real work,
but skulks through the land thinking only to fill his insatiate
belly by begging. But I will tell you something, and I think   210
it will come to pass: If he comes to the house of good Odysseus,

---

190 ... *had boxed it in*: Ithakos, Neritos, and Polyktor ("much-possessing") are said in the scholia to be the
       founders first of Kephallenia, then of Ithaca, who gave their names to the island and to Mount Neriton on
       Ithaca. Polyktor is the name of the suitor Peisander's father (Book 18), but it is probably not the same man.
       The *Odyssey* itself gives us no more information about Ithakos, Neritos, and Polyktor.
194 *Melanthios son of Dolios*: "blackie," son of "tricky."

many a footstool hurled around his head from the hands
of real men will break his ribs as he is pelted through the house!"

So Melanthios spoke, and as he passed, in his madness,
215 he kicked Odysseus on the hip with his heel. Yet he did not drive
him from the path. Odysseus held his ground and pondered
whether he should leap on Melanthios and club him to death,
or whether he should seize him around the waist, raise him up
and dash his brains on the ground. But he endured, holding back
220 from his intention.

The pig herder, looking Melanthios in the face,
rebuked him, and he prayed aloud, holding up his hands: "Nymphs
of the spring, daughters of Zeus, if ever Odysseus burned
thigh bones in your honor, wrapping them in rich fat of sheep
or goats, then fulfill for me this prayer—that that man might
225 come back! May some spirit guide him! Then he would
dispel the hollow show that you insolently now put on,
wandering always through the city while the wicked herdsmen
destroy the flocks."

Melanthios answered the goatherd: "Well, well,
what a word this sly dog has said . . . Some day I will take you
230 on a well-benched black ship far from Ithaca, so that you might
bring me much wealth. I wish that Apollo of the silver bow might
strike Telemachos in the halls, today, or that the suitors might kill
him—just as I hope that the day of Odysseus' homecoming has been
lost in some far land!"

So speaking, Melanthios left them there
235 as they slowly walked along. But Melanthios himself went quickly
forward and soon arrived at the house of the king. He went in at once
and sat down among the suitors, opposite Eurymachos, who liked
him especially. The attendants served Melanthios a portion of meat,
and the revered housekeeper brought in some bread and put it down
240 before him to eat.

Odysseus and the good pig herder stopped when
they came close to the palace, and around them came the sound
of the hollow lyre—it was Phemios striking the chords
to sing before the suitors. Then Odysseus took Eumaios by the hand
and said: "Eumaios, surely this is the beautiful palace
245 of Odysseus, easy to recognize and to pick out from among many.
There is building upon building, and the courtyard is built with wall

and coping, and the double doors are well fenced. No man could
equip it better. I notice that inside the house many men are feasting,
for the savor of flesh rises above it, and from inside the lyre sounds,
which the gods have made as companion to the feast."   250

                              Then you said
in reply, O Eumaios, my pig herder: "You recognize it easily,
because you are not a stupid man. But come, let us consider
how things will be. Either you go in to the busy household first
and join the company of the suitors, and I will remain here—
or if you want, you stay here and I will go in first. But don't   255
stay long, or someone may see you out here and throw something
at you, to drive you off. I urge you to consider these things."

    Then the much-enduring good Odysseus answered him:
"I know, I do see. You are giving advice to one who knows.
But you go ahead, and I will stay behind. I am no stranger   260
to beatings or to being knocked about. My spirit is a daring one
because I have suffered so many evils on the waves and in war.
Let this be added to what has gone before. There is no way
to hide a greedy belly—so destructive!—which brings so many
evils to men, on account of which benched ships are fitted   265
out to sail across the restless sea, bringing misery to the enemy."

    They spoke to one another in this fashion, when the hound
dog Argos,° lying there, raised his head and pricked up his ears.
Odysseus, of enduring heart, had reared him long ago, but had
little joy of him before he went to sacred Ilion. In earlier   270
times the young men used him to chase wild goats and deer
and hares, but now, his king gone, he lay neglected on a pile
of excrement poured out by mules and cattle and piled up
in front of the gates, until Odysseus' slaves could take it away
to dung the master's wide fields. There the dog Argos lay,   275
a mess of fleas, but still, when he saw Odysseus standing near,
he wagged his tale and pricked up his two ears. Yet he did not
have the strength to move closer to his master.

                              Looking aside,
Odysseus wiped away a tear, hiding it from Eumaios,
and right away he asked him: "Eumaios, it is odd that this dog   280
lies here in excrement! He has a good shape, but I cannot
know this clearly, whether he has speed of foot to match

---

268 *Argos:* "speedy."

his beauty, or whether he is like all those table-dogs that their
masters keep for show."

           Then you answered, O Eumaios my
285 pig herder: "This is the dog of a man that has died in a far land.
     If he were in form and action as when Odysseus left him
     and went to Troy, you would quickly be astonished at his
     speed and strength. No creature that he startled in the depths
     of the thick woods could escape him, and he was a superior
290 tracker. But now he is in wretched way. His master has perished
     in a foreign land, and the careless women do not take care
     of him. Slaves, when their masters are not about, no longer
     want to do what they are supposed to. For Zeus, whose voice
     is heard afar, takes away half the worth of a man when
295 the day of slavery takes him."°

           Then he went straight into
     the house and among the proud suitors, but the fate of black death
     took Argos when he had seen Odysseus in the twentieth year.

     Godlike Telemachos was by far the first to see
     the pig herder coming into the house, and swiftly he nodded,
300 calling him to come to his side. Eumaios looked around him
     and took a nearby stool on which the carver sat when he cut
     the many pieces of meat for the suitors as they feasted
     in the hall. He placed it on the other side of Telemachos'
     table and sat down himself. A herald took a portion of meat
305 and set it before him and some bread from the basket.

     Coming right after him, Odysseus entered the palace
     in the likeness of a wretched beggar, an old man leaning
     on his staff, his repulsive clothes hanging from his flesh.
     He sat down on the threshold of ashwood° just inside the doors,
310 leaning against a pillar made of cypress wood that once
     a carpenter had expertly planed and trued to the measuring-line.

     Telemachos spoke to the pig herder, calling him over,
     and he took a whole loaf from the very beautiful basket,
     and all the meats that his hands could hold in their grasp:
315 "Take these things to the stranger and give them to him.

---

295 *takes him*: That is, slavery ruins one's moral fiber so that carelessness and treachery come easily.

309 *ashwood*: Earlier in this book, it is made of stone.

FIGURE 17.1 Argos recognizes Odysseus. Odysseus squats on a rock, his staff at his side, while Argos grovels before him. The doors of Odysseus' palace stand closed behind him. The face of Odysseus seems deliberately mutilated, no doubt from fear of the image's power. Relief on a Roman sarcophagus, third century AD.

Tell him to beg among the suitors, going among them
one and all. Shame is not a good thing for a man in need."

So he spoke, and the pig herder went when he heard
Telemachos' command. He stood beside Odysseus and spoke
320   to him words that went like arrows: "Telemachos, O stranger,
gives you these things, and he says that you should go
through the suitors and beg, one and all. He says that shame
is not a good thing for a beggar."

The resourceful Odysseus replied:
"King Zeus, I pray that Telemachos be blessed among men.
325   May he have all that his heart desires."

He spoke and took
the food in both his hands and set it down there before his feet
on top of his disgusting pouch. He ate while the singer sang
in the halls.

When he had eaten, the divine singer stopped,
and the suitors broke into an uproar throughout the halls.
330   But Athena, standing close to Odysseus the son of Laërtes,
urged him to beg for bread from the suitors so that he might
see which were righteous and which were lawless. Yet even
so she was not minded to save a single one of them from
destruction.

Odysseus began to beg of each man singly,
335   working from the right, extending to each his hands
as if he had long been a beggar. Some took pity and gave
him something, and they marveled at him. They asked
one another who he was and where he came from.

Then Melanthios the goatherd spoke to them: "Listen
340   to me, suitors of a glorious queen—I have something to say
about this stranger. I have seen him before. The pig herder
has brought him here. I am not sure where he claims to come from."

So he spoke, and Antinoös reproached the pig herder, saying:
"O you most distinguished *swine* herder, why have you brought
345   this man to the city? Don't we have enough homeless wretches
coming by as it is—annoying beggars, wreckers of the feast?
Don't you think it is bad enough that they gather here and consume
the wealth of the king? and now you bring in *this* man?"

And you answered, O my pig herder Eumaios: "Antinoös,
though you may be noble, you have not spoken properly.   350
Who of himself goes out and summons a stranger to come
from somewhere else, unless it is one of those who benefit
the people—a prophet or a healer of ills or a builder with wood,
or even a divine singer who might delight with his song.°
These men are called all over the boundless earth, but you would   355
never summon a beggar who would only wear you down.
You above all the other suitors are always hard toward Odysseus'
slaves, and especially to me. But I don't care, so long as the judicious
Penelope lives in these halls—and godlike Telemachos."

    The shrewd Telemachos answered him: "Be quiet! Don't answer   360
that man with a long speech. It is always the habit of Antinoös
to provoke to anger in an evil way, and always with his harsh words.
And he eggs-on others to do the same!"

                    Telemachos spoke,
and he said to Antinoös words that went like arrows:
"Antinoös, truly you take care of me as a father does his son.   365
And now you propose that I drive the stranger from this hall
with a dismissive word. May no god bring this to pass!
No! Take something and give it to him. I do not begrudge it,
for I myself ask you to give it. Don't worry about my mother,
nor any other of the slaves who are in the house of the divine   370
Odysseus. But I don't think this is what bothers you. You would
rather eat than give to another!"

                    Then Antinoös said in reply:
"Telemachos, you fat mouth, without restraint in daring—such
words you have spoken! If all the suitors should hand him as much
as I have, this house would be free of him for three months!"   375

    So he spoke, and he took the footstool on which
he was accustomed to rest his shining feet while feasting,
and he showed it beneath the table.° But all the others gave
the beggar something, filling his pouch with bread and meat.

    Soon Odysseus was about to go back to the threshold and eat   380
what the Achaeans had given him, but first he stood beside Antinoös

---

354 *his song*: Our earliest evidence that such singers as Homer himself and craftsmen were itinerant workers in
     Greek society.

378 *the table*: That is, his generous gift to the beggar would be to throw a stool at him.

and said: "Give me something, my friend. You don't seem
to me to be the worst of the Achaeans, but the best. You have
the air of a chieftain. Therefore you ought to give me a better
385 portion of bread than all the others. I will celebrate you over
the broad earth.

       "You know once I lived in a house among men,
a rich man in a rich house. And I often gave to a wanderer,
no matter who he was or with whatever need he came. I had
countless slaves and many other things by which men live well
390 and are called rich. But Zeus, the son of Kronos, ruined it all.
I suppose he wanted to. He forced me to go with far-traveled
pirates into Egypt, a long journey, so that I might perish.
Stationing my beaked ships near the river Egypt, I then ordered
my trusty companions to stay beside the ships and guard them.
395 I ordered scouts to go to places of outlook. But giving in to
insolence, confident in their strength, they quickly plundered
the very beautiful fields of the men of Egypt. They carried off
the women and little children, and they killed the men. Soon
a cry came to the city. Hearing the cry, the Egyptians came
400 at the crack of dawn. The whole plain was filled with foot soldiers
and horses, and the shining bronze.

       "Then Zeus who delights
in the thunderbolt cast a panic among my companions, and no one
dared to stand his ground. There was evil all around. The Egyptians
killed many with their sharp bronze, and others they captured
405 alive, to work for them by force. But they gave me to a guest-friend
who happened to come by, to take me to Cyprus, to Dmetor
the son of Iasos° who ruled with power in Cyprus. Having suffered
greatly, I have now come here from there."°

       Antinoös answered
him and said: "What spirit has brought this anguish here,
410 this sorrow to the feast? Stand off over there in the middle,
away from my table—or you may quickly come to a *bitter*
Egypt and Cyprus! You are a bold and shameless beggar.
You come up to everyone in a row, and they give recklessly,
because there is no restraint or pity in giving freely of another's
415 wealth, because each man has plenty beside him!"

---

407 *son of Iasos*: Dmetor means "subduer"; nothing else is known about him.

408 *from there*: This story is very close to the story earlier told to Eumaios (Book 14), so as not to alert the pig
    herder to the beggar's true identity. Odysseus' other false tales are rather different.

Then the resourceful
Odysseus drew back and said: "My, my—I see that your wits
do not match your excellent looks. You would not give even
a grain of salt from your own house to one who asked—you who
sit at another's table would not dare to take a piece of bread
and give it to me, though you have plenty at hand?"   420

So Odysseus spoke,
and Antinoös grew still more angry in his heart. Looking beneath
his brows he spoke words that went like arrows: "I don't think
that you will leave this hall is such good shape, for you speak
insulting words."

So he spoke, and picking up the footstool
he threw it, hitting Odysseus at the base of his right shoulder,   425
where it joins the back. But Odysseus stood firm like a rock,
Antinoös' cowardly blow did not stagger him. Odysseus shook
his head in silence, pondering evil deep in his heart. Then he went
back to the threshold and sat. He put down his well-filled pouch.

Then he spoke to the suitors: "Listen to me, you suitors   430
of a glorious lady, so that I may say what my heart urges.
There is no pain of heart, nor sorrow, when a man is struck
fighting for his possessions, either for his cattle or his white sheep.
But Antinoös has struck me on account of my wretched belly,
that ruinous thing that gives so many evils to men. And if there   435
are gods and Erinyes° for beggars, may death's black end come
to Antinoös before his marriage."

Then Antinoös, the son of Eupeithes,
said: "Sit still and eat, O stranger, or go someplace else.
Else the young men will drag you through this house for the things
you say, taking hold of your foot or hand, and they will strip   440
off all your skin!"

So he spoke. But all the other suitors were exceedingly
indignant, so that one of the many young men would say: "Antinoös,
you did wrong to strike this miserable beggar, and a danger
if perhaps he turns out to be a god from heaven. For the gods wander
the cities in the likeness of strangers from abroad, taking on every   445
kind of shape, witnessing the violence and righteousness of men."

---

436 *Erinyes:* Originally punishers of crimes against one's mother or father, but here
     simply the spirits of revenge.

So spoke the suitors, but Antinoös paid no mind
to their words, while in Telemachos' heart the pain grew great
at the blow. Yet he shed no tear to the ground from his lids.
450 He shook his head in silence, contemplating the evil he would do.

The judicious Penelope heard of the man being struck
in the hall, and she said to her female slaves: "I wish that Apollo,
famous for his bow, would strike *him*!"

                                  Eurynomê, her waiting woman,
then said to her: "Would that our prayers could come true . . . Then
455 not one of these men would make it to Dawn on her beautiful throne."

The judicious Penelope answered her: "Nurse, they are all
enemies, for they contemplate evil. But Antinoös especially
is like black fate. Some wretched stranger wanders through the house,
begging from these suitors, for necessity compels him. All the others
460 fill his pouch and give him gifts, but Antinoös throws a footstool
and hits him at the base of his right shoulder!"

                                  So she spoke among
her women slaves, seated in her room,° and Odysseus sat and ate.
Then Penelope called the good pig herder to herself: "Go, worthy Eumaios,
and bring the stranger here so that I may greet him and ask him
465 if perhaps he has heard of Odysseus with the steadfast heart,
or seen him in person. For he seems to me be a much-traveled man."

Then you answered her, O Eumaios my pig herder: "I wish
that the Achaeans would keep silent, my lady, for the things
that he says would delight your heart. I had him beside me
470 for three nights, and for three days I kept him in my hut,
for he came to me first when he sneaked away from his ship.
But he has not yet finished telling his tale of woe. Even as when
a man looks on a singer who sings to mortals songs of longing
that the gods have taught him, and so the man desires to hear
475 whatever the singer sings—just so did that man charm me, sitting
in my halls.

          "He says that Odysseus is an ancestral guest-friend
of his father, and that he lives in Crete, where the lineage of Minos lives.

---

462 *her room*: Although the layout of Odysseus' house is hard to reconstruct, this room appears not to be the
      upper chamber to which Penelope earlier retired, but another room on the ground floor off the hall where
      she can hear and perhaps see what is happening in the big room (*see* MAP VI, J).

He came here from there, suffering terribly as he wandered along.
He declares that he heard about Odysseus, that he is near,
in the rich land of the Thresprotians—alive. And that he has 480
a large treasure to bring home."

The judicious Penelope then answered:
"Come, call him here, so that I myself may speak to him directly.
As for the suitors, they can take their pleasure sitting by the door
or here in the house, since their hearts are merry. Their own
possessions lie untouched in their own houses—bread and sweet 485
wine, which their house servants may consume. But they swarm
all day long in *our* house, butcher cattle and sheep and fat goats,
and they feast and drink the flaming wine carelessly, and much
is used up. For there is no man such as Odysseus was to ward off
ruin from this house. If Odysseus comes and arrives in the land 490
of his fathers, he will swiftly take vengeance on these men
for their violent acts!"

So she spoke, and Telemachos sneezed
loudly. All the room resounded with the astonishing sound.
Penelope laughed, and at once she spoke to Eumaios words
that went like arrows: "Come! Call the stranger here beside me. 495
Do you not see that my son has sneezed at my words?° Therefore
the death of every one of the suitors is certain, and not one
of them will escape death and fate. And I will tell you something
else, and you take it to heart: If I think that this beggar speaks
the truth in what he says, I will give him a cloak and a shirt, 500
beautiful clothes."

So she spoke, and the pig herder went off
when he had heard her instructions. He stood nearby the beggar
and spoke words that went like arrows: "Old man—stranger—
Penelope, Telemachos' mother, summons you. Her spirit bids
her to make inquiry about her husband, for she has suffered 505
terribly on his account. And if she thinks that everything that you
say is true, she will give you a cloak and a shirt, which you certainly
need. As for feeding your belly, you can go through the land begging
and he who wants to will give you something."

Then much-enduring
good Odysseus answered him: "Eumaios, I will tell all the truth 510

---

496   *at my words*: A sneeze is always a good omen.

right away to the daughter of Ikarios, the judicious Penelope.
For I know a lot about her husband. We suffered misery together.
But I am afraid of this crowd of hostile suitors, whose insolence
and power reaches the iron sky.° Just now, when I was going
515 through the hall doing nothing bad, this man struck me and hurt me.
But Telemachos did nothing to ward off the blow, nor did anyone
else. For this reason, ask Penelope to wait in the halls until
the sun goes down, although she is eager. Then let her ask me about
her husband's day of return, giving me a place nearer the fire.
520 For my clothes are in rags, as you well know, because I first
approached *you* as a suppliant."

          Thus he spoke, and the pig herder
went off when he heard these instructions. Penelope spoke to him
as he crossed over the threshold: "You have not brought him,
Eumaios. What does the wanderer mean by this? Does he fear
525 someone so very much? Or is he otherwise ashamed in this house?
It is a bad thing for a beggar to feel shame."

          Then you answered her,
O Eumaios my pig herder: "He speaks as is right, what any other
man would think who tried to avoid the insolence of haughty men.
But he asks that you wait until the sun goes down, and for yourself
530 too it is much better, my lady, to speak alone with the stranger
and to hear what he has to say."

          Then the judicious Penelope said:
"This stranger is not stupid. He sees how things might go.
There are no other mortal men, I think, who in their insolence
devise such idiocy."

          Thus she spoke, and the good pig herder went off
535 into the crowd of suitors after he had told her everything. He promptly
spoke to Telemachos words that went like arrows, holding his
head close to him so that the others would not hear: "My friend,
I am off to look after the pigs and the other things there,
your livelihood and mine. You take care of things here. Keep
540 yourself safe first of all, and let your mind be careful that nothing
happens to you. For many of the Achaeans intend evil. May Zeus
destroy them all before any ill befalls us!"

---

514 *iron sky*: It is not clear what he means by "iron sky." Homer calls the sky "bronze" in the *Iliad* (Books 3, 17).
      Perhaps he means that the sky is a metal dome over the earth, bronze for the heroic age (the world of the
      Iliad), and iron for the Iron Age (the world of the *Odyssey*).

And shrewd Telemachos
then answered him: "So it will be, father.° You go off, once you've
had your evening meal. In the morning come back, and bring
the beautiful sacrificial victims. Let me, and the deathless ones,   545
take care of things here."

So he spoke, and the pig herder sat down
again on the well-polished chair. When he had satisfied his spirit
with food and drink, he went off toward the swine. He left
the courts and the hall, filled with banqueters. And they took delight
in the dance and in song. Already evening had come on.   550

---

543 *father*: A term of affectionate regard.

BOOK 18. *Presents from the Suitors*

A public beggar came up who liked to beg throughout the city
of Ithaca. He stood out for his greedy belly, always eating
and drinking. He had no strength or force, but he was bulky
to look at. His name was Arnaios.° His revered mother gave it
5 to him at birth. But everyone called him Iros, because he ran
around bringing messages when someone summoned him.°

He came now and tried to drive Odysseus from his own
house as, reviling him, he spoke words that went like arrows:
"Get away from the doorway, old man, if you don't want
10 to be dragged out by the foot! Do you not see that everyone
is winking at me, that they are urging me to drag you out?
Still, I'd be ashamed to do so. But get out, unless you want
this quarrel to get to fists—fast!"

                                    The resourceful Odysseus then said,
looking from beneath his brows: "Are you mad, man? I've done
15 you no harm, or even spoken to you. I don't envy anything
that any man gives you, not even if he gives a great deal.
This threshold is big enough for the two of us, and you ought not
to be envious of others. You seem to me to be a wanderer, just as
I am. Soon our luck will turn around! But don't threaten me
20 with your fists, or you will make me angry. Although I am
an old man, I will wet your chest and lips with blood. And then
I would have a greater peace tomorrow. I don't think that you'll be
coming back a second time to the house of Odysseus, son
of Laërtes!"

Then the vagrant Iros grew angry and said:
25 "Bah! what a slick talker this filthy dog is—like some old
kitchen hag. But I will devise evil for him. I will smash him
from both sides, and scatter all his teeth from his jaws
onto the ground, as if he were a pig ruining the crop! So now

---

4 *Arnaios*: Probably (appropriately) "getter."

6 *summoned him*: Iris was the divine messenger in the *Iliad*, a role played by Hermes in the *Odyssey*.

gird yourself up so that all these men here can see our fight.
But . . . how could *you* fight with a younger man?"   30

So they heartily
exchanged harsh words on the polished threshold before
the high doors. The strong and mighty Antinoös heard the two,
and, laughing smugly, he spoke to the suitors: "My friends,
I don't think that the like has ever happened in earlier times!
Some god has brought such sport into this house. The stranger   35
and Iros are actually threatening to go at it with their fists.
Well, let's quickly egg them on!"

So he spoke, and they all
sprang up, laughing, and gathered around the beggars dressed
in rags. Antinoös, the son of Eupeithes, spoke to them: "Listen
to me, noble suitors, to what I say. We have these goat   40
stomachs lying in the fire, which we are preparing for dinner,
which we have stuffed with fat and blood. Whichever of these
two is victorious and proves the stronger, may he stand up
and himself take whichever one of these stomachs he wants.
And he will always dine with us, and we will not allow   45
any other beggar to mix with us and beg."

So spoke Antinoös,
and his proposal pleased them. But resourceful Odysseus, plotting
a trap, said: "An old man, afflicted by pain, cannot fight
a younger man. But my stomach, urging me to evil, drives me on—
so that, I guess, I will be overcome by his blows. But come now,   50
all of you swear a great oath—that no one, showing favor
to Iros, will bring aid to him and wickedly strike me with
a heavy hand, and so by violence subdue me to this man."

Thus he spoke and they all swore not to hit him, just as he asked.
And when they had sworn and accomplished their oath,   55
then the strong and mighty Telemachos spoke up: "Stranger,
if your heart and spirit are pushing you to beat up this man,
well, don't be afraid of any of the other Achaeans. Anyone
who touches you will have to take on many. I am the host here,
and these two chieftains, Antinoös and Eurymachos, both   60
sensible men, agree."

So he spoke, and everyone praised what he said.
Then Odysseus tied up his rags about his private parts, and he showed
his thighs, beautiful and strong, and his broad shoulders became

obvious, and his chest and his strong arms. Athena stood next
65   to him and filled out the limbs of the shepherd of the people.

  All the suitors marveled exceedingly, and thus would one say,
looking to the man standing nearby: "Well, I think that our Iros
will soon be a *non*-Iros! Now he is bringing an evil on himself!
Did you see that old man's thigh showing from beneath his rags?"

70   Thus they spoke, and Iros' spirit was shaken. Even so
the servants girded him up and by force led him out, terrified.
His flesh trembled on his limbs. Antinoös berated him, he spoke
and addressed him: "Better, O braggart, that you were not alive,
or had never been born, if you tremble at this man and fear him so.
75 Look, he is an old man afflicted by all the pain that has come
upon him! But I will tell you something, and I think that it will
come to pass. If this fellow beats you and proves the stronger,
I will throw you into a black ship and send you to the mainland,
to the chieftain Echetos,° the mangler of all men, who will slice
80 up your nose and cut off your ears with the pitiless bronze.
And he will claw out your balls and give them to the dogs
to eat raw!"

  So he spoke, and still more trembling took hold
of Iros' limbs. They dragged him out into the middle. The two men
raised up their hands. Then the much-enduring good Odysseus
85 pondered whether he should hit Iros so that his breath-soul
would leave him as he fell, or whether he should give him a light
blow and stretch him out on the ground. As he thought this over,
this seemed to him to be the best plan—to deliver him a light
blow so the Achaeans would not notice anything special about him.

90   So the two of them put up their hands, and Iros drove
at Odysseus' right shoulder, but Odysseus hit Iros on the neck
beneath the ear, smashing all the bones inward. Immediately
the red blood ran from his mouth, and he fell stretched out
in the dust with a moan. He gnashed his teeth and kicked
95 the ground with his feet. The noble suitors raised up
their hands, keeling over with laughter.

                                    Then Odysseus took Iros
by the foot and dragged him out the door until he came
into the court and the gates of the portico. He set him down,

---

79 *Echetos:* "holder," probably a folktale bogeyman.

leaning him up against the wall of the court, and Odysseus
put his staff in Iros' hand and spoke to him words that went   100
like arrows: "Sit there now and ward off your pigs and dogs,
and do not be lord of strangers and beggars, you scoundrel,
unless you want something worse to happen to you!"

He spoke and he threw his miserable pouch, riddled with
holes, suspended by a twisted strap, over Iros' shoulders.   105
Odysseus went back to the threshold and sat down. The suitors
went back inside, laughing sweetly, and they greeted Odysseus,
saying: "May Zeus, and the other deathless gods give you,
O stranger, whatever you want and is dear to your heart,
for you have put a stop to this insatiate man's begging   110
over the land. We'll quickly gather him up and send him
to the mainland—to the chieftain Echetos, the mangler
of all men!"

So they said, and the good Odysseus took joy
in these words of omen. Antinoös set a large stomach filled with
fat and blood beside him. Amphinomos took two loaves of bread   115
from the basket and set them before him, and he toasted
Odysseus with a golden cup, saying: "Hail to you, sir stranger—
father! May good fortune come to you in future times, though
now you are steeped in many evils."

The resourceful Odysseus said
in reply: "Amphinomos, you seem to me to be a reasonable man.   120
Your father was too, for I have heard of his high fame—the report
that Nisos of Doulichion was a fine man, and a wealthy one too.
They say you are sprung from that man, and you seem a fellow
of measured speech. For this reason I am telling you something,
and please understand me and hear what I am saying. The earth   125
nourishes nothing more feeble than a man, of all the things
that breathe and crawl upon it. For a man thinks that nothing
bad will ever happen in the future, so long as the gods give him
physical prowess and make his knees nimble. But when
the blessed gods bring sorrow, he bears that too, though   130
reluctant, with a steadfast heart. For such is the cast of mind
of the men who are upon the earth— to bear the day that
the father of men and gods brings upon them.°

---

133 . . . *upon them*: That is, man's mind, what he thinks and feels, is subject to as much change as is brought by
the succession of days; you cannot tell where things are going. Life is unpredictable, and you must go where
circumstances take you.

"Once I had
the promise of being a rich man among men, but I did many
135 foolish things, giving way to my might and great power,
trusting in my father and in my brothers. So let no man
at any time be lawless, but let him always keep in silence
whatever gifts the gods give. For I see the suitors doing
foolish things—wasting wealth and disrespecting the wife
140 of a man who I don't think will be long away from his friends
and the land of his fathers. No, he is near! But may a spirit
lead you forth to your house, so that you do not meet up
with him when he returns to the beloved land of his fathers.
For I do not think that he and the suitors will part without
145 bloodshed, when he comes back under his roof."

So Odysseus spoke,
and after pouring a drink-offering he drank the honey-sweet
wine. He placed the cup back in the hands of the marshaller
of the people. Amphinomos went through the house
sorrowful at heart, bowing his head, for his spirit foresaw evil.
150 Even so he did not escape fate: Athena bound him to be killed
at the hands of Telemachos, beneath the might of his spear.

Amphinomos went back and sat down on the same
chair from which he had arisen. Then the goddess flashing-eyed
Athena put the notion in the heart of the daughter of Ikarios,
155 the judicious Penelope, to show herself before the suitors
so that she might set their hearts a-flutter and earn greater
honor from her husband and her son than before.°

She gave a forced laugh and spoke, addressing her slave
woman: "Eurynomê, my heart urges me, unlike before, to show
160 myself to the suitors, although I despise them. Also, I would like
to have a word with my son that will be to his advantage—
that it would be better if he not mix at all with the proud
suitors, who speak kindly, but then afterwards plan evil."

Eurynomê, the housemaid, then said to Penelope:
165 "Yes, you have said everything that is right, my child.
Go then and reveal this word to your son. Do not conceal it.
But first you must wash your skin and oil your face.
Don't go as you are with your face stained by tears.

---

157 *than before*: Penelope is, of course, unaware of her husband's presence, but he is her husband nonetheless.

It's a bad thing to be grieving constantly without end.
Now your son has come of age. You prayed to the gods   170
to see him grow a beard!"

        The judicious Penelope then answered her:
"Eurynomê, do not try to persuade me, though you love me,
to wash myself and anoint my skin with oil. For the gods
who inhabit Olympos took away all my beauty when
that man went in the hollow ships. But summon Autonoê   175
and Hippodameia, would you, so that they may stand beside
me in the hall . . . I will not go in alone to the men, for that would
be immodest."

        So she spoke, and the old woman went through
the halls to tell the women and urge them to come. Then the goddess
flashing-eyed Athena had another thought. She poured out   180
sweet sleep on the daughter of Ikarios. Penelope leaned back
and slept there on her couch, and all her joints were relaxed.
In the meanwhile the beautiful goddess poured out ambrosial
gifts so that the Achaeans would be amazed to see her.
First she cleansed her beautiful face with an ambrosial unguent,   185
the same substance that the fair-crowned Kythereia° uses to anoint
her skin whenever she goes into the lovely dance of the Graces.
And she made her taller and statelier to look upon, and she
made her whiter than new-sawn ivory.

        After doing these things,
the beautiful goddess went off, and the white-armed serving   190
girls came from the hall, talking as they came. And sweet sleep
released Penelope. She rubbed her cheeks with her hands and said:
"Truly, in my deep wretchedness a soft sleep has enfolded me.
I wish that the chaste Artemis would send so soft a death
on me right away, so that I waste my life away no more,   195
going around in sadness, longing for the many-sided goodness
of my husband, who was by far the best of the Achaeans."

    So saying, she descended from the shining upper chamber,
and not alone, for the two serving girls followed her. When the good
woman came to the suitors, she stood beside the doorpost of the well-built   200
hall, holding before her face a glimmering veil. A trusted serving
girl stood on either side of her. And just then Penelope's glow

---

186 *Kythereia*: Aphrodite, because she was sometimes said to be born on the island of Cythera off the south
    coast of the Peloponnesus.

loosened the knees of the suitors. Their hearts were clogged with
lust—each man prayed he might be the one by her side in bed.

205   But she addressed Telemachos, her own dear son: "Telemachos,
I don't think that you have your wits about you, as once you did.
When you were a child you were better at devising clever
counsel. Now that you are big and have come to the full
measure of youth, so that someone who looked only at your stature
210 and good looks—one from a far country—would say that you
were the offspring of a wealthy man—but *now* your thinking is no
longer correct, nor your cast of mind! I mean, what is this
going on in the halls? You allowed a stranger to be abused
in this fashion? How would it be if this stranger, while sitting
215 in our house, should suffer some harm through vicious
mishandling? Then shame and disgrace would fall on *you*
among men."

        Then shrewd Telemachos answered her:
"My mother, I do not blame you for being angry. But I now know
and understand some things in my heart—what is good and what
220 is evil, whereas before I was a child. Still, I cannot make all
things come out right. The suitors sit at my side—one here, one
there—and they divert my will. They do have an evil purpose.
There is no one to help.

                        "But I can tell you that this battle between
the stranger and Iros did not work out according to the suitors'
225 plan—for the stranger proved the stronger! I wish—O father
Zeus and Athena and Apollo—that the suitors in our house
were thus subdued, all nodding their heads, some in the court,
some inside the house. And that the limbs of each man were
loosened, just as Iros now sits against the doors of the court
230 nodding his head like a drunk, and he cannot stand on his feet
or go off home to wherever he used to go because his limbs
are loosened."

        They said such things to one another. Then
Eurymachos had something to say to Penelope: "O daughter
of Ikarios, judicious Penelope! If all the Achaeans throughout
235 Iasian Argos° were to get a look at you, still more suitors

---

235 *Iasian Argos*: Evidently he means the Peloponnesus, but the phrase only appears here in Greek literature.
Iasian may be cognate with *Ionian*, according to a tradition that the Peloponnesus once was populated
by Ionians.

would be dining in your house starting right at dawn, because
you surpass all women in beauty and stature, and in your
balanced mind within!"

      Then the judicious Penelope answered him:
"Eurymachos, I think that the deathless ones destroyed all
my excellence, both of beauty and form, when the Argives   240
went to Ilion, and my husband Odysseus went with them.
If that man were to return and take control of my life, my fame
would be greater and fairer. But as it is, I suffer, for some spirit
has set in motion many evils against me. Yes, when he was leaving
the land of his fathers, my husband gripped me by the right wrist   245
and said: 'My wife, I do not think that all the Achaeans
who wear fancy shin guards will return from Troy safe and unhurt.
For they say that the Trojans are valiant fighting men, good
with the spear, and shooters of arrows, and herders of swift-footed
horses that quickly decide the great battles of an evenly   250
balanced war. I don't know if some god will save me,
or whether I will be cut off there in Troy. So take charge
of everything here. Remember my father and my mother
in the halls, just as now—and still more when I am gone.
But when you see a beard sprouting on our son, then marry   255
whomever you wish, and leave the house.'

      "That's what he said,
and now all is being brought to pass. The night will come
when a hateful marriage will fall to my lot—wretched me!—
whose happiness Zeus has taken away. But this dread pain
comes to my heart and spirit, for you have been suitors   260
in such a way as never before. Those who want to court a lady
of good birth, a daughter of wealth, and who wish to compete
one with another—well, they bring in cattle and strong
flocks, a banquet for the friends of the bride, and they give her
glorious gifts. But they do not eat the substance of another   265
without recompense!"

      So she spoke, and the much-enduring good
Odysseus rejoiced, because she extorted gifts from the suitors
while charming their spirits with honeyed words, having
other things in mind. Then Antinoös, the son of Eupeithes,
spoke to her again: "O daughter of Ikarios, judicious Penelope,   270
whoever of the Achaeans wishes to bring gifts in here—receive
them! For it is not kind to refuse a gift. But we will not go

FIGURE 18.1 Penelope. Wearing a modest head cover (what Homer means by "veil"), she is seated on a stone wall, staring pensively at the ground, thinking of her husband. This is a typical posture in artistic representations of Penelope—legs crossed, looking downward, hand to her face (Figures 2.1, 19.1, 20.1). Roman copy in marble (perhaps first century BC) of a lost Greek original, probably in bronze, c. 460 BC.

to our lands, nor anyplace else, before you marry whoever
is best of the Achaeans."

    So spoke Antinoös, and his word pleased
the others. Each man ordered his herald to bring in gifts.   275
Antinoös' herald brought in a long gown, embroidered,
very beautiful. There were twelve brooches in it, all of them gold,
fitted with curved clasps. For Eurymachos a herald quickly
brought in a complex chain, golden, strung with amber beads,
like the sun. For Eurymedon two aides brought in earrings   280
consisting of three dark drops. A great grace shone from them.
From the house of Peisander, son of the chief Polyktor, an aide
brought a necklace, a wonderfully beautiful jewel. Other
of the Achaeans brought other beautiful gifts.

    Then Penelope went
up to her chamber, a goddess among women, and her servants   285
carried the beautiful gifts behind her.

    Meanwhile the suitors delighted
themselves by turning to the dance and lovely epic song as they
awaited the coming of night. They were still having fun when
black night came on. Quickly they set up three braziers
in the halls, to give them light. Round about inside they put dry   290
kindling, seasoned long since, hardened, recently split by the bronze,
and they mixed in fatwood.° The female slaves of long-suffering
Odysseus kindled the fires in turn.

    Then the Zeus-nourished
resourceful Odysseus spoke to them: "You slaves of Odysseus,
a lord long gone, go into the house where your chaste lady resides.   295
Sit by her side and twist yarn for her. Delight her as you sit
in her chamber, or card the wool with your hands. I will take
care of the fire for all these men, even if they go on to await
the coming of Dawn on her beautiful throne. They will not
outdo me, for I am a man who has suffered much."   300

    So he spoke, and they broke into a laugh,° glancing at one
another. Then pretty-cheeked Melantho insulted him shamefully—
Dolios fathered her, but Penelope had raised and cherished

---

292 *fatwood*: Pine with a high pitch content.
301 *broke into a laugh*: Laughter in Homer is nearly always hostile.

FIGURE 18.2 The suitors bring presents.   Penelope sits on a chair at the far right, receiving
the suitors' gifts. The first suitor seems to offer jewelry in a box. The next suitor, carrying a staff,
brings woven cloth. The third suitor, also with a staff, carries a precious bowl and turns to speak to
the fourth suitor, who brings a bronze mirror. Athenian red-figure vase, c. 470 BC.

her as her own child, giving her playthings that delighted her heart.
Even so Melantho felt no sorrow for Penelope, but she consorted
with Eurymachos and had sex with him.

                     Melantho insulted
Odysseus with reviling words: "Stranger—you wretch! You seem
out of your mind! You do not want to go to a blacksmith's
house, or to a public lodging, but here you blather on boldly
with many men, and you have no fear in your heart. Either you
are drunk, or maybe this is your ordinary state of mind,
that you babble idly? Or are you so full of yourself because
you beat the beggar Iros? Be careful that some other, better
than Iros, does not quickly stand up and beat you about the head
with his powerful hands and send you out of the house,
hard head streaming a lot of blood!"

                Looking from beneath
his brows the resourceful Odysseus said: "I shall soon go over
there and tell Telemachos what you have said, you *bitch*,
so that on this very spot he might cut you limb from limb."

    So speaking he frightened away the women with his words.
They went through the house, and the limbs of each were
loosened in terror. For they feared he meant just as he spoke.

    Odysseus took his stand beside the blazing braziers,
giving light to the room and looking on all the men. His heart
pondered other things, things that were not to be left unfulfilled.

    But Athena did not allow the proud suitors to leave off
at all from their offending insolence, so that pain might sink
yet deeper into the heart of Odysseus, son of Laërtes.
Eurymachos, the son of Polybos, began to speak to them,
jeering at Odysseus, and raising a laugh among his companions:
"Hear me, suitors of a famous lady, so that I may say what
the spirit in my chest urges me to say. This man has not come
into Odysseus' house without the guidance of some god.
Just so, it seems to me that there is a glare of torches from him—
or, from his head, for there is no hair on it—not a single strand!"

    He spoke, and at the same time he called out to Odysseus,
the sacker of cities: "Stranger! You know, if you want to work
for hire, I could take you on in the outermost fields. I can
guarantee the pay, gathering stones for walls and planting

340 tall trees. There I would provide you with food all year round,
and I would give you some clothes and sandals for your feet.
But because you have learned only evil deeds, you will not
want to take a job, for you'd rather beg through the land
so that you can feed your insatiate belly."

                                          The resourceful Odysseus
345 said in reply: "Eurymachos, I only wish that the two of us
could have a labor contest in the springtime when the days
are long, at mowing a field. Yes, I would have a curved scythe,
and you would have the same, and there would be plenty of grass
so we could test ourselves against it—and we would not eat
350 anything until late evening. Or, I wish that there were cattle
to drive—the best, tawny, large, both well fed on grass, of a like
age, of a like power to bear the yoke, of exhaustless strength . . .
and that there were a field of four acres, and that the soil
should yield before the plow. *Then* you would see me, whether
355 I could cut a continuous furrow to the end. Or yet, I wish that
the son of Zeus should stir up a war in some quarter today,
and I had a shield and two spears and a bronze helmet fitted
to my temples: Then you would see me mixing with the foremost
fighters, and you would not babble, taunting this stomach of mine.

360   "But you are too insolent. Your mind is cruel. You think
that you are a great and powerful man because you associate
with few men, and hardly from the best class. If Odysseus
were to come and return to the land of his fathers, quickly
those doors over there, wide as they may be, would not
365 be wide enough for you as you fled away."

                                          So Odysseus spoke,
and Eurymachos grew still more angry in his heart. Looking
from beneath his brows, he spoke words that went like arrows:
"You filth! I shall soon work evil on you, because you blather
on boldly with many men, and you have no fear in your heart.
370 Perhaps you are drunk, or maybe this is your ordinary state
of mind, that you babble idly? Or are you so all puffed up
because you beat the beggar Iros?"

                                          So speaking, he picked up a stool,
but Odysseus hunched down at the knees of Amphinomos
of Doulichion, in fear of Eurymachos—and the stool hit
375 a cupbearer on the right hand. His wine-jug fell to the ground
with a clang, and the bearer groaned and fell backwards

in the dust. The suitors broke into an uproar through the shadowy
halls, and one would glance at his neighbor and say: "I wish
that the stranger had perished elsewhere on his travels,
before he came here. Then he would not have caused us so
much trouble. Now we are arguing about beggars! There is
no sweetness in the noble feast now, while bad things
are on the rise."

Then the resolutely strong Telemachos
spoke to them: "Come good friends, you are out of control!
You no longer conceal that you have eaten and drunk. Some
god drives you on. So go to your homes and take your rest,
now that you have eaten well—I mean whenever the spirit
moves you. I'm not chasing anyone out."

Thus he spoke,
and everyone sat stunned and marveled at Telemachos,
for he had spoken boldly. Then Amphinomos spoke
and addressed them, the glorious son of prince Nisus,
son of Aretias: "My friends, one would never grow angry
at what was justly said, nor reply with wrangling words.
So, don't abuse the stranger or any other of the slaves who live
in the house of godlike Odysseus. But come, let a cupbearer
fill our cups for a drink-offering so that we can pour
out an offering and go home to bed. And let us leave the stranger
in the house of Odysseus for Telemachos to take care of.
It's *his* house that he has come to."

So he spoke, and the word
was pleasing to them. Brave Moulios, a herald from Doulichion
and aide to Amphinomos, mixed a wine-bowl for them.

He distributed the wine to all, coming to each in turn.
They poured out an offering to the blessed gods, then drank
the honey-sweet wine. When they had completed the offering
and had drunk as much as each man wanted, they went
off each one to his own home to take their rest.

380

385

390

395

400

405

BOOK 19. *Odysseus' Scar*

The good Odysseus was left in the hall, pondering death for the suitors
with the help of Athena. At once he spoke to Telemachos words
that went like arrows: "Telemachos, you must store away the weapons
of war inside, absolutely all of them. Trick the suitors with soft
5   words when they notice that the armor is gone and ask you about it.°
Say: 'I have taken them down out of the smoke, because they
no longer have the same appearance as when Odysseus left them
and went off to Troy, but they are corroded, to the extent that the breath
of the fire reached them. Also, and even more, a spirit has put this
10 in my breast, the thought that when you are drunk a fight might
break out among you. You might wound one another and bring
shame to the feast and the suit for my mother's hand! For the iron
draws a man to it.'"

So he spoke, and Telemachos obeyed his father.
He called over the nurse Eurykleia and said to her: "Nurse, shut up
15 the women in their rooms while I put away my father's weapons
in the storeroom, the beautiful weapons which the smoke
is corroding as they lay uncared for throughout the house since
my father went away. I was just a little tyke then. But now I want
to put these things away so that the breath of fire won't get to them."

20   The nurse Eurykleia answered him: "I only wish, child,
that you would take thought for the running of the house, and guard
all your possessions. But come, who will get a light and carry it
for you? For you do not allow the female slaves to precede you,
who might have given you light."

The shrewd Telemachos answered her:
25 "This stranger will do it. I will not allow a man to be idle who
eats my bread, even though he comes from a long way off."

So Telemachos spoke, for her words had gone like arrows.
Eurykleia shut the doors of the stately hall. Odysseus and his brilliant
son, the two of them, sprang up and carried off the helmets and bossed

---

5   *about it*: In fact, the suitors never ask about the armor.

shields and the sharp-pointed spears. Pallas Athena went before them,   30
carrying a golden lamp° that made a very beautiful light.

Then suddenly Telemachos spoke to his father: "O Father,
truly this is a great wonder that my eyes behold! Surely the walls
of the house and the beautiful beams and the cross-beams of fir,
and the pillars that reach up high, seem as if they blaze with fire.   35
Surely, there is some god within, of those who hold the broad sky."

The resourceful Odysseus said in reply: "Be quiet! and check
your thought. Don't ask questions. This is the way of the gods
who hold Olympos. But you go on to bed, and I will stay here
behind so that I may challenge the slave women and your mother,   40
who will weep and ask me about everything."

So he spoke,
and Telemachos went through the hall, lit by the light of blazing
torches, to go to his chamber and lie down, where he was accustomed
to rest. Sweet sleep came over him as he lay down and awaited
the shining Dawn. But the good Odysseus was left behind in the hall,   45
pondering death for the suitors with the help of Athena.

The judicious
Penelope then came out of her chamber, looking like Artemis or golden
Aphrodite. Servants set down a chair for her near the fire, where
she liked to sit, worked with coils of ivory and silver. The craftsman
Ikmalios° once had made it, and he fitted beneath it a built-in   50
footstool for the feet. A fleece was thrown over the chair.
There the judicious Penelope sat. Her white-armed female
slaves came from the women's hall. They began to take away
the abundant food, the tables, and the cups, from which the too-bold
men had been drinking. They cast the embers from the braziers   55
down onto the floor, and they piled lots of dried wood
on the braziers, for illumination and heat.

Then Melantho for a second
time scolded Odysseus: "Stranger, will you continue to be a nuisance
to us through the night, roaming about the house? Will you spy on

---

31 *lamp*: This is the only time that a lamp (a wick in a vessel) is referred to in all of Homer. Otherwise lighting is
    always provided by torches. Lamps disappear from the archaeological record after the end of the Bronze Age
    (c. 1100 BC) and do not reappear until the seventh century BC. But perhaps their use continued in a cultic
    context: This is the lamp of Athena.

50 *Ikmalios*: Probably "beater," as of one working metal; the name occurs only here.

60 the women? Why, get outside, you rogue, and enjoy your dinner
there! Either that or be smashed with a torch and go out that way!"

But the resourceful Odysseus looked from beneath his brows
and said: "Good woman, why do you come on so against me with
an angry heart? Is it because I am filthy, and I wear ragged clothes
65 around my skin, and I go around the country begging? But I cannot
help it. Beggars and wanderers are like that. You know, once
I lived in a house among men, a rich man in a rich house,
and I often gave to a wanderer, no matter who he was or with
whatever need he came. I had countless slaves and many other things
70 by which men live well and are called rich. But Zeus, the son
of Kronos, ruined it all—I suppose he wanted to. Beware that
you too, woman, do not lose all the glory through which you stand
out among the slaves if your mistress becomes angry with you,
or if Odysseus returns. There is still room for hope. And already
75 his son is such as *he* was, by the favor of Apollo—Telemachos.
He will be aware of any sexual play among you women.
He is no longer the child he was."

So he spoke, and judicious Penelope
overheard him. She rebuked Melantho and addressed her, saying:
"Don't think, you hussy—you shameless bitch!—that your
80 outrageous behavior is unknown to me! With your *own* head you will
wipe away its stain!° You knew full well—because you heard it
from me myself, that I wanted to ask the stranger in my halls
about my husband. I suffer *so* . . ."

She spoke, and then she addressed
Eurynomê: "Eurynomê, bring a chair and put a fleece on it so that
85 the stranger can sit down with me and tell me his tale, and listen to me.
I want to question him closely."

So she spoke, and Eurynomê quickly
brought in a well-polished chair and set it down, and she threw
a fleece over it. That is where the much-enduring good Odysseus sat
as judicious Penelope began to speak: "Stranger, I would like
90 myself to ask you something first. Who are you among men,
and where do you come from? Where is your city and your parents?"

---

81 *away its stain:* The expression comes from the custom of wiping the blood off the sacrificial knife onto the
sacrificial victim, as if to divert the guilt for killing onto the victim itself. As used by Penelope here, the
figure means that Melantho will *not* succeed in transferring guilt, but the guilt will fall on the head of the
doer of the deed—herself.

The resourceful Odysseus then said in reply: "My lady, no
mortal on the boundless earth could find fault with you. Truly your
fame reaches the broad heaven, as does the fame of some excellent
chieftain who like a god rules amidst many powerful men, upholds   95
justice, and the black earth bears wheat and barley, and the trees
bristle with fruit, the flocks multiply unceasingly, and the sea
provides fish—all from his fine leadership as the people prosper
under his rule. For which reason ask me about anything—I am
in your house—but do not ask about my family and the land   100
of my fathers. You will fill my heart more with pain as I think
on such things. I am a man of many sorrows. Nor is it right
that I sit in another's house moaning and wailing, for it is a poor
thing to grieve continuously. Don't let any of your slaves be angry
with me, or you yourself, because you say that I swim in tears   105
because my heart is made heavy by wine."

                              The judicious Penelope
then answered him: "Stranger, I think that the deathless ones
destroyed all my excellence, both of beauty and of form, when
the Argives went to Ilion, and with them went my husband, Odysseus.
If that man were to return and take control of my life, my fame   110
would be greater and fairer. But as it is, I suffer. Some spirit
has set in motion many evils against me. Whoever are strong
in the islands DOULICHION and SAMÊ and wooded ZAKYNTHOS,
and those who live in clear-seen ITHACA itself—these men court me,
though I am unwilling, and lay waste to the house. For this reason   115
I pay no attention to strangers, nor to suppliants, nor to heralds,
who are workers for the public good. In longing for my dear
Odysseus I waste away my heart.

                              "But these suitors hasten
on the marriage, though I have woven a bundle of tricks. A spirit
suggested to me first of all that I set up a great loom in my halls   120
to weave a robe, fine and wide. I right away spoke among the suitors:
'Young men, my suitors, because the good Odysseus has died,
be patient, though you are eager for my marriage, until I finish
this robe—I would not want my spinning to come to nothing!
It is a burial shroud for Lord Laërtes, for the day when the ruinous   125
fate of dreadful death will take him. In this way no one of the Achaean
women will be angry with me, saying that he lay without a shroud
who once was rich.'

                              "So I spoke, and their proud hearts agreed.
I wove at that great loom all day long, but at night, with torches

FIGURE 19.1 Melian relief with Odysseus and Penelope. A curious series of small, shallow relief sculptures with flat backs were produced on the island of Melos from about 470 to 416 BC, called "Melian reliefs" (compare Figure 20.1). Details were once painted in, but the paint is now mostly gone. They usually show narrative subjects from Greek myth. They were perhaps made for wooden boxes, an inexpensive imitation for reliefs made in more expensive materials, such as ivory. Many have holes for attachment. But their true purpose is unknown.

In this relief, Odysseus wears his typical felt traveler's cap. He is "heroically nude" from the waist down, but carries a pouch and a staff, just as Homer describes. He speaks to the demure Penelope, who typically casts her eyes to the ground.

In 416 BC, Melos was taken by Athens in the Peloponnesian War. The men were killed and the women and children sold into slavery, bringing to an end the production of Melian reliefs. Painted terracotta, c. 450 BC.

beside me, I unraveled it. And so for three years I deceived   130
and beguiled the Achaeans. But when the fourth year came on
as the seasons advanced, as the months raced away, as the many
days came to completion, then, thanks to my women slaves—
those uncaring bitches!—they came in and caught me. They loudly
reproached me.   135

      "And so I finished the robe, although I didn't want to—
but because I was forced to. And now I cannot escape the marriage.
I cannot find a way out. Furthermore, my parents want me to marry,
and my son is impatient as he sees the suitors devouring his livelihood.
By now he is a man and fully capable of taking care of a household
to which Zeus grants glory.   140

      "So tell me of your family, where you
are from. For I don't think you sprang from an oak, as the old story
tells it, nor from a stone!"°

      The resourceful Odysseus said in reply:
"Revered lady, wife of Odysseus son of Laërtes, will you *never*
stop asking me about my family? But I will tell you—and you will
cause me to suffer more pain than I already do. For that is the way   145
things are, when a man is gone for so long from his country
as I have been now, wandering through the many cities of men,
suffering always. Even so I will tell you what you ask and inquire about.

      "There is a land called CRETE in the middle of the wine-dark sea,
beautiful and rich, surrounded by water. Many men live there,   150
numberless, and ninety cities. One tongue is mixed with another.
There dwell the Achaeans, the great-hearted True-Cretans,
the Kydonians, and the Dorians divided into three tribes,
and the good Pelasgians.° The greatest city is KNOSSOS,
where Minos ruled in nine-year cycles,° he who conversed with   155

---

142   *... a stone*: A proverbial expression apparently referring to myths of the origin of humans from oak trees or
     from stones. Penelope means that the beggar has real life-blood ancestors and now has come the time to
     reveal them.

154   *... Pelasgians*: The Achaeans are the Mycenaean Greeks, under the leadership of Idomeneus; the True-
     Cretans are the aboriginal inhabitants, the descendants of the Minoans; the Kydonians live near the river
     Iardanos in the northwest of the island; the Dorians are, strangely, mentioned only here in all of Homer,
     the inhabitants of the Peloponnesus during the Classical Period (Sparta was a Dorian state) and the
     predominant group in Crete during the eighth century BC; the Pelasgians are a mysterious unidentified
     aboriginal people.

155   *nine-year cycles*: Perhaps to correspond with a ritual festival cycle; or the phrase could mean "when he was
     nine years old."

great Zeus. Minos was the father of my father, great-hearted Deukalion.
Deukalion bore me and King Idomeneus.°

                            "Now Idomeneus went off
to Troy in his beaked ships together with the sons of Atreus.
My famous name is Aithon,° the younger by birth—Idomeneus
160 was older and a better man. There in Crete I saw Odysseus. I gave
him the gifts of guest-friendship. The strength of the wind drove
him to Crete as he made for Troy, knocking him off course
near CAPE MALEA. He docked his boats in AMNISOS, where there is
a cave of Eileithyia,° in a harbor where the water was rough,
165 and he barely escaped the storm. Odysseus went straight to the city
and asked for Idomeneus. He said that he was his guest-friend,
beloved and respected. But it was now the tenth or the eleventh
day that Idomeneus had gone off to Ilion in his beaked ships.
So I took him to my house and entertained him well, with kindly
170 welcome, and I drew from the abundance in my house. To the rest
of his companions, who followed with him, I gathered up
and gave out barley from the public store and flaming wine
and cattle to sacrifice, so that they might satisfy their hearts.
The good Achaeans remained there for twelve days, for the great
175 North Wind held them back. You could not even stand on the land!
Some hard spirit had aroused it. But on the thirteenth day
the wind subsided, and they put to sea."

                            He spoke on, knowing how
to make the many falsehoods in his tale seem like truth,
and Penelope's tears ran when she heard him, and her skin melted
180 from her tears, as when snow melts on the peaks of the high
mountains that East Wind has melted, when West Wind has scattered it.
The rivers fill with running water as the snow melts—even so her
beautiful cheeks melted as she poured down tears, lamenting
her husband, who even then sat there beside her.

                            But Odysseus took
185 pity in his heart for his own weeping wife, though his eyes stood

---

157 *Idomeneus*: In his earlier false tale to Eumaios (Book 14), Odysseus claimed to be the illegitimate son of
     a Cretan nobleman by a concubine; now he has gone up the social scale and is brother to the king himself.

159 *Aithon*: "with-a-dark-complexion."

164 *of Eileithyia*: There is, in fact, a cave of the birth-goddess Eileithyia in the harbor of Amnisos on Crete,
     which received cult offerings between the third millennium and the fifth century BC (c. 3000-450 BC).
     The name Eileithyia appears on the Linear B tablets and is sometimes explained as Greek "she-who-makes-
     one-come," that is, the child, but it may be a nonGreek name for the Great Mother goddess of nature and
     fertility. Her cult is testified by primitive figurines found all over the Near East from a very early time.

like horn or iron, unmovable between his lids, and cunningly,
he hid his tears. When she had had her fill of tearful wailing,
she answered him right away and said: "Now, stranger, I think
I will put you to the test to see if you truly entertained my husband
with his godlike companions in your halls, as you say. So tell me,   190
what kind of clothes was he wearing? And what kind man was he,
and tell me of the companions who followed him."

         Then the resourceful
Odysseus answered her: "Woman, it is hard for one who has been
so long gone to speak of this. It is already the twentieth year since
he went off and left my country, but I will tell you as I remember it.   195
The good Odysseus wore a purple cloak, woolen, doubled.
It had a brooch made of gold with twin sheaths,° and it was delicately
worked on the front. A dog held a spotted fawn with his forepaws,
staring at the fawn as he strangled it. Everyone who saw it was
amazed, how although made of gold the dog held down the fawn   200
and throttled it. The fawn writhed with its feet, striving to escape.
I noted the shirt around his skin that shone like the skin of a dried
onion, so soft it was, and it glistened like the sun. I can tell you,
the women marveled at him!

       "But I will tell you something else,
and you take it to heart. I do not know whether Odysseus wore   205
this garment about his skin when he was at home, or whether
one of his comrades gave it to him as he went on the swift ship,
or whether perhaps a guest-friend gave it to him—for Odysseus
was guest-friend to many. There were few of the Achaeans
who were his equal. I gave him a bronze sword and a fringed   210
shirt of double fold—beautiful, purple-dyed—and I respectfully
sent him on his way in his well-benched ship.

       "And his herald,
who was a little older than Odysseus, followed behind. And I will
tell you about this herald, what kind of man he was. He had round
shoulders, and a dark complexion, and he was curly-haired.   215
His name was Eurybates.° Odysseus honored him above all his
companions, because they were of a like mind."

        So Odysseus spoke,
and he stirred in Penelope the desire to weep still more, because

---

197 *twin sheaths*: Into which two pins fit, to close the brooch.

216 *Eurybates*: He figures in the *Iliad* as Odysseus' herald.

she recognized the sure token that Odysseus had described.
220 When she had had her fill of tearful wailing, then she answered him
with these words: "Now, stranger, though before you were pitiable,
now you are a friend in my halls and we respect you. For it was
I who gave him these clothes that you describe, folding them
and removing them from the storage chamber, and I added
225 the shining brooch as a treasure. But I will never again receive
that man coming home to the land of his fathers. Truly Odysseus
went forth with an evil fate when he journeyed in a hollow ship
to see that cursed Ilion, not to be named!"

                        Then the resourceful
Odysseus said to her in reply: "O woman, honored wife
230 of Odysseus, son of Laërtes, don't stain your beautiful skin
any more with tears, and do not despair at heart, wailing for your
husband. I do not blame you at all. Any woman weeps when she
has lost her wedded husband, to whom she has borne children after
mingling in love, though her husband was different from Odysseus,
235 who they say was like the gods.

                        "But give up your weeping, and listen
to what I have to say. I will tell you truly and I will not conceal it.
I have heard that Odysseus will return home soon, that he is now
in the rich land of the Thresprotians—that he is alive! He has
acquired many fine treasures, begging through the land, but he lost
240 his entire crew and his hollow ship on the wine-dark sea when he left
the island of Thrinakia. Zeus and Helios were angered with him,
for his companions had killed the cattle of Helios. And so they
were all destroyed on the foamy sea, but a wave tossed
Odysseus, riding the keel of the ship, onto the dry land, the land
245 of the Phaeacians, who are close kin with the gods.°

                        "The Phaeacians
heartily honored him, like a god, and they gave him many gifts
and wanted themselves to send him home unharmed. And Odysseus
would long since have been here, excepts that it seemed better
in his heart to gather riches wandering over the broad earth.
250 Odysseus knows beyond all other mortal men the pathway
to riches, nor could any other compete with him.

---

245 *the gods*: Odysseus conflates the wreck off Thrinakia with the wrecked raft off Phaeacia and so avoids
having to talk about Kalypso!

                                          "So Pheidon,
chief of the Thesprotians, told me the tale. And he swore to me,
pouring drink-offerings, that the ship was launched and the men
ready who would take Odysseus to the land of his fathers.
But he sent me off first, for there happened to be a ship   255
of Thesprotians that was going to Doulichion, rich in wheat.
And Pheidon showed the riches that Odysseus had gathered.
They would support a man's children up to the tenth generation,
so many treasures lay in the house of the king. But Odysseus,
Pheidon said, had gone to Dodona to hear the advice of Zeus   260
from the god's high oak, whether being gone so long he should
return openly or in secret.

                        "And so he is safe and will return soon—
very soon. He will not long be far from his friends and the land
of his fathers. All the same, I will swear you an oath. May Zeus
be my witness first of all, the highest and best of the gods,   265
and the hearth of noble Odysseus to which I have come:
All these things shall come to pass that I say. In the course
of this very month Odysseus will come home, as the old moon
wanes and the new one appears."°

                        The judicious Penelope answered
him: "I *wish* that what you say would come to pass. Then you   270
would quickly come to know of our friendship, and receive so many
gifts from me that someone, meeting you, would say you were blessed.

   "But this seems to me how things will turn out: Odysseus
will never return to his home, nor will you obtain a convoy
from here, because there are not such masters in the house as   275
Odysseus was among men—if he ever lived!—who can send away
and receive respectable guest-friends. Still—slaves, will you
wash this man and prepare a bed for him? And spread on a bedstead
robes and shining blankets so that he may arrive nice and warm
to Dawn on her golden throne. At dawn, bathe him and oil him,   280
so that he may take thought for dinner inside, with Telemachos,
sitting in the hall. And all the worse for any man who commits
any abuse against this stranger! That man will accomplish nothing
more here, though he is exceedingly angry.

                        "For how, O stranger,
will you know if I excel other women in wit and in a discreet mind   285

---

269   ... *appears*: When the new moon festival of Apollo will be held, the day of doom for the suitors.

if all unkempt and dressed in rags you sit in our halls to dine?
Humans don't live long. And everyone calls down pain in times
to come on him who is mean-spirited and hard-hearted,
and when he is dead everyone makes fun of him. But if one
290 is blameless and has a blameless heart, then strangers
spread his fame far and wide among all humans, and many call
him a real man."

       The resourceful Odysseus then said in reply:
"Lady, wife of Odysseus, the son of Laërtes, truly cloaks and shining
blankets became hateful to me on the day when first we turned
295 our back on the snowy mountains of Crete, sailing in a long-oared ship.
No, I will lie as I have been used to rest through sleepless nights.
Many are the nights I have slept on a foul bed awaiting shining Dawn
on her beautiful throne. Nor do baths for the feet give me pleasure.
And no woman will take hold of my foot of those who are servants
300 in this house—unless you have some ancient old lady, wise in her
years who has suffered as many pains in her heart as have I.
One such as that could touch my feet."

       Then the judicious Penelope said:
"Dear stranger, never has a wanderer from far away come into
my house whose words are more sensible. You are welcome here,
305 so wise and prudent is everything that you say. I have an old woman,
wise from her years, of good sense, who nourished and suckled
that wretched man—Odysseus—whom she took into her arms
when her mother first bore him. She will wash your feet, though
she is weak with age.

       "So get up now, wise Eurykleia, and wash
310 the feet of one of like age to your king! Even such as his are this
man's feet, and even such are his hands. For mortals quickly
grow old when their fortune is ill."

       So she spoke, and the old woman
hid her face in her hands, and she poured down hot tears, and she spoke
a word of lamentation: "O Odysseus, my child, I am in despair
315 about you. Surely Zeus has hated you above all humans, although
you are god-fearing. Never before has any mortal burned so many
fat thigh pieces to Zeus who delights in the thunderbolt, nor killed
so many perfect beasts as you killed in his honor, praying that you
might reach a sleek old age and raise your glorious son. But now
320 he has altogether taken away from you alone the day of your
homecoming. I suppose that the women of these strange and distant

lands mocked him when he came to their glorious houses, just as
these sluts mock you here, all of them. Is it to avoid their insult
and shameless words that you won't allow them to wash your feet?
Well, the daughter of Ikarios, prudent Penelope, asks me to do it,   325
and I am not unwilling. I'll wash your feet, for our Penelope's sake
and for your own. The heart within me is moved with sorrow.
But come now, listen to the word that I say—Many long-suffering
strangers have come here, but not ever do I think I have seen a man
so like another as you are like Odysseus in your stature, in your voice,   330
and in the shape of your feet."

                    Then the resourceful Odysseus said
in reply: "Old lady, that's what everybody says who has seen
the two of us with his own eyes, that we are remarkably like
one another, as you shrewdly observe."

                         So he spoke and the old
woman took the shining cauldron in which she was going to wash   335
his feet, and she poured in a quantity of cold water, then hot on top,
while Odysseus sat far away from the hearth. But quickly he turned
toward the shadows, suddenly realizing that, as she touched him,
she might notice his scar, that everything would come out into the open.

   She washed him, coming in close to her king, and immediately   340
she recognized the scar, which once a boar had driven in with
his white tusks when he went to Parnassos, to Autolykos°
and his sons, the noble father of his mother, who surpassed all
men in thievery and in the swearing of false oaths. For the god
Hermes himself had given him this gift, to whom Autolykos burned   345
the pleasing thigh bones of sheep and goats, and the god befriended
him with a ready heart.

                   Autolykos happened to come to the rich land
of Ithaca and found that his daughter had recently borne a son.
Eurykleia placed the child on his knees just after he had finished
dinner, and she said to him: "Now come up with a name that you can   350
give the dear child of your child, who has long been prayed for."

   Autolykos replied and answered: "My son-in-law and daughter,
give this boy the name that I say. I come as a man *who has been*

---

342 *Autolykos*: "true wolf," a speaking name reflecting his character, similar to Odysseus' in all its negative
     aspects. In *Iliad* 10, Autolykos is said to have stolen a boar's tusk helmet from a certain Amyntor. Parnassos
     is a high snow-capped mountain in Phocis; Delphi is built on the southern slopes of Parnassos.

angered [*odyssamenos*]° with many, both with men and women over
355 the much-nourishing earth. Therefore let the name of the child
be *Odysseus*, a signifying name. And when he comes of age let him
come to the great house of his mother's family at Parnassos, where my
possessions are. I'll give him some and will send him home in joy."

For this reason Odysseus came, so that Autolykos could
360 give him glorious gifts. Autolykos and the sons of Autolykos clasped
his hands in welcome and spoke honeyed words. Amphithea,
my mother's mother, took Odysseus in her arms and kissed his head
and both his beautiful eyes. Autolykos called out to his noble sons
to prepare a meal, and they heard his command. Right away they
365 brought in a five-year old ox. They skinned and dressed the animal
and cut it into quarters. They cut these up skillfully and pierced them
on spits. They roasted and divided up the pieces. Thus they feasted
all day long until the sun went down, nor did the spirit of any lack
in the equal feast. When the sun set and the shadows came on,
370 then they lay down to rest and took the gift of sleep.

When early-born
Dawn appeared with her fingers of rose, they went off on a hunt,
the hounds and the sons of Autolykos too, and with them went
the good Odysseus. They went up the steep mountain of Parnassos,
covered in forest, and soon they came into its windy valleys.
375 Helios was just then striking the fields as he rose from softly
gliding, deep-flowing Ocean when the beaters came into a gorge.
Before them went the hounds, tracking the scent, and behind
them came the sons of Autolykos, and with them the good Odysseus,
close on the hounds, brandishing his long-shadowed spear.
380 Now nearby in a dense thicket lay a huge boar. The strength
of the wet winds did not penetrate this thicket, nor did shining
Helios strike it with his rays, nor could the rains pierce through—
so thick it was!—and there was a huge mass of fallen leaves.

Then around the boar came the noise of the feet of men and dogs
385 as they pressed on in the chase. He charged from his hiding place,
his hair bristling and standing up, and he glanced fire from his eyes
as he stood right before them. Odysseus was first to rush up, holding
his long spear in a powerful hand, eager to hit him, but the boar
got in first and struck him above the knee, charging on him sideways,

---

353–354   *who has been angered*: The Greek is *odyssamenos*, punning on the name of *Odysseus*, but we are unsure
of the meaning of *odyssamenos*: Either it means "the man who has been angered" or it means "the man
who makes others angry." In reality, the name of Odysseus is probably not Greek.

and with his white tusk he tore away much of the flesh. But he did   390
not reach the man's bone. Odysseus with his sure aim hit the boar
on the right shoulder, and straight through went the tip of the shining
spear. The boar fell in the dust with a cry, and his spirit fled away.

The sons of Autolykos busied themselves with the boar,
and they skillfully bound up the wound of handsome Odysseus,   395
like a god, and they stopped the black blood by a spell. Quickly
they returned to the house of their dear father. Autolykos and the sons
of Autolykos doctored him well and gave him glorious gifts
and soon sent him rejoicing to the lovely land of his fathers,
to Ithaca. Odysseus' father and revered mother were very happy   400
to see him return and they asked him about everything and how
he got the scar. He told them all the truth, how when he was hunting
a boar wounded him with its white tusk, when he went into Parnassos
with the sons of Autolykos.

　　　　　　　　　Touching this scar with the flat of her hands,
feeling over it, Eurykleia knew what it was, and she dropped his foot.   405
His leg fell into the basin and the bronze resounded. The bowl
tipped on its side and all the water ran out on the ground.
Joy and terror overcame her mind at the same time, and her two eyes
filled with tears, and her voice grew full.

　　　　　　　　　　Taking hold of Odysseus' chin
she said: "Truly you are Odysseus, my child! And I did not   410
recognize you before I had handled my king all over." So she spoke
and glanced over at Penelope, wanting to tell her that her dear
husband was in the house. But Penelope could not see her,
nor understand, because Athena had turned her thoughts aside.

Odysseus, feeling for the old woman's throat, seized it   415
with his right hand and with his other pulled her in close to him
and said: "Old lady, why do you want to destroy me? You yourself
nursed me at your tit. Now after suffering many pains I have returned
in the twentieth year to the land of my fathers. But because you
have found out and a god has placed this in your heart—keep quiet!   420
Let no one else in these halls take notice. For I will tell you this,
and I think it will come to pass: If some god allows me to take
the bold suitors, I will not spare you, though you were my nurse,
when I kill the other slave women in the my halls."

　　　　　　　　　　The thoughtful Eurykleia
then said: "My child, what a word has come from your lips!   425

FIGURE 19.2 Eurykleia washing Odysseus' feet. The old woman, wearing the short hair of a slave, is about to discover the scar on Odysseus' leg. The bearded Odysseus, dressed in rags, holds a staff in his right hand and a stick supporting his pouch in his left. He wears an odd traveler's hat with a bill to shade his eyes. Attic red-figure drinking cup by the Penelope Painter, from Chiusi, c. 440 BC.

You know how my strength is steadfast and unyielding. I will be
as steady as hard stone or iron. I will tell you something else,
and you best take account of it. If some god allows you to overcome
the bold suitors, then I will tell you in detail which women
in the halls dishonor you, and which are guiltless."   430

                                Then the resourceful
Odysseus said in reply: "Old lady, why will you tell me who they are?
There is no need. I can see for myself and I will come to know
about each. So keep your tale to yourself. Turn it over to the gods."

    So he spoke, and the old woman went through the hall to get
water for his feet, because all the first had spilled. When she had washed   435
him and anointed him richly with oil, Odysseus again moved
his chair over closer to the fire, to warm himself, and he concealed
the scar beneath his rags.

                                Then the judicious Penelope was first
to speak: "Stranger, this little further thing will I ask you. Then soon
it will be the hour for pleasant rest, for him at least on whom   440
sleep can come, though one is troubled at heart. But for me some
spirit has given measureless sorrow. All day long I come to the end
of grieving, mourning, looking to my household tasks and those
of my attendants in the house. When night comes, and sleep
takes all, I lie on the bed. Then sharp anxiety, crowding around   445
my crowded heart, disquiets me as I mourn. As when the daughter
of Pandareos, nightingale of the green wood, sings beautifully
at the beginning of spring as she sits among the thick leafage
of the trees, and in thickly trilling notes pours out her many-toned
voice in mourning for her dear son Itylos, whom once she carelessly   450
killed with the bronze, the son of King Zethos—even so my heart
is pushed this way and that, whether I should stay with my son
and see that everything is safe—my property, the slaves, and the great
high-roofed house—respecting the bed of my husband and my reputation
among the people, or whether I should follow whoever is best   455
of the Achaeans in his suit, and has offered countless wedding-gifts.°

    "So long as my son was a child and of empty mind, he would
not let me marry and leave the house of my husband. But now that

---

456   ...wedding-gifts: The story of Pandareos and his daughter, who unintentionally killed her own child, the son of
       Zethus, king of Thebes, is unknown from other sources. A rather different story is known from the Athenian
       tradition. The obscure point of comparison seems to be that, as Pandareos' daughter bewailed her unintentional
       homicide, so Penelope may have to bewail her own son if the suitors kill him because she refused to marry.

he is big and has reached the measure of maturity, he begs me
460   to retreat from the hall, impatient over his wealth that the Achaeans
consume. But come, listen to this dream of mine, tell me what you
think. Twenty geese were out of the water and eating wheat
in my house, and I warmed with joy looking at them. Then a great eagle
with bent beak came from the mountains, and he broke the necks
465   of all of them and put them to death. They were scattered in piles
throughout the halls. Then he arose into the bright sky. But I wept
and was sorry, although it was a dream, and the Achaean women
with their fine hairdos gathered around me as I piteously complained
that the eagle had killed my geese.

                              "Then the eagle returned
470   and sat down on a projecting roof beam, and with the voice
of a mortal man he restrained my weeping, and he said: 'Courage,
daughter of far-famed Ikarios! This is not a dream, but true reality,
a vision of what will come to pass. The geese are the suitors,
and I who once was the eagle, a bird, am now your husband
475   returned, who will impose a bitter doom on all the suitors.'
So he spoke, and then sweet sleep released me. I looked about,
and I saw the geese in the halls eating wheat beside the trough,
just as they usually do."

                              Replying to her the resourceful Odysseus said:
"Lady, there is no way to turn aside the meaning of this dream,
480   for Odysseus himself indicates how he will bring this about—
destruction for the suitors, for all of them, is plain to see. Not one
of them will escape death and the fates!"

                              Then the judicious Penelope
said: "Stranger, surely dreams are baffling and hard to interpret,
and they do not fulfill all things for all men. For there are two
485   gates of strengthless dreams. The one is made of horn, and other
of ivory [*elephanti*]. Those dreams that pass through sawn ivory, they *cause
harm* [*elephairontai*], bringing things that do not come to pass. Those that
pass outside through the gates *of horn* [*keraôn*], they *are accomplished* [*krainousi*]
as true, when some mortal sees them.° But I don't think that this

---

489   ... *sees them*: The symbolism of the gates of horn, through which true dreams pass, and the gates of ivory,
        through which false dreams pass, has never been explained. In the Greek, however, Homer is punning on
        similar sounding words, as he punned on the name of Odysseus.

dread dream came from there—though it would have been welcome   490
to me and to my son.

      "But I will tell you something, and you take
it to heart. The dawn already comes on of an evil name, which
will cut me off from the house of Odysseus. For now I will set up
a contest of the axes, which Odysseus used to set up in a row
in his halls, like the props of a ship when you are building it,   495
twelve in all. He would stand a good distance away and shoot
an arrow through them.° Now I will set up this contest for the suitors.
Whoever shall string the bow in his hands most easily and shall
shoot through all twelve axes, I will follow him, leaving this house
of my wedded life, this very beautiful house, filled with livelihood.   500
I think I will remember it in my dreams."°

                 The resourceful Odysseus
said in reply: "Lady, revered wife of Odysseus, son of Laërtes,
no longer put off this contest in your halls. The resourceful Odysseus
will be here before these men, handling the well-polished bow,
shall have strung it and shot an arrow through the iron."   505

                The judicious
Penelope then said: "Oh, if you could but wish to sit beside me,
in my halls, stranger, and delight me, then sleep would never be poured
over my eyes! But there is no way that human beings can go forever
without sleep. The deathless ones have appointed a proper time
for each thing upon the fruitful earth. I will go to my upper   510
chamber and lie down on my bed, which has become a bed
of wailing, mixed always with my tears, ever since Odysseus

---

497 *through them*: We cannot reconstruct how this contest worked from the information Homer gives us, and
     perhaps he did not understand it himself. What does he mean by "shoot an arrow through them"? In line
     505, he says that the shot will pass "through the iron." Some think that this means that the socket holes of
     the ax heads are lined up to make a kind of tunnel, but the bow shot would then be very close to the ground
     if the blades of the ax heads are embedded in the ground. Another explanation is that these are votive axes
     with handles that terminated in a ring of iron to hang them from (but real votive axes were always small).
     Perhaps the ax heads, then, are set into the earth, forming at their upper end a tunnel of iron rings through
     which Odysseus shoots.

501 *. . . in my dreams*: Why Penelope should decide at just this moment to hold a suitor contest and marry the
     winner has never been explained. She has just heard the prophecy of Theoklymenos, the beggar's report,
     and now the dream, then goes ahead as if Odysseus' return were not imminent. Some interpreters have
     thought that Homer has used a version of the story in which Odysseus and Penelope plotted together to
     kill the suitors. In any event, Homer needed to move his story along and for that Penelope needed to set
     the contest.

went off to see that evil Ilion—not to be named! There I shall
lie down. You too lie down in the house, either spreading your
515 bedding on the floor, or have the slaves set up a bed for you."

     So speaking she went up to her shining upper chamber,
not alone, but with her went the other female attendants. When
she came to the upper chamber with her women attendants,
she wept then for Odysseus, her dear husband, until
520 flashing-eyed Athena sent sweet sleep onto her lids.

BOOK 20. *A Vision of Doom*

The good Odysseus lay down to sleep in the forehall. He stretched
out an undressed cow's hide, and over it he spread several fleeces
of sheep the Achaeans had butchered. Then Eurynomê threw
a cloak over him, once he lay down.

Odysseus lay there

sleepless, contemplating evil things for the suitors in his heart.   5
The slave women came out of the hall laughing with one another,
the women having sex with the suitors, bad girls having a good time.
Odysseus' heart was stirred in his breast, and he contemplated
in his heart and spirit whether he should jump up and kill every one
of them, or whether he should let them have sex with the proud   10
suitors yet one last time. His heart howled within—as when a bitch
stands over her tender pups and growls when she sees a man
she does not know and is eager to fight—even so his heart growled
within, indignant at the evil before him.

Still, he struck his breast

and he rebuked his heart, saying: "Endure, my heart! You withstood   15
a thing more hideous than this on that day when Cyclops, unrestrained
in strength, ate your strong companions. But you kept at it until
your intelligence led you from the cave where you thought you
would die."

So he spoke, scolding his own heart in his breast,
and his heart remained bound within him to endure to the end.   20
But he himself tossed here and there. As when a man before
a blazing fire swiftly turns a stomach filled with fat and blood
this way and that, and he is eager that it quickly roast, even so
was Odysseus turned this way and that as he contemplated how
he might place his hands on the shameless suitors, being one   25
against many.

Then Athena came close to him from heaven,
and she took on the appearance of a woman. She stood over his

head and she said: "Why are you awake, most ill-fated of all mortals?
This is your house, and here inside this house is your wife,
30 and your child, such a man as anyone would pray to be his son."

   The resourceful Odysseus answered her: "Yes, goddess,
you have said all this as is right. But my spirit ponders greatly
in my breast, how being alone I can place my hands on the unholy
suitors. For they are always inside, in a crowd. Also, I wonder about
35 this even more—if I kill them by the will of Zeus, and yourself, where
will I flee? I urge you to consider these things."

                                        Flashing-eyed Athena
then answered him: "You *are* obstinate. Many a man puts trust
in a worse companion, one who is mortal and doesn't know
so many things as I do. I am a goddess! I will guard you always
40 in every danger. I shall tell you clearly: If fifty bands of mortal men
were to surround us, eager to kill us through the deeds of Ares,
still you would drive off their cattle and their strong sheep.
But let sleep take you now. There is trouble in staying awake
all night long. You will now come forth from all your troubles."

45   So she spoke, and she poured sleep over his eyelids. She herself,
the beautiful goddess, went to Olympos. When sleep came on Odysseus,
loosening the cares of his heart, loosening his limbs, his wife awoke,
true at heart. She wept, sitting on the soft bed, but when her heart
had its fill of weeping, the goddess among women prayed first
50 of all to Artemis: "O Artemis, revered goddess, daughter of Zeus,
I wish you would strike me in the breast with one of your arrows
and take away my life right away. Or that a storm-wind would snatch
me up and carry me over the murky ways and cast me out
at the mouth of back-flowing Ocean . . . even as the storm winds did
55 once snatch up the daughters of Pandareos.° The gods had destroyed
their parents and they were left orphans in the halls, but shining
Aphrodite took care of them with cheese and sweet honey
and sweetened wine. Hera gave them beauty and cleverness
above all other women, and holy Artemis gave them height,
60 and Athena taught them to accomplish glorious things with their labor.
While Athena went to high Olympos to ask for the fulfillment

----

55 *Pandareos*: The following story is unattested in any other source, like the story about the daughter of Pan-
   dareos in Book 19, which it resembles. Pandareos' daughter, the nightingale, is not mentioned, and they do
   not seem to be the same story. Penelope is evidently selecting different accounts of the catastrophes that
   came to the daughters of Pandareos to illustrate her feelings on two separate occasions.

of a blossoming marriage for them, going up to Zeus who delights
in the thunderbolt, who knows all things well, both what is fated
and what is not fated among mortal men. Meanwhile spirits
of the storm snatched away the daughters of Pandareos and gave   65
them to the terrible Erinyes to deal with . . . Even so do I wish that those
who live in Olympos might blot me out. Or that Artemis with her fine
tresses would strike me so that I might pass beneath the hateful earth
with Odysseus before my mind, and never gladden the thoughts
of a lesser man.   70

      "Yet when someone weeps all day, deeply grieved
at heart, and then at night sleep possesses him—this is an evil that can
be tolerated, for sleep causes you to forget all things, the good
and the bad, when once it casts a veil over the eyelids. But some evil
spirit sends dreams on me as well. Last night there slept
with me one just like he was when he went off on campaign.   75
And my heart rejoiced, because I did not think it was a dream,
but that it was real."

      So she spoke, and promptly Dawn came on her
golden throne. As Penelope wept, the good Odysseus heard her voice,
and he mused. He imagined that she had recognized him and now
she stood at his head. He gathered up the cloak and the fleeces   80
in which he had slept, and he set them on a chair in the hall,
and he took the cowhide outside and put it down. Then he prayed
to Zeus, raising his hands: "Father Zeus, if you gods have willingly
brought me over land and sea to my country, after you had tormented
me exceedingly, let someone of those who are awaking utter a word   85
of good omen inside the house, and may some other wonder appear
from Zeus outside."

      So he said in prayer, and Zeus the counselor heard him.
Immediately he thundered from gleaming Olympos, from the high
clouds, and the good Odysseus rejoiced. A woman grinding
at the mill uttered a word of omen from inside the nearby   90
house where the mills belonging to the shepherd of the people
were set up. There, twelve women in all performed their tasks,
grinding barley to meal, and wheat too, the marrow of men.
The others had gone off to sleep because they had ground their
portion of wheat, but she was not yet done, for she was the weakest.   95

   She stopped her mill and said, a sign for the king: "Father Zeus,
who rules over gods and men, you have thundered from a starry sky

where there is no cloud anywhere.° Surely this is a wonder that
you show to some man! So fulfill now for even wretched me
100 the words that I speak: May the suitors take their pleasant feast
in the halls of Odysseus for the very last time on this day—they who
have loosened my limbs with bitter labor as I grind the barley.
May they now dine their last!"

So she spoke, and the good Odysseus
rejoiced at the word of good omen and the thunder strike of Zeus.
105 He thought vengeance on the guilty had already begun.

The other female
slaves in the beautiful house of Odysseus gathered together and stoked
up the untiring fire in the hearth. Telemachos rose from his bed,
a man like a god, and he put on his clothes. He set his sharp sword
around his shoulder. He bound the beautiful sandals beneath his shining
110 feet and he took up his mighty spear, tipped with sharp bronze.

He went to the threshold and stood there, and he called
out to Eurykleia: "Dear nurse, have you shown honor to the stranger
in our house, with a place to sleep, and food, or does he lie there
uncared for as usual? That's the way it is with my mother,
115 although she is sensible enough. She *madly* gives honor
to the worthless of mortal men, then sends off the better man
after dishonoring him."

The shrewd Eurykleia answered him:
"You ought not to blame her, my child, for she is guiltless.
The stranger sat there and drank wine for as long as he wanted,
120 but he said that he was not hungry for food, when she asked him.
And when he thought of lying down to get some sleep, Penelope asked
the women slaves to set up a bed. Still, like someone who is wholly
miserable and afflicted by bad luck, he did not want to sleep
on a bed with covers. He slept in the forehall, on an undressed
125 cowhide and the fleeces of sheep. We spread out a cloak over him."

So she spoke, and Telemachos went forth through
the hall holding his spear, and his two swift dogs followed along.
He went off to the place of meeting to join the Achaeans
who wear fancy shin guards. Meanwhile, Eurykleia, a goddess
130 among women, the daughter of Ops the son of Peisenor, called

---

98 *anywhere*: The millworker sees no clouds, although we have just been told that Zeus thundered "from the
high clouds" (lines 88–89)!

out to the female slaves: "Come here girls! I want some of you
to go around and sweep the house and sprinkle the floors,
and throw covers, purple ones, over the well-made chairs.
I want others of you to sponge down all the tables, and clean
the wine-mixing bowls and the nicely made two-handled cups.   135
Others, I want to go off to get water from the spring, and bring
it back quickly. The suitors will not be away from the hall for long.
They will come very early, because today is a festival day for all."°

So she spoke, and they listened to her and obeyed. Twenty
of them went off to the black water of the spring, the others   140
worked skillfully throughout the house. Then the servants of the
Achaeans came in, who well and skillfully split up logs of wood.
The women returned from the spring. After them came the pig herder
driving three pigs, by far the best he had.° Eumaios let them graze inside
the beautiful enclosure, and himself spoke to Odysseus with honeyed   145
words: "Stranger, do the Achaeans look at you with any more regard,
or do they still dishonor you in the halls, as they did before?"

The resourceful Odysseus then said in reply: "I wish
that the gods would pay back this offense, Eumaios. These men
behave violently and rashly in another's house, and they have   150
no shame."

They were saying things like this to one another
when Melanthios, the goatherd, came up close to them, leading
she-goats that were the best in all the herds—dinner for the suitors.
Two herders followed along with him. He tied up the goats beneath
the echoing portico, and he addressed Odysseus with mocking words: 155
"Stranger, are you *still* causing trouble here in the hall, begging
from men? Will you not be gone? I do not think that we can ever
part company before having a taste of one another's fists! You beg in an
unbecoming fashion. Aren't there *other* banquets of the Achaeans?"

So he spoke, but the resourceful Odysseus did not answer him.   160
In silence he shook his head, thinking evil things deep inside. Then,
third, came Philoitios,° a leader of the people, bringing a barren

---

138   *day for all*: The celebration is the new-moon festival for Apollo, the archer god, when all the suitors will die,
      killed by Odysseus' arrows.

144   *. . . he had*: Usually the suitors consumed one pig a day (Book 14), but this is a special day, a feast day
      "for all."

162   *Philoitios*: "desirable fate."

heifer and fat she-goats. Ferrymen had brought them over from
the mainland, who also ferried other men—whoever came to them.

165   Philoitios tied-up the animals beneath the echoing
portico, then he himself stood by the pig herder and asked:
"Who is this stranger who has recently come to our house,
pig herder? From what men is he said to be sprung? Where
are his family and his native fields? Poor fellow, he seems to me
170 in appearance like a king! But the gods bring misery to men
who wander far, when the gods spin a fate of sorrow, even
for chieftains."

        Then Philoitios greeted Odysseus by extending
his right hand, standing beside him, and he spoke words that went
like arrows: "Greeting, sir stranger. May you be happy in times
175 to come, though now you are oppressed by many evils. Father Zeus,
there is no other god more destructive than you. You do not
take pity on men, even when you yourself have begotten them,
but you mix them up with evil and savage pain. I broke out
in a sweat when I saw this man, and my eyes were filled
180 with tears as I think about Odysseus,° because I think that
that man too is clothed in such rags and that he wanders lost
among men—that is, if he is still alive and sees the light of the sun.
But if he is dead and has gone down into the house of Hades,
then woe is me for the blameless Odysseus, who set me over
185 his cattle when I was still little, in the land of the Kephallenians.°
Now they grow past counting, and no one could have done better
with them than I have, for they have bred like ears of wheat.
But strangers drive them off for themselves to eat, and they do not
care for the son of the house. Nor do they tremble at the anger
190 of the gods. They want to divide up the wealth of the king who is gone.

        "As for myself, my heart keeps turning this over in my breast—
it is an evil thing while the son is still alive to go off to some
other people with the cattle, to a land of strangers, but it is still
more shivery to remain here and suffer woes, being in charge
195 of cattle that are just given over to others. I would long ago have
fled to some other of the powerful chieftains, for the situation here

---

180 . . . *Odysseus*: Those closest to Odysseus see something familiar in the beggar and compare his condition
        with that imagined for Odysseus. Athena has not transformed Odysseus into a different person, but only
        aged him magically.

185 *land of the Kephallenians*: He seems to mean the mainland where Odysseus kept his herds, not the island of
        Kephallenia. In the Iliad (*Il.* Book 2), the Kephallenians are all those under Odysseus' control and come
        from Ithaca and neighboring islands and part of the mainland.

has become intolerable. Yet still I think of that unfortunate one—
if perhaps he will return and scatter the suitors in his house."

The resourceful Odysseus then said: "Cow herder, because
you do not seem to me to be a base man, or one without wits,   200
I see myself that you have an understanding heart. I will therefore
speak out and swear a great oath. Now be witness, Zeus above all
the gods, and this table friendly to guest-friends be witness,
and the hearth of noble Odysseus to which I have come—
Odysseus will come home while you are still here! You will   205
see him with your very own eyes, if you want, as he kills
the suitors who lord it over his property."

Then the cow-herding man
said to Odysseus: "I hope, stranger, that the son of Kronos will bring
this to pass. Then you would see what my strength is, and how
my hands obey." And Eumaios too prayed to all the gods that   210
the wise Odysseus would soon return to his house.

Thus they spoke
to one another, but in the meantime the suitors schemed on the death
and fate of Telemachos. Then a bird flew on their left, a high-flying
eagle that held in its claws a timid pigeon. Amphinomos began to speak
to them and he said: "This plan will not run to our liking, this murder   215
of Telemachos. So let us think of the feast!"

So spoke Amphinomos,
and his word was pleasing to them.° They went into the house
of godlike Odysseus and placed their cloaks on the chairs
and seats. Then they butchered large sheep and fat goats,
and they butchered fat pigs and a cow from the herd. They roasted   220
the entrails and distributed them, and they mixed wine in wine-mixing
bowls. The pig herder handed around cups. Philoitios, a leader
of the people, passed around bread in a beautiful basket,
and Melanthios poured the wine. They reached out their hands
to the good things that lay before them. Telemachos, pressing   225
his advantage,° gave Odysseus a seat inside the well-built hall
next to the stone threshold, placing nearby a shabby stool

---

217 *pleasing to them*: Amphinomos is the "good" suitor, who here definitely cancels plans to murder Telemachos.
     Earlier (Book 16) he dissuaded the others from a new plot to kill Telemachos before they had consulted the
     gods. Now an omen has come indicating they should abandon that plot.

226 *his advantage*: The advantage comes from his knowledge of who the beggar really is. Telemachos can estab-
     lish Odysseus in the hall under his protection, in preparation for the attack on the suitors.

FIGURE 20.1   Melian relief with the return of Odysseus.   In this "Melian relief" (compare
Figure 19.1). Penelope sits on a chair, her legs demurely crossed and her head buried in sorrow.
The hatless Odysseus, disguised as a beggar, takes her by the forearm. He is in "heroic nudity" but
with a ragged cloak over his arms and back. He holds a staff in his left hand from which his pouch
is suspended. Behind Penelope is the beardless Telemachos, and at his feet probably Eumaios the
pig herder, seated on the ground and holding a staff, his hat tossed back. The last figure on the left is
probably Philoitios, the cow herder from Kephallenia. Terracotta plaque, c. 460–450 BC.

and a tiny table nearby. He set portions of the entrails beside him
and he poured out wine into a golden cup.

                       Telemachos said
to Odysseus: "Sit here now and drink wine with the men.   230
As for the insults and blows from the suitors, I will myself
ward them off. This is no public house, but the house of Odysseus!
And he obtained it for me. And you suitors—restrain your minds
from insults and blows, so that no strife or quarrel arise!"

    So he spoke, and they all bit their lips and were amazed   235
at Telemachos because he had spoken so boldly. Then Antinoös,
the son of Eupeithes, spoke up, and he said: "Let us accept
these harsh words of Telemachos, O Achaeans, though he boldly
threatens us in his speech. Zeus the son of Kronos simply
did not allow it—otherwise we would have put an end to him   240
in these halls, however smooth a talker he might be."

    So spoke Antinoös, but Telemachos paid no attention to his words.
Meanwhile the heralds were leading the holy sacrifices
to the gods through the city, and the Achaeans with their long hair
gathered together beneath a shady wood belonging to Apollo   245
who shoots from a long ways off. When they had roasted the outermost
flesh and drawn it from the spits, they divided up the portions
and had a splendid feast. They gave the same portion to Odysseus
as they received themselves, for Telemachos, the dear son
of godlike Odysseus, commanded that it be so.   250

                       But Athena did not
permit the noble suitors to pull back completely from bitter
insolence, so that still more anger might invade the heart
of Odysseus, son of Laërtes.

                    There was a certain man among
the suitors whose heart was lawless, Ktesippos by name,°
and he lived in SAMÊ. Trusting in his vast wealth, he courted   255
the wife of Odysseus, who had long been away. Now he spoke
to the noble suitors: "Listen to me, proud suitors, to what I say.
This 'guest' has for a long time had an equal portion, as is only
proper. It is not a nice thing for Telemachos to disappoint
his guests, whoever comes to this house—nor is it just!   260
But come, I will give a gift of guest-friendship so that he may

---

254 *Ktesippos*: "possessor of horses."

give a present to the bath-woman, or to some other of the female
slaves in the house of godlike Odysseus . . ."

So speaking
he threw the foot of an ox with his powerful hand, taking it
265 from the basket where it lay.° Odysseus avoided the hoof, quickly
leaning his head to the side, and in his heart he smiled a bitter
smile. The ox's hoof struck the well-made wall.

Telemachos
reproached Ktesippos with this word: "Ktesippos, I think this
turned out rather well for you. You missed the stranger—
270 he avoided the missile, or I would have struck you in the gut
with my sharp spear. Then instead of your wedding feast,
your father would be busy preparing your funeral feast here
in this land. So we'll have no unseemly behavior in my house!
I know and am aware of everything, the good and the bad.
275 Before I was a child. All the same, we still endure to see these
acts of yours—the sheep slaughtered and wine drunk and bread
eaten. It is a tough thing for one man to hold back many.

"But come, give up your plans to do me harm. If you want
to kill me with the bronze, I'd prefer it—I would rather die than
280 constantly behold your indecent acts. Strangers maltreated and the
female slaves dragged off unwilling through the beautiful halls!"

So he spoke, and they all fell into silence. Finally, Agelaos,°
the son of Damastor, spoke: "My friends, one would never grow
angry at words justly spoken, and reply with hostile words.
285 So, don't maltreat the stranger, nor any other of the female slaves
who live in godlike Odysseus' house. But to Telemachos and his
mother I would speak a gentle word, in the hopes that it finds
favor in the hearts of both. For as long as you hoped
in your hearts that the resourceful Odysseus would return
290 to his home, for so long it has been no blame that you waited
and restrained the suitors in your house. That was much better,
in case Odysseus *did* return and came back to his house. But now
it is clear: He won't be returning. So come on, sit down beside

---

265 *where it lay*: Probably the less desirable parts of the sacrificial animal, like the hooves, were kept in a basket
for those lowest in rank. By throwing an ox-hoof at the beggar Ktesippos is saying that this is his proper
fare, not the meat given him by Telemachos.

282 *Agelaos*: "leader of the people," first mentioned here. He is important in Book 22 as a leader of the suitors'
resistance to Odysseus after the deaths of Eurymachos and Antinoös.

your mother and tell her that she must marry whoever is the best
man and has provided the most gifts. That way you may enjoy   295
your paternal inheritance in peace, eating and drinking—
and your mother can take care of the house of another."

The shrewd Telemachos answered him: "Not, by Zeus—
O Agelaos—and by the sufferings of my father, who has either
perished far from Ithaca or wanders around lost, have I delayed   300
my mother's marriage. I encourage her to marry whom
she wishes, and I offer her gifts past counting. But I am ashamed
to expel her unwilling from the house by a peremptory command.
May the god never bring this to pass!"

           So spoke Telemachos,
but among the suitors Pallas Athena stirred up an unquenchable   305
laughter, and she turned their minds askew. They laughed
with alien lips, and they ate meat that dripped with blood.
Their eyes were filled with blood, and they wanted to wail
but could make no sound. Theoklymenos, who had the air
of a god, spoke to them:° "Ah, you wretched men, what is this evil   310
that you suffer? Your heads and faces are wrapped in night,
and your knees beneath. A wailing blazes forth—your cheeks
are bathed by tears—the walls drip with blood, and the beautiful
rafters. The forehall is filled with ghosts, and the court is filled too,
as they long to go to Erebos beneath the gloom. The sun is gone   315
from the sky, and a dread mist has fallen over all."

           So he spoke,
and they all laughed sweetly. Eurymachos, the son of Polybos,
began to speak to them: "This stranger is mad!—recently coming
in here from someplace else. Throw him outdoors quickly,
lads, to go his way to the place of assembly, because here   320
he finds it like night."

           Theoklymenos, who had the air of a god,
then said: "Eurymachos, I do not ask you to give me guides
for my way. I have eyes and ears and my two feet and a mind
in my breast that is well fashioned. With these I will go outdoors,
because I see that an evil is coming upon you that no one   325
of you suitors can escape or avoid—those of you who commit
senseless folly, insulting men in the house of godlike Odysseus."

---

310 *spoke to them*: Theoklymenos has not been heard of since Book 17, when Telemachos brought him to the
    palace, where he has presumably been all this time. After this scene, he disappears.

So saying, he went out of the stately house and came to Peiraios,°
who happily received him.

                              Then all the suitors, looking at one another,
330 began to provoke Telemachos by making fun of his guests. Thus would
one of the proud young men say: "Telemachos, no one is more
unfortunate in his guests than you. You keep this filthy beggar here,
always after some bread or wine, knowing neither the deeds of peace
nor of war, a burden upon the earth. And this other one, he stood up
335 to make a prophecy! But if you will listen to me, it would be much
better to throw these 'guests' in a boat with many benches and send
them to the Sicilians° where they will bring in a worthy price."

So spoke the suitors. But Telemachos paid no attention
to their words. He watched his father in silence, always on the alert
340 until Odysseus should place his hands on the shameless suitors.

In the meanwhile, the daughter of Ikarios, judicious Penelope,
had placed her very beautiful chair over against the suitors and had
heard what each man said in the halls.° They had made ready their
meal in the midst of laughter—a sweet and satisfying meal, for they
345 had butchered many animals. Never could a meal have been less
welcome than that which a goddess and a mighty man were about
to set before the suitors. But first *they* contrived deeds of shame.

---

328 *Peiraios*: A member of Telemachos' crew on the journey to Pylos, to whom Telemachos had earlier
entrusted Theoklymenos (Book 15).

337 *Sicilians*: This is the earliest extant reference to the Sicilians, who were presumably non-Greeks—
slave-traders—living in SICILY. Greek settlement in Sicily was somewhat later than Homer's time.

343 *in the halls*: She seems again to be sitting in an adjoining room that allows her to see and hear what is
happening in the big hall (see J, Map VI).

BOOK 21. *The Contest of the Bow*

The goddess flashing-eyed Athena put it into the mind
of the daughter of Ikarios, the judicious Penelope, to set up
the bow and the gray iron in the feast-hall of Odysseus,
to be a contest and the beginning of death.°

She went up the steep
stairs of her house, and she took the bent key in her strong hand—   5
beautiful, made of bronze, and the handle was of ivory.
Then she descended from her chamber with her attendant
women to a storeroom at the far end the house.° The treasures
of her king lay there, bronze and gold and well-worked iron.
There was the back-bent bow° and the quiver that held   10
the arrows. Within were many arrows, the bearers of pain, a gift
that his guest-friend Iphitos, the son of Eurytos, had made him,
a man like the deathless ones.

They met in Lacedaemon.
The two of them came on one another in Messenê,° in the house
of the war-minded Ortilochos.° Odysseus had come after a debt   15
that the whole people owed him, for the men of Messenê
had stolen three hundred sheep from Ithaca in their ships
with many benches, and the herders along with them. On their
account Odysseus had come a long distance on an embassy
while still a youth, for his father and the other elders had sent   20
him forth. Iphitos, for his part, had come in search of twelve mares
that he had lost, with mules at the teat. They were about to become
death and fate for Iphitos, when he came to the proud-spirited
son of Zeus, the great Herakles, experienced in many deeds.
Herakles killed Iphitos in his own house—in cold blood!—   25

---

4   *beginning of death*: For the nature of this contest, see note on line 497, Book 19.

8   *the house*: For a possible reconstruction of the layout of the house, see MAP VI.

10 *back-bent bow*: A very powerful type of bow invented on the plains of central Asia consisting of a stave faced
    with horn on the front and backed with sinew.

14 *Messenê*: Here evidently a town in LACEDAEMON.

15 *Ortilochos*: The name of the father of Diokles at whose house in PHERAI, in the southern PELOPONESSUS,
    Telemachos stayed (Books 3, 15), perhaps the same man.

FIGURE 21.1 Herakles.   Herakles was the greatest hero in Greek myth, known as much for his beneficent deeds as for his betrayals and treacheries. He belonged to an earlier generation than the Trojan fighters; his son Tlepolemos of Rhodes fought on the Achaean side. By the sixth century BC he is usually shown wearing a lion's skin, as here, and carrying a primitive club. He was also a famous bowman. Corinthian water jar c. 575 BC.

although Iphitos was a guest-friend, and he had no respect
for the will of the gods, nor for the table that Herakles set before him.
He killed Iphitos and kept the single-hoofed horses in his halls.°

It was while asking for these mares that Iphitos met Odysseus
and gave him the bow that earlier great Eurytos had carried.   30
When Eurytos died he had left it to his son in the high-roofed
halls. And Odysseus gave Iphitos a sharp sword and a powerful
spear, the beginning of affectionate relations of guest-friendship,
though they never sat at the same table. Before that the son
of Zeus° killed Iphitos, the son of Eurytos, a man like the deathless   35
ones, who gave the bow to Odysseus. Odysseus never took it
when he went to war in the black ships, but he kept it in his halls
as a reminder of a beloved guest-friend, and he used it on his own land.

The beautiful woman arrived at the chamber and stepped
on the oak threshold that a carpenter had once skillfully planed   40
and made true to the line, and fitted in doorposts and set
in them shining doors. She promptly loosened the strap
on the door-knob. She put in the key and with sure aim she shot
back the bolt.° As a bull bellows when grazing in the meadow,
even so the beautiful door panels bellowed, struck by the key,   45
and they swiftly opened wide before her. Then she stepped out
onto the high floor° where the chests lay in which fragrant
clothing was stored.

Standing up tall, she took down from a peg
the bow and the bright bow-case that surrounded it. She sat down
there and placed it on her knees, and she wept shrilly. She took   50
out the bow of her king. When she had had her fill of tearful
moaning, she went off to the feast hall and the bold suitors,
with the back-bent bow in her hands and the quiver for arrows.
There were many sorrowful arrows within it. Beside her,

---

28   *in his halls*: According to the story reconstructed from later sources, Autolykos, the maternal grandfather
     of Odysseus, had stolen the mares from Eurytos, a famous bowman from Oichalia (perhaps somewhere in
     the Peloponnesus) and entrusted them to Herakles for safe-keeping. Iphitos came to Herakles for help in
     finding the mares, not knowing that they were in Herakles' possession. Herakles lured him to the rooftop,
     pushed him off, and kept the horses.

34–35   *son of Zeus*: Herakles.

44   *bolt*: The double door is double-locked. First Penelope must untie a thong attached through a hole in the
     door to a bolt on the inside. This thong is tied to a knob or handle on the outside. Untying the thong releases
     the bolt inside. The key is not like a modern key, but is a large device with an ivory handle. By now inserting
     the key into a second hole in the door, Penelope shoots back the bolt that holds the door locked.

47   *high floor*: Apparently the storeroom has a built-in raised floor.

55 assistants carried a chest in which was a quantity of iron
and bronze, the armor of her king. When the beautiful woman
came to the suitors, she stood beside the doorpost of the well-made
house, and she held her shining veil before her cheeks.
A faithful assistant stood at either side.

                                        Immediately she spoke
60 to the suitors and said: "Listen to me, you noble suitors who afflict
this house with your constant eating and drinking, while the man
of the house has been a long time gone. You have not found
any better excuse to plead than that you wanted to marry me
and make me your wife. Well, then—come on suitors, since this
65 appears to be your prize!

                          "I will place before you the great bow
of godlike Odysseus. Whoever strings the bow most easily
in his hands and shoots through all the twelve axes—I will
follow him, leaving this house of my wedded life behind,
this very beautiful house, filled with livelihood that I now will
70 see only in my dreams."

                          So she spoke, and she urged Eumaios,
the good pig herder, to set out the bow and the gray iron°
for the suitors. Bursting into tears, Eumaios took them and set
them down. In another part of the room the cow herder wept too
when he saw the bow of his king.

                                    Then Antinoös reproached them
75 and spoke, calling out: "You fools! Bunglers! Thinking only of today!
You wretches—why do you *now* pour down tears and get this
woman all excited? She already has enough troubles, for she
has lost her dear husband. Sit down and eat in silence, or go
outside and wail. But leave the bow here—a decisive contest
80 for the suitors. But I do not think it will be easy to string this bow.
For there is no man among all those here such as Odysseus was.
I myself saw him, and I remember him well, although I was
just a little boy."

                    So he spoke, but his heart in his breast hoped
that he could string the bow and shoot through the iron. Yet he
85 was to be the first to taste an arrow from the hands of the noble

---

71 …*iron*: The axes, evidently also in the storeroom and carried in the chest along with the "armor of her king."

Odysseus, whom even then, sitting in the hall, he disrespected,
and Antinoös urged on his companions too.

                        Then the strong, mighty
Telemachos spoke to them: "Well, Zeus the son of Kronos
has just knocked the senses from me. For my dear mother,
although she is a woman of understanding, says that she will follow   90
along with another and leave this house! That makes me laugh,
and I am glad in my senseless mind. Come, suitors, since *this* is
the prize, a woman unique in all Achaea, and in holy Pylos,
and Argos, and in Mycenae, and in Ithaca itself, and on the dark
mainland . . . But you know this yourselves! Why do I need   95
to praise my mother?

            "Come, do not put the matter off with excuses.
Let us no longer turn away from the drawing of the bow, so that
we may see the outcome of this matter. I myself will first try the bow.
If I succeed in stringing and shooting through the iron, then it won't
bother me at all if my revered mother leaves this house,   100
going with another—and I will be left behind alone to wield
the beautiful battle-gear of my father."

                   He spoke and he flung down
the purple cloak from his shoulders. He stood up tall. He took
off the sharp sword from his shoulders. First of all he set up the axes,
digging a single deep trench for them all, and he made the trench   105
true to the line. Then he tamped down dirt around the axes. All were
amazed when they saw it, how expertly he set up the axes,
though he had never before seen them. Then Telemachos went
and stood on the threshold and began to try the bow. Three times
he made it quiver in his eagerness to string it, and three times   110
his strength gave out—although he wanted in his heart to string
the bow and shoot through the iron. And now for the fourth time,
when he tried, he *would* have strung it, but Odysseus nodded
his head and held him back in his eagerness.

                     The strong, mighty
Telemachos then said: "Sure, in days to come I will no doubt   115
be said to be a coward and a weakling, or I am still too young
and I do not trust in the power of my hands to defend myself
from some man's attack, if he is the first to take offense.
But come, you who are greater in strength than I—have a try
at the bow, and let us finish this contest."   120

So speaking, he placed
the bow on the ground, leaning it against the jointed polished
door, and nearby he leaned the sharp arrow against the curved
tip of the bow. Then he went and sat down on the chair from
which he had arisen.

Antinoös, the son of Eupeithes, spoke to them:
125 "Get up, all you of our company! In a row, from left to right,
beginning with the place where the cupbearer pours the wine."

So spoke Antinoös, and his word was pleasing to them.
Leiodes stood up first, the son of Oinops,° who inspected the entrails
of victims for them. He always sat next to the beautiful wine-mixing
130 bowl in the innermost part of the hall.° He alone hated the foolish
shenanigans of the suitors and was indignant at their antics.
It was he who first took up the bow and the sharp arrow. He went
and stood on the threshold and tried the bow, but he could not
string it. His arms grew tired as he pulled the string with his soft,
135 delicate hands.

Leiodes spoke to the suitors: "My friends,
I can't string it. Let someone else try it. This bow will rob the spirit
and breath many of the best men, because it is much better
to die than to live on, ever missing the mark on account of which
we always gather together here, waiting, day after day. Many
140 a man hopes in his heart and is eager to marry Penelope,
the wife of Odysseus. But when he has tried his hand at the bow
and has seen the outcome, then let him pursue some other
of the Achaean women with their fine gowns, showering them
with wedding gifts and hoping to win one. Then Penelope should
145 marry him who offers the most presents and comes as her man
of destiny."

So he spoke, and he put down the bow, leaning it up
against the jointed well-polished door, and he leaned the sharp arrow
up against the curved bow-tip. Leiodes sat back down in the seat
from which he had arisen.

---

128 *Leiodes . . . Oinops*: "smooth" the son of "wine-face," that is, the weakling son of a weakling father, first
heard of here.

130 *of the hall*: He inspects the entrails of sacrificed animals looking for "signs" of good and bad luck in their
shape. The wine-mixing bowl (*krater*) that Leiodes sits beside was ordinarily kept on the floor.

But Antinoös reproached him and spoke
and called out: "Leiodes, what a word has escaped the barrier   150
of your teeth! Fearful, horrid—I am angry to hear it. You say this bow
will 'deprive many of the best men of spirit and life'—just because
you can't string it! But your revered mother did not beget you
to be strong enough to draw a bow and shoot arrows. Others
of the noble suitors will quickly string it."   155

So he spoke and he called
to Melanthios, the goat herder: "Look sharp, Melanthios,
light a fire in the halls,° and put a great stool beside it, and throw
a fleece on the stool, and bring in a big cake of lard that they keep
in the house. Then we young fellows may warm the bow, and rub
it with fat, and so make trial of the bow, and bring this contest   160
to an end."

So he spoke, and Melanthios quickly built the restless
fire. He brought in a stool and set it down, and he spread
a fleece over it. Then he brought in a large cake of lard that was
in the house. The young men warmed and tried their hand at the bow,
but they could not string it, for they were much too weak.   165

Antinoös and godlike Eurymachos remained to try to string the bow,
but meanwhile Odysseus' cow herder, Philoitios, and his pig herder,
Eumaios, went together at the same time out of the hall.

The good Odysseus himself went forth from the house after them.
When they got outside the gates and the court,° Odysseus spoke   170
to them with honeyed words: "Cow herder, and you, O pig herder,
shall I tell you something, or should I keep it to myself? My spirit
urges me to say it. Are you such men as would defend Odysseus
if he should suddenly come from somewhere and some god should
bring him in? Would you help the suitors or Odysseus? Speak how   175
your heart and spirit commands."

The cow herder then said: "Father
Zeus, if this hope should ever come to pass, that this man should
come, and some spirit should lead him—then you would know what
my power is and how my hands obey!" In a like manner Eumaios

---

157   *in the halls*: Not on the hearth, which is already burning to keep the house warm, but in a brazier.

170   *the court*: That is, they are in the street.

180 prayed to all the gods that the resourceful Odysseus would return
to his home.

　　　　　When Odysseus knew with certainty their minds,
he immediately spoke to them in reply: "I am here at home then!
After suffering much I have returned in the twentieth year
to the land of my fathers. I see that I have arrived in answer
185 to your desires, alone of the slaves. For I have heard of not one
other praying that I return home again.

　　　　　　　　　　　　　"But to you two I will
tell the truth, how it will be if a god grants that I take down
the proud suitors. I will give you both a wife and give you
property and a house built close to mine. You two will be
190 the companions and brothers to Telemachos. But come, I will
show you a clear sign so that you may know for certain
and have trust in your hearts—the scar that a boar once
gave me with his white tusk when I went with the sons
of Autolykos to the slopes of Parnassos."°

　　　　　　　　　　　So speaking he parted
195 the rags to show the huge scar. When the two men saw it
and realized what it meant, they wept and threw their arms
around war-minded Odysseus. Rejoicing, they began to kiss
his head and shoulders, and in the same way Odysseus kissed
their heads and hands.

　　　　　　　　And the sun would have gone down
200 as they wailed, if Odysseus himself had not put a stop to it
and said: "Cease from your weeping and wailing, or someone
may come out of the feast-hall and see, and tell those inside.
Go in one by one, not both together. I'll go in first, and you after.
And let this be the sign: All the other noble suitors will not
205 allow that the bow or the quiver be given to me, but you, good
Eumaios, when you are carrying the bow through the house,
place it in my hands, and tell the women to close the tightly fitting
doors of their hall. If one of them should hear the groaning
and the fighting of men going on inside our walls, let them
210 not rush outdoors, but remain in silence at their labor where
they are. And you, good Philoitios, I'm asking to shut up the doors
of the court with a bolt and swiftly throw a cord upon it."

194　…　*Parnassos*: It is not obvious how Philoitios and Eumaios would have known about the scar.

So speaking he went into the stately house. He went
over to the stool from which he had arisen and took his seat.
The slaves of Odysseus went in as well. Eurymachos was holding   215
the bow in his hands, warming it on this side and that in front of
the flame of the fire. But even so he was unable to string it,
and his bold heart groaned mightily within.

                        With a burst of anger
Eurymachos spoke and said: "Well! There is grief here for me
and grief for all of us! It is not so much the marriage that I regret,   220
though that does make me sad. There are many other Achaean
women, both here in Ithaca itself, surrounded by the sea, and in other
cities. But if we fall so far short of godlike Odysseus, seeing
that we cannot string his bow—this will be a reproach for men
to learn about in times to come."   225

                   Antinoös, the son of Eupeithes,
then answered him: "Eurymachos, it will not be so, and you yourself
know it. For today is a festival throughout the land of the god,
the sacred feast. Who then would bend a bow? So put it down
quietly, in peace. As for the axes—what if we let them all
stand as they are? For I don't think that anyone is going to come   230
into the house of Odysseus, son of Laërtes, and steal them!

    "But come, let the cupbearer pour wine in the cups for a drink-offering,
and let us put aside the bent bow. In the morning tell Melanthios,
the goatherd, to bring in she-goats, those that are the best
in the herds, so that we may lay thigh pieces on the altar   235
to Apollo, famous for his bow. Then we may try our hands
at the bow and put an end to this contest."

                 So spoke Antinoös,
and his word was pleasing to them. The heralds poured out
water over their hands, and the young men topped-up the bowls
brim full of drink. They served out wine to all, first pouring   240
out wine for the drink-offering into the cups.

               When they had
made the drink-offerings and drunk as much as they wanted,
then the resourceful Odysseus spoke to them with a crafty mind:
"Hear me, suitors, of a famous lady, so that I may say what
my heart urges me to say. I ask Eurymachos especially   245
and godlike Antinoös, for he has spoken in accordance
with what is right—yes, put down the bow for now, turn it

FIGURE 21.2 A Centaur abducting a Lapith woman.   Perhaps the Centaur is Eurytion and the woman Hippodameia, the bride of Peirithoös. The sculpture comes from the west pediment of the temple of Zeus at Olympia, Greece, one of the most celebrated sculptural groups to survive from classical Greece. Here the Centaur has the body of a horse. He is fully bearded but has a bestial pug nose. He places his left hand on the woman's breast and in his right clasps her waist as she struggles against him. By c. 460 BC when this sculpture was made, the myth of the battle between the Lapiths and Centaurs was taken as an allegory of the Greek triumph over Persia, the Greek enlightenment over the cruel, bestial, and barbarous East, and hence an appropriate subject to decorate the temple of the king of the Greek gods at Olympia. Marble, c. 460 BC.

over to the gods. At dawn the god will give strength to whomever
he wishes. But come, give *me* the well-polished bow so that
among you I can try the strength of my hands, to see if I still   250
have strength such as once I had in my supple limbs. But the sea
and bad food have brought me low."

So he spoke, and all of them burst
out angrily, fearing that he might string the well-polished bow.
Antinoös reproached him and called out: "Ah, you wretched
wanderer, you've lost your mind completely! Are you not   255
content that you dine at your ease among this proud crowd,
and you lack nothing of the feast, and you hear our words
and our speech? There is no other stranger or beggar who hears
our words! Sweet wine has wounded you, which has done
harm to others too, whoever takes it in gulps and drinks more   260
than he should.

"Wine drove the Centaur, the famous Eurytion,
mad in the hall of great-hearted Peirithoös, when Eurytion went
to the Lapith land. When his mind was driven mad by wine,
in his madness he did an evil act in the house of Peirithoös.°
Distress took hold of the heroes, and they leaped up and dragged   265
Eurytion outdoors through the gateway, and they cut off his ears
and nose. He went off driven mad in his mind, bearing his madness
in the madness of his heart. From that arose the quarrel between
the Centaurs and men, but it was for himself, heavy with wine,
that he first discovered evil.   270

"And thus do I predict a *big* pain for you,
if you string the bow! For you will not meet anyone with kindness
in our land, but we will send you right away in a black ship
to the chief Echetos, the most cruel of all men. There you will
never save yourself. So drink up at ease, and do not contend
with men who are younger than you!"   275

Then the judicious Penelope
answered him: "Antinoös, it is not a pretty sight, nor is it just,
when you mistreat Telemachos' guests who come to the house.
Why, do you think that if the stranger should string the great bow

---

264 *Peirithoös*: Peirithoös was king of the Lapiths. The Centaurs, whom Homer may not think of as half-horse,
     half-men, came, to the wedding party, got drunk, and attacked the bride and her attendants, beginning the
     war between the Lapiths and the Centaurs.

of Odysseus, trusting in his strength and power—that he will
280 take me to his house and make his wife? I don't think *that* is
what he has in mind. So let no one of you from fear of this sit
here at table grieving at heart—it is really not fit and proper."

Eurymachos, the son of Polybos, then said in reply: "Daughter
of Ikarios, judicious Penelope, it's not that we think that the man
285 will lead you to his house—that would hardly be right!—but we
fear the talk among men and women. At some time one
base Achaean may say, 'Weaker men by far are courting the wife
of a noble man, and they can not string the well-polished bow.
Then some *beggar* came wandering along and easily strung
290 the bow, and he shot through the iron!' So they will say—
and this will be a disgrace for us."

Then the judicious Penelope said:
"Eurymachos, there can never be a good reputation among the people
for those who dishonor and consume the house of a great man.
How do you rate *that* disgrace? This stranger is tall and well built,
295 and he says he is the son of a noble father. But come, give him
the well-polished bow so that we may see. I will say this,
and I think it will come to pass—if he strings the bow, and Apollo
grants him glory, I will give him a cloak and a shirt, fine clothes,
and I will give him a sharp spear to ward off dogs and men
300 and a two-edged sword. I will give him sandals for his feet,
and I will send him wherever his heart and spirit urges."

Then the shrewd Telemachos answered her: "My mother,
as for the bow, there is no one of the Achaeans who has more
right than I to give it or refuse it to whomever I wish—not anyone
305 who claims rule in rocky Ithaca, nor anyone in the islands toward
horse-pasturing ELIS. Of those, not *anyone* will force me against
my will, not even if I want, say, to give the bow to the stranger to carry
off with him—

"But go now into the house and attend to your affairs,
your loom and your distaff, and command your attendants to join
310 in the labor. The bow is a matter of concern for men, and especially
for me. For I have the power in this house."

In astonishment Penelope
want back into the house, for she had much taken to heart the wise
words of her son. She went into her upper chamber with her

attendant women, and she wept then for Odysseus, her dear husband,
until flashing-eyed Athena cast sweet sleep on her eyelids. 315

Now the good pig herder had picked up the bent bow
and was carrying it, and all the suitors were crying out in the halls.
And one of the arrogant young men would say: "Where are you
taking the bent bow, you loathsome pig herder, you madman?
Soon the swift dogs will devour you near your swine, alone and apart 320
from men, the dogs that you yourself raised!—if Apollo will
be gracious to us and the other deathless gods!"

So they would say,
and the pig herder put the bow back where he got it, being afraid,
because many were shouting in the feast-hall. Then Telemachos
from the other side shouted out in a threatening manner: 325
"Old man, bear the bow onward! You will not do well to obey
everyone here. Though I am younger, I will chase you to the field,
pelting you with stones! I am greater in strength. I only wish I had
as much power in the strength of my hands over the suitors who
are in my house—then I would soon send many a one in hatred 330
from our house. They are the devisers of evil." So he spoke,
and all the suitors laughed sweetly at him, and they relaxed their
harsh anger toward Telemachos.

But Eumaios carried the bow
through the hall and, coming up to war-minded Odysseus,
he placed the bow in his hands. Then Eumaios called out 335
to the nurse Eurykleia: "Telemachos calls you, good Eurykleia,
to bar the closely fitting doors of the feast-hall. And if any
of the women hears a groaning or racket from the men who are
within our walls, don't let them run outside. They should stay
in silence at their work." 340

So Eumaios spoke, and Eurykleia knew
what he meant. She closed the doors of the stately feast-hall.
Philoitios leaped up and went outside in silence. He barred
the gates of the court with its thick walls. Now there was a cable
for a beaked ship in the portico, made of papyrus, with which
he tied up the gates. Then he himself went inside. He went over 345
to the stool from which he had arisen, and he sat down. He looked
over to Odysseus, who was handling the bow, turning it round
and round, trying it this way, then that, in case worms had eaten
the horns while the king was away.

And thus would one say, looking
350 to his neighbor: "Say there, he is a connoisseur and a sly rogue with
a bow. Perhaps he has a similar one lying back in his home?
Or maybe he is thinking of making one. See how he handles it
in his hands, turning it this way and that—this bum, learned in evil!"

And another of the arrogant young men would say:
355 "May this fellow be as successful in other matters as he is about
to be in stringing the bow—"°

So spoke the suitors. But the resourceful
Odysseus hefted the great bow and looked it over carefully—
even as when a man skilled in the lyre and in song easily
stretches the string around a new peg, making the twisted
360 sheep gut fast from both ends, so Odysseus without trouble
strung the great bow. Holding it in his right hand, he tried
the string. It sang sweetly beneath his touch, like the sound
of a nightingale.°

But a great anger took hold of the suitors, and they
lost color in their skin. Zeus thundered aloud, showing forth a sign.
365 The much-enduring good Odysseus rejoiced then, because
the son of crooked-counseling Kronos° had sent him a sign.
He took up the swift arrow, which lay beside him on the table,
all by itself. The others lay inside the hollow quiver, which
the Achaeans were soon to taste.

Taking the arrow, he laid it on
370 the thick part of the bow and drew back the bow-string
and the notched arrow, still sitting on his stool, and he fired
the arrow, aiming carefully. He did not miss a single hole,°
but the arrow, heavy with bronze, went straight out through
the doorway.

---

356 *stringing the bow*: That is, may he be *un*successful in other affairs, as I hope he will be unsuccessful in string-
ing the bow.

363 *nightingale*: Many commentators have suggested that the singer must at this moment have twanged the
string on his lyre.

366 *crooked-counseling Kronos*: Kronos led the revolt of the older gods against Ouranos (Sky), waiting for his
father in ambush, then castrating him. For his deviousness he was called "crooked-counseling."

372 *a single hole*: The Greek here is highly obscure, but the fact that Odysseus fired while sitting on a stool might
agree with the theory that the ax-heads were buried by the blades in a trench with the haft-holes lined up so
that the shooter could shoot the arrow "through the iron."

Odysseus spoke to Telemachos: "Telemachos,
the stranger who sits in your halls brings no shame upon you.   375
I did not miss the mark, nor did I have to work a long time to string
the bow. My strength within is still steadfast, not as the suitors
contemptuously mock me. But now it is time to make dinner
ready for the Achaeans, while there is still light, and after that
we must make sport in a different way, with song and lyre.   380
For those are the companions of a feast."

                     He spoke and nodded
with his brows. Telemachos put on his sharp sword, the dear son
of godlike Odysseus, and in his hand he took up his spear. He stood
beside the chair at his father's side, armed in gleaming bronze.

BOOK 22. *The Slaughter of the Suitors*

And then the resourceful Odysseus stripped off his rags,
and he leaped up onto the great threshold, holding his bow
and his quiver filled with arrows, and he poured out the swift
arrows before his feet. He spoke to the suitors: "Now at last
5   this mad contest comes to an end. And now for another
target, which no man has yet struck. I will know if I can
hit it and Apollo give me glory!"

He spoke, and he aimed
a bitter arrow at Antinoös, who was about to raise up a beautiful
two-eared cup, made of gold. Antinoös held it his hands
10   so that he could drink the wine. Death was not in his thoughts,
for who among many diners could think that one man, even if
he were strong, would fashion for himself evil death and black
fate by taking on so many?

Taking aim, Odysseus hit him
in the throat with his arrow, and the point went straight through
15   the tender neck. Antinoös sank to one side, and the cup fell
from his hand when he was struck. Immediately a thick jet
of the blood of this man came through his nostrils. He quickly
kicked the table away from him, hitting it with his foot, and he
spilled his food on the ground, and the bread and roast meat
20   were befouled.

The suitors fell into an uproar throughout the house
when they saw that man fall. They leaped from their chairs,
driven in fear through the house, looking around everywhere
along the well-built walls. But there was no shield or strong spear
to be had. They railed at Odysseus with angry words: "Stranger,
25   you shoot at men at *your* cost! You will never engage in a contest
again! Your destruction is certain now! You have killed a man
who is by far the best of the young men in Ithaca. Therefore
the vultures will devour your flesh!"

So spoke each man, because
they did not think that the beggar had killed Antinoös on purpose.

The fools! They did not see that the cords of doom were fixed
upon them.

       The resourceful Odysseus spoke to them,
looking from beneath his brows: "You dogs, you did not think
that I would ever return home from the land of the Trojans,
so you wasted my house. You sleep with the women slaves
by force, and you court my wife while I am still alive, having
no respect for the gods who dwell in the broad sky. Nor do you
think there will be blame among men in time to come. The cords
of doom are fastened over you now—one and all!"

                     So he spoke,
and a green fear fell on all of them, and each man looked about
to see how he might flee dread destruction. Eurymachos alone
dared answer: "If you really are Odysseus of Ithaca returned,
then this is just, what you say that the Achaeans did—many
acts of out-and-out folly in your halls, and many in the field.
But that man who was the cause of it all—Antinoös—is already dead.
It was *he* who encouraged these acts, not so much through desire
or need for the wedding, but having other things in mind,
which the son of Zeus was not about to bring to pass—that
throughout the land of well-settled Ithaca *he* be the boss
and that we might lie in wait for your son and kill him. Now he
lies dead, as was his fate.

           "But you should spare your own people!
And after this we will go through the land and gather recompense
for all the wine that has been drunk, and all the food that
has been eaten in your halls. And each man of us will pay
in compensation the worth of twenty oxen. We will repay in bronze
and gold until your heart is warmed. It is hardly surprising
that, until then, you are angry."

          The resourceful Odysseus looked
at him from beneath his brows and said: "Eurymachos,
not if you were to give me all the wealth of your fathers—
as much as you now have, and if you were to add more to it
from someplace else—not even then would I hold back
my hands from slaughter, before I have avenged every
arrogance of you suitors. Now you have two choices: to fight
or to flee, if anyone wants to avoid death and fate. But I don't
think that any of you will escape utter destruction."

30

35

40

45

50

55

60

So he spoke,
65 and their knees were loosened where they stood, and their hearts
dissolved. Eurymachos spoke for a second time, to the suitors:
"My friends, this man will not restrain his invincible hands,
but because he has taken the well-polished bow and the quiver,
he will continue to shoot from the polished threshold until he kills
70 every last one of us. Let us remember our courage! Draw your
swords and turn over the tables against the deadly arrows.
Let us mass against him in hopes that we can get him away
from the threshold and the door. Then let us go through the city
and quickly raise the alarm. Then this man will soon have fired
75 his last arrow!"

So speaking, Eurymachos drew his sharp bronze sword,
edged on both sides, and he leaped on Odysseus, screaming terribly.
But at the same time the good Odysseus loosed an arrow
and hit Eurymachos in the breast beside the nipple, and the swift
missile was fixed in his liver. The sword fell from his hand
80 to the ground, and tumbling across the table he doubled over
and fell. He knocked the food to the ground, and his two-handled cup.
He hit the ground with his forehead, in agony of spirit, and with both
feet kicked the chair and overturned it. A mist poured over his eyes.

Then Amphinomos rushed on the bold Odysseus,
85 coming straight at him, and he drew his sharp sword in hopes
he might drive Odysseus from the doorway. But Telemachos got
Amphinomos first, throwing from behind and hitting him with
the bronze spear right between the shoulders. Telemachos drove
the spear through his chest, and Amphinomos dropped with a thud,
90 striking the ground with his full forehead. Telemachos leaped back,
leaving the long-shadowed spear still in Amphinomos, for he feared
that one of the Achaeans might rush on him and stab him
with his sword, or deal him a blow as he stooped over the body.

Telemachos moved at a run and came quickly to his dear father.
95 Standing beside him, he spoke words that went like arrows:
"Father, I will bring you a shield and two spears and a bronze helmet
well-fitted to your temples, and when I come back I will arm myself.
I will likewise arm the pig herder and the cow herder. It is better
to be in armor."

In reply the shrewd Odysseus said to him: "Run,
100 bring it, so long as my arrows hold out. I am afraid that they will
push me from the door, because I am just one."

So he spoke,
and Telemachos obeyed his dear father. He went off to the storeroom
where the famous weapons° lay. From there he took up four shields,
eight spears, and four helmets made of bronze with thick horse-hair
crests. He carried them out, and quickly he came to his dear father.   105
He first of all cloaked his own flesh in bronze. Likewise
the two slaves put on the handsome armor, and they stood beside
war-minded Odysseus, the man of many devices.

And Odysseus,
so long as there were arrows, took aim and fired at the suitors
in his house, one by one, and they fell one on top of the other.   110
But when the king ran out of arrows to fire, he leaned the back-bent
bow up against the shining side-walls of the vestibule near
the doorpost.° He himself put the shield with four layers around
his shoulders, and on his powerful head he placed the well-made
helmet with horse-hair crest, and the crest nodded terribly   115
from above. Now there was a rear-door in the well-made wall
of the feast-hall, and hard by the threshold of the well-built feast-hall
was a passage into the hall, closed by well-fitting doors. Odysseus
ordered the good pig herder to watch this passage, taking his stand
nearby, for there was but a single approach.   120

Then Agelaos spoke
to the suitors, making his words clear to all: "My friends,
won't somebody go out by the rear door and inform the people
so that the alarm can be quickly sounded? Then this man would
soon be done with his bowmanship!"

Melanthios the goat herder
then answered him: "That's not possible, god-nourished Agelaos.   125
For it is fearfully close to the beautiful doors of the court,
and the opening to the hall is dangerous. One man could hold off
all of us there, if he is strong. But come, I will bring armor
out of the storeroom for you to arm yourselves. For it is within,
and no place else I think, that Odysseus and his glorious son have   130
put the armor."°

---

103 *weapons*: This seems to be a separate storeroom from where the bow was kept because Telemachos does not
     use a key to open it. Later he regrets not locking the door. See Map VI.

113 *doorpost*: This vestibule would be located at D in Map VI, which helps to clarify the following description.

131 *the armor*: That Telemachos and Odysseus earlier removed from the walls. But we are not told how
     Melanthios knows where this armor is.

FIGURE 22.1 Odysseus shoots the suitors.   Dressed in rags, his pouch at his side, he pulls back the powerful back-bent bow. Behind him stand two of the slave girls, one anxiously holding her chin in her hand, the other anxiously holding her hands before her.

FIGURE 22.2 Death of the suitors. This is other side of the cup from Figure 22.1. All the suitors, situated around a dining couch, are in "heroic nudity" but carry cloaks. On the left a suitor tugs at an arrow in his back. In the middle a suitor tries to defend himself with an overturned table. On the right a debonair suitor, with trim mustache, holds up his hands to stop the inevitable. Athenian cup, c. 450–440 BC.

So saying, Melanthios went out by the rear door
and down the side-hall to the storerooms of Odysseus. There
he took up twelve shields and as many spears and bronze helmets
with thick horsehair crests. He went off with these and quickly
135   brought them and gave them to the suitors. And then Odysseus'
knees were loosened, and his heart melted, when he saw the suitors
putting on armor and wielding long spears. Now the task appeared
immense to him.

But he quickly called to Telemachos words
that went like arrows: "Telemachos, truly some woman
140   in the halls is rousing up evil battle, or it is Melanthios!"

Then the shrewd Telemachos answered him: "O father, it is
I myself who made this mistake—there is no one else to blame.
I left the tightly fitting door of the storeroom ajar. Someone
has made better sense of the situation than we have. But come,
145   good Eumaios, close the door of the storeroom and find
out who of the women has done this, or is it the son of Dolios,
Melanthios? as I think."

Thus they conversed with one another,
and in the meanwhile Melanthios, the goat herder, went again
to the storeroom, to get some beautiful armor, but this time
150   the good pig herder saw him. Being near to Odysseus,
he said: "Zeus-nurtured son of Laërtes, much-resourceful
Odysseus, there is that vile man whom we already suspect,
going to the storeroom. Tell me truly—should I kill him,
if I prove the stronger, or shall I bring him here to you
155   so you might take payment for the many crimes that he has
planned against this house?"

The resourceful Odysseus then
answered him: "Telemachos and I will hold the proud suitors
inside the feast-hall, no matter how fierce they become.
You two bind Melanthios' feet behind him and his hands above,
160   and throw him into the storeroom. Tie boards to his back, then
bind a woven rope to his body, and hoist him up a high pillar—
bring him up near the rafters. Let him stay alive a long time.
That way he will suffer the more."

So he spoke, and they heard him
and obeyed. They went to the storeroom and, inside, Melanthios
165   did not notice them. He was looking for armor in the deepest

recesses of the chamber. Philoitios and Eumaios stood on either
side of the doorposts, waiting. When Melanthios the goat herder
came over the threshold, he carried in one hand a beautiful helmet
and in the other a broad ancient shield sprinkled with rust
that had belonged to the fighting man Laërtes, who wore it   170
when he was young. Then it lay in the storeroom, and the seams
of its leather straps were loosened.

                Philoitios and Eumaios leaped on
Melanthios. They seized and dragged him by the hair inside
the storeroom. They threw him, terrified, on the ground, and they
bound his feet and hands with dread bonds, mean and tight. Bending   175
his legs behind his back—as the son of Laërtes, the much-enduring
good Odysseus, had advised—they then bound a woven rope
to his body and hoisted him up a high pillar, near the rafters.
And Eumaios said in mocking tones: "Now, I think Melanthios,
you will watch the whole night through, lying in as soft a bed   180
as befits you. Nor will you fail to see the early-born Dawn,
the golden-throned, rising from the streams of Ocean, at a time
when you are accustomed to bring in your she-goats to the dandies
to make their feast in the house."

                And so they left him there,
stretched in tight bonds. Then the two slaves put on armor   185
and closed the shining door. They went back to war-minded
Odysseus, the man of many devices.

                There they stood, breathing
fury. There were but four of them on the threshold, and within
the hall were very many men—brave men! But Athena, the daughter
of Zeus, came close to them in the likeness of Mentor, in appearance   190
and in voice.

                Odysseus saw and was heartened, and he said:
"Mentor, ward off ruin! Remember me, your dear comrade,
and all the good things I have done for you. Furthermore, you are
the same age as I." So he spoke, knowing that it was really
Athena, the rouser of the people.   195

                On the other side of the room
the suitors were raising an uproar in the halls. First Agelaos,
the son of Damastor, rebuked Athena: "Mentor, don't let Odysseus
wheedle you with fancy words to fight against the suitors
and defend himself. For I think that this plan of ours will come

200   to pass in just this way—once we have killed these men, father and son,
then you too will perish along with them, for such deeds as you
think you can pull off in these halls. You will pay with your head!
And when we shall have stripped you of all your power through
the bronze, all the possessions that you have both inside
205   and outside we will add to those of Odysseus. Nor will we
allow your sons to live in their halls, nor your daughters,
nor your faithful wife to live openly in the city of Ithaca!"

So he spoke, and Athena grew still more angry in her heart,
and she reproached Odysseus with angry words: "Apparently,
210   Odysseus, your steady strength and your bravery are no longer
the same as when you fought without end for nine years against
the Trojans for the sake of high-born Helen of the white arms.
You killed many men, then, in the dread contendings, and it was
through a plan of yours that the broad-wayed city of Priam
215   was taken.° How then can you come back to your house and your
possessions and grumble that you must be brave against
the suitors? But come, friend, stand beside me and behold
the deed, so that you might see what sort of man is Mentor,
the son of Alkimos, to repay kindness in the midst of the enemy."

220   She spoke, but by no means gave him a completely decisive victory.
She continued to make trial of the strength and valor of Odysseus,
and of his noble son. She herself flew up to the roof-beam of the smoky
feast-hall and sat there in the form of a swallow.

But the suitors were
pressed on by Agelaos, the son of Damastor, and by Eurynomos—
225   and Amphimedon, and Demoptolemos, and Peisander the son
of Polyktor, and war-minded Polybos. These were by far the best
of the suitors in valor of those still alive and fighting for the sake
of their breath-souls. The bow and the thick-falling arrows had already
cut down the others.

Agelaos spoke then, addressing his words
230   to everyone: "Friends, now this man will hold back his invincible
hands! Mentor has gone off after mouthing his empty boasts,
and they are left alone at the outer doors. Let us not all throw
our long spears at the same time, but—you six—throw first
in the hopes that Zeus will grant that Odysseus be struck

---

215   *was taken*: The Trojan Horse was Odysseus' idea.

FIGURE 22.3 **Odysseus with his spear.** In "heroic nudity," with a cloak about his shoulders, wearing a traveler's skullcap, the bearded Odysseus raises his spear against the suitors. Bronze relief on the cheek piece of a horse from the second century AD, found at Hexamila on the Hellespont, near Troy.

235 and that we win glory. Don't worry about the others once
this man falls!"

So he spoke, and the others eagerly threw their
spears, just as he said. But Athena made most of them
fly in vain. One man hit only the doorpost of the well-built
feast-hall, another hit the close-fitting door. The ash-spear
240 of another, heavy with bronze, struck the wall.

When they had
dodged the spears of the suitors, then the resourceful good
Odysseus began to speak to his companions: "My friends,
now I give the word—cast your spears into the crowd of suitors,
who are anxious to kill us, in addition to their earlier crimes!"

245   So he spoke, and they all threw their sharp spears, taking
careful aim. Odysseus killed Demoptolemos, Telemachos
killed Euryades, the pig herder killed Elatos, and the cow herder
killed Peisander—all those four bit the vast floor with their teeth,
and the surviving suitors fled into the innermost part of the feast-hall.

250   Odysseus and his men rushed forward and snatched the spears
from the corpses while the suitors eagerly threw their sharp spears,
but Athena made them fly mostly in vain. One man hit the doorpost
of the well-built feast-hall, another hit the close-fitting door.
The ash-spear of another, heavy with bronze, struck the wall.
255 But Amphimedon hit Telemachos on the hand by the wrist,
a glancing blow, and the bronze broke the surface of the skin.

Ktesippos grazed Eumaios on the shoulder, throwing over
his shield with a long spear, but the spear flew on and fell
to the ground. Then the crafty war-minded Odysseus and his men
260 threw their sharp spears right into the crowd of the suitors.
City-sacking Odysseus hit Eurydamas, Telemachos got Amphimedon,
and the pig herder hit Polybos.

Then Philoitios struck Ktesippos
in the chest, and the cow herder said, boasting over him:
"Son of Polytherses, you lover of insult, I don't think you will again
265 give into foolishness and talk your big words. We'll let the gods
have the last say—they are stronger by far. This is *your* gift of guest-
friendship, to match the hoof that once you gave to godlike Odysseus,
when he begged through the house."

So spoke the herdsman
of the bent-horned cattle. Then Odysseus wounded the son of
Damastor, taking him on in the hand-to-hand with his long spear.   270
Telemachos wounded Leiokritos, the son of Euenor, getting him
in the soft underbelly and driving the bronze straight through.
Leiokritos fell forward onto the ground and hit the earth with full face.

Then Athena spread out her man-destroying goatskin
fetish high from the rafters, and the hearts of the suitors were   275
aghast. Some ran off through the feast-hall like a herd
of cattle that the nimble stinging black fly falls upon and drives
along in the season of spring when the days are long.
Even as vultures with their crooked talons and their curved
beaks come from the mountains and dart upon smaller birds   280
who fly low over the plain beneath the clouds, and the vultures
pounce on them and kill them, and valor or flight is useless,
and the men in the field rejoice watching the chase—even so
did Odysseus and his men set upon the suitors throughout the house,
striking them from the left and from the right. A repulsive groaning   285
arose from them as their heads were smashed, and all the floor
ran with blood.

But Leiodes° ran up to Odysseus and took hold
of his knees, and, begging, he spoke words that went like arrows:
"By your knees I beg you, Odysseus! Respect me and take pity!
I say that I have never done any harm to the women in the house,   290
neither in word nor in deed. I tried to hold back the other suitors
whenever any one would do such things. But they would not
listen to me and keep their hands away from foul deeds. And so
they have met an unpleasant fate for their loutish behavior.
But I, who am just a soothsayer, will lie low along with them   295
although I have done nothing—so true it is that there is never
any ultimate thanks for deeds well done."

The resourceful
Odysseus looked from beneath his brows and said: "If you are
the soothsayer among these men, you must often have prayed
in the halls that my sweet homecoming be a long ways off,   300
and that my wife might follow you and give you children.
For this reason, you will not escape sorrowful death!"

---

288 *Leiodes*: He was the first to try to string Odysseus' bow (Book 21).

So speaking
he took up in his powerful hand a sword lying there that Agelaos
had thrown to the ground when he was killed. He drove the sword
305 through the middle of Leiodes' neck, and the seer's head was mixed
with the dust even as he still spoke.

But Phemios, the singer,
the son of Terpes, avoided black fate because he sang for the suitors
from compulsion. He stood holding the clear-toned lyre
in his hands close beside the rear door. His mind pondered two
310 courses—either to slip out of the feast-hall and take a seat on
the well-built altar of great Zeus, the god of the court,° where
Odysseus, the son of Laërtes, had burned the thigh bones of many
cattle—or whether he should rush upon Odysseus and entreat him.
This seemed to be the better course: to take hold of the knees
315 of Odysseus, the son of Laërtes.°

So he put down the hollow lyre
on the ground, in between the wine-mixing bowl and the chair with
its silver rivets, and he rushed to Odysseus and clasped his knees,
and, begging, he spoke words that went like arrows: "By your knees
I beg of you, O Odysseus—respect me and take pity! It will
320 be trouble for you in times to come if you kill a singer—I who
sing to gods and humans. I am self-taught, but a god has breathed
into my heart the many pathways of song. And I seem to sing
by your side as by the side of a god. So don't be eager to cut
my throat! And Telemachos, your own son, will confirm these things—
325 that I never came willingly or through desire to your house
to sing to the suitors after their feasting. But they were many,
and strong, and they forced me to come here."

So Phemios spoke,
and the strong and mighty Telemachos heard him and quickly
he spoke to his father, standing near him: "Don't do it! Don't
330 slice him with the bronze, for he did nothing wrong. And let
us spare the herald Medon too, who always took care of me
in the house when I was little—unless Philoitios or the pig herder
has already killed him. Or perhaps he went up against you
as you raged through the house?"

---

311 *of the court*: Still in classical times, Greek houses usually had an altar in the open courtyard dedicated to Zeus of the Court (*Herkeios*), a protective spirit that defended the household.

315 *of Laërtes*: To clasp the enemy's knees was a sign of abject submission all over the ancient world.

So he spoke, and the intelligent
Medon heard him. For he lay crouching beneath a chair. He had   335
clothed himself in the skin of a newly flayed ox, trying to avoid
black death. Quickly he arose from beneath his chair and swiftly
he threw off the ox-hide. Then he rushed forward and clasped
the knees of Telemachos, and, begging, he spoke words that went
like arrows: "My friend, this is me—do not strike! And tell your father   340
not to cut me down with the sharp bronze in the greatness of his power,
being angry with the suitors who consumed the possessions in his halls.
And—the fools!—they did not honor you."

Then the resourceful
Odysseus said with a smile: "Take courage, for Telemachos
has protected and saved you, so that you might know in your heart,   345
and that you might tell others, that good deeds are better than bad ones.
But go outside the halls and sit outside in the court away from
the slaughter—you and the renowned singer—so that I can go
through the house and do what is required."

So he spoke and the two
men went outside the feast-hall, and they sat down on the altar of great   350
Zeus, looking around, expecting death at every instant. And then Odysseus
looked around his house to see if anyone of the men were hiding,
still alive, trying to avoid black death. He saw them all fallen
in the blood and the dust, the great mass of them, like fish
that the fishermen has dragged out of the gray sea up on the curving   355
shore in the mesh of their nets, and they all lie in piles longing
for the waves of the sea, and the burning sun takes away their
breath—even so, the suitors lay in piles on top of one another.

Then the resourceful Odysseus spoke: "Telemachos, come:
call out the nurse Eurykleia, so that I can say the word that is   360
in my mind."

So he spoke, and Telemachos obeyed his father.
Shaking the door,° he spoke to the nurse: "Come out here, old lady,
you who are in charge of the female slaves throughout our halls.
Come! My father calls you, because he wants to say something."

So he spoke, but she did not reply. Then she opened the doors   365
of the stately feast-hall and came forth. Telemachos led the way
before her. She found Odysseus with the corpses of the dead,

---

362   *shaking the door*: By the knob to which the thong was attached.

splattered with blood and filth like a lion that comes from feeding
on a cow in the field, and all its chest and its cheeks on both sides
370 are covered in blood, and he is terrible to look upon—even so
Odysseus was splattered with blood on his feet and hands.

When Eurykleia saw the corpses and the endless blood,
she began to exult for joy, for she saw what great deeds had
been done. But Odysseus restrained her and held her back
375 in her eagerness, and he spoke to her words that went like arrows:
"In your *heart*, old woman, take joy, but restrain yourself
and do not cry out for joy. It is not holy to boast over the corpses
of the dead. It is the fate of the gods that has overcome them,
and their own evil deeds. They honored no one of the men
380 who walk on the earth, neither wicked nor good, whoever
would come to them. And so through their folly they have come
to a shameful end. But come, tell me about the women in the halls—
which ones disrespect me and which ones are innocent."

The dear nurse
Eurykleia then answered him: "Well, child, I will tell you the truth.
385 There are fifty slave women in your house, whom we have taught
to do their work, to card wool and to bear the lot of slaves.
Of those, twelve are utterly without shame, honoring neither me
nor Penelope. Telemachos has only recently grown up, and his mother
would not allow him to rule over these slave women. But come,
390 I will go upstairs to the shining chamber to tell your wife,
on whom some god has cast sleep."

The resourceful Odysseus then
answered her: "Don't awaken her yet, but order the women to come
here, those who have committed these indecencies."

So he spoke,
and the old woman went through the feast-hall to make her
395 announcement to the women, and to order them to come. Odysseus
called Telemachos and the cow herder and the pig herder to himself,
and he spoke words that went like arrows: "Start to carry
out the corpses, and have the women help you. Then clean
the beautiful chairs and the tables with water and porous sponges.
400 When you have set the whole house in order, lead out the women
slaves from the well-built feast-hall to a place between the round-house°

---

401   *round-house*: We cannot say what the purpose or nature of this building was.

and the handsome wall of the court. There, cut them down
with your long swords until you have released the breath-souls
of all of them, and they have forgotten all about the sex that they
enjoyed with the suitors—sleeping with them in secret."   405

                              So he spoke,
and the women came all in a group, weeping gruesomely, pouring
down hot tears. First they carried out the corpses of the dead
and set them down beneath the portico° of the well-walled court,
leaning them up against one another. Odysseus himself gave
the orders, hastening on the work, and the women were compelled   410
to carry out the bodies. And they cleaned the very beautiful chairs
and the tables with water and porous sponges. Then Telemachos
and the cow herder and the pig herder scraped the floor of the tightly
built house with hoes. The slave women carried out the scrapings
and placed them outdoors. When they had set all the feast-hall   415
in order, they led the women forth from the well-built chamber
to the place between the round-house and the handsome enclosure
of the court, and there they confined them in a narrow space from which
they could not escape.

                  The shrewd Telemachos was the first to speak
to them: "Let me not impose a clean death on those women   420
who have heaped insults on me and my mother and slept with
the suitors."

        So he spoke, and he tied one end of the cable of
a blue-prowed ship to a great pillar of the portico and the other
to the round-house, stretching it up high so that no one could reach
the ground with her feet. As when long-winged thrushes or doves fall   425
into a snare set in a thicket as they launch themselves toward their
resting place, but hateful is the bed that gives them welcome—even so
the women held their heads in a row, and around the necks of all
of them were placed nooses so that they might die most piteously.
They writhed a little with their feet, but not for long.°   430

                              Then they brought
out Melanthios into the forehall and the court, and they cut off
his nose and ears with the cruel bronze. They ripped out
his groin and fed it raw to the dogs, and they cut off his hands

---

408 *portico*: Evidently this is the same as the forehall.

430 *for long*: We cannot reconstruct the details of this execution or see how in practical terms it was carried out.

and feet in their furious anger.° They then washed their hands
435 and feet and went into the house, to Odysseus. The deed was done.

Odysseus spoke to the dear nurse Eurykleia: "Bring in
sulfur, the driver-away of evils, old lady, and bring fire to me
so that I may purify the feast-hall. You tell Penelope to come
here with her attendant women. Order that the remaining female slaves
440 come into the house."

The dear nurse Eurykleia then spoke: "You have said
everything, my child, that is right. But come, I will bring you clothes,
a cloak and shirt so that you don't have to stand in the feast-hall
with your broad shoulders wrapped in rags. This is hardly appropriate."

Then the resourceful Odysseus said in reply: "First make a fire
445 in the halls." So he spoke, and the dear nurse Eurykleia did not
disobey. She brought fire and sulfur, and Odysseus purified
the feast-hall and the house and the court.° The old lady went
through the beautiful house of Odysseus to make her announcement
to the women, to command them to come. They came forth from their hall
450 carrying torches in their hands. They swarmed around Odysseus
and embraced him, and they kissed his head and shoulders and hands
in loving welcome. Then sweet desire for weeping and wailing took
hold of him, for he recognized each one of them in his heart.

---

434 *furious anger*: We do not learn who exactly performs these mutilations.

447 *and the court*: Ghosts do not like the smell of sulfur, and the feast-hall is at the moment filled with ghosts.

BOOK 23. *Husband and Wife*

The old woman went into the upper chamber, laughing loudly,
to tell her mistress that her dear husband was within the house.
Her knees were nimble, and her feet were swift beneath her.

She stood over the head of Penelope and said: "Wake up,
Penelope, my child, so that you might see with your own eyes   5
that which you have hoped for every day! Odysseus has come
and reached his home, though returning late. He has killed
the proud suitors who plundered his house and ate his animals
and threatened his child with violence."

       Then the judicious Penelope
answered her: "My dear nurse, the gods have made you *mad*,   10
for they can easily remove one's wits even if you are highly sensible,
even as they can put the simple-minded on the road to understanding.
It is they who have harmed your wits, although you were of sound
mind before. They have struck you. Before you were temperate
in your heart. And why do you mock me, who have a heart full   15
of sorrow, by telling me this wild tale and rousing me from a sweet
sleep that has covered over and bound my eyes? For I have never
slept better than this, ever since Odysseus went off to see that
cursed Ilion, a place not to be named.

      "But come, go back downstairs
to the women's quarters. If any other of the women who attend   20
me had come to me and told me this story and waked me up
from sleep, I would quickly have sent her back with much
ill-feeling to the women's quarters. But in this you shall profit
from your old age."

     Then the dear nurse Eurykleia answered her:
"I do not mock you, my child, but truly Odysseus has come   25
and arrived at his home just as I say—the stranger whom everyone
despised in his halls. Telemachos knew long ago that he was
in the house, but in his wisdom he hid his father's purpose until
Odysseus could take revenge on the violence of the haughty men."

30   So Eurykleia spoke, and Penelope was thrilled, and she leaped
      from the bed and embraced the old lady, and she poured down tears
      from her eyelids and spoke words that went like arrows: "But come,
      tell me truly, dear nurse, if he has really come home, as you say, how
      he was able to put his hands on the shameless suitors, being alone
35   when they were always inside in a crowd?"

                                        The dear nurse Eurykleia
      then answered: "I didn't see it, and I do not know—only I heard
      a groaning of them as they died. We women were sitting
      in the innermost part of our well-built chambers, terrified,
      and the well-fitting doors shut us in until your son Telemachos
40   called me to come forth from the women's quarters. For his father
      had ordered him to summon me. Then I found Odysseus standing
      in the midst of the corpses of the dead. They lay around him,
      covering the hard-packed ground, and they lay on top of one another.
      It would warm your heart to see it! Now they are all gathered
45   together near the gates to the court, and your husband is cleansing
      the beautiful house with sulfur, and he has kindled a great fire.
      Odysseus ordered me to fetch you. Do follow along, so that the two
      of you can enter into joy, for you have suffered many evils.
      Now at last has your longtime hope come to pass. Your husband
50   has come home alive, he has found you and his son in the halls.
      As for the suitors who did him dirt, he has taken vengeance
      on them, one and all, in his house."

                                  The judicious Penelope answered her:
      "Dear nurse, do not boast loudly over them, laughing. You know
      how welcome Odysseus would appear to everyone in the halls,
55   and especially to me and my son, whom the two of us bore.
      But this story cannot be true as you tell it. Perhaps one of the gods
      killed the bold suitors, paying them back for their infuriating
      violence and their evil deeds. They would not respect *anyone*
      of men who walk on the earth, neither good nor bad, whoever
60   should come to them. Therefore they have suffered evil for their
      folly . . . but Odysseus has lost his homecoming, far away from
      the land of Achaea, and he himself has perished."

                                              The dear nurse
      Eurykleia then answered her: "My child, what a word has escaped
      the barrier of your teeth! That your husband, who is inside the house
65   beside the hearth, would never come home! Your mind is always
      unbelieving! But come and I will tell you another clear sign—
      the scar that once a boar etched in with his white tusk—I recognized

FIGURE 23.1   Melian relief with Penelope and Eurykleia.   The mourning Penelope sits in a traditional pose with her hand to her forehead and her legs crossed. Her head is veiled. Here she stares gloomily downwards, seated on a padded stool beneath which is a basket for yarn, while the ancient Eurykleia, her head veiled, her fist clenched, tries to persuade her that her husband has returned. The purpose of these terracotta reliefs, found in different parts of the Roman world, is unclear. Roman Relief, first century AD.

it when I was washing him. I wanted to tell you, but he laid
his hands on my mouth and in the great wisdom of his heart
70 would not let me speak. But come! I will put my life at stake
if I am deceiving you, so that you can kill me with a pitiable death!"

Then the judicious Penelope answered her: "Dear nurse, it is
hard for you to understand the counsel of the gods who last forever,
no matter how wise you may be. But all the same, let us go to
75 my son, so that I can see the dead suitors, and see who killed them."

So speaking, she descended from the upper chamber. And her mind
rushed this way and that, whether she should interrogate her husband
from a distance, or whether she should stand beside him and kiss
his head and take hold of his hands. And when Penelope went into
80 the chamber and crossed the stone threshold, she took her seat
opposite Odysseus in the glare of the fire against the farther wall.
He sat down against a tall pillar, looking down, waiting to see
if his excellent wife would say something when she saw him with
her own eyes.

She sat in silence for a long time, and amazement came
85 upon her heart. Now she would look in full gaze at his face, now she
would fail to recognize him because of the foul clothing that he wore.

Telemachos reproached his mother and spoke and called her out:
"Mother of mine—*cruel* mother! With an unfeeling heart! Why do
you stay apart from my father and not sit by his side and exchange
90 words with him and converse? No other woman would so harden
her heart and stand apart from her husband who after suffering many
pains came on the twentieth year again to the land of his fathers.
Your heart is always harder than a stone!"

Then the judicious Penelope
answered him: "My child, the heart in my breast is amazed,
95 and I cannot say a word, neither to ask a question nor to look him
in the face. If this truly is Odysseus, and he has come home,
surely we will know each other even better. For we have special
signs that we two alone know, kept secret from others."

So he spoke, and the much-enduring good Odysseus smiled,°
100 and quickly he spoke to Telemachos words that went like arrows:
"Well, Telemachos, let your mother put me to the test in the halls.

---

99 *smiled*: The only time in the *Odyssey* where Odysseus smiles.

Then she will soon know all the better. For now, she scorns me
because I am filthy. I have evil clothes about my flesh, and she does
not think that I am he. But as far as we ourselves are concerned,
let us consider what will be the best course. If someone kills   105
one man in the land, even one who has few supporters left behind,
he still flees, leaving his family and the land of his fathers.
But we have killed the cream of the city, those who were the best
young men in Ithaca. I think we should think about this."

The shrewd Telemachos said in reply: "You yourself should   110
look to this, dear father. For they say that your counsel is the best
among men and that not any other of mortal men could contend with you.
As for ourselves, we will follow you eagerly, and I don't think
that we will be lacking in bravery, as far as our strength permits."

Then the resourceful Odysseus said in reply: "I will tell you   115
what seems to me to be the best plan. First of all, wash yourselves
off and put on clean shirts, and order the female slaves in the halls
to put on clean clothes too. Then have the divine singer with his
clear-toned lyre lead a merry dance for us, so that someone coming
along and hearing the sound will think that a wedding feast   120
is going on, either someone going along the road or someone
who lives nearby. I don't want news of the death of the suitors
to get out through the broad city before we ourselves can go out
to our well-wooded farm.° There we can take thought about
what advantage the Olympian places in our hands."   125

So he spoke,
and they heard and obeyed him. First they washed themselves
and put on clean shirts that the women provided. Then the divine
singer took up his hollow lyre and roused in them the desire
for sweet song and the noble dance. The great hall resounded
all about the feet of the men and women with beautiful waists   130
as they danced. And thus someone who heard the hoopla from
outside the house would say: "Looks like someone has married
the much-courted lady—cruel woman! She did not have the daring
to preserve the great house of her wedded husband to the end,
until he returned."   135

Thus would one say when they did not know what
had happened. Then Eurynomê, the housekeeper, bathed great-hearted

---

124 *well-wooded farm:* He means the farm of his father, Laërtes, mentioned several times before, where, in fact,
he goes.

Odysseus in his house and anointed him with olive oil, and she threw
around him a cloak and a shirt. Then Athena poured out abundant
beauty, making him taller to see and more robust. And from
140 his head she made locks to curl down like the hyacinth flower.
As when a man overlays silver with gold, a man whom Hephaistos
and Pallas Athena have taught every kind of craft, and he fashions
lovely works—even so did Athena pour out grace on Odysseus' head
and shoulders.

He emerged from the bath like in appearance to
145 the deathless ones. He sat back down in the chair from which he had
arisen, directly opposite his wife, and he said to her: "You are
a strange woman! To you beyond all women those who live
in Olympos have given a heart that cannot be softened. For no other
woman would dare to stand apart from her husband, who after
150 suffering many sorrows came to her in the twentieth year in the land
of his fathers. But come, nurse, prepare a bed for me so that I can get
some rest. Her heart—it is like iron!"

The judicious Penelope then spoke
to him: "Well, *you* are a strange man. I am not acting proudly,
nor do I make light of you, nor am I so amazed,° but I know well
155 that you looked the same then, when you left Ithaca, traveling in your
long-oared ship. But come, make up the stout bedstead for him,
Eurykleia, and put it outside the well-built chamber that Odysseus
himself built. Set up the stout bedstead there and put bedding on it,
fleeces and cloaks and bright blankets."

So she spoke, putting her husband
160 to the test. But Odysseus, bursting with anger, spoke to his sensible
wife: "Woman—truly you have uttered a grievous word! *Who* has
moved my bed elsewhere? That would be hard to do even for one
highly skilled, unless some god should come down himself
and easily will it to be in another place. But no living man, no matter
165 how young and strong, could easily have moved it, for a great
sign is built into the decorated bed. *I* made it, and no one else.

"There was a bush of long-leafed olive growing inside my
compound, flourishing and vigorous. It had the thickness of a column.
I built my chamber around the olive, working on it until it was done,
170 making the walls of close-set stones, and I fitted a roof overhead,

---

154 *so amazed*: Amazed, perhaps, at his transformation, meaning that she *should* recognize him now that he
      looks like he did when he left her, but still she holds back. But her reply is obscure.

and I installed joined doors, close-fitting. Then I cut off the leafy
branches of the long-leafed olive and, trimming the trunk up
from the root, I skillfully polished it with a bronze adze.
I made it straight to the line, thus making the bedpost.
I bored it all with the augur.° Beginning from this I worked   175
everything smooth until it was done, inlaying it with gold
and silver and ivory. And I stretched ox-hide cords, stained red.

"Thus I tell to you a sign. But I do not know at all, woman,
whether my bedstead is still in place, or whether someone
has cut from beneath the trunk of the olive and set the bedstead   180
someplace else."

So he spoke, and he loosened her knees
and melted her heart, for she recognized the sure signs that
Odysseus had told her. Weeping, she ran straight toward him
and threw her arms around the neck of Odysseus and she kissed
his head and said: "Don't be angry with me, O Odysseus,   185
for in all other things you were the wisest of men. It is the gods
who gave us this sorrow, who didn't want us to enjoy our youth
together and come to the threshold of old age. So do not be angry
with me for this, nor resent me, because I did not welcome you
when I first saw you. Always the heart in my breast was filled   190
with shivering that someone should come and deceive me
with his words. For there are many who devise evil things.

"No, not even Argive Helen, the daughter of Zeus, would have
lain in love with a man from another people if she had known
that the warlike sons of the Achaeans would bring her home again   195
to the dear land of her fathers. It must be some god that prompted her
to that shameful act. For she did realize in her mind the dread
blindness° from which, at the first, the sorrow came to us too.

"But now, because you have told the clear signs of our bed,
which no other mortal but one has seen—you and I and our   200
attendant, the daughter of Aktor,° whom my father gave me
at the time I came here, who guarded the doors of our strong bridal
chamber. So you have persuaded me, though I am hard of heart."

---

175   *with the augur*: To drill holes for the oxhide thongs that create the mattress, that he mentions in line 177.

198   *. . . dread blindness*: The Greek word is the untranslatable *atê*, which refers to the act of divine intervention,
      the delusion thus caused, and the disaster that follows.

201   *daughter of Aktor*: Not mentioned elsewhere; perhaps Eurynomê is meant.

So she spoke, and she stirred in Odysseus still more
205 the urge to weep, and he cried, holding his beloved wife in his arms,
she who was true of heart. As welcome as the land appears
to swimmers, whose well-built ship Poseidon has smashed on the sea
as it was driven on by wind and rough waves—few escape
the gray sea by swimming to the mainland, and a thick crust of brine
210 has formed around their flesh, and gladly have they gone forth
onto the land, fleeing evil—even so was her husband welcome
to Penelope as she looked upon him, and she would not let loose
her white arms from his neck.

                      And Dawn with her fingers of rose
would have appeared as they still lamented if flashing-eyed Athena
215 did not have another thought. She held back the night at the end
of its course so that it was long, and she stayed golden-throned
Dawn at the streams of Ocean, and she would not allow Dawn
to yoke her swift horses Lampos and Phaëthon,° which are the colts
that draw her car, that bring light to men.

                          And then the resourceful
220 Odysseus addressed his wife: "Wife, we have not yet come
to the end of our trials. There is still measureless labor ahead of us,
long and hard, that I must see through to the end. For thus did
the breath-soul of Tiresias prophesy to me on that day when
I went down into the house of Hades to learn of the homecoming
225 for my companions and myself. But come, let us go to our bed,
woman, so we might take pleasure in sweet sleep."

                           The judicious
Penelope then answered him: "We can go to bed any time you
want, for the gods have brought it about that you have come back
to your well-built house and the land of your fathers. But because
230 you have thought of this, and a god has put it into your heart—
come, tell me what *is* this trial. In time to come, as I think,
I will learn of it. To know it at once is not a worse thing."

The resourceful Odysseus then said in reply: "Strange woman!
Why do you insist that I talk of such things? Alright, I will tell you,
235 and I will hide nothing. You won't be happy about it, nor am I
myself happy about it.

---

218 *Lampos and Phaëthon:* "light" and "shining," speaking names reminiscent of the nymphs who looked after
    Helios' cattle on Thrinakia (Book 12), *Phaëthousa* and *Lampetiê.*

"Tiresias advised me to go forth through
the many cities of men, holding in my hands a well-fitted oar,
until I come to people who do not know what the sea is,
nor do they eat food mixed with salt, nor do they know of ships
with painted red cheeks, nor of well-fitted oars that are the wings   240
of ships. He gave this very clear sign to me, and I will not
conceal it. When another traveler, coming upon me, should say
that I have a winnowing-fan on my strong shoulder, then
he ordered that I fix the oar in the earth and perform holy sacrifices
to King Poseidon—a ram and a bull and a boar that mates   245
with sows—then go home and perform holy sacrifices
to the deathless gods who inhabit the broad sky, to all of them,
one after the other.

          "And Tiresias said that a gentle death would
come to me from the sea,° which will kill me when I am
overcome in a vigorous old age. And around me all the people   250
will be prosperous. Tiresias said that all this would come to pass."

     The judicious Penelope then answered him: "If the gods
are going to bring about a better old age, there is hope that
you will find an escape from evil."

          Thus they spoke such things
to one another. In the meanwhile Eurynomê and Eurykleia   255
prepared the bed of soft covers by the light of blazing torches.
When they had busily made the stout bed, the old nurse went
back to her chamber to lie down, and Eurynomê, the lady
of the bedchamber, led Odysseus and Penelope on their way
to the bed, holding a torch in her hands. After she had led them   260
to the bedchamber, she withdrew. The couple gladly came to the place
of their ancient marriage bed.

          In the meanwhile, Telemachos
and the cow herder and the pig herder stopped their feet
from the dance, and they stopped the women, and they themselves
went to bed in the shadowy halls.   265

---

249   *from the sea*: It is not clear whether this means "away from the sea," inland, or whether it means as the
       result of something "coming from the sea." Taking the second interpretation, later tradition reported that
       Odysseus' son Telegonos (by Kirkê, of whom Homer has no knowledge) mistakenly killed him with a spear
       tipped with a stingray barb "from the sea," but this is hardly a "gentle" death.

But when Odysseus and Penelope
had had their fill of the joy of love-making, they entertained
one another by telling tales to one another. She, a goddess
among women, told of all the things she endured in the halls,
beholding the destructive crowd of the suitors who on her account
270 butchered many animals, both cattle and fat sheep, and a huge
amount of wine was drawn from the jars. And Odysseus recounted
all the agonies that he had brought on men, and all the labor that
he himself in sorrow had to endure. She took pleasure in hearing him,
nor did sleep fall on her eyelids before he had told her all.

275   He began by telling her how he overcame the Kikones,
then came to the rich land of the Lotus Eaters. And all that
Cyclops did, and how he took revenge for his strong companions
whom Cyclops ate, whom Cyclops did not pity. And how he came
to the island of Aiolos, who received him openly and sent them
280 on their way. But it was not his fate to come to the dear land
of his fathers just yet, for a storm wind snatched him up and carried
Odysseus on the fishy sea, groaning deeply.

                                    And how he came
to Telepylos, the town of the Laestrygonians, who destroyed his ships
and killed his companions who wore fancy shin guards, one and all.
285 Odysseus alone escaped in his black ship. And he told about the trickery
and craftiness of Kirkê, and how he came in his benched ship
to the dank house of Hades to make inquiry of the breath-soul
of Theban Tiresias, and he saw all his comrades and his mother,
she who gave him birth and raised him when he was small.

290   And how he heard the voices of the Sirens, who sing without
cease, and how he came to the Planktai° and dread Charybdis
and Skylla, from whom no other men ever escaped unharmed.
And how his companions killed the cattle of Helios and how Zeus
who thunders on high hit his swift ship with a fiery thunderbolt,
295 and his noble companions died every one. Only he alone escaped
the black fates.

                    And how he arrived to the island of Ogygia
and the nymph Kalypso, who kept him in her hollow caves,
and wanted him to be her husband, and nourished him and said

---

291 *Planktai*: The "clashing (rocks)," a danger that threatened Jason, which Odysseus does not actually
     encounter, but that Kirkê tells him about (Book 12).

that she would make him immortal and ageless for all his days.
But she did not persuade the spirit in his breast.   300

                                        Then he came
to the Phaeacians, as he suffered terribly, who heartily honored him
as if he were a god, and sent him on his way in a black ship
to the land of his fathers, after giving him a mass of bronze
and gold and fine cloth.

                                This was the last thing he said before
sweet sleep, the looser of care, settled upon him, loosening   305
the cares of his heart. But flashing-eyed Athena had another thought.
When she judged that Odysseus had taken sufficient pleasure
from mingling with his wife, and from sleep itself, she immediately
roused from Ocean early-born golden-throned Dawn, who brings
light to men.   310

                        Odysseus arose from his soft bed and he gave a command
to his wife: "Woman, surely we have had our fill of trials, both of us,
you here and me crying about my troublesome homecoming. But Zeus
and the other gods bound me with sorrows far away from the land
of my fathers, although I was eager to return. Because we have
both come to the marriage bed that we both wanted so much,   315
I want you now to take care of the possessions that are in the house.
As for the flocks that the proud suitors have wasted, I shall restore
them through raids, and the Achaeans will give some,° until they
fill up all my pens. But now I must go to my well-wooded farm,
to see my noble father, who grieves bitterly for me. To you, woman,   320
I give this charge, though you are in any event a sensible woman.
Right away, at the time of the rising sun, a report about the suitors
I killed will get out. You go up to your upper chamber with your
attendants and wait there. Look on no man and ask no questions."

    He spoke and put on his beautiful armor around his   325
shoulder, and he roused Telemachos and the cow herder and
the pig herder, and he pressed them all to take up war gear
in their hands. They obeyed him and armed themselves
in bronze. And they opened the gates and went out. Odysseus
was in the lead. Already the sun shone on the earth, but Athena   330
covered them in night and led them swiftly forth from the city.

---

318 *give some*: He means those peoples under his direct control: Responsibility for allowing the suitors to
behave as they did implies responsibility for making good the damage.

BOOK 24. *Father and Son*

In the meanwhile Kyllenian Hermes° called forth the breath-souls
of the suitors. He had a wand in his hands—beautiful, golden—
with which he enchants the eyes of those he wishes, while
he awakes others from their sleep, whomever he wishes.
5   He drove them on with it, and gibbering they followed.
As when bats in the depths of a wondrous cave fly around gibbering,
and then one falls from the rock in the chain in which they cling
to one another, even so the breath-souls went off gibbering.
And Hermes the Deliverer led them over the mildewy ways.

10   And they came to the streams of Ocean and the White Rock,
and they went past the Gates of Helios and the Land of Dreams.
Quickly they came to the meadow of asphodel, where the breath-souls
were, the images of men who are done with their labor.°
They found the breath-soul of Achilles, son of Peleus, and of Patroklos
15   and of noble Antilochos and Ajax,° who was the best in form
and muscle of all the Danaäns, after the noble son of Peleus.

So these were swarming around Achilles when the breath-soul
of Agamemnon, son of Atreus, filled with sorrow, came up close.
Around him were gathered all those who had died and met their fate
20   together with Agamemnon in the house of Aigisthos. The breath-soul
of the son of Peleus first addressed him: "Son of Atreus, we thought
that you above all fighting men were dear to Zeus who delights
in the thunder, and for all your days, because you ruled over many
powerful men around the land of the Trojans, where the Achaeans

---

1   *Kyllenian Hermes*: Because he was born on Mount Kyllenê, in the Peloponnesus, according to later accounts.
Only here in Homer is Hermes called Kyllenian, and only here does he appear as the *psychopompos*, or "soul-
guide," who leads the breath-souls to the other world. He does, however, serve an analogous function in the
Iliad, when he leads Priam through the night into the camp of the Achaeans (Book 24), and in the *Odyssey*
when he meets Odysseus on the otherworldly island of Kirkê.

13   *...labor*: Asphodel, a pretty blooming herb, is often associated with the underworld and was planted on
graves. The White Rock, not mentioned elsewhere, is somewhere in the other world, as are the Gates of
Helios and the Land of Dreams.

15   *...Ajax*: Heroes of the Trojan War, all killed in battle. Patroklos is Achilles' friend. Antilochos is the son
of Nestor. (Big) Ajax is the son of Telamon and the best fighter after Achilles, whose breath-soul turned
away in anger from Odysseus in the underworld because Odysseus had cheated Ajax of the arms of Achilles
(Book 11).

suffered so horribly. But it was your fate that death would claim you   25
prematurely, before your time, the fate that no one born can escape.
I wish that, still enjoying the honor that was yours, you had met
death and found your fate in the land of the Trojans. Then all
the Achaeans would have made you a tomb, and for your son
you would have won great glory in the times to come. But as it is,   30
fate has decreed that you be taken in a most pathetic death."°

    The breath-soul of the son of Atreus answered the breath-soul
of Achilles in this fashion: "Most fortunate son of Peleus! Achilles,
like to the gods, who died in Troy far from Argos—around you
others were killed, the best of sons of the Trojans and the Achaeans,   35
fighting over your corpse.° You lay in a whirl of dust, mighty in your
power, forgetful of your horsemanship. But we fought all day long
and would never have left off the fight if Zeus had not stopped it
with a storm. Then, when we had carried you from the war to the ships,
we lay you down on a bier and cleansed your beautiful flesh   40
with warm water and anointing oil. The Danaäns poured
out abundant hot tears, and they cut their hair. Your mother came
from the sea, along with the immortal nymphs of the sea, when
she heard the news. A wondrous cry arose over the sea,
and a trembling took hold of all the Achaeans. Then would they   45
have sprung up and rushed to the hollow ships had not a man
with vast experience of olden days held them back—Nestor,
whose counsel always seemed best in earlier times. With good
intentions he spoke and addressed them: 'Stay now, Argives—
don't flee, young men of the Achaeans! His mother has come   50
from the waters with her deathless nymphs of the sea in order
to see the face of her dead son.'

             "So Nestor spoke, and the great-hearted
Achaeans held back from their flight. Then around you the daughters
of the Old Man of the Sea stood, weeping piteously,
and they clothed you with their deathless garments. The Muses,   55
all nine of them, singing in antiphony with their beautiful voices,
sang the threnody. Then you could scarcely have seen a dry eye
among the Argives, so deeply did the clear-toned Muse stir
them. For seventeen days and nights we lamented you—
both deathless gods and mortal men. And on the eighteenth   60
we gave you to the fire. We killed many well-fatted sheep

---

31 ... *death*: The breath-soul of Achilles seems only now for the first time to encounter the breath-soul of
    Agamemnon, although ten years have passed.

36 *your corpse*: Seemingly Achilles has not heard the story of his death before.

FIGURE 24.1 Ajax carries the body of Achilles from battle. The figures are labeled. Big Ajax was usually credited with saving Achilles' corpse from the battle, although the *Odyssey* does not say so. Ajax here wears a helmet, breast-plate and shin-guards, but his genitals are exposed. He carries a spear. A naked Achilles, killed by an arrow fired by Paris, is suspended over his shoulder. From the handle of the famous François Vase, signed by the potter Ergotimos and the painter Kleitias. Athenian black-figure wine-mixing bowl, c. 570 BC.

around you, and cattle with crumpled horns. You were burned
in the clothing of the gods, and with rich unguent and sweet
honey. Many of the Achaean fighting men danced an armed
dance around the fire as you burned, both foot soldiers and drivers   65
of cars. And a great cry arose.

     "But when the flame of Hephaistos
had put an end to you, in the morning we gathered together
your white bones, O Achilles, and placed them in unmixed
wine and oil. Your mother gave you a golden two-handled
vase. She said it was a gift of Dionysos, the work of the justly   70
renowned Hephaistos. Your white bones lie within it, glorious
Achilles, mixed with those of the dead Patroklos, son of
Menoitios. But in another jar lie the bones of Antilochos,°
whom you honored above all your other companions, once
Patroklos was dead.   75

    "And around them the holy army of spear-bearing
Argives heaped up a great and handsome tomb on a projecting
headland on the broad Hellespont, so that it could be seen
by men from far over the sea, both those who live now
and those who are to come after.°

     "Your mother asked the gods
for beautiful prizes, and she set them out in the middle   80
of the contestants' arena for the best of the Achaeans.
Before now you have been at the burials of many fighting men,
when, at the death of some king, young men tie a belt around
their middles and prepare for the competition. Still, had you
seen that sight, you would most have marveled in your heart,   85
such beautiful prizes did Thetis, the goddess whose feet are
of silver, set out on your behalf. For you were very dear
to the gods. And so, though you have died, your name lives on,
and your fame will always be great on the lips of men, Achilles.

  "But to me!—what was the sweetness in having survived   90
the war? For Zeus had in mind a wretched death for me
on my return at the hands of Aigisthos and my ruinous wife!"

---

73 *Antilochos*: The son of Nestor, killed by Memnon, an Ethiopian king, in the post-Homeric tradition. It is odd
 that Homer mentions him here. Perhaps in some other version of the poem Antilochos had a close relation-
 ship with Achilles, or Patroklos has even replaced him in this tale.

79 *come after*: There was, in fact, a barrow near the Hellespont called the "tomb of Achilles," but we cannot be
 sure that Homer refers to that here. The barrow may have been so called after this passage.

They spoke to one another in this fashion, then Argeïphontes
the guide came up close to them, leading down the breath-souls
95 of the dead suitors. The two—the souls of Achilles
and Agamemnon—marveled when they saw them, and they
went straight toward them. The breath-soul of Agamemnon,
son of Atreus, recognized the dear son of Melaneos, the famous
Amphimedon, for Amphimedon was a guest-friend, having his
100 house on Ithaca.

The breath-soul of the son of Atreus spoke first:
"Amphimedon, what has happened to you that you come
down here beneath the black earth—all of you picked men,
all of the same age? If one were to pick the best men in the city,
one would not choose otherwise. Perhaps Poseidon overwhelmed
105 you in your boats, arousing savage winds and high waves?
Or did enemy men harm you on the land while you were
rustling some cattle, or beautiful flocks of sheep, while they
fought for their city and their women? Tell me, because I am asking!

"I tell you that I am a guest-friend to your house. Don't you
110 remember when I came there to your house along with godlike
Menelaos to recruit Odysseus, to get him to follow us to Ilion
in ships with fine benches? It took us a full month to cross
over all the wide sea, for we could hardly persuade Odysseus,
sacker of cities."

Then the breath-soul of Amphimedon answered:
115 "Most glorious son of Atreus, king of men, Agamemnon,
I remember all of these things, Zeus-nourished one, just
as you say. And I will tell you all this exactly, how my evil
death came to be.

"We courted the wife of Odysseus, who was gone
for so long a time. She would neither refuse the hated marriage,
120 nor accept it, but instead contemplated death and black
fate for us. She contrived this trick in her mind: She set up
a great loom in her halls and wove before it, work very fine
and large. And she said to us: 'Young men, my suitors, though
godlike Odysseus has died, be patient in your eagerness
125 for my marriage. Wait until I finish this robe. I don't want
my spinning to go for nothing! It is a shroud for Lord Laërtes,
for that day when the dread fate of woeful death will take him—
so that none of the Achaean women in the land reproach me if he
were to lie without a shroud, this man who once had much in life.'

"So she spoke, and our trusting spirit was persuaded.   130
By day she would weave at the great loom, but at night
she set up torches and unwove. Thus for three years she beguiled
us by a trick, she deceived the Achaeans. But when the fourth
year came and the seasons rolled around as the months passed by,
and many days came to completion, then one of the women,   135
who knew well, told us, and we caught her unweaving
the glorious robe. And so she finished it by compulsion,
all unwilling.

          "When Penelope showed us the robe that she had
woven on the great loom, like to the sun or to the moon
after washing it, even then some evil spirit brought Odysseus   140
to the outskirts of the land, to where the pig herder lived.
There too came the son of godlike Odysseus, returning from
sandy Pylos in his black ship. The two of them, planning black
death for the suitors, came to the famous city—Telemachos first,
and then Odysseus came along after. The pig herder brought him   145
dressed in vile clothes, like a miserable beggar, an old man
leaning on a staff. He wore wretched clothes about his flesh,
and not any one of us knew who he was, so suddenly returned.
We attacked him with evil words and threw things at him.
But he endured in his own house with a steadfast heart, although   150
he was struck and insulted.

          "But when the mind of Zeus who carries
the goatskin fetish roused him, he with the help of Telemachos
took up all the beautiful armor and laid them away in the storeroom,
and he locked the bolts.° Then in his great cunning he urged
his wife to set up his bow and the gray iron to be a contest   155
for us ill-fated men, the beginning of our destruction.°

"No one of us was able to string the powerful bow—we didn't
even come close! But when the great bow came into Odysseus'
hands, then we all cried out that the bow not be given
to him, no matter what he should say. Telemachos alone urged   160
him on and told him to take it. When much-enduring godlike
Odysseus had received it in his hand, he easily strung the bow
and shot it through the iron. Then he went to the threshold

---

154 *locked the bolts*: This is not mentioned in Book 19.

156 *. . . destruction*: In fact Odysseus did not conspire with Penelope to set up the contest of the bow, but this is
     the way it seems to Amphimedon. Also, there was a lapse of time between the finishing of the shroud and
     the return of Odysseus, but to Amphimedon they seemed to happen at the same time.

and stood there, and he broadcast the swift arrows before him,
165 looking around with a terrible stare. Then he hit chief
Antinoös, and he shot his arrows, rife with groaning, at the others,
taking careful aim. And they fell thick and fast. Then it was clear
that some god was their helper, for right away rushing through
the house they killed men left and right in their rage. And an awful
170 moaning arose as heads were smashed, and all the floor ran
with blood.

      "And so, Agamemnon, we died, and even now
our bodies lie uncared for in the halls of Odysseus. For our friends
in every man's home know nothing of this, those who might wash
the black blood from our wounds and lay out our bodies with wailing.
175 For that is the gift due the dead."

                        Then the breath-soul of the son
of Atreus spoke: "O happy son of Laërtes, much-devising
Odysseus! Truly, *you* got a wife of great goodness! How good
were the brains in blameless Penelope, the daughter of Ikarios,
that she never forgot Odysseus, her wedded husband! The fame
180 of her virtue will never die. The deathless ones will fashion for men
on earth a pleasing song about the faithful Penelope.° Not like
that did the daughter of Tyndareus° fashion her own evil deeds—
killing her wedded husband! The song about *her* will be hateful
among men! Why, she brings a bad reputation to all womankind,
185 even on her who does the right thing."

                        And so they spoke to one
another in this fashion, standing in the house of Hades
beneath the depths of earth.

                        As for Odysseus and his men, when
they went down from the city, they came quickly to the beautiful
farm worked by Laërtes, which once Laërtes had won for himself,
190 and much had he labored upon it. There was his house.
Huts ran all the around it in which the slaves ate and sat
and slept, those who did his bidding. Among them was an old
Sicilian woman who took kindly care of the old man there
at the farm, far from the city.

---

181   ...*Penelope*: Like the *Odyssey*.

182   *daughter of Tyndareus*: Klytaimnestra.

Odysseus spoke to the slaves,
and his son: "You now, go inside the well-built house. Quickly   195
butcher the best of the pigs for dinner. In the meanwhile I will
put my father to the test, to see if he recognizes me and knows
me by sight, or whether he does not recognize me because I have
been gone such a long time."

So saying he gave his battle armor
to the slaves. They went swiftly into the house, and Odysseus   200
went near the fruitful orchard in his search. He did not find Dolios
as he went down into the great orchard, nor did he find
any of Dolios' slaves, nor his children They had gone off
to gather stones for a wall around the vineyard, and Dolios
was their leader.   205

Then Odysseus found Laërtes in the well-tended
garden, digging around a plant. He was dressed in a rotten
shirt—patched, unsuitable!—and around his shins he had tied
stitched oxhide shin guards to ward against scratches.
He had put gloves on his hands to protect him from brambles,
and he wore a goatskin cap on his head, nourishing his sorrow.   210

When the much-enduring godlike Odysseus saw Laërtes, worn
out with old age, he stood beneath a tall pear tree and with great
sorrow in his heart poured down tears. Then he debated
in his mind and heart whether he should kiss and embrace his father,
and tell him everything—how he came back to his native land—   215
or whether he should first question him and put him to the test
on every matter. As he thought about this, this seemed to him
to be the better course—first to test his father with mocking words.°

With this in mind, the godlike Odysseus went straight to his father.
Laërtes kept his head down—he was working the soil around   220
a plant. His glorious son stood beside him and said: "Old man,
I don't think that you lack skill in tending a garden. Your care
is good, nor does any plant—not a fig, a vine, an olive, a pear tree,
nor any garden-plot in all the field—lack for care. But I will
tell you something else, and do not become angry—you yourself   225
receive no good care! Why, you bear a gloomy old age and you

---

218   *mocking words:* It is not clear what Homer means by this and many have complained about what appears
needless cruelty toward Laërtes. But Homer's narrative is driven by a deep pattern: Odysseus always
"tests" the principal figure of the episode, then reveals his true identity, whether this be Cyclops, Kirkê,
the suitors, Penelope, or Laërtes.

live in this wretched squalor, and you dress in foul clothes!
Not because of your idleness does your master not take care
of you, nor do you look like a slave in stature or form—
you look like a king! Like one who, when he has bathed
and eaten, sleeps in a soft bed. For this is the way of old men.

"But come, tell me this, and tell it straight out: Whose slave
are you? Whose orchard do you care for? Tell me this truly
so that I may know full well, if truly we have come to Ithaca,
as a man I just met told me as I came here. But he didn't
show himself very obliging. He did not condescend to tell
me of each thing, nor did he listen to me when I questioned
him about a guest-friend of mine, whether he was still alive,
or whether he had died and gone to the house of Hades.

"I will tell you right out, so please pay attention and listen:
I once befriended a man in my own native land who came
to our house, and never did any man of strangers from a far
country come as a more welcome guest-friend. He said he was
an Ithacan, that Laërtes the son of Arkeisios was his father.

"Well, I took him to my house, and I entertained him
with kindly welcome from the rich store within the house,
and I gave him gift-tokens, as is appropriate. I gave him seven
talents of gold and a wine-mixing bowl made all of silver,
embossed with flowers, and twelve cloaks with a single fold,
and as many coverlets, and as many beautiful cloaks, and as many
shirts on top of those, and four very fine-looking women skilled
in fine handiwork, whom he himself chose."

Then his father
answered him, pouring down tears: "Stranger, truly you
have come to the land that you ask about. Violent and reckless
men are in control of it. I'm afraid that you gave all those gifts
for nothing, the countless gifts that you gave. But if you had
found Odysseus alive in the land of Ithaca, he would have sent
you on your way after reciprocating with many gifts and fine
entertainment. That is only right for him who began the kindness!

"But come tell me this, and tell it truly—how many years
has it been since you entertained that man, your unfortunate
guest-friend, my own son—if in fact he ever existed!—
Fated to bad luck! Either fish ate him on the sea, far from his friends

and the land of his fathers, or he became prey to wild animals
and birds on the land. Nor did his mother weep over him   265
after preparing him for burial, nor his father—those who gave
birth to him. Nor did his wife, who was courted with many gifts—
the judicious Penelope—bewail her husband on his bier, closing
his eyes, as is appropriate. For that is the gift due the dead.

    "And now tell me this truly, so that I may know: 270
Who are you among men? Where is your city and your parents?
Where have you moored your swift ship, the one that brought
you and your godlike companions here? Or did you come
as a passenger on someone else's ship, who put you out
and then went on?"   275

              The cunning Odysseus then answered him:
"I will tell you everything exactly. I am from Alybas,
where I live in a glorious house. I am the son of Apheidas,
son of king Polypemon. But my own name is Eperitos.
Some spirit drove me here from Sikania against my will.°
I moored my ship in the fields far from the city. But as for Odysseus,   280
this is the fifth year since he left from there and departed the land
of my fathers. Luckless man! But the birds were of good omen
for him on the right hand as he left, so I was glad to send him on,
and he was glad to go. Our hearts hoped to meet again
in guest-friendship and to exchange glorious gifts."   285

                      So he spoke,
and a dark cloud of anguish descended on Laërtes. Taking black
dust in both his hands, he poured it out over his gray hair,
groaning deeply. But Odysseus' heart was stirred, and a bitter pain
shot up through his nostrils as he looked on his father.

    Then Odysseus sprang forward and embraced him and kissed   290
him and said: "That man, about whom you ask, dear father, is me—
come in the twentieth year of absence to my native land!
But restrain your wailing and your tears. I will tell you something,
though haste is of the essence: I have killed the suitors in our house,
taking revenge for their insolence and their evil deeds!"   295

---

279 . . . *my will*: The improvised names in this false story suggest riches, though Laërtes does not pick up on
    the meaning of the names: *Alybas* is probably the same as *Alybê*, a source of silver (*Il.* Book 2); *Apheidas* is
    "unsparing" (that is, generous); *Polypemon*, "one who has suffered much" (to obtain his riches); *Eperitos*,
    "the chosen one." *Sikania* is Sicily.

FIGURE 24.2 Odysseus and his father, Laërtes. Odysseus, wearing his felt traveler's cap, lovingly embraces his father. Fragment from a Roman marble sarcophagus, second century AD.

Laërtes answered him and said: "If surely you have come
as Odysseus, my son—give me a clear sign now so that I can
be persuaded."

And the cunning Odysseus said in reply: "Well, first
take a look at this scar, which a boar gave me with his white tusk
on PARNASSOS when I went there. You and my honored mother   300
sent me there to Autolykos, my mother's father, so that I could
claim gifts that he had promised and agreed to give me when
he came here. And come, I will tell you the trees which once you
gave to me in the well-ordered garden, and I while just a child
was asking you about every single thing as I followed you through   305
the garden. We came past these very trees, and you named every
one of them and told me about each one. You gave me thirteen
pear trees and ten apple trees and forty fig trees. And you promised
to give me fifty rows of vines that ripen at different times.
And on them are clusters of all kinds, whenever the seasons   310
of Zeus weigh them down from above."

So he spoke, and Laërtes'
knees were loosened beneath him and his heart melted
when he recognized the sure signs that Odysseus told him.
He threw his powerful arms around his dear son, and godlike,
much-enduring Odysseus caught him as he fainted.   315

But when he revived and his spirit was gathered again into
his breast, immediately Laërtes spoke in reply: "Father Zeus,
truly the gods are at home in high Olympos, if in reality the suitors
have paid the price for their crass insolence. But now I fear terribly
in my heart that soon all the Ithacans will assemble here against   320
us and that they will send messengers everywhere to the cities
of the Kephallenians."

The resourceful Odysseus said to him in reply:
"Courage! Don't worry about any of this. But let us go to the house,
which lies close to the orchard. I sent Telemachos ahead,
and the cow herder and the pig herder, to prepare a dinner   325
as soon as possible."

When they had spoken to one another,
they went to the beautiful house. When they came to that good
house, they found Telemachos and the cow herder and the pig
herder cutting up the abundant meat and mixing the flaming wine.
Meanwhile the Sicilian attendant washed great-hearted Laërtes   330

in his house and anointed him with olive oil, and around him
they cast a beautiful cloak. And Athena, standing nearby, filled out
the limbs of the shepherd of the people, and she made him taller
and stouter to look upon.

          He got out of the bath. His son stared
335 with amazement when he saw him up close—like the deathless gods!—
and he spoke words that went like arrows: "Father, surely someone
of the gods that live forever have made you greater in size
and stature to look upon."

          The sensible Laërtes spoke to him:
"I only wish, O father Zeus and Athena and Apollo, that I were
340 such as I was when I captured Nerikos,° the well built citadel,
on a promontory of the mainland, when I was king of the Kephallenians.
And I wish that I had stood yesterday in our house, wearing armor
on my shoulders—stood with you as you beat back the suitors.
Then I would have loosened the knees of many in the halls, and you
345 would have rejoiced in your heart."

          So they spoke to one another
in this fashion. When everyone had ceased from his labor and made
ready the meal, they all sat down in a row in the seats and chairs.
They were about to set their hands to the food when the old man
Dolios drew near, and with him were the sons of that old man,
350 tired from their work in the fields. Their mother, the old Sicilian
woman, had gone out and called them in, she who nourished them
and took care of the old man in a kindly fashion, now that old age
had taken hold of him.

          When Dolios and his sons saw Odysseus,
and appreciated what this meant, they stood amazed in the halls,
355 and Odysseus, speaking gentle words, said: "Old man, sit down
and eat. Give up your wonder. Long have we waited in the halls,
eager to set our hands to the food, expecting you to come at any time."

    So he spoke, and Dolios went straight to Odysseus with both hands
outstretched, and he took Odysseus' hand and kissed it on the wrist,
360 and he spoke words that went like arrows: "My beloved master—
at last you have returned to us who longed greatly for you,
but thought that we would never see you again. And now the gods

---

340 *Nerikos:* It is not clear where this is.

themselves have brought you here. Hail to you, and greetings!
May the gods grant you happiness! But tell me this truly so that
I may know—does the judicious Penelope know that you have   365
returned, or shall we send a messenger?"

                     The resourceful Odysseus
then answered him: "Old man, she knows already. Why be busy
with this?"

    So he spoke, and Dolios sat down immediately
on a polished stool. In a similar way the sons of Dolios gathered
around great Odysseus, and they greeted him with words   370
and clasped his hands. Then they sat down in a row beside Dolios,
their father. So they were busy with the meal in the halls.

    Meanwhile, Rumor, the messenger, went swiftly everywhere
through the city, telling of the awful death and fate of the suitors.
The people heard it all at once and gathered from every corner,   375
with moaning and groans, in front of Odysseus' house. Each carried
his own dead from the house, and they buried the corpses. Those
who had come from other cities, they sent to their homes, placing
them on swift ships for seamen to carry. They themselves then
gathered into the place of assembly, sad at heart.   380

                   And when they
were gathered and assembled into a group, Eupeithes° stood up
and spoke to them. For a violent grief lay upon his heart for Antinoös,
the first man that godlike Odysseus had killed. Weeping for him,
he spoke and addressed the assembly: "My friends, truly this man
has contrived a monstrous deed against the Achaeans. Some he led   385
forth in his ships, many men and noble, but he has lost his hollow
ships and he has destroyed his people, and others he has killed—
by far the best of the Kephallenians—when he came back. So come,
before this man gets quickly to PYLOS, or to shining ELIS where
the Epeians are strong. Let us go, or in times to come we will   390
be covered in shame! For this is a disgrace for men to learn
who are yet to be—if we do not take revenge for the deaths
of our children and brothers. At least for me life would no longer
be a sweet thing, for I would rather die at once and be among
the dead. Let us go then, before Odysseus and his men get away   395
from us and cross over the sea!"

---

381 *Eupeithes*: "easily persuading," aptly named, the father of Antinoös, who appears here for the first time.

So he spoke, pouring down tears.
And pity seized all the Achaeans. Then Medon the herald came up
in their midst, and the godlike singer from the house of Odysseus,
when sleep had released them.° They took their stand in their midst,
400 and those around were astounded to see them.

Then Medon, a wise
man, spoke to them: "Now listen to me, Ithacans—Odysseus did not
perform these deeds without the help of the gods! I myself saw
an immortal god, who stood next to Odysseus in the likeness
of Mentor. First he would appear as an immortal god, egging
405 him on, and then he would charge through the hall striking terror
into the hearts of the suitors. They fell thick and fast!"°

So he spoke,
and a green fear took hold of everyone. Then among them spoke
Lord Halitherses,° the old man, the son of Mastor. He alone saw
before and behind. With the best of intentions he spoke and addressed
410 them: "Through *your own* wickedness, my friends, these things have
come to pass! You would not believe me! Nor would you believe
Mentor, shepherd of the people, that you should stop your sons
from their madness.° Instead they performed a monstrous deed
in the viciousness of their folly, wasting away someone's possessions
415 and disrespecting the wife of an excellent man. They said he would
never return! And now it has happened. Believe what I say: Let us
not go off, so that no one find an evil that he has brought on himself."°

So he spoke. But they leapt up with loud cries, more than half
of them. The others remained seated together. For Halitherses'
420 word was not pleasing to their hearts—and so they followed
Eupeithes. Quickly then they put on their armor. When they had
placed the gleaming bronze about their flesh, they gathered
in a group in front of the city with wide dancing-places. Eupeithes

---

399 *released them*: The herald and the singer seem to have taken a nap after the slaughter!

406 *thick and fast*: The differences between Medon's descriptions of Athena's intervention and the poet's are small, arising from Medon's desire to show that divine interference was decisive in Odysseus' victory.

408 *Halitherses*: Perhaps "sea-bold," he was introduced in Book 2 when he predicted that Odysseus would soon return. At first the gathering in the place of assembly has appeared to consist of the families of the dead suitors, but now it seems to include the Ithacan populace.

413 *… madness*: Mentor, whose form Athena takes to accompany Telemachos on his journey and to aid Odysseus in the slaughter of the suitors, appears only once in the *Odyssey* in his own person: in Book 2 when he advises the suitors to give up their depredations.

417 *on himself*: This is an important Odyssean theme, that some of the misfortunes that befall a man are fated, but some he brings on himself. Zeus makes this point in Book 1.

in his foolishness was their leader. He thought that he would avenge
the death of his son, yet he himself would not return home—   425
for now he would meet his fate.

But Athena spoke to Zeus the son
of Kronos: "Father of us all, son of Kronos, highest of rulers,
tell me when I ask: What purpose do you hide within? Will you
rather make evil war and the dread din of battle, or will you
establish friendship between the two parties?"   430

Cloud-gathering Zeus
then said in reply: "My child, why do you ask and inquire about
these matters? Was this not your plan all along? that Odysseus
should return and take vengeance on these men? Do what you
want, but I will speak as seems right to me. Now that godlike
Odysseus has taken his revenge on the suitors, let them swear   435
a solemn oath, and let him be chieftain for all his days.
And let us for our part bring about a forgetting of the death of their sons
and brothers. Let them love one another as before, and let there
be wealth, and let peace abound."

So speaking he roused up Athena,
who was already eager, and she went down in a rush from the peaks   440
of Olympos.

Now when Odysseus and his companions had put
aside the desire for honey-sweet food, the much-enduring godlike
Odysseus began to speak: "Let somebody go out and see
if they are coming near." So he spoke, and a son of Dolios went out,
just as he commanded. He went to the threshold and stood,   445
and he saw the suitors' kin coming near.

Quickly he spoke words
to Odysseus that went like arrows: "They are close by. Let us arm
quickly!" So he spoke, and they rose up and put on their armor.
Odysseus and his men were four,° and there were the six sons
of Dolios. Among them, too, Laërtes and Dolios, although advanced   450
in age, also put on armor, forced now to fight. And when they
put the shining armor about their flesh, they opened the doors
and went forth. Odysseus was in the lead. And Athena, the daughter
of Zeus, came near to them in the likeness of Mentor, both
in form and voice.   455

---

449 *four*: Odysseus, Telemachos, and the two herders.

The much-enduring godlike Odysseus rejoiced
when he saw her, and right away he spoke to Telemachos, his dear
son: "Telemachos, now you will learn, when you have come
to where the best men are tested in battle, how not to bring
disgrace on the race of your fathers who in earlier times were
460   superior in strength and courage over the entire earth."

                                              The sensible
Telemachos then replied: "You will see, if you want, dear father,
that in my present state of mind I will bring no disgrace on your house,
just as you say!"

        So he spoke, and Laërtes was glad and he said:
"What a day this is for me. Dear gods! I am so glad! My son
465   and my son's son compete with one another in valor!"

      Standing beside him the flashing-eyed Athena said:
"Son of Arkeisios, by far the dearest of all my companions,
make a prayer to the flashing-eyed virgin and to Zeus the father,
then brandish your long-shadowed spear right away, and hurl it."

470   So spoke Pallas Athena and breathed great strength into him.
Then Laërtes made the prayer to the daughter of great Zeus,
and right away he brandished his long-shadowed spear, then hurled it.
He struck Eupeithes on his helmet with bronze cheek pieces.
The helmet did not stop the spear, but the bronze went straight
475   through. Eupeithes made a thud when he hit the ground
and his armor clanged about him.

                     Then Odysseus and his glorious
troop fell on the foremost fighters. They stabbed with their swords
and their spears, sharp at both ends. And surely now they would
have destroyed all of them and taken away their day of return,
480   if Athena, the daughter of Zeus who carries the goatskin fetish,
had not shouted out and put a stop to the people: "Hold off
from savage war, O Ithacans, so that you may be separated
as quickly as possible without bloodshed!"

                   So spoke Athena,
and a green fear took hold of them. When the goddess spoke,
485   then all of their arms flew from their hands and fell to the ground.
They turned toward the city, longing for life. Then much-enduring
godlike Odysseus cried out terribly as he gathered himself
together and swept on them like a high-flying eagle.

And then the son of Kronos threw down his flaming bolt
of thunder, and it fell at the feet of the flashing-eyed daughter   490
with the mighty father. The flashing-eyed Athena said to Odysseus:
"Son of Laërtes, nourished by Zeus, resourceful Odysseus—cease!
Stop this quarrel of leveling war, or Zeus, the son of Kronos,
whose voice is heard from a long ways off, will grow angry."

So spoke Athena, and he believed her, and he rejoiced   495
in his heart. Pallas Athena, the daughter of Zeus who carries
the goatskin fetish, appearing in the likeness of Mentor in form
and voice, drew solemn oaths for all time from both parties.

Bibliography

EDITIONS (TEXTS IN HOMERIC GREEK)

Demetrius Chalcondyles, *editio princeps*, Florence, 1488

William Walter Merry and James Riddell, *Odyssey I–XII* (2nd edition, Oxford, 1886)

D. B. Monro and T. W. Allen, *Homeri Opera* (*Odyssey*, 2nd edition, Vols. III and IV, Oxford, 1917: the basis for this translation)

H. van Thiel, *Homeri Odyssey* (Hildesheim, 1991)

P. von der Mühll, *Homeri Odyssea*, (Munich/Leipzig, 1993)

SOME ENGLISH TRANSLATIONS

S. Butler, *The Odyssey* (London, 1900)

A. T. Murray, *Homer: Odyssey* (Cambridge, MA/London, 1919); revised by G. Dimock, 2 vols. (Cambridge, MA, 1995)

R. Lattimore, *The Odyssey* (Chicago, 1968)

R. Fagles, *The Odyssey* (New York, 1997)

R. Fitzgerald, *The Odyssey* (New York, 1998)

S. Lombardo, *The Odyssey* (Indianapolis, 2000)

GENERAL WORKS ON HOMER

F. A. Wolf, *Prolegomena ad Homerum* (Halle, 1795; English translation, Princeton, 1985)

J. T. Kakridis, *Homeric Researches* (London, 1949)

A. J. B. Wace and F. H. Stubbings, *A Companion to Homer* (London, 1962)

G. S. Kirk, *The Songs of Homer* (Cambridge, UK 1962)

J. Griffin, *Homer on Life and Death* (Oxford, 1980)

I. Morris and B. B. Powell, *A New Companion to Homer* (Leiden, 1997)

J. Latacz, *Troy and Homer: Towards a Solution of an Old Mystery* (Oxford, 2004)

R. Fowler (ed.), *The Cambridge Companion to Homer* (Cambridge UK, 2004)

B. B. Powell, *Homer* (2nd edition, Malden/Oxford, 2007)

M. Finkelberg, *The Homer Encyclopedia* (Malden/Oxford, 2011)

INFLUENTIAL READINGS AND INTERPRETATIONS

U. von Wilamowitz-Möllendorff, *Die Heimkehr Des Odysseus: Neue Homerische Untersuchungen* (Berlin, 1927)

Woodhouse, W. J., *The Composition of Homer's Odyssey* (Oxford, 1930)

A. Thornton, A., *People and Themes in the Odyssey* (London 1970)

M. I. Finley, *The World of Odysseus* (New York, 1978)

D. L., Page, *Folktales in Homer's Odyssey* (Cambridge, MA, 1973)

J. S. Clay, *The Wrath of Athena: Gods and Men in the Odyssey* (Princeton, 1983)

W. B. Stanford, *The Ulysses Theme: A Study in Adaptability of the Homeric Hero* (Oxford, 1983)

G. Dimock, *The Unity of the Odyssey* (Amherst, 1989)

H. Bloom, ed., *Homer's Odyssey* (New York, 1996)

COMMENTARY

Heubeck, A. et al. *A Commentary on Homer's* Odyssey, 3 vols. (Oxford 1988–1992)

TEXT AND TRANSMISSION

T. W. Allen, *Homer: The Origins and Transmission* (Oxford, 1924)

J. A. Davison, "The Transmission of the Text," in Wace and Stubbings (1962), 215–233

HOMER AND ORAL TRADITION

M. Parry (intro. by A. Parry), *The Making of Homeric Verse* (Oxford, 1971)

G. S. Kirk, *Homer and the Oral Tradition* (Cambridge UK, 1976)

B. B. Powell, *Writing and the Origins of Greek Literature* (Cambridge UK, 2003)

E. Bakker, *Poetry in Speech: Orality and Homeric Discourse* (Ithaca NY, 1997)

J. M. Foley, *Homer's Traditional Art* (University Park PA, 1999)

A. B. Lord, *The Singer of Tales* (2nd edition, Cambridge MA, 2000)

DATING THE HOMERIC POEMS

R. Janko, *Homer, Hesiod and the Hymns* (Cambridge, 1982)

B. B. Powell, *Homer and the Origin of the Greek Alphabet* (Cambridge UK, 1991)

HOMER AND THE NEAR EAST

M. L. West, *The East Face of Helicon* (Oxford, 1997)

B. Louden, *Homer's* Odyssey *and the Near East* (Cambridge, 2011)

THE *ODYSSEY* AND ART

D. Buitron and B. Cohen, eds. *The Odyssey and Ancient Art: An Epic in Word and Image* (New York, 1992)

Credits

Pronouncing Glossary/Index

I have included names in the text together with a pronunciation guide, except for names where the pronunciation is obvious. I give the meaning of the names, where this is clear; many of the names in Homer are "speaking names," that is, they reveal the role of the character in the narrative and, in many cases, appear to be made up for the occasion. The meaning of many other names is opaque or unknown. I give the number of the Book in which the name appears, together with the page numbers, except for common names such as "Apollo," "Achilles," or "Paris," where I give the Book numbers followed by *passim*. *Il.* means that the reference is found in the *Iliad*, *Od.* that it is found in the *Odyssey*.

A

Achaeans (a-**kē**-ans. Akhaians), a division of the Greek people, Homer's word for the Greeks at Troy, 26; (*Od.* 1–5, 8–24) *passim*

Acheron (**ak**-er-on. Akheron), "sorrowful," river of the underworld (*Od.* 10) 207

Admetos (ad-**mē**-tos), "invincible," king of Pherai in Thessaly, son of Pheres, husband of Alkestis (*Od.* 4, 11) 107, 218

aegis (**ē**-jis), "goat skin," a shield with serpent border used by Athena and Zeus (*Od.* 2, 3, 6, 13) 64, 67, 132, 259

Aeneid (ē-**nē**-id), poem by Vergil on founding of Rome, late first century BC, 20

Aeschylus (**ē**-ski-lus, **es**-ki-lus) (525–456 BC), Athenian playwright, 22, 36; (*Od.* 1, 3, 11) 39, 75, 223

Aethiopians, "burnt-faced," a people who dwell in never-never land in the extreme south, where Poseidon and Zeus sometimes visit (*Od.* 1, 4, 5) 37, 84, 120

Aetolia (e-**tō**-li-a), district north of the Corinthian Gulf, where were the cites of Pleuron and Kalydon (*Od.* 14) 276, 279

Agamemnon (a-ga-**mem**-non), son of Atreus, brother of Menelaos, leader of Greek forces at Troy, 13, 21, 27, 29, 30, 32; (*Od.* 1, 3, 4, 8, 9, 11, 13, 14, 24) *passim*

Agelaos (a-ge-**lā**-os), son of Damastor, one of the suitors (*Od.* 20, 22) 374, 375, 395, 399, 400, 404

Aiaia (ē-ē-a), "earthland," island home of Circê (*Od.* 9–12) 170, 194, 212, 233

Aiakos, son of Zeus, father of Peleus, king of Aegina, judge in the underworld (*Od.* 11) 227

Aietes (ē-**ē**-tēz), "man of earth," king of Kolchis in Aia, brother of Kirkê, father of Medea (*Od.* 10, 12) 196, 235

Aigisthos (ē-**jis**-thos), son of Thyestes, lover of Klytaimnestra, murderer of Agamemnon, killed by Orestes, 13, 29, 30; (*Od.* 1, 3, 4, 11, 24) 38, 39, 46, 47, 72–75, 97, 99, 223, 420, 423

Aigyptios, "Egyptian", an Ithacan elder (*Od.* 2) 52, 53

Aiolos (**ē**-o-los), 31; (*Od.* 10, 11, 23) 190–192, 217, 230, 418

Aison (**ē**-son), father of Jason, son of Kretheus and Tyro (*Od.* 11) 218

Aithon (**ē**-thon), name assumed by Odysseus when in disguise on Ithaca (*Od.* 19) 352

Ajax (Aias), (1) son of Telamon, the "greater Ajax," half-brother to Teucer, ruler of Salamis (*Od.* 11, 24) 225, 227–229, 420, 422; (2) son of Oïleus, the "lesser Ajax," ruler of the Locrians, 35; (*Od.* 1, 3–5, 11, 24) 48, 69, 70, 97, 98, 113, 225, 227–229, 420, 422

Alexander the Great (356–323 BC), 6, 22

Alexander, another name for Paris (which see), 1, 6, 22, 35

Alexandria, city in Egypt founded by Alexander the Great, 6, 7; (*Od.* 4) 93

Alexandrian scholars, 7

Alkestis (al-**kes**-tis), most beautiful of the daughters of Pelias, wife of Admetos, died for her husband (*Od.* 4, 11) 107, 218

Alkinoös (al-**kin**-o-os), "strong of mind," king of the Phaeacians, father of Nausicaä, who entertains Odysseus, 33; (*Od.* 6–9, 11, 13) *passim*

Alkmenê (alk-**mēn**-ē), daughter of Elektryon, wife of Amphitryon, mother of Herakles, 36; (*Od.* 2, 11) 55, 219

Allen, T. W., editor of the Oxford Classical Text of Homer, 18

alphabet, a writing that can be pronounced, 3, 5, 9, 14–17, 19, 22;

Alpheios, the largest river in the Peloponnesus and the god of this river (*Od.* 3, 15) 81, 286

Alybas, (**al**-i-bas), Odysseus claims this name in the false tale to his father (*Od.* 24) 429

ambrosia, "immortal," food of the gods (*Od.* 4, 5, 12) 95, 112, 115, 235

Amphiaraos (am-fē-a-**rā**-os), a seer, participated in the Kalydonian boar hunt, one of the seven against Thebes swallowed by the earth (*Od.* 11, 15) 221, 288, 289

Amphilochos (am-**fil**-o-kos), son of Amphiaraos, brother of Alkmaon, participant of the expedition by the Epigoni against Thebes (*Od.* 15) 289

Amphimedon (am-**fim**-i-don), "around-protecting," the suitor who was a guest-friend to Agamemnon (*Od.* 22, 24) 400, 402, 424, 425

Amphinomos (am-**fin**-o-mos), the "good" suitor of Penelope, from Doulichion, killed by Telemachos (*Od.* 16, 18, 20, 22) 309–311, 335, 336, 344, 345, 371, 394

Amphion (am-**fī**-on), son of Zeus and Antiopê, husband of Niobê, musician brother of Zethus, one of the twin founders of Thebes (*Od.* 11) 218, 219

Amphitritê (am-fi-**trī**-tē), a Nereid, wife of Poseidon (*Od.* 3, 5, 12) 68, 123, 234, 235

Amphitryon (am-**fit**-ri-on), descendant of Perseus, husband of Alcmena (*Od.* 11) 219

Analysis, an approach to Homer that wishes to divide his texts into constituent parts that once had an independent existence, 3, 9, 10, 12

Analyst, a scholar who wishes to identify the small parts of which Homer's poems are made, a follower of F. A. Wolf, 10, 11, 13

Anatolia, "sunrise," the westernmost protrusion of Asia, modern Turkey, synonymous with Asia Minor, 21

Anchialos, "close-to-the-sea," a Taphian, father of Mentes (*Od.* 1) (*Od.* 1, 8) 43, 50, 155

Antikleia (an-ti-**klē**-a), daughter of Autolykos, wife of Laërtes, mother of Odysseus (*Od.* 11) 212, 216

Antilochos (an-**til**-o-kos), son of Nestor of Pylos, a suitor to Helen, killed by Memnon (*Od.* 3–5, 11, 24) 69, 88, 111, 225, 420, 423

Antinoös (an-**tin**-o-os), "wrong-thinker," leader of the suitors in Odysseus' palace (*Od.* 1, 2, 4, 16–18, 20–22, 24) *passim*

Antiopê (an-**tī**-o-pē) mother of Amphion and Zethus (*Od.* 11) 218, 219

aoidos (a-**oi**-dos, pl. *aoidoi*), Greek word for such oral poets as Homer and Hesiod (contrast with "rhapsode"), 12, 30, 32, 33; (*Od.* 8) 152

Aphrodite, Greek goddess of sexual attraction, related to Inanna/Astartê/Ishtar, equated with Roman Venus, 3, 33; (*Od.* 4, 8, 17–20) 82, 90, 159–162, 315, 337, 347, 366

Apollo, god of plague and archery, sponsor of the Trojans, (*Od.* 3, 4, 6–9, 11, 15, 17–19, 21, 22, 24) *passim*

Arcadia (ar-**kād**-i-a), mountainous region in the central Peloponnesus (*Od.* 6) 129

Archaic Period, c. 800–480 BC, 22

Ares (**air**-ēz), Greek god of war, 33; (*Od.* 8, 11, 14, 16, 20) 155, 159–162, 211, 227, 270, 307, 366

Aretê (ar-**ē**-tē), queen of the Phaeacians, mother of Nausicaä, 33; (*Od.* 7, 8, 11, 13) 140, 143, 146, 147, 150, 164, 221, 222, 250, 251

Argeïphontes (ar-jē-i-**fon**-tēz), "Argus-killer," epithet of Hermes (*Od.* 1, 5, 7, 8, 10, 24) 38, 40, 110, 112, 114, 143, 162, 200, 202, 424

Argive (**ar**-jīv) plain, in eastern Peloponnesus, 26; (*Od.* 3, 4, 11, 17, 23) 73, 88, 92, 221, 316, 415

Argo, "swift," ship of Jason (*Od.* 12) 235

Argolid, the easternmost lobe of the Peloponnesus, including the Argive plain, Mycenae, Tiryns, Epidaurus, and Troizen (*Od.* 4) 99

Argos, "plain," city in the Argive plain in the northeastern Peloponnesus, 4, 26; (*Od.* 1, 3, 4, 15, 17, 18, 21, 24) *passim*

Ariadnê (ar-i-**ad**-nê), "very holy one," Cretan princess, daughter of Minos and Pasiphaë who helped Theseus defeat the Minotaur (*Od.* 11) 221

Aristophanes (ar-is-**tof**-a-nēz) (448–380 BC), Athenian writer of comedies, 7

Aristophanes of Byzantium (c. 257–180 BC), Homeric scholar in Alexandria, 7

Aristotle (384–322 BC), Greek philosopher, 8, 22

Asopos (ā-**sō**-pos), the largest river in Boeotia; god of that river who was father to Antiopê (*Od.* 11) 218

Astyanax (as-**tī**-a-naks), "king of the city, " son of Hector and Andromachê, known as Skamandrios to his parents, thrown from walls of Troy (*Od.* 3) 70

Atlas, a Titan, son of Iapetos and Klymenê, father of Kalypso and Maia; holds up the sky (*Od.* 1, 7) 38, 146

Atreus (**ā**-trūs), king of Mycenae, son of Pelops, brother of Thyestes, father of Agamemnon and Menelaus, 29; (*Od.* 1, 3–5, 9, 11, 13–15, 17, 19, 24) *passim*

Attica (**at**-ti-ka), region in central Greece where Athens is located, 74

Augeias (ow-**jē**-as), king of the Epeians in the days of Nestor's father Neleus (Homer does not mention the famous episode where Herakles cleaned his stables) (*Od.* 15) 286

Augustus (ow-**gus**-tus) (63-BC–AD 14), originally called Octavian, first Roman emperor, 24

Aulis (**ow**-lis), port in Boeotia from which the Trojan expedition set sail, 4, 24, 26

Autolykos (ow-**tol**-i-kos), "true wolf," rogue and thief, son of Hermes, father of Antiklea, grandfather of Odysseus (*Od.* 11, 19, 21, 24) 212, 357–359, 379, 384, 431

B

basileus (ba-**sil**-ā-us, plural *basileis*), "big man, chief," 27

Bellerophon (bel-**ler**-o-fon), Corinthian hero, grandson of Sisyphos, tamed Pegasus and killed the Chimaira, 9; (*Od.* 1) 45

Bias (**bi**-as), brother of the famous seer Melampous, 20; (*Od.* 11, 15) 220, 289

Black Sea, also called Pontos, 6

Boeotia (bē-**ō**-sha), "cow-land," region north of Attica, where Thebes was situated, 26

Boötes (bo-**ō**-tes), "plowman," a constellation (*Od.* 5) 118

Bronze Age, c. 3000–1200 BC, 21, 24, 26, 27; (*Od.* 2, 3, 11, 13, 19) 52, 66, 217, 227, 258, 347

Byzantium, Greek colony at the entrance to the Bosporus (= later Constantinople), 7, 18

C

Caucasus Mountains, at the eastern end of the Black Sea (*Od.* 11) 210

Centaurs (**sen**-towrs), half-human, half-horse creatures (*Od.* 21) 386, 387

Chalcis, "bronze," "copper," the principal settlement (with Eretria) on the island of Euboea, 4, 5

Chaos (**kā**-os), "chasm," the first thing that came into being, 30, 31; (*Od.* 10) 208

Charis, "charm," personification of the quality, the wife of Hephaistos in the *Iliad* (*Od.* 8) 159

Charybdis (ka-**rib**-dis), dangerous whirlpool, opposite Skylla, said to be in the Straits of Messina (*Od.* 12, 23) 236, 240, 241, 246, 418

Chios (**kē**-os), Greek island near Asia Minor, often claimed as Homer's birthplace, 3; (*Od.* 3) 71

Chloris, wife of Neleus, mother of Nestor (*Od.* 11) 219, 220

Cimmerians (si-**mer**-i-anz), live across the river Ocean, where Odysseus summons the spirits of the dead (*Od.* 11), 31; (*Od.* 11) 210, 225

Corcyra (cor-**sīr**-a), modern Corfu, an island off the northwest coast of Greece, identified with Phaeacia in the *Odyssey* (*Od.* 13) 255

Corinth (**kor**-inth), city on isthmus between central Greece and the Peloponnesus, 27; (*Od.* 1, 11) 45, 230

Crete, largest island in the Aegean, home of Odysseus according to several false tales, 4, 21, 22, 33; (*Od.* 3, 11, 13, 14, 16, 17), 19) 72, 75, 221, 228, 257, 270–272, 300, 328, 351, 352, 356

Cumae (**kū**-mē), site of earliest Greek colony in Italy, north of the bay of Naples, 5

Cyclades (**sik**-la-dēz), "circle islands," around Delos in the Aegean Sea 4; (*Od.* 3–6, 15) 71, 97, 113, 131, 294

Cyclopes (sī-**klōp**-ēz, sing., Cyclops), "round-eyes," rude one-eyed giants, including Polyphemos (*Od.* 1, 6, 7, 9) 40, 126, 145, 172, 173, 177, 180, 181, 187

Cyclops (**sī**-klops), "round-eyed," rude one-eyed giant Polyphemos whom Odysseus blinded 31; (*Od.* 1, 2, 6, 7, 9, 10, 12, 13, 20, 23, 24) *passim*

Cyprus, large island in eastern Mediterranean, home of Aphrodite, 4; (*Od.* 4, 8, 17) 84, 162, 326

Cythera (**sith**-e-ra), island south of the Peloponnesus, sometimes said to be the birthplace of Aphrodite (*Od.* 8, 9, 18) 159, 171, 337

D

dactylic hexameter, the meter of Homer, six feet per line 2, 3, 16, 35

Danaäns (**dān**-a-anz), descendants of Danaös, one of Homer's name for the Greeks (*Od.* 1, 4, 5, 8, 11, 24) 48, 90, 104, 107, 120, 153, 168, 225, 227, 228, 420, 421

Dardanelles (= Hellespont), straits between the Aegean Sea and the Propontis (= Sea of Marmora), 4, 22

Dark Age, c. 1150–800 BC, 22

Deïphobos (dē-**if**-o-bos), brother of Hector and Paris who took up with Helen after Paris' death (*Od.* 3, 4, 8) 70, 90, 167

Delos (**dē**-los), "clear," tiny island in the center of the Cyclades, where there was a cult of Apollo and Artemis, who were born there 4; (*Od.* 5, 6, 15) 113, 131, 294

Delphi (**del**-fī), sanctuary of Apollo at foot of Mount Parnassus, where Apollo slew Python (*Od.* 8, 11, 19) 153, 230, 357

Demeter (de-**mēt**-er), daughter of Kronos and Rhea, mother of Persephone, goddess of the grain harvest (*Od.* 5) 113

Demodokos, oral singer at the court of the Phaeacians (*Od.* 8, 13) 152, 153, 158, 159, 165–167, 249

Demoptolemos, a suitor of Penelope (*Od.* 22) 400, 402

Deukalion (dū-**kāl**-i-on), son of Minos, father of Idomeneus, king of Crete, and of Odysseus in one of his false tales (*Od.* 19) 352

Dia (**dī**-a), another name for the island of Naxos (*Od.* 11) 221

Diokles (**dī**-o-klēz), rich king of Messenian Pherai, whose sons Ortilochos and Krethos were killed by Aeneas in the *Iliad* (*Il.* 5); Telamachos and Peisistratos stay at his house en route to Sparta (*Od.* 3, 15, 21) 81, 286, 377

Diomedes (dī-ō-**mēd**-ēz), son of Tydeus (who fought in the Seven Against Thebes), a principal Greek warrior at Troy (*Od.* 3, 4) 71, 73, 90

Dionê (dī-**ōn**-ê), feminine form of "Zeus," a consort of Zeus at Dodona (*Od.* 14) 273

Dioscuri (dī-os-**kūr**-ī), "sons of Zeus" and Leda, Kastor and Polydeukes, brothers of Helen (*Od.* 11) 220

Dmetor (d-**mē**-tor), "subduer," a king of Cyprus mentioned by Odysseus in a lying tale (*Od.* 17) 326

Dodona (do-**dōn**-a), site of oracular shrine of Zeus in northwestern Greece (*Od.* 14, 19) 273, 355

Dolios, an aged servant of Penelope, father of the unfaithful Melantho and Melanthios (*Od.* 4, 17, 18, 22, 24) 105, 319, 341, 398, 427, 432, 433, 435

Dorians, a division of the Greek people (*Od.* 19) 351

Doulichion, one of the Ionian islands (*Od.* 1, 9, 14, 16, 18, 19) 45, 169, 273, 276, 302, 305, 310, 335, 344, 345, 349, 355

E

Echephron (**ek**-e-fron), a son of Nestor (*Od.* 3) 78, 79

Echetos, "holder," a wicked king who lives on the mainland (*Od.* 18, 21) 334, 335, 387

Echineos (e-**kin**-e-os), a Phaeacian nobleman (*Od.* 7, 11) (*Od.* 11) 222

Eidothea (ē-**do**-the-a), daughter of Proteus, the Old Man of the Sea (*Od.* 4) 93, 95

Eileithyia (ē-lē-**thī**-ya), "she who makes one come," goddess of childbirth (*Od.* 19) 352

Elatos (**el**-a-tos), one of the suitors (*Od.* 22) 402

Elis, a territory in the northwest Peloponnesus, 4; (*Od.* 3, 4, 6, 13, 15, 21) 77, 102, 129, 257, 291, 388

Elpenor (el-**pēn**-or), companion of Odysseus who died after falling from Kirkê's roof (*Od.* 11, 12) 211–213, 233

Enipeus, a river in Thessaly, a tributary of the Peneius (*Od.* 11) 218

Epeians, population of Elis, on the one hand (also called Eleians), and of Doulichion and the Echinades islands, on the other (*Od.* 13, 15, 24) 257, 291, 433

Epeios (e-**pē**-os), builder of the Trojan Horse (*Od.* 8, 11) 166, 227

Ephesus (**ef**-e-sus. Ephesos), city in Asia Minor, site of a great temple to Artemis, 4, 7

Ephialtes (ef-i-**al**-tēz), a giant who stormed heaven, one of the Aloads (*Od.* 11) 220

Ephyra (**e**-fir-a), a city on the Selleïs River in Thresprotia (*Od.* 1, 2) 45, 62

Epikastê (epi-**kas**-tē), mother/wife of Oedipus of Thebes (*Od.* 11) 219

Erechtheus (e-**rek**-thūs), an early king of Athens (*Od.* 7) 142

Erinys (er-**i**-nis), *or plural*, Erinyes (er-**in**-u-es), the underworld punisher(s) of broken oaths; the fulfillers of a curse (*Od.* 2, 15) 57, 287, 289

Eriphylê (er-i-**fī**-lê), sister of Adrastos, wife of Amphiaraös, mother of Alcmeon (*Od.* 11, 15) 221, 288, 289

Erymanthos, mountain range in northwest Peloponnesus, abode of Artemis and wild boars (*Od.* 6) 129

Eteoneus (et-tē-**ō**-nūs), an attendant of Menelaos (*Od.* 4, 15) 82, 83, 283

Euboea (yū-**bē**-a. Euboia), long island east of Attica, site of vigorous Iron Age community where the alphabet seems to have been invented, 4, 5, 12, 17, 26; (*Od.* 3, 4, 7, 8) 71, 97, 142, 150, 158

Eumaios (yū-**mē**-os), "seeker after good," Odysseus' loyal swineherd (*Od.* 13–17, 19–22) *passim*

Eumelos (yū-**mē**-los), son of Admetos and Alkestis (*Od.* 4) 107

Eupeithes (yū-**pē**-thēz), "good at persuasion," father of the suitor Antinoös, he led an attack against Odysseus and was killed by Laërtes (*Od.* 1, 4, 16–18, 20, 21, 24) 49, 102, 103, 309, 327, 333, 339, 373, 382, 385, 433, 434, 436

Euripides (yū-**rip**-i-dēz) (480–406 BC), Athenian playwright, 22; (*Od.* 11) 218, 219

Europa (yū-**rōp**-a), daughter of Agenor, brother of Kadmos, seduced by Zeus in the form of a bull, mother to Minos (*Od.* 7, 11) 150, 228

Euryades (yū-ri-**a**-dēz), one of Penelope's suitors (*Od.* 22) 402

Euryalos (yū-**rī**-a-los), a Phaeacian noble who taunts Odysseus (*Od.* 8) 155, 156, 163

Eurybates (yū-**rī**-ba-tēz), Odysseus' herald (*Od.* 19) 353

Eurydamas (yū-rī-**dā**-mas), one of Penelope's suitors (*Od.* 22) 402

Eurydikê (yū-**rid**-i-kē), wife of Nestor in the Odyssey (*Od.* 3) 79

Eurykleia (yū-ri-**klē**-a), "wide-fame," Odysseus' nurse, who recognized his scar (*Od.* 1, 2, 4, 17, 19–23) 50, 51, 62, 105, 314, 346, 356, 357, 359, 360, 368, 389, 405, 406, 408–411, 414, 417

Eurylochos (yū-**ril**-o-kos), a comrade and relative of Odysseus, the instigator of disobedience (*Od.* 10–12) 197–199, 201, 205, 210, 238, 241, 243, 244

Eurymachos (yū-**rim**-a-kos), a leading suitor (*Od.* 1, 2, 4, 8, 15–18, 20–22) *passim*

Eurymedon (yū-**rim**-e-don), "wide ruling," one of the suitors (*Od.* 7, 18) 140, 341

Eurymedousa, "wide-ruling," Nausicaä's aged waiting-maid (*Od.* 7) 139

Eurynomê, Penelope's housekeeper and chambermaid (*Od.* 17–20, 23) 328, 336, 337, 348, 365, 413, 415, 417

Eurynomos (yū-**rin**-o-mos), suitor of Penelope (*Od.* 2, 22) 52, 400

Eurypylos (yū-**rip**-i-los), a king of Mysia, son of Telephos (*Od.* 11) 226, 227

Eurytion (yū-**rit**-i-on), a centaur who drank too much and was mutilated (*Od.* 21) 386, 387

Eurytos, a king of Oichalia, father of Iphitos, the famous bowman (*Od.* 8, 21) 158, 377, 379

Evans, Arthur (1851–1941), British archaeologist, excavated Knossos 21

F

Fates, see also Moerae, 25; (*Od.* 1, 2, 4, 5, 14, 19, 23) 44, 62, 97, 111, 270, 362, 418

folktale, traditional tales that are neither myths nor legends, 25, 28–31; (*Od.* 9, 18) 179, 180, 334

formula, a building block in the formation of oral verse, 12, 14

G

Gaia (**ghī**-a), "earth," sprung from Chaos, consort of Ouranos, mother of the Titans, 31; (*Od.* 7, 11) 150, 228, 230

Geraistos, southernmost point of Euboea (*Od.* 3) 71

Gerenian, obscure epithet applied to Nestor (*Od.* 3, 4) 68, 72, 74, 77–79, 87

Giants, "earth-born ones," sprung from the blood of Uranus that fell on Gaia, 2; (*Od.* 7, 10) 140, 145, 194, 195

Gorgon, terrifying head of Medusa (*Od.* 3, 11, 13) 67, 232, 259

Gortyn, city in south-central Crete (*Od.* 3) 75

Graces (Charites), attendants of Aphrodite, imparters of feminine charm (*Od.* 6, 8, 14, 18) 126, 162, 275, 337

Greek alphabet, invented c. 800 BC, 3, 16, 17, 22

H

Hades (**hā**-dēz), "unseen," lord of the underworld, son of Kronos and Rhea, husband of Persephonê, 31; (*Od.* 3–7, 9–12, 14, 15, 20, 23, 24) *passim*

Halios, "of the sea," a son of Alkinoös (*Od.* 8) 155, 163

Halitherses, "sea-bold (?)," friend of Odysseus and advisor to Telemachos (*Od.* 2, 17, 24) 57, 58, 60, 315, 434

Hebê (**hēb**-ē), "youth," married to Herakles on Olympos (*Od.* 11) 230

Hector, greatest of the Trojan warriors, married to Andromachê, killed by Achilles, 28; (*Od.* 3–5, 8) 70, 90, 111, 167

Hekabê (**hek**-a-bē), wife of Priam, queen of Troy, mother of Hector (*Od.* 8) 167

Helen, daughter of Zeus and Leda, husband of Menelaos, lover of Paris, 35; (*Od.* 4, 5, 8, 11, 14, 15, 17, 22, 23) 82, 85, 86, 88–90, 92, 100, 120, 167, 220, 224, 267, 282–285, 316, 400, 415

Helios, sun god, 29–31; (*Od.* 1, 5, 8, 10–12, 19, 23, 24) 37, 113, 159, 160, 196, 214, 235–238, 241, 243–245, 354, 358, 416, 418, 420

Hellas, "land of the Hellenes" (*Od.* 1, 4, 11, 15) 48, 104, 107, 226, 283

Hellê (**hel**-lē), daughter of Athamas and Nephelê, sister of Phrixus, fell from the golden ram into the Hellespont (*Od.* 5) 121

Hellenistic Period, 323–30 BC, 22

Hellenistic, referring to Greek culture between Alexander's death in 323 BC and the ascendancy of Rome, 22; (*Od.* 13) 252

Hellespont, straits between the Aegean Sea and the Propontis (Sea of Marmora, = the Dardanelles), 4; (*Od.* 22, 24) 401, 423

Hemera (**hēm**-er-a), "day," one of the first beings, daughter of Erebos and Nyx (*Od.* 10) 208

Hephaistos (he-**fēs**-tos), Greek god of smiths, son of Zeus and Hera or Hera alone (*Od.* 4, 6–8, 11, 15, 23, 24) 101, 135, 142, 159, 160, 162, 227, 284, 414, 423

Hera (**her**-a), "mistress(?)," daughter of Kronos and Rhea, wife and sister of Zeus (*Od.* 4, 8, 11, 12, 14, 15, 20) 97, 160, 165, 230, 231, 235, 273, 284, 286, 366

Herakles, son of Zeus and Alkmenê, the strongest man who ever lived (*Od.* 2, 3, 6, 8, 11, 15, 21) 55, 72, 129, 157, 158, 218, 219, 230, 232, 286, 377–379

Hermes, "he of the stone heap," son of Zeus and Maia, Greek god of travel, tricks, commerce, and thievery (*Od.* 1, 2, 5, 7, 8, 10–12, 14–16, 18, 19, 24) *passim*

Hermionê (her-**mī**-o-nē), only daughter of Helen and Menelaus, whose marriage coincided with Telemachos' visit to Sparta (*Od.* 4) 82

Herodotus (her-**od**-o-tus) (c. 484–425 BC), Greek historian, 6, 22

Hesiod (**hēs**-i-od), Greek poet, eighth century BC, composer of *Works and Days* and *Theogony*, 16, 17, 22, 30, 31; (*Od.* 3, 9, 10) 68, 172, 208

Hippodameia, Peirithoös' first wife, raped at the altar by the hairy Centaurs (*Od.* 18, 21) 337, 386

Hittites (**hit**-ītz), Indo-European Bronze Age warrior people in central Anatolia, their capital was Hattusas near modern Ankara (*Od.* 11) 227

Homer, composer of the *Iliad* and the *Odyssey*, eighth century BC, see also, *aoidos*, Cyclic Poems, Troy, 1–22, 24–31, 33–35; (*Od.* 1, 3–5, 7–9, 11–15, 17–21, 23, 24) *passim*

Homeric Hymns, c. seventh-fifth centuries BC, oral dictated texts celebrating the gods, 3

Homeric Question, really "Homeric Investigation," into the origin of Homer's texts, 8, 11

Horus, the child of Isis and Osiris, after whom the island of Pharos is named (*Od.* 4) 93

Hypereia (hi-per-ē-a), "land beyond the horizon," a fanciful name designating the Phaeacians' original home (*Od.* 6) 126

Hyperion (hi-**per**-ion), "he who travels above," epithet and synonym of Helios, 29; (*Od.* 1, 12) 37, 237, 238, 241, 244, 245

I

Iasion (i-**as**-i-on), consort of Demeter, father of Ploutos (*Od.* 5) 113

Iasos (i-**a**-sos), (1) father of Amphion, grandfather of Chloris, Nestor's wife (*Od.* 11); (2) father of Dmetor, king of Cyprus, in a lying tale of Odysseus (*Od.* 11, 17) 219, 326

Idomeneus (ī-**dom**-i-nūs), grandson of Minos, leader of the Cretan contingent at Troy (*Od.* 3, 13, 14, 19) 72, 257, 271, 276, 351, 352

Ikarios, father of Penelope, brother to Tyndareos (*Od.* 1, 2, 4, 11, 16–21, 24) 46, 48, 53, 55, 107, 108, 224, 311, 330, 336–339, 357, 362, 376, 377, 388, 426

Ikmalios, a carpenter, maker of Penelope's fancy chair (*Od.* 19) 347

Ilion, another name for Troy, 25; (*Od.* 2, 8–11, 14, 17–19, 23, 24) 52, 58, 166, 168, 170, 190, 212, 222, 267, 271, 321, 339, 349, 352, 354, 364, 409, 424

Ilos (ī-los), of Ephyra, from whom Odysseus tried to obtain poison for his arrows (*Od.* 1) 45

Imbros, island in the northeast Aegean, 4

Ino (ī-nō), daughter of Kadmos and Harmonia, sister of Semelê, becomes Leukothea (*Od.* 5) 121, 124

Iolkos (ī-**olk**-us), city in southeastern Thessaly, home of Jason at the head of the Gulf of Pagasae (= modern Volo) (*Od.* 11) 218

Ionia, the west coast of Asia Minor, 4, 14

Ionians, a division of the Greek people (*Od.* 18) 338

Iphiklos, Thessalian father of Protesilaos, a fast runner (*Od.* 11, 15) 219, 220, 289

Iphimedeia (if-i-me-**dē**-a), "mighty mistress," mother by Poseidon of Otos and Ephialtes (*Od.* 11) 220

Iphthimê (**if**-thi-mê), "comely," sister of Penelope whose form Athena took on in dream to Penelope (*Od.* 4) 107

Iros, a beggar on Ithaca (*Od.* 18) 332–335, 338, 343, 344

Ismaros (**is**-ma-ros), city in Thrace, sacked by Odysseus (*Od.* 9) 170, 174

Ithaca, off the northwest coast of Greece, home of Odysseus, one of the Ionian Islands, 4, 27, 30–33; (*Od.* 1–6, 8–24) *passim*

Ithakos, one of the men who built the public fountain on Ithaca (*Od.* 17) 319

Itylos, son of Zethus, whom a daughter of Pandareos killed and bewailed as a nightingale (*Od.* 19) 361

J

Jason, son of Aeson, husband of Medea, leader of the Argonauts (*Od.* 1, 10–12, 23) 45, 190, 196, 218, 235, 418

K

Kadmos (**kad**-mos), "man of the East," founder of Thebes (*Od.* 5) 121

Kalypso (ka-**lip**-so), "concealer," nymph, daughter of Atlas, who kept Odysseus for seven years on her island Ogygia at the navel of the sea, 29, 31, 36; (*Od.* 1, 5, 7–9, 12, 19, 23) *passim*

Kassandra, beautiful daughter of Priam and Hekabê, a priestess of Apollo (*Od.* 12) (*Od.* 1, 3, 4, 5, 11) 48, 70, 97, 98, 113, 224

Kastor ("beavesr"), (1) son of Tyndareos and Leda, brother of Polydeukes, on of the Dioscuri; (*Od.* 11, 14) 220, 270 (2) a Cretan noble in one of Odysseus' lying tales (*Od.* 14) 220, 270

Kaukones (kau-**kō**-nēz), an obscure group who seem to have lived someplace in Elis (*Od.* 3) 77

Kaystrios (ka-**is**-tri-os), a river in Asia Minor, 4

Kephallenians (kef-al-**ēn**-i-ans), all those under Odysseus' control from Ithaca and neighboring islands and part of the mainland (*Od.* 20, 24) 370, 431–433

Kirkê (**kir**-kē), daughter of Helios, enchantress who entertained Odysseus for a year on her island, 31; (*Od.* 10) 194, 201, 203

Kleitos (**klē**-tos), "famous," grandson of Melampous, carried to Olympos by Dawn (*Od.* 15) 289

Klymenê (**klī**-me-nê), "famous," one of the heroines of olden times that Odysseus meets in the underworld (*Od.* 11) 221

Klytaimnestra (kli-**tēm**-nest-tra), "famed for her suitors," or "famed for her cunning," daughter of Tyndareos and Leda, sister of Helen, wife of Agamemnon, whom she killed, then was herself killed by Orestes, 29, 30, 32; (*Od.* 3, 11, 24) 74, 223, 224, 426

Klytoneos (kli-**tō**-ne-os), "famed for ships," one of the three sons of Alkinoös (*Od.* 8) 155

Knossos (**knos**-sos), principal Bronze Age settlement in Crete, where labyrinthine ruins have been found (*Od.* 19) 351

Kreon (**krē**-on), "ruler," (1) a king of Thebes, brother of Oedipus' wife Epikastê, father of Megara, wife of Herakles, whom Odysseus met in the underworld (*Od.* 11) 219

Kronos, child of Ouranos and Gaia, husband of Rhea, overthrown by his son Zeus, who imprisoned him in Tartaros, 31; (*Od.* 1, 3, 4, 8–10, 12–17, 19–21, 24) *passim*

Ktesippos (ktēs-**i**-pos), "horse-acquiring," one of the suitors of Penelope (*Od.* 20, 22) 373, 374, 402

Ktimenê (ki-**tē**-men-ē), sister of Odysseus (*Od.* 15) 292

Kydonians, an autochthonous Cretan ethnic group (*Od.* 3, 19) 75, 351

Kyllenê (ki-**lēn**-ē), mountain in Arcadia, where Hermes was born (*Od.* 24) 420

Kythereia (ki-ther-**ē**-a), "she of the island of Kythera," another name for Aphrodite (*Od.* 8, 18) 159, 337

L

Lacedaemon (las-e-**dēm**-on), the Eurotas furrow in the southern Peloponnesus, bounded by Mt. Taygetos in the west and Mt. Parnes in the east (*Od.* 3–6, 13, 15, 17, 21) 76, 82, 92, 104, 109, 129, 263, 264, 281, 317, 377

Laërtes (lā-**er**-tēz), father of Odysseus, husband of Antikleia (*Od.* 1, 2, 4, 5, 8–24) *passim*

Laestrygonians (les-tri-**gōn**-i-anz), cannibal-giants who destroy all Odysseus' ships save one, 31; (*Od.* 10, 23) 193–195, 418

Lamos (**lā**-mos), probably the founder of the Laestrygonian city Telypylos (*Od.* 10) 416

Lampos, "shiner," one of Dawn's horses (*Od.* 23) 416

Laodamas (lā-**od**-a-mas), a Phaeacian, son of Alkinoös (*Od.* 7, 8) 144, 155–157, 163

Laomedon (lā-**om**-e-don), early king of Troy, father of Priam (*Od.* 5) 109

Lapiths (**lap**-iths), Thessalian tribe led by Peirithoös that defeated the Centaurs (*Od.* 21) 386

Leda (**lē**-da), wife of Tyndareos, mother of Helen, Klytaimnestra, Kastor, Polydeukes (*Od.* 11) 220

legend, "things that must be read," stories of famous early men and women, 24, 32; (*Od.* 11) 218, 220, 221, 232

Leiodes (lē-**ō**-dēz), a soothsayer suitor of Penelope (*Od.* 21, 22) 382, 383, 403, 404

Leiokritos (lē-**o**-kri-tos), an Ithacan suitor of Penelope, killed by Telemachos (*Od.* 2, 22) 55, 60, 403

Lemnos, island in the Aegean, associated with Hephaistos, where Philoktetes was abandoned (*Od.* 3, 8) 72, 159, 160

Lesbos, island in the Aegean, near Troy, 4; (*Od.* 3, 4, 17) 71, 93, 317

Leto (**lē**-tō), mother of Apollo and Artemis, supporter of Troy (*Od.* 6, 7, 11) 129, 131, 150, 220, 230

Leucothea (lu-**koth**-e-a-a), "white goddess," a sea-goddess, formerly the mortal Ino, who gave Odysseus a magic sash (*Od.* 5) 121

Libya, a fertile country in North Africa (*Od.* 4, 14) 84, 272

Lord, Albert B. (1912–1991), student and assistant to Milman Parry, author of *The Singer of Tales*, 10–14

Lotus Eaters, tempted Odysseus' crew with a drug that removes all longing to go home (*Od.* 9, 23) 171, 418

Lycia (**lish**-i-a), region in southwest Anatolia, 4, 9; (*Od.* 5) 120

Lydia, a region in western Anatolia centered on Sardis, 4; (*Od.* 11) 230

M

Magnesia (mag-**nēz**-i-a), a territory in northern Greece around the Gulf of Pagasae, whose capital was Iolcus (*Od.* 11) 218

Maia (**mī**-a) "mid-wife," a daughter of Atlas, mother of Hermes, one of the Pleïades (*Od.* 14) 277

Maira (**mī**-ra), one of the famous women of olden times that Odysseus sees in the Underworld (*Od.* 11) 221

Malea, the southernmost cape of the Peloponnesus where ships are blown off course (*Od.* 3, 4, 9, 19) 74, 97, 99, 171, 352

Mantios, "prophet," son of Melampous, grandfather of Theoklymenos (*Od.* 15) 289

Marathon, plain near Athens where Persians were defeated in 490 BC (*Od.* 7) 142

Maron, Thracian priest of Apollo at Ismarus (*Od.* 9) 174, 175

Medea (me-**dē**-a), witch from Colchis, daughter of Aeëtes, wife of Jason (*Od.* 1, 10, 12) 45, 196, 235

Medon (**me**-dōn), a herald loyal to Odysseus (*Od.* 4, 13, 16, 17, 22, 24) 103, 104, 257, 305, 309, 311, 318, 404, 405, 434

Medusa (me-**dūs**-a), "[wide]-ruling," one of the three Gorgons, beheaded by Perseus (*Od.* 11) 232

Megapenthes (meg-a-**pen**-thēz), "great of sorrow," bastard son of Menelaos (*Od.* 4, 15) 82, 283, 284

Megara (**meg**-a-ra), wife of Heracles, killed with her children (*Od.* 11) 219

Meges (**me**-jēz), chieftain from Doulichion (*Od.* 1) 45

Melampous (mel-**am**-pus), a king of Argos, a famous prophet who tried to steal the cattle of Iphiklos on his brother Bias' behalf (*Od.* 11, 15) 218–220, 287, 289

Melanthios (mel-**an**-thi-os), "blackie," treacherous supporter of the suitors (*Od.* 4, 17, 20–22) 105, 319, 320, 324, 369, 371, 383, 385, 395, 398, 399, 407

Melantho, "black," treacherous maid-servant in Odysseus' house, sister of Melanthios (*Od.* 4, 18, 19) 105, 341, 343, 347, 348

Memnon, a son of Dawn, king of Ethiopia, ally of the Trojans in postHomeric epic, killed by Achilles (*Od.* 3–5, 11, 24) 69, 88, 111, 225, 227, 423

Menelaos (men-e-**lā**-os), king of Sparta, son of Atreus, husband of Helen, brother of Agamemnon, 28, 35; (*Od.* 1, 3, 4, 8, 9, 11, 13–15, 17, 24) *passim*

Menoitios, son of Aktor, father of Patroklos (*Od.* 24) 423

Mentes, Athena disguises herself as this Taphian traveler to appear to Telemachus (*Od.* 1, 14) 41, 43, 46, 50, 278

Mentor, "advisor," Ithacan adviser to Telemachos; Athena often takes on his form (*Od.* 1, 4, 17, 22, 24) *passim*

Mesaulios, a servant of Eumaios (*Od.* 14) 278

Mesopotamia, "land between the rivers," the Euphrates and the Tigris, 16, 21

Messenia (mes-**sēn**-i-a), territory in the southwest Peloponnesus (*Od.* 6, 8, 15) 129, 158, 286

Methonê (mē-**thō**-nē), a city on the west side of the Magnesian peninsula where very early poetic inscriptions have been found, 5

Mimas, a mountain on the coast of Ionia opposite Chios (*Od.* 3) 71

Minoans, Bronze Age inhabitants of Crete (*Od.* 19) 351

Minos (**mī**-nos), Cretan king of Knossos, son of Zeus and Europa, husband of Pasiphaë, judge in the underworld, 21; (*Od.* 5, 7, 11, 17, 19) 113, 150, 221, 228, 328, 351, 352

Minyans, inhabitants of Orchomenos, followers of Minyas (*Od.* 11) 219

moly (**mo**-lē), magic herb that protects Odysseus from Kirkê (*Od.* 10) 200

Moulios, aide to the suitor Amphinomos (*Od.* 18) 345

Mouseion, "temple of the Muses," in Alexandria, Egypt, 6

Muses, the inspirers of oral song, a personification of the oral tradition, 6, 32; (*Od.* 24) 421

Mycenae (mī-**sēn**-ē), largest Bronze Age settlement in the Argive plain, home of the house of Atreus, 21, 22, 27, 32; (*Od.* 2–4, 21) 55, 73, 75, 99, 381

Mykalê (**mik**-a-lē), a mountain ridge on the western coast of Asia Minor opposite Samos, 4

Mykenê (mi-**kē**-nē), eponymous heroine of Mycenae to whom Antinoös compares Penelope, 36; (*Od.* 2) 55

Myrmidons (**mir**-mi-dons), "ants," followers of Achilles (*Od.* 3, 4, 11) 72, 82, 226

Mysia, territory surrounding the Troad (*Od.* 11) 227

N

Naiads (**nī**-adz), water nymphs (*Od.* 13) 252, 260

Naples, "new city," a Greek colony in southern Italy, 5

Nausicaä (now-**sik**-a-a), "ship-girl," Phaeacian princess, daughter of Alkinoös and Aretê, who helped Odysseus, 31, 32; (*Od.* 6) 126–129

Nausithoös (now-**sith**-o-os), "swift in ships," king of the Phaeacians who ruled before his son Alkinoös (*Od.* 6, 7, 8) 36, (*Od.* 6, 7, 8) 126, 140, 168

Naxos, one of the Cycladic islands (*Od.* 11) 221

Neaira (ne-ē-ra), mother by Helios of two nymphs who cared for the cattle of Helios on Thrinakia (*Od.* 12) 237

nectar drink of the gods (*Od.* 5) 112, 115

Neleus (**nē**-lūs), son of Poseidon and Tyro, father of Nestor, founder of royal house of Pylos (*Od.* 2–4, 11, 15) *passim*

Neoptolemos (nē-op-**tol**-e-mos), "new-fighter," son of Achilles, also called Pyrrhos, "red" (*Od.* 3, 4, 11) 70, 72, 82, 226

Nereus (**nē**-rūs), son of Pontos and Gaia, wise Old Man of the Sea (*Od.* 1, 3, 13) 40, 68, 251

Nerikos (**nēr**-i-kos), a city sacked by Laërtes when he was young (*Od.* 24) 432

Neriton, a mountain on Ithaca (*Od.* 9, 13, 17) 169, 260, 319

Neritos, an Ithacan who helped build the well on the island (*Od.* 17) 319

Nestor, garrulous septuagenarian chieftain of Pylos, 4, 5; (*Od.* 1–6, 10, 11, 15, 17, 24) *passim*

Nisos (**nī**-sos), father of the suitor Amphinomos, from Doulichion (*Od.* 16, 18) 310, 335

Noëmon (no-ē-mon), "thoughtful," an Ithacan who lent his ship to Telemachos (*Od.* 2, 4) 63, 102

nostos (plural *nostoi*) "homecoming" of the heroes from Troy, a genre of oral song, 27, 28

nymphs, "young women," spirits of nature (*Od.* 6, 9, 12–14, 17, 23, 24) *passim*

Nyx (nux), "night," sprung from Chaos (*Od.* 10) 208

O

Oedipus (ē-di-pus), "swellfoot," son of Laios and Epikastê, married his mother, killed his father (*Od.* 11) 219

Ogygia (ō-**gij**-ya), Kalypso's island (*Od.* 1, 6, 7, 12, 23) 40, 131, 146, 248, 418

Oichalia (ē-**kāl**-i-a), a city variously located, over which Eurytos ruled (*Od.* 8, 21) 158, 379

Oïkles (**o**-i-klēz), grandson of Melampous, father of Amphiaraos (*Od.* 15) 288

Oïleus (o-**ī**-lūs), father of Little Ajax, from Locris (*Od.* 4); 97

Olympos, the highest mountain in Greece, in northern Thessaly (*Od.* 1, 3, 4, 6, 8, 10–12, 14, 15, 18–20, 23, 24) *passim*

Onetor (o-**nē**-tor), "beneficial," father of Odysseus' helmsman (*Od.* 3) 74

Orchomenos (or-**kom**-en-os), major Bronze Age site in northern Boeotia (*Od.* 11) 219, 225

Orestes (or-**es**-tēz), son of Agamemnon and Klytaimnestra, who killed his mother and her lover Aigisthos to avenge his father, 29, 30, 32; (*Od.* 1, 3, 4, 11) 38, 46, 47, 72, 75, 99, 225

Orion (ō-**rī**-on), a hunter, lover of Dawn, turned into a constellation (*Od.* 5, 11) 113, 118, 220, 228

Orsilochos (or-**sil**-o-kos), "well-skilled in all ways of battle," Odysseus killed him in one of his fictitious tales (*Od.* 13) 257

Ortilochos (or-**til**-o-kos), king of Pherai in Messenia (*Od.* 3, 15, 21) 81, 286, 377

Ortygia (or-**tij**-ya), "quail island," where the sun turns and Artemis killed Orion, equated in classical time with Delos, birthplace of Apollo and Artemis (*Od.* 5, 15) 113, 294

Ossa, mountain in Thessaly bordering Macedon, piled on Olympos and Pelion by the Otos and Ephialtes in order to reach heaven (*Od.* 11) 220, 221

Otos (**ō**-tos), gigantic brother of Ephialtes who attempted to pile Olympos and Pelion on Ossa in order to reach heaven (*Od.* 11) 220

Ouranos (**ou**-ra-nos), "sky," consort of Gaia/Earth," castrated by his son, 31; (*Od.* 21) 390

P

Palamedes (pal-a-**mēd**-ēz), son of Nauplios, clever enemy of Odysseus, perhaps the name of the inventor of the Greek alphabet, 15, 16

Palestine, the southern portion of the eastern end of the Mediterranean Sea, named after the Philistines, same as Canaan, 22

Pallas (**pal**-as), an epithet for Athena (*Od.* 1–4, 6–8, 11, 13, 15, 16, 19, 20–24) *passim*

Panathenaic Festival (pan-ath-en-**ē**-ic), annual festival to Athena at Athens where the *Iliad* and the *Odyssey* were performed, 9

Pandareos, father of unnamed daughters who suffered greatly (*Od.* 19, 20) 361, 366, 367

Panopeus, a town in Phocis (*Od.* 11) 230

Paphos (**pāf**-os), city in Cyprus, sacred to Aphrodite (*Od.* 8) 162

Paris, son of Priam and Hekabê, lover of Helen

Parnassos, Mount (par-**nas**-os), behind Delphi (*Od.* 19, 21, 24) 357–359, 384, 431

Parry, Milman (1902–1935), American classicist, creator of the oral-formulaic theory of Homeric composition, 10–14, 34

Patroklos (pa-**trok**-los), son of Menoitios, Achilles' best friend, killed by Hector, 26, 28; (*Od.* 3, 11, 13, 24) 69, 225, 266, 420, 423

Peiraios (pē-**rē**-os), a member of Telemachos' crew (*Od.* 15–17, 20) 297, 308, 315, 316, 376

Peirithoös (pē-**rith**-o-os), son of Zeus by Ixion's wife, king of the Lapiths, foe of the Centaurs (*Od.* 11, 21) 232, 386, 387

Peisenor (pē-**sē**-nor), (1) grandfather of Eurykleia (*Od.* 1, 2, 20) 50, 62, 368; (2) an Ithacan herald (*Od.* 2) 53

Peisistratos, youngest son of Nestor, Telemachos' guide (*Od.* 3, 4, 15) 67, 77–79, 81, 83, 87, 88, 282, 284–287

Pelasgians, "peoples of the sea," an unknown people or peoples who lived in Greece before the Greeks came (*Od.* 19) 351

Peleus (**pē**-lūs), grandson of Zeus, son of Aiakos, husband of Thetis, father of Achilles (*Od.* 5, 8, 11, 24) 120, 153, 225, 226, 228, 420, 421

Pelias (**pel**-i-as), son of Poseidon and Tyro, twin of Neleus, father of Alkestis (*Od.* 2, 11) 55, 218

Pelion, coastal mountain on the Magnesian peninsula in southeastern Thessaly near Iolcus, abode of the Centaurs (*Od.* 11) 220, 221

Peloponnesian War (431–404 BC) (*Od.* 19) 350

Peloponnesus (pel-o-po-**nēs**-us), "island of Pelops," the southern portion of mainland Greece linked to the north by the narrow Isthmus of Corinth, 4, 26

Pelops (**pē**-lops), son of Tantalus, defeated Oenomaüs and married Hippodameia, father of Atreus and Thyestes, grandfather of Agamemnon and Menelaos, eponymous here of the Peloponessus (*Od.* 4, 11) 82, 230

Penelope, "duck," daughter of Ikarios, niece of Tyndareos, mother of Telemachos, faithful wife of Odysseus, 27, 30–32; (*Od.* 1, 2, 4, 5, 8, 11, 13–24) *passim*

Periboia (per-i-**bē**-a), mother by Poseidon of Nausithoös, father of Alkinoös (*Od.* 7) 140

Periklymenos, a son of Neleus, brother of Nestor (*Od.* 11) 219, 220

Perimedes (per-i-**mē**-dēz), one of Odysseus' companions (*Od.* 11, 12) 210, 238

Pero (**pē**-rō), daughter of Neleus, sister of Nestor, loved by Bias (*Od.* 11, 15) 219, 220, 289

Persê, daughter of Ocean, mother of Kirkê by Helios (*Od.* 10, 12) 196, 235

Perseus (**per**-sūs), "destroyer(?)," (1) son of Zeus and Danaë, beheaded Medusa, married Andromeda, founded Mycenae; (2) a son of Nestor (*Od.* 3) 78, 79

Phaeacia (fē-**āsh**-a), the island of Scheria, where Nausicaä lives, equated with Corcyra, 31; (*Od.* 6, 19) 138, 354

Phaeacians, a fabulous people inhabiting Scheria at the edge of the world (*Od.* 5–9, 11, 13, 16, 19, 23) *passim*

Phaëthon (**fē**-e-thon), "shining," one of Dawn's two horses (*Od.* 23) 416

Phaethousa (fā-e-**thu**-sa), "shining," one of the daughters of Helios put in charge of his cattle on Thrinakia (*Od.* 12) 237

Phaidimos (**fēd**-i-mos), "famous," king of the Sidonians (*Od.* 4, 15) 101, 284

Phaidra (**fēd**-ra), "bright," daughter of Minos, sister of Ariadnê, consort of Theseus (*Od.* 11) 221

Phaistos (**fē**-stos), city in south central Crete (*Od.* 3) 75

Pharos, an island one day's sail off Egypt (*Od.* 4) 93, 108

Pheai (**fe**-ē), a city of unknown location (*Od.* 15) 291

Pheidon (**fē**-don), king of the Thresprotians who hosted Odysseus (*Od.* 14, 19) 273, 355

Phemios (**fēm**-i-os), "the man rich in tales," an *aoidos* who sang for the suitors, 32, 33; (*Od.* 1, 4, 8, 17, 22) 42, 48, 103, 152, 320, 404

Pherai, in Messenia, where Peisistratos and Telemachos stay on their journey to Sparta (*Od.* 3, 4, 15) 81, 107, 286

Pheres (**fer**-ēz), father of Admetos (*Od.* 11) 218

Philoitios (fil-**oi**-ti-os), "desirable fate," cowherd who helps Odysseus kill the suitors (*Od.* 20–22) 369–372, 383, 384, 389, 399, 402, 404

Philoktetes (fi-lok-**tēt**-ēz), inherited bow of Herakles, bit by a serpent and abandoned on Lemnos, killer of Paris

Philomeleides (fil-o-mel-**ē**-dēz), king of Lesbos (*Od.* 17) 317

Phocis (**fō**-sis), region in central Greece, where Delphi is (*Od.* 3, 7, 11, 19) 75, 150, 230, 357

Phoenicia, the coast of the Eastern Mediterranean, modern Lebanon, 4; (*Od.* 4, 13, 14) 84, 258, 272

Phoenicians, "red-men," from the dye that stained their hands, a Semitic seafaring people living on the coast of the northern Levant, 14, 15; (*Od.* 4, 13, 15) 84, 101, 257, 294, 295

Phorkys (**for**-kis), an ancient sea-god, son of Pontos and Gaia, father of the monster Skylla (*Od.* 1, 13) 40, 251, 260

Phrixus (**frik**-sus), son of Athamas and Nephelê, brother of Hellê, escaped on the back of a golden ram (*Od.* 5) 121

Phrontis, helmsman of Menelaos (*Od.* 3) 74

Phrygia (**frij**-a), region in Asia Minor, home of fertility religions, 4; (*Od.* 11) 230

Phthia (**thī**-a), region in southern Thessaly, home of Achilles, 26; (*Od.* 4, 11) 82, 226

Phylakê (**fil**-a-kē), a city in Thessaly, homeland of Protesilaos (*Od.* 11, 15) 219, 220, 287

Phylakos (**fil**-a-kos), Thessalian father of Iphiklos, grandfather of Protesilaos, imprisoned Melampous (*Od.* 15) 287, 289

Pieria (pi-**er**-i-a), "fat," region in Thessaly near Mt. Olympus, home of the Muses, where the gods land when coming down from Olympos (*Od.* 5) 110

Plato (428–348 BC), Greek philosopher, 8, 18, 22

Polites (pol-**ī**-tēz), a companion of Odysseus (*Od.* 10) 198

Polydamna, Egyptian wife of Thôn who gave Helen drugs (*Od.* 4) 89

Polykastê, daughter of Nestor who prepared a bath for Telemachos (*Od.* 3) 79, 80

Polyktor, "much-possessing," one of the suitors of Penelope, from Ithaca (*Od.* 18, 22) 341, 400

Polyneikes (pol-i-**nēk**-ēz), son of Oedipus, brother of Eteokles (*Od.* 15) 289

Polypheides (pol-i-**fē**-dēz), a prophet, father of Theoklymenos (*Od.* 15) 289

Polyphemos (pol-i-**fēm**-os), "much famed," the Cyclops blinded by Odysseus, 30, 31; (*Od.* 1, 6, 7, 9, 13) 40, 138, 141, 181–186, 251, 260

Pontonoös (pon-**ton**-o-os), Phaeacian herald (*Od.* 7, 8, 13) 144, 152, 250

Porson, Richard (1759–1808), British classical scholar

Poseidon (po-**sīd**-on), son of Kronos and Rhea, Greek god of the sea, 30, 31; (*Od.* 1–9, 11, 13, 23, 24) *passim*

Priam (**prī**-am), king of Troy, son of Laomedon, husband of Hekabê, father of Hector and Paris, 23, 24, 35; (*Od.* 3, 5, 8, 11, 13, 14, 22, 24) *passim*

Prokris (**pro**-kris), daughter of Erechtheus king of Athens, wife of Kephalos who killed her accidentally (*Od.* 11) 221

Protesilaos (pro-tes-i-**lā**-os), son of Iphiklos, first man to die at Troy (*Od.* 11) 220

Proteus (**prō**-tūs), shapeshifting prophetic old man of the sea (*Od.* 4) 94, 100

psychê (**sī**-kē; plural *psychai*, **sūk**-ī), (1) "breath, soul," the ghost that survives the death of the body, 34; (*Od.* 5) 111

Psychopompus (si-ko-**pom**-pus), "soul-guide," see Hermes

Ptolemies, Macedonian/Greek dynasty who ruled Egypt from 334–30 BC, 6

Pylos (**pī**-los), Bronze Age settlement in the southwest Peloponnesus, kingdom of Nestor where important archaeological remains have been found, 4, 21; (*Od.* 1–6, 11, 13–17, 20, 21, 24) *passim*

Pyriphlegethon (pi-ri-**flej**-e-thon), "river of fire," in the underworld (*Od.* 10) 207

Pytho, Homer' name for Delphi (*Od.* 8, 11) 153, 230

R

Rhadamanthys (rad-a-**man**-this), brother of Minos; judge in the underworld (*Il.* 14); (*Od.* 4, 7) 100, 140

rhapsode, "staff-singer," performers who memorized written poetry, especially Homer (contrast with *aoidoi*), 9

Rhea (**rē**-a), a Titaness, wife of Kronos, 31

Rhexenor (reks-**ē**-nor), son of Nausithoös king of the Phaeacians, brother of Alkinoös, father of Admetê (*Od.* 7) 140, 143

Rhodes (**rōdz**), Aegean island near southwestern tip of Asia Minor

S

Salamis (**sal**-a-mis), island near the port of Athens (*Od.* 4) 97

Salmoneus (sal-**mōn**-ūs), son of Aiolos, father of Tyro, grandfather of Neleus (*Od.* 11) 217

Samê (**sa**-mē), "hill," one of the Ionian islands, later Kephallenia (*Od.* 1, 4, 9, 15, 16, 19, 20) 45, 103, 169, 281, 293, 302, 305, 349, 373

Samos (**sā**-mos), "hill," island in the east Aegean (*Od.* 4) 103, 108

Samothrace, island in the north Aegean, 4, 7, 8

Scheria (**sker**-i-a), island of the Phaeacians, equated with Corcyra (*Od.* 5–7, 13) 110, 126, 142, 253, 255

Schliemann, Heinrich (1822–1890), German archaeologist, escavated Troy and Mycenae, 21–24, 27

scholia, "little lesson," marginal notations in literary texts that explicate point of interest, 8; (*Od.* 17) 319

sêmata lugra, "baneful signs," inscribed on a tablet given to Bellerophon (*Il.* 6), the only reference to writing in Homer, 9

Semites, "descendants of Shem," a son of Noah, peoples of the Near East speaking a language with triconsonantal roots, including Assyrians, Babylonians, Hebrews, Phoenicians, 14, 15

Sidon (**sī**-don), Phoenician city in the Levant, 4, 14; (*Od.* 4, 13, 15) 84, 258, 294

Sidonians, a Homeric word for the Phoenicians (*Od.* 4, 15) 84, 101, 284

Sikania, a name for Sicily or part of Sicily (*Od.* 24) 429

Sintians, early inhabitants of the island of Lemnos who took care of Hephaistos when he was thrown from heaven (*Od.* 8) 159

Sirens, creatures who through the beauty of their song lured sailors to their deaths, 32, 33; (*Od.* 12, 23) 234, 237–239, 418

Sisyphos (**sis**-i-fos), son of Aeolus, perhaps the real father of Odysseus, punished in the underworld (*Od.* 11) 230, 231

Skylla (**skil**-la), "puppy," many-headed monster who attacked Odysseus, 31; (*Od.* 12) 235, 236, 240–243, 246

Skyros (**skir**-os), island west of Euboea where Neoptolemos was raised (*Od.* 11) 226

Solymi, a tribe of warriors in Lycia defeated by Bellerophon (*Od.* 5) 120

Sophocles (496–406 BC), Greek playwright, 22; (*Od.* 3, 11) 69, 219, 225

Sounion, the southernmost cape in Attica, where Menelaos' helmsman died (*Od.* 3) 74

Sparta, city in the southern Peloponnesus (*Od.* 1–4, 6, 11, 13, 15) 40, 46, 53, 59, 62, 82, 225, 263, 286

Stratios, a son of Nestor (*Od.* 3) 78, 79

Styx (stiks), "hate," a river in the underworld (*Od.* 5, 10) 115, 207

symposium, "drinking party," (*Od.* 11) 224

Syria, the territory surrounding the upper Euphrates, 4, 14, 15; (*Od.* 15) 294

Syriê, Eumaios' island birthplace (*Od.* 15) 294

T

Tantalos (**tan**-ta-los), an early king of Lydia who fed his son Pelops to the gods, one of the damned in the underworld (*Od.* 11) 230

Taphians, pirates who roam the western seas (*Od.* 1, 14) 41, 43, 50, 278

Taygetos (tā-**ig**-e-tos), "big," a mountain range between Messenia and Lacedaemon (*Od.* 6) 82

Telamon (**tel**-a-mon), son of Aeacus, half-brother of Peleus, father of Big Ajax (*Od.* 4, 11, 24) 97, 225, 227, 228, 420

Telemachos (tel-**em**-a-kos), "far-fighter," son of Odysseus and Penelope, 28, 30, 32; (*Od.* 1–6, 11, 13–24) *passim*

Telemos, the seer of the Cyclopes (*Od.* 9) 187

Telephos, a son of Herakles, father of the Trojan-fighter Eurypylos (*Od.* 11) 226, 227

Temesa (**tem**-es-a), a town in southern Italy, a source of copper (*Od.* 1) 43

Tenedos (**ten**-e-dos), an Aegean island near Troy, 4; (*Od.* 3) 71

Tethys (**tē**-this), a Titan, wife of Ocean (*Od.* 4) 100

Theagenes (thē-**aj**-e-nēz) (sixth century BC), early Greek allegorizer, 6

Thebes (thēbz), principal city in Boeotia, unsuccessfully attacked by seven heroes, destroyed by their sons 3, 36, (*Od.* 4, 11, 15) 85, 218, 219, 289

Themis (**them**-is), "what is laid down," "law," a Titan, sponsors asseemblies (*Od.* 2) 54

Theoklymenos, "known to the gods," mysterious prophet who warns the suitors of their doom (*Od.* 15, 17, 20) 289, 290, 296, 297, 315–317, 375

Theseus (**thē**-sūs), son of Poseidon and Aithra, killer of the Minotaur, consort of Ariadnê (*Od.* 11) 221, 232

Thessaly, region in Greece south of Mt. Olympus, 4, 26

Thetis (**the**-tis), a daughter of Nereus, wife of Peleus, mother of Achilles (*Od.* 11, 24) 227, 423

Thoas, a leader of the Aetolians, whom Odysseus tricked out of his cloak (*Od.* 14) 279

Thoön, a Phaeacian (*Od.* 8) 155

Thrace, region northeast of Greece, 30 (*Od.* 8) 162

Thrasymedes (thras-i-**mē**-dēz), a son of Nestor (*Od.* 3) 67, 78, 79

Thrinakia (thrin-**āk**-i-a), island where Helios kept his cattle, equated with Sicily (*Od.* 11, 12) 214, 236, 237, 354

Thucydides (thu-**sid**-i-dēz) (c. 460–395 BC), Athenian historian, 6, 18, 22

Thyestes (thī-**es**-tēz), son of Pelops, father of Aigisthos (Klytaimnestra's lover), brother of Atreus (*Od.* 4) 97, 99

Tiamat (**tē**-a-mat), Babylonian monster of chaos, 31

Tiresias (ti-**rēs**-i-as), blind prophet of Thebes (*Od.* 10–12, 23) 207–209, 211, 212, 215, 225, 241, 416–418

Tiryns (**tir**-inz), Bronze Age city in Argive plain, part of the kingdom of Diomedes, associated with Herakles, 27

Tithonos (ti-**thōn**-os), brother of Priam, beloved of Dawn, given eternal life without eternal youth, turned into a grasshopper (*Od.* 5) 109

Tityos (**tit**-i-os), tortured in the underworld by vultures because he attacked Leto (*Od.* 7, 11), 150, 228, 230

Tlepolemos (tlē-**pol**-e-mos), a son of Herakles, leader of the Rhodian contingent (*Od.* 21) 378

Tritogeneia (trit-o-gen-**ē**-a), an obscure epithet of Athena (*Od.* 3), 77

Troad, the area around Troy, at the entrance to the Dardanelles, 4

Troy, in northwestern Asia Minor, 4, 22–27, 29, 32; (*Od.* 1–5, 9–17, 19, 22, 24) *passim*

Tydeus (**tī**-dūs), son of Oineus, father of Diomedes, fought at Thebes (*Od.* 3, 4) 71, 90

Tyndareos (tin-**dar**-e-us), Spartan king, husband of Leda (*Od.* 11, 24) 220, 426

Tyre, Phoenician city in the Levant, 14

Tyro (**tī**-ro), mother of Neleus and Pelias, grandmother of Jason (*Od.* 2, 11) 55, 217, 218

U

Ulysses, Roman name for Odysseus (*Od.* 1) 38

W

Wolf, Frederick August (1759–1824), German classicist who formulated the modern Homeric Question, 9, 16

X

xenia (ksen-**ē**-a), "guest friendship," the conventions that govern relationships between host and guest (*Od.* 9) 176, 177

Z

Zakynthos, the most southerly of the Ionian Islands (*Od.* 1, 9, 16,19) 45, 169, 302, 305, 349

Zenodotus (zen-**od**-i-tus) (third century BC), Alexandrian commentator on Homer, 7

Zethos (**zē**-thos), son of Zeus and Antiopê, twin brother of Amphion, co-founder of Thebes (*Od.* 19) 361